CAMP ALIEN

GINI KOCH

DAW BOOKS, INC.

DONALD A. WOLLHEIM, FOUNDER

375 Hudson Street, New York, NY 10014

ELIZABETH R. WOLLHEIM
SHEILA E. GILBERT
PUBLISHERS

www.dawbooks.com

First Printing, May 2016
1 2 3 4 5 6 7 8 9

DAW TRADEMARK REGISTERED
U.S. PAT. AND TM. OFF. AND FOREIGN COUNTRIES
—MARCA REGISTRADA
HECHO EN U.S.A.

PRINTED IN THE U.S.A.

ACKNOWLEDGMENTS

As always, so many to thank and so little page space. But, as you can see by the size of this particular book, I'm going to go for it anyway.

Thanks again for both the patience of Job and amazing editorial direction to the fantastic Sheila Gilbert. Bows and cries of "I am not worthy" to my awesome agent, Cherry Weiner, my amazing crit partner, Lisa Dovichi, and the best and fastest beta reader in the West, Mary Fiore. As always, wouldn't have made it through this book with any shreds of sanity left without you four ladies and I love all of you for putting up with me in all the various ways you put up with me.

Love and thanks as always to all the good folks at DAW Books and Penguin Random House, to all my fans around the globe, my Hook Me Up! Gang, members of Team Gini new and old, all Alien Collective Members in Very Good Standing, Members of the Stampeding Herd, Twitter followers, Facebook fans and friends, Pinterest followers, the fabulous bookstores that support me, and all the wonderful fans who come to my various book signings and conference panels—you're all the best and I wouldn't want to do this without each and every one of you along for the ride.

Special love and extra shout-outs to: my awesome assistants, Colette Chmiel and Joseph Gaxiola for continuing to fight the good fight of keeping me on schedule and somewhat coherent; Edward Pulley for allowing me to steal Joseph away all the time with good grace; Edward Pulley again for amazing and inventive Poof creations; Museum of Robots for giving me the excitement of a licensing deal made better because it's with such an awesome company; Scott Johnson for continuing to allow me to stay at the nicest bed & breakfast spot in San Diego that's also the oasis of calm in my book tours; Doug & Gen Cook for the opportunity to be "home" while on book tour; Beth Bartlett, Jan Robinson, Lisa Dovichi, Patience Fones, Kay Johnson,

Andrea Hippauf, Kevin Bowman, Koleta Parsley, Mariann Asanuma, Vicki & Richard Kung, Stephanie and Craig Dyer, Chrysta Stuckless, Kelly Mueller, Anne Taylor, Michael & Mandi Shelton, Terry Smith, Christina Callahan, Lynn Crain for bestowing beautiful, supportive, wonderful, and delicious things upon me; Robert Palsma for continuously liking everything I do; Michele Sharik, Brian Pituly, and Brianne Lucinda for going long distances to see me; for a ton of physical labor and emotional support, special love to Duncan & Andrea Rittschof; Adrian & Lisa Payne, Duncan & Andrea Rittschof, and Hal & Dee Astell for always showing up and making every event all the better for your presence; and especially to the Authors of the Stampeding Herd—Barb Tyler, Lisa Dovichi, Hal Astell, Sue Martin, Teresa Cutler-Broyles, Phyllis Hemann, Terry Smith, Marsheila Rockwell, and Lynn Crain—I literally would not have finished this book without the competition with and support from all of you, and I'm proud to pound hooves with all y'all.

Always last in the listings but first in my heart, thanks to my husband, Steve, who learned a lot of new drink recipes for me in order to ensure that I kept on writing, and our daughter, Veronica, who both encouraged me and kept me grounded. You both truly complete me and give me all the inspiration anyone could ever need.

THERE'S AN OLD ADAGE—be careful what you wish for. I've already learned that it's true—wonder for one moment if your life could be more interesting and "Whoomp! (There It Is)", you're killing a newly formed superbeing and discovering aliens are real, on the planet, and total hotties.

Of course, that was so Twelve Operations Ago. I've gotten used to the excitement that is now my daily life, sorta, and the fact that, when push comes to shove, my brand of outside-the-box thinking and ability to just go with the crazy will save the day. It never ceases to amaze me, but at the same time, I know not to complain about things working out the way I've hoped they would. Well, mostly the way I've hoped they would.

Of course, many times what I've hoped would happen has, but with catastrophic side effects no one had predicted. Okay, almost all the time. But sometimes, it's kind of nice to see that little cosmic joke explode into someone else's face.

The Mastermind has been unmasked on national and international television, and our side stopped his latest bid to end the world. Go team.

Oh, sure, he killed a lot of people we cared about and many innocents along the way, but that's just par for the old Course O' Evil. All things considered, and if we ignore that we hate even losing one person on the Side Of Right, we've kept the body count pretty low. At least for our side. It's not nearly high enough on the evil side, but we do persevere.

However, as our luck would seem to constantly have it, the Mastermind and seven of his cronies escaped. Always the way, am I right?

On the supposedly plus side, this has left my alien husband the new President of the United States, which makes me the First Lady. The fact that I keep on being shoved into these public-facing positions where everyone knows I'm going to blow it and yet still acts totally surprised when I do is just the way the cosmos amuses itself, at least insofar as I can tell.

Of course, if you're going to inherit a position after the former owner of said position and half of his staff were murdered by your most dedicated enemy, there's no one better than Jeff to take control and keep the populace calm and functioning. And we can but hope that my role will be small and not televised. Again and again and again. You know, just to mix it up and be different from all the other times.

Oh, who am I kidding? We all know it's going to be the Kitty Messes Up Again Show for the foreseeable future. But no worries, I have a plan.

What is that plan, you ask? I'm going to channel The Cars and let the "Good Times Roll" while at the same time accepting that when Aerosmith sings about someone being "Crazy," they're singing about their Number One Fan. Who is me. In case you, like so many others, haven't been paying attention.

After all, what could possibly go wrong?

Yeah, I'll wait while everyone stops rolling around the floor laughing and catches their breath. Because Murphy and his Law are pretty much my copilots.

CHAPTER 1

"EXCUSE ME, President Martini, but we have a situation. It seems the Planetary Council is requesting foodstuffs that, ah, we don't actually have on hand."

This whispered, worried statement was coming from the head of the White House's household, the Chief Usher, Antoinette Reilly.

She was an attractive black woman, a few years older than Jeff, and she'd been wearing a constantly worried expression for the past week. I'd met her before this, when the now-late President Armstrong was the man in charge, and she'd never seemed as ready to request immediate leave as she had been in the week and a half since his death.

And she wasn't the only one. We were already clearly stressing out the staff of the White House beyond their obvious expectations, and we hadn't even officially moved in yet.

"What could they possibly want that we don't have?" Jeff asked, just as quietly.

"It's, ah, considered a delicacy. Apparently. Only we would need to import it from, ah, the Alpha Centauri system, and even if we could do so easily, Chef is flat-out refusing to make it. And," Antoinette looked over to me, "ah, I can't blame him."

Took the leap. "Oh my God, Alexander wants to have the horrid Alpha Four boiled tapeworms dish, doesn't he?"

Antoinette nodded. "Madam First Lady, could you please help?"

"The formality of this new stage of my life is literally going to kill me. Can I order you and the rest of the staff to call me Kitty and have a hope of it sticking?"

Antoinette smiled. It was the first smile I'd seen her crack in a week, so go me. "Possibly in private. But right now, we need your help. Formally."

Nodded, and turned to look down the long conference table. "Excuse me, Alex?"

Emperor Alexander, Ruler of the Entire Alpha Centauri System—at least as far as anyone on Earth other than those of us who actually understood the political system over there knew—nodded his head toward me in a regal manner. "Yes, Kitty?"

"Dude, you're asking for food that makes humans literally want to barf their guts out. It's a no-go. And anyone else requesting personal national or planetary specialties, up to and definitely including haggis, need to run those requests through me. So that I can say no in the nicest possible way."

"That wasn't what we were going for," Antoinette said quietly.

"No problem, Kitty. But they're really delicious," Alexander said, sounding far more like what he really was— Jeff's and his cousin, Christopher White's, younger relative who we'd put onto the throne of Alpha Four—than the Ruler of the Free Alpha Centauri Worlds.

"Dude, gag me. Seriously. Never speak of those things again in my or any other human's presence and we'll continue to love you." Turned back to Antoinette. "Learn this now—I may have been forced to be the American Centaurion Ambassador, but don't for one moment think that I enjoyed the job. I get far better results by living by the cat motto of asking for exactly what I want. And that includes being the FLOTUS. By the way, FLOTUS really makes me feel like I'm costarring in a *Finding Nemo* spin-off as the chipper strip of seaweed that helps the gang save the day."

Antoinette was now clearly trying not to laugh. Or cry. Possibly both. Gave it even odds either way. "Duly noted, Madam First Lady."

"The less said about what movie that title makes me think I'm starring in, the better."

"*Best Little Whorehouse in Texas*?" Tim Crawford, the Head of Airborne for Centaurion Division, aka the guy doing what remained my favorite job on my entire resume, asked with a quiet snicker.

"Got it in one."

Antoinette heaved a sigh. Had to figure I was going to generate that in her for the foreseeable future. She was a nice, smart, competent, capable woman, and I felt bad about stressing her out. However, we were still in Major Crisis Mode, and therefore me not being me wasn't in our best interests.

"So, now that we've had an entire week to collect ourselves, what do we do?" It was the day after the third day of State Funerals, otherwise known as the day we buried our friend and the late President of the United States, Vincent Armstrong, and this question was coming from, of all people, his widow, Elaine.

The Former First Lady wasn't normally included in matters of state, but we were possibly the most unconventional politicians the world had ever known, the former unwilling Vice President and even more unwilling President, also known as my husband, Jeff Martini, wanted her input, and the man who'd murdered her husband and so many others was still at large. As such, Elaine had joined Team Megalomaniac with gusto.

Frankly, the Current First Lady wasn't normally included in this stuff either, but—under the variety of circumstances that had, in just over six short years, moved me from a happy-go-lucky marketing manager into being a superbeing exterminator, the Head of Airborne, the Co- then Head Ambassador for American Centaurion, and now the wife of the President of the United States—my husband valued my input, and so my input would be inputted. This was a fast-track career path that college had definitely not prepared me for.

"Jeff needs to fill a variety of Cabinet posts and then some," Charles Reynolds said. He was the Head of the CIA's Extra-Terrestrial Division. He was also my best guy friend since ninth grade. He'd been the focus of the Mastermind's insanity, and since Clifford Goodman and his Goon Squad had escaped after Operation Epidemic, that meant we needed to keep Chuckie very safe while listening carefully and acting on his input.

"Starting with Vice President," my mother said. She wasn't saying this as my mother, of course, but as the Head of the Presidential Terrorism Control Unit. Yeah, my friends and family were definitely representing in the higher levels of government.

"Angela's right as always, and we need to assign Embassy staff as well," Doreen Coleman-Weisman said. She'd been raised in the American Centaurion Diplomatic Corps and was now our Ambassador, since I couldn't do the job any longer. "I realize you're going to say that you want me to choose, but under the circumstances, I want your input, Jeff, as well as Kitty's. And everyone else's, too, Chuck's and Angela's in particular."

"I think we're avoiding a key issue," Evander Horn said. He was a handsome black man in his late fifties and the Director of the FBI's Alien Affairs Division. "And not just because Doreen doesn't want my input specifically." He grinned at her and she laughed.

"What's that, Vander?" Jeff asked.

Horn pointed to the end of the table where Alexander and the rest of the Planetary Council were sitting. "The people who accidentally triggered the Mastermind's doomsday attempt. They came here for a reason, and we're not even sure what that reason is."

CHAPTER 2

ALEXANDER NODDED. "Yes, I suppose everything has been rather ... jumbled. Rohini, if you would?"

This was directed to one of the two Shantanu, meaning one of the two giant, colorful penguin people in attendance. I'd liked Rohini from the moment we'd met him during Operation Civil War, and it wasn't a surprise that he was functioning as Planetary Team Spokesbird. He reminded me very much of Alpha Four's version of Winston Churchill, Councilor Leyton Leonidas, and our own Stealth Diplomat, Top Field Agent, and All-Around Ladies' Man, the Former Supreme Pontifex of our Earth A-Cs, Richard White.

White was sitting next to Rohini, meaning he was far down the table from me, but of those in the room, he had the closest ties to the Alpha Centauri system, since he'd been born on Alpha Four.

Rohini put his flippers onto the table. "Our earlier stated intent, to ask Earth to join the greater galactic community, is the main reason we are here. However, we want Earth to join with us because we fear two things—repeated Z'porrah attacks and contact with other alien life from systems far from both of ours."

The Z'porrah were an ancient race of dinobirds who had a deep-seated hatred of the Ancients, who were an ancient humanoid race of shape-shifters. Both races had meddled around with Earth and the inhabited Alpha Centauri planets, with the Ancients winning the overall war. However, we'd found Ancient turncoats working for the Z'porrah on several planets, including Earth. So the concern about the Z'porrah wasn't surprising.

"What indication do you have that other sentient races might be contacting you or us?" Chuckie asked, covering the surprising portion.

"Since our solar system repelled the Z'porrah so forcefully, we have received numerous transmissions from planets around the galaxy. Apparently the Z'porrah are very unpopular."

"Shocker." Could tell by the expressions of several White House staffers in the room that I wasn't the one who was supposed to be speaking right now. Oh well, they might as well learn how we rolled, also right now. "So, while we can appreciate the need to show a united front, honestly, we have bigger issues at home that we need to fix first."

"I agree with Kitty," Jeff said. "Not that we want to insinuate that the concerns of the Planetary Council aren't important to us. They are. But if there is no immediate threat, we need to get our own house in order. There's going to be tremendous fallout from the situation Cliff Goodman's insanity put us in."

Alexander nodded. "We agree and understand. And, with your permission, we will stay as long as we are able to assist you in any way, up to and including proving that we weren't responsible in any way for the so-called Alien Virus our mutual enemy released on your unsuspecting populace."

Alexander had gotten really good at the political speak. Nice to know he'd been spending his time learning, not being a jerk, not that this was a big surprise.

"So, since I'm reassured that we aren't offending the Planetary Council or not paying attention to an imminent threat, who are you thinking of for Vice President, Jeff?" Vander asked.

Jeff looked down the table at Senator McMillan. He was the senior senator from Arizona, a good friend, and one of the few honest politicians we knew. "Don?" Jeff asked hopefully.

McMillan shook his head. "I'm tempted, Jeff, don't get me wrong. But honestly, if I'd wanted to be Vice President, I'd have been Vince's running mate instead of you. And as the President Pro Tempore of the Senate, I can do a lot more good for your presidency by staying put."

This wasn't a new sentiment. Jeff had been trying to ha-
rangue McMillan into taking the Vice Presidential position
for the past several days. McMillan standing firm was in
keeping with his personality and beliefs, so couldn't really
argue. Even though his wife, Kelly, was an alumna from the
same sorority as me and I really liked her, meaning I'd have
a pal in the White House.

"You need to ensure that whoever you put into the position is either an existing politician or high enough up in a
government agency to be a name the public would know,"
Nathalie Gagnon-Brewer said. She would know—she'd
been the wife of a Representative who'd become our good
friend, Edmund Brewer. He'd been murdered by Cliff's
people during Operation Sherlock. And the fact that two
out of the three men who'd been mentoring Jeff in how to
be a good politician were dead at our enemy's hands wasn't
lost on me. I'd assigned extra guards to McMillan during
Operation Epidemic and had insisted they remain indefi-
nitely.

"What about you, Nathalie?" Jeff asked, clearly not joking.

She shook her head. "I'm a naturalized American, Jeff. I
cannot become President and, sadly, as we have just seen,
the Vice President is truly a heartbeat away from the Presidency."

Jeff looked at Vander, who shook his head with a grin. "I
know that look, Jeff, so let me say no on behalf of myself
and Chuck, too. Neither of us is high enough up in our re-
spective agencies to take the job."

"Oh, I wasn't thinking of Chuck for Vice President," Jeff
said.

Everyone at the table stared at him, some with their
mouths open. James Reader, the Head of Field for Centaurion Division, the Head of Alpha Team, and my other best
guy friend since I'd joined up with the gang from Alpha
Four, found his voice first. "Why the hell not?"

Jeff grinned at Chuckie's hurt look. "Because I already
have a job that Chuck's by far the best qualified to cover.
Due to Goodman's virus, we have an opening—I want
Chuck to take over the CIA."

"I'm already the Head of the E-T Division, Jeff,"

Chuckie said, sounding confused, which was a rarity along the lines of a blue moon.

Jeff shook his head. "I want you in charge of it all, Chuck. As of right now, you're the Director of the Central Intelligence Agency."

CHAPTER 3

"I WHOLEHEARTEDLY APPROVE," Mom said without missing a beat.

"Me, too," Serene Dwyer said. She was the Head of Imageering now, and, after Christopher, was the strongest imageer we had. She was also a closet troubadour, meaning she could affect anyone with her voice, facial expression, and body movements. She'd started the A-C version of the CIA, manned solely by our much-maligned and quite eager to represent troubadour population. Other than me, no one outside of their organization knew they existed.

Horn and McMillan both nodded. "You accepting, Chuck, or do we have to coerce it out of you?" Horn asked with a grin.

"Ah, I accept," Chuckie said, sounding slightly dazed. "You're sure, Jeff?"

"No. I'm positive." Jeff shrugged. "I want the best person for the job. And that's you. For a variety of jobs, really, but this is the one where we need you most—the CIA has been our main source of infiltration for years, and you're the only thing that's stood between them and us, and the American people, for far too long. Clean the house—it's yours now."

"Logical choice," McMillan said. "Though you'll be accused of cronyism."

"Yeah?" Jeff looked around the table. "I expect it. In fact, I welcome it."

"Why so?" Horn asked.

"Because I plan to tell the press—two of whom are in the room with us already—the same thing that I'm going to say now." Jeff nodded toward Mister Joel Oliver, who'd been the laughingstock of the reporting world until we'd been shoved out of the extraterrestrial closet during Operation Destruction, and Bruce Jenkins, who'd joined Team Alien during Operation Defection Election.

They were the only press allowed unlimited access to us, and that meant that they were now the envy of all their peers. Of course, most of the press corps didn't know about the action that naturally followed in our wake. If and when they did, Oliver and Jenkins would probably have a lot less peer envy to deal with.

"And that is, Mister President?" Oliver asked, microphone for his recording device aimed straight at Jeff.

"As events have shown, the government and all of its agencies has been infiltrated by people bent on destroying everything good about our country, starting with her people. I refuse to allow that on my watch. Therefore, I'm going to be putting people I know I can trust into positions of power. And anyone who doesn't like it can go find Cliff Goodman and bring him back to stand trial for treason and mass murder. Do that and I'll listen to your complaints. Otherwise, this is now my show, and I'm going to run it in a way that both protects and benefits all the people of the United States and the world at large both."

"God he's Presidential," Tim whispered to me. "You sure he's not a troubadour somewhere?"

"No, he's just being himself."

Jeff, who was the strongest empath in the galaxy, picked up how proud of him I was. At least I figured him turning to me and giving me a very private smile to mean that he'd picked it up. He turned back to the room. "Doreen, let's deal with the Embassy before we deal with the rest of my nominations."

She nodded. "Okay, I agree with our former Ambassador that Benjamin Vrabel should be moved into the role of Defense Attaché." Heads nodded around the table.

Vrabel wasn't his real last name, but it was the one we were using for anything public-facing. His real last name was Siler. He was the son of one of the many female Brains Behind the Throne baddies we'd had to deal with, Madeleine Siler Cartwright, and the original Mastermind for our world, Ronald Yates, aka the in-control superbeing Mephistopheles. Yates was actually Richard White's father, and therefore Jeff and Christopher's grandfather, and had been a skirt chaser of the highest order, meaning there were a lot of Yates progeny out there.

I'd met the Yates-Mephistopheles superbeing during Operation Fugly, aka my introduction to what was really going on in the world, and I'd killed Mephistopheles, right after the Yates portion had died, but right before Mephs could join with me. I'd met Siler during Operation Defection Election, however, and, due to what his fab parental units had done to him, he aged very slowly. He had other interesting talents, too, and we'd determined he had probably been the first A-C and human hybrid on Earth.

Siler had been saved by his uncle, Cartwright's brother, Hubert Siler, and had been trained in the fine art of assassination. So putting him into the Defense Attaché position hadn't been a hard sell to anyone, including Siler himself. He'd lost a lot during Operation Epidemic, just as the rest of us had, and having a safe place to raise his adopted daughter, Lizzie, was high on his list of New Job Must-Haves.

"I'm also going to listen to things I've heard Kitty say over the years," Doreen shared next, "and ask that Richard White take an official role as our Public Relations Minister."

This earned a lot of shocked looks around the table. The only reason Christopher wasn't arguing this was because he wasn't at this meeting—he'd just become a father and was at the Embassy with his wife and child. Not that Christopher thought his father was a loser, but he was hyperprotective of White, even though White routinely proved he was able to kick butt and take names better than anyone else.

However, White looked surprised by Doreen's announcement. "Ah, I'm retired."

Doreen shook her head. "As our Supreme Pontifex? Yes, you are. As an active participant in the protection of our people and adopted country? You're as involved as Kitty is. And she's right—you're the best diplomat we have. And I know that, far too often, what we need is going to be better achieved if an older, white man asks for it."

This was a point no one could argue. "Richard, I'll still grab you to kick butt as necessary."

"Which will be never." Malcolm Buchanan was part of

the P.T.C.U. and had been assigned by my mother to protect me and my daughter, Jamie, since we'd first come to D.C. He now protected my almost seven-month-old son, Charlie, too, and, somewhat grudgingly, Jeff and the rest of our extended group of friends and family.

Buchanan was built like Jeff—big, broad, and good looking, only he had straight brown hair and blue eyes—and even though he was a human he had what I felt were Dr. Strange powers. If he didn't want you to see him, you didn't see him, and so forth. Frankly, I'd forgotten he was in the room until he'd spoken.

Of course, Jeff's first appointment had been to put Buchanan in charge of all White House security, and the first thing Buchanan had done was insist that Walter Ward, the A-C who was the Head of Security at the Embassy, be moved into the White House to set up an extremely secure net around the entire complex. Meaning both that the White House complex would become even more secure than it had ever been before, and I'd be watched like a hawk 24/7. Always the way.

"Whatevs. Anyway, Richard, I really agree with Doreen—it's time to stop pretending you're retired in any way and just accept that all the haters are going to do what they can to keep us apart."

White laughed. "Well, when the First Lady puts it that way, who am I to argue? Paul, your thoughts?"

This was directed to Paul Gower, Reader's husband and the current Supreme Pontifex. Gower had been White's adjunct when I'd first joined up, but it had been clear from Day One that White had been grooming Gower to take over the head religious role. Gower was big, black, bald, and beautiful, and he also missed being in on the action because, like me and Jeff, he was sidelined a lot because of his role within the A-C's internal government.

"I think it's a good choice, Richard," he said seriously. "If Raj has no objections."

Rajnish Singh was an A-C troubadour originally from New Delhi Base. He was Serene's second in command in the secret A-C CIA. And he was the current Public Relations Minister.

"He won't mind," Jeff said before Raj could reply. "He's moving into the White House."

"Thanks, Jeff," Raj said. "In what position? Press Secretary?"

"That had been my first thought," Jeff said. "However, I've gone over the various roles that we have empty, and, barring any meaningful objections from anyone in the room, I'd like to have you take on Chief of Staff instead."

This earned gasps from the humans in the room. Chief of Staff ran the entire business side of the White House. This would make Raj literally the most important man here, after Jeff. But no one offered any objections.

"Then who will fill the Press Secretary position?" Raj asked.

"You pick," Jeff said. "That's part of your job now."

Raj nodded and, troubadour or not, trying to hide it or not, I could tell that he was incredibly flattered.

Jeff turned back to Doreen. "Who else?"

She sighed. "He's going to object to it, but I really want Christopher to stay on as the Embassy Chargé d'Affaires and as the Primary, as well. As in, he'll be the main point of contact for the Embassy with any of the Planetary Council, as well as helping me with all the day-to-day running of our diplomatic mission."

Jeff sighed. "He won't like it."

"You two have been joined at the hip for long enough," Gower said. "He can get over to you in less than a minute, Jeff."

"Wow, I'm totally reminded of when we first moved here and you said almost the exact same thing about my not wanting to be too far from James."

Jeff laughed. "Fine, fine, I'll be a big boy. And you're right—he's the best qualified for those positions, and we need continuity of some kind at the Embassy."

"I'd like Abigail Gower to stay on as one of our Cultural Attachés, and Mahin Sherazi to take the other Cultural Attaché role," Doreen went on.

Jeff nodded. "I agree."

"Who's going to take Walter's place as Head of Security?" I asked.

"I've consulted with Embassy staff, and Denise Lewis feels, based on the security discussions she's been leading with Base Security worldwide, that moving Melissa Gunnels from Sydney Base to the Embassy is the right choice.

I've interviewed her, and I agree. So, barring any objections, Missy's going to take that role."

"Good choice." I honestly felt that it was, even though Missy and I hadn't gotten along all that well the few times I'd interacted with her. That was due to the fact that the "me" she'd met the first time had been Other Me during Operation Bizarro World. Apparently Other Me had impressed, and I'd messed up and ruined that initial good will. Oh well. We'd fix it. Somewhere along the line. "Tito's coming to the White House, right?" I wanted Dr. Tito Hernandez close by, period, and not just because he was an amazing doctor—he was also a highly trained mixed martial arts fighter and incredibly smart.

He was sitting next to his future mother-in-law, Queen Renata from Beta Twelve, aka the Planet of Getting Less Pissed Off Daily Amazons. They were both being troopers and not demanding that we get to their main concern, which was that the two princesses, Rahmi and Rhee, had gone off on a secret mission during Operation Epidemic and were still missing and unaccounted for. Tito and Rahmi were engaged, and with Renata on Earth, they might be able to speed up the longest engagement in recent memory. If, you know, we could find Rahmi and Rhee, among others.

Tito smiled. "Yes, Kitty. We've already discussed it, and Magdalena is going to remain in the Embassy—she's more than qualified to run their medical. Jeff's already appointed me. I don't have all my staff on board yet, but two of them will make you very happy."

But before Tito could tell us who was going to make my day, my phone rang. Checked—an unknown number. Showed it to Jeff before I answered, because anonymous callers to my cell phone tended to indicate one thing and one thing only—enemy action was about to be perpetrated against us.

CHAPTER 4

"HELLO?" Chose to go with the simple answer, in case this was, as I so often hoped, AeroForceOne telling me that, against all the odds, I'd won a private meet and greet with Steven Tyler and Joe Perry.

"Madam First Lady, how good it is to hear your voice."

As per usual, though, this wasn't AeroForceOne, nor was it a voice I recognized. Ansom Somerall, one of the heads of Gaultier Enterprises, meaning one of our most likely sworn enemies, had been my Mystery Caller at the start of Operation Epidemic. But I'd saved his number to my phone, and this definitely wasn't his voice. It sounded faintly European.

In addition to the politicians, U.S. agency and Centaurion Division personnel in the room, we also had two lobbyists with us—Lillian Culver and Guy Gadoire. Lillian was the head lobbyist for the weapons industry and Guy was the same for tobacco. Guy spoke in a French accent we all thought was faked. But since Guy and his husband, Vance Beaumont, were both here in the room, this wasn't Guy on the line.

"And to whom do I have the pleasure of speaking?"

"We've never met. Yet. However, I believe I have something that you are very interested in."

Decided that pretending to be the FLOTUS was a waste of effort. It was clearly time to toss on my Megalomaniac Girl cape and make the leaps so near and dear to every cackling madman's or crazed evil genius' heart.

During Operation Epidemic we'd lost the five

flyboys—Jerry Tucker, Matt Hughes, Chip Walker, Joe Billings, and Randy Muir. Not to death, but to capture. By an invisible helicarrier created by one Gustav Drax. Rahmi and Rhee, under the lead of our deep cover agent, Camilla, had gone after them. Plus several security teams—P.T.C.U., Secret Service, and Centaurion Division Field—had all disappeared as well. I took the leap.

"Gustav Drax, what a thrill it is to hear your voice."

The entire room stiffened and started paying full attention—Tim, since it was his team that was captured, Lorraine and Claudia, the Captains on Alpha Team who were married to Joe and Randy respectively, and Tito and Queen Renata, in particular.

Buchanan shoved off the wall he was leaning against and trotted over. As he'd done in the past, he shoved a small blinking device into my phone's audio jack. Then he nodded to the other security folks in the room, all of whom pulled out their phones and started listening. So much for privacy. And apparently this was a new and improved model—the last time I'd had the special blinky receiver in my phone it had only worked as a tracer. Nice to see us always using the newest tech.

Of course, Chuckie was one of those listening, and he had his phone between his ear and Jeff's. Noted that this was happening around the room. No privacy at all. So much for that plan of mine to run off with Drax.

Sincerely hoped this new tech was also getting a GPS fix on where Drax was, but figured we'd find out he was in a lead-walled room or something, because I knew exactly how our luck rolled.

Drax chuckled. "I was told you weren't that . . . intuitive."

"Yeah, well your intel is coming from what's essentially a petulant child. Stephanie and I have never had a close relationship because, and I'm just spitballing here, she thinks I'm as much of a bitch as I think she is."

Received a lot of WTF looks from the room, a look of utter horror from Antoinette, and a look of "that's my girl" from Mom. Chose to focus on Mom thinking I was handling things fine.

"Ah . . . yes. I had heard you were blunt."

"That I am. Why are you calling me?"

"Well . . ." He paused, presumably for breath or to cackle evilly. Decided I didn't feel like drawing this out.

"Let me tell you why you're calling." Got even more WTF looks from everyone other than Mom who, like the rest of the Security Team, was listening to this on her own phone. "Your sales pitch was an unmitigated failure. Not only did you fail to impress the potential customers, but you lost your invisible commando force to capture. They're singing like the Mormon Tabernacle Choir, by the way, and who can blame them?"

"As to that—"

"Then you kidnapped five Navy pilots and their very expensive planes. Which is, last time I checked, an act of war against the United States. Since those were my flyboys you inconvenienced, it's also an act of war with American Centaurion."

"That wasn't my—"

"Intent? I'm sure it wasn't, dude. You can't be as stupid as your sales pitch makes you seem. You also captured a variety of security personnel from the Rocky Mount train station, which included American government antiterrorism teams, Secret Service teams, and Centaurion Division teams, compounding your acts of war against the United States and American Centaurion. And now you're hoping that the new regime is going to want to laugh this all under the rug."

"Ah . . ."

"Yes?"

"Oh, you're letting me speak. I wasn't sure. I wouldn't say that the term 'act of war' applies here. No one has been harmed."

"Oh, I think I can look over at a war hero sitting in the room with me and get confirmation that the capture during peacetime of our five pilots is enough for the President to push the button down in your general direction." Looked at McMillan, who nodded emphatically.

Drax cleared his throat. "Be that as it may, I was calling to suggest an exchange."

"Excuse me while I laugh long and loudly. We're going to find you, dude. Whether we bomb the hell out of you when we find you is the Question of the Hour. You may think you have bargaining chips, but we aren't giving you your commandos back, ever. We're not giving you anything, unless we decide—horrific first impressions aside—that you're not an enemy or an idiot. So don't try asking for one *million* dollars, either."

"Ah, no, that wasn't my intent."

Raj and I exchanged a look. He was listening in with Evalyne, the head of my Secret Service detail. Evalyne, like most of the humans in the room—including those I'd have insisted didn't possess a sense of humor they were aware of—all controlled snickers of some kind. The A-Cs, for the most part, however, looked blank, as did the Planetary Council.

Raj nodded at me then jerked his head toward the Planetary Council while he raised an eyebrow. Mouthed "I love you" to him, then returned to my call.

"See, Gustav, may I call you Gustav?"

"Ah—"

"Super. Gustav, here's the thing. I realize that your accent tells me you're not from America. It sounds like it could be Eastern Bloc, German, Polish, or originating from any number of countries, which totally fits with the whole Mysterious Arms Dealer idiom you're going with. However, even if you're from the most backward country in the world, you'd have gotten the joke I passed just a moment ago."

"You were joking?"

"No. I was referring to a very successful movie from years ago. Lines from that movie have been used and reused so many times that I'd bet that even in the rain forest, if I said that line, the people who live there would laugh or put their pinky up to their mouth."

"What does a finger have to do with this?" Drax sounded totally confused. His tone matched the expressions of half of the room—the alien half, other than Raj and the few other troubadours in the room.

"It's proof, as if I needed it, that you're not actually from a foreign country. And I don't think you're from anywhere else on Earth, either, in part because that movie was a worldwide hit and in other part because you've literally come out of nowhere, and it's hard to believe that a major player in the arms dealing business hasn't hit *someone's* radar by now."

"You think I'm an American?"

"Hardly. There's not an American alive who'd have missed that line. No, the only people I know who routinely don't pay attention to our popular culture are, with very few exceptions, aliens. Just like you are."

CHAPTER 5

THERE WERE A LOT of gasps from the room. Heard Drax draw in his breath. But now it was time to put my sales experience to work. Once the offer was made, the big question asked, or the definitive statement given, the next person who spoke lost. So now it was time for Drax to speak, because I wasn't going to utter another sound.

While we waited I pantomimed that I wanted paper and a writing implement of some kind. Three tries later, Len Parker, who was my driver and part of my Security Squad, figured out what I wanted and trotted a pad of paper and a pen over to me.

Scribbled my request, ripped the paper off, and handed it to him. He nodded, grabbed the nearest A-C, they linked hands and the A-C made them disappear. Well, not really. A-Cs had hyperspeed, and that meant they could move faster than humans could see.

Scribbled another note and waved it at Buchanan. He came over again, took the note from me, then took the pen from me, wrote a big "DUH" on the paper, and handed both back to me. So they were indeed tracing this call. A girl just liked to be sure and all that.

Len and his A-C helpmate were back well before Drax had made a sound, with Rudolph "John" Wruck in tow. We'd originally thought Wruck was one of the many Ronald Yates offspring out there, either a pure-blooded A-C or an A-C and human hybrid.

However, Wruck wasn't a Yates offspring. Nor was he fully A-C or human. As I'd just discovered during Operation Epidemic, Wruck was actually an Ancient.

Originally we'd thought that the Ancients had died out. How wrong we were. They, like our mortal enemies, the Z'porrah, were still around and kicking. Most of the kicking seemed to happen in the Alpha Centauri and Earth systems, too. And while the Z'porrah had turncoat Ancients on their side, Wruck wasn't one of those, either.

He'd been on the ill-fated mission that had included LaRue Demorte Gaultier. As we'd finally learned when I'd changed universes during Operation Bizarro World, LaRue was a turncoat Ancient. She'd murdered the other Ancients on her team then formed an alliance with Yates, becoming the True Power Behind The Throne for every Mastermind.

At least, she thought she'd murdered all of her team.

Wruck had played dead then hidden himself away, to heal up and figure out how to take LaRue down. Technically, LaRue had been killed at the end of Operation Destruction, but our Evil Genius League was quite good, and they'd created cloning, for themselves, of course. So there was at least one LaRue clone out there now.

However, I wanted Wruck so that he could help me confirm what planet Drax might be from.

Scribbled quickly while I waited for Drax to speak and pointed at the paper. Wruck looked at what I'd written, nodded, then pulled Buchanan aside. They had a quiet conversation while the rest of us listened to "The Sound of Silence." Only Simon and Garfunkel weren't actually singing. No matter how much I whined, I hadn't been able to convince Antoinette or Jeff to let me have music piped into every room in the White House.

Wruck came back to me, took the pen, and wrote several words. He circled one of them. Took a look and gave him a thumbs-up.

Had to hand it to Drax—he was good at this silence game. Either that or he'd hung up and I'd missed it. Or Camilla had used this time to make whatever move I sincerely hoped she was in a position to make. Hadn't made a reference to her or the princesses under the wild hope that the three of them weren't actually captured but were instead using radio silence so as not to give themselves away.

Drax cleared his throat. "Ah, are you still there?"

"Yep."

More silence. Had a feeling it was making him

uncomfortable. Certainly hoped so. Buchanan gave me the thumbs-up sign. I waved the "DUH" paper at him and he nodded. Good. We had Drax's location pinpointed. Go team.

"Why are you not speaking?" Drax definitely sounded out of his element. Good.

"I'm waiting for you."

"For me to what?"

"To share what planet you're from."

"I'm from Earth."

"Dude, that's so clearly a lie that there's no child on this planet who'd fall for it. If you weren't an alien, you'd have protested that already, not sat there hoping I was just joking. I wasn't. You're an alien, and you're not from this solar system. Nor are you from the Alpha Centauri system. So, give me your name, rank, planetary system number, planet designation, and how many light-years from home you happen to be."

"Or what?"

"Or I hang up, we find you, and kill you and anyone else with you. Including if someone with you happens to be Stephanie. Who isn't doing you or herself any favors with this little stunt. Her uncle just became the President. This is the time for her to come in from the cold, share how she was being used by manipulative older men, and throw herself onto the country's mercy while asking her uncle very nicely for a presidential pardon. Now is not the time to, once again, show how she's hooked up with an enemy of the state who we are, make no mistake, going to find and very likely destroy."

"Unless?" Drax asked hopefully.

"Unless you give me a good reason not to. Which you, so far, have not."

"What if I can provide the person you want most in the world?"

"Just who would you think that would be?"

"Clifford Goodman."

Contemplated my reply. But Drax confirmed that his salesmanship was as bad as I felt it was. "You *do* want him, don't you?" he asked. Managed not to try to high-five anyone, but only just. In part because I wasn't sure who would high-five me back, and I also didn't want to give Antoinette a heart attack.

"Oh yes, we're very interested in him. I'm just curious as to how you're going to hand him over to us."

Truly didn't think that Drax was working with Cliff, in part because Drax's Sales Pitch of Doom had been the reason Cliff's train attack hadn't really worked fully as expected during Operation Epidemic. And Stephanie had cut ties with Cliff on national and international television at the end of Operation Epidemic. So it was truly doubtful that Cliff was hanging out at Chez Drax to lick his wounds and plan revenge.

"I have my ways."

Couldn't help it, I snorted. Loudly. "Oh, dude, please. Your 'ways' are Stephanie, and her knowledge is now obsolete. There's no way that Cliff and his cronies are anywhere she thinks they are. She already told him she was giving him up. They've cleared out and are in a brand-new hiding place."

"Drax Industrial has more resources than you've seen." He sounded huffy. It was cute.

"I'm sure." Ensured I sounded bored. "Look, dude, let's try this another way."

"What way are you suggesting?"

"You show us that this was all just a big misunderstanding. You return all of our people that you're holding, ensuring that not even one of them has been harmed or has even a single hair out of place, return our planes and such in the same perfect working condition, and then we nicely let you do a normal person sales pitch."

I got a lot of WTF looks from lots of people. But Kevin Lewis, who was Mom's right hand in the P.T.C.U. and had been the Embassy Defense Attaché just until this past week, wasn't one of them. He nodded emphatically, then leaned over to Mom and whispered in her ear, presumably telling her he knew where I was going with this offer.

Kevin was a former pro football player, black, gorgeous, with the greatest smile and teeth, and literally bags of charisma. He'd been part of our team since the start of Operation Drug Addict, and he was able to get onto my wavelength pretty easily.

Jeff had been jealous of Kevin and how hot and smart I thought he was. For about five minutes, until he'd learned that Kevin was married. His wife, Denise, who was blonde and fair-skinned, but otherwise matched him in looks, smile, and charisma, now ran the Embassy School and Daycare Center.

While most of the kids who were under Denise's care were all younger than Jamie, the Lewis kids were several years older. Raymond and Rachel were beautiful blends of their parents, and they'd both inherited the smiles and the bags of charisma, too. Tried not to feel disappointed that I wouldn't be able to just go up to the daycare area and see all the kids whenever I wanted. However, I had another megalomaniac to deal with, so shoved the maternal part of me to the side for the moment.

"How do I know you won't just try to incarcerate me?" Drax finally asked.

Damn, Drax actually could think. Bummer. Looked to Kevin again. He nodded. "Because I give you my word that we won't. Both you and Stephanie can come here without worry. The first time."

"What do you mean?"

"I mean that I'm used to people being sneaky bastards, Gustav, and that if you and Stephanie think that you're going to fool us and come in here and create mayhem, you're both sadly mistaken. We won't arrest either one of you or fill you full of lead, but if either one of you so much as twitches in a manner deemed threatening, all bets are off, and your heads will be, too."

Waited again.

"Ah," Drax said finally, "I don't really understand you."

"So few ever do, Gustav. So few ever do." Though, frankly, a human would have caught most of this. Not only was Drax an alien, I truly didn't think he'd been on Earth all that long. "So, this generous offer of you returning our people and planes without issue or harm then you getting a chance to share the wonder that is Drax Industrial with us isn't going to stay on the table for long. You literally have until I hang up."

"What happens if I say no?"

Looked to Buchanan and held up the DUH paper with a questioning look. He nodded emphatically. Good. We had Drax for certain.

"You and Stephanie die."

CHAPTER 6

WHILE WE WAITED for Drax's reaction to this, Culver waved at me. She had a pad and pen, too, and she had one word written on the paper she was holding up. Nodded—she was right, I'd forgotten a key point.

"Ah..." Drax said finally. "That seems rather... extreme."

"Does it? This from the guy who irradiated commandos and had them attack the President of the United States in order to make an introduction. Just out of curiosity, dude, what's your version of sedate?"

"Madam First Lady, clearly we got off on the wrong foot."

"Yeah, we did. Speaking of which, was Stephanie trying to put crossbow arrows into a variety of our friends—such as Don McMillan, Gideon Cleary, and Lillian Culver—on your order, using her own wacked-out initiative, or by suggestion of Thomas Kendrick from Titan Security?"

The room went very still, though there were a lot of heads swiveling back and forth between Culver and me. She rolled her eyes and winked at me. Yeah, no matter how much I might want to pretend this woman was still the Joker, if she was, she'd joined up with the rest of the Suicide Squad and was working with Batman to destroy a much bigger threat.

Of course, by mentioning Titan I was giving Drax an out. What he'd do with it was going to be the most interesting part of this entire conversation.

While we waited Drax out, Buchanan stepped out of the room. Wondered what was going on. Didn't have long to wait. He came back, looking seriously pissed. Wrote on my pad of paper and it wasn't good news. Drax had some kind of GPS scrambling going on. Our agents had indeed gone to where we'd identified Drax as being only to find an empty warehouse. It had been searched by P.T.C.U. and Field agents and they'd all found exactly nothing.

Wrote back. Buchanan scribbled that, yes, he'd had them search for invisible things, too, using the goggles we'd gotten off of the No Longer Invisible Commandos. Nada.

Didn't let this throw off my groove. This just meant that Drax actually did have some tech we might want to use.

Wruck, who was still standing behind me, leaned over and read what Buchanan had written. He nodded to me, then pulled Buchanan out of the room.

Drax cleared his throat. "I see that your people hit a warehouse."

Didn't let this throw off my groove either. "We did. What of it?"

"I wasn't there. But that means you're tracing this call."

"Does it?"

"Ah . . . yes?"

"Because, so far as I know, you just confirmed that you felt that 'my' people hit a warehouse you're monitoring."

"Yes?"

"Which is, let's face it, rather suspicious, isn't it, Gustav?"

"I don't understand you."

"I've mentioned that I'm used to that already. I'll talk slower. You were monitoring a warehouse, which is suspicious, since that begs the question of why you were so monitoring. So, I'm going to ask that beggar. Why?"

He cleared his throat. "Ah . . ."

"Could it be because you expected 'my' people to go there to find your own sweet self?"

"Could be," he said slowly. "I have enemies."

"Yeah, color me just shocked that a man of your total finesse isn't popular with everyone." Decided not to mention that us not finding Drax at the first location was just going to make those searching for him even more eager to find him quickly as well as ensuring that they'd be far more pissed off. Why spoil Buchanan's fun? "So, what's your offer?"

"Offer? Ah, do you mean my offer to exchange prisoners?"

"No, that's still not going to fly."

"But you haven't found me."

"We're willing to be Avis."

"Excuse me?"

"We're always willing to try harder. Seriously, Gustav, you're not a human. Stop pretending that you are, it's getting tiresome." Time to utilize the intel I'd gotten from Wruck. "So, my guess, and this is just a guess, mind you, is that you're a Vata from Vatusus. A planet near the galactic core," I added for the rest of the room.

Heard what sounded like a crashing sound. "Hang on!" Drax shouted, from what sounded far away. Waited a few seconds while I enjoyed the shocked looks on almost everyone's faces, then he was back. "Sorry about that."

"Shock and surprise will make you drop your phone, won't it?"

"Ah . . . what planet were you talking about?"

"Your home one. The one where the natives are able to mentally connect with technological things. As in, you think you're using your mad skills to track us. Only, I have to give you a major duh on this one, dude. We're in the White House. What a total shocker. And, regardless of your capabilities or not, you're not learning anything at all about us that you didn't already know. You're not the smartest Vata on the hill, are you?"

Wruck and Buchanan were back. They both looked rather pleased. Hoped this meant that our resident Ancient was able to reverse engineer a Vata's mental signature.

"I'm a technological genius!" Drax said finally, sounding insulted and freaked out. I had that effect on people.

Buchanan wrote on my notepad.

"Sure you arc. Look, Gustav, I'm going to give you one last chance. What, exactly, would you and Stephanie like to do in order to get out of the situation you've dug yourselves into? Your next words will, literally, decide your fate."

Something about my tone, the situation, or the realization that I somehow knew about a planet almost no one on Earth had ever heard of before must have gotten through to him. He heaved a sigh. "I don't have your people."

Buchanan looked ready to go into action. Put my hand up. "What do you mean?"

"I mean that, yes, I had them. Only they're gone. As is my helicarrier."

"The invisible helicarrier, right?"

"Yes, that's the one."

Looked up at Buchanan who shook his head. Looked to Chuckie, who shook his head as well. So, Camilla hadn't checked in and, if she'd engineered the Great Helicarrier Escape, she should have advised us by now.

"So, who took all your prisoners and your fancy-shmancy S.H.I.E.L.D. tech?"

He sighed again. "The person you named a little earlier—Thomas Kendrick."

CHAPTER 7

I COULD TELL THAT everyone in the room wanted to be freaking out. But since I was on a call they were all listening to, the humans managed to act like the A-Cs and keep quiet. Didn't expect this to last.

Decided to do everyone a favor. "Gustav, hang on, I'm going to put you on speakerphone. You're now live to the room." Well, to the part of the room that might not have been listening in already. Antoinette would now get to hear everything, lucky her. "So, let me ask you this—are you sure?"

"Yes, sadly, I am. Thomas was here, I went to check on something he'd ordered. When I came back, he was gone, as were all the prisoners and the helicarrier."

"Where's Stephanie?" Wondered if she was trading up or not.

"With me."

Interesting. "Did she see anything?"

"Ah, no. She wasn't . . . here when it happened."

"You mean this happened when Stephanie and I were on TV last week, don't you?" In other words, at the end of Operation Epidemic, when we were revealing Cliff to be the Mastermind to the world news organizations.

"Yes," he admitted.

"Dude, why did you wait so long to contact us?"

"Ah . . . you were busy?" He sounded like he knew this was as lame said aloud as he feared.

"And just how did you think you were going to bluff us into giving you the Invisible Commandos back when you don't, in fact, have anyone we actually want?"

He sighed. "I was hoping to have them back by the time

you agreed to do whatever deal you were going to agree to do."

Buchanan was talking quietly to Jeff and Chuckie, since they no longer had to listen to my conversation via Chuckie's phone. Wasn't so fully focused on my Standard Opening Gambit Call that I couldn't pick up words here and there. Buchanan felt that, with what Wruck had given him, they actually had Drax and Stephanie surrounded and he wanted the go order.

"Yeah, that's not exactly working out for you. Guys, before you do whatever it is you want to do, I think we need to ask Lillian if this is in character for Kendrick."

"It's not," she said firmly. "He's not your friend, but he's not an idiot, either. No one could come to the U.S. government right now offering invisible tech and not immediately be assumed to be responsible for the terrorist attack on Rail Force One."

"And no one's come forward," Fritz Hochberg said. He was the current Secretary of Defense, though he, like so many others, felt that he'd failed at his job completely over the past couple of weeks. "We have had absolutely no chatter about anyone having Drax Industrial tech, an invisible helicarrier in particular."

"Nor have we received any offers of hostage exchange," Horn added. "None of the Agencies have heard any word about our captured people."

"Oh, so it's the old enemy of my enemy is my enemy thing again."

"Isn't that the enemy of my enemy is my friend, Madam First Lady?" Drax asked, sounding confused again.

"Depends on what you're used to, Gustav. Look, I'm being hella nice here. What, exactly, now that most of your cards are on the table, do you actually want?"

"I wanted to become the main armaments dealer to the United States and her allies," he said, sounding frustrated. "I have tech that you all can use."

"You mean you brought tech from another world that works here and are trying to pass it off. Gotcha."

"No, this is my tech."

"Dude, I don't even have to see your face to be able to tell that you're lying. Again, this is me exercising more patience than any other person in the room. One last chance—what is it that you want, what you really, really want?" Now I wanted to hear the Spice Girls. Well, that wasn't going to be happening during White House briefings, so I'd have to belay any musical enjoyment for a while.

Drax was silent again while I heard Jeff agree that, should Drax not give me the answer I was looking for, whatever it was, Buchanan could give the go order.

"To work with you to get my tech and your people back."

"Gosh, was that so hard? I guess male Vata are as big on protecting their dignity as male humans and A-Cs."

"I'm not . . . oh, fine, yes. I'm from another planet. Does that change anything?"

"It makes me a lot more interested in meeting you." And clearly it changed things for Jeff, Chuckie, and Buchanan, since Jeff nodded and Buchanan trotted out of the room, Wruck going with him.

"That's a good thing?"

"Oh, yes. Gustav?"

"Yes?"

"What you do next will determine the next many things that will happen to you. I'd strongly recommend that you think long and hard about your reactions."

"My reactions to—" He stopped speaking. There was a lot of noise in the background. Was pretty sure I heard a woman making a fuss in the background.

Looked over to Jeff. "I wasn't done."

He shrugged. "I'd like to have that meeting, baby. Face-to-face."

The sounds of struggle and capture were still going on. "I want to actually verify where Thomas Kendrick is, and if he's still a human or not."

Chuckie nodded. "Ahead of you." He grinned. "My first act as the Director."

Tito and some of our scientists at the Dulce Science Center had created the Organic Validation Sensor, or OVS, which looked like the wands security folks used at airports to do the closer body checks, only with a lot more blinking lights. We had a lot of these now, and most Field teams carried small ones with them because androids had been an unwilling part of our lives for far too long now.

"If you do it without a warrant, that will cause some issues," Culver shared.

Chuckie shook his head. "It's non-invasive, and, frankly, he won't know it's happening."

"Using the old 'manipulate the gasses' ploy?" I asked Jeff quietly.

"Yep. Sometimes it's effective. And yes, I realize it leaves us open. Right now, I'll worry about impeachment later."

"Stop acting like that's a good option," Chuckie said.

Jeff shrugged. "That will depend on who I choose as Vice President, won't it?"

"Kitty," Wruck said via Drax's phone, "we have Drax and Stephanie in custody. Would you like them brought to the White House or somewhere more secure?"

"Oh, I'd say we're pretty secure here, so let's bring them in. I'm assuming everyone's checked them for bombs and such?"

"Yes, they've been thoroughly searched."

"Excellent. Why did you go on the raid?"

He chuckled. "Because I know how to deal with Vata. And Benjamin knows how to deal with Stephanie."

"Oh, it's a party. Great, hopefully he's coming back with you."

"Yes, we'll be to you shortly." He hung up.

Chuckie's phone beeped and he grunted. "Interesting. Lillian, I believe we're going to need your help."

"Thomas objected to being violated?" she asked, sarcasm knob heading toward eleven.

"No, actually, as we said, he had no idea he was scanned. He's eighty-nine percent organic, meaning he's a human. However, that means we need to have him come here willingly. I'd like to ask you to ask him to join us."

"Now?" She had her phone out.

"Yes, since Drax is on the way here."

"Which I'm sure you don't want me to mention."

"Exactly. If he's willing to come, though, please tell him that we have a security team standing by to escort him. For his safety, of course."

"Of course." She stood up and stepped away. Chose not to get up and try to hear what she was saying. Culver had more than proved she was on our side. Kendrick, on the other hand, had not.

However, I still had my Megalomaniac Girl cape on. "What do you think the odds are that the person who stole

Drax's helicarrier wasn't actually Kendrick but an android version of him working for the New Crazy Eights?"

"You're sticking with that moniker?" Chuckie asked.

"Yeah, there are—with the five remaining Original Crazy Eights, the LaRue and Reid clones, and Cliff—eight of them. At least, I hope it's only eight."

"Better than the Unmagnificent Seven Plus Their Leader, so I'll live with it. And yes, to answer your question, I think there's a strong likelihood."

"I think it's a fifty-fifty shot," Culver said, coming back into the room. "I know for a fact that Thomas is interested in integrating Drax Industrial's tech into Titan Security."

"Integrating normally means a corporate merger, buy-out, or contracts," Reader said. "Not blatant theft."

Culver nodded. "Thomas is bold, but if what Drax described really happened, I'd have a hard time understanding his motivation. If it was to rescue captured people and return them to the U.S. and American Centaurion governments—and thereby become a hero and garner favorite vendor status—he should have done the rescue and return days ago."

"Stealing a helicarrier, five Navy supersonic jets, five Navy pilots, and a host of U.S. and Centaurion security personnel at the same time doesn't say subtle, either. That's a baroque supervillain move. I realize the dude was in the military, but heads of major corporations rarely decide to go all Rambo and handle these kinds of things alone."

Chuckie nodded. "Hence why we want him to come visit the White House. Lillian?"

"He's amenable. And sounded rather thrilled. He asked me if I'd negotiated a new contract for Titan with all of you. I gave him a vague reply, but that seemed a good mindset for him to have."

"That doesn't sound like someone who's just taken off with my team," Tim said. "That sounds like a normal person reaction."

"We'll find out soon enough," Jeff said. "They should all be back here soon."

"Why isn't the security team back already?" I asked. They'd clearly been taking gates—which we'd already had installed all over the White House—and should have been back almost immediately after the raid.

"They're triple-checking the prisoners," Chuckie replied. "And going over Drax's compound and such before bringing terrorists back to hang out with the remaining living members of America's leadership."

"Wow, dude, no need to get touchy. I was just asking."

"While we wait," McMillan said, presumably to prevent Chuckie and me from snapping at each other, "let's get back to important things, Mister President. You need to pick your Vice President, and you need to pick him or her now."

CHAPTER 8

JEFF NODDED. "You're right, Don." He looked down the table. "Gideon?"

This earned a lot of shocked looks from pretty much everyone at the long table other than the Planetary Council. Cleary was the current governor of Florida and had started out as our enemy because he'd been working for the Mastermind. Only he hadn't known that Cliff Goodman actually was the Mastermind, and, politics being what it was, Cleary had become our ally over the course of the last few Operations. Had to hand it to Cliff—he'd really brought people together, one way or the other.

Cleary looked the most shocked, but then he shook his head. "I can't accept, Jeff. For a variety of reasons."

"Not the same party being only one of them," McMillan said.

Cleary nodded. "Even if we wanted to try to be the first bipartisan administration in recent history, there are more reasons that I can't accept." He looked at me. "You know why."

I did. "You're tainted."

Cleary nodded. "Exactly. No one—not you, not the people around this table, not the American people, and not the international community—will ever be able to be sure that I'm not still working for the Mastermind. If anything were to happen to you, Jeff, even if it was just a hangnail, suspicion would instantly fall on me."

"Not necessarily," Jeff said.

Reader shook his head. "Gideon's right, Jeff."

"He's proven himself," Jeff protested.

"He has, but that won't matter," I said. "Public opinion is hard to control, and I can guarantee that our enemies will want to create as much havoc as they can. And this would give them an easy opening."

"Exactly," Cleary agreed. "Let's say that you give me whatever tests that make everyone here, all your key people, feel confident that I'm not a risk. There will still be nothing you can do to prevent the press from constantly asking if I'm just lying in wait. The speculation will increase to the point where I'll be accused of being the Mastermind, of having engineered Vince's death, just so that I could fool you into making me your Vice President."

"It would be a good plan," Chuckie said, eyes narrowed.

Cleary managed a chuckle. "Exactly. Mister Reynolds is, rightly, a suspicious man who would need about one shred of evidence to believe it, and he's now the Director of the CIA. I know what his first order will be if you appoint me, Jeff. I honestly don't want to turn my life into that kind of media circus, let alone live the rest of my life under the suspicion and scrutiny that all your people would *have* to have for me. Like Don, I can do more good for you by staying Governor, and it will also be far better for me, both personally and professionally."

"You're just going to run against me next time out anyway," Jeff said with a laugh.

Cleary shook his head. "No, Jeff. And not just because we've become friends. But by helping out Cliff Goodman, I've ensured that I can never be President—and I can also never be one heartbeat away from the office either."

Jeff heaved a sigh. "Fine. I can tell that everyone agrees with you." He ran his hand through his hair. "We have so many roles to fill."

"That's what someone trying to kill all the leaders does to a country," I said. "But you have plenty of good options, Jeff."

"You can't make Kitty your VP," Tim said with a grin. "Though I'm sure you want to."

"And before you suggest Mortimer Katt," McMillan said, before Jeff could confirm or deny my VP-ness, "you might as well appoint your wife because choosing her uncle isn't going to do you any political favors."

"You're reading me too well, Don. Unfortunately, we have a lot of openings in the Joint Chiefs. I could move Mort there," Jeff suggested hopefully.

"He's not of high enough rank, even though he was just promoted to Lieutenant General," Mom said. "Unfortunately. And neither are any of the military personnel you're used to working with, Jeff."

Serene cleared her throat. "Ah, Jeff? You've just appointed a Chief of Staff and the Director of the CIA. Why don't you take a few moments and have a private discussion with them? And Kitty." She sounded sweet but I could tell she was using her troubadour talent, because all the heads around the table nodded and no one argued that I didn't need to be a part of this little meeting.

"That's a good idea," Jeff said, sounding relieved. He stood and so did Chuckie, Raj, and I.

"Why don't we have Alpha Team along, too?" I suggested, as I slung my purse over my shoulder. White House meeting or not, First Lady or not, by now I'd learned to keep Ol' Trusty with me all the time. "And Richard. They're the people you're the most used to working with."

Jeff nodded. "Fine. Everyone else relax. Antoinette, is food going to be ready soon?"

"Yes, Mister President. In fact, Chef says that it should be ready to be served in five minutes."

"Good. Why don't you escort our guests to whatever dining room we'll be using?"

"What about Thomas?" Culver asked.

"In light of the fact that Kitty's theory is likely to be correct," Chuckie said, "have him and his escorts taken to the dining room, too."

White house staff I didn't know by name yet appeared out of nowhere and, as Antoinette led the way, helped usher everyone out.

"This is a gigantic room that, despite our trusting everyone and all that, could be bugged. Let's go elsewhere." Considered where. "How about the Rose Garden?"

"Works for me." Jeff took my hand, Raj grabbed Chuckie's, Serene took hold of Tim, Gower grabbed Reader, and we headed off, White, Lorraine, and Claudia following. We were in the pretty garden in less than a second. "Now, why do you want to do this so secretly?"

Looked at Serene. "Because I think some of us already have ideas of who you should put where and why."

She smiled. "We do. Jeff, in the downtime we've had, Imageering has done thorough background checks on all of your current cabinet members and those who might be under consideration for posts."

"Really?" Reader sounded surprised. "I didn't give you that order."

"I know, James," Serene said calmly. "You were busy. My team was already in place after helping Kitty to reveal Cliff as the Mastermind. I just had them focus on a wider net."

Knew for a fact that she hadn't really used Imageering, but had used her A-C CIA team. Which I wholeheartedly approved of. "James, just take it as one for the win column and relax. Jeff, you appointed Raj as your Chief of Staff. These recommendations are part of his job."

"Good point." Jeff looked at Raj. "So, what do you recommend?"

Raj grinned. "I thought you'd never ask. Honestly, I was expecting to be the Press Secretary, so I don't have this as thought-out as I would have if I'd realized you were moving me here. However, I do have some suggestions. Charles, if you object to any of these, just speak up."

Chuckie nodded. "Will do."

"Fine. Let's start with the easy ones. Appoint Nathalie Gagnon-Brewer to Secretary of Transportation. That section was run by one of our biggest enemies and so needs someone who will be willing to ferret out all the bad seeds. These people helped murder her husband. She'll find them."

"I can agree with that," Jeff said.

"Next, put Colonel Marvin Hamlin in as the Secretary of Homeland Security."

This earned some shocked looks from everyone other than Serene, me, and White. "I agree." Now the shocked looks were turned toward me. "Look, the dude may be anti-alien, but he's got the goods, and it would be nice to have someone in that role who can't be fooled by the next Mastermind to come along."

"He's been reinstated with full rank and honors," White added. "And is being hailed as a hero by the entire military. If he were of high enough rank, he'd be the man to put into the Joint Chiefs."

"He's not, though," Raj said, "and we need him in this position. He can work his way up, and I believe he'll want to."

"He's far less anti-alien than he was," Serene added. "It's amazing how your feelings change when you see the face of the real enemy."

"He's also up for Brigadier General," Chuckie said. "Jeff, that decision will be yours."

"You don't have to tell me twice, I'll approve it. But that means he won't be able to move into the Cabinet post."

"True enough," Raj said. "We'll circle back on Hamlin, then. The next one will be tricky. But, I believe I have a way around Angela's legitimate concerns. I suggest that you request that Mortimer Katt be made a four-star general."

"That could work," Reader said. "They're nominated by the President, after all."

"It's a double jump in rank, though," Claudia pointed out.

"In less than a week," Lorraine added. "Will that be allowed?"

"We jumped our First Lady up several levels without question way back when," White said with a smile. "I'm certain that Mortimer has the regard of his peers."

"I'm just going to bet that Centaurion Division is a little looser than the Marine Corps." Most of the guys snorted laughs. Ignored them. "But I'm with you, Richard—Uncle Mort being the uncle by marriage to the President is a reason that will probably fly in military circles."

"Then that solves the issue of who the Chairman of the Joint Chiefs will be," Raj went on. "Under the circumstances, I doubt anyone in the Marine Corps is going to argue with this. They'll see it as you having a strong relationship with the Corps, relative by marriage or not."

"What about Hamlin?" Jeff asked. "Can we jump him enough to get him into the Joint Chiefs?"

"No," Chuckie said flatly. "Frankly, I'd bet that, awards or not, he'll be willing to take Homeland Security."

"That's not where he really belongs." Got the group's attention, go me. "Look, if we're asking for what we want and hoping that no one's going to tell us no, then let's put the right people in place everywhere. And if we have to make him give up his military career—again, I might add— then let's give him what I know he wanted all along. Make him the Secretary of Defense."

"Then what happens to Hochberg?" Jeff asked. "Fritzy's done a good job."

"He has, however, he feels like he's failed," Chuckie said. "And that's going to affect him."

"He's trustworthy," Raj went on. "In fact, out of most of the existing Cabinet members still alive, he's probably the most reliable. He was a four-star general in the Army. He's also shown no signs of working against Vince or you, and nothing links him to any anti-alien groups or interests, either."

"So, why are we shoving him off, then?" Jeff sounded frustrated. "You're telling me that my best man needs to go because we have someone else we think we like better?"

"No," Raj said, Troubadour Tones set to Soothe. "I'm saying that I want you to move your best man into another position."

"What would a former military man be better at than Secretary of Defense?" Jeff asked.

Couldn't help it, the Inner Hyena took over. While everyone stared at me—Raj and Serene clearly trying not to laugh as well—got myself under control. "This from the man who used to be in charge of all of Centaurion Division's military? I know where Raj is going with this, and I agree that it makes sense."

"What makes sense?" Jeff asked.

"Making Fritz Hochberg your Vice President."

CHAPTER 9

"**O**H." Jeff was quiet for a moment. "That does make sense, actually. I hadn't considered him because I wanted him to remain in the position he was already in."

Chuckie was looking up into the air. A quick glance confirmed that he wasn't looking at anything—he was thinking. "I like it," he said finally. "You give him a much-needed boost of confidence, and put even more people we can trust into key positions. You earn Hochberg's loyalty and show all of those who aren't your intimates that you'll move the best person for the job up, regardless of existing friendships." He nodded and looked back at Jeff. "I say do it, just be sure that you tell him why you're asking him so late, because that information will matter to him. Greatly."

"That also means Jeff will have made positive moves for Army, Air Force, and Marine Corps personnel. I think we need to look at the Navy for something, anything, just 'cause." Knew suggesting the flyboys all get Cabinet posts was out. Tried not to worry about them and the others who were missing. Failed.

Everyone nodded. "I'll think of someone," Raj said with a grin.

"Super. By the way, have you checked Fritzy out like Raj did, Secret Agent Man?" Hey, just because he seemed good, I didn't want to discover we'd missed something.

Chuckie grinned. "Yeah. After your trip to another world, I investigated him. I investigated Monica Strauss, too, but since she's dead, we have no more worries there. But Hochberg checked out just as Raj said."

"Speaking of Secretary of State, though, that needs to be

someone really good with the diplomacy, and while I'd suggest Richard he already took a job with the Embassy."

White chuckled. "I believe Jeffrey putting his uncle into the position would create the same havoc as him assigning that position to his wife. However, Missus Martini is right—that position is as important as your Vice President."

"Vander," Reader said. "It's a perfect position for him."

Chuckie nodded slowly. "I can agree with that."

"Vander's the one who said I needed higher profile people," Jeff pointed out.

"For VP," Tim said. "But not for the other positions. Though, honestly, I think we need him in Homeland Security, because based on all of this, that's still open."

"It's a much lower Cabinet rank," Jeff said.

"Not after last week it isn't," I pointed out. "Let's face it, we're going to want to focus on our plethora of homegrown terrorists. I think Tim's right—put someone we know has the goods into that position and let him *make* it a higher-ranking post."

"Put him there," Chuckie agreed. "He'll be more likely to agree to it, and Tim and Kitty are both right."

Raj nodded. "I can agree with that as well. Before we look at Secretary of State, though, are you satisfied with the rest of Vince's Cabinet? And we still have slots open in the Joint Chiefs of Staff."

"I'll ask Mort for his recommendations on the Joint Chiefs," Jeff said. "And my answer to the rest of Vince's Cabinet and other assignments is to ask you and Chuck which of them we need to cut loose immediately and which ones we should keep."

"Get rid of Marion Villanova immediately if not sooner."

"I'll do a workup with Mister Reynolds," Raj said.

Chuckie shook his head. "Seriously, why the formality all of a sudden?"

Looked where Raj was. "Oh. Because we're about to have visitors." Elaine and Mom were heading for us, our Secret Service details with them. Shocking no one, the Secret Service agents all had long-suffering expressions.

"Why do you persist in running off without us?" Joseph, the head of Jeff's detail asked when they all reached us.

"We're impetuous." This earned me the "really?" look from every single one of the Secret Service. Chose not to let it harsh my groove. The Secret Service fanned out, Joseph and Evalyne staying nearest to us.

"Sorry to barge in," Elaine said. "But Angela felt you might want my input, so we came under the guise of letting you all know that Thomas Kendrick is here and everyone's eating without you."

Mom nodded. "You're discussing people that Vince might have talked about in private with his wife. It seems prudent to ask Elaine her impressions before you make commitments you can't take back easily."

"Ooh, Mom, love where your head's at." Since I'd honed my Recap Girl skills a lot over the past few years, I brought them up to speed on our suggested nominations.

"Those all sound good to me," Mom said. "Elaine?"

She nodded. "I agree about Fritzy and the others, and also about ensuring that Marion Villanova is no longer around. Monica relied on her—and Monica was a good enough Secretary of State to work for two Presidents—but I've never liked her."

"Proving that you're a woman of taste and refinement."

Tim jerked. "You know, supposedly she was dating Langston Whitmore."

Claudia and Lorraine looked at each other. "If she was, she sure wasn't around when we went to get him to confess on the news," Lorraine said.

"And he never mentioned her," Claudia added. "At all."

"They're both gay and closeted," I reminded everyone. "They're pretending to date each other, and I honestly thought they were going to get married to double down on the charade, but they're clearly not pretending at all in private."

"Okay, great, we know that," Tim said patiently. "But her boss is dead and her 'boyfriend' almost died. So where the hell is *she*?"

"On it," Lorraine said. She and Claudia kicked up the hyperspeed and disappeared. The Secret Service didn't even blink. This should have been flattering to me, but it was just a reminder that my every move was being watched and everyone was focused on ensuring that I'd never see any action ever again. Haters.

"That never stops being . . . odd," Elaine said. "So, while we wait for the Captains to return, I'd like to go over the remaining personnel with Mister Singh and Mister Reynolds. I'm certain we need to remove some others, just in case. Starting with the Secretary of the Treasury, but he won't be the only one."

Jeff groaned quietly. "I'm running out of people I know and trust who can move into these positions."

Elaine patted his arm. "It will be fine, Jeff. You have a strong team. They'll be able to sort things out."

"We need a Secretary of State," Jeff said. "Badly. And as far as I can tell, we have no ideas."

Looked at Mom, who had a look on her face I was familiar with—her I've Practically Spelled It Out For You look. Considered this while Elaine, Raj, and Chuckie started to quickly go over the Cabinet and White House staffers. Elaine knew all of them. And had details on all of them, too, as well as recommendations. Clear, concise, and well-thought-out recommendations.

Cleared my throat and got their attention. "Ah, Elaine, have a couple quick questions."

"Certainly, Kitty. What?"

"What did you do before Vince became the President? For work, I mean."

"Oh, well, I was an attorney. I worked for several large firms and two Fortune Fifty corporations. None of those on your watch list."

"Not where I was going with this, but good to know. You stopped because of Vince's political career?"

"Because of his presidential run, really. He needed my full focus."

"Gotcha, and I can see how that would be." Jeff had certainly needed mine. "What's your undergrad degree in?"

"I had a double major—Urban Planning and Public Affairs with a minor in Public Policy, in addition to Psychology. But it looked like all I'd be able to do was teach, which is why I got my law degree. Why?"

"What colleges?"

"University of Illinois at Chicago for my undergrad degrees, Harvard for law. Again, why?"

"Both of those are good schools." Looked at Mom. "Will it cause a lot of problems?"

She shrugged. "Probably. However, you're all nothing if not unconventional. And it will quell a variety of rumors."

"Like Jeff being the one who had Vince killed? Yeah, I can see that."

Jeff was looking at us, eyes narrowed. "My blocks are up, so all I'm getting is that you're really excited, baby. And that Angela's amused by all of the rest of us being slow on the uptake. And Elaine's confused. Like the rest of us."

"Sorry, let me clear it all up for you. Elaine's your new Secretary of State."

CHAPTER 10

WHILE EVERYONE OTHER than Mom stared at me openmouthed, I took the opportunity to sniff some roses. I mean, why not?

Elaine recovered first. "I, ah, think that would be met with a great deal of . . . resistance."

"Nope," I said as I stopped sniffing. "I can promise you that, right now, Congress is likely to approve pretty much everything Jeff wants."

"Why would you think that?" Chuckie asked. "It seems remarkably naïve."

"I'm not naïve, I'm realistic. And we have a slew of aliens snorking down whatever Chef's prepared that tell me that what Jeff wants, Jeff gets."

"The Planetary Council isn't here to control our government," Jeff protested.

Managed not to roll my eyes. "Of course they are, Jeff. At least, they're here to influence it. They weren't here to kill anyone and force a takeover or anything like that. But they were indeed coming to have a chat with our President and his VP about getting Earth involved in galactic politics. Trust me, that means they have an agenda. And there's not a single politician on the Hill who won't realize that. And there's also not a single one who will want to be seen as working against you. They all remember Operation Destruction."

"True enough," Chuckie said.

"So, they'll let you appoint whoever the hell you want, providing that person isn't clearly an enemy of the state or totally bonkers by D.C. standards, which gives you wide range. They'll wait until the Planetary Council leaves before they start actively working against you. In other words, the moment the Galactic Police are gone, it'll be back to political business as usual."

"Leonidas knows this, even if Alexander doesn't," Chuckie added. "I'd assume he's banking on it."

"Ah, Elaine, do you want the job?" Jeff asked.

She looked at Mom. "That's why you brought me out here?"

Mom shrugged. "So many times, the best man for the job is a woman. Sometimes that woman has been overlooked because she was being a good wife. But right now, the country needs the right leadership. Not people who want it, necessarily, but those who will actually do with the power as they should."

"Senator McMillan always says that you have to do what you know is right, even when you might not want to, unless you can know the hearts and minds of those who would or could take your place."

"Don's a good man. I . . . I'd like to know his opinion on this, before I say yes or no."

"Figured you would." Mom held out her phone. I read the text on it before Elaine did. *Elaine Armstrong is a bold and wonderful choice for Secretary of State. If you can convince her, I can convince Congress.*

Elaine seemed overwhelmed. "If this helps you make your decision, I'd appreciate it if you said yes," Jeff said gently.

She smiled and looked up at him. "It does. Yes, Mister President, thank you, I'll take the position."

Tim's phone beeped. "Glad we have that settled. We need to get through the rest of this, then Chuck, Raj, and Elaine need to go through the entire White House staff pronto. Per Claudia and Lorraine, Marion Villanova has disappeared."

"I'm renaming the Super Group to the Noxious Nine."

"Duly noted," Chuckie said with a laugh.

Reader's phone beeped. "What Tim said. And, per Buchanan, Drax is here."

"Time to keep the party going, apparently." Turned to Elaine as some of the others started off. "Is it too forward of me to ask you to move your stuff into a room you'd prefer here at the White House?"

If getting asked to become the Secretary of State had shocked her, this request of mine definitely took that shock all the way up to eleven. "Ah . . . what?"

Heaved a sigh. "I'm already stressing Antoinette and the rest of the staff out of their minds. And it's only been a week and we aren't moved in yet. I can't imagine what it's going to be like for them by next week, but either they need help or I need help."

Elaine laughed and patted my hand. "Sorry, I already put a deposit down on an apartment at the Cairo, based on Nathalie's suggestion. We're going to be neighbors."

I'd been shocked when Nathalie hadn't moved out of the building where her husband had been murdered. But she'd said that Edmund had loved it there so much that she couldn't bear to leave it. Apparently this was true, and she was starting the Washington Widow's Wing. Sincerely hoped there weren't going to be more residents there any time soon.

"Oh well, it was worth a shot."

"I don't know why you're worried. Your Pierre will solve everything."

"But he's the Embassy's Concierge Majordomo. I can't make him the Chief Usher here. So what role could he have?"

"First Lady's Chief of Staff," she replied without missing a beat. "Or White House Social Secretary. You get your own Press Secretary, too, and you're in charge of the Chief Floral Designer, the Executive Chef, and so on."

"You're kidding."

"No." She smiled. "You have almost as many positions to fill as Jeff does."

"Gee, how lucky can you get?"

"So, go get your man away from that other woman."

Burst out laughing. "I'll definitely have to fight Doreen for him. Especially since I don't have a suggestion for who could replace him." And the Embassy needed Pierre as much as I did. Maybe more than I did—Pierre was not only the most competent man on Earth, he was also the only one in the Embassy not changing roles or having his life upended in some way.

Elaine shrugged. "You'll figure it out, Kitty. I have total faith in you." She squeezed my hand. "Just like you do in me." She kissed my cheek. "Thank you for the vote of confidence. I think this is what Vince would have wanted."

"I'm sure of it."

Everyone else started off now, Elaine and Jeff discussing something extremely political that I decided I didn't need to know about.

Noted Serene and Mom, mostly because they weren't going inside and, in fact, weren't even facing the way the others were—they were looking off in the distance. Looked where they were as I went to join them.

There was someone coming toward us from the South Lawn. Due to what had just gone on, any White House tours had been suspended until the government was back in order. So all tourists and visitors were supposed to be kept out. Yet there was a woman getting nearer.

As I reached Mom and Serene I realized a couple of things. The woman coming toward us looked like me and she was wearing a pink linen suit. I'd owned a suit like that, six years ago. A suit exactly like it, in fact. And I'd been wearing that suit when my first superbeing formed in front of me and Operation Fugly started. And she, in point of fact, didn't just look like me —she looked *just* like me.

Of course, memory shared that we'd discovered someone else wearing the exact same outfit during Operation Fugly—the robot who'd been with Ronald Yates, presumably to be put into action to kill my mother once I was dead. And my mother was here, and that meant that I had a really good guess for who the Kitty-Bot was aiming for. My mother was dead in Bizarro World, and I'd thought she was going to die here during Operation Epidemic. Mom was not getting killed on my watch, especially not due to something made to look like me.

Despite all that had happened, I'd kind of forgotten about my personal robot or android or whatever she actually was, probably because I'd only seen "me" in a picture and the robot had never been seen again.

But there "I" was right now, striding along, making a beeline for the Rose Garden.

"You seeing what I'm seeing?" I asked Mom as I rummaged around in my purse.

"I am. You know, I'd forgotten about this, don't ask me why."

"Was just berating myself for the same forgetfulness, Mom."

"It's a good copy. That suit's as bedraggled as I always remember it being when you wore it."

"You're hilarious, Mom. Serene?" Found my iPod. In this situation I didn't want to risk my phone. Plugged in my earbuds.

"Yes, Kitty?"

"Go get Chuckie, as fast as possible, and ensure that no one allows Jeff or anyone else politically important out of the White House. Whatever that Kitty-Bot has in mind, I can guarantee it isn't good, and Chuckie's the only one who knows how to deactivate these things before they go boom." Of course, I knew how to deactivate them in a different way.

"Ah, what are you going to be doing, Kitty?" Serene asked, though, to her credit, I could see she was poised to run.

Because I was enhanced from the mother-and-child feedback that had happened when Jamie was born—since Jeff had been altered by the Surcenthumain, aka the Superpowers Drug, that our enemies had snuck into him, Jamie had been altered, too—I was kind of an A-C now. No double hearts, but all the other bells and whistles.

So I definitely had the hyperspeed and the super strength. I knew what the Kitty-Bot had been programmed to do before, and I doubted anyone had altered her programming all that much now.

Clipped my iPod to the waist of my skirt, put in my ear buds, dropped my purse, selected my I Still Got It playlist, and hit play. I was in my FLOTUS colors, meaning an iced blue suit, cream blouse, and sensible cream pumps. Kicked off my sensible pumps. The FLOTUS clothes would just have to adapt or die.

"I'm going to be kicking android or robot, depending, butt." Then I took off, straight for the android version of me, with Rachel Platten's "Fight Song" in my ears.

CHAPTER 11

THE KITTY-BOT SAW ME coming, stopped striding with purpose, then started running right for me. In her pumps. So she wasn't really programmed to be me, which was something of a relief.

Figured the Secret Service would be planning to get involved, which meant I needed to get the Kitty-Bot away from the Rose Garden and back into the middle of the South Lawn, so when she exploded the blast wouldn't hurt anyone.

We were running at each other like we were jousting, only without horses and lances. So, okay, maybe not just like jousting, but along similar lines. Didn't have a lot of time to do math, but either she wasn't trying as hard or I was faster, because I'd judged where we should have met and we were farther from the Rose Garden than I'd figured we'd be. One for the win column.

I'd fought androids during Operations Assassination and Destruction, and I remembered how hard they could hit. But much of their abilities depended upon which android model they were. And, based on time alone, the Kitty-Bot was, hopefully, an older, less advanced model.

Of course I didn't want to just slam into the Kitty-Bot. When I was close enough I launched myself into a tackle. Got her around the waist and we flew backward, for her, forward for me. Realized why football players preferred to do this kind of work in padding, but forged on and did my best to channel rugby players and mixed martial arts fighters.

We went down with me on top. She didn't tuck her head, but said head hitting the ground didn't even make her blink.

She didn't feel as hard as either Bryce Taylor or Leslie Manning had. She didn't feel like Sandra the Android, either. I hadn't fought with either John Butler or Cameron Maurer—though Maurer had held me up in the air with one hand when he was choking me—so I couldn't compare her to them. But, in my limited experience, she didn't hurt to hit nearly as badly as the other androids had.

She smelled of pine, which was a really weird perfume to go with, but who was I to question android perfume choices? Perhaps she'd gotten the special scented oils at her last tune-up.

"What are you doing?" the Kitty-Bot shouted as she hit at me. She sounded like me. How extra-special. She hit hard, but not as hard as I was used to. We rolled around, though I was able to ensure that we rolled away from the Rose Garden. Was also fairly sure that my skirt had ripped.

"Stopping you from whatever you're planning." Roll, hit, roll, hit. Heart's "Kick It Out" came on my airwaves. At least my iPod and earbuds were hanging tough. Did my best to kick while we rolled, but I miscalculated and the Kitty-Bot rolled so she was on top of me and got me pinned.

She started to hit me, but I'd been in this situation before and didn't even need Tito to shout instructions. Got my arms up over my head so she was only hitting my forearms. Hit her hard with a knee to her back and she went forward. Used my pelvis to throw her off, shoved hard at her with my hands while she was moving, then leaped up from the ground to my feet, just like they did in the movies: from my back, no hands. Really and truly hoped someone, anyone, was witness to this—the skills were working exceptionally well, and that usually meant no one I wanted to impress was around to see them. The fact that I heard my suit jacket rip was irrelevant to the coolness of the move.

Got out of my wrecked jacket, then grabbed her with the intent to try to rip one of her arms off. Didn't work, mostly because she pulled out of my hold.

"Get your hands off me. I have a message for the President."

"You can share it with me. I'll make sure he gets it." Slammed a front ball kick into her midsection. My skirt definitely ripped on that one.

She staggered back a couple steps. She might not have

been as hard as the other androids, but she was still more painful to hit than any human or alien, and I *had* hit a lot of those over the past years.

Went for the tackle again. She wasn't really ready to block it, meaning I was able to grab her. But this time I wasn't able to bring her to the ground, so we were grappling while standing up and sort of flinging each other around without letting go.

She threw me off of her. I didn't go sailing, like I had with other androids. So either the Kitty-Bot wasn't trying all that hard, or I was right—she was an older model. For all I knew, she wasn't really an android, just a robot, though I'd look to Chuckie and Serene for the distinction, if there even was one.

Landed in a crouch that would have made every kung fu instructor I'd ever had glow with pride and claim to be the one who'd taught me to do it. The Kitty-Bot, meanwhile, spun and headed back toward the Rose Garden. Interesting. The mission appeared to be all for her. Of course, Mom, my Secret Service detail, Serene, Chuckie, Reader, Tim, and Tito were all here, between her and the Rose Garden, so maybe she was just going to try to blow up the maximum number of participants.

Launched myself at her and caught her from behind this time. We went to the ground again. This time, though, I wasn't going to allow her to get into a better position. Grabbed her head and put it into a lock.

Before I could decide if I was willing to pull her head off or not, Chuckie ran up with a pen. I'd have made a smartass comment but we'd learned that pens fit into the android ears and were able to hit the off switch.

He jammed the pen into her ear. Nothing happened.

"What are you doing?" she shouted. "That hurts!" She managed to pull the pen out.

Chuckie looked confused. "I know I hit the right spot."

"Dude, I have nothing for you other than that the Kitty-Bot is still fighting me and I'm going to have to rip her head off unless you come up with something else."

"I have a message for the President," she shouted. "Stop trying to stop me! I'm the wife of the Vice President and I need to get inside."

As she said this she managed to get out of my necklock

and bucked, tossing me into Chuckie. He didn't go down and steadied both of us, but the Kitty-Bot was heading for the others.

Mom stepped out in front and my stomach clenched. "Who am I?" she asked the Kitty-Bot.

"An enemy of the state." The Kitty-Bot pointed her left arm at Mom, like it was a gun.

At that, my Secret Service detail converged on the Kitty-Bot as one. She went down under a dogpile of sturdy, serviceable suits. There were six of them, four of them men, and she'd had trouble with just me.

Sure enough, they subdued the Kitty-Bot. "Go team." Tried to go over to the others but Chuckie kept a firm hold on me. He also gently pulled my earbuds out, right in the middle of Social Distortion's "Don't Drag Me Down."

"Love how you told Serene to keep everyone politically important inside and yet you charged the android."

"She's impersonating *me*. Did we ever tell you about her?"

"No, you didn't." Chuckie didn't sound happy about this.

Filled him in fast on the whats and wherefores, as few of them as we had. "So, I think she's here to kill Mom."

"I think she's here to kill the President. She wasn't trying to kill you. But if she's really an older model, that might explain why the off switch isn't in the same place on her as it is on the other androids."

"If she is an android. She seems far less . . . realistic then they all were and are."

The Secret Service had the Kitty-Bot standing up and her hands were cuffed behind her. She looked roughed up, which wasn't surprising. But she didn't look upset. Realized she'd kept the same expression on her face the entire time—determined concern.

"Robots and androids are pretty close, Kitty."

"But they're not the same. And the Kitty-Bot seems much more like a robot."

Reader came over to us. Chuckie didn't release his hold on me, and Reader didn't seem to disapprove. "Yates was into robotics, but most of those connections were into Titan. Though not all."

"I need to speak to the President," the Kitty-Bot said. "I have an urgent message for him."

"You're going to tell it to me," Mom said, voice radiating authority.

"You are an enemy of the state. All enemies of the state must be destroyed. I can only share my information with the President."

"That's it." I wrenched out of Chuckie's hold and slipped past Reader. "It's head ripping time." Got in front of Mom. "Who the hell am I?"

The Kitty-Bot didn't blink. "An enemy of the state."

My brain nudged. She'd said something when I was fighting her and talking to Chuckie. And if she was a robot, versus an android, that meant her programming was far less sophisticated. "Who *is* the President?"

"The President of the United States."

"Right, we're outside his house, we're clear on which President you want. What's his *name*? We can't let you through to see the President unless you can properly identify him."

The Kitty-Bot blinked. Clearly I'd said something that registered. "I'm the wife of the Vice President and I have an urgent message for President Vincent Armstrong."

CHAPTER 12

EVERYONE GAPED AT HER, other than Chuckie and Reader, who'd joined us. "We'll discuss your throwing yourself in front of danger later," Chuckie said, in a tone that indicated he was talking to everyone else more than he was talking to me. "Kitty, your thoughts?"

Waited. The Kitty-Bot didn't speak. "I think that Antony Marling did far better work, that's what I think."

"If this is the same thing we saw six years ago with Ronald Yates at the Pueblo Caliente courthouse, then she's not only older, but she was created for one reason only, and that was to blow up," Reader pointed out.

"But to blow up a specific person. And apparently that person is no longer my mother."

Mom stepped up next to me. "Thanks for the protective shield, kitten." She studied the Kitty-Bot. "It's good enough to fool for a few seconds, and that's all a recognition bomb needs."

"Recognition as in it's triggered by seeing the person targeted?"

"Yes." Mom's eyes narrowed. "So I'm clearly not the target. It's had plenty of time to register me, you, all of us here. We're all close enough that we'd be killed by almost any conventional bomb. So none of us is the target."

"No, Vince is." Thought about that. "So," I said to the Kitty-Bot, "is your message also for the Vice President, your husband?"

She cocked her head at me. "The Vice President should be in the room with the President when I share my urgent message."

"Gotcha. Anyone else?" I asked nicely, while I ignored the many WTF looks I was getting from everyone other than, interestingly enough, Tito.

"No," the Kitty-Bot said. "My message is for the two of them only."

"Who am I?" Tito asked nicely.

The Kitty-Bot swiveled her head toward him in a very non-human and also non-android way. She stared at him. "I don't know."

"Well, I'm your friend," Tito said. "I'm here to help you achieve your mission. So are many of these others."

She looked at all of us. "Those two are enemies of the state," she said, looking at me and Mom.

"We have them contained, so they can't stop you. Where's your off switch?" Tito asked.

"What do you mean?"

"The President and Vice President aren't here," Tito said, still keeping his tone pleasant and friendly. "We're here to assist you. And we're thinking you might need to rest, while we find them. So, you might want to power down. But if you do, we want to be able to turn you back on, wake you up, at the right time."

"Oh." The Kitty-Bot blinked slowly. "When will they be back?"

"We don't know," Tito said. "And you look like you've come a long way to deliver your message."

At this both Reader and Chuckie looked at the Kitty-Bot more closely. "Take a sniff," I said to them. "Tito's right, I think."

"I have," the Kitty-Bot said to Tito. "The President was not where he was supposed to be. I had to locate him."

"You walked the whole way?" Tito asked.

"Yes, sixty-nine-point-five miles."

Chuckie jerked. "She smells like pine. And that's exactly how far it is to Camp David from the White House via conventional means."

"You mean via highways and such."

Tito nodded. "You stayed on the roads?" he asked the Kitty-Bot.

"Near them. I . . . don't know the area very well."

"Meaning she wasn't programmed for this, necessarily,"

Reader said. "She's just clear enough on her goal that she's adapted and gone to the next most obvious place."

"Serene, we need to contain the Kitty-Bot in some way, and you're going to have to be the one in charge of that." The Kitty-Bot's head swiveled back toward me. "Serene can help you rest correctly."

"I'm not supposed to rest until I deliver my urgent message to the President."

"Yeah, but he's not here. We don't know where he is. No one does. So, you should plan to wait a while."

"Can you tell us how to help you power down?" Tito asked. "That way you won't be worn out when it's time to deliver your message."

"That . . . makes sense." The Kitty-Bot seemed to reach a decision. "If you are really here to help me, tell me what my message is."

We were all quiet. Thought about what the actual message would be. It would be short, because Jeff was an A-C and therefore no one who knew that would program any robot for a lengthy monologue. Doubted anyone else had a better guess, other than maybe Tim. This was, after all, my area of expertise.

"Your message is: Goodbye."

The Kitty-Bot blinked. "That is correct." Her head swiveled back to Tito. "My system controls are in my lower back. All items should be clearly labeled."

"Can you turn yourself on and off?" Tito asked, sounding concerned.

"No," she said slowly. "I don't think so."

He nodded. "Don't worry, we'll make sure you're woken up when it's time to deliver your message."

She nodded and Tito went to her back. He fiddled around, Chuckie and Reader watching him. "Huh, it's very clearly marked. Goodnight," he said to the Kitty-Bot, still nicely. Then he flipped whatever switch and she went still and "dead." She looked like C-3PO did when he powered down. There but not there.

"Well, this is going to give me all the nightmares I'll ever need. Let's get her somewhere safe."

Serene was on her phone, and I saw a floater gate shimmer into existence nearby. Four Field teams arrived, along with six Dazzlers and a stretcher. "This one needs to go into a strong containment chamber," Serene said. "We have no idea how it's armed or what will trigger it, but it's turned off right now."

The Kitty-Bot was removed. The icky feeling didn't leave me when she did. Always the way and totally par for my personal course.

"How did the two of you know what to do and say?" Tim asked. "I seriously had no real guesses. And I'm kind of shocked that Chuck didn't get there first."

"Chuckie was dealing with keeping me from getting killed, and you weren't on the team when we first saw the Kitty-Bot."

"Neither was Tito, and he was hired on a lot later," Tim pointed out.

Tito shrugged. "It's clearly not an advanced android. The sentience level wasn't there, let alone the facial expressions, and, in fact, she wasn't even able to identify that she was a copy of Kitty. That indicates relatively simple programming."

"Meaning that if we found the right trigger phrases . . ." I shrugged. "We're just good at guessing, go us."

"How did you know the message?" Mom asked.

"Because whoever found and set up the Kitty-Bot knows that the 'Vice President' is an A-C, meaning he can move fast enough to escape the blast. So two syllables would be it, max."

"That seems less . . . baroque . . . than Cliff would have managed," Chuckie said.

"Which is part of the reason why I'm kind of sure it's not Cliff or any of his immediate cronies behind this. I don't think Drax is behind it, either, or anyone from our favorite Corporations of Evil."

Got the crowd's attention, go me. "Who do you think *is* behind it?" Mom asked.

"Someone too dead to make alterations."

CHAPTER 13

EVERYONE STARED AT ME. "Excuse me?" Chuckie asked finally.

Heaved a sigh. "Look, we're forgetting something really key." More blank stares. "Why are we no longer interested in whatever Monica Strauss had going on?"

"Because she's dead," Reader said as if this was obvious, which, in that sense, it was.

"Right. But Other Me didn't trust her at all, and Elaine Armstrong didn't, either, from what she said."

"But Monica Strauss *is* dead," Serene said.

"Yes, but that doesn't mean that she's not the one who put the Kitty-Bot into action."

There was silence. "I think I speak for everyone," Tim said finally, "when I say that I have no idea what you're getting at."

Always the way. "I'll just pretend you're all still in shock about there being another me around. Again. Okay, so, let's pretend that all that happened this past week didn't. The Mastermind didn't roll his Doomsday Plan, no one died, and it's business as usual. In fact, let's pretend that it *is* a week ago. We don't know that Stephanie's trying out for a recurring role on a CW series based on DC Comics characters. We don't know that Drax exists. NASA Base isn't in jeopardy. It's Washington Business As Usual."

"Okay," Serene said slowly. "And?"

"And . . . Strauss was a political animal. She wanted to be the President. She was our first suspect when Operation Epidemic started going beyond weird. Maybe she also wanted to be or was an Apprentice."

"So?" Chuckie asked, sounding as if the wheels were turning but definitely needed more oil to run smoothly.

"So, what plan did Straus have in play a week or so ago? Or, more importantly, what meeting was Armstrong supposed to be having at Camp David in the past few days?"

Mom jerked. "Peace accords. There are issues in the Middle East, you know, as there always are. The Israeli Prime Minister and the President of Iraq were supposed to be here to try to work things out. That was canceled the moment the President's train was attacked and is supposed to be rescheduled, now, once Jeff feels confident he can preside."

"Was Jeff supposed to be there, too, for these talks?" Because if so he hadn't mentioned it to me.

"Yes, but he'd insisted that he wasn't going to bring his family and would be spending each night at home. As the Vice President and the father of two small children, that was approved, and the gates make it safe and easy to achieve. Mostly we didn't want Charlie to create . . . issues, and no one was naïve enough to think that if Jeff was going to be sleeping there that you and the children would just stay home and behave."

"I'll be insulted for our family later, Mom."

"Not an insult, kitten. We just all know you."

"Blah, blah, blah. So, anyway, was Strauss supposed to be there?"

"No," Mom said. "She was supposed to be in D.C. to keep things running. I'd have been there, though."

"And we have a perfect little plan. 'I' show up with an urgent message. There is no way in the world Jeff wouldn't insist on my being let in, and you'd support it, too, Mom. Then the wife of the Vice President, aka an alien, and the daughter of the Head of the P.T.C.U. blows up the President, VP, and the visiting dignitaries. Strauss takes over and gets rid of the A-Cs, or has them so on the run that they have to do whatever she wants in order to keep from being deported or put into concentration camps."

"But you would be alive to prove that it wasn't you who did it," Tim pointed out.

"Yes, presuming she didn't have assassins in play to kill me or similar."

"And we should never assume that," Chuckie said. "Even with the protections you've . . . had."

"Yeah." Did my best not to think about what had happened to those protections. "But I'd be so busy scrambling while my husband and mother had just been murdered that, let's face it, I'd be out of control and so would the rest of us."

Reader nodded. "I can easily see you saying something that would have gotten us all in trouble, and I'm not trying to be mean."

"No, I agree with you. Plus, whenever this plan was put into effect, Cliff was still running things. But I don't think he had a real hand in this."

"Why not?" Tim asked.

"Because it's counter to what he wanted," Chuckie replied. "I think it's safe to go with the idea that Strauss was vying to become the Mastermind."

"I agree, Secret Agent Man. I think she might have been in the Apprentice Tryouts, but this says 'I'm done listening to you.'"

"So, now what?" Evalyne asked. "Do we assume it's all over? Or do we assume there are more attacks put in motion by a dead woman?"

"Never assume it's over, that's my motto." Heaved a sigh. "But this part of it is over for now and, before you all get in line to bawl me out, save it for later. I know I need to change clothes and probably shower. But first I need to race to the Embassy and be sure my children aren't being kidnapped by a robot that looks like me."

"Stay here," Mom said. "I contacted the Embassy while you were having your little rumble. Everyone's fine, the Embassy and the children are secure, and everyone's on high alert. Missy is monitoring for 'you' coming into the Embassy any way other than via gate or a presidential cavalcade. The Embassy is in lockdown other than for gate traffic. She'll alert every authority known to God if 'you're' seen coming in from the streets. And that goes for everyone else who might be a duplicate. Right now, we're only to access the Embassy via gates or advise Missy otherwise."

"Okay and thanks for being a good grandma, Mom. Clothing change time it is."

Serene was looking at her phone. "I'll go with you, Kitty, to help you change."

"So will we," Evalyne said.

"No. Look, I'll be inside the freaking White House and, unless there's another Kitty-Bot in there, I just want to change and pretend we're normal people. Serene is the Head of Imageering—I'll be fine."

"Fine," Mom said with a sigh. "This ended far better than I'd thought it would. Let's get back inside and get back on track, since we have Drax and Kendrick both to deal with."

"Yeah, please reassure Jeff that I'm fine and just want to change and all that."

Chuckie nodded. "We'll try, but I doubt he'll take our words for it."

"Oh, distract him by filling him in on all the new fun."

Grabbed my discarded shoes and purse, then we all trotted inside and Serene and I went off for the room Jeff and I had been sleeping in.

It wasn't the room we'd actually be living in—we'd had our things put into a guest room this morning, because we didn't want to rush Elaine out. But it gave me someplace to go.

Fortunately, Serene knew where the room was. I wasn't comfortable finding my way around here yet, and since I wasn't going to be living in this room for the next years, I hadn't worried about memorizing its location.

We got inside and headed into my closet. "Okay, what's going on?" I asked her quietly while I stripped off my totally wrecked FLOTUS clothes and put my iPod and earbuds carefully back into my purse.

"I heard from Lorraine and Claudia. And they texted me, not Tim or James, because they want us, you and me, to join them." Serene showed me her phone. There was a picture of what I presumed was Marion Villanova's apartment.

The apartment was, to put it nicely, completely trashed.

"This looks like a job for the police," I said. "Not us."

"Lorraine and Claudia insist that they feel something's wrong and want us there," Serene said. Stared at the pictures as Serene scrolled through. Every room in Villanova's apartment was ransacked. And yet, the girls were right—something looked wrong.

"It's too staged," I said finally. "That's what's bothering the girls, I think. But it also means we'll be going to an active crime scene, and the girls are already at one."

Serene chuckled and texted something. Another picture appeared. Two sets of hands in plastic gloves. "I instituted a policy that all Field agents must carry evidence gloves with them over a year ago," Serene said. "I have enough with me to cover us, as well."

"You rock. Think we can do it fast? They're only going to give me so much time before someone comes asking why it's taking me so long to get back downstairs."

"I just sent James a message saying that I'm having you shower, possibly even take a bath, to calm you down and all that. That gives us a little more time. Hyperspeed will handle the rest."

"Even getting out of our carefully guarded doors?"

She grinned. "I understand there are tunnels and lots and lots of secret ways in and out. We don't actually have to hit a tunnel—we're just going to use the deliveries entrance."

Contemplated what to wear. Comfort and the realistic thought that I'd be far less easily spotted if I wasn't dressed as the First Lady won the day. Dressed at hyperspeed. Back to normal—jeans, Converse, and a t-shirt—in a couple of seconds, with no clothing accidents. One definitely for the win column.

To help with anonymity, I didn't choose a band shirt, even though not rolling with Aerosmith on my chest seemed like a bad omen. There was a plain black t-shirt in the closet, and I chose that.

Whether this was something that I'd brought over with me was a mystery. At the Embassy and all other A-C facilities, the Operations Team, aka the Elves, handled all things like this. Of course, I and a miniscule select few knew that there was no "team" or elves plural. There was one being—a Black Hole Universe being on the run for crimes against protecting the younger races, with the biggest hard-on for Free Will ever.

Whether or not Algar was going to take over the housekeeping and dry cleaning duties for the White House was unclear, and I hadn't had a lot of time to ask him. And now was definitely not the time, since Serene wasn't in Algar's Tiny Inner Circle.

Made sure I had all I could possibly need in my purse, my Glock and several clips included, then put my purse over my neck and I was ready to go.

Serene grabbed my hand and we took off, zipping

through the White House, down stairs, past a lot of humans, but no A-Cs. We had to do some backtracking and avoidance to be sure that we weren't seen by an A-C, since they could see us at hyperspeed. But we managed it, and were outside and off the White House grounds in less than a minute.

Hyperspeed being what it was, it took us only a few seconds to reach Georgetown and the building where Villanova lived. Serene steered us into an alleyway near it, though, where we were hidden. "I want to let them know to open the door for us so we aren't seen," she said.

Took a cautious look around while she did so. Didn't see anything out of the ordinary for the area. Due to the university, Georgetown had a high student population, but it also had its share of young professionals and D.C. movers and shakers. I tried to spot anything amiss, but everything looked as it should.

"Ready." Serene and I put on our plastic evidence gloves, and she grabbed me again. We zipped into the building and up the stairs, to where the next of the day's strange events awaited.

CHAPTER 14

THE GIRLS WERE WAITING FOR US, so we got inside Villanova's apartment without having to stop.

"Interesting fact number one," Lorraine said without preamble, "is that this is the same building that Langston Whitmore lives in."

"He's not here," Claudia said. "He's still in the hospital, recovering. We checked his apartment, though, and nothing's disturbed from when we were there a few days ago."

"Okay." Looked around and stepped through the mess carefully while Serene gave Lorraine and Claudia the recap of what had happened while they were here. She did it at hyperspeed, meaning I pulled out my phone and earbuds and put music on immediately. Hyperspeed speech made most humans physically ill to hear, and I didn't need to leave DNA evidence here.

Hit random play and, with the sounds of Miss Li's "Come Over to My Place" protecting me from nausea and my phone in my back pocket, I examined the place.

It was a small apartment, all things considered. You entered into the living room with a small dining room to your right that connected to the kitchen, which connected to another room that looked to be Villanova's home office. That room and the living room connected to a small hall, where one found the guest bathroom and the quite spacious bedroom, which had its own full bathroom attached.

Everything that could be on the floor appeared to be. And yet, I could step through it fairly well, without stepping onto anything. There was a path, and it was easy enough to spot.

"What's wrong with this scene?" I asked as Serene finished and I lowered my volume so I could hear them talking clearly. I'd gotten the A-C enhanced hearing, too, and because I wanted music at any and all times, I'd ensured that I could listen to it and hear the sounds of approaching danger at the same time. "Aside from the ransacked version of the yellow brick road?" Fittingly, Elton John's "Goodbye Yellow Brick Road" came on my personal airwaves.

"It's staged," Claudia replied. "I'm sure you could see that when you looked at the pictures we sent over." Serene and I both nodded.

"Nothing's broken," Lorraine said. "That's what's bothering you. In addition to the path, I mean. This was carefully done."

"Huh. So, that begs the very obvious question of why did someone bother?"

"Why do you think?" Serene asked. "And I mean you, Kitty. As in, what's your gut reaction?"

My Megalomaniac Girl cape was already on. Took the leap. "I think Villanova did this herself. That's why nothing's broken and why there's an easy enough path to follow. She didn't want to trash her stuff and she didn't want to step on any of it, either, presumably to ensure she didn't leave a footprint somehow."

"I agree," Serene said. "So the next question is, why did she do this?"

"She's either running to Cliff or she's running away," Lorraine suggested.

"Or she's running to someone else," Claudia said. "There are plenty of options."

"And not just Drax or Kendrick," Lorraine said. "We checked with the agents who picked Kendrick up, by the way, and there was no sign of Villanova at Titan."

"Okay," I said as I worked my way through the apartment, "Illegal Search" by LL Cool J providing accurate background tunes. "So, running to Cliff seems like an easy choice." Went into the kitchen and opened the fridge. It wasn't empty but it wasn't full, either. Jeff was an old TV shows junkie, and I liked mystery shows a lot. There was milk and I looked at the expiration date. "Or not."

"What have you found?" Claudia asked.

Opened the milk to be sure and slammed the top right

back on as fast as I could. Hyperspeed for the win. "This milk is two weeks out of code and smells it." Dug through the rest of the fridge. Much food was rotting or out of code.

Checked out the freezer. It was empty other than four filled ice cube trays.

"So, she took off well before Operation Epidemic started. Meaning we have to ask ourselves why. And we also have to ask if she was involved in what Monica Strauss was planning, as in, is she part of Utilize the Kitty-Bot?"

"No idea," Lorraine said. "There are no computers or notebooks with information around. There's no incriminating evidence at all, other than this mess."

"Though I'd bet on yes," Claudia said.

Closed the freezer and looked around as my music changed to "Mary Jane's Last Dance" by Tom Petty and the Heartbreakers. "Why trash her apartment? She must be expecting the police to drop by. But why?"

"Because she's disappeared?" Serene asked.

There was a paper shredder in the office that connected to the kitchen. Went to that and opened it up. Lots of shredded things were in it. "Hold that thought. Need a trash bag."

One was found and produced and we emptied the shredder's contents into it. Handed that to Lorraine. "Enjoy the puzzle."

She had her mouth open, probably to provide a witty comeback, when we all heard a noise and froze. It was the sound of the door being unlocked.

We closed the door that connected the kitchen to the office, but not tightly, so we could see through it. Got it closed just as the outer door opened.

Fortunately, we were all trained operatives, because the fact that we all didn't gasp was impressive.

Christopher stepped inside, closing and locking the door behind him.

CHAPTER 15

CHRISTOPHER LOOKED AROUND. "Come out, come out, wherever you are." We didn't move. He rolled his eyes. "Kitty, Jeff told me to come over and find out what you all were up to."

Opened the door. "Oh. So you're not an evil bad guy? Crushing news. We were about to really have to question whether we'd gotten the right Mastermind and all that."

"Hilarious. Look, your husband is aware of what you're doing because he knows you. I'm here to ensure that when something goes wrong, you have backup. And before the three of you on Alpha Team try to add words to the glares you're all shooting at me, there's no one who can get you guys out of here and *to* a good alibi faster than me. But it's nice to see that you're taking out the trash for the apartment's resident. That's thoughtful breaking and entering."

"Oh, fine, good point." While Lifehouse crooned "Wrecking Ball" in the background, brought Christopher quickly up to speed, including why we had the Bag of Shredded Possibly Information, while Serene gave him evidence gloves and he put them on and Claudia wiped down the door and anywhere else he might have touched on this floor.

Once all that was done, he zipped through the apartment, checking everywhere while "Story of My Life" by Smash Mouth started.

"Okay, everything's on the floor," he said as he rejoined us approximately five seconds later. "No idea why she did that, but there's nothing in any drawer, cabinet, or closet. It's all on the floors. I checked under the bed, though, and there's nothing there but some dust."

"Other than the kitchen," Lorraine said. "It's kind of trashed, but the only things dumped out and around aren't breakable."

"Yeah, there's nothing broken anywhere," Claudia added.

"Nothing," Christopher agreed. "So obviously this is staged."

"Yeah, as I mentioned already. We're at the 'why do this' part of the festivities."

"Why leave the shredder full?" Serene asked. "She dumped everything else."

"Who knows?" Christopher shrugged. "But since she clearly had time to throw away whatever was in there, I think it's unlikely that it's going to be of interest to us."

My brain nudged. Cop shows were very clear on a certain point.

Went back to the freezer, put the stopper in the sink, and dumped the ice cubes out. Ran warm water over them.

"What are you doing?" Christopher asked.

"She could have something hidden in these."

"Who hides things in ice cubes?"

"You need to catch up on pop culture." Pulled something out of the water. "Fast."

The girls took a look. "That looks like a diamond," Claudia said.

"It is a diamond." Searched through the rest of the sink. Found three more diamonds. "So, one diamond per ice cube tray, presumably. Interesting." Filled the trays back up and put them into the freezer.

"Why are you doing that?" Christopher asked.

"Because no one does all this—trash their own place then take off—while leaving diamonds in their ice," Lorraine said.

"So Kitty's making ice so whoever's supposed to get those diamonds doesn't think someone else has them," Claudia added. "Oh, and duh."

"Whatever," Christopher muttered.

"If I were going on the run, I'd sure as hell take my loose diamonds with me. That she didn't indicates they're here as a payment for someone. Either to do something or to not do something."

"Assassins?" Claudia suggested.

"I don't think so. I mean it's very possible, but it seems a little . . . complex." Felt another pang. A week ago I'd have asked Siler or Buchanan to contact the Dingo and Surly Vic and just asked them. But a week ago they'd been alive. Right up until they'd both sacrificed themselves to save me. Their last act of protection.

Serene put her arm around my shoulders. "We can ask Benjamin about it," she said gently.

Leaned my head against hers. "I miss them."

"I do, too. I didn't know them as well as you, but we did . . . interact. Now and then."

Presumed this was when the A-C CIA had either crossed into the Dingo's territory or had needed his help. He'd liked Serene, and I was sure that he'd known what she was up to far longer than I had.

Swallowed hard and pushed the sorrow away. Now wasn't the time to mourn. Now was the time to think, and if I could add thinking like the Dingo and Surly Vic to my repertoire, so much the better for me and mine.

As "Assassin" by John Mayer came on, I gave it a shot. "Could be for an assassin to kill me so I'm not around to say that the Kitty-Bot isn't really me. But if that's the case, he or she is late and working really cheap, because these diamonds can't be worth all that much, and anyway, Villanova has to know that Strauss is dead."

"Are you sure those are real diamonds?" Christopher asked.

"I have an uncle who's a jeweler. Yes, I'm sure."

"Just verifying, no need to be snippy."

"I'm not the one who pulled you away from Amy and the baby, stop snarling at me."

"Sorry." His voice was softer. "Jeff wants you back at the White House as fast as possible, you know, Kitty."

"I know." Stared at the diamonds in my hand. "These are nice but . . ."

"But what?" Serene asked.

"But they're not huge and they're not uncut. I'm wondering if they're actually from jewelry that Villanova owns herself."

Lorraine zipped off and was back quickly. "I found this in the rubble." She had what looked like an engagement ring without the stone in her palm.

"That would account for one of the stones, but not the others."

"This was the only thing that was missing a stone that I could find."

"I could search again," Claudia offered.

"No . . . you know, Strauss is dead, but clearly what she was planning isn't."

"We have the, as you call it, Kitty-Bot at Dulce," Serene said. "That plan was clearly rolling."

"Right. So, is her loyal assistant who is definitely not on the side of right continuing the plan on her lonesome? As in, are these other three diamonds from Strauss' personal collection?"

"We can only find that by breaking into her home and checking," Christopher said. "Which I'm sure you'll have us do shortly, but you cannot be involved in that. You have a couple minutes more here, and then I have to get you back to the White House."

"That's fine. Hang on, though. Don't talk, not for a second or two." Had to get all the questions rushing into my mind into a semblance of order. Closed my eyes. It helped somewhat. "Dream On" by Aerosmith helped more. Because I had one overriding issue. "The milk."

"Excuse me, what?" Christopher asked. "Sorry to speak out of turn, try to forgive me."

"It'll be hard, but I'll give it a shot." I thought better running my yap, after all. "The milk has been out of code for much longer than we've known that crap was going down. The empty freezer indicates that Villanova wasn't planning on being around for a good long while, so she cleared her freezer out. Veggies and such can rot quickly, and everything else in the fridge looked random, as in, bought at one time or another, but none of it being bad or not is an issue—we all have veggies that have gone bad because we forgot about them, and we all have ancient bottles of something or other shoved into the back of the fridge."

"Not all of us," Christopher said.

"Don't even try to make me believe you cook, dude. And yeah, yeah, the Elves handle all things for the A-Cs. However, I'm talking humans. Regardless, milk tends to be on the money in terms of when it goes bad. And every shopper checks the expiration date—unless it's the last quart in the market, no one buys milk that's going out of code the next day."

"What does it prove?" Lorraine asked.

"That whatever's going on with Villanova has nothing to do with what just went on with all of us this past week. But very probably has a lot to do with what we just went through with the Kitty-Bot, because that plan appears to have kicked off about two weeks ago, since that's how long the milk's been out of date, so how long Villanova's been gone. And while I'm no forensics expert, I imagine it'll show that the dust has been gathering for a little while."

"So she went shopping and then took off?" Christopher asked. "Who would do that?"

"More like she'd gotten food to last her a few days since she'd cleared out her freezer already and then was given the go order. The milk isn't full, she'd drunk some of it."

"I can see what you've said," Serene said slowly. "But doesn't Villanova know that Strauss is dead? I mean, this plan is, like the milk, out of date."

"Good question. Just like the one you asked earlier—was someone supposed to come search this apartment because Villanova has 'disappeared'?"

"That's the only thing that makes sense," Christopher said. "Meaning the expectation would be that the police would be here."

"Possibly, but never sell our enemies short in the Cray-Cray Buffet of Insane Ideas Department. And that also begs this question—does Villanova, in fact, know that Strauss is dead, or is she somewhere remote enough that she's not aware of the new world order?"

"She'd have to be pretty remote to miss everything that happened," Christopher said.

"Or too busy," Claudia offered.

Serene shook her head. "I don't think you roll a takeover plan and never communicate with your team. Plans go wrong all the time, and these people work in politics, where they *know* things don't go as planned. So, is Villanova running the plan even though Strauss is dead? And if she is, what does she actually hope to achieve? For herself, I mean."

"She could be in hiding," Lorraine said. "As in, she's not working the plan but doesn't think she can come back here for whatever reason."

"Come Back Home" by Two Door Cinema Club came on. Hoped it wasn't prophetic. "Add this to the growing Questions List—what other aspects of the plan the Kitty-Bot is a part of did Straus and Villanova have in play two weeks ago? And what else might be coming?"

The others looked like they might be ready to join in the conversation when we all heard the same sound we'd heard before—someone was coming into the apartment. Again. Apparently prophecy was in the air.

CHAPTER 16

WE WERE STILL IN the kitchen but we zipped into the office. Considered possibilities and realized that there was no way the water in the trays was frozen. Shoved the shredder into the kitchen, ran to the freezer and dumped out the water in the ice trays, put them back, and skedaddled back to the others. Hyperspeed was truly the best because this only took me about a second. Then I did what I had before—I closed the office door, leaving it open a crack.

Christopher took my hand as I shoved the diamonds into one of the inner pockets of my purse, hoping that I hadn't blown it by taking them out of the ice. Then again, if they were a payoff to someone to kill me, or whatever, it was better to not have said payoff available to said potential assassin. Everyone else linked up, just in case whoever was on the other side wasn't the next person Jeff was sending to bring his errant wife home.

The door opened slowly. Far more slowly than when Christopher had been on the other side. But then, an A-C picking a lock, especially the former Head of Imageering, would be fast at it, and Christopher had undoubtedly been working at hyperspeed.

Because I was enhanced I could see people moving at the normal hyperspeed level, so Christopher's entry had seemed normal to me.

But this entry was far slower, slower than a normal human's would have been. Meaning whoever was breaking in or returning home was being especially cautious.

The person on the other side finally stepped through the doorway. It was a man about Chuckie's size, average looks, with short blond hair and a messenger bag slung over his shoulder. He was also wearing gloves, leather ones, and since it was the end of May, it wasn't because he was cold. I didn't think I knew him, but he was vaguely familiar.

Since my earbuds were in, any noises my phone might make would only be heard by me. Risked it and took a few pictures of whoever this was.

He walked to the kitchen and I waited to discover if he was going for the freezer. But he wasn't. What he wanted was the shredder.

He pulled the lid off and made a sound of disgust. "Unreal. How did I get talked into this?"

Recognized his voice. Not exactly, but I knew I'd heard it before, and I knew for sure now that I'd seen him before. Where this had been and who he was were, however, still not coming to me.

"The Chauffeur" by Duran Duran came on and I realized exactly who this was. Figured my using this as a reason for Jeff to allow me to pipe my music throughout the White House wasn't going to fly, but I planned to hold it in reserve, just in case.

I was looking at Evan, Armstrong's former limo driver. Evan had been Armstrong's driver for years, but during Operation Destruction he'd been proven to be a little suspect in the trustworthy department. Armstrong hadn't fired him so much as handed him off to someone else. Senator Zachary Kramer, as faded memory did me a solid and shared a relevant fact when I actually needed it.

I'd been in the Washington Wife class with his wife, Marcia, but while she'd been friends with that in-crowd, things had changed—me being friends with most of that in-crowd that was still alive, mainly—and now the Kramers were officially anti-alien. Meaning Kramer's driver was fake breaking into Strauss' apartment to gather the shredded materials we'd already snagged. Which suggested a connection between Kramer and Strauss, which wasn't really shocking in any way.

Of course, I couldn't tell any of the others who this was, at least not out loud. And it probably didn't matter—we needed to ensure that we weren't spotted here.

Evan didn't seem to have any curiosity about looking for another shredder, which was good for us. Instead, he went right to the freezer and grabbed the ice cube trays. "Are you kidding me?" He tossed them back in and slammed the freezer door. "How did I get stuck with these idiots?"

He heaved a sigh and pulled something out of the messenger bag. It looked like a thermos. Took pictures of it in case it was actually a nuclear reactor or a bomb while "Black Coffee in Bed" by Squeeze kept me calm and focused.

He unscrewed the lid and carefully splattered the contents around the room. Said contents looked like blood. Once done he closed up the thermos, put it back into his messenger bag, and left, leaving the front door just slightly ajar.

We waited a few moments. "We need to get out of here right now," Christopher said in a low voice. "And we have to be sure we don't touch any of that blood."

"Why was Evan tossing blood around?"

"Who cares?" Christopher asked. "Because he's in on whatever's going on. We need to go. Now. And be sure not to step in any of the blood."

Turned my music off and put my phone into my purse, just in case. We walked carefully to the front door, then linked back up and left at hyperspeed, Christopher leaving the door ajar in the same way Evan had.

Once the five of us were out, he kicked it up to his Flash level and we were all back in my room at the White House in less than a minute.

"Who was that?" Serene asked while we all gagged. Christopher's top speed was hard on everyone other than Jeff.

Shared the wonder that was Evan and his connection to the Kramers, which meant they were likely connected to Strauss and Villanova. "Christopher, you need to get back to the Embassy. Lorraine, Claudia, go with him. Get Hacker International working on piecing together whatever's been shredded. Clearly it's key."

"Kitty, you need to take a shower," Serene said. "We used you taking a bath as an excuse for why you've been gone. It's only been about thirty minutes, but that's almost too long."

"Hyperspeed shower here I come. See you three later."

They zipped off and I zipped into the bathroom and took

the fastest shower of my life. Didn't wash my hair because I figured I could use the excuse of blow-drying it as a reason for my being so absent. And, despite everything, figured a good brushing would solve most issues.

Serene had clothes out for me, a navy skirt and pumps with an iced blue top, and I got into them quickly but carefully. While I brushed out my hair and put it up in a banana clip, we discussed what we knew and concluded we knew a lot and nothing at the same time.

"We need to get anything Elaine has on Evan out of her."

"That'll fall more to you than me," Serene said. "Honestly, right now, the two of us need to get back into political mode, and fast."

"Only sort of. We have the head of Titan here as well as Drax. We're just in *that* What The Hell Is Going On mode, versus this other What The Hell Is Going On mode. Speaking of which, what's our story for what happened with the Kitty-Bot?"

"I checked with Tim while you were showering. Suspected intruder issue that was handled is the official word. I don't know that you'll even be asked about it—the Planetary Council has been mingling, and most of what everyone's talking about are Jeff's personnel announcements and the Drax situation."

"As long as no one suggests the Kitty-Bot as my replacement, I'm good with it."

She laughed. "I'll get my people on the Kitty-Bot What The Hell problem. We're better suited to that than the Titan and Drax issues."

"Which is your polite way of saying that the FLOTUS can't be caught up in all the intrigue and illegal B&E that's going to go on."

Serene shot me a very innocent look. "Kitty, we would never do anything illegal." She sounded totally honest and completely ditzy.

Laughed and hugged her. "You're really our best secret weapon."

She hugged me back. "Have to take care of my family."

We headed downstairs. Serene either had the White House layout memorized or was a lot better with spotting the signage, because we reached the dining room where everyone else was without issue. Spent the time regressing my mindset back to what it had been before the Kitty-Bot appeared. I had to FLOTUS up and take one for the political team, and I had to do it now.

We separated, and I went over to where Thomas Kendrick was. Unsurprisingly, he was with Culver, Gadoire, and Vance. Tito was also there, and he nodded to me, meaning that he'd double-checked Kendrick and he was indeed a real human.

Everyone asked if I was alright, said I was, and that was that. Presumably because Kendrick had been here waiting for a good forty-five minutes or more and no one wanted any more delays. Worked for me.

"Madam First Lady, thank you so much for inviting me into your new home," Kendrick said as he stood up and we shook paws. No joy buzzer or similar in his hand. One for the win column.

"Kitty," Vance said as he stood, too, "I'm sorry, but I need to grab you for just a moment. It's a point of etiquette that our new First Lady might be unaware of," he added with a gracious smile for the others. Then Vance took my arm and led me out of the room.

"What point of etiquette am I unaware of? I mean besides all of them."

"None, I just wanted to tell you what we've gotten out of Thomas while you were out of the room doing whatever it is that you were really doing that we're all going to pretend was taking a bath and calming down from a false intruder alert."

"Really?" Tried not to sound shocked. Failed, based on Vance's expression.

"Yes, really," he said, sarcasm knob easily at eight and heading for nine. "We're not idiots and we're on your side. And he'll tell us things he might hold back from the rest of you."

"As always, not trying to insult you or the skills."

"Whatever. Anyway, Lillian got him onto Drax Industrial right away. Thomas knows about the Invisible Commandos, and he told us that he had no idea that was Drax's sales pitch. He's horrified, and has been subtly cutting ties. He did say that if Jeff wants him to keep an eye on Drax, he will."

"I have just so, so much trouble believing that the head of Titan Security is our friend. I'm sure it's possible, but it's still a leap."

Vance shrugged. "He's not Antony Marling. You know how it works here."

"I do. I also know he's pals with the heads of Gaultier and YatesCorp."

"You're pals with one of the other heads of Gaultier."

"Stop using your evil logic on me. So, do you guys believe him?"

"Well, Jeremy Barone does." Jeremy was the brother half of a brother-sister Field team. He was the empath, his sister Jennifer was the imageer. She was now Jennifer Barone-Gaekwad, but she was still working with us and was on-site at the White House, too. "He was hanging out nearby, and he gave me the signal that Thomas wasn't lying. He could be wearing an emotional manipulator, of course, but until he's strip-searched, we don't have any way of telling. But Jeremy thinks he got enough emotions to feel confident that Thomas isn't wearing a blocker or an overlay."

"Or he's testing out the next level of Titan tech. But, fine. That gives me a lot to work with."

Vance grinned. "That's what I'm here for."

Decided that, regardless of what my role was now, I was still the Head of Recruitment for Alpha Team. And that meant I could hire as I saw fit. And, per Elaine, I had a lot of staff positions to fill. And we had at least two evil plots working, and more always loomed on the horizon. It was time to fill the ranks.

"Um, Vance?"

"Yeah?"

"By any chance, are you interested in a job?"

CHAPTER 17

VANCE STARED AT ME for a long moment. "What kind of job? I don't want to run off to retrieve a briefcase while being shot at again. I'll do it, but I don't want to."

"That's not what I meant, but good to know that you're always willing. No. I need a First Lady's Chief of Staff along with a Social Secretary and Press Secretary. Or, as I think of it, I need a Pierre. I don't think it's right for me to rip him away from the Embassy, though."

"I agree. He's the only one there who isn't changing jobs or having massive life upheavals."

"Wow."

"What?"

"It's literally like you read my mind."

"I'll be thrilled if I'm reading this right. You want me to be, what, your Chief of Staff?"

"Yeah, I do. I really do."

Vance stared at me again. "Why?" he asked finally.

"Because you, like Pierre, know all the right things to do, who's zooming who, what to do in all the social situations. You dress like you just stepped out of the pages of *GQ*, you know everyone, and you're smart enough to make everyone think you're not smart at all. I have no idea why you were even *in* the Washington Wife class—you didn't need it."

He grinned. "I take it every time it's offered. So does Abner. It's how we help our spouses meet new players, Kitty. Darcy likes having ringers in the class, and she also likes our money, so she doesn't let on to the new students that she's known us for years."

Blinked. "Wow. That hadn't even occurred to me. But it's brilliant, really."

"Thanks. You mean it? This isn't a joke job offer?"

"When have I ever offered you a joke job? When have I offered anyone a joke job?"

He shrugged. "I just want to be sure."

"Be sure. Do you want the job?"

Vance hugged me. "Hells to the yeah. And I don't even care what it pays."

Hugged him back. "Thanks. Get to work. In addition to having no knowledge of what your salary is, I also have no freaking idea what I'm supposed to be doing in that dining room."

He laughed. "You mean besides eating and determining what's going on at Bad Guy Central?"

"Right. I'm great on the Megalomaniac Girl side of the house. The FLOTUS side on the other hand . . ."

Vance put his arm around my waist and headed us back. "Oh, don't worry, my chipper strip of seaweed . . . Your Mister Beaumont has you covered."

Managed to control the Inner Hyena, but only barely. "Thank you, Jeeves."

He grinned. "This is going to be fun. As for what you do, just sit and eat. This isn't a formal gathering, and everyone in here is aware of how you roll, plus those who don't know you well think you had a scare before the intruder was handled. But definitely eat. The food's great."

"Got it, I'm a scared bunny. Do I get to sit next to Jeff?"

"No, not right now. And just be you, no bunny needed. You're going to sit with us, and keep Thomas entertained. Trust me on this one."

"That is now your job, dude. To be the guy I trust."

Vance stopped walking, took his arm from around my waist, and looked at me seriously. "I promise I won't let you down."

"Thanks."

"Speaking of which . . . you said you needed a Chief Floral Designer, right?"

"Yep. Along with God alone knows what else."

"Probably a Decorator or similar. I'm going to get in touch with Pierre and tell him that, as of right now, Akiko Designs only works for American Centaurion and the

White House and have him ensure that's the case by the time we're done with this lunch." He was texting like mad as he said this. "Also, and don't take my head off for this suggestion, but I think you can cover two jobs with one person if you hire Abner to be your Decorator and Chief Floral Designer."

Let that one sit on the air for a long moment. "Excuse me? The Akiko thing I have no issue with. The Abner thing on the other hand . . ."

Vance shrugged while still texting. "He's Lillian's husband, he's an artist, and he, like me, knows the movers and shakers. In case you're unsure, Lillian is, by now, one hundred percent on your side, which means Abner is as well." He looked up with a wicked little gleam in his eyes. "Besides, it'll kill, just *kill*, Marcia Kramer."

"Make it so, Jeeves, immediately if not sooner." Had a thought. "We need to ensure that we're watching her husband like a hawk, too. He was Gideon's VP replacement after we rescued the Cameron Maurer android, and even though Gideon's now on our side, I can't imagine that Kramer has joined him." Particularly after my extracurricular activity at Villanova's apartment.

"He hasn't. Like Marcia, he's bitter that they've been shoved out of the in-crowd in order to move you guys in. Zachary is definitely anti-alien and anti-you."

"Always nice to be able to keep one enemy for life, right?"

Vance grinned. "I'm glad Guy and I moved out of that circle, and I know Lillian and Abner are as well. She'll be thrilled with this, by the way. It will show her massive influence over you and your husband without her actually influencing anything. So it's a win for both of you."

"I hire so exceptionally well."

"I totally agree. I've texted Abner. He's possibly crying he's so excited. He's also on his way here to join us. I'll let Lillian know privately, just in case."

We joined Kendrick, Culver, and Gadoire, and, as suggested, I ate with them. Well, I ate the meal everyone else had already had while they lingered over dessert so I wouldn't eat alone. Jeff was with McMillan, Chuckie, Elaine, Raj, and Mom. Those members of Alpha Team present were with White and the Planetary Council. Decided to let

Vance worry about seating arrangements and get some food into me.

As promised, it was excellent. Apparently I now ran Chef's life. As long as he continued to refuse to serve Alpha Four Boiled Tapeworms and continued to make food like I was consuming, he could count on only seeing me when I wanted to filch extra foodstuffs or lick the bowls. So, possibly regularly, but I wasn't planning to cramp Chef's style. He was a culinary genius. Shared this with Vance, who agreed we were keeping Chef on staff.

While I ate with probably a lot less social grace than the others around me had, in part because I was hurrying to be polite and in part because I was starving, so happy to shovel the food in, Culver and Vance kept the conversation flowing. Kendrick again proclaimed his love for all things alien and his horror at the depths Drax was willing to stoop to.

Wondered where Drax, Stephanie, Buchanan, Wruck, and Siler were. Not in this room. Wasn't sure how long we should leave them, because every minute we were eating and chatting was a minute the flyboys, the princesses, Camilla, and all the security agents were under an enemy's control. Planes and helicarriers could be replaced. The people couldn't be.

Or, rather, they could be.

Eyed Kendrick as I finished up my lighter-than-air chocolate mousse that I was going to demand that Chef make on a daily basis. Kendrick was a good-looking man—his father had been in the Marines and his mother was Vietnamese—and he was former military himself and, other than Culver, he still tended to hang with military folks.

Kendrick had the buttoned-down, crisp, intense look so many former military people had. The Department of Defense had essentially put Kendrick in charge of Titan. But that didn't mean he was a good guy—the DOD had been as infiltrated as every other government agency.

Of course, he was also part of the YatesCorp, Gaultier Enterprises, and Titan Security Unholy Trinity, which indicated nothing good. Then again, I'd just hired two people I'd have said were my bitter enemies not all that long ago and, technically, half of those around the table had, at one point in time, been against us. So that only proved that Kendrick was working in D.C. like the rest of us.

There was nothing for it. Time to do what I did best and see what reactions I garnered. Jeff was far too busy, but Jeremy was still close by. Waited until I'd made eye contact with him, then sent what I hoped was a clear emotional signal to be paying close attention. He nodded and shifted in his chair so that he was turned more toward us.

"Thomas, I have a question."

"Sure, Kitty, what?" I'd thankfully gotten him to stop calling me anything formal. Maybe there was hope for the White House staff, though I doubted it.

"What're Titan Security's thoughts about the android situation worldwide?"

CHAPTER 18

TO KENDRICK'S GREAT CREDIT, he didn't immediately try to pretend he had no idea what I was talking about.

"Well, that's kind of dicey to answer," he said after a moment's shocked pause.

"Why?"

"Because my predecessor, the man who built up Titan to become a global power, was the man who created them. So, it's a natural question for you to ask. Realistically, I should know where any existing androids are."

"Yes, you should. So, where are they?" Managed not to ask if he knew about the Kitty-Bot, but it took effort. I'd save it for later, when I needed to really get a reaction from the crowd.

He sighed. "I don't know. I have no idea how he hid the information—not only were all the Alphabet Agencies given full access to search his files, but once I took over, that was one of the main areas I focused on. We have literally zero information on how to make an android, let alone where the existing ones were or are."

Managed not to say that I didn't believe this, in part because Jeremy sent me a text which, being the Worst First Lady in the World, I looked at. Kendrick wasn't lying. Meaning that Cliff, under the auspices of his then-role at Homeland Security, had probably searched first, found whatever he needed, taken it, and wiped the rest clean. Always the way.

Of course, that didn't mean that Kendrick wasn't still a slimy evildoer working against us. But it lowered the slime level potential.

"So . . . what about emotional blockers or overlays?"

My having tossed out the Android Question already meant that Kendrick wasn't nearly as surprised by this. He nodded. "Titan created them. Under Marling's tenure."

"And yet you know about them."

"I do. However, as with the rest of what I'd call our anti-alien tech, the data is gone. However, I've been looking into it." He nodded toward Lillian. "It was suggested that determining how to effectively counter those devices would be something American Centaurion would appreciate."

That Culver had given him this idea wasn't a surprise. That Jeremy was again texting that Kendrick wasn't lying was the surprising part of all of this.

"I think we'd prefer that they all be found and neutralized at the source, but we'll take what we can get."

Kendrick sighed. "Kitty, I realize that Titan Security went out of its way to create horrific weapons of mass destruction. It also created genuinely useful weapons and tech that were used against most of the people here unlawfully. And I also realize you have no reason to trust me. But I'd like to do what I can to earn that trust."

"Works for me. When was the last time you saw Gustav Drax?"

"The day before your ill-fated rail trip to Florida."

"No time after that?"

"No. We were supposed to have a meeting a week ago, but his office called to cancel."

Managed not to react to this and, to everyone else's credit, those nearby didn't react either. "So, what's your take on Drax?"

"I think anyone who drops invisible commandos onto the President's train as a sales pitch is an idiot," Kendrick said dryly.

"Join the club on that one, but I'd really like to know what you thought of him before then. I know you were interested in getting some of his tech."

"I was interested in merging his company into Titan. He has some amazingly advanced tech—things we're trying to create but aren't close to yet. Maybe if Antony Marling were still alive, and not trying to bring down the government, what Drax Industrial has wouldn't be as interesting, but since I'm not the same kind of genius as Marling was, we could use a mind like Drax's. At least, that's what I'd thought."

"Why did the DOD put you in charge of Titan, then?"

Kendrick shrugged. "I'm former military, I understand what we need on the ground and so forth, and I'd spent time dealing with various suppliers. I had the right résumé to take over a company like Titan. But what I don't have is the creative genius of someone like Marling."

"Think of it like comparing artists," Culver suggested. "Or musicians. You can try to imitate Mozart, but you won't *be* Mozart, and the listener will know the difference."

"Exactly," Kendrick agreed. "There's only one Leonardo da Vinci."

"Michelangelo didn't suck."

He chuckled. "No, he didn't. But I'm not at that level. I'm better than the people painting the dogs playing poker or putting Elvis onto velvet, but I'm not up to the grand master level. And without that spark of true genius, I'm not able to lead Titan like Marling did. And while I'm sure you're glad about this from one side, from the other, that means that the advances Marling would make naturally are lost to us."

"That's why you were interested in Drax?"

He nodded. "He has that spark, at least as far as I've seen. Clearly that spark comes with a side helping of madness, but I didn't realize that. Then. I'm clear on it now."

"What can you tell us about his invisibility stuff?"

"Not as much as I'd like." Kendrick shrugged again. "He's using an irradiation process. I'd prefer to have something that was more easily turned on and off."

"So, let's move off of Drax for a moment. If Titan doesn't have the data to be able to recreate androids or to create emotional overlays and blockers and such, then who has it—Gaultier or YatesCorp?"

Kendrick looked uncomfortable. "Ah . . ."

"Answer the question, Thomas," Culver said gently.

He nodded. "I think it's with Gaultier, honestly."

This jibed with all that we'd discovered. However, there was no guarantee Kendrick was telling the truth, Jeremy or no Jeremy.

Jeff wandered over. "Excuse me, folks, need to steal my wife away for a moment."

I stood. "Back in a bit. At least, I assume." Gave Vance a

look I hoped he'd interpret to mean that he should keep grilling Kendrick. Then Jeff put his arm around me and led me out of the room.

"Nice work, baby," he said when we were out of earshot. "Jeremy let me know you were interrogating Kendrick, so I paid attention."

"Was that safe for you to do with this many people around? I don't want to have to give you adrenaline—I think witnessing that might give Antoinette a heart attack."

Jeff grinned. "I appreciate the concern, baby, but I'm fine. Since you handled that robotic version of yourself, no one's panicking or getting ready to do anything overly emotional. All things considered, other than excitement from various new appointees along with anxiety about their being able to do a good job, it's pretty relaxed in there."

"I'd call you a liar, but it does kind of seem calmer than what we're used to."

"I don't expect it to last."

"Sorry about the Kitty-Bot Incident."

Jeff hugged me. "I know you, baby. That you ran headlong into danger without me there is something I'm used to. I don't like it, mind you, but I *am* used to it. From what Chuck told me, I'm glad I had Tito go with the others to help you."

"Oh, you're why he was there? Yeah, good call, he figured out how to talk to the Kitty-Bot faster than anyone else."

"That's not why I sent him."

Looked up and tried not to look or feel guilty. Failed. "I wasn't hurt. A little banged up, but I'm fine now."

Jeff sighed. "I know, baby. And I'm not angry with you. For that."

"I needed to help." Didn't say where and with what, just in case.

Jeff grinned. "I know." He nuzzled my head. "I'm not really mad at you for anything. As I said, I know you. But back to the matter at hand. Kendrick's not against us. Not sure how for us he is, but when you forced him to talk about Gaultier and YatesCorp, what I picked up was frustration, anger—directed at the people running those companies—and feelings of betrayal and fear. If he was in bed with them, I don't think he is anymore."

"Or else he's wearing the next-level emotional overlay and is laughing at us right now."

"Maybe. But his reactions when you had him talking about Drax were more interesting."

"Yeah? How so?"

"His overriding emotions were embarrassment and disappointment. I think he liked Drax and was excited to be looking to merge the companies. Drax has let Kendrick down and put him in an awkward situation, and Kendrick doesn't like that."

"Interesting. You may not have gotten this, but Kendrick says that he hasn't seen Drax since before we got onto Rail Force One."

"Huh. Well, let's go see what Buchanan, Siler, and Wruck have gotten out of Drax. And Stephanie."

"You going to be okay seeing her?"

He shrugged. "She's made her choices. She came through for us when we needed her to."

"After trying to kill several of our friends. And me. Just in case you didn't remember."

Jeff hugged me. "Of course I remember, baby. Believe me, I'm aware of all that Stephanie's done. But you and Chuck both think she wasn't really trying to kill anyone."

"She was really trying to kill Cliff, but I can't argue with that particular sentiment. And considering when, where, and how she attacked me, Lillian, Len, and Kyle, killing us might have indeed been her hoped-for outcome. One way or the other, I can promise you that I'm willing to kick her ass if I have to."

"I know. I'm just hoping you won't have to. I assume a lot will depend on what Drax does. I pulled you away so that we could interrogate him before it seemed like you were done with Kendrick because I know we'll need to compare stories sooner than later. And," he pulled me into a nearby alcove, "because I've wanted to do this for at least two hours."

With that, he pulled me into his arms and kissed me. Jeff was the God of Kissing and there was something arousingly illicit about kissing in the White House when we had a million high-level people waiting on us all over the place.

Jeff's lips and tongue owned mine as always, and also as always, I was ready to go for doing the deed right here, right now, meetings and intrigue be damned.

He ended our kiss slowly, eyes smoldering. "I'd love to do exactly what you want, baby. But duty calls."

"I'm so sick of duty."

Jeff laughed and hugged me. "Me too. But we have to do it anyway."

"Yeah, I'm clear that missing getting to have sex every hour on the hour is our lot in life. Doesn't mean I have to enjoy it."

He grinned. "Always nice to know that your laser focus on the priorities remains intact."

"Every minute of every day, Jeff."

He nuzzled my head. "Right back atcha, baby. Now, let's get to the next vital meeting and interrogation."

CHAPTER 19

JEFF AND I STARTED OFF AGAIN. I wasn't good with mazes, and while the White House wasn't the most confusing setup in the world, it was huge, and without the tasteful placards on the walls I'd have had no idea where I was at any given time. Even with the tasteful placards I was having trouble. As before, decided I didn't need to focus on the rat maze right now. There were other things to focus on.

"If you can be sure Drax is or isn't lying, and if he's still convinced Kendrick took the helicarrier and all our people, then we have an android on the loose." And a robot in custody. Lucky us.

"Maybe more than one. And that means we're going to have to have security details we can trust on Kendrick. Probably on others, too."

"You seem calm about all of this."

"I am. We've dealt with the androids before; I feel confident that we can handle them again. The Planetary Council have heard of Vatusus, but it's not somewhere they've gone. Other than their own solar system and ours, no one from Alpha Centauri has gone elsewhere."

"That seems odd, considering how so many of them are space-worthy."

"As you like to point out, baby, we're out in the boondocks of the galaxy, and they're not much better off. It's a long way to the next inhabited star system, at least as far as they know, and as of yet, no one's been interested in trying."

Looked up at Jeff's expression. "Oh. So that's it. They want us to join them on interstellar exploration. That's what they mean by us joining the galactic community, isn't it?"

"NASA's going to be happy," Jeff said with a chuckle. "Because Alexander's ready to give us schematics to build the ships we'll need for that endeavor. But we need to deal with our own situations first."

"I agree. We can worry about the final frontier later. Right now, I really want to meet Gustav Drax, late of Vatusus and the Galactic Core."

We found Buchanan waiting for us just outside what I realized was Jeff's old office, as in, the office for the Vice President. Jeff's things were still in here, and it was weird to realize that, very shortly—possibly this afternoon—we'd be moving his stuff into the Oval Office and Hochberg's things in here.

"You sure it's okay that you're not in there?" I asked Buchanan.

He nodded. "Drax and Stephanie are secured. Stephanie isn't here, by the way. She was too violent for us to bring into the White House complex. We have her secured under the Pentagon."

"Seriously?"

"Yes. She's an A-C, a confirmed terrorist, and, frankly, needs to be in solitary for a while to consider her sins and options."

"Oh, Mom told you to take her there, didn't she?"

"She did. And she's right. You're going to get far more truth out of Drax without Stephanie around." Buchanan sighed. "Honestly, if it turns out that she's the one behind the idea of dropping invisible commandos onto Rail Force One, it won't surprise me."

"She's a female A-C, and they're all hella smart. Though that move was hella stupid."

"Which may have been her intent. Don't for one moment assume that she's helping Drax for anything but her own ends. She also hates all of you with a passion." He looked at Jeff. "When you do go to see her, I think you'll need to go in there with the understanding that your niece is a lost cause. Frankly, I think the only reason she didn't run off with Kendrick when he took the helicarrier was that she was with us at the center of the action, versus with Drax."

"I think she wouldn't have, because I sincerely think the Kendrick that took the helicarrier was an android. Meaning our people are in a lot more danger, because I'd assume that android took the helicarrier right back to Cliff."

Jeff nodded. "What Kitty said." He heaved a sigh. "And I'm as prepared for what Stephanie's going to be like as I can be." He cocked his head. "There are only three people in there?"

Buchanan nodded. "Wruck knows how to handle Drax, and Siler's in there to help him. By contrast, I needed eight Field teams to keep Stephanie under control. Hence her current location."

"Works for me. We'll interrogate her later. And before either one of you try to tell me that I won't be there, let me mention that I'm Megalomaniac Girl and you're not keeping me away. I will pull rank and confirm it with my mother if I need to, and I can guarantee Mom will want me along."

"Probably. We'll argue later. Ready to meet our newest alien, Mister and Missus Chief?"

"Wow, you're not going for the Full Title Experience?"

Buchanan chuckled. "Not when we're alone."

"He doesn't think I've earned the respect that goes with the title yet," Jeff said.

Buchanan shook his head. "No. Honestly, I think you're the best possible choice we could have for President. However, no man is infallible. And, who knows? There may be a time when you have to hear truth from someone who isn't awed by you in any way."

"Yes, that totally sounds like respect," Jeff said, sarcasm knob heading for eleven.

"It is, though, Jeff. Malcolm works outside of the approved system. And that includes our approved system."

"Yes and speaking of that, Missus Chief, we're going to have a nice, long, and rather nasty talk about the stunt you pulled earlier."

Managed not to ask him which stunt he was talking about. "Totally looking forward to that, Malcolm. Promise. Though I have to say that you not calling me First Lady anything is a huge relief."

Buchanan grinned. "I know. I do know you." He looked at Jeff. "Both of you. But let's focus on the prisoner at hand."

Jeff cocked his head again, and once again I could tell he

was focused on his empathic talent, meaning his blocks were down. He was quiet for a good long minute, then grunted. "Drax isn't wearing an emotional overlay of any kind. I already know what you, Siler, and Wruck feel like. Drax is, interestingly enough, as easy to read as any other ape-based or similar humanoid for me."

"Cool, that probably means he's susceptible to the Good Cop/Bad Cop routine. For the record, I'm going to be bad cop because I do it better than you do for a variety of reasons." Jeff not being able to lie being the biggest.

"Can't argue with your judgment, baby."

To his great credit, Buchanan didn't share his thoughts on this, but his expression said that he argued with my judgment on a daily, if not hourly, basis. Instead, he opened the door. And we were treated to an interesting sight.

Drax had metal plates at the sides of his temples, and they looked organic, as if he'd been born with them, not had them implanted later in life.

Wruck had shifted one of his arms to look like a set of space-aged funky forceps, and had them on the plates in Drax's temples. Drax looked frozen. Not dead, necessarily, but immobile.

Other than the metal in his head and his wide-eyed, frozen expression, Drax looked exceptionally human. He had long, black hair that was pulled away from his face — presumably by Wruck — that would hide the plates at his temples effectively. He was a little smaller than Jeff or Buchanan, slightly larger than Siler. Skin tone was one that could merely be olive or could indicate a multiracial background. In other words, he looked like he was a human and could be from pretty much anywhere.

"Um, John, I'm going to go under the assumption that you haven't killed Drax here."

"No, I haven't. You can control a Vata by running the right electrical current through their system. I'm doing that."

"You rock. Can he hear and all that?"

"No. I have him in stasis mode."

"Awesome. Jeff, how could you feel him?"

"No idea, but I could. He's frightened as his overriding emotion, but there's frustration, disappointment, hope, many others in there."

"Interesting," Wruck said. "I can't feel emotions, so I didn't realize that he could still feel during this time."

"You've frozen the neural impulses that control movement of all kind," Jeff said. "But that doesn't appear to freeze the brain's ability to think and feel."

"I find this fascinating, but I can guarantee that we have to belay the scientific discovery for later. So, Nightcrawler and Martian Manhunter, let's let our newest alien buddy out of stasis and hear what lies he plans to tell."

"The Vata aren't a race filled with guile in the first place, but I can force him to tell the truth if need be," Wruck said. "The advantage of being an older race and knowing younger races' weaknesses."

"Wow. So, are you and the Z'porrah the oldest races around?"

"No, we're not, but we're among the oldest. The Vata aren't a young race, nothing like the races in this and the Alpha Centauri solar systems. But they're not as old as we are, and we take care to keep eyes on all of those races we consider on our side of the Great War."

"There is so much more I want to ask you about all of that, but, as with the stasis and empathic discussion from a minute ago, sadly, we must deal with the situation at hand. I want to point out that this statement was me totally being the FLOTUS. That's my last FLOTUS statement for a while, but I really wanted it noted."

"Duly," Buchanan said, sarcasm knob definitely at eleven.

"Do we need to tie up Drax in any way before he's released from stasis?" Jeff asked. "Because I don't want my wife hurt, in case no one's sure of why I'm asking."

"A-Cs are stronger and faster than Vata," Wruck said. "I'm keeping hold of him when I wake him from stasis—I won't allow anything to happen to Kitty."

Jeff grunted. "Great, another one."

"Another one what?"

"Another one I have to keep an eye on," Jeff muttered, and I could tell he was having a jealousy reaction. Flattering but likely very inaccurate. Our Martian Manhunter wasn't looking for love—he was looking for family, which we'd now given him.

Wruck chuckled. "Yes, I'm very fond of her. Though not

in the way you're concerned with." He smiled at me. "Though I could be convinced. But since I know she'd ask me to shift to become you, I don't believe you have anything to worry about."

Siler nodded. "And this is why your enemies hate you, Kitty. You have a rare ability to turn those who are either against you or neutral to your side."

"Well then, let's see how the Friendship Skills are working today. John, please release the Drax Kraken."

CHAPTER 20

COULDN'T SEE WRUCK do anything differently with his Forceps Arm, but all of a sudden Drax blinked and drew breath. It was weird and creepy in a totally Frankenstein's Monster kind of way.

Drax jumped when he saw us. "What? How did I get here?"

"We have our mysterious ways. Let's just pick up our conversation from where we left off a little while ago."

"You're the First Lady?"

Looked around the room. "Am I the only woman in here and does my voice not sound somewhat familiar?" Chose not to ask if he'd seen me on TV only a week ago—maybe he hadn't been watching Stephanie's fifteen minutes of fame.

"Ah, yes. I'm just . . . disoriented. What's being done to me is . . . addling."

Still wasn't convinced that Drax was the sharpest Vata in the drawer, but now wasn't the time to insult his intelligence. Was sure he'd give me good reason to do so soon enough.

"Good. We want honesty, and I have a bet that I'm going to get that faster if you're addled than if you think you're somehow being smooth and fooling me."

Drax wasn't so addled that he couldn't shoot me a dirty look. "This is hardly the way to begin a partnership."

Couldn't control myself. I snorted. Loudly. "Dude, you have chutzpah, I'll give you that. But right now, the idea of partnership isn't looking too good for you." Sat at the edge of the desk. "Tell me how you met Stephanie."

He blinked. "What?"

"Stephanie. I want to know how you found her or how she found you."

"Why?"

"Because she wants to know," Jeff snarled. "That's why."

"You don't want to know about my products?"

Heaved a sigh. "Oh, we do. However, we have other questions that take priority. The one I asked is our top issue. So, answer or go to the nasty jail where we create something that puts you in stasis forever."

"It's not hard to create," Wruck said helpfully. "I could help design one quickly and easily."

"Super-duper. Gustav, get with the program."

"Fine. I'm just not clear on why this matters. I realize she's your niece," he said quickly to Jeff. "But how we met seems irrelevant. Before you berate me, though, I put out an ad. She answered it. I hired her."

Couldn't speak for the others, but this wasn't actually the answer I'd been expecting. "Um, excuse me?"

"A want ad. I know you use them in this country. Why is this shocking?"

"You placed an ad for an A-C who was willing to learn to ride a motorcycle and shoot at people with a crossbow in the local paper?"

"Ah, no. I placed an ad on the dark web for an assistant willing to do whatever it takes to help a business succeed."

Buchanan grunted as he texted. "We need Reynolds in here."

"Chuckie knows about the dark web. Trust me. I got the full details about it from him a long time ago. And despite the temptation to go onto it and just see what was out there, he convinced me it was a bad idea." Presumably because he was the dude at the CIA who was in charge of monitoring it at that time, but that didn't need to be shared right now.

"So, you advertised for an assistant in the same place where people are hiring assassins and making drug trades? And my niece responded to it?" Jeff asked, sounding like this was the worst news about Stephanie he could have imagined. Proving that, at his core, Jeff was a tad naïve.

"Yes." Drax shrugged. "Much business is conducted there."

"It is," Siler said. "And Stephanie being on the dark web

isn't a surprise." He cocked his head at Drax. "Was your ad the one that asked for a person of taste and refinement who also understood the political infrastructure of the world?"

"Yes, that was my ad." Drax sounded rather proud.

Siler shook his head. "Who applied for your job, aside from Stephanie?"

"Ah . . ." Drax now looked embarrassed.

Made the leap. "Oh, my God. That ad was so unlike how business really rolls on the dark web that no one who had a clue would have touched it, right, Nightcrawler?"

He grinned. "Got it in one. That ad was considered to be a terrible entrapment attempt by law enforcement."

Drax looked hugely offended. "I am a legitimate employer and I have excellent opportunities for those who choose to work with me!"

The office door opened and Chuckie joined us. "You called?" he said to Buchanan.

"Chuckie, meet our own Booster Gold! He's not from the future but otherwise the similarities are amazing. He's the one who advertised on the dark web."

Chuckie gaped at me for a moment. "You mean the 'taste and refinement' ad?"

Wasn't shocked for a moment that Chuckie knew what I was talking about. Something like this ad would have been the dark web's version of the best joke meme ever—everyone would have passed it along to their buddies and clients for the shared hilarity. "I do. I do indeed."

Chuckie gave in to the Inner Hyena. And when he did, so did Buchanan and Siler. And me, of course, because I didn't want Chuckie and the others to laugh their heads off alone. Jeff, being the President and all, merely grinned, but managed to keep from laughing. Out loud.

"And Stephanie answered that ad?" Chuckie managed to ask between fits of laughter.

"She did," I confirmed, managing not to snort while I said it. Go me for the Decorum Win.

"This isn't funny," Drax said, sounding beyond offended.

"No, it's hilarious. Seriously, are all Vata this dim?"

"It's different there," Wruck said. "Their abilities make them far more comfortable with electronics than other animated beings."

"So, the metal plates, those are organic?"

Wruck nodded. "They are. All Vata can mentally connect with any electronic device. There are tremendous restrictions put upon them when they travel to other worlds."

"Which I'll just bet Gustav here was ignoring."

"I was not! I am not here to abuse my power. I've taken our Oath and I will not stray from it, no matter the cause." He sounded deeply offended and deadly serious.

We all stared at him. "Um, Martian Manhunter? I want to say that Gustav is lying like a wet rug, but what are your thoughts?"

"He's probably not lying. It's literally their religion," Wruck said.

"What is?" Jeff asked. "Oh, and he's not lying, thanks for asking."

"So sensitive, must be all the pressure of high office. John, you were saying?"

"That they cannot interconnect without permission unless the stakes are literally life and death, and their religious text outlines what life and what death. In detail. They spend their youth learning what is and isn't an appropriate reason to integrate. As a Judeo-Christian equivalent, a Vata integrating into a system without permission is pretty much like breaking all the Ten Commandments at once. The penalties for breaking their Oath are high—Vata have been hunted down and sent to a prison world in their system for abuse."

"How Alpha Four of them." This earned me blank looks from Wruck and Drax but knowing nods from the others. "So, seriously, Drax hasn't learned the bomb codes or where all the bodies are buried or anything?"

"If I'd done that, why would I need to ask you to work with me?"

We were all quiet. I assumed the others were, like me, trying to figure out the answer to Drax's pertinent and obvious point.

Chuckie broke our silence. "I have a question. Why are you here? And I don't mean here in this room. I mean here on Earth?"

Drax looked embarrassed and mumbled something.

"Excuse me? None of us could hear that. Try again." Noted that Wruck was concentrating. "John, is everything okay?"

Wruck nodded. "I'm encouraging honesty."

"Thought you said they had no guile," Jeff said.

"Not much, as a race. However, they're good about dragging out the answers. I'm speeding up the process."

"How so?" I asked.

"By hurting me," Drax snapped. "But fine. I'm the youngest son of the Potentate, and since I have thirteen brothers and seven sisters older than me, there's literally nothing on Vatusus for me to do. I wanted to make my mark, to do something grand. Earth is beginning to gain quite a reputation—your dealings with the Z'porrah have impressed many." He shrugged. "So, I thought I'd come here, set up shop, and see what I could accomplish where no one knows me."

"Wait," Chuckie said. "Are you saying that you're part of the ruling family of your country?"

"Oh, no," Drax said nonchalantly. "Of my planet."

CHAPTER 21

JEFF GROANED. "Only us. These kinds of things literally only happen to us. John, can you verify if what he's saying is true?"

Wruck shook his head. "I've been on Earth far too long, and Vatusan politics was never a great interest of mine. However, when I left, there was only one ruling family for all of Vatusus. And Vata in general and their royal family in particular believe in having as many offspring as possible."

"You're saying you can't tell?" I asked Jeff.

"I really wanted confirmation from someone else for this, the political system on Vatusus in particular, but yeah, baby, I can tell. He's telling the truth."

Drax looked frustrated. "Of course I am! I believe on Earth I would be called a prince. However, I eschew the title."

"You do?" Chuckie represented the shock in the room well.

"Yes. I'm the youngest of twenty-one children. Do you have any idea what my role on Vatusus would be?"

"Get married and have twenty kids?" Hey, it was worth a shot.

"Worse. All I did was attend parties."

"Wow, are the Kardashians from Vatusus, do you think?"

"What do you mean?" Drax asked.

"I mean I think I'm making a FLOTUS decree that all aliens working on my side need to watch some damn television. Anyway, Gustav, lots of people would think just partying all day long was the best."

"That was my *job*. Going to parties. Being charming.

Being funny. But I couldn't say anything where anyone could take offense. I couldn't do anything. I couldn't entertain on my own because that would indicate favor, and I couldn't do that. Plus, I couldn't think. I design things—I know you think that I stole my designs to bring them here, but I didn't. I just wanted to be . . . important, in a real way. Somewhere that I'd fit in."

"Jeff, is he lying?"

Jeff heaved a sigh. "No. He's still not. I've been monitoring him and I can feel him as well as I can feel everyone else. He's telling the truth, and I don't sense that he's hiding anything, either."

Felt bad for Drax. Knew I shouldn't—he could still be an enemy somehow—but I couldn't help it. He wanted to be meaningful and didn't really have the training to do so. He was fumbling around like a really enthusiastic puppy, but puppies weren't evil. They needed training to be good dogs, but treats and love worked better than beatings and cages for that.

"Put him back in stasis," Jeff said to Wruck, who nodded. Drax went back to the Dead But Alive look.

"Why did you do that?" I asked. "If he's telling the truth, then he's not a bad guy. An idiot, to be sure, at least in terms of how to impress, but not bad."

"It's déjà vu all over again," Jeff said.

"What is?" Chuckie was again speaking for the room.

"Kitty's ready to adopt him," Jeff said. "And don't tell me you can't tell, Chuck. I don't think we need this. We have too much on our plate right now to focus on befriending this guy."

"Actually, we do need him," Buchanan said. "At least if we want to stay ahead of our ever-growing list of enemies."

Wruck nodded. "Vatusus is far ahead of Earth and Alpha Four."

"And that," Chuckie said, "means that even if Drax is the worst weapons creator on his planet, he's likely still better than anyone here."

"Kendrick indicated such, too."

Jeff grunted. "You're close to bringing Kendrick in out of the cold, too, baby, I can tell."

"You said he was telling the truth, too, Jeff."

"This is her skill," Siler said, rather gently, presumably before Jeff and I could get into some sort of domestic dispute that, to me, made no sense. "I said it before you questioned Drax. This is what we want. You want another alien on your side. Let me mention that while Drax may be the twenty-first child, he's still royalty, and that means his parents probably care about what happens to him."

"They might care even if he's not royalty, but yeah. Vatusus in general might care, too. Jeff, why are you so against him?"

Jeff heaved a sigh and ran his hand through his hair. "Honestly? I'm not. I'm just kind of tired."

"Of adding in allies?" Wruck asked carefully.

Jeff shook his head. "No. I'm thankful everyone in this room is here, even Drax, if I'm honest. I'm just tired. Literally. And that's making me want to, I don't know, hunker down and not add in anything or anyone else new into the mix."

"That's normal," Chuckie said quietly. "You're allowed to be stressed."

"Not really. Especially not after the last week or so that we've had. But I can already tell why Presidents go gray so fast."

"You'll just look distinguished." And probably even hotter than he did now, if such could be believed.

Jeff laughed. "Thanks, baby, I needed that. So, what do we do with our newest royal exile?"

"I think we find out if he can tell if a person is an android or not."

The men all looked at me. "How would we test him?" Chuckie asked.

"We have two androids and the Kitty-Bot. Dress the Kitty-Bot in what I'd wear, have him see if she's real or not. Same with the Cameron Maurer and John Butler androids."

"If the Kitty-Bot's in any condition to be seen," Chuckie said. "You kind of went to town on her."

"I resent her very existence, so sue me." And, reality said that I hadn't damaged the Kitty-Bot all that much. That Chuckie had probably been a lot more focused on the Double Kitty Chick Fight in general as opposed to specific wasn't all that surprising. Decided that pointing this out would only be likely to make Jeff jealous and/or give Chuckie a mood swing and migraine combo, which we really didn't need.

"He should be able to tell," Wruck said, presumably to stop our potential bantering or bickering. There was a lot of that going on in the room. Chose not to be bitter. Yet. "Though Vata are not used to ever trying to connect to others' minds. They connect to others' electronics and computer systems and similar, but not the people themselves. So he may not actually know *how* to tell."

"Surely we aren't the only planet that has androids or robots on it," Chuckie said.

"No, however, if they're considered sentient beings, then the Vata would not try to connect with them without their permission."

"No time like the present to find out if Drax has the skills or not."

Jeff's phone beeped. He groaned. "Actually, it's past time for me. Raj just let me know that I've been absent too long and I need to get back and keep the country running."

"Do I have to go back, too?"

"No. Raj says that Vance is handling whatever you should be. Am I right in that you hired him?"

"Yes, he's my Chief of Staff. Thank me for that later, because I can guarantee that Vance is going to FLOTUS better with five minutes on the job than I'll ever be able to. We can discuss all the fun changes later because yes, I have to hire more staff, too. Get back to Presidenting and I'll handle things here."

"I'll ride herd on her," Buchanan said. "You want Reynolds with you or here?"

"Both places?" Jeff didn't sound like he was joking.

"One Chuckie-Bot coming up."

"Not funny," Chuckie and Jeff said in unison.

"Too much caffeine, guys?"

"We're ignoring you, Kitty. Though we all know that's dangerous." Chuckie sighed. "You have three extremely competent men here, two of whom I trust to kill someone first and determine if they were really an enemy later. I'll go with Jeff."

"Works for me." Hugged Chuckie, who seemed to need it, gave Jeff a longer hug and a quick kiss, then he grabbed

Chuckie and they zipped off to do important things. Turned back to the others. "Let's wake Drax up again."

Siler put up his hand. "Before we do that, I want to hear your plan."

"Beg pardon?" Tried to look politely confused.

Siler snorted a laugh. "You have a plan, I know it. It's probably a crazy plan, but even if it's somehow sane, I want to know what it is."

"Seriously, I want to do exactly what I said—I want to see if Drax can tell if someone's an android or not."

"I'd like to know if it was really Thomas Kendrick who stole his helicarrier first," Buchanan said. "Since that's a high priority and we have personnel missing."

"I know. But the Kitty-Bot appeared on the White House lawn. Sure, it could be an elaborate ruse to make us think that Kendrick's not involved, but that's overly complex even for our enemies. Barring Kendrick wanting to show her off and show his control over her, I doubt it, especially since she came to us from Camp David."

Siler and Buchanan both looked like migraines were on the horizon. "Let's deal with what's in front of us first," Siler suggested.

"Fine," Buchanan said. "That means Missus Chief here. What did you find when you left the White House grounds? Oh, and before you try to lie about it, I know because your husband was aware of where you were and he advised me. Something about my security measures needing improvement."

"Sorry to get you in trouble, Doctor Strange." Did a fast recap of what we'd found in Villanova's bizarre faked crime scene. "I have no idea where Evan went, since we didn't follow him and I came right back here instead."

"If you somehow think that gives you a pass, Missus Chief, you're sadly mistaken." Buchanan looked pissed, but I didn't think it was with me.

"Malcolm, what's upsetting you?"

"We should have kept eyes on him. And I forgot."

"Gosh, it couldn't be because we were literally facing the end of the world as we knew it, was it? We all forget, even you. But he's back on our radar and working with someone—presumably Villanova—on a plan. Whether it's the plan that Strauss had going already or a different plan, though, I can't be sure. But my money's on them following the old plan and just trying to adapt."

"Is whatever those people are doing related to the missing helicarrier situation?" Wruck asked. "Because if not, we need to prioritize."

"And we need to let Drax out of stasis. Just to be nice."

"You're sure he's not lying?" Siler asked Wruck.

"The Vata have little guile, as I said. Their ability to connect to electronics means that they can connect to each other that way as well, albeit via the electronics. Their planet is very . . . wired, for want of a better description."

"As if their planet really *is* a worldwide web?"

Wruck smiled at me. "Essentially, yes. Meaning that the Vata are used to plugging in and interacting this way as easily as interacting in person. It's hard to hide when you're all linked together, so they don't. There are always rogues who are willing and able to buck the norms, but in Drax's case, the norm he's bucking doesn't seem to be truth-telling."

"Jeff confirmed it, and, honestly, he's tried to lie, and he's as bad at it as most of the A-Cs are. We have a handful who lie well, you're one of them, Nightcrawler, but overall, most A-Cs can't lie convincingly to an infant, let alone anyone else, and Drax seems firmly on that side of the alien house."

"Then I'm with Kitty," Siler said. "Let him out."

Buchanan nodded and Wruck let go. Drax blinked and returned to the Land of the Living. "I really hate it when you do that," he grumbled. "What did I miss? And where did the President and your friend go?"

Before I could answer, my phone rang. Checked before I answered. "Malcolm, get your blinky phone thing out again. It's a blocked number, and since Gustav's in the room with us and Stephanie is locked up nice and tight, it's likely a new player in our continuing Game of Lunatic Throne Lovers Anonymous."

CHAPTER 22

BUCHANAN TOSSED ME THE TRACER, I inserted it into the phone's headphone slot, then hit answer. Buchanan, Siler, and Wruck all pulled out phones and began listening in—the Privacy Police on the job again. Wruck's phone was near to Drax's ear. Had no idea why Wruck felt it was time to share with our Visiting Vata, but I wasn't in a position to argue.

A very tiny part of me held out hope for this being Aero-ForceOne because it could happen if I really believed. "Hello?"

"Missus Martini?" Unfamiliar woman's voice, pleasant. The hope that it could be AeroForceOne stayed alive.

"Yes?" Probably sounded too eager. But you know, I didn't want anyone thinking I wasn't excited to win a private meet and greet with Steven Tyler and Joe Perry.

"Hello. We haven't met before. My name is Talia Lee. We have a mutual friend, Janelle Gardiner from Gaultier Enterprises." This was not AeroForceOne.

"Hope is dead."

"Excuse me?"

"Oops, was that my Out Loud Voice? Um, nice of you to call, I guess. I don't know that I'd call Janelle Gardiner a friend, but you do you and all that."

Per Vance, Lee did indeed call Gardiner her bestie. She was the head lobbyist for the firearms lobby, and therefore also the National Rifle Association's best friend forever. And this would be, if my intel was correct, the very first time she'd ever contacted anyone from American Centaurion, we who used guns a whole lot. My Dealer of Death Bingo Card was filling up.

"Ah . . ." She paused. I'd stunned her into silence, go me. "I'm calling because I have information that you might find interesting."

"I doubt it."

"*Excuse* me?"

"Damn. Out Loud Voice again? Ignore that. What information are we talking about?"

Noted the men's reactions. Siler was cracking up silently. Buchanan had a long-suffering look that I felt sure he'd learned from watching Jeff's and Chuckie's reactions to my doing things like this. Wruck appeared interested. And Drax looked horrified by, I presumed, my utter lack of decorum. Well, he'd learn that it wasn't just for him. Perhaps that was why Wruck was sharing his phone, to bring Drax along into the program sooner as opposed to later.

"Well, several things, really." She seemed flustered. Needed to control my Out Loud Voice. Possibly.

"And they would be?"

"You have an underage criminal you're protecting."

At this, Siler's amusement disappeared. Because the said supposed criminal was his adopted daughter, Lizzie. She, like Siler, was using Vrabel as her official name for any who were asking. And she wasn't a juvenile delinquent so much as a kid who'd stuck up for the underdogs and kicked the butts of many kids who were connected to Very Important People. People like Lee here, whose son, niece, and nephew were all in the ranks of Those Whom Lizzie Schooled.

"Oh, Talia, that's so last week ago. Besides, we have no idea who you're talking about."

"Elizabeth Jackson."

"Noted when your buddy Ansom Somerall called me before my husband had to take over the Presidency of the United States. In case you're not clear, we have no such juvenile with us and we're tired of you all trying to create stress when we already have more than enough."

"She's dangerous."

"So are dogs but, you know, if you train them right—"

"This is a serious issue!"

"Oh, blah, blah, blah. Seriously, if this is why you're calling, we're done." Had a feeling they were still on the Lizzie is a Bad Girl kick because Amy Gaultier-White had just given birth and therefore they considered her vulnerable. My gut was quite confident that the Gaultier Enterprises Board of Directors and their Dealers of Death buddies wanted to get rid of Amy and blame it on Lizzie. Therefore, and despite all that had gone on, the extra guards I'd put onto Amy were still there, and she was safe in the Embassy.

However, it paid to be sure. Grabbed a pen from Jeff's desk, wrote on a convenient notepad, and shoved it at Buchanan. Who nodded. Good. The security was still set to Extra Crispy at the Embassy.

"Well, that's not all."

"Oh goody. I'm breathless with antici- . . . *pation*."

"Ah, good."

She hadn't gotten my *Rocky Horror Picture Show* reference. My disdain knew no bounds. Clearly Lee and I were not destined to "get on." A heartbreaking shocker I'd somehow have to manage to recover from.

"Still waiting here." Wrote on the pad and shoved it at Siler. Who nodded and zipped off at hyperspeed. For all I knew, Lee was sending a drone or a bomb or the invisible helicarrier to bomb the hell out of us and just wanted to be sure of where I was.

Siler was back and indicated that the skies were clear and we were not under imminent attack.

"I'm sorry, I'm just having trouble understanding you."

"Get in line, Talia. My time—it's limited. As is my patience. Much to do when an insane home-grown terrorist goes to town and wipes out a great deal of the power structure of your country and all that. Cut to the chase or stop wasting my time. Is that clear enough?"

"Ah, yes. Well, the other information I have is that Thomas Kendrick is creating robots designed to take the place of a variety of high-level politicians and businesspeople. Including you."

Half a day ago, this would have been scary news. As things stood now, all this made me do was figure that by coming here Kendrick had cut his ties with the rest of the Land Sharks—what I called the now-heads of Gaultier Enterprises, Titan Security, and YatesCorp—even if he didn't know it.

"Gosh. That *is* interesting news. What proof do you

happen to have?" There was silence on the other end of the phone. Hit my mute button. "You know, I just have to say that I am freaking sick and tired of being considered the stupidest link in the chain. I mean, it's helpful and all that, but come *on*."

Lee cleared her throat. "Proof?"

Took the phone off mute. "Yes, proof. In this country we love to have some before we convict anyone. And I, personally, like to have more to go on before I release the hounds and shock troops to arrest someone."

"Arrest?"

"You've just made an accusation of treason against the head of Titan Security. What, exactly, do you think I'm going to do with that information should it somehow prove to be correct?" Hit mute again. "She cannot be this stupid, can she?"

"No," Buchanan said. "Assume entrapment. Focus on the call. Rant later."

Nodded and once more took the phone off mute. And waited. For a good thirty seconds.

"Are you still there?" Lee asked. Wasn't sure if she was up on the Sales Tip of the Ages or just unsure if I'd hung up. Which I was tempted to do, but I took one for the team and stayed on the phone.

"I am, still here, waiting for you to share what proof you have that Thomas Kendrick is acting in a treasonous manner."

"We've seen the robots."

"And *I've Seen The Saucers*. But since I doubt we're about to go see Elton John together, let's have you share more actual information. Who is 'we' that is co-accusing?"

"What does Elton John have to do with this?"

"Possibly as much as Thomas Kendrick, since you're awfully short on details, facts, or anything resembling information. Start with who the 'we' is that makes up the 'you' that is so concerned for the safety of the world."

"Janelle, myself, Ansom, Amos Tobin, and several others I don't believe you've met yet." Tobin was the head of YatesCorp.

"Quinton Cross?"

"Oh. I'm sorry, you must not know. Quinton passed away. Due to the Alien Flu."

"It's not the Alien Flu. It's the disease Clifford Goodman created and released on an unsuspecting populace, which he called the Alien Flu. However, that disease was human-made. Let's be sure that you and the rest of 'we' keep that very, very straight."

"Ah, yes, yes, I'm sorry."

"And condolences on your loss." Losing Cross probably meant that the ick factor in the world had gone down, but that wasn't an appropriate thing for the First Lady to say, so I wasn't going to say it. To Lee. To Amy? Hells to the yeah, I'd be sharing this news with her as soon as possible.

"Thank you. That does sort of bring me to the last thing on my list. With Quinton gone, we need to shore up the Gaultier Enterprises Board. We'd really like Amy Gaultier to take her place with them now."

"It's Gaultier-White now. And why are you telling me this?"

"You're her oldest friend, she's married to your husband's cousin, and we can't reach her. If you'd pass along the message and let her know, we'd appreciate it."

"Talia, you know what's interesting to me about this request?"

"What?"

"That it's you making it, not, say, Janelle or Ansom or anyone else connected with Gaultier."

"Janelle and Ansom are still too broken up over losing Quinton to handle these kinds of calls," she said quickly. "I'm helping out."

"How good of you. Thanks for the heads up, I'll be sure to share the message as soon as I can."

"Wonderful. Thank you for your time, I hope we get to meet in person soon." She hung up before I could say goodbye.

Made sure the call was dead then handed my phone to Buchanan so he could retrieve his tracker. "Well, that was interesting."

"I personally liked how she avoided telling you who all those making up 'we' was for as long as possible," Wruck said.

"Guaranteed it's everyone she named and probably the rest of the Dealers of Death that aren't actually sitting in the White House with us." Whether the Kramers were part of "we" was something I figured we'd find out soon enough.

"I'm more interested in the robot," Buchanan said.

"I'm more interested that she called it a robot and not an android, personally. There's a distinction and I think it's important. And remember that Eugene Montgomery was fed the robots story to get him to help out the wrong side during Operation Sherlock."

"I honestly didn't realize that bringing Lizzie to the Embassy would have caused all of this," Siler said, sounding angry and worried.

"It didn't, it just gave them something else to barrage us with. Trust me, this would be going on with or without you two in the Embassy. But it's good to know that they're still going for the Juvenile Delinquent Gambit."

"So, does this mean that Kendrick's off the suspects list?" Buchanan asked carefully.

"Still fifty-fifty."

"He stole my helicarrier," Drax said huffily. "I don't believe that indicates you should trust him."

"Yeah, about that . . . Gustav, how'd you like to get onto my good side?"

CHAPTER 23

WE EXPLAINED OUR suspicions about there being an android version of Kendrick about, and also shared that there actually was a Kitty-Bot as well as a couple of friendly, in-control androids.

Drax seemed amenable to seeing if he could determine if someone was or wasn't an android or robot. Buchanan made some calls and the androids were requested.

The Cameron Maurer android was living in D.C. with his mother, Nancy. They had four Field teams assigned to them on a 24/7 basis and Nancy checked in with us regularly. However, we didn't do a lot of study on Maurer, because, frankly, it was already hard enough on his mother, and we saw no reason to make things harder.

The Colonel John Butler android, on the other hand, was at the Dulce Science Center in New Mexico, since that was the main A-C Base of Operations for Centaurion Division. Butler had agreed to as much study and testing as we wanted to do, so him staying at Dulce made sense.

Both androids had been able to retain enough of their humanity that they were now more Data from *Star Trek: The Next Generation* than *The Terminator*. So far, they were the only ones we'd been able to capture and keep from self-destructing, but the hope was that we could hot-wire other androids and save them, too.

The decision was made that it was safer to do Android Identification Testing at Dulce than at the White House or the Embassy. But before Drax was allowed over there, Buchanan wanted Reader's approval, not to mention Jeff's, Chuckie's, Tim's, Serene's, Gower's, and my mother's. To say that Buchanan wasn't trusting was to say that ice was cold and water wet.

"But how can you be sure that the Thomas who took my helicarrier isn't the man who's sitting in another part of the white House right now?" Drax asked.

"That, Gustav, is the question of the hour. Tell me, truthfully, what did you think of Kendrick before the stolen helicarrier incident?"

"I liked him. He was enthused about and interested in everything I could bring to his company. It was exciting, my first big potential client. We were discussing a merger," he added rather wistfully.

"He mentioned that, too. So, did he act differently when he came to see you, when the helicarrier was stolen?"

Drax looked thoughtful. "You know . . . now that you put it that way, yes, he seemed a little off. Frankly, I thought it was because of all the drama that was going on here."

"Why did he come to see you during that drama? What reason did he give?"

"We'd had a meeting planned already. But when he arrived he said he didn't want to discuss the merger but instead wanted to get some of my invisible tech to test out . . ." Drax looked pissed. "And so he took my invisible helicarrier when I went to get him a small handheld tracker. That was a joke, wasn't it? Something I was supposed to laugh at?"

"Well, whoever took the helicarrier is laughing. Whether that's the real Thomas Kendrick or an android under someone else's control is the question. Did you ever meet Clifford Goodman, or did Kendrick ever mention him to you?"

"The lunatic who tried to kill everyone? No, no one other than Stephanie had ever mentioned him. She was afraid of him until—" Drax looked like he was sorry he'd said this.

"Until what? Or, should I ask, until you gave her what tech?"

"She has a personal protection suit. It increases her strength and natural abilities, and assists her with things that don't come naturally."

"That's why she was so hard to control," Buchanan growled.

"And why she can ride a motorcycle so well." Though

Serene had already proved that A-Cs with enough will could find the way to manage human machinery. And suit or no suit, I was sure that Stephanie had had the will. "Why didn't you want to tell us about that, Gustav?"

"It's still experimental, and I don't want you to take it from her and reverse engineer it."

We all jerked. "That's why they took the helicarrier. It's not just for the hostages, not that anyone has given us a ransom demand. They have fighter jets and an invisible helicarrier carrying God alone knows what tech. It's why they haven't attacked us with it, yet, too. They're still too busy learning from it."

"Which again points to Titan," Drax said.

"It does, that's true."

"Do you think whoever took my tech and your people, be it Thomas or someone else, is creating androids of the hostages?" Drax asked.

The rest of us stared at each other. The looks of horror on the men's faces probably matched my own. "Gustav," I said finally, "we hadn't considered that horrible option until you just mentioned it, but it just moved to the top of the list of what I think our enemies are doing."

"Do you mean 'our enemies' as in yours, or as in yours and mine?" Drax sounded rather hopeful.

Heaved a sigh. "Yours and ours. Clearly whoever took your tech isn't doing it to give it special upgrades and return it to you." Only the A-Cs did things like that. And while we did have traitors in the A-C midst—Stephanie currently being Example A—it wasn't likely that an A-C had engineered this particular heist. Possible, but improbable.

"So how do we tell if Kendrick is for us or against us?" Siler asked. "I mean, I have ways, but they're unpleasant."

"To put it mildly, I'm sure. But if he's essentially being framed, that wouldn't be a wise course of action." Looked at Buchanan. "You haven't heard from our mutual friend?"

"Not since the last time I told you about." When Camilla had sent a weird message—*Staying longer on Spring Break, getting lots of souvenirs*. Which had told all of us, Buchanan and Chuckie included, nothing.

But thinking about Camilla reminded me of something. She'd been in deep with Drax before I'd pulled her out to supposedly help save the day at the end of Operation Epidemic. "Ah, Gustav, did anyone other than Stephanie answer your ad on the dark web?"

"Yes," he said with more than a little defensiveness. "A very competent woman. She has a very different role than Stephanie does."

"You mean you don't have two chicks shooting arrows at your prospective clients? I almost want to ask why not."

"Because Stephanie was functioning as my bodyguard in addition to assisting in creating a demand for our products."

"Wow, I guess they have marketing on Vatusus. Because that was a truly impressive spin for what Stephanie was actually doing. So, what's this other woman's name?"

"Marguerite Gautier. Her family is French, though she's an American."

Managed not to react, but this was necessary only because my father liked old movies and I'd watched many with him growing up. Marguerite Gautier was the name of Greta Garbo's character in *Camille*, which was basically Camilla's name. And it was close enough to Gaultier that it was likely she was getting double duty or more from the alias.

"Where is Marguerite now?"

"She had a family emergency—I believe her mother had contracted the disease. Of course I let her leave to go home and care for her parents."

"Of course. Why would I think that a guy who has his bodyguard shooting crossbow arrows at half of D.C. wouldn't be a kind and caring employer who puts the needs of his employees first?"

"Yes, I do. It's a Vata strength, something we pride ourselves in on Vatusus."

"I see they lack sarcasm on Vatusus, though. But, whatever. So, Marguerite left and you haven't seen her since?"

"No. She told me she'd advise me when it was safe for her to return to work. After all, the disease was quite contagious. It was very valiant of her to go home and risk exposure, but she's a loving person, and brave as well."

Brave I could agree with. Loving I had yet to see from Camilla, but I was sure she was capable of the emotion. Clearly Drax had been completely fooled by her, though without Jeff, Jeremy, or another empath, we didn't have confirmation that he was telling the truth.

"And you're here now, so if she's trying to call, the phone's just ringing."

"My phone was confiscated."

"Figure of speech. Okay, so what did Marguerite do for you?" Might as well find out what Camilla was doing there. After all, no one in the know was willing to tell me, so getting the information out of Drax, in front of Buchanan, was kind of Ironic Justice. Which I still felt should be the title of a monthly comic.

"She was in charge of expansion. She was brokering the deal between Drax Industrial and Titan Security."

Of course she was. But whether this meant that she was finding out just how bad it was before the CIA, NSA, FBI, and all of Centaurion Division did a raid, or whether she thought Kendrick and Drax were both on the up and up and wanted us to reap the benefits of their merger I didn't know. And I also knew that I had no way of knowing without being able to ask Camilla straight out. Which was currently not possible.

"So, what about your other employees?"

"I don't have any others."

"We only found him and Stephanie," Siler confirmed.

"Do you have hyperspeed?" Why not? Everyone else from other solar systems seemed to.

"No, not as your people do. But my machines build themselves."

"Want to explain that more clearly? Are you saying that you've got robots in your factory?"

"Not as such, not like you're talking about. But Vata can mentally connect to electronics and such. It's not that difficult to merely show the machine what it is I want it do to or create."

"Every day. I learn something new every, single day. At least this is new information I could not possibly have known before, so there's that. So, seriously, no other staff? No henchmen hanging about to do the dirty work or just the heavy lifting?"

"No, I have machines for that."

"I see the future, and it's all *Terminator*."

"Nothing attacked us," Buchanan said, eyeing Drax suspiciously.

"Because you didn't find me at my factory. You found me at my home."

"It was a lair," Siler said. "Trust me. Total lair."

"Nightcrawler, you complete me. Sharks and such?"

"No, but they're probably on order."

"So, who helped you design your home, Gustav?"

"Stephanie," he admitted. "I liked her design suggestions."

"I'll bet they were quite grandiose." Siler nodded emphatically but I kept the Inner Hyena at bay. Just. "So, I didn't ask before—where is the Supervillain Lair and where is the actual factory?"

"The Supervillain Lair is in the Ivy City neighborhood," Buchanan shared. "It's a converted warehouse."

"Right in the middle of D.C.? Seriously? And no one's noticed?"

"Yep," Siler said.

"I keep a low profile," Drax said with a sniff.

Siler grinned. "True, at least on the outside. Though the warehouse the agents went to first was in the middle of Turkistan. Be happy we have gates."

"Always am. So, Gustav, where's the factory?"

Drax made sure to look at Siler and Buchanan when he answered. "Across the street."

CHAPTER 24

DRAX HAD A RATHER SMUG EXPRESSION, which contrasted nicely with the shocked and embarrassed looks from Buchanan and Siler.

The Inner Hyena got a snort out of me, but I managed to keep the rest inside. "So, I assume everyone was far too busy with Stephanie to check out the surrounding buildings?"

"Nice spin," Buchanan said as he texted.

"I'll take it," Siler added.

"Sending agents to the area now." Buchanan looked up. "What might they be facing?"

"Not much, since they won't be able to get into the factory without me," Drax said. "The building won't let them in."

Let that sit on the air for a moment. "Ah, Gustav? Are we to assume that you mean the building has some form of sentience?"

"Not as any of us do. But it's computerized and automated, and I told it not to allow anyone in if they're not with me. That includes Stephanie and Marguerite."

"You know, Alpha Four had some weird smart metal, it's what their Unity Necklaces are made out of. Think it's the same?"

"Similar," Wruck answered. "Different worlds have different properties."

"So, like, there are worlds with sentient dirt and water and such?"

"Yes. Most are more like the metals in the Unity Necklaces and those from Vatusus. Very few elements can actually reason and communicate, though there are some planets that have such, of course."

"Oh, of *course*. And, oh my God, we are so not ready for the Greater Galactic Community. Plus, the learning is starting to get to that point where I feel like I'm back in college. College was great, but I'm really not ready to go back for my Masters in Alien Planetary Geology."

"You'll be fine," Wruck said loyally. "As a species humans are amazingly adaptable, and you personally, Kitty, are a prime example."

"John's my favorite. But back to the fun of Gustav's thinking metal, because I'd rather deal with the problem at hand than the myriad problems just waiting for us out there in the great unknown."

"I've had the agents hold," Buchanan said. "In case the building decides to be nasty."

"It won't," Drax said. "I don't have it programmed to be violent. Well, not as long as they don't actually get in."

"Fantastic. Malcolm, please keep those teams on hold. The ramifications of all of this are just awesome, aren't they? No wonder Titan wanted to do a merger. Which, I have to add, makes it more unlikely that Kendrick is the one who stole the helicarrier. Why steal one thing when there's so much more you can get just by playing nicely with others?"

"I have to agree," Buchanan said. "Did Kendrick know that you were the creator?" he asked Drax.

"Of course. And he was also aware that I had . . . safeguards . . . so that no one else could access my building. Though he wasn't aware of what they were. I didn't share that I was from another planet."

"Wise, under the circumstances. Did he suspect, do you think?" If he had, Kendrick hadn't mentioned it to me.

"No, he believed I was from Eastern Europe and didn't try to determine my country of origin."

"Why weren't those safeguards on the helicarrier?" Wruck asked. "It seems . . . foolish to have left them off of what had to be your most expensive piece of equipment."

Drax heaved a sigh. "I had to allow the helicarrier to function with human personnel. My temporary help were going to have to think on their feet, so to speak, so I turned off the sentience, as you'd put it."

"Can you turn it on from a distance?" Hey, it didn't hurt to ask.

"No. I've tried, believe me."

A thought occurred. "How in the world did you get all the equipment to build a helicarrier and anything else you have? And how did you get to this planet in the first place?"

Drax stared at me. "I brought it all with me," he said finally. "I thought that was obvious."

Time for the rest of us to stare back. "How?" Buchanan asked finally. "And when?"

"In my ship." Drax said this as if it, too, was obvious. "And about two years ago."

So probably during Operation Defection Election, meaning we were all focused on Sandy and the Superconsciousness Seven and, perhaps, not paying attention to anyone else arriving. However, that didn't seem likely—we were all about monitoring for suspicious activity. And by "we" I meant every world government all the time. Sandy and Friends would have had the governments on higher alert, too.

"What ship? I'm asking because no one, anywhere, has mentioned that a spaceship arrived from parts unknown and landed here. We're picky about things like that here on Earth. We tend to notice. And complain."

Drax shrugged. "We have good cloaking. I came when there were other beings here, I do know that. They left me alone, however."

"Superconsciousness someones?"

"Yes, I think so, at any rate. They were rather . . . insubstantial. We've heard of them, of course, but haven't seen them. They don't come to the Galactic Core, for whatever reasons."

"Count your blessings. Okay, so where is your ship hidden? And if you say it's in the middle of D.C. I'm literally going to take some Advil and go lie down for the rest of the day."

Drax chuckled nervously. "No, of course not. Well, not the *middle*. I don't think."

Buchanan and I exchanged a look. "I'm sure I'm going to hate this, Missus Chief."

"Me, too. So, Gustav, where is your cloaked spaceship hanging out?"

"There's a large hospital complex that's undergoing major renovation that has a parking structure that's not being used and hasn't been torn down yet. My ship is on top of that."

"So . . . your spaceship is parked at the old Walter Reed hospital complex? And no one's noticed? I shudder to think how the press is going to play this when that ship *is* found." Because I was certain that it would be found. At the worst possible moment for Jeff's presidency. Because that was how our luck rolled.

"We need to handle all of this, quickly and quietly," Siler said.

"Nightcrawler, you've read my mind. Stephanie can wait. Testing androids can wait. You three take Drax and get that spaceship stored at Andrews as fast as humanly possible and by humanly I mean Christopher and by possible I mean faster than the Flash."

"What are you going to be doing?" Buchanan asked.

"I'm going to go back to the others, verify that no one needs me, and go to the Embassy to see my children. Because this day has made me want to hunker down and cuddle my kids for some weird reason." A potential robot impersonator getting near enough to fool my children being only one of those reasons. Because, after all, if there was one, who was to say there weren't more Kitty-Bots out there? Or Jeff-Bots? Or Whomever-Bots? That we hadn't seen them yet seemed more a matter of time than proving there weren't any more around.

"Fine," Buchanan said, in a tone that indicated that, as per usual, it really wasn't. "I'm having the boys meet you."

"Works for me." Of all my personnel, the ones most likely to roll with whatever I really wanted to do were Len and Kyle. I was all kinds of happy they were taking over the FLOTUS Babysitter post for a while.

"Are you going to have him restrain me?" Drax asked, indicating Wruck.

Contemplated all the options and heaved a sigh. "No."

"You're far too trusting," Siler said. "Not that I think he's lying about being on our side. But still. I don't want to find out we're wrong."

"Oh, no worries. I have a plan." Looked around. "Any Poofs or Peregrines available, please come to Kitty."

CHAPTER 25

THE ROOM WAS SUDDENLY loaded with a lot of fluffy cuteness and feathered beauty.

Poofs were small, fluffy animals with black button eyes, no visible ears and tails due to fur fluff, and were basically the cutest things in existence. Everyone else thought they were Alpha Four animals. However, I knew they were really from the Black Hole Universe and had been brought here by Algar. In addition to being the most adorable things around, Poofs were able to go Jeff-sized with a mouth full of razor-sharp teeth.

The Poofs attached to whoever named them, and they sort of chose what they considered a name. I looked at this as a way to determine when we really had a new ally or not.

Peregrines, on the other hand, were indeed Alpha Four animals, and resembled peacocks and peahens on steroids. The males were colorful, the females all white. In addition to being fierce fighters, Peregrines could also go chameleon and were, therefore quite good at stealth protection. They also used their keen animal senses to determine friend from foe as best as they could.

The Peregrines reported to me, and, as such, I was the one who named them. All of them. Any new Peregrine chicks who were born were brought to me for their Royal Naming Ceremony. At least, that was what Bruno, the Head Peregrine, had told me, and who was I to argue?

Since the Peregrines tended to be in Stealth Mode until needed and the Poofs had the ability to all be in my purse or in someone's pocket without you even feeling their weight, for all I knew the easily twenty-five Poofs and eight

Peregrines who were in here with us had been with us all along.

Buchanan, Siler, and Wruck all knew about and possessed their own Poofs—Wruck had gotten his the day before, as a matter of fact—so they weren't freaked by the sudden Animal Kingdom Arrival.

Drax, on the other hand, apparently had not been briefed on our animal situation. Because he jumped and gave a little shriek. "What are those?"

"Protection and insurance." Knelt down. "Thanks for coming, Kitty would like a word."

Got their full attention and a blast of the Sea of Animal Love. Never an issue and made me feel a whole lot better. "First off, can anyone confirm for Kitty if Gustav here is someone Kitty and Jeff should trust?"

They all stepped back and began conversing.

"Excuse me," Drax said, "but are you actually talking to those fluffy things and those birds?" He sounded amazed and freaked out.

"Metal being sentient, it's no big. Me being Doctor Doolittle? That's somehow the biggest shock in the multiverse."

Of course, what I wasn't sharing was that while the animals could always understand me and I could absolutely understand them when they wanted me to, when they didn't, it was just so much mewling, purring, squawking, and scratching. Which was what they were doing now.

Waited. Some things were worth taking time, and verifying if someone was or wasn't a real ally was right up there at the top of the list. Wruck took the time to explain the situation to Drax. Wruck had only joined up with us in the past week, so this new information was top of mind for him. He was rather proudly showing off his Poof, which he'd named Vaya, which apparently meant "calm" in Ancient.

Buchanan's Poof, presumably not wanting him to look Poofless, jumped onto his shoulder. "Help the others, Killer," Buchanan said with a grin. The Poof purred, rubbed against his neck, then jumped down with the others, though Vaya stayed with Wruck.

Siler merely grinned. He actually had three Poofs, something I'd discovered only about a day ago. Apparently the Poofs had adopted him, the Dingo, and Surly Vic without my knowing during Operation Epidemic—basically, once

Lizzie had gotten a Poof, those three had had Poofs appear, clamoring for attention which they'd duly received, since even hardened assassins couldn't resist the cuteness that was the Poofs.

But their Poofs had been off helping with the rest of the Poof Herd during the endgame of Operation Epidemic, so they hadn't been there to prevent Annette Dier from torturing all three of them and murdering the Dingo and Surly Vic.

Shoved the sorrow thinking about this gave me away again. Sure, they'd been the top assassins in the world. But they'd become my Uncles Peter and Victor, and they'd died to protect me. They'd had a kind of Viking funeral, but it wasn't enough. I didn't know what would be enough. Time, maybe. Though I doubted it.

At any rate, the two other Poofs had attached to Siler. Which was probably nice for him and Lizzie both. They hadn't been able to have pets, because pets tend to cramp the Assassin Lifestyle. But Poof abilities meant you could have a herd of Poofs and, as long as you had meat for them to eat and a convenient litterbox, they were incredibly easy to care for.

The animals seemed to reach a consensus, and Bruno came forward. Squawked, scratched the carpet, flapped wings, squawked again, then cocked his head at me.

"Ah, gotcha. And yes, before anyone gets mouthy, I'll translate." Bruno shot me a wink and I gave him a scritchy-scratch between his wings while I talked. "The animals think Gustav is okay, but they aren't really sure because they hadn't had a lot of time to check him out. They feel that Stephanie is absolutely no good—so score one for you again, Malcolm—and because Gustav was associated with her, they aren't sure about him. The suggestion is that you guys will travel with several Poofs in addition to your own, as well as four Peregrines, and the animals will observe and report."

"Works for me," Buchanan said.

"You're taking security direction from animals?" Drax asked.

"Sentient ones. So, you should be able to relate, seeing as you have smart metal hanging about and all that. And my animals all can and do think for themselves." Gave the

Poofs pats and the rest of the Peregrines their scritchy-scratches, then stood up as there was a knock at the door and Len and Kyle came in. "So, you guys handle the Drax stuff, and we'll convene later."

We all left the Vice President's office together, but since we were in the West Wing, the Spaceship Recovery Team left us and zipped off, Siler providing both hyperspeed and his own form of chameleon camouflage. While the boys and I walked slowly back to the Top Level Meeting in the White House, I filled them in on what had been transpiring.

I'd met Len and Kyle in Las Vegas during the fun festivities that had happened right before my wedding. They'd helped me avert disaster, and, despite being on the USC football team—Len as quarterback and Kyle on the line—and expecting very promising pro careers, they'd opted to join the CIA immediately out of college instead of going into the NFL. As Kyle liked to joke, they'd just chosen a different Alphabet Agency to align with.

Chuckie had hired them and assigned them to be my driver and bodyguard. The boys were smart and brave and, as Len liked to say, Trojan Football was always there to help.

Because it was Len and Kyle and they weren't going to bawl me out, I also told them all about the trip to Villanova's apartment and my concerns about the Kramers being involved in some way, as well as my fun phone call from Talia Lee. I was extremely good at being Recap Girl, so I was done before we reached the conference room we'd been in before lunch. Or else the boys had been wandering the White House complex with me in order to get all the pertinent details. Still wasn't sure where I was in here, so that was quite possible.

"So, what is it you really want to do?" Len asked as I finished up. "Right now, I mean. In the grand scheme of things, I know you want to foil the bad guys."

"Honestly? I really want to go see Jamie and Charlie and pretend none of this is going on."

"That doesn't sound like you," Kyle said. He blushed. "I don't mean I don't think you're a good mom, Kitty. You are. I just can't believe you don't want to get in on the action."

"Well, I did that already. I can't go with Malcolm and the others on Mission: Move That Ship. I also can't go on Mission: Examine Drax Industrial's Swell Digs. I know without asking that Jeff wants more than the three of us to be the ones to talk to Stephanie. The Android and Kitty-Bot comparisons are happening in Dulce and I know without asking that if I go there without Jeff or James I'll be hearing about it for a long time. And I'm willing to leave the determination of whether or not Kendrick has an android that stole the helicarrier to wiser minds."

"You are?" Len asked. Kyle's expression of shock matched Len's.

"Yes, because the real action right now is at the Zoo. Well, so to speak."

"What do you mean?" Kyle asked.

"I had the girls give the pictures we took at Villanova's apartment to Hacker International. And they also have the stuff from the shredder. If there's anything to be found or learned in regard to that situation, it's there, not here."

The boys looked at each other, then back at me. "You're sure there's been an android of Kendrick created and that it's the android that fooled Drax," Len said. "That's why you aren't interested in interrogating him anymore."

"And you know that Jeff can monitor you if you're in the complex," Kyle added. "But with all that's going on, he might not be able to when you're at the Embassy."

"Oh, don't sell Jeff short. But it's nice to know that both of you think I'm using seeing my children as an excuse to do things that the menfolk don't want me to."

Len shrugged. "We know you, Kitty."

"I'm going to resent that. I can't deny it, but I can and do resent it."

"You'd better let Jeff know before we leave," Kyle said. "I don't think he's going to want you to go."

Heaved a sigh. "Probably not. I'm so not ready to be the FLOTUS."

"He's not ready to be the President," Len said. "But he's doing it well, and you are, too. Better than either of you think."

"Yeah, it's been like a week. I guarantee that we're not doing as well as most people think we should, and I literally cannot wait for the media who don't like us to start their reporting." The boys looked at each other. "Oh goody. It's started already?"

Kyle nodded. "Raj said that no one is allowed to show

you or Jeff any media, and we're to try to keep it away from Mister Reynolds, too."

"Chuckie hasn't had a mood swing or migraine since the fun Train Ride O' Doom."

"Doesn't mean he's cured," Len pointed out. "Just that he had so many other things going on that he was forced to focus."

Considered this. "You know, I wonder if Cliff getting outed to the world has helped with Chuckie getting better. Because stress and pressure was what seemed to trigger him most of the time these past long months."

"Maybe." Len shrugged. "That's Tito's job, really, Kitty, not yours."

"I'd rather work on Chuckie's issues than the political stuff."

"Shocker." Like everyone else in my circle, Kyle had a sarcasm knob. "And a week without an episode doesn't equal cure, Kitty. It just means that he could be better, or a worse attack is just around the corner."

"Wow, thanks for that, Mister Sunshine." Though I had to admit that Kyle was, sadly, probably right. "Anyway, let's get what needs to be done for the Presidential Dog and Pony Show here then get over to the Embassy."

We rounded a corner and went into the room everyone had been in before. It was completely devoid of people.

CHAPTER 26

THE EXPRESSIONS ON the boys' faces said that this was not what they'd expected. "Uh, maybe they went back to the dining room?" Kyle suggested.

So, we went there. No people. The room was all cleaned up, though, and ready for the next gigantic meal.

"Maybe we're being punked? Because that makes as much sense as what usually goes on in our lives."

"I kind of doubt it." Len looked around. "I don't see anyone hiding behind the drapes."

"Maybe they left us a message," Kyle suggested.

So we trotted back to the meeting room to see if anyone had left us a note or something. Nada. It was neat and tidy, though. If we'd been in the Embassy, I'd just have assumed the Elves had cleaned up. But humans did the work here, and none were around or about.

"Okay, before I start panicking, any guesses as for who's gone where and why?"

"They weren't in the West Wing," Len said, voice tight. "We went through there to get you and come back and we'd have spotted everyone, even if they were in a room."

"And we should have heard them even if we didn't see them," Kyle added. "There would be no reason to go to the East Wing. That's your area, Kitty, where the First Lady runs things."

"Maybe Vance wanted them to check something out over there?"

"Why take everyone?" Len asked.

"No clue. Um, link up, I think it's time to do the

hyperspeed check of the entire building, because I'm not spotting any White House staffers anywhere, either."

Right before we took off I felt something nudge my leg. Looked down to see Bruno there. He bobbed his head, fluffed his feathers, and squawked quietly.

"What's the word?" Len asked. The boys were less freaked out by my Dr. Doolittle talents than most others. Yet another one of their sterling qualities.

"Huh. Well, the first word is 'phones,' as in we all have them and Bruno is wondering why we haven't bothered to send a text or make a call, but the second word is East Wing, as it turns out. They're over there to watch a movie or similar. Apparently. I have no clue. But everyone is fine. And not missing us." Well, not missing me. Which was both okay and sort of disappointing. Focused on the okay side.

The okay side shared that I had two people with me who were legitimately assigned as protection who were also game to actually do something and break the rules, and no one around to tell me not to do something. I wouldn't have long—sooner rather than later, someone would want to know why I wasn't coming to join the rest of them. But I'd have long enough. Besides, who knew when I'd ever get an opportunity like this again?

But, what was I going to do with it?

Had no ideas other than to head to the Embassy complex and visit Hacker International, which now seemed anticlimactic. I could get there without permission any time. However, I was out of clever ideas for what things to do that no one wanted me to do.

Was about to give up and let my one golden opportunity pass me by, when my phone beeped. Bruno looked smug. Ignored him. "Huh, Stryker has intel."

Stryker Dane was the unofficial head of what I'd nicknamed Hacker International—a group of the top five hackers in the world. Stryker was also the author of the "Taken Away" series, where he wrote about being abducted by aliens. He wrote good fiction, basically.

Chuckie had ferreted out that Stryker Dane was Eddy Simms and found where he lived—Pueblo Caliente, just like us—when we were in high school, and even though Stryker was a decade older than us, he'd become one of Chuckie's closest confidants. I'd known Stryker just as long, of course, and had found out where he'd been living and working during Operation Destruction—Andrews Air Force Base. Due to a variety of circumstances, he and the rest of Hacker International had ended up living with us in the Zoo portion of the Embassy complex.

But these days we had the True Number One Hacker in the World living with us as well—Chernobog the Ultimate, thought to be a boogeyman myth until we'd had her existence confirmed during Operation Infiltration. We'd found her during Operation Defection Election and, because of the deal I'd brokered, she was considered officially dead and was happily living in the Zoo—under watchful guard— and finally using her talents for good.

Made the call and put it on speaker so the boys could hear. "Hey, Eddy, how're they hanging?"

"Well like always, Kitty. Look, all that stuff you sent over? It's interesting."

"I figured. I want to know how interesting it is."

"Very interesting. First off, she shredded the file folders as well as the documents. We put those together first because there was less and it was easier and faster to do. But all the folders were marked and the names are all indicative of robotics research."

"Robotics versus androids?"

"Yes. There is a distinction." Could hear voices in the background. Arguing. Which was The Way of Hacker International. "Chernobog says they're distinctly different, so they are," Stryker said with finality.

"I agree. I don't want the nuance, so don't tell it to me. But since all we have are folder titles, while this is interesting, I don't get why you're excited."

"I'm excited because we have more than titles. But before I get to that, you should know that we monitor the police bands. An anonymous tip was called in about a possible abduction. The police are at the scene."

"K-9 squad?"

"No, and you should be thankful, because those dogs know your scent and they'd actually incriminate you."

"Good point, not that we did anything wrong."

"No? You stole shredded classified documents." Stryker sounded smug.

"Yeah? How do you know that?"

"I know because we've gotten them all put back together, not just the folders, because the A-Cs assigned to us are excellent."

I was impressed. I'd had no idea Stryker was capable of buttering someone up, but apparently he had hidden depths.

"True enough. So, what's the word?"

"The word is that the shredded documents are schematics for robots. Robots who are supposed to imitate people."

"Always nice to be right. So, what else?"

"We could make a functioning robot from these—I have no idea what this information was doing at the home of the Assistant to the Secretary of State, but these papers shouldn't have been there. The police feel, just like you guys did, that something's off at the crime scene and that it's staged. However, no one's seen Marion Villanova for over two weeks, and so they're investigating it as a missing persons case while also trying to figure out what's going on. The blood is hers, by the way, and there's a lot of it."

"A full thermos, as memory serves."

"Right, that's a lot. Enough to insinuate that she's dead."

"Or else she's been donating blood on a regular basis until they had enough."

"I'm not following you."

"Evan came to the apartment today. Not two weeks ago, not one week ago, but today. He searched for what we'd already taken, found nothing, tossed the blood around, and then, and only then, did the police get their anonymous tip. They were waiting until she'd given enough blood to the cause to ensure that police would feel that she was potentially dead before her body left the apartment."

Heard voices again. "Yeah, okay, everyone agrees."

"I didn't realize I was on speaker."

"You're not, we're just all hooked into the call. Only I can talk to you, though."

"How extra special."

"What we don't agree on is why. This makes no sense, really. A scene staged as much as this one is—it's highly suspicious. The police aren't sure what's going on, but they know it's something fishy, fishier than an abduction."

"Maybe that's the goal. And don't ask me what that goal is. My job in this scenario is to try to figure that out, but it's not like I know the plans, I just have to foil them."

More voices. "Chernobog says she has every faith in you."

"Boggy's my favorite. Okay, so the police are as suspicious as we are, and we can now make robots from the shredded papers. It's more than we had."

"Why leave diamonds in ice cubes?" Len asked. "That seems stupid and pointless both."

"They were left there to be found. Evan looked for them, so he was expecting to find ice cubes in those trays and presumably the diamonds inside them."

"But why? Clearly it wasn't a payment to him, because he did the rest of whatever he viewed his job to be."

"What's this about diamonds?" Stryker asked before I could reply. "No one mentioned diamonds."

"They must have forgotten about them." Or figured I hadn't wanted Hacker International told about them. Explained the four diamonds I'd found and how. "Why do you care?"

"I care because the robot brains need diamonds to function."

We stared at each other as Kyle's phone beeped. He grunted. "Mister Reynolds just asked if we're okay." His phone beeped again. "And now there's Mister Buchanan, verifying that we're not idiots. I told them both we're in here, talking, and will join the rest of them in a little while."

"It's hard having two bosses, I know," Stryker said, sympathy oozing. "Chuck can be quite the pain to deal with and, frankly, sometimes Jeff can be worse."

"Yeah, yeah, and all your bosses are slave drivers and you know better than they do—"

Stopped speaking. The boys stared at me and it was silent on the phone. "What?" Len asked finally.

"Two bosses. What if Villanova and Evan have two bosses? Or more? Or a new boss who took over once Strauss was dead? What if they're in it together somehow and trying to play or appease those different bosses?"

Everyone was quiet, a shocking thing, really. A-Cs were normally silent when thinking, but humans weren't always. Hacker International in particular liked to run their yaps almost as much as I liked to run mine.

"That could be," Stryker said slowly. "But if so, who are their bosses and what's really going on?"

"The boss they liked was Strauss," Len said.

"Why do you say that? Not arguing, just asking."

Len shrugged. "Because they were already rolling it and always could have come to you for help, meaning they were happy to be involved."

"Precedent has been set for enemies coming to me for help, so . . ."

"Villanova's been her assistant for as long as you've been in D.C., right?"

"Longer."

"You think this was rolling when it was because that's when Strauss gave the go order. So, why keep it going now that she's dead?"

"If you think it's to honor her, I don't buy it."

"No, I think someone else knew about it, and is making Villanova and Evan continue the plan."

"Kitty," Stryker said, "the robot schematics are general for the most part, however, they have two significant things that stand out beyond their needing diamonds to function—they're all supposed to explode and they're all for women."

"Seriously?"

"Yeah. The 'original prototype' was a female. We figure that's the Kitty-Bot."

"Why have them built only to explode?" Kyle asked. "That seems awfully wasteful."

Shrugged. "Of the diamonds, yeah, but it's effective otherwise. We've already figured out how they were going to use the Kitty-Bot. It's not a leap to assume that a woman's going to be able to get closer to certain people or in certain situations than a man."

"Agreed," Stryker said. "But there are a couple that are very specific, and we know this because they were named."

"Really? Who?"

"Janelle Gardiner and Amy."

"Amy who?"

"Amy Amy. Our Amy."

CHAPTER 27

M **ANAGED NOT TO GET** too angry. Well, that was a lie. Was really angry, but decided to save it for when I was really going to need it. "Is Amy safe?"

"Yeah, we've verified. She and Becky are in their rooms and Christopher's there and has been since we figured out that she was called out, which was right before I called you. They have security in with them as well as all over the Embassy. And your dad is there with them, too."

"Great." Pondered. Realized I was still me and needed to talk to think. "Okay, so is Talia Lee on that list by any chance?"

"No, the only names are Amy Gaultier and Janelle Gardiner. Not to say that they aren't planning more, because it certainly seems like they are. But those are the only names called out. The rest are in code, and we haven't cracked the code yet." Voices in the background. "Yeah, yeah. The guys think we'll have it cracked by tomorrow."

"Okay, speed it up, speaking as Boss Number Three. So this explains why Talia called me instead of having Janelle call."

"It does?" Len asked.

"Yeah. They rolled the Kitty-Bot, and for all I know they're ready to roll the Janelle-Bot. Maybe they wouldn't have but Quinton Cross just died. Now is a perfect time for either Somerall or Gardiner to solidify power. That's why they suddenly want Amy to 'take her place' on the Board—they can get her alone that way and do the robot switch. Then she goes back to the Embassy and blows it up. No idea who or what Gardiner is going to blow up, but be assured that it's something. Then Somerall controls all of Gaultier free and clear of real competition."

"They'll use Lizzie as the excuse for the bomb, too," Kyle said angrily.

"Yeah. Okay, Eddy, anything else?"

"Not yet."

"Okay, then can you track Janelle Gardiner and determine where she is?"

"Hang on, Chernobog is on it." Waited a minute or so during which time I contemplated options. "Yeah, got it. She's supposedly at home, at least that's where her phone is." He gave me the address.

"Thank you. Keep me posted as events warrant. We'll be over there in a while." Hung up and dropped my phone into my purse. "Guys? I think we need to pay a call on Janelle Gardiner."

"Who do you want to take with us?" Len asked.

"Just you two." Looked at Bruno. "And our Attack Peregrine. And any Poofs who might be wanting to go on an adventure." Checked my purse. Harlie, the Head Poof, and Poofikins, my Poof, were in there, along with several others. "Excellent. Poofs are on Board. Do you guys have evidence gloves on you by any chance?"

"We do," Len said, as he picked up Bruno. "Serene told us to have them on us at all times, and that's CIA policy anyway."

"I have extras," Kyle said.

"Awesome, I'll want a pair." With that I grabbed his hand and Len's, then I hypersped us back to the West Wing and went out the same way the Spaceship Recovery Team had. There were no A-Cs around and we zipped past the few humans guarding the exterior of this part of the complex far faster than they could see.

Clearly we were going to need to up the White House security, regardless of whatever was supposedly already in place, because I'd gotten out twice and, so far, in once with no issues. Siler had gone chameleon, meaning that team wasn't advising anyone that they were going out of the complex, and Lorraine and Claudia had mentioned no issues, so I wasn't the only one dashing to and fro with no hindrance. While this was helpful for me and the rest of the team today, wasn't sure that I wanted anyone with hyperspeed just able to waltz in and out, especially since there was no guarantee that Stephanie was the only traitor A-C around these days.

Hyperspeed was hard on humans—the normal reaction when it was over was to barf your guts out, if you hadn't already passed out midway through. Tito was amazing, though, and he'd created our own Hyperspeed Dramamine. Every human agent we had now took it regularly, which included our specifically assigned Secret Service teams, too. The boys, needless to say, never missed a dose.

Fortunately, Kyle had recorded the address and I let him lead, since I still got lost in D.C. without a map, a GPS, and someone else to give me directions. So I provided the speed and Kyle steered.

Interestingly, Gardiner lived in Georgetown, just like Whitmore and Villanova. She wasn't in an apartment but her own three-story house. Which happily had a backyard with a lot of flourishing old trees and bushes, meaning it was well hidden from prying eyes.

Stopped running and we slunk around to the back door while putting on our plastic gloves. Listened hard but didn't hear anyone. Knocked softly. No answer. Tried the door. Unlocked. Not a good sign.

Opened the door slowly and carefully to find ourselves in the kitchen. It was clean and neat and no one was there. Closed the door behind us and checked the fridge and freezer. Both looked normal and nothing was ridiculously out of code, though Gardiner ate a lot of frozen and prepared meals. I could relate—my fridge had looked a lot like this before I'd joined Centaurion Division.

"If she's been taken or changed, it was recently," I said softly.

Len nodded and pointed to the milk. It went out of code two weeks from now, meaning that it had to have been purchased recently.

We worked our way through the house, Bruno perched on Len's shoulder. The house wasn't huge, and we only took a few minutes to find nothing and no one on the first or second floors. Kitchen, living room, bathroom, and utility room were on the first floor. The second one had two bedrooms and one bathroom. One of the bedrooms appeared to be where Gardiner slept and one was her home office. Checked the shredder—nothing in it.

The third floor had another bathroom and a playroom for the children I was pretty sure Gardiner didn't have. It also had another bedroom, and it was in here we finally found something of interest. Mainly, Janelle Gardiner.

She was fully clothed in a typical business suit, shoes included, and lying on top of the bed, hands crossed over her stomach. Makeup was on and her hair was done. Her eyes were closed but she wasn't breathing.

Went to her and touched her neck. No pulse. But her eyes opened.

The boys and I jumped and yelped, proving that our Stealth Skills were sadly lacking.

What I was fairly sure was the Janelle Gardiner Fem-Bot turned its head toward me. "Who are you?" Sounded like I remembered Gardiner sounding.

"A friend. Who are you?"

"Why are you here?" She sat up without using her arms or legs in any way. Either Gardiner had Abs of Steel or we were definitely talking to her Fem-Bot.

"Ah, we came to get you."

"Why? Is it time?"

"Um, yes?"

She swung her legs over the side of the bed and stood up. Whatever this Fem-Bot was supposed to do, it wasn't fool anyone into thinking that she was a real human being. The Kitty-Bot had been far more lifelike in her movements.

Which might mean that whoever made this Fem-Bot wasn't who made the original model. And perhaps they weren't as talented as the original design team.

"Where are the others?" the Gardiner Fem-Bot asked.

"Downstairs." Whatever was going to happen, us being on the ground floor was probably the best choice.

The Gardiner Fem-Bot nodded and headed off, us trailing her. Noted that Bruno hadn't bothered to go chameleon, meaning that either the Fem-Bot was trustworthy, which I highly doubted, or else he didn't feel the need to waste the effort to pretend he wasn't here.

We reached the ground floor and the Fem-Bot headed to the kitchen. Thought she was going to head outside but instead she grabbed a butcher knife from the block on the counter and swung around. "You're not supposed to be here."

"True enough!"

She swung at me. I ducked, and tried to kick her legs out. But I was in FLOTUS clothes and they just weren't really made for action. Landed on my butt.

Kyle bent his shoulder and slammed into Gardiner as if she was the opposing team's wide receiver. She hit the counter and bounced off, still waving the butcher knife around.

Len managed the sweep I hadn't been able to pull off, and she went down. He helped me up, fast, and we started to back out of the kitchen as the Fem-Bot leaped to her feet. In pumps, no less. I was impressed. Doing the moves in pumps was, as the last ten seconds had proved, still beyond me.

We were blocked from the back door, but the front one was available. "Boys, let's get out of here."

Kyle shoved me and Len behind him. Grabbed Kyle and pulled him back, just in time, as the Fem-Bot swung at him again. "I'm supposed to protect you," he said as I used my enhanced strength and threw him behind me.

"Not if it means you're going to die."

"You're not clear on this whole 'you have a security team in place to protect you' thing, are you?" Len asked as he grabbed me and tossed me to Kyle, who was by the front door.

This just meant that the Fem-Bot went for Len, which was no better than her swinging at Kyle. But Len had something Kyle hadn't—Bruno.

CHAPTER 28

BRUNO SAID SOMETHING very nasty in Peregrine and flew, claws first, into the Fem-Bot's face. Len, meanwhile, karate chopped the arm holding the butcher knife. She didn't let go and her arm didn't break, but the knife was now a lot farther away from Len's body. She kicked at him, though, and sent Len flying back into me and Kyle.

We slammed into furniture but the Fem-Bot was focused on Bruno, who was now on her head and managing to avoid the butcher knife.

Len grabbed a nearby end table and threw it at her. He still had his quarterback moves, because he hit her square in the chest. Kyle, meanwhile, helped me to my feet as the Fem-Bot chopped at and through the end table. Clearly her butcher knife was packing quite the punch.

Once I was upright, the boys grabbed the couch and threw it at her. This knocked her back into the kitchen and blocked her a little, too.

"Dudes feathered and otherwise, it's time to *go*."

Kyle flung the door open and I grabbed both boys as Bruno disengaged and flew after us and the Fem-Bot leaped the couch like a gazelle. A gazelle with a butcher knife, but whatever. Noted that the Fem-Bot's face was repairing itself right before we ran outside. The Fem-Bot followed us, still waving the butcher knife around. Made sure Len had Bruno, then hit the hyperspeed button.

I'd been on the track team in both high school and college as a sprinter and hurdler. Sprinters who looked behind them lost their races, so I rarely if ever did so, in part because whenever I did look behind me, it proved that the adage was true.

However, I couldn't help it, I had to see what the Fem-Bot was doing.

I looked back just in time to see the front door to Gardiner's house close, and there was no sign of the Fem-Bot in the street. Meaning she was probably going back upstairs to wait for whatever her trigger was. Or she was cleaning up the mess. Could go either way. But this might mean that Gardiner herself was still alive.

We could search for her, but who knew if someone had spotted us coming out of her house before I'd managed to take us to hyperspeed.

"We need to get back to the White House," Len said.

"It's as if you read my mind. Kyle, steer us home."

We got back more quickly than we'd gotten to Gardiner's thanks to the total adrenaline rush being attacked by a Fem-Bot with a butcher knife had given me. Got us back to where we'd been before we'd left—just outside the meeting room. It was still devoid of anyone, so that was one for the win column.

"What do we tell who?" Len asked shakily.

"No one and nothing, yet." Took a deep breath and let it out slowly. "No, that's stupid. But I don't want to tell Malcolm because I don't want to get yelled at. Same again for Jeff and the other guys." Plus, I didn't want any of us going up against the Bots without some kind of plan and a whole lot of protective gear.

"Whatever's going on, it's bad," Kyle said. "We should tell someone."

Decided to go for what would definitely be the lesser of all the evils and called Stryker. "I need Chernobog to hear this," I said by way of hello.

"Long time no talk and hi to you, too. You want speaker or just her hooked in?"

"Hooked in. Just her and the five of you. No A-Cs or other visiting guests."

Heard speaking and other noises in the background. "Got it. Go ahead, just the six of us are on with you, and I asked the others to leave the room for the time being."

"Great. The boys and I just found the Janelle Gardiner

Fem-Bot. She's currently at the address you gave us for Gardiner herself. Unlike the Kitty-Bot, she doesn't act all that human, and she's also self-repairing."

"That would be a Level Four, then," Chernobog said. "The Kitty-Bot is Level One. There are five levels indicated."

"Wow, how lucky can we get? Look, I want someone checking this out, but, honestly, I don't want to get yelled at for going to Gardiner's apartment in the first place. What can you guys do or suggest?"

"Since we know where a robot is," Henry Wu said, "I believe we can do a trace." Henry had doctorates in various sciences and was the best software guy out there. "Starting now to see what we can find."

"That's the spirit, Doctor Wu! What else do you guys have for me? Deactivation codes?"

"No, Kitty, that's the bad news." This was Ravi Gaekwad, the current King of Hacker Hill because he'd married a Dazzler in the form of Jennifer Barone. He was also our best reverse engineer, among other things. "The codes that have worked on all the androids so far are not working on the Kitty-Bot, we already tried that in a joint experiment with Dulce. As far as we can tell, whatever codes activate or deactivate the robots, it's different from those that work on the androids."

"And we haven't been able to identify any codes that will work," Yuri Stanislav said regretfully. Yuri was Russian, blind, and the only one of the hackers who worked out. I'd never asked him if he realized that the others all looked like various forms of Unhealthy Body Type or if he was keeping himself fit because he thought the others were all hardbodies, too. "Chernobog has created amazing algorithms to test an almost infinite variety of potential codes, so if she can't find it, it's possible that their codes can't be found."

"Oh, he's so sweet, isn't he?" Chernobog said fondly. "Assume that it will take longer than we would like. And also assume that these may be far more low tech than we're expecting as well."

"Low tech can sometimes be far more effective than high," Big George Lecroix agreed. Big George was from France and had a voice for radio. He wasn't TV material, but he could have made a fortune doing voiceover work.

"For all we know, the only real deactivation is the switches in their backs, if all the robots are created in the same way as the Kitty-Bot is. Are you sure you don't want to get Centaurion Division involved?"

"Kind of yes, kind of no." I really and truly didn't want to get yelled at and I also didn't want anyone tackling the Fem-Bot alone. "Something's going on, and I'd rather have the Fem-Bot watched than intercepted so we have a chance of following her. Plus, she was tougher than the Kitty-Bot, and I don't want anyone getting hurt."

"We can observe and track," Chernobog said. "Easily. Henry has definitely found the robot where you felt she would be. Does her being on the third floor of the building indicate anything?"

"That she's back exactly where we found her."

"Excellent. We'll keep her monitored, and we'll get eyes and ears into the house and, before you fret, we'll do it from a distance. Drones are wonderful things."

"Kitty shouldn't hear any more," Len said quickly. "Run this through me and Kyle."

"Only," Kyle added.

"As you wish, the CIA will have the lead," Chernobog said cheerfully. "Go back to your exciting meetings and bring us back some White House souvenirs."

"Um, you'll probably get to come over once things are settled."

"I don't leave the complex because I'm 'dead,' remember? I'd like a set of towels."

"I'll get someone right on that, Boggy." We hung up before the rest of Hacker International could make requests of things they wanted me to filch for them. Heaved a sigh. "Let's join the others. Play it cool. Jeff may know that we've been up to something, but let's make sure no one else does. Try thinking about flowers. It usually doesn't work, but hope springs eternal."

Considered going to the East Wing using the slow hyperspeed, which always sounded like an oxymoron but wasn't, but decided the boys and I needed time to gather ourselves, so we walked. Slowly. Because it was me, Len had to lead so that we'd get to where we were going.

Happily, when we reached the theater we found it packed with everyone who'd been in the other meetings.

They weren't watching a movie, however, at least not one released by Hollywood. They were watching what appeared to be a how-to video for building a Faster Than Light spaceship. Which explained their rapt interest and why none of them were really missing the three of us.

Jeff was standing near the back, and we managed to grab him and pull him out without disturbing too many people.

Figured the best defense was a good offense. "Why didn't you tell us where you were going? The boys and I nearly had heart attacks thinking you'd all been snatched up by the invisible helicarrier or something."

"Sorry, baby. Alexander suggested we take a look at what they're offering us because Chuck said that I might need to create a new Cabinet post for Interstellar Relations, and I honestly didn't think you'd be done with Drax already."

"Oh. Um. Good point. He's probably right." The offensive seemed to be working. Or my thinking about gladiolas was, for once, doing the job I wanted it to.

"Yeah, that was the general consensus."

Filled Jeff in on what we'd learned from Drax, leaving out what the boys and I had just learned about the Fem-Bots. "So, while I could sit and gaze, it doesn't really seem like you need me here."

Jeff ran his hand through his hair. "You want to go to the Embassy, don't you?"

"Yeah, even though I'm sure this video is truly exciting. Did we get the Elves over here, by the way? It's hella neat and tidy in the last two rooms you guys were in."

"Not that I know of, but I haven't actually talked to William about it." William Ward was Walter's older brother and in charge of all Security for all of Centaurion Division worldwide, meaning he was the one who assigned the Operations Team. His predecessor, Gladys Gower, had known about Algar. But I hadn't been able to ask William if he knew about our King of the Elves or not.

"Well, I'll check with him when I'm home. I mean, at the Embassy."

"Yeah, I'm not comfortable here, either."

"You will be," Antoinette said, as she joined us. "To answer the First Lady's question, no, we haven't had American Centaurion personnel here cleaning up. The staff is just quite efficient."

"No insult intended. Frankly, it's a compliment. They were almost as fast as the A-Cs, which is impressive."

Antoinette smiled. Managed not to faint. "I'll pass along your compliment. However, we have had a request to allow your personnel to help you move in fully, under the idea that the President will feel more comfortable. Which we've agreed to. Your things have been moved into the Master Bedroom, both from the room you were in here and from your Embassy. The new Secretary of State's things have been relocated to her new apartment as well. Rooms have been selected for your children, as well. We left that to your people—the person I spoke to was quite adamant that they needed to make certain . . . arrangements."

"Yes, thank you, they do." Things like creating an empathic isolation chamber where Jeff and Jamie could go if they needed to regenerate. And God alone knew what Charlie might need, other than a room with everything weighted down. Figured Algar had fixed things up properly and if he hadn't, well, I was going to the Embassy anyway.

Antoinette seemed expectant. Did my best to come up with what she might be expecting me to do right about now, because it was clear that I was the one who she was being expectant with.

"Ah . . . am I okay to go up and, um, check the new rooms out?"

Another smile! Score one for my FLOTUS skills. "Yes, if you'd like I can take you there." This offer seemed perfunctory rather than hopeful.

"Oh, I'm sure Jeff needs you here more than I do. The boys and I will be fine."

Antoinette nodded. "As you wish. Mister President, I believe your being out of the room has been noticed."

As she said this, King Benny came out. "There you are. Emperor Alexander wanted to know if all was well."

King Benny was a giant walking otter from Beta Eight. His real name was Musgraff but because he looked like Benedict Cumberbatch to me, I'd called him King Benny, and because of who I was presumed to be on Beta Eight, the name stuck.

He hadn't brought his ceremonial wooden antlers that he wore as a sign of office, but otherwise, he was dressed as I was used to—leather boots, a codpiece, and fur.

"We'll be right back." Jeff straightened up. "Musgraff could I ask a favor?" He sounded extremely formal and rather regal, too.

King Benny bowed deeply. "You have but to ask Leo—ah, Jeff." Almost all of us who'd gone on an unplanned visit to the Alpha Centauri system had God names. Jeff's was Leoalla, mine was Shealla. But we'd asked King Benny not to use those names here, and he was doing his best to comply.

"Can you accompany Kitty while she takes a look at our new living quarters? I'd appreciate someone helping back up Len and Kyle."

"Absolutely, it will be my honor."

Jeff grinned. "Thanks." He leaned down and kissed me. "Be good, baby."

"Ha ha, I consider this a challenge, you know."

He laughed. "I'm sure you do," he said quietly, so only I could hear. "However, with King Benny along, you're not going to be able to go onto the streets. Again. For a third time. I'll expect a full report when we're able to be alone with just our core team." With that Jeff and Antoinette went back into the theater.

"Why does Jeff think we need King Benny's help?" Len asked quietly.

"He thinks that I won't do anything he'd consider stupid or foolhardy with King Benny along." Clearly Jeff knew I'd already done something stupid and foolhardy and was, therefore, taking steps to ensure that didn't happen again. Took King Benny's arm and hooked mine through it. "But Leoalla isn't clear on just how sneaky Shealla can be."

King Benny nodded. "I presume Leoalla expects you to try to leave the complex in order to protect your world?"

"Indeed he does. And you're supposedly along to stop me."

"I would not go against what a God believes to be the best course. And I will, of course, offer my services as guard or warrior, as Shealla needs."

"And that, my beloved King Benny, is why Jeff's chosen wisely. At least as far as I'm concerned."

CHAPTER 29

WE WALKED UPSTAIRS to check out where we now lived. A couple of thoughts occurred and I pulled my phone out.

"Yes, Madam First Lady?" Walter said as he answered.

"Oh my God, Walt, we're losing that immediately. It's Kitty. All the time. Period. I'll give you that when we need to impress someone the full title is all that it should be. But otherwise? You call me Kitty or I replace you with an android."

"But titles matter." This was true, at least for Walter. Titles mattered a lot to Walter. And I liked Walter a lot. And he'd almost whined that statement, and Walter wasn't a whiner. And I'd let him use titles for me when I was the Ambassador.

"Fine. But can we choose something that doesn't make me feel uncomfortable?"

"I doubt it, because you are the First Lady, and I know you're uncomfortable with the job and the title."

Heaved a sigh. "Good point. I really don't like the 'madam.'"

"How about Chief First Lady?"

Considered my options. They seemed remarkably few. "It'll do."

"Thank you. So, Chief First Lady, what can I do for you?"

"Can you tell me where Len and Kyle and other key personnel are sleeping now?"

"All Embassy personnel who are now White House personnel will have rooms on the third floor of the White House residence. Those rooms haven't been used for staff for many years, but not to worry—the rooms have been refurbished and refitted and their things have been moved in, just as yours have."

"Wow. Efficiency is our watchword, isn't it?"

"Yes. I'd have had this done last week but we all felt that it was wrong to rush out the Former First Lady."

"True enough. We've rushed her right out, now."

"No. We've moved the new Secretary of State into her new apartment right next to the new Secretary of Transportation."

"Walt, can you please ask William to put Field agent teams onto the Cairo and make sure that our new Secretaries aren't harmed?"

"Already done, Chief First Lady. We also have security on every other newly appointed person and their immediate families. The Chief of Staff is advising us as the President makes his assignments. He also advised that you're also making appointments and that protection will be assigned to your new hires as well."

"I hire so well. Thanks, Walt. Can you please thank Raj when next you two speak and also let Pierre know that I'm going to be coming over to the Embassy in a little bit?"

"Yes, and we have gates in every residence bathroom, as well as in other areas of the complex."

"Super-duper, glad we're keeping to our theme of escape via the toilet."

"We do our best. Please note that there are no gates in any washroom that's too old, mostly due to space issues and concerns that the gates could harm anything historic. There are also none in any public bathrooms, as a precaution."

"Someone needs to give me a map. Of everything, really."

"Noted. I'll assign a team. We also have all gate activity in the White House complex being monitored twenty-four-seven by my team and by Embassy Security as well."

"Security is Job One, got it. And well done."

Walter and I hung up as we reached the Master Bedroom. One of the interesting things about the White House was that you were allowed to change things around in the living areas. As long as they weren't considered part of the museum or a historical portion or whatever, you could make changes.

And changes had been made.

The last time I'd been in here—near the end of Operation Epidemic, less than two weeks ago—the suite had had five rooms, one of which had been the huge dressing room and two of which were bathrooms. There had also been a huge bedroom suite and a living room.

The bathrooms and the dressing room were the same. But the bedroom and living room were altered.

A portion of the master bedroom had been turned into a nursery, similar to the nursery setup in the Embassy. Chose to assume that Algar expected Charlie with us for a few months longer, as opposed to being given a "have more babies" hint.

A part of the living room, on the other hand, had been converted into an isolation chamber. And, as with the nursery, it copied what we'd had in the Embassy. In fact, it was a duplicate, with a king bed and a twin bed, complete with all the necessary medical equipment, and it was all in white. The headboard for the king bed was very familiar.

Examined this carefully but chose not to say anything.

The rooms had been redecorated, too. Most of the White House was very Old World, or at least as Old World as a young country like ours could manage. But everything in the Master Suite was now very reminiscent of what Jeff had grown up in. We were in Martini Manor D.C.

Of course, the Martini family's complex in Florida was still more on the sleek and high-class hotel setup. But these rooms were more like theirs than the rooms at the Embassy, and definitely snazzier than standard A-C housing. While the general setup of the Master Suite was like our much beloved Human Lair back at Dulce, the interior was all Top Dawg A-C.

Wondered for a moment if Lucinda and Alfred had had anything to do with this. But it was unlikely that Algar was taking decorating tips from Jeff's parents. More like he'd created what they'd wanted years ago, and was just duplicating the theme. Intentionally, I was sure.

"The Operations Team is amazing," Kyle said, as we looked at everything.

"They are," I agreed. I considered the fact that Algar had tens of thousands of people convinced that there were a huge number of A-Cs who worked in Operations to be far more amazing than the fact that he could redo the White House in a matter of minutes. Walls were one thing. Fooling all of the people all of the time was much harder.

"This is so different from how we live on Beta Eight," King Benny said, sounding awed.

"Every world is different. We still have people living similarly to how yours do, they're just not around here."

We finished staring at where I was going to be living for the next couple of years and went searching for what room had been assigned to Jamie. Found the room assigned to Charlie first, though, across the hall and down a little. It was called the West Bedroom, which made no sense since it was in the middle. But I'd stopped arguing with how the names were assigned here days ago. Antoinette had shared that the West and East bedrooms were to the west and east of the Yellow Oval Room, which they were across the hall from, as if this explained everything. I'd quickly decided that the White House Staff were their own special kind of crazy and made the decision to humor them.

At least, I assumed this room was for Charlie, since it was decorated as a combination of Junior Science Wizard and Future Sports Star. In Bizarro World, the room that Charlie and Max—"my" sons—shared had been decorated very much like this.

Of course, the Poof Condo, dog beds, and Peregrine hammocks in here indicated one of my children was going to be living in this room. And since said room was not all pink, it clearly wasn't Jamie's.

"I guess the Operations Team expects you and Jeff to get busy," Len said.

"Um, yeah."

We wandered out and found that Jamie was in the East Bedroom, which was sort of connected to the West one by a small hallway and a ginormous closet. We could confirm that this was Jamie's room because it was a fabulous Shrine to Pink and loaded with more Poof Condos, dog beds, and Peregrine hammocks than Charlie's room.

"Think she'll ever outgrow her love of pink?" Kyle asked.

"One can dream. But, you know, as long as it's her choice, whatever color she wants." I just hoped she wasn't going to be disappointed—this room was actually smaller than the room she'd had at the Embassy.

"See?" Len said encouragingly. "You're a great mother."

"If you're one with the Operations Team's suggestion that Jeff and I need to grow our family, I don't want to hear about it right now. I'm still not managing the two I have all that well—the idea of three is almost terrifying."

We wandered out and down the hall. The family dining room and kitchen were across from the Master Suite, the kids' rooms were across from that oval room, and the Treaty Room and Lincoln Bedroom were also on the Master Suite side.

All these other rooms looked like the rest of the White House—old and expensive. It didn't seem like the Operations Team had touched them other than to put in gates in their bathrooms, as confirmed by the boys and my ability to see the small red dab of paint on the bottom of every wall that indicated a gate was there.

Kyle was explaining the red dots and the gates to King Benny when we headed across the hall again. The Queen's Bedroom was across from the Lincoln, and we peeked into it. To find that it was decorated just like the other bedrooms—in Early American Martini Manor.

"Who's supposed to be in here?" Kyle asked, interrupting himself from his own explanation.

"I have no idea. Maybe my parents?"

"Doesn't look like it's set up for them," Len said. "I mean, I thought this room was supposed to be for your overnight guests if the Lincoln Bedroom was taken. So I can see them staying here in that case, but this looks set up for someone to live here permanently."

King Benny sniffed. As in sniffed like an animal would. "Whoever it is, I believe their things indicate a female."

Was about to comment on the mystery and King Benny's sense of smell when my phone rang. Happily, it wasn't an anonymous number. "Hey, Lizzie, what's up?"

"Kitty? All my stuff is gone!" Lizzie sounded frantic. "I went to my room to get something and nothing's there. Is something wrong? Is my dad okay? Are you guys kicking me out?"

I hadn't known her long, but I'd never heard Lizzie this panicked, and she'd been trained by Assassination International. Then again, if I'd gone to my room and discovered everything missing, I'd be freaked out, too.

Looked around again. There was something on the bed that seemed personal. "Ah, Lizzie? Do you happen to own a stuffed animal that looks very much like a skunk?"

"It is a skunk. My dad got that for me so I'd have something to hold when . . ."

"When you had nightmares?" I asked gently.

"Yeah. How did you know? I don't remember showing it to you."

"You didn't. But, I'm looking at it right now."

"How?"

"How? With my eyes. Why is the better question. And the answer is that, apparently, the Operations Team has decided you're supposed to live in the White House."

CHAPTER 30

WE QUICKLY DECIDED that us getting to the Embassy was now Job One. Lizzie and I got off the phone, and we decided to test out the gate in her about-to-be new bathroom.

Gates looked like what we all walked through at the airport security check, but they had the ability to send you thousands of miles in seconds. The main gate hub was the Crash Site Dome, where the Ancients' ship had crashlanded. I hadn't had time to ask Wruck what he thought about this, but basically, the half-life of the Ancients' power source was impressive and kept the Dome powered and cloaked.

There were gates in every airport worldwide, even the tiniest ones. There were gates now in pretty much every train station and bus station, according to Christopher, because of me and Jeff. But whatever. More gates meant more mobility, right?

All the gates were programmable, but they all reset to send whoever walked through them to the Dome as a safety measure. However, the ones in the White House all reset to the Embassy, under the probably quite accurate idea that most of us would want to go to the Embassy in case of trouble, or just to visit.

So, we didn't have to do anything. We just walked through, as if we were going to walk through the wall, only we landed in the Embassy's basement, not smashing our faces. Len went first with Bruno, then King Benny, then me, with Kyle bringing up the rear. I was in between the boys, some for protection but mostly because the gates had made me nauseous from Day One with Centaurion, and I hated going through, especially if Jeff wasn't around to carry me.

However, I had a semihysterical teenager to get to, so I bit the bullet and walked through like a big girl. The journey was so short that my stomach only had a moment to consider making a fuss before it was over.

We headed upstairs to the kitchen to find Lizzie with Pierre. And a plate of Lucinda's brownies. Pierre had gone with the age-old Delicious Foodstuffs To Calm The Nerves Ploy. Proving again that my view of him as the most competent man in the world was dead-on.

King Benny, like the rest of the Planetary Council, was sleeping at the Embassy, and neither Lizzie nor Pierre had an issue with a giant walking otter. Lizzie actually seemed relieved to see him and gave him a big hug, which he returned. Of course, he was like a giant stuffed animal, in that sense, so score another one for us bringing over someone comforting.

The boys and I each grabbed a brownie while Pierre ordered up some pickled mackerel from the Elves and made King Benny's culinary day.

As Pierre explained the "ask for it when the door is closed, then open the door and what you want is there" magic of how the Elves worked to King Benny, who apparently hadn't ever asked before, I hugged Lizzie. "It'll be fine." Kept one arm around her shoulders while I scarfed my brownie. Oh, sure, Chef's food had been awesome. But Lucinda's brownies were the best on, at least, two planets. And I'd been active and had to think a lot since I'd last eaten. Snagged another brownie.

"Why does the Operations Team want me to leave the Embassy?" Lizzie asked, sounding slightly better than when we'd been on the phone.

"I have no idea. But your stuff is there. You got the biggest room, too. Well, for the kids."

Pierre got glasses of milk for all of us while we all ate more brownies. "I'm wondering, Kitty darling, if the assumption isn't that our Lizzie will function as your au pair. Or possibly even your ward."

"Like Robin was Batman's ward?"

"Exactly."

"But my dad is here," Lizzie said. "And he's working in the Embassy. He's not planning on leaving."

"No, he's not. But his job is going to mean that he's busy . . ." Considered things. Specifically, who was likely to have made this decision. And I sincerely doubted said individual was either human or A-C. "You know, I think it's going to be fine. I'm going to go up and see Jamie and Charlie. I think we'll all go back together, okay? You can get settled and talk to your dad when he's back."

"Back from what?"

"Yet another mission." Felt that I was right, but wanted to be sure. And there was really only one way to do that. Besides, I wanted to verify some other things, too. "Len, Kyle, King Benny, you guys stay here with Lizzie. I'll be back soonish and I'll call if I need help with the kids."

With that, I zipped off to the top floor. Where Jeff and I had lived since we'd been moved to D.C. Until yesterday.

Opened the door carefully, but no one was there. Apparently Doreen and Irving hadn't been moved in here yet.

Went into the master bedroom and checked on the beds in the isolation room—the headboard for the king bed in particular. It was definitely different than it had been, just slightly, but this headboard was vitally important, and I'd paid a lot of attention to it once I'd discovered that fact.

Headed into the closet. The hamper was there, though nothing else was. Sat down and looked at it. "I thought the stationary cube was for the Embassy."

The Z'porrah had littered our world with power cubes—things that looked like bright white and golden Rubik's Cubes. However, they allowed you to move anywhere, anyhow, as long as you could see your location in your mind and had the cube set up properly.

The Poofs had confiscated all but two of the power cubes during Operation Destruction. Cliff had had one of the power cubes—presumably the one LaRue had brought with her from her planet—and we'd gotten that one from him, finally, at the end of Operation Epidemic. But there had been another one, one had been hidden in plain sight—in the headboard of the bed in the Embassy's isolation room. A headboard no one had paid attention to for a long time.

Until I'd gotten the Poofs and Peregrines to admit to where this last cube was. Then I'd used it, along with Gladys, on a commando mission. She'd died on that mission.

I blinked back tears and, as I did, a rakishly handsome dwarf with unnaturally bright green eyes appeared, sitting cross-legged on the hamper. Algar smiled at me. "No. It's for you."

"Why?"

He shrugged. "You use it best. And let's not kid ourselves—you're going to remain active, wife of the most powerful man in the world or not. As today's events have amply shown."

"That power's open to debate, but I'll let it slide. And, thanks, I think, for moving the headboard into my room. So, um, will you be handling the cleaning at the White House?"

"Not so much, no. It would . . . disrupt the natural functioning there. But, to reassure you, yes, you can talk to me in your closet, just like you did last week."

"I didn't know for sure if you were there."

"But you picked up the penny."

"For good luck. And thank you for that luck. Why do you want Lizzie at the White House? Is something going to happen to Siler?"

"I like her. She's a lot like you. Only her parents weren't good."

"Yes, I kind of figured, since they were willing to kill her and all that. You like a lot of people, as far as I can tell. But you're not trying to have them all live with me."

"Her adoptive father brought her to *you* for safety. Not to the Embassy, but to you."

"He brought her to the Embassy because it's the most secure building around."

"Not anymore. The White House complex can now be said to be as secure."

"Shields have been installed?"

"They have indeed."

"Okay, that's great, but Siler didn't bring Lizzie to me forever. He brought her because he was on a mission and she needed to be somewhere safe. And before you say it, yeah, I get it. He's on a mission right now, and she's a teenager. Someone needs to be keeping an eye on her and she also needs to go to school. Denise is great, but she's got a room full of little kids to be taking care of, and Lizzie doesn't strike me as wanting to go into teaching as her life's work."

"Exactly."

"But shouldn't she, I don't know, sleep in the same place as her father?"

"Yes, if her father was home every night. But he won't be, even though he'll be working at the Embassy. He's one of your best operatives—you won't be able to sideline him."

"He's not about to die or something, is he?" Wasn't sure if I could handle it if Algar said yes.

"There is no fate, so could he die right now? Yes. Could he live for decades more? Yes. The future's always changing, and I've told you that if you want to discuss time, you need to talk to Charles."

"And then you snapped your fingers and disappeared. Fine, I'll let that drop. Is our going out into the greater cosmos going to cause problems for you?"

"Not any more problems than you all normally create. I'm not the one who was programmed not to allow that."

"Alexander took those restraints off of ACE."

"He did, but programming is hard to overcome."

"I'll have a chat with ACE."

"If you like."

"Using my own free will and all that."

"Good. Something else managed a bit of free will today."

"You mean the Kitty-Bot, don't you?"

"I do."

"Do you mean the Janelle Gardiner Fem-Bot as well?"

"I don't."

"So those are hints, but I'm not feeling sharp enough to catch it all. For all I know, Villanova and Evan are also using their free will."

"They are."

"Super. So are all the Dealers of Death." Algar nodded. "So, any chance you can do me a solid and tell me if Drax is trustworthy?"

"That's what you want to waste a favor on?" Algar actually seemed mildly shocked.

"I'd really rather waste it by asking you what all's going on, how many different actions are in active motion against us right now, if all the actions are being run by Cliff

Goodman, where my flyboys, Camilla, and the princesses are and if they're okay or not and what I need to do to rescue them, and what to do to get the White House staff to not hate me, but I'll settle for what I can get."

"Many things are going on, many actions are in motion, though you won't know about most of them for a long time, you've again harmed your biggest enemy far more than you know and, because of that, other enemies are striking while he's weak and you're focused incorrectly, I can't help you with rescues other than to tell you that, as always, time is of the essence, and just be you, you charm most people even though you don't realize it."

"Wow. That was . . . helpful. Sort of." Considered what he'd said that was key. "You said I was focused incorrectly. So, what should I be focused on?"

"Camping." And with that, Algar snapped his fingers and disappeared.

CHAPTER 31

"YOU DRIVE ME CRAZY," I said to the hamper. "But I appreciate the hints. I think. I do appreciate that I'll see you at the White House."

Got up and looked around the closet. Didn't see anything that indicated I should pick it up, so headed out of the apartment and to the elevator.

Went down to the third floor and into the daycare center. Jamie knew I was here, of course—she'd always had an uncanny ability to know when people she loved were nearby, and with ACE inside of her, that ability was strengthened.

ACE had been created by Alpha Four to keep the A-Cs, Jeff in particular, on Earth. We'd discovered him, and I'd originally filtered ACE into Gower during Operation Drug Addict. But due to what ACE had done to protect Earth during Operation Destruction, he'd been pulled away to face whatever kind of trial a superconsciousness could face.

Naomi Gower-Reynolds had saved ACE at the same time as she was sacrificing herself and becoming a superconsciousness of her own. ACE, Algar, and I were the only ones who knew that Naomi was still alive, though not in any earthly sense of the word, at least insofar as I could tell. Had my suspicions that Jamie knew, too, but actively chose not to ask.

Since returning to us, ACE had been housed inside of Jamie, which was protection for both of them. The downside was that I couldn't just chat with ACE like I had in the old days. Now, I had to wait for Jamie to be asleep, and it didn't hurt if I was asleep, also. So, these days, my chats with ACE tended to be kind of freaky, which was really par for my particular course.

However, Algar's veiled warning or not, I wasn't here to chat with ACE. I was here to get my kids.

Jamie ran over, arms outstretched for hugs, and I grabbed her, picked her up, and hugged her tightly while giving her plenty of kisses. Shoved any thoughts of bad things away—Jamie was easily as sensitive as Jeff, possibly more so, and I didn't need her worried about fake mothers and robots blowing up. Sure, she had powerful blocks installed in her mind by both Jeff and Christopher, but I wasn't positive that she kept them up all the time.

The next to hit me were the animals, of which we had a tonnage. In addition to my parents' three cats and four dogs—all of whom probably now considered themselves to belong to Jamie—we also had any unattached Poofs not on duty, any available Peregrines, and all the ocellars and cho-chos, the Beta Eight foxcats and pigdogs we'd brought back with us at the end of Operation Civil War.

The ocellars were a rusty orange color, with some blacks, browns, and yellows for highlights. They had elongated, pointy ears and extremely bright blue eyes, looked a little foxy and a lot like caracals, but in the same way that the Peregrines looked a lot like peacocks—similar and yet stronger, a lot more human-level intelligent, and just a little more alien. Ocellars were the same size as Peregrines without the tail-feathers.

Chochos, on the other hand, were about the size of an extra-large German Shepherd but with noses that were more squat and broad than elongated, long claws on their paws, tusks that stuck out just like a boar's, bristles instead of whiskers, and curlicue tails. They looked dorky but in a totally cute way.

The alien animals did time on the first floor of the Zoo whenever we did open viewings of our own personal Galactic Menagerie. However, things being what they were, we hadn't had the Zoo open for a couple of weeks now. And whenever they weren't on exhibit, the animals slept in our rooms or were at daycare with Jamie.

The realization that I was going to be bringing an entire alien petting zoo into the White House hit me. There was no way my children were going to accept that the animals weren't moving with us. Frankly, the animals weren't going to accept it, either.

Decided I'd worry about that later as I petted every

furred or feathered body that I could reach. After all, there had to be some upside to the FLOTUS gig, and if my mark on the White House was going to be really fantastic luxury kennels, then so be it.

"You're here a little early," Denise said cheerfully as she joined us and the other daycare kids came over for hugs. "Charlie's still napping."

Checked my watch as I put Jamie down. We were indeed now into later afternoon. Early to get the kids for dinner, but, under the circumstances, that worked for me because I had no intention of going back to the White House any sooner than I had to. "Well, I can probably get him and keep him asleep."

Enjoyed hugging all the kids. Wasn't looking forward to having to ask permission to visit now, nor the idea that I'd be dragging along a million security personnel. Of course, I'd managed to leave all my Secret Service detail in the White House for most of the afternoon while I'd been elsewhere, so perhaps I was worried for nothing.

"Oh," Denise said, "Jeff called and asked me to remind you that you're needed back at the White House and can't hide out here."

"I need a new husband."

She shook her head. "Chuck sent me a text saying the same thing as Jeff. So I think you're out of luck on your options."

"Thanks, traitor."

Jamie looked up at me. "You're funny, Mommy. You know Missus Lewis isn't a traitor."

"That's true, I do, and you're right, I was teasing her." Chucked Jamie under her chin. "Shall we get your brother? All our things are moved into the new house where we're going to live for a while, and I can't wait for you to see your room."

Instead of excited, which I'd expected, Jamie looked worried. "Where is Lizzie going to stay?"

Interesting. Well, it wasn't like it was going to be a secret. "Lizzie has a room at our new house, too, right down the hall from you."

"Yay!" Jamie jumped up and down and clapped her hands. "Lizzie's going to stay with us forever!"

Denise and I exchanged another look. Denise knelt

down and hugged Jamie gently around her shoulders. "You know that Lizzie's daddy won't want her to live with someone else forever."

"Oh, he can live with us, too," Jamie said. "I like Uncle Benjamin. He's neat."

"Yes, he is. So, let's get Charlie and go downstairs. King Benny is here, too."

At this all the kids gasped, even Raymond, who at ten was the eldest in our school and daycare combo. All the kids had met the Planetary Council, and while they seemed to like everyone and were very interested in Rohini and Bettini, the other Shantanu in the Council, King Benny was definitely the Daycare Favorite. As a giant walking otter, his Cuteness Level started at eleven.

"Can we go see him, please, Mommy?" Rachel begged, clearly speaking for all the kids.

Denise looked at me and raised her eyebrow questioningly.

Pulled out my phone and sent a text to Len, asking him to get the A-Cs assigned to Animal Duty revved up and ready to transport. "Sure, why not? Pierre has special, dinner-ruining treats in the kitchen, too."

"Oh, good." Denise laughed. "Hopefully you mean Lucinda's brownies."

"I do, indeed, and the grown-ups need a treat, too." I mean, I'd only had a few brownies and hadn't even finished my milk. I was still hungry. "Ah, Pierre says that they'll come up to us, so let's get ready for Special Snack Time."

While Denise got the kids in order, I went and got Charlie. To find Wilbur, my personal chocho, curled up next to Charlie's crib. This wasn't a surprise, really. Wilbur adored Charlie, and if Charlie wasn't with me or Jeff, Wilbur was right by his side.

Patted Wilbur. "What a good chocho you are."

Wilbur honk-barked very softly to share that I was the greatest and that he was on the guarding case and all things were secure in the baby sleep chamber.

Charlie was indeed still asleep, clutching his Poof, and looked angelic, as children do when they're sleeping. Even though human genetics were supposedly always dominant in hybrid children, and Jamie did look pretty much exactly like me, I could really see Jeff in Charlie.

Stroked his hair, then I lifted him and his Poof up into my arms. The Poof grumbled a little, but Charlie stayed asleep, though he did nestle his head into my neck.

"Come on, Wilbur," I whispered. "We're going on a trip." Wilbur got up and trotted happily at my heels.

All the kids had their own Poofs, and most of the families of our Embassy Daycare Kids had their own Peregrines now. The ocellars and chochos hadn't gone forth and multiplied enough to ensure that everyone had their own foxcat or pigdog yet, but that seemed to be just a matter of time.

The kids were in a semicircle on the floor, all looking expectant. Other than Jamie, who was getting her things ready to go, meaning getting all the animals prepped for departure. This wasn't something that a little girl of four and a half would normally be in charge of, but Jamie was as effective with the animals as I was. Wasn't sure if this meant she had my Dr. Doolittle talent or if she just loved the animals so much that they wanted to do whatever to please her, but the outcome was that they all behaved like well-trained animal citizens for her.

"When did he go down?" I asked Denise softly, as Jamie got the cats and Poofs into their luxury carrier on wheels, aka the Feline Winnebago.

"Late, so don't worry. He was really using his talents today." She looked a little worried. "He lifted Dudley."

Dudley was our Great Dane and therefore the largest animal we had, since he was even bigger than the chochos.

"Wow. Is Dudley okay?"

"Yes, as are the other animals. He, ah, did the animals in order of their weight. He started with the cats, then the ocellars, then Duchess, Dottie, and Duke, then the chochos, and then Dudley."

Duchess was our pit bull, Dottie our Dalmatian, and Duke was our Labrador. Duke might have been close to the chochos in weight, but I had a feeling that Charlie was being far more accurate than was good for anyone's peace of mind.

"Um . . ."

"Yeah." Denise shrugged. "The animals didn't seem to mind . . . too much. And Wilbur loved it."

"I think Wilbur is genetically disposed to love anything Charlie wants to do, potentially ever."

She laughed as Len, Kyle, Lizzie, Pierre, King Benny, four gigantic platters of brownies, and three gallons of milk arrived.

The kids were all great and waited until the new arrivals had put the food down on the lunch tables. Then they all sort of mobbed King Benny.

It reminded me of when Jeff and Christopher and I had arrived at Martini Manor during Operation Drug Addict and the kids had spotted them. King Benny was doing what Jeff had—picking the kids up, hugging them, tossing them carefully in the air and catching them. Got a sad, misty feeling—Stephanie had been there and she'd mobbed her uncles, too. Right before she'd shared with me that Jeff and I would never be allowed to be married.

She'd been fifteen then, and even though she'd been a little too old for the mob scene she'd still participated willingly.

And now? Now she'd spit at Jeff and Christopher before she'd hug them. Which was, all things considered, odd. Because she had me to blame for everything. So why hate on her beloved uncles when a convenient scapegoat was right there? Why desert her entire family? It was the rare A-C who could or would do that willingly. I could only come up with a handful.

My brain nudged while I ate another brownie and watched the kids and King Benny have such a nice time. Algar had said I should be focused on camping, which I hated. But if I thought about all that had gone on today, the Kitty-Bot had come from Camp David, where a peace treaty meeting was supposed to be happening.

But we'd captured the Kitty-Bot, so why would Camp David matter in the same way now?

Answered my own mental question—because Algar had said that other enemies would be striking while Cliff was weak. As in more than one. And I doubted he meant them as a group, per se, because Algar enjoyed giving fiddly little clues based on music, lyrics, and wordplay.

As in and as always, there was more than one plan going on.

So maybe the question was—which plan was Stephanie in on?

CHAPTER 32

WHILE THE KIDS enjoyed King Benny and Jamie excitedly shared with Lizzie that Lizzie would be lucky enough to be living with us forever and ever and Lizzie managed to feign excitement about this, I sent a text to Amy.

I was sort of surprised that the response I got was that she, Christopher, the baby, and my dad came down to the daycare center along with about half of the Field teams that had been assigned to Amy's protective detail. Dad was holding Becky, and I had the distinct impression that he and my mother had totally claimed the Maternal Grandparent Rights, for which I was happy and not jealous.

Amy's father had murdered her mother. Chuckie had known this for a long time but Amy and I hadn't. What we had known was that her mother's body had barely been in the ground before her father had married his secretary—who happened to be LaRue Demorte, Ancient Turncoat to the Stars.

Herbert Gaultier had been the Big Bad behind Operation Confusion, when Jamie had been born. Christopher had had to kill him, in fact, to stop him from killing Amy and the rest of us, too. Fortunately, Amy was so appalled by what her father had become that this was merely part of their courtship ritual.

My parents had stepped in and, since Amy had been my friend since ninth grade, become her second set of parents. This worked out well because Christopher's mother, Terry, had been murdered by the Yates-Mephistopheles in-control superbeing when he and Jeff were ten, so Alfred and

Lucinda felt they were Christopher's second set of parents. Basically, White had to fend off my parents and Jeff's both in order to get to spend time with his grandchild. He seemed okay with it, at least so far, though Becky was only a week old, so time would tell.

King Benny and Denise made much over Becky while Amy pulled me and Christopher aside. "Okay, I want all the details and I want them now," Amy said without any preamble.

"You should be upstairs, resting," Christopher countered, shooting Patented Glare #1 at me. Christopher was the unquestioned Glaring Champion of the World, and I figured he needed to keep in practice, since he'd spent most of this past week smiling at his first child.

Amy snorted. "As if. Kitty was embroiled with saving the world before Jamie was hours old. By that standard, we're slackers. I've had over a week of relaxed new mother time, and while I'm all for extending that, I'm not willing to let our enemies destroy us simply because you think I'm a delicate freaking flower."

Amy didn't actually look like a wilting flower. She'd had a very good birth—fast, since A-C babies came fast—and without complications, so totally unlike mine with Jamie. What she hadn't done was mutate like I had, so while she still looked great, she wasn't back to a prepregnancy state. Close, though, so I wondered if she might have a mutation that was slower to arrive.

Christopher had shot himself up to the max with Surcenthumain, and the Surcenthumain in Jeff's bloodstream was what had affected me when Jamie was in utero. The expectation was that Amy would have mutated like I had, but so far, other than looking really good, she didn't look like anything else had changed, and the doctors said that nothing had. Meaning that was a worry for another day.

"That's my girl, Ames. And Christopher, chill. Frankly, the last thing we want is to give anyone a chance at Amy. However, forewarned is forearmed, and all that sort of blah, blah, blah." Did my Recap Girl thing again and caught them up on all I knew. "You two now know more than Jeff and Chuckie do, so do me a solid and come up with ideas and action plans so that I can look like a winner when I share this with them."

Amy nodded slowly. "You're sure that there's more than one plan going on?"

"There always is," Christopher replied. "So that's always the safe bet."

"Exactly. Meaning, it would help to determine what the plans are or who's running what or similar."

Amy cocked her head. "Do you think that Villanova is the one who triggered the Kitty-Bot?"

"I think that's part of what we should probably call the Strauss Initiative, so yes."

"What about Janelle?" Amy asked. "Do you think there being a robot version of her is part of the same plan?"

"Not sure," I admitted.

"I'd think it is," Christopher said slowly. "Because of what you mentioned when you filled us in—Eugene was triggered into action via a robots take over people plan."

"Yeah, we'd thought that was a ruse, but if it wasn't, then Strauss had this going even during the Sith Apprentice Tryouts that were Operation Sherlock."

"That makes sense," Amy said. "I mean, who's to say there's only one Sith?"

"There are always two," I said automatically. "The Master and the Apprentice."

"You spend too much time with the hackers." Amy shook her head. "That's not what I meant. I mean—who's to say that there weren't two Masters?"

Christopher and I stared at her. "Ah, what?" he asked finally.

She rolled her eyes. "Come on, you guys. Kitty, this is normally your side of things. I'm suggesting that Monica Strauss was never working with Cliff Goodman, or if she was, she was faking him out. I think she was a Mastermind in her own right—the robot stuff makes it likely. And you've said how Ronald Yates was sleeping with anything that moved. So, maybe he slept with her early, she found out what was going on, and she distanced herself from Reid and Cliff and the others, but took what she could use from Yates and ran with it."

"But we never had her on radar all this time," Christopher said after a few moments of shocked silence. "We didn't even distrust her until the other Kitty made it clear that she suspected Strauss of being anti-alien."

"So what? Cliff had his crazy one-sided fight going on with Chuck. He probably could have taken over easily if he hadn't been so bent on playing a chess game that Chuck wasn't even aware he was involved with. Maybe Strauss didn't have anyone she was trying to screw over, and she just wanted to get to become the President without ever having to be elected."

"Ames, you're on fire. Clearly having a baby was great for you. That makes sense, a ton of sense. Meaning that Villanova was always doing the double agent thing for Strauss."

Amy shrugged. "Just like Camilla does for us."

"Cliff was always looking for our double agents . . ." Had to formulate what I was thinking into coherent words.

"What?" Amy said after a few seconds. "I know that look."

"What if Cliff figured out that Strauss was about to make her Mastermind move? Maybe that's why he rolled Operation Epidemic when he did—because we'd not only given him a great patsy in the Planetary Council, but if he didn't kill her in a way that didn't look suspicious, then she'd win."

"That means the action at Camp David was key," Christopher said. "Because that's where the Kitty-Bot was waiting."

"Meaning what?" Amy asked. "The Kitty-Bot's been captured. That plan is over now, right?"

"No, I don't think so." And not just because Algar had told me I had to go camping. "They've been doing their level best for years to keep you out of Gaultier and off the Board, and all of a sudden it's your rightful place? That's to get you alone and turn you into a robot. For all we know, they have the Amy-Bot ready to go and are just waiting to do the switch when you and Gardiner are in the same room."

"Sounds like Ansom," Amy said. "He's all about getting things to do double-duty. But that doesn't indicate they're following Strauss' plan."

"How did they get the robot schematics?"

"She might have given them to several people," Christopher said. "After all, Eugene had them, and he'd gotten them from Pia Ryan."

"Who'd gotten them from Marion Villanova, most likely. Meaning that I think we're safe for right now to assume that anyone working on the Stepford Wives Plan is working the plan Strauss had going in some way."

"Meaning that we're still out the person who took the helicarrier and our people." Christopher shot Patented Glare #4 at the room in general.

A large number of A-Cs who'd drawn the short straws appeared and got the dogs, chochos, and occllars onto leashes, because we all kept up the fiction that the animals behaved when semi-restrained.

Watched the kids while this was going on. They were still all about the King Benny Experience and were admiring Becky along with him. None of them felt the need to break off to exchange withering banter with an adult, not even Lizzie, who was about the age Stephanie had been during Operation Drug Addict.

Lizzie was so different from Stephanie, though, and not just because she was a human. In some ways she and Stephanie were alike, of course. But not in the ways that mattered most.

My brain nudged, rather insistently. "You know what? We need to get over to the White House pronto, because I think I need to share a theory with our core team. And I need to do it fast."

CHAPTER 33

OF COURSE, fast was a relative term when dealing with children and animals.

Christopher went first, to ensure that the White House was prepared for the onslaught of fur and feathers we were bringing with us and to get Jeff and Chuckie ready to pull everyone into yet another meeting. Sent Mom a text requesting her help with this and why I felt I needed the floor.

Once we got an all clear from Christopher, the A-Cs on Animal Transport Duty headed off. Then it was time for the rest of us. Amy had Becky, King Benny carried Jamie—earning her the total envy of all the rest of the kids—and Dad took Charlie, who'd woken up thankfully without issue and also thankfully without wanting to telekinetically lift anyone or anything for the moment. Technically the boys had me, though Len went before me and Kyle went last, to ensure I went through.

Score one for the Elves—in the time I'd been gone they'd installed the First Kennels by converting what had been the Game Room on the third floor to the Luxury Kennels. Apparently Algar liked the animals as much if not more than he liked me, because they had the nicest digs of anyone so far. Not that I minded. My father totally approved, too, which was definitely one for my personal win column.

The A-Cs on Animal Duty had the bedroom that attached to the kennels, and it was set up nicely so that four could sleep while four were awake. It was quite military in that sense, but they didn't seem to mind. At least, I took them telling me that they'd actually won the right to get to be on White House duty and were lording it over their comrades to mean they were happy with the setup. Of course, that might have been said for Dad's benefit. Dad thought Animal Patrol was one of the best gigs an A-C could get. Needless to say, all the pets loved him. Wasn't so sure about the A-Cs who worked this gig, and had a feeling most of them thought Dad was just this side of crazy due to his demands that the pets be treated like everyone else and therefore needed to be appeased.

Naturally, after we put the animals into their living quarters and requested they stay there at least until Antoinette went home for the night, we had to show the kids their rooms. All three of them seemed delighted, particularly Charlie who apparently no longer wanted to be in the nursery.

Managed not to have my feelings hurt by this. Well, not too much. Mostly because I had no time to wallow in anything, since we now had the issue of who in the world was going to watch the kids over here when Jeff and I were working. Maybe other First Families had their action stop at six p.m. every day, though I doubted it, but we certainly ran 24/7 far too often.

"I can handle this, kitten," Dad said, as we all looked over Lizzie's room and Jamie pronounced it okay because it had a Poof Condo, dog beds, and Peregrine hammocks. "I'm happy to spend extra time with my grandchildren, all three of them." Lizzie looked at Dad suspiciously.

"He's not kidding. My parents consider Amy and my other best friend from high school, Sheila, to be their 'other' daughters. We adopt quickly in this family."

Dad put his arm around Lizzie's shoulders. "We're all for as many grandchildren as we can get, including those who arrive a little later."

Vance chose this moment to join us. "Ah, I see you're ready for the First Family's Nanny to come on duty."

We all stared at him. "You took mind reading classes?" I asked finally.

He grinned. "Let's just say that I'm well aware of how you roll and that I've spent a lot of time talking to Pierre this afternoon."

"Who'd you get?" Amy asked. "Because it's going to be hard to beat Denise Lewis at this."

"Well, Denise isn't being beaten, so to speak," Vance replied. "She's still who will have the First Children during regular daycare and schooling hours, at least until they're ready for the Sidwell Friends School."

"The where?" I asked.

"It's one of the best local private schools," Amy said. "Loaded with children whose parents are hugely influential."

"*The* best, as far as I'm concerned," Vance said. "It's one of the few places where First Children tend to go. And where yours will be going."

"Normally our children school within our community," Christopher said, shooting Patented Glare #3 at Vance.

Who ignored it. "Do they? How nice for those children who aren't the children of the President of the United States. The children of the President of the United States, however, will be going to the Sidwell Friends School. As will the Lewis children. And as will Lizzie."

"What?" she asked.

"School," Vance said. "You'll be at the high school when sessions resume. You're already enrolled as, per Pierre, the ward of the First Lady. Expect to have your cachet increased from what it was at your other school. You're welcome."

Lizzie's jaw was still hanging open. I shut it gently. "You already know Vance, Lizzie. Think of him as Our Pierre in the White House and just roll with it. What else have you magically handled while I wasn't around? And please tell me it's everything." Made a mental note to not be around more so that Vance could work.

"Plenty, but you can just lose the idea that I'm going to cover as FLOTUS all the time."

"Wow, I suddenly hate your mind reading skills."

"I'm sure you do. However, I've gotten your double in place, which was simple, since Francine already has experience with that from what I've been told. Finding Jeff's is harder, but Raj feels confident we'll be able to find someone out there in the greater A-C community who can fit the bill."

"Um, what?"

"Doubles," Amy answered. "All the presidents have them. So the double goes to a gala when the President is having a tryst or having a top level meeting, things like that." Clearly Amy was on the Vance Wavelength.

"Oh. Like *Dave*. Gotcha."

"I suggest you watch that movie, and several others I have listed for you, carefully," Vance said. "Take notes, even. You'll need the information, though it seems unlikely that Jeff's going to be chasing interns around."

"Let's be safe and make all the interns old, ugly, and stupid."

"Nice try. They'll be young and bright, and half of them will be A-Cs, so rest easy. At any rate, I also have your press secretary handled, chosen out of the selection of troubadours Raj suggested. Colette will be briefed by Raj tonight and will be fully on the job tomorrow."

"Have I ever met Colette?"

"Doubt it. She's been working with Raj and Serene a lot, though."

"Ah, I'm sure she'll be great." Based on the Raj and Serene Connection, I was sure that she was in the A-C CIA, and that meant probably really efficient. "So, who's the nanny, then?"

"Nadine, who I know you do know. She's also been working with Raj and Serene, but she loves kids, so I think she's a great choice."

Nadine had been the A-C troubadour assigned to double Serene during Operation Infiltration. I knew and liked her, and that she was also in Serene's Secret Club seemed obvious. Meaning a really well-trained A-C likely willing to take the smart risks would be watching my children. I was good with this.

"Okay, she's awesome."

"I'm glad you think so." Nadine came in with Francine and another woman I didn't know. The third could have been their sister, though—same Dazzler gorgeous, same blonde hair, similar features. As I thought about it, she probably was their sister. After all, I'd never asked Francine and Nadine if they were related. "You're Colette, aren't you?"

She dimpled. "Good guess."

"Which sister are you, oldest, middle, or baby?"

"Baby." Colette laughed. "Francine's the middle, so she tries harder. You're good."

"No, I'm really slow, but sometimes I can catch on."

Francine grinned. "Oh, don't sell yourself short. We never said we were sisters."

"Yeah, you only all look a lot alike." Different enough to double me and Serene, who were not all that similar seeing as she was a typical Dazzler and I was not. Better looking than me by far, but the beauty of doubles was that as long as they were close enough, expectations covered the rest.

"Better late than never," Nadine said with a smile. "Now, it's time for me to take over as nanny and for you all to get back to the business of running this country."

Of course, we didn't leave immediately, seeing as I had to kiss and hug the kids goodbye several times, plus go over what they should and shouldn't have, do, and all that jazz. Then they had to hug and kiss King Benny goodbye even more than they had me. Did my best not to be bitter. Happily, Pierre had whipped up a schedule of how we did things and Nadine was a quick study. Plus the kids liked her, which was an added bonus. Oh sure, not as much as they liked King Benny, but I was getting the feeling that no one was going to compare to King Benny in the short or long run.

"I know I'm not needed downstairs," Dad said. "I'll help Nadine so you can relax fully, kitten."

Amy was torn between staying with Nadine or coming with us, but Christopher put his foot down about Becky being around a ton of people. So Amy stayed with Dad, Nadine, and the kids, and it was decided that she would be on the phone with Christopher, listening in on anything of importance and adding in as needed.

"I thought Raj was supposed to fill you in before you started," I said to Colette as the rest of us, King Benny included, headed back downstairs.

"He'll go over it all tonight, but since I'm living here now, I came over early to get settled in."

"We're all in a room together," Francine said, before I could ask. "The Operations Team did a great job."

"Yeah, they always do. Are you two sharing?" I asked Len and Kyle.

Len nodded. "Yep, we're used to it."

"And there's plenty of sitting rooms and stuff around here when someone has to hang the sock on the door," Kyle added, then blushed bright red.

Francine and Nadine giggled, but Colette gave Kyle a look I could only think of as interested. Well, both he and Len were smart, and intelligence was *the* Dazzler weakness.

Managed to control the Inner Hyena. "Good to know. Good to know. It'll be a change from the Embassy, though. No Elves here, at least not on a regular basis."

"Yeah," Len said quickly, presumably to keep us off the sock topic. "None of the White House staff live on the property anymore, but they used to. But there's staff here around the clock."

"Meaning that all of you need to remember that you're no longer in a secured facility," Vance said. "And I don't mean from a guns and bombs standpoint, because I know that shielding was put onto the entire complex. I mean that the walls will have ears and all of you need to restrict yourselves to casual chat about nothing when you're not in closed-door meetings."

Heaved a sigh. "Well then, I hope we're meeting everyone in a room like that, because I what I need to discuss is definitely not for the general public at large."

CHAPTER 34

WE WERE BACK in the big meeting room from earlier in the day. Had a sense of déjà vu—nothing like what I'd had during Operation Civil War, but still, the total feeling that I'd been here before doing this exact same thing was strong.

Of course, there were actually more people in here than we'd had before. Supposedly everyone had the high security clearances by now, even Abner Schnekedy, who was sitting with Culver, who had wisely kept her maiden name for business. Vance hadn't been kidding—Abner seemed to be almost vibrating from the thrill of being here. Well, better to have someone keen on the job, especially since I certainly wasn't winning the New Job Excitement Challenge.

Happily, the rest of Jeff's cabinet had been selected while I wasn't around and, other than nodding and waving at those now in the Inner Circle, nothing else was required of me in regard to this.

Chuckie was sitting between Jeff and Mom. He passed me a sign—the "keep quiet" sign. Meaning now wasn't a good time for me to share anything I was thinking.

"We have about thirty minutes before dinner," Mom said. "Kitty, we're discussing the Camp David peace talks."

Almost opened my mouth, but Chuckie shot me a quick glare and I managed to control myself. "Okay, when are they happening?"

"We feel it's imperative to get those back on track as soon as possible," Hochberg, who was sitting on Jeff's other side, said. He looked a lot better than he had earlier, which was good—clearly the promotion to VP had been an ego-booster.

"After we make good on the promise we made to Club Fifty-One," Raj said. "We did say they'd get a thank-you ceremony." Club 51 was the most vocal of the anti-alien organizations out there. But Raj had managed a brilliant switch at the end of Operation Epidemic, and he was right—we did need to make good.

"Do we really think any of them will show up?" Hey, it had to be asked.

"I think so," Chuckie said. "Some of them, anyway."

"They're spread out all over the country—how will we manage a ceremony that doesn't give them an excuse to complain that we made them spend a fortune to get to the ceremony?" Hadn't realized I was coming into this meeting to be Negative Nelly, but someone had to ask the hard questions.

"There are ways," Jeff said. "However, I think this is something that can go to committee." Heads around the table nodded. "Great. Folks, I think I'd like to take a break before dinner and actually take a look at the Oval Office. Fritzy, I've been advised that my things are out of your office, so if you want to take a little time to see if you want a different chair, now's the time." This earned chuckles from the room. "I'd also like to do a small religious ceremony in the Oval Office, which is restricted to immediate family."

The nice thing about religion was that most normal people felt that it wasn't their place to tell someone else how to worship. So the room divided up fairly quickly, with Antoinette taking most people into a parlor for predinner drinks while the rest of us went to the Oval Office. I had Colette and Francine stay with the majority of the Planetary Council, but Alexander, being a close enough family member, was coming with us. Which was fine with me.

Mom didn't allow the Secret Service to join us, which of course meant an argument. Jeff said that Len and Kyle could be there as security, and Evalyne and Joseph subsided, mostly because Mom pointed out that we were inside the White House and could probably manage not to be killed in the next thirty minutes.

Once we were in the Oval Office, Jeff jerked his head at

Chuckie, who tossed some scanners to Raj, Lorraine, and Claudia, who all went over the room at hyperspeed. "All clean," Lorraine said as they finished up.

"Now," Claudia added. "It wasn't clean earlier."

"I had the Operations Team check, and the moment our security was in here we had Dulce scan the complex as well," Reader said.

"Tons of bugs," Tim said. "Most of them homegrown, but not all."

Chuckie rubbed the back of his neck. "I had this place swept yesterday."

"There are a lot of people coming in and out, Vance just gave me the 'speak softly and only in rooms you know are safe' lecture. But, since we are safe in here, Jeff, is there really a ceremony you want to do?"

"Yeah, baby, there is. It's brief, and then you can tell us what you've been wanting to tell us for at least an hour."

He looked at Gower, who walked over to Jeff and put his hand over Jeff's hearts. "Lead well and true, always do what you know to be right, protect the weak and helpless, and never capitulate to evil." Gower took his hand away and stepped back.

"That was it?"

Jeff grinned. "Told you it was short."

"We don't stand on a lot of ceremony," Gower added with a laugh.

"Don't try to lie to me, I had a Royal Wedding, remember?"

"Should I hook Amy in now?" Christopher asked.

"As long as your phone isn't tapped, yeah."

Chuckie put his hand out and Christopher tossed his phone over. Chuckie plugged something into it, grunted, unplugged, and tossed the phone back. "Clean. Kitty's was, too. So we have that going for us."

Chose not to mention that Chuckie was now the head of one of the agencies most responsible for phone taps. Why spoil the mood? "So, can I finally tell you guys what I've been thinking?"

Christopher put his phone on Jeff's desk. "I'm here," Amy said. "Not on speaker on my side."

"Go ahead, baby. You can start by explaining just what you and the jocks were doing earlier today."

"Give us guilt if and only when someone says that we were spotted. Otherwise, we've discovered at least part of what's going on."

Gave everyone the Recap Girl Update on what the boys and I had discovered, including that Hacker International was on the case, and that we felt that Strauss had been going for Mastermind status.

"So, you think that Villanova and Evan, Armstrong's former driver, are in charge now?" The way Chuckie asked, he didn't think that.

Which was fine, because I didn't either. "No. I think they're trying to continue a plan that should have been aborted the moment Strauss died. Meaning someone else is likely to think they can take over like Strauss would have. As for who, my money's on Zachary Kramer."

"Not Cliff?" Jeff asked.

"No. I don't think Cliff's involved with the Fem-Bot craze at all."

"Timing would indicate that he isn't, and I think Kitty's right," Chuckie said. "Cliff rolled his last action because the timing was good and necessary, both. Meaning he'd figured out what Strauss had planned and also thought she had an excellent chance of success."

"Fritzy wasn't wrong—those peace talks need to happen soon," Mom said. "It would be nice to be able to stop whatever they have planned before we have foreign dignitaries here."

"Right, totally agree, and I have some thoughts about that, including that Kramer's probably now in bed with Ansom Somerall and at least some of the Dealers of Death who aren't in the White House with us right now. But what I've been wanting to discuss has nothing to do with this. I want to tell you who I think has the invisible helicarrier and all our missing people."

"Who?" Jeff asked.

"The person who's the opposite side of Lizzie's coin."

CHAPTER 35

THE ROOM STARED AT ME. "I'm lost," Jeff said. Most heads nodded.

"Me too, Kitty," Chuckie said.

"I'm with you," Amy said via speakerphone. "But only because of what we were discussing right before you suddenly had a burning desire to come back to the White House."

"I'm not," Christopher admitted.

"That's because of your emotional attachments. Okay, look, I was thinking about Lizzie because she's a great kid, and she shouldn't be."

"Why shouldn't she be?" Jeff asked, sounding almost as protective as he did whenever he perceived even the slightest threat to Jamie or Charlie.

"Okay, follow me. Lizzie's parents were traitors. They wanted her to join them in their plan to literally kill half the world. She refused because she knew they were evil. At age eleven she was not only willing to defy her parents but she was willing to die in order to try to save the world. Meaning she's braver than adults several times her age."

"That's never been in dispute," Chuckie said.

"Right. So, she was rescued by an assassin, and yet she's still fighting on the side of right. And I'd bet that Siler's a lot more willing to be a good guy because Lizzie sees him as a hero and, in fact, *expects* him to be a hero. And she's still a great kid, still brave, still fighting for right. She had to leave her cushy school because she was protecting people weaker than herself."

"So who's her opposite?" Jeff asked.

"Seriously? Only Ames has this one? Stephanie. Stephanie is Lizzie's opposite. And not just because she's an A-C and Lizzie's a human. Stephanie only had one parent who was a traitor, not two. And yet . . ."

"She was being influenced by Clarence," Christopher said. Most of the other A-Cs nodded. Serene and White, however, did not. Had a feeling they'd joined Amy on my side of the thinking.

"Yeah? Let's look at a different scenario than the one we've all been buying for years. Stephanie was the one who gave Christopher and all the other men on Alpha Team key chains that had bugs in them, which were used against us for at least a year. We'd always thought that she'd been duped into doing so by her father."

"Well, of course," Jeff said. "She was just a teenager."

"Yeah? Lizzie was *eleven*. But let's continue on my little path here. What if we're wrong? What if the Original Clarence didn't actually dupe her? What if he brought her over fully way back when?"

"How?" Gower asked.

"Maybe she heard something or saw something she shouldn't have and confronted her father. Sure, most of you are terribly trusting, but Stephanie doesn't seem to suffer from that particular failing." Stephanie was a Dazzler, after all, and even those Dazzlers considered dumb as posts by the others were still MENSA material for humans. Meaning she'd have been able to put two and two together without trouble. "There was more than enough going on that Clarence was privy to, after all, so the chances are high that she caught something."

"Okay," Reader said slowly. "Let's say you're right. Are you going where I think you're going?"

"God, I hope so. I'm saying that this means that she's done all that she's done against us of her own free will."

"I have trouble buying that," Jeff said, sounding angry and dismissive.

"Because you still see her as a little girl and you love her. And she's been exploiting that for a really long time. Look, I never considered Clarence all that bright for an A-C, and while he was ambitious, he was always willing to go up the ladder by being someone's muscle or employee. Clarence wasn't an independent thinker. TCC isn't really, either, but he hasn't been tainted, so he's sweet and caring, but still, very willing to follow. But, what if Stephanie isn't like her father in that way? What if she is, in fact, quite a strong, independent thinker?"

Could see the wheels turning in Chuckie's mind. More people in the room looked as if they were considering this. Jeff and Christopher, however, were flat-out rejecting, based on Patented Glare #5 coming from Christopher and a glower from Jeff that was at least going for the Bronze in the Glare Olympics.

Forged on. "Stephanie knew where all of Cliff's hideouts were. And that means she had access to all of his information. Maybe she'd been spending all her time after disappearing not hiding from him due to fear, but hiding from Cliff so that she could gather all the intelligence she possibly could."

"Let's say she has," Mom said slowly. "Where are you going with this line of thought?"

"Stephanie has all of Cliff's data, or all that she could get her mitts on, which was probably a lot. He didn't think she was all that smart—you can tell by how he treated her. He thinks he's smarter than LaRue, too. Frankly, he thinks he's smarter than everyone, that's why he had to try to destroy Chuckie. So it's likely he didn't take the precautions around her that he should have."

"Meaning she had access to the androids," Tim said. "And she had access to Drax, too. So she could set the Kendrick Android to steal the helicarrier and whoever else was around."

"Welcome home, Megalomaniac Lad. That is exactly what I mean. I think the reason we can't find the invisible helicarrier is that the person who had it stolen hasn't had an opportunity to get it. She was still faking Drax out—why not, after all? Get all the tech from him you can, just like you did with Cliff. And then we raided them and she's now in the supermax prison without a way to tell the android or androids what to do next."

"It fits," Chuckie said. "It fits well, honestly."

White nodded. "I believe that Missus Martini is, as is so often the case, probably correct."

"But . . . but she was just a kid," Jeff protested. "She didn't know any better."

Alexander cleared his throat. "I realize that I'm essentially an outsider in this situation, but if you remember, my brother was a traitor. He always coveted the throne, and hindsight shows me that he was a traitor from a young age. I believe that the excuse of 'not knowing better' is a weak one, Jeff. And as a strong leader, you know this to be true."

"Alex is right. Lizzie was eleven and she knew better. Stephanie was probably around fifteen, because I don't think she was in on this until after I hit the Centaurion scene, and I know that she still loved you and Christopher when I first met the family. So she was definitely old enough to know better, Jeff. You're going to have to accept that Malcolm's right—she's a lost cause and likely our current biggest threat."

Serene cleared her throat. "I've had people researching the extended Martini family, since we have known traitors among them. Kitty's theory is more than a theory, Jeff. We have proof that Stephanie's been involved for at least as long as Kitty thinks."

"What proof and why didn't you give this to me before?" Jeff snapped.

Serene walked up to him and got as in his face as she could, seeing that he was a good few inches taller. "I am the Head of Imageering and James is the Head of Field. You are not." Her voice was icy and radiated authority, easily as much as Jeff, Christopher, or Reader ever had. "You are also compromised. Therefore, I had absolutely no need to tell you anything. I'd like you to remember that when you ask me anything again, ever, at any time."

Jeff blinked. "Ah . . ."

"And Serene shatters the glass ceiling just that quickly. Can I make a guess as to what Serene's proof is?"

Serene turned to me and smiled. "Of course, Kitty."

"I think Stephanie was the first test subject for the emotional manipulators. She's an empath, right?" Jeff and Serene both nodded. "And yet she had no idea that Cliff was two-timing her. I realize he was good at hiding his emotions, but no one is *that* good, at least not without help. But Stephanie didn't pick up anything, including, I think, that Jeff and Christopher still loved her."

"How could she not pick that up?" Jeff asked. "She can manipulate her blocks, we taught all the kids how."

"She wore the manipulators," Christopher said, coming over to the Side of Megalomania. "And since she was the test subject, they probably tested an internal overlay on her, too, somewhere in the last couple of years."

"Yes," Serene said. "We've found a trail on the emotional overlays. It's taken us time because we lost all our data during the ... internal attack. However, we've been working on this for almost three years now. The overlays came after the emotional blockers, but not as far behind as our experiences would indicate. However, an S.V. was listed as the initial tester in every case that we've found. It's not rocket science to assume those initials stand for Stephanie Valentino."

"Could be Sylvia, of course," I said. "But I sincerely doubt it. Because your sisters love you, Jeff. And their kids do, too. All but the ones turned against you by their fathers."

"You know it's plural?" Jeff asked, sounding like he was going to need adrenaline.

"Not confirmed yet," Serene said. "Stephanie is confirmed, but no others."

"So where does this leave us?" Reader asked.

"It leaves us with a traitor to interrogate. I don't want Jeff and Christopher in the interrogation, though."

"Who, then?" Reader shot me a fast grin. "I'd better be involved."

"Of course. You, me, Serene, Chuckie, Siler, and Malcolm. You know, you get to be Good Cop and the rest of us will cover all the other Bad Cop levels."

"That's fine," Mom said. "Only that has to be tabled for now." She got the room's attention and shot us all a look that could only be described as long-suffering.

"What?" Jeff sounded lost. "This is important. Especially if they're right, and I can feel that everyone here thinks they're right."

"It may be important, but not in the greater scheme of things." Mom's tone was brisk and no-nonsense. Wondered how many times she'd had talks like this with presidents. Figured more than she'd ever be allowed to tell me. "This issue is a family issue. A domestic issue at the most. But right now, the country needs strong leadership—not to have their President fretting over his delinquent niece. Those peace talks have to happen, and soon. We must show that this country is back to functioning properly, or we become vulnerable to not only enemy nations but enemy planets. And I'm not saying this as your mother-in-law—I'm saying it as the Head of the P.T.C.U. The terrorist is incarcerated. That's good enough for the moment."

"But we have people still missing," Claudia said quietly.

"I realize that," Mom said, rather gently. "But five of those people would be the first to tell you that there's a proper order to things and that ensuring that the country they've sworn to protect is secure is job one, and ensuring that the world won't blow up tomorrow is job two. Stephanie and their rescue would be job three."

"The princesses would say that honor demands that we handle the peace talks first, too. However, the nice thing is that not everyone has to do the same thing at the same time."

Mom shot me a look I was familiar with—her "let's see what you're going to try to fool me with this time" look. "You're going to need to be at Camp David, Kitty. For a variety of reasons, not the least of which is a message I received from Mossad earlier today."

"No argument, Mom. But I can guarantee that I don't need to help Raj figure out logistics for the Club Fifty-One shindig, nor am I going to be needed to set up the peace talks."

"You need to be seen," Mom said, using her long-suffering mother voice. "At more things than you want to be."

"See, this is why I'm so glad I hired Vance. Because I have a nifty solution to that problem, and precedent appears to have been really set for it, too."

CHAPTER 36

NO ONE LIKED THE IDEA of Francine covering for me at anything that was considered low FLOTUS involvement, but no one could argue against the logic either.

Happily, before we could really get into a fight about this, it was time for dinner. Per Nadine, the children and the adults with them were eating upstairs in the Family Dining Room. Tried to get permission to go up and eat with them, but was instantly overruled by pretty much everyone.

As with lunch, I wasn't allowed to sit near to Jeff. He had his part of the giant table, I had mine. Chuckie was on my side of things this time, which was a switch. Had a feeling he was on Kitty Wrangling Duty, but then again he might have wanted to grill Kendrick, since I had Vance on my other side and Culver, Abner, Kendrick, and Gadoire nearby. Nathalie and Horn had also joined us, though, so that was nice.

The food was even better than it had been at lunch. "Does Chef do midnight snacks?" I asked Vance.

He grinned. "I'll find out. I'm sure that your private kitchen is stocked."

"I haven't rummaged through it yet. I haven't really investigated the complex yet."

"Well, give it time."

As we ate and chatted about totally inconsequential things—other than Kendrick, who was having a very intense conversation with Chuckie and Culver about all things Titan Security and how they were pro this administration—my mind wandered as it so frequently did. And it wandered to its favorite wandering place—thinking about where Jeff and I could have sex in this place.

Our new bedroom was obvious, and the kids' rooms were out completely. But there were a lot of other options. Made the decision that doing it in the Oval Office had to be Job One. Figured I could not possibly have been the first person to have thought of this, but had no way of asking how well cleaned the furniture was, at least not without giving Antoinette a heart attack. Oh well, I'd just have to risk it in the name of science and all that jazz.

The next question was when. Right now was, sadly, out. Besides, the kids were going to want some serious Daddy Time, and Lizzie probably needed to feel accepted and wanted, too. And lord knew when we were going to get all these people out of here. Decided I'd better table all the potential sexy times thinking for later, because it was hard to concentrate.

Realized Jeff had caught something of what I was thinking, because he caught my eye from far, far away and gave me a very slow, sexy smile. Okay, maybe we'd just stay up late.

Was interrupted from the only fun thoughts I'd had in ages by a question from Horn. "Kitty, are you keeping your Cause?"

"I think so, yeah." The Cause was improving college security for coeds and doing antirape education and more for the male students. Kyle was really in charge of the Cause because he'd instituted a Best-in-Class version at USC. "Unless that's going to create problems for some reason."

"No, I think it's a good choice," Horn said. "I was going to suggest that you give Gideon an official position with the Cause."

"Um, he's already a Governor."

"But this is something that he could do as well, my dove," Gadoire said. "And it would give Gideon much happiness, to be still shown to be, ah, important to your administration."

Looked at Vance. "Your thoughts?" Noted the others, Abner in particular, looking at Vance with a lot of admiration.

Vance nodded. "I agree that we don't want Governor Cleary to feel shoved aside. And, I'm also certain that this will drive Senator Kramer nuts."

"Make it so."

"You really don't care for them, do you?" Abner asked.

"No, not really. Unlike some people who started off in an adversarial position to me," all of whom were eating with me right now, technically Horn included, "the Kramers chose to become virulently anti-alien. I find it hard to like people like that."

"Zachary isn't your friend," Culver said, interrupting her side conversation.

"And I wouldn't put anything past Marcia," Nathalie added. "She's very . . . focused on rising up."

Someone else had been focused on rising up politically. Cameron Maurer's wife, Crystal. And she hadn't divorced him yet, even though she knew he was an android and they were living in separate states. This bore some investigation, and clearly I needed to give Mrs. Maurer a call or pay a visit, sooner as opposed to later.

Chuckie's phone beeped before anyone else could comment. He read his text, grunted, and showed it to me. Buchanan and the rest were back and needed to see Chuckie, me, Jeff, Reader, Tim, and Serene immediately. Chuckie started texting those being requested.

Fortunately, we'd just finished dessert. "I'm sorry, gang, but a couple of us are needed in a private meeting. Vance, what's the proper way to excuse myself?"

He laughed. "Just like that is fine for your friends, Kitty." Noted Kendrick looking pleased at being included in the general "friends" assessment. "Just graciously grab whoever else you need and we'll all be good here." He leaned closer. "I'll ensure that everyone leaves sooner as opposed to later."

"You're the best, Vance. By the way, give some thought to what we could ask Nancy Maurer to do. I'd love to have her on my staff in some way if she's willing."

Chuckie and I stood and excused ourselves, and the others requested did as well. Jeff sort of left Hochberg, Elaine, and Mom in charge of his end of the table. Decided that I'd leave all of this to Vance and stop worrying about it.

We went to the Oval Office at hyperspeed. Definitely the right place to have sex, but not right now, unless Jeff and I were going to institute an Orgy Policy which I knew without asking Jeff was totally against.

Buchanan and the rest of the Spaceship Recovery Team were there. They also had a Special Guest Star—Colonel

Arthur Franklin, the man in charge of Andrews Air Force Base.

"Arthur, it's nice to see you. I hope, anyway."

He laughed. "Always good to see you, Kitty. And I'm here because I wanted to discuss our special equipment issue with all of you."

Jeff looked at Buchanan. "Did you find what you were looking for?"

"Yes. Right where Drax said it would be."

"I'm not a liar," Drax said huffily. "And the rest was *not* my fault."

"Dude, that tends to be my line. What happened?"

Siler looked like he was trying not to laugh. Buchanan looked pinned. Wruck looked interested. And Drax looked defensive. Franklin, on the other hand, looked rather excited.

"Are we safe to assume that the ship did not uncloak where the general populace could see it?" Chuckie asked.

"Oh yes," Franklin said. "Prince Gustav's ship is safely housed in one of our larger hangars. One restricted to top security clearances only."

"So it's Prince Gustav now? What gives? You said you eschewed the title."

"I did and do," Drax muttered. "I'm not the one insisting on calling me that."

"I suggested it," Wruck said. "Under the circumstances."

"What circumstances?" Jeff asked, sounding annoyed. "I'd like answers, gentlemen, not innuendos. As everyone's told me every minute of every hour of the last few days, I have a country to run."

Tim and I exchanged a look. "You think?" he asked.

"Oh, I do, I really do. Can I take a guess?"

"Sure," Buchanan said tiredly. "I'm willing to bet that you're going to be right, Missus Executive Chief, because what's going on is definitely in your wheelhouse."

"Super. So, how many Vatusan ships came searching for their Runaway Royal?"

"Are you kidding me?" Jeff asked.

"No, and only two," Franklin said. "They were kind enough to remain cloaked and are also parked in our hangar. There's room there for the stolen helicarrier, too, should it ever be found."

"You know, Vata were explained to us," Tim said. "Why can't you just mind-connect with your helicarrier and bring it back?" he asked Drax.

"I created it to be fully invulnerable to humans and Vata alike. Meaning I can't connect to it because I have its system blocked from external influence. And if I can't reach it, no one else can, either."

"This was confirmed by the four Royal Retainers," Franklin said.

"Four?" Jeff asked. "I thought you said there were two ships."

"There were," Buchanan replied. "But they're a lot smaller than what I think you're expecting. Drax's ship is reasonably large, presumably because he was bringing materials with him. The ships that the retainers are in? Those are about the size of a seven-forty-seven."

"They could have flown something the size of this planet with only two on board," Drax said. "We connect to our ships to fly them. It's, for us, a simple process, much easier than having a large crew. That was why and how I could come alone and use the interior space to carry my materials."

"And they came here from the Galactic Core?" Chuckie asked.

Wruck nodded. "They're faster than the Z'porrah."

"And we've experienced how fast the Z'porrah ships can jump. So, let's ask the twenty-four-thousand-dollar question: what is it the retainers want?"

"To ensure that His Royal Highness is safe and well," Franklin said. "But they plan to stay here. Because that's their job—to babysit your arms dealer."

"He's not our arms dealer," Jeff said. Drax looked hurt and Jeff grunted. "Not officially and not yet, at any rate. Where are they, these retainers?"

"At the only place we could put them where they wouldn't cause more problems," Siler replied cheerfully. "The Alpha Centaurion Embassy."

CHAPTER 37

"I'M MISSING ALL the good stuff. I was just there and chose to come here when I could have stayed longer and met our newest surprise guests. I'm bitter."

Jeff sighed. "Yes, I realize being in the White House is a letdown."

Felt bad. "Well, no. But my particular style isn't suited to our new gig."

"You said that when we took over the Embassy, and everything worked out," Jeff said.

"So to speak," Chuckie added.

"Et tu, Brute?"

"You know that she's right and that all our enemies are going to exploit this weakness, too," Reader said. "Kitty's every evildoer's Enemy Number One."

"Et tu, Brute Two?"

"What do you suggest?" Jeff asked, sarcasm knob heading for eleven. "That I explain that my wife isn't going to be around a lot because she's off leading the armed forces?"

"That could work," Franklin said with a laugh. "But you can all relax. Frankly, the Vata were very pleasant, apologetic, and cooperative. I didn't get the impression they were here to cause trouble. They're here because they've been searching for their missing prince for two years. Your Concierge Majordomo said to tell you that all is being handled."

"Sounds about right for the timeline, and Pierre's a national treasure. So, what did you find at Drax Industrial's Sentient Headquarters?"

"Pretty much what he said we'd find," Buchanan replied.

"But we left everything there. The building's secure and it doesn't appear to attract a lot of attention."

"Far less like a lair than his home," Siler added. "Reminiscent of any factory you've ever seen, albeit extremely high tech. It's clear he's a tinkerer."

"As long as no one's shooting at us from the catwalks, I'm good. So, Iron Man here has the skills, at least as far as we can tell?"

Siler chuckled. "I liked Booster Gold better."

"Well, the jury's still out on which one he gets to keep. Maybe both. I like to mix it up and keep everyone guessing."

Buchanan rolled his eyes. "Yes, you do. And it appears that Drax does have the Iron Man skills, so to speak. He now also has official babysitters. They said they weren't leaving unless or until he was leaving."

"Do they look any different from Drax?"

"They aren't relatives, if that's what you mean," Franklin said.

"No, she means can they pass for humans or not," Siler said. "And yes, they can. Their hair is long just like his is. Hides the plates."

"Did you have time to do the robot and android tests?"

"No," Drax answered. "I was quite willing and still am, but my family interfered. Just as they always do." He sounded as bitter and teenaged as I'd ever heard Stephanie or Lizzie sound. Interesting. Figured I should find out how Vata aged sooner as opposed to later.

"Parents worry about their children. Oh, speaking of which, Nightcrawler, Lizzie's been moved into the White House. Apparently the Elves feel that she needs the stuffy yet stable environment the White House will provide. And she's enrolled at the Sidwell Friends School. If you have any issues, take it up with Vance and Pierre and good luck complaining to the Elves."

He looked surprised but not displeased. "That's good, I guess. I kind of thought that we'd be staying in family quarters together, though, at the Embassy. Like we have been for the last few days."

"As did we all. However, wiser heads and all that. Apparently she's now my ward. Don't ask me, I don't make these decisions. I apparently have people to do that."

"And yet she's unhappy," Jeff muttered to Chuckie.

"She's adaptable, but sometimes it takes her a while," Chuckie replied. "You know how she is about wealth, she gets it from her father."

"I'm in the room and I'll be offended for me and Dad both later on. So, here's my question—are there any other Vata ships on our horizon?"

"I asked," Franklin said. "Multiple times and in various ways. The reply was a consistent no. They've found Prince Gustav, he's safe and happy on Earth, that information has been relayed home, and they're staying to guard him and help him with whatever it is they think he's doing here."

"Does this happen to other Presidents?" Jeff asked. "I mean that seriously."

"Some have it worse, some have it better, but I can tell you that President Johnson definitely went through something like this," Chuckie said. "When your emissaries first arrived."

"Good point." Jeff ran his hand through his hair. "So, do we announce this?"

"You don't have to," Franklin said. "I'd talk to Mort and Hammy about it, but I'd imagine they'll both counsel that you keep this quiet. The Vata are in the Embassy. Keep them there for now and all should be well. Great choices, moving Mort and Hammy into the positions you did, by the way."

"I'd have moved you in, too, but everyone insisted we needed you to stay at Andrews."

"They were right. And I'm glad to be there—I find my job very rewarding, since I can confirm that I'm helping on a daily basis. Not everyone can say that." He clapped Jeff on the shoulder. "You're doing a great job. I realize the weight of the world is on your shoulders, but you'll handle it and then some."

Franklin said goodbye and that he'd be in touch and we should feel free to call him day or night. Then Serene escorted him to the Executive Washroom where he took a gate back to the base.

"Now what?" Tim asked.

"Now Alpha Team takes him to Dulce," Jeff nodded at Drax. "Do the tests Kitty wants done."

"Take the other Vata to do the tests, too."

This earned me looks. "Why?" Reader asked.

"Five metal heads able to talk to electronics are better than one. Maybe one of them will catch what Drax doesn't."

"That's a security risk," Chuckie said. "Having Drax in Dulce is a huge risk in the first place. Four other Vata there is a potential breach of epic proportions. And before you mention the religious aspect, I heard it already, and while I respect the idea of their beliefs, we've seen too many wars fought in the name of religion on this planet for me to trust that these Vata aren't willing to do wrong against us if they feel it's right for them."

"I'd argue this, but I conceded your point," Drax said. "The only way for us to earn your trust, however, is for you to allow us to do so."

"He hasn't launched the missiles," I pointed out. "None of them have. I know you're not a trusting person, Chuckie, but there has to be a middle ground."

"There is," he said. "In the middle of Groom Lake."

"That works," Reader said. "You want us doing that tonight?"

"No, everyone needs some rest," Jeff said. "Drax has been here two years and, as Kitty said, he hasn't blown us up. I'm willing to err on the side of trust, at least at this level. Take him to the Embassy and keep him with you," he said to Siler.

"I'll go, too," Wruck said.

"Please, and thank you. Can you handle all five of them if you have to?" Jeff sounded worried.

Wruck nodded. "I can. Shape-shifting has its advantages."

"Where do you want me?" Buchanan asked.

"I'd say here, but I'll try to keep an eye on my wife tonight. So, the Embassy might be the better choice."

"I agree." Buchanan shot me a half-smile. "Try to stay out of trouble for a few hours, will you, Missus Executive Chief?"

"Everyone's a hater."

"We'll stay at the Embassy, too," Reader indicated himself and Tim. "Serene, here or Dulce?"

"I'll go to Dulce and get the Groom Lake test area set up for us."

"I'm still living in the Embassy," Chuckie pointed out.

"So I'll be there, too." He sighed. "I need to find somewhere else to live now, though." Jeff opened his mouth and Chuckie put up his hand. "The Director of the CIA cannot live at the American Centaurion Embassy, Jeff."

"Or the White House, so don't suggest that either, Jeff. But it's fine, I know where you're going, Chuckie, never fear." Sent a text to Pierre, who said he'd handle the request with the Elves immediately.

"And where is that?" Chuckie asked.

"The Cairo. With Nathalie and Elaine. We already have the building under guard, and you'll like it, it's very cool. The Operations Team will handle it, you'll just need to sign whatever lease. Oh, and make sure that they install gates in your apartment and in Nathalie's and Elaine's, too."

"Oh, will do, Boss Lady." He laughed. "But that's a good compromise, honestly. If they have a vacancy."

My phone beeped. "They do, and you're in."

"That fast?" Chuckie sounded shocked.

Jeff grinned. "We move fast, remember?"

CHAPTER 38

IT WASN'T ALL THAT LATE but we were all that tired and more. So everyone headed off to either their rooms or their residences. The Planetary Council was briefed about the Vata at the Embassy, and they were all on board with the new arrivals and also about not sharing that said new arrivals were here with anybody else.

Raj was living in the White House along with the other A-C White House personnel, so he and Antoinette took care of getting everyone out and headed home. Not that we wouldn't see most if not all of them first thing in the morning, but we liked to pretend our lives were normal occasionally.

Since Dad and her grandchildren were there, and his wife and child were also, Mom and Christopher came upstairs with us. "So, what does Malcolm want me to have plausible deniability for?" she asked.

"Shouldn't we not mention that until we're in a room without bugs?"

Mom shot me a look. "What was bugged?"

"The Oval Office," Jeff replied. "And Chuck said he swept it yesterday."

"Plus Vance gave us the Walls Have Ears speech on the way down," Christopher added.

"I'm so proud. That was a Kitty-ism at its finest."

Mom and Christopher both grimaced—her at the state of things, him at me—and she pulled out her phone and made a call. "Kevin, have Security do a full sweep of the White House complex, the Embassy, and Dulce. Probably the Cairo, too. Yes. Yes, I know they were checked yesterday. Today, the Oval Office had an infestation." She barked a laugh. "Yeah, exactly, why would we expect that?" Laughed again. "Oh, good point. Yes, keep me posted." She hung up and heaved a sigh.

"What would you expect?" Christopher asked.

"That no one coming in would be bringing bugs in with them. Kevin suggests Kitty's purse be thoroughly searched."

"And he's probably not wrong. Mom, who could be bringing bugs in? This place is supposedly secure."

"It's also gigantic, and any system can be gamed. You do it all the time."

Christopher and I looked at each other. "Several times today, as a matter of fact," he shared.

"Traitor."

"I'm with Kitty, Angela, about the security, even though my wife and cousin are clearly stating that I'm an idiot to think we're safe. Who should I be firing?" Jeff sounded tired and worried, not that I could blame him. Put my arm around his waist. He was incredibly tense. Hugged him and he put his arm around my shoulders. Felt him relax a bit.

"Neither one of us thinks that, Jeff."

"What Kitty said," Christopher added. "We just both know that we got out easily enough, meaning someone else can get in. So, like Jeff asked, who should we be wary of, Angela?"

"Everyone. No one." Her phone beeped. "God, I love hyperspeed and A-C efficiency. Per Kevin, there are no bugs anywhere in the complex. The Embassy is clean as well. Bugs were removed at the Cairo from, and I'm sure this will totally shock you, the apartments of Nathalie Brewer and Elaine Armstrong." Mom was texting almost as fast as Tim usually did. "Kevin feels that the only reason there aren't bugs at the apartment Charles will be in is because no one knows he's moving in there yet."

"Geez. Elaine was just moved in. By the Operations Team."

"Yes, but then they left. I'd assume that every single Alphabet Agency had teams sneak in here to plant those bugs in the Oval Office. And of course your many enemies would have done so, as well. I'm having agents sent to the homes of every one of Jeff's new appointees and also to the homes of those few that are holdovers from Vince's regime."

"How would they do that? We were all here, right here, today."

Mom shot me a look I was quite familiar with—her "don't try to lie to *me*, missy" look. "Not everyone was 'right here' all day, as Christopher and you *just* mentioned, and those who were here were busy. The staff is still reeling from Vince's death, so if they saw someone who looked like they should be here, they'd ignore it. The Secret Service is spending all its time trying to keep you and Jeff from being killed. They're focused far too internally right now."

"Sorry." I was. All the Secret Service agents we'd dealt with, save one, were awesome, and I didn't want to make their lives even harder and more dangerous than they already were.

"They'll adjust to how you are, I'm sure," Mom said. "However, today, I'd think it was easy to get someone in here. My guess for when the bugs were planted is when you were fighting a robot on the South Lawn."

"I have a hard time believing that Strauss was planning to overthrow the government in concert with every single protective agency we have."

"No, but it's obvious we were being watched. An opportunity arose, and apparently everyone took advantage of it."

"They could have done it when we were in the theater and Kitty and the others were in my old office, too," Jeff said. "Frankly, we gave these people plenty of opportunities. Bottom line is that we need to make sure that we aren't breached that easily again. Bugs are bad, but they're nothing compared to bombs or poisons."

"I'll have a talk with your Secret Service staff, all of them, not just the ones you know best. I plan to have Jeremy Barone with me while doing that briefing, too. I've requested that he leave the Embassy detail and move in here, and he's agreed."

"That's great, but I have to ask—why would the Alphabet Agencies be spying on us? And I don't want derisive looks. I'm serious. Now that Cliff's gone, they're all on our side, aren't they?"

"Kitten, this is politics. That you're still somehow surprised by it is both sweet and worrying. However, look at it like friendly fire—they're listening to guard and to, you know, catch something they can use for blackmail, what's called influence in this town."

"Gotcha. Friends and enemies all want to listen in and take advantage of us. Wow, this is the best job in the world."

"Tell me about it, baby," Jeff said with a sigh. "I just want to see the kids and Sol and pretend we're a normal family for a few minutes."

"Ask and ye shall receive."

Of course, it wasn't quite as simple as that, mostly because no one was in Lizzie's room, Jamie's room, or Charlie's room. Christopher checked the supposedly unoccupied rooms—no one. Belayed panic even though no one was in the rooms on our side of the hall, Master Suite included.

Mom wasn't worried and headed us to the Family Dining Room where, happily, everyone we were searching for was waiting for us, Jamie and Charlie in their standard A-C-issue pajamas of blue bottoms and white tops. Mom also refrained from saying "duh" to me, but I could tell she wanted to.

Jamie and Charlie were thrilled to see their Daddy *and* their Nana Angela. They gave me perfunctory kisses but definitely wanted more of Jeff and Mom's time than mine. Again chose not to be bitter. After all, if King Benny had come upstairs with us, Mom and Jeff would be playing Second Bananas to him anyway.

"Jamie and Charlie have already had their baths and brushed their teeth," Nadine said.

"Super. Where are you sleeping?" I asked her as I sat down next to her and Dad, who was now also not of interest to his grandchildren, at least for the moment. Christopher settled next to Amy and took Becky from her. She gave a happy baby gurgle and snuggled up to her father and Christopher got a look on his face I recognized well, since I saw it on Jeff's face all the time—the happy glow of loving on his child.

"Well, we've been discussing that." Nadine nodded her head toward Amy and Lizzie. "I'm kind of surprised that you have Charlie in his own room already at only seven months."

"Seriously, that wasn't my idea. The Elves set the room up and he really seems to like it."

"Oh, he does, Mommy," Jamie said. "Just like I like my room."

"That's great, sweetie, but Charlie is still a baby. And babies need their mommies and daddies nearby."

"But you are nearby," Jamie said. "Aren't you?" She looked worried.

"Yes, we are. Just across the hall." The ginormous hall, but still right across it. Didn't know what to say that wouldn't make Jamie nervous. "But, um . . ."

Jeff kissed Jamie's head. "You stayed in the nursery for a long time, Jamie-Kat. We just think that maybe Charlie should, too."

Jamie shook her head. "Charlie will be fine."

Looked at my son, who was grabbing Mom's nose. "Maybe. But Mom, what do you think?"

Mom kissed Charlie's forehead. "I think that whatever makes you and Jeff feel safe is the right choice, kitten. But, frankly, as Alfred and Lucinda have told your father and me more than once, with hyperspeed and a good baby monitor, it doesn't take long to reach your child."

This was true. In fact, Alfred and Lucinda's bedroom at Martini Manor was quite far away from their children's rooms. Sure, the isolation chamber they'd had to install for Jeff was in their bedroom. Just as the isolation chamber here was now in our suite of rooms.

"And the pets are guarding us all the time, Mommy, you know that," Jamie reminded me. She held up her Poof. "Mous-Mous is always on the case."

"True, the Poofs are ever-vigilant." I hoped and presumed. Felt a feathered nudge. "As are the Peregrines, dogs, cats, ocellars, and chochos." Why risk hurting anyone's feelings? "Well, why don't we see how it goes? Charlie can always come into the nursery if he wants to, and if he's happy in his own room, you're right, we'll hear him if need be. Which brings me back to the question of where Nadine's sleeping."

"I was thinking I should be in Charlie's room, honestly," she said.

"I think you should be in Lizzie's room," Jamie said. "That way, Lizzie will have a friend to talk to."

Lizzie looked more than a little weirded out, not that I could blame her. Jamie was quite advanced to begin with, and her tendency to share things in a way that made it seem like she was mind reading or seeing the future was freaky, even to me and Jeff. Maybe mostly to me and Jeff.

"Lizzie's a big girl," Jeff said. "Bigger than you. That should mean she gets her own room and doesn't have to share."

"But all the big girls and boys are sharing," Jamie said. "Upstairs and here, too. You and Mommy share, too, Daddy."

"It's fine," Lizzie said. "There's room in my room 'cause it's totes big. Nadine can stay with me if you guys want."

Christopher handed Becky to Amy. I blinked and he was gone. Blinked again and he was back. "There are two beds in Lizzie's room now. When we came upstairs there was only one. So, I guess that means the Operations Team got the message."

"Okay, um, well, I guess that's settled then. Lizzie, are you sure you're okay with this? We have plenty of room and the other bed can go in Charlie's room just as easily as yours."

"No, really, it's fine, Kitty. Promise."

Had a feeling that something had happened while we were downstairs, but had no good way to ask in front of the kids. "Well, it's bedtime for the two who get to sleep in their rooms alone, then."

Jeff handed Jamie to Lizzie. "Okay, Charlie first." He took our son from Mom. "Back soon, Jamie-Kat. Enjoy your special time."

With that we headed to Charlie's room. "Any guess for what's going on?" I asked him quietly.

"A little. Tell you once Charlie's in bed."

"Oh good. More mystery. Just what today needed."

CHAPTER 39

EVEN THOUGH IT WAS A NEW, strange place, doing our regular bedtime ritual was soothing. We tucked Charlie in, sang songs to him, and made sure that his Poof and Sugarfoot the cat were both on his bed. Duchess was already settled in her dog bed and Wilbur was in his, right next to hers. They were on one side of Charlie's crib. The two Peregrine hammocks were on the other side, already filled by a younger set of Peregrines, Mork and Mindy, who had attached to Charlie pretty early on.

Two ocellars and some random Poofs were in here, too, lounging in their Poof Condo. I knew without asking that the moment Jeff and I left the room that they'd be on the bed, but we all chose to pretend that they'd stay where they were supposed to.

Baby monitor set up, songs all sung, we kissed Charlie goodnight and headed out, our half of his baby monitor in Jeff's pocket.

"Before we get Jamie, seriously, what's going on?"

"I can't be sure, baby, but I think that Jamie's picked up Lizzie's anxiety."

"She doesn't seem anxious to me. I mean, anymore. She was freaked earlier, which was totally understandable, but why be anxious now?"

"Because her adopted father isn't here. He's at the Embassy and that means that, to her, she's alone again."

"But she has us. I mean, seriously, Pierre and Vance have announced her as my ward."

"Yeah, but she isn't convinced that she's got us for the

long haul." Jeff ran his hand through his hair. "Like you said earlier, she's been through a lot."

"True, though Nightcrawler isn't deserting her. He was disappointed that she wasn't going to be in the family suite with him. I think he was as confused as I was by the Elves moving Lizzie in here. Jamie, on the other hand, plans for her Uncle Benjamin to move into the White House with us at some point."

Jeff grunted. "I have no objection, but he's currently Embassy staff so that doesn't really work. Meaning that Lizzie's going to be living separately from her father, and that has to feel like desertion, or at least a loss."

"And right after she's lost the Dingo and Surly Vic, too." Just like I had.

"Yeah. Two of the men she knew as her new family are dead and gone, and she didn't get to say goodbye to them."

"And her father almost died, too. And, regardless of who's sleeping where, he's off doing things that are dangerous again, and what happens to Lizzie if something happens to him? I mean, obviously, she stays with us and remains with and within our family, but she doesn't know that, does she?"

"Ah . . ." Jeff had a funny look on his face and he wasn't really looking at me.

Turned around to see Lizzie standing there. Couldn't read her expression. "I was coming to tell you . . ," She stopped, scrunched up her face, then threw herself into my arms and started sobbing.

I was shocked, but I'd been a teenaged girl before, and the right course of action wasn't that hard to come up with. Hugged her tightly and rocked her a little. "It's okay," I said quietly when her crying slowed down. "It's hard to have your life upended once, let alone twice. And now for the third time."

Jeff put his arms around both of us. "Like Kitty said, it's okay. Your father is part of our family, and that makes you part of it, too. Forever. I promise."

Lizzie was still crying but she relaxed more and more. Finally her body felt normal. Kissed the top of her head. "You won't be alone again, or deserted, or anything like that. In fact, get used to not getting a lot of alone time, just because that seems to be how A-Cs roll. They're big on the once in, never out mindset. And family is who you choose, too. Like I told you, my family is larger than it seems. Amy, Chuckie, Sheila, Brian . . . my parents consider all of them family. And you're now part of that, too. Besides, you're apparently the big sister Jamie's always dreamed of."

She managed a laugh. "Thanks. I hope. I'm sorry. Jamie and Charlie are awesome. I was coming to tell you that Jamie had Nadine, Sol, and Angela tuck her in and . . . heard you . . . and . . ."

I was still holding her but I hugged her again. "Heard us discussing possible outcomes."

"Yeah."

Tried to think of what would really make her feel like everything was really alright. "It's okay. No matter what Mister Dash may be doing, Megalomaniac Girl and Superman will always need your help."

She took her face out of my neck and smiled at me. "Quick Girl is always ready for action."

Jeff chuckled. "Good. I hope the action Quick Girl is ready for right now, however, is bedtime."

"She's almost fifteen."

"And I'm the President and I make the rules, and tonight our teenager is going to bed early."

"It's okay. Nadine and I are going to compare places in France we've been. She and her sisters are from Euro Base. They don't sound French, but they are. That's totes weird, isn't it?"

Couldn't help it, I laughed. "That, in a nutshell, is life with A-Cs."

"I think I should be offended somehow," Jeff said, looking a little hurt, as we broke out of our group huddle.

"Nah. You get used to it. After a while at least."

Lizzie grinned. "That's what Mister Dash says." She heaved a sigh. "I miss my dad."

"He misses you, too. We'll get through the current madness and then things will settle down." Oh, sure, I was probably telling a real whopper, but a girl could dream, right?

"I don't think things ever settle for you guys, but that's okay. Keeps things interesting, right?" Lizzie seemed almost back to normal.

"Yeah. You want to wash up in our bathroom before we go back to the others?"

She shook her head. "I'm supposed to go to bed, remember? I'll wash up in my own bathroom. You think Nadine will need to sleep with Charlie?"

The way she asked told me the right answer to give. "Nope. If he can't handle being alone we'll move him right into the nursery. We're kind of overprotective that way. I'd have all three of you in the master suite with us but, you know, people would talk."

She giggled, and Nadine chose this time to join us in the hallway. Nadine gave me a little nod, then she put her arm around Lizzie's shoulders. "Let's get into bed and talk ourselves to sleep."

They headed off to their now shared room and Jeff put his arm around me. "Well handled, baby."

"You, too. I guess this is our *Sound of Music* moment."

"I actually get that reference, and yeah, I think so. Teenagers need parents and older confidantes they can trust, too. And if that means Lizzie wants our nanny to be her roommate, I'm good with that."

We went back to the dining room. "Ames, what in the world did we miss while you guys were here and we were downstairs?" Took Becky from Christopher and gave her a snuggle. Seeing as she was only a week old, she couldn't share that she'd really prefer to be in a room by herself now and had to put up with me giving her attention.

Amy shook her head. "I have no idea, honestly. But Jamie spent a lot of time telling Lizzie how she was going to live with you guys forever and ever. I think it might have freaked her out. It kind of freaked me out a little."

"Well, Jamie's not wrong," Jeff said. "Siler's got a more stable job with us now, but if today is any example, we're stretching the definition of stable."

"Yeah, not every day is like this, let's all please remember, but I can see why the Elves wanted Lizzie here."

"It'll keep him here, too," Christopher said.

"What do you mean?" Jeff asked.

Christopher shrugged. "He's spent decades as a globe-trotting assassin. Settling in one place can't feel natural to him."

Considered this. "Good point. But he doesn't seem restless."

Christopher snorted. "Kitty, he's been here, what, a week? Right after almost dying and all of us taking down Cliff. It's not like we wouldn't all kill for some downtime. But once we finally get it, then what? Is he really going to settle into our version of embassy life? Or is he going to go back to the profession he's had for longer than any of us in this room have been alive?"

"No bet, honestly. But we don't have to decide that tonight. And, as embarrassed as I am to say it, I'm as tired as the kids. I think I want to take advantage of all the help and turn in early."

"I second that," Jeff said.

"We can take a hint." Amy laughed. "You two just want to have sex in the White House, don't try to lie to me."

"You don't know me."

Both Christopher and Amy cracked up and Jeff grinned. "Caught us. Go home. Get some rest."

Amy sent a text to the half of her protection detail that was in the White House, and they zipped into the dining room to escort the White family home. Amy insisted on taking her child back, despite the fact that I offered to let Becky test out the nursery. Always the way.

As they left Mom and Dad came back. "Jamie's happily in bed with more animals than I cared to count," Mom said. "And now your father and I are going to get out of your hair."

"You want to spend the night in the Lincoln Bedroom?" Mom shrugged. "No. We've done it before."

"Wow. Really?"

She laughed and kissed my cheek. "Really."

The nearest bathroom, meaning the nearest gate, was in our suite, so we all headed for the living room, since we scored those two bathrooms—private and guest. Jeff calibrated the gate, Mom and Dad hugged us both, then they stepped through, doing the Slow Fade Mambo that still made my stomach as queasy to watch as it did to experience.

Mom sent me a text to let me know they were safely home, and I finally relaxed.

Jeff rubbed the back of my neck. "What do you want to do now, baby?"

Looked up at him. "Oh, I don't know. What do *you* want to do?"

He smiled slowly, getting the Jungle Cat About To Eat Me look on his face. I loved that look. It was potentially my favorite look of his. "Well, I do have a couple of ideas."

CHAPTER 40

WE TROTTED INTO the ginormous dressing room–closet combo, taking Charlie's monitor with us. Got out of our clothes quickly, tossed them roughly near the hamper, and got down to the most important business of the day.

In the olden days, before children, we'd take a long time on foreplay. Tonight—in deference to how many people were on this floor alone and because we hadn't really tested the soundproofing yet—not so much.

Jeff had me in his arms, with my legs wrapped around his waist, in short order. While he busied himself with licking, biting, and kissing my neck and breasts, I did my part by grinding against him.

Charlie made sleeping baby sounds, we paused to be sure he was staying asleep and, when he did, we went for it.

Jeff slipped inside me and it was hyperspeed sex, which sounds disappointing but was totally awesome the way Jeff did it. We were thrusting together at speeds fast enough to burst into flames, but I burst into orgasm instead.

Wailed sharply and loudly, but Charlie didn't wake up and no one came running into our rooms to see if a cat in heat was dying in here. So, one definitely for the win column.

Still inside me, Jeff headed us out of the closet and into the bed.

"Nice bed," he purred at me. "Comfy."

"How can you tell?" I managed to gasp out. "You're on top of me."

He grinned. "Best way to test the bed, baby." Which he did by ratcheting me right back up to the brink while he nipped and nibbled my breasts.

Orgasm number two took longer to arrive, but I had no complaints, since I could and did grab his awesome butt—what I thought of as his perfect thrusters—and got more actively involved in the proceedings.

We were like this for a good long while, during which time Jeff flipped me on top of him so that my second orgasm could hit while he was bucking into me and squeezing my breasts at the same time.

Collapsed onto him as my body shuddered and I managed to moan against his neck. He rolled on top of me again, still inside me, basically proving he was the man for the sex job each and every time. Then we were back to a fast rhythm that, despite the prior excellent outcomes, got me right back to the edge almost immediately.

I was close, and I could tell he was, too, when he flipped my legs up to his shoulders and grabbed my hands and held them down at my sides. In this position I really couldn't move, but I could wail, and I did, as he sent me flying over the edge again.

This time Jeff came with me and it felt like my climax went on forever. But finally both of our bodies slowed down, he let my legs drop, rolled off me, and pulled me next to him.

I snuggled my face into the hair on his chest. "Nice way to break in part of the room."

He chuckled as he nuzzled my head. "Well, we'll wait for tomorrow to break in the shower."

"Oh, I'll hold you to that."

"Good." He heaved a sigh. "Want to hear my plan for the rest of the night?"

"Sure."

"We sleep for a couple of hours, then, once we're sure everyone's really asleep around here, we go follow through on that great idea you had earlier."

"Oooh, love this plan!"

Jeff zipped out of bed, got Charlie's monitor from the closet, we verified that he was breathing just fine, then we got into the adult version of the standard-issue night clothes and cuddled together. Couldn't speak for Jeff, but I was out like a light. Happily, a dreamless, deep-sleeping light.

True to his word and the plan, Jeff nuzzled me awake sometime later. Checked out what Mister Presidential

Clock had to say—three a.m. Perfect. The entire complex should be and should remain asleep.

We found slippers in the closet because the Elves never failed to deliver. Found some lovely bathrobes with the Presidential Seal on them, so we took the hint and put those on, too.

Did a fast check through our rooms and noted that while we had Poof Condos, Peregrine hammocks, and doggy beds, what we did not have were any animals in said beds. Which was fine for tonight, but something I hoped would be rectified in the future.

We kept the lights off—A-Cs had great night vision and, since my enhancement, so did I. Slipped Charlie's baby monitor into the pocket of my robe. Considered taking my phone or purse, and decided against it. This was literally the only time Jeff and I had had alone together in what felt like weeks, even though that wasn't reality, and I didn't want to waste it on texts or late night phone calls from crazed lunatics. The crazed loons could leave a voicemail.

Checked on Charlie and Jamie, just in case. They had tons of animals with them, and everyone was sleeping soundly, though Duchess and Wilbur both looked up when we peeked in on Charlie, and Duke and Dottie did the same when we checked on Jamie.

Listened at Lizzie's door. Sleep sounds only. Checked in on them as well. Dudley was in here, snuggled on the bed with Lizzie, and he gave us a "go away, you're disturbing us" look. Nadine was asleep, too, and any missing animals were in here.

Thusly reassured that our family was soundly and safely asleep, we hypersped through the complex and to the Oval Office. There were Secret Service agents scattered throughout, but we zipped past them. After the third one we were both trying not to giggle and snicker like little kids sneaking out behind their parents' backs and had to take a couple giggle breaks in closets so we didn't give ourselves away.

Had to do some doubling back to avoid a few A-C Field agents who Jeff knew on sight and I, of course, could only say were A-Cs because they were really great looking. Didn't see anyone, A-C or human, too close to the Oval Office—most of them had been in the living quarters area, which, at this time of night and with nothing going on, made some sense. Unlike when I'd done similar with Serene, it was kind of fun to be "naughty" like this with Jeff, and certainly the most fun I'd had here outside of what we'd just done in the bedroom.

Once in the Oval Office, we didn't turn on the lights, because there was no point. And we didn't want to get caught. Besides, we were being illicit in our own home, so to speak, and turning on the lights would be staid and boring and undoubtedly alert someone who would come in at the wrong time.

Jeff locked the door and chuckled. "That was fun, but I think we should be worried about security."

Couldn't help it, I still had the giggles. "I know, right? It's easier to slip past our guardians than it ever was to get past my dad, let alone my mom."

Jeff grinned. "Well, then I'll enjoy this because I didn't know you when you were having to sneak in late."

"Works for me. I'd suggest raiding the liquor cabinet but I like you alive."

"I appreciate that, baby." He took my hand and led me to the sofas in the center of the room. "So," Jeff purred as we took off our robes and slippers, "where's your pleasure?"

"You have to ask? I'm totally disappointed in you."

He laughed, picked me up, and put me onto the desk, with my butt right at the edge. "I just wanted to be sure."

"I'm positive that we're doing it on the *Resolute* desk or I'm knowing the reason why and asking who's replaced my husband."

Jeff grinned, then pulled my pajama bottoms down and off while also sliding my t-shirt up and over my breasts. First he spent some time on my breasts again, probably because he hadn't brought me to orgasm this way yet tonight and, so far, his record was unblemished.

His hands, teeth, tongue, and lips were still the Best in Show and I was howling my usual howls of happiness in short order. Then, his talents confirmed, Jeff trailed down over my stomach, spread my legs, and really went to town.

Grabbed his head and just sort of held on while he reminded me once again why it was great to be his woman. When we were like this Jeff liked to see how often he could make me climax in a concentrated amount of time. The location and his skills ensured that the answer was "a lot." I lost count somewhere after three and coherency shortly thereafter.

But all fantastic things come to an end. In this case, that meant a new fantastic thing, as Jeff headed his mouth for my neck, then straightened up and slid the best part of him inside of me. He had his forearms keeping my thighs spread while he held onto the desk and he started slamming into me in at ever-increasing speed.

We went on like this for a long, fantastic while, until I was on the edge of the precipice. Jeff pulled me up, our torsos now tightly together, him still deep inside me, and that did it.

Grabbed his shoulders and screamed, but his mouth covered mine and muffled my shouting as he took us over the edge again together.

His body shuddered as much as mine and he returned my shout, which, since we were still kissing, was really erotic. My hands wrapped around his back as our bodies shook in time together.

Finally, though, we were both calm and still. Jeff picked me up and sat us down in his chair. "You know, I hear that I need to hire a secretary and several interns. You interested in the jobs?"

"Oh yeah, but only if I get to sleep with the most powerful man in the world in order to get and keep the positions."

Jeff lifted and turned me so that I was straddling him. "Mmm," he said, right before he kissed me again, "let's just see how well you interview."

CHAPTER 41

ABOUT AN HOUR OR SO later we were finally fully satiated, I'd landed any and every job I wanted, and we were ready to head back upstairs to get a little more sleep before the kids woke up.

Having had sex in more than one place in the White House somehow made it feel more welcoming—less like a gigantic, imposing structure and more like someplace with a ton of cool possibilities for illicit sex with my alien sex-god husband.

Jeff chuckled as we pulled our nightclothes back on, slippers and robes included. "Glad you feel at home here now, baby."

"Oh, give yourself all the credit for that, Jeff, trust me." Would have said more but I saw something out of the corner of my eye and stopped talking to focus on it.

The Oval Office had several windows and a door leading outside that also had windows in it. We hadn't bothered to pull the drapes because it was dark, it was the middle of the night, we hadn't turned a light on in here, there was foliage around, and supposedly the grounds were secure.

But now I was wondering if that had been wise, because I was sure I'd seen something outside.

Jeff picked up that I'd gone from relaxed and sexually fulfilled on a global level to tense and wary on a very personal level. He took my hand. "What is it?" he asked softly.

"Not sure," I replied in kind. "I'd swear I saw something outside the window."

"Something or someone?"

"Not sure. Movement, I guess. Like the bushes were moving. But there's no wind."

We both looked at the various windows. "I don't see anything."

"Yeah, I don't either. Now. I think we might have to break down and get closer to the glass."

"Me not you."

"Hells to the no. Us together, Mister President, or you not at all and I call the Secret Service and make them happy that we're behaving." So to speak. And not really, since I had my pajamas, slippers, and baby monitor on me, and that was it. Now I kicked myself for leaving my phone and purse in our bedroom.

Jeff's mouth opened, presumably to tell me that he wasn't going to let me risk myself, either, when he slammed his mouth shut and turned toward the door that led outside. Looked where he was. The door handle was turning, slowly.

Prepped myself to run and could feel that Jeff was ready, too. Tugged him down, so that we were crouched behind the couch, and turned down the volume on the baby monitor, just in case. Better some protection than none because even the fastest A-C could still be hit with a bullet, and while Jeff was fast, he wasn't Christopher when it came to speed.

Had to figure that whoever was coming in was a human. An A-C would have already been inside by now with the door shut and locked behind him or her.

The door opened wide enough to allow someone of normal size to enter, then it closed quietly. But no one was there.

Some people might have made the leap that the White House was haunted. Those people wouldn't have just been on the Murder Train with a bunch of Invisible Commandos a week ago. I figured we had three guesses for what was in here with us, and the first two weren't going to count. The real bummer was that I knew that I had the goggles in my purse that would allow me to see who this was. However, hyperspeeding to get them wasn't in the cards, because there was no way I was leaving Jeff alone in here and I knew without asking he felt the same way about me.

Did the double-finger point to my eyes and the door, then indicated we needed to split up. Jeff had just fought invisible dudes, too, and he'd spent most of that fight unable to see them, whereas I'd had said goggles on, so he didn't argue.

We stayed crouched down. The robes were a deep, dark blue, meaning that they weren't going to give us away like the white t-shirts we both had on under the robes. We were, all things considered, fairly stealth, even though we had no idea if whoever our Invisible Friend was happened to be looking at us or not.

Jeff went to the left and around the couch, so he was nearer to the outside door. I went straight, toward the desk, both of us breathing shallowly and moving as quietly as possible.

A desk drawer opened and I leaped for it. Slammed into what really felt like legs. Whoever I hit yelped. Sounded female, though I couldn't be positive.

However, I didn't have a great hold and, whoever it was, they managed to kick me away. Jeff was up and now on the other side of the desk, and while he was swinging like a champ, it's hella hard to hit what you can't see.

The outer door opened, wide this time, and it didn't close. "She's outside!" Got up and ran after the presumed her. Could see some of the foliage moving, so went that way, Jeff right behind me.

He caught up to me and grabbed my hand. "Where are we going?"

"After our intruder."

He pulled me to a stop. "I can't see anything that tells me where that person is. I can't feel them, either, meaning they're wearing an emotional blocker. And if they have a gun or a projectile of some kind, we're far too exposed."

Couldn't argue because it was clear that we'd lost the trail. "Fine, let's go back inside."

We turned to go back when a light shone in our eyes. "Halt," a man said, "who goes there?"

"Oh my God, seriously? Who gave you that line? And who the hell do you think's going here?" Put my hand up to shield my eyes.

"Don't move or I'll shoot," said whoever this was who'd never seen either me or Jeff before.

Of course, that meant that this guy had threatened Jeff's wife, and Jeff wasn't a man who was ever cool with that. He let go of me and tackled the guy at hyperspeed. Jeff was also stronger than the average A-C, and they were all stronger than humans. Our clueless guardian went down.

He lost the flashlight and it rolled away. Went and got it and played the light around.

Jeff had someone who was dressed like a Secret Service agent down and under control. So I looked to see if I could spot any tracks. Could and followed them a little way, but lost the trail again and decided my husband would probably appreciate the support, so I went back.

Jeff had the guy up, arms twisted behind him. "Just who the hell are you?" Jeff growled as I put the flashlight onto this guy's face.

"I've never seen him before, but that means nothing. I can't recognize half of the Field agents, including guys I've technically known for years."

"I'm with the Secret Service and you're under arrest."

"Have to hand it to him, he's dedicated. An idiot, but dedicated. So that has to count for something."

"Can you see if he has a walkie or a phone, baby? Before I break his neck just because I don't necessarily think we want murderous idiots on our security team."

"Oh, he didn't shoot," I said as I patted the guy down.

"He was about to," Jeff's growl was on Rabid Dog. This didn't bode well for the dude he was holding.

Found a walkie and hit the talkie part. "Yo, um, who's on the other end of this thing?"

"Identify," a man's voice replied.

"Sorry, you first, dude. We're a tad untrusting right now." Sure, the guy Jeff had might be Secret Service. Then again, he might be working with the invisible cat burglar. And that would mean his pal on the other end wasn't a friendly.

Heard voices in the background as a different voice came on. "Is this Cyclone?" Different male.

"Depends. Who are you?"

"This is Rob. From Cosmos' security detail." Meaning the second in command of Jeff's security detail. Which begged a question, and that question was, where was Joseph, the head of Jeff's detail?

"Rob! Great to talk to you, buddy. You totally don't sound the same in person as you do on this walkie."

"Noted. Confirm it's you, please."

"Blah, blah, blah. Yes, this is Cyclone. Cosmos has hold of the absolute beginner who, per Cosmos, was ready to shoot me. I may be spitballing here, but I think you guys might want to come out and verify that our captive is actually on our team, seeing as someone just broke into the Oval Office."

"Where are you?" Rob asked, sounding freaked.

"Um . . . not on the South Lawn, I don't think. Not in the Rose Garden, either. We're kind of in some trees."

"Found them," Joseph said from behind me. "Turn on the lights outside the West Wing, Rose Garden area." Suddenly it was quite bright out, even though we were still under some trees and in some bushes.

"Took you long enough," Jeff said.

"That's not fair to anyone on our details," I said before Joseph could reply.

"Thanks. I'd ask what you two are doing out here," he said to us, "but I've known you both long enough to know that I don't actually want the answer."

"You kind of do because someone invisible just broke into the Oval Office and I think it was a chick."

Joseph nodded. "I heard." He looked at the guy Jeff had and sighed. "He's one of us."

Jeff let him go, not all that nicely, since he shoved the guy away from himself and me both. "And he's fired. Move him to the counterfeiting side, because he's off White House duty as of this minute. And, before anyone argues, I'm the strongest empath on this planet, I can feel what he was feeling, and he was going to shoot Kitty first and ask questions later. He's gone. Now."

"Agreed." Joseph barked some orders into his walkie and more Secret Service agents arrived and carted our trigger-happy night watchman off.

"This is just like at the airport at the start of Operation Drug Addict."

Jeff grunted. "Don't remind me."

"Actually, I think I should, as in, we have people all around willing to do bad things against us and many times they're pawns, not power pieces on the chessboard. Joseph, don't just reassign whoever that was. I really want to be sure that he wasn't turned against us. Check him for Club

Fifty-One affiliations, affiliations with anyone on our Enemies List, whatever. Run him anywhere and everywhere and don't let him out of sight of anyone we can actually trust."

Joseph nodded and barked more instructions, to Rob as far as I could tell.

"Why?" Jeff asked me quietly. "Your feminine intuition?"

Jeff called it that, Mom called it my gut, and I did, too, sometimes. But really, it was just what I was good at. "I guess. My Megalomaniac Girl sense is tingling."

"Let's get you two back inside," Joseph said. He cocked his head and I knew he was listening to someone via his earpiece this time. "Thanks. Cosmos and Cyclone are contained. Will relay that Cutie-Pie, Challenger, and Comet along with the menagerie and the nanny are okay."

"Nice to know that Lizzie's got her own call name." Hoped she didn't mind being both on the Secret Service Nickname Roster and on Santa's Reindeer Team at the same time.

Joseph shrugged. "Mister Beaumont made it clear that she's part of your family now."

The rest of Jeff's Secret Service detail, minus Rob, and all of mine arrived now and began escorting us back into the White House. "Don't you guys ever get to sleep?"

"Tonight we chose to stay in the complex to ensure that nothing went wrong," Evalyne said, sarcasm knob definitely turned way past eleven. "You see how well we managed that."

"Do you think we should just all resign tomorrow?" Phoebe, the second in command of my detail, asked. Had a feeling she was only half-kidding.

"Oh, stop being such Drama Llamas. Everyone's fine, right? At least per what I heard Joseph confirm."

"Yes, through no fault of yours or ours," Joseph said.

"Look, I'm not going to be all apologetic because, as I see I have to mention again, we had an invisible intruder in the Oval Office and she was trying for something in the *Resolute* desk. Since I doubt that this is the start of *National Treasure Three*, and since we have the man who does the invisible irradiation in our custody *and* our people confirmed that all was well and extremely secure at his factory,

I think we need to ask ourselves just who was willing to ir-
radiate themselves to become the new Super Stealth Supervillain Henchperson and who they're actually working for.
And I think we need to figure this out sooner as opposed to
later."

"Agreed." Only the man who said this wasn't anyone escorting us. And he sounded pissed.

CHAPTER 42

CHUCKIE HEAVED A SIGH. "One night. Couldn't you two have waited one night before breaking every rule? Just one?"

"Playboy is on the scene," Joseph said into his walkie, presumably to Rob again, who was also presumably the one who'd called Chuckie over in the first place.

"Oh, Secret Agent Man, you've joined Team Drama Llama, too?"

Jeff grunted. "Long story, Chuck."

"I doubt it." Chuckie rubbed the back of his neck. Realized he was essentially in his nightclothes, too, meaning he'd been advised and taken a gate without bothering to dress. Felt bad. And like we were having a sleepover. "I'm fully capable of guessing what the short story is, but I'm trying not to embarrass everyone else."

"Whatevs. Let's go to the Oval Office, get some cocoa, and we'll tell you what happened. The exciting-to-everyone parts."

"I heard it," he said as we went inside. "Was anything taken?"

"How, literally, would I know?" Jeff asked. "I haven't opened the desk or put anything in it. The move was done by the Operations Team and unless we want them awake and over here to do a search, I have no idea."

Went to the desk and looked at the open drawer. "There's nothing in here. Meaning this probably has a false bottom or something that I'll let Chuckie find."

Chuckie came over and looked the drawer over.

"Actually, no. There's no false bottom in this particular drawer. It's just a drawer, and an empty one."

"I think I got her before she had a chance to grab anything, honestly."

"Meaning she didn't know where whatever it was she was looking for actually is. Jeff, we'll search the desk in a minute." Chuckie turned to Joseph and Evalyne. "No one got hurt that we know of, and that means no one gets fired or gets to quit tonight. However, I want to know why the shield isn't up on the complex."

"We have too many going in and out at all hours," Evalyne said. "We've had several talks today with White House, Embassy, and Dulce Security. While we *can* put up shields on the complex, we can only do so when we're in a State of Emergency, because otherwise the business of keeping the White House running would come to a complete halt."

Chuckie heaved a sigh. "That makes sense. I don't like it, but it is what it is." He pulled out his phone and made a call. "Serene, hi and sorry to wake you. Oh? Well, good I guess. Look, we need to equip the entire Secret Service staff at the White House and those assigned to the Martini family with goggles. Yes. Per Kitty, someone invisible broke in. Huh. Not as far as I know, but it's interesting that you ask because Kitty said she thinks it was a woman. Yeah. Yeah. Yes, please clear it with them but tell them both that if they want to say no they should think again." Chuckie laughed. "Thanks, you're my favorite, too."

He hung up and turned back to me and Jeff. "Serene was up early to work with the androids and check on the Kitty-Bot. She'll get Dulce on the goggles situation. Until further notice, those are going to need to be standard-issue and I'll want all the agents wearing them—Field and Secret Service both—until we have our invisibility problem solved."

"Who shouldn't say no?" Hey, I had to ask.

"Reader and Tom Curran, the Director of the FBI. Serene's advising both of them of what's going on. Technically because it's domestic this would fall to Tom's agency, but I'm here and I'm not ceding authority for all the reasons you can think of."

"Works for me," Jeff said.

"Don't forget Homeland Security," Joseph said.

"I'm not, believe me. Look, we apologize, again, for being in the Oval Office at night. However, as I understand it, I can go anywhere in the complex that I want, whenever I want, without a babysitter. Supposedly we're safe in this place. That I was in here, with my wife, when someone broke in says a lot more about our lack of security measures, or our enemies' willingness to take risks, than it does about either Kitty or me being 'naughty.'"

"We care more that you both were outside of the building, chasing after the intruder, than that you weren't in your bedroom," Evalyne said.

"We're both basically ex-military and, frankly, we're also both trained. I realize that we're important, but so is stopping whoever was in here to try to plant or steal whatever."

Chuckie jerked. "Plant. There were bugs in the desk. Maybe whoever broke in was either coming to retrieve what they'd planted or they were trying to plant another, since we cleaned this place out, again, earlier."

"Makes sense." Jeff looked around. "We're heading back to the residence section. Feel free to actually get some sleep. But ensure that the agent who was ready to shoot Kitty is held in solitary while his background is being dug into, because I can guarantee we're going to want to question him later."

Our details escorted us to the second floor of the residence anyway. We didn't really talk while we walked along. Jeff and Chuckie were both mad, though not at each other or me as far as I could tell. The Secret Service were mad with us, but it was clear they were more upset with themselves. Hated that we made these people feel so inadequate so often, when they were really awesome. They just weren't A-Cs. And we just weren't plain folks anymore.

Once we were upstairs the Secret Service left us, after asking us to do them a solid and try not to get into trouble. There were other agents standing outside of each bedroom door. They hadn't been here earlier, but had a feeling they were going to be a standard feature from now on.

It was close to dawn, but now I was tired, and I could tell both men were tired, too. We had a brand-new nanny and, as far as I was concerned, Nadine was going to get to really show off the skills.

Verified with the two agents outside of Lizzie's room that she and Nadine were still asleep, asked them to give Nadine the "you get to take care of the kids until we can drag up" message, then went into the Lincoln Bedroom. Into its closet.

Found the hamper. "Could you make up the room for Chuckie, please and thank you? I'm sure he'll need clothes and such and whatever else to make him feel comfortable sleeping here for a few hours and all that jazz."

Turned around to see a suit and all the trimmings hanging up. "You're the best."

Left the closet and tugged Chuckie into the room. "Get some sleep. The Operations Team has it set up for you. The adrenaline's wearing off and we all look like sleepwalkers."

Chuckie looked uncertain.

"Do it," Jeff said. "Please. Let's be in a situation where we can at least pretend we're fresh when we go over this."

Chuckie nodded. "You win because I'm exhausted."

"Meet us in the Family Dining Room. It's on this floor. I'm sure one of the really angry Secret Service Agents will be happy to escort you there."

He barked a laugh. "I'm sure I can find it without trouble. What time?"

"Whenever we wake up," Jeff said. "Or are woken up. My money's on the latter."

"Mine, too. Goodnight Jeff, Kitty. Please have sex in your room, only, for the remainder of what we're going to laughingly call the rest of the night."

"You don't know us."

Chuckie managed a grin. "Sometimes I feel like I know the two of you better than anyone else. Sometimes you're both enigmas. Keeps life interesting." He closed the door and we headed down the hall.

"When am I ever an enigma?" Especially to Chuckie.

"Never, really," Jeff said. "And I doubt I am, either." He sighed. "I wish there was someone, anyone, we could fix him up with."

"Romance? Right now?"

"Definitely right now. He's over you romantically, but it wouldn't take much to push him back. And I enjoy having him as my friend now, so I'd really like to avoid that."

"Chuckie would never, Jeff, you know that."

"I do, but I also know that he's crushingly, heartbreakingly lonely. And that loneliness only abates a little when he's with us, and by us I mean our extended family and those in the Embassy." Jeff shook his head. "He wasn't like this before he fell in love with Naomi, and certainly not while they were together. But since she died . . ." He sighed again. "It's been worse since we went to Beta Eight. He's still not recovered from that."

"He's doing better."

"The past week or so? Yeah. But he's also just hanging on in some ways. And I have no idea what either one of us can do for him."

"Me either."

This was the thing that pushed me over the edge of tired to exhausted, though. Jeff picked it up, of course, and he picked me up. We were at our door, so that was convenient. He carried me inside, and I was too tired to make a wedding night joke. Kicked my slippers off before he laid me onto the bed, robe still on.

He lay down next to me, his robe still on, too. He wrapped his arm around me, and I snuggled up against him and let his double heartbeats lull me right to sleep.

We actually got a few hours of good sleep before Raj drew the short straw and had to come in and wake us up.

We dragged out of bed and into the shower. Despite our desires we decided to wait to test the shower out until we were confident half of the White House Staff wasn't standing outside in the hall.

Happily, the Elves had hung a rather lovely velour tracksuit up on my side of the closet. It was iced blue, because apparently now at least seventy-five percent of what I had to wear had to be in "my color." But it wasn't a business suit, and I put it on with great joy. Plus I could wear my blue Lifehouse t-shirt and Converse with this, so win all the way around.

Jeff, naturally, was in the Armani Fatigues—black Armani suit and tie, crisp white shirt. There were jeans hanging on his side of the closet, but he ignored them as if they were an affront to humanity instead of something made for comfort that also really showed his amazing butt off well. But, I was too tired to argue, so saved that fight for another day.

Nadine had the kids fed, dressed, and entertained, so that was definitely one for the win column. Chuckie joined us along with Raj, Vance, and Reader, who looked as tired as the rest of us, in the Family Dining Room. Frankly, only the kids looked well rested, but it was more important for them to get a good night's sleep, so I consoled myself with that.

Breakfast for the adults was being whipped up, so after the kids got hugs, kisses, and snuggles from all of us, Nadine and Lizzie took them down to the East Sitting Room which was, as far as I was concerned, about to become the First Family Playroom. Figured I'd ask the Elves for that later, though.

Our food arrived as the kids left. The people serving us were all nice, but they were staff, not our people. So we waited to talk about anything of importance until they were gone, meaning until we were done eating. Which was okay because the food was great and, from the way we were eating, we were all starving.

"I miss the Elves," I said as the last person left, carrying the last of our dirty dishes into the kitchen. I was still a little hungry. "I think we need to adjourn to our living room."

We did, and Jeff and I filled everyone in on what had transpired earlier in the morning. There was, when we got right down to it, very little to tell.

"Well," Reader said when we were done, "we can investigate, but I think what Chuck put in place already is the best option. We'll have all the goggles needed today."

"We need to come up with the spin for the press," Raj said.

"Security sunglasses." Everyone looked at me. "What? That sounds cool enough and it's technically true."

"I sometimes forget you were in marketing," Chuckie said with a small smile. "I think that will work well enough."

Talk turned to what else we did and didn't know. Sadly, the consensus was that we really didn't know a lot. "The bottom line is, as Angela said last night, we need to get those peace talks back on as soon as possible." Reader grimaced. "We've had agents all over the Camp David area. They found a little evidence that the Kitty-Bot was there, but it was slight. Basically, she wasn't doing much while she was waiting."

"Robots usually don't. I mean, they're made to sit there

until they're needed or activated. Androids, too, since I still vividly remember Sandra the Android and she was definitely a sleeper." And, as an android, had possessed quite the unpleasant personality. Wondered if that was how we could tell if someone was an android—because they were high on the nasty person scale. Chose not to mention this theory at this time, in part because I didn't want to be told I was crazy this early in the day.

"I sincerely think we're going to find that the android and robot programs are different," Chuckie said. "But that's down the road, even if that road is only a couple of days away."

"I totally agree with that theory."

"That's nice, but we need things we can focus on right now," Jeff said.

"Really?" Vance asked. "That's what you're waiting on, focus? Why? The answer is obvious."

CHAPTER 43

"**N**OT TO ANYONE HERE," Jeff said dryly. "So enlighten us as to what we're supposed to focus on."

"Your jobs," Vance said flatly. "Not the jobs you want to do, but the actual jobs you actually have now. What everyone needs to do is get comfortable with their official assignments. Jeff, Congress will be approving your appointees tomorrow, or at least beginning the process, which will be sped up, under the circumstances. But all those people are brand new to their positions, just like you are. As much as stopping the bad guys is important, I suggest that we spend the next few days actually focused on doing the mundane parts of our jobs. Like learning what they are."

No one could really argue with this level of logic, so we didn't. We chatted some more, but the bottom line was that Vance was right, and we all dispersed to do what we could with what we currently had. Even though Chuckie probably had the most work to do, since he had to clean out the CIA, Jeff and Raj both wanted him at the White House, so they went to get him a temporary office.

I currently had Vance, so I was in far better shape than I probably had any right to be. "I've contacted Nancy Maurer as requested," he said when we were alone.

"Super. I need a snack." Got up, grabbed my purse because I learned from my mistakes, and headed back to the dining room. Well, the kitchen, actually. Because there was a fridge and I was all about testing to see if Algar had provided Elf Service here.

Vance followed me. "I'd mention that you're going to gain weight but I guess you're lucky that way."

"It's from running around after bad guys." And probably my enhancement, but that wasn't important right now. Dumped my purse on the table and headed for my goal. "So, what did Nancy say?"

"She's going to be your Social Secretary. It's a job she's well suited for, and she's excited to do it. And we already had security on the Maurers, at least on Nancy and Cameron, so we got those folks their goggles and that's all set."

"Awesome. A Coca-Cola, please and thank you." Opened the fridge with all the digits crossed. There was a frosty Coke in an ice-cold bottle. The good stuff up from Mexico. "You are the *best*," I whispered as I grabbed my Coke. "So," I said as I closed the door and grabbed some handy donuts on the counter, "um, what should I be doing?"

"Besides scarfing junk food?" He shrugged. "Work on your theories, because I know you'll be doing that anyway. But I'm going to pull your core team in, and we're going to go over the thing you're most concerned about—image and how we control yours."

"Let's do it, because I'm basically terrified of what the press is going to do when they get a load of me. Want a soda?"

"Sure, I'll take a Coke, too."

Turned to the fridge. "Another Coke, please and thank you." Opened the door, took the Coke, gave it to Vance. "Hope still lives."

Reader popped his head in. "Figured I'd find you here, girlfriend."

"I'd be offended but I'm too thrilled that the Elves took the refrigerator contract for the White House to complain. What's up?"

"Want to go over your image issues."

"We're handling that," Vance said.

Reader eyed him. "*Are* you? Well, that's nice. You'll be handling them with me involved."

"*Are* we?" Vance asked in that way that indicated a cat-fight of epic proportions was about to start.

Remembered that Reader had been jealous of my budding relationship with Vance during Operation Sherlock, just like I'd been jealous that he and Tim had private jokes with people I hadn't met. Thought we'd gotten past that, but it had been a trying couple of weeks for everyone.

Cleared my throat and, happily, they both looked at me. "Dudes, while I'm all kinds of flattered that you're both sort of ready to fight over me, let's all take deep breaths and remember that I love you both and in different ways. And I need you both, also in different ways."

They didn't look convinced. Forged on. "James, Vance is covering being Pierre for me, a desperate need I know you can relate to, since you're the reason we have Pierre with us in the first place. Vance, James is a lot like you, only he kicks butt better than almost anyone and has never met a skill he can't master faster than anyone else. You're alike, but not duplicates of each other. So, let's all try to get along. Neither one of you is being replaced by the other. Ever."

Tim's turn to pop in, which was good timing, at least in my opinion, since Reader and Vance were still giving each other side-eye while trying to pretend to me that they weren't ready to kick the other one in the shins. "Hey, figured I'd find you here."

"Now I'm starting to get offended." Consoled myself by starting in on one of my donuts. "I didn't even know you were here."

"I wasn't. I came over to appeal to the only person in authority who might care that my team is still missing in action and might, conceivably, want to do something about it."

"Wow that sort of sells everyone else short."

"Yeah, well, I have five guys who are gone, and they're not the only ones still missing. I was just downstairs talking to Tito, Melanie, and Emily, and they all agree a little focus on finding the princesses would be nice, too."

"Why are Melanie and Emily here?"

And why hadn't they come to say hi? They were Lorraine and Claudia's mothers and, right after my own mother and Chuckie's mom, I liked them best, as mothers went. Lucinda had moved up in my esteem over the years, but she still wasn't in the same category as Melanie and Emily for me.

The guys all stared at me. Tim recovered first. "Oh, that's right. Tito never got to tell you. They're part of his White House Medical Staff. They and their husbands have moved here, up on the third floor with the rest of your twenty-four-seven staff."

"Awesome! And is that what we're calling our people who live here with us?"

"Yes," Vance said. "Because the normal staff rotates depending on time of day. They used to live here, but that was a long time ago. However, because of your administration's specific needs and requirements, things are reverting in some ways."

"Nice spin, and Len mentioned that to me yesterday, so, don't faint, I already knew this. But back to Tim's accurate concerns—we can talk about doing our jobs and all that, but we have people missing, and every day they're gone is a day they're in danger of some kind."

"And potentially being turned into androids," Tim added. "Which I'm not okay with in case no one's clear."

"We're all clear and, despite your insinuations, we all care," Vance said. "But in the earlier meeting you missed it was decided that everyone would do their jobs. What is your job, just out of curiosity?"

Tim glared at Vance. Not up to Christopher's standards, but then, who was? "I'm the Head of Airborne for Centaurion Division. Which I'm pretty sure you know."

"I do. I was just wondering if you did. Since you seem remarkably dependent upon Kitty to do all the heavy thinking."

"Wow, Vance, let's not be in Attack Dog Mode with these guys, okay?"

Vance heaved the Sigh of the Long-Suffering. "They, like you, refuse to accept that you have a job that's considered vitally important in our government. I'm not saying that you can't help out. I'm not insane, and I realize that you'll be doing your best to lead whatever charge your boys here are going to be coordinating. But at the same time, does anyone, anyone at all, realize that the First Lady of the United States has to represent at peace talks in a few days? Anybody? Or is it *just* me?"

Tim and Reader stared at Vance. "We need her help," Tim said finally. "I'm good at it, but no one thinks like the crazy people like Kitty does."

"And part of why I'm here is the upcoming peace talks," Reader added. He looked at me. "Attack dog is right. Where was this fight in him when, you know, actual fighting was taking place?"

"Vance serves in other ways."

"Look," Vance snapped, "I'm a lover, not a fighter. But

you're on my turf, and Kitty hired me, and it's my damn job to make her look not just good but fantastic. She, more than any other First Lady, has the scrutiny of the world on her, thanks to that freaking lunatic Cliff Goodman. Ergo, you two either get with the program or get out. For God's sake, don't you have bloodhounds or something you can set to sniffing?"

I jerked. "Holy crap. Someone get Thomas Kendrick and Lillian Culver here, faster than fast."

CHAPTER 44

INSISTED THAT WE STAY in the Family Dining Room because I felt that Coca-Cola and donuts were now vital to my process. Plus, fewer people were likely to hear Vance, Reader, and Tim bickering with each other.

So I snacked and the three men snarled and snapped at each other while we waited for Kendrick and Culver to arrive. Interestingly enough, Vance was handling both Reader and Tim with relative ease. Clearly the verbal sparring and such was his forte. Good.

On the plus side, when someone in the White House asks for a meeting, most people race to get right there, and Kendrick and Culver were no exceptions. Reader having floater gates sent to them helped, too. They were dressed as I was used to—Culver in her signature red, Kendrick in the Typical Washington Wear for Men, a navy suit.

Once the usual pleasantries were done, got right to it. "Thomas, you have all kinds of tracking devices, right?"

"Of course."

"Great. Got anything called a bloodhound? Or something that does what a bloodhound would do?"

He nodded. "A variety of options. Why?"

"We have missing people. Screw the planes and helicarrier. I mean, if we can find them, super-duper. But we have humans and aliens missing that we'd all like back. And so far, no one, neither you nor Drax, have suggested we use your equipment to find them. Why is that?"

"Titan's Bloodhound Tracker requires two things—the DNA of the missing person and a relative idea of where that person is. Without both, the BT is useless. We have generalized trackers, of course, but they're used more to determine if the specified target or targets is or are there."

"Beg pardon? Lots of words. Made individual sense, but . . ."

"He's being political," Culver said. "Thomas, Kitty doesn't care for political. It's why we're meeting here, not in her office. Speak plainly."

"Apologies. These trackers are made for warfare. You send them in to make sure that there are or aren't living things, such as people, where you've targeted to bomb or send strafing fire or whatever. They don't find a specific person — they find if a person is in the vicinity of the specific radius."

"What's the square mileage of the BT?" Reader asked. "We're clear the others don't do what I think it is Kitty wants, but the BT sounds like it's exactly what we need."

"A ten-mile radius, tops. We're working on refinements, but something like the BT is of far more use to covert and clandestine ops, and they've been far more focused on things that help or hinder A-Cs."

"I literally cannot wait for the list of who's been asking you for what, Thomas, and I mean that in such a totally nasty FLOTUS way you can't even imagine. By the way, I know you have a spying device called a Tarantula. Is there anything those things can't get into?"

"Anything shielded by what the A-Cs use for shielding. Other than that? They're small but powerful, and they 'sleep' as a sphere. They can move as a sphere, as well, if need be. If air can get in, it's likely the Tarantulas can, too."

"How many BTs do you have?" Tim asked.

"Megalomaniac Lad, it's lovely that your confidence is back and we're once again on the same wavelength."

Kendrick shook his head. "Not enough for what I'm sure you're going to suggest. They're very costly to create, and we haven't sold any yet. I have a handful of prototypes, but that's it. Not enough to blanket the world and wait."

"Can they find something that's mostly inanimate? Like smart metal?"

"I have no idea. We haven't tried that. Like I said, the demand hasn't been there. Yet."

"That's okay, it's here now. James, check with Serene. Really need to know if the experiments she's running are completed and what the outcomes are." He nodded and started texting. "In the meantime, Thomas, was any Titan tech, any at all, even the littlest bit, in Drax's helicarrier?"

He looked thoughtful. "Nothing that really mattered for the running of the ship."

"What *was* in there?"

"Group communications. He was using Titan tech to ensure that his strike force could stay in contact with each other. Not the most advanced technology we have, but it's stable and effective."

"That tech is not in our control, though," Tim pointed out. "So we can't track on it."

"Someone had to be flying the thing," Reader said. "Were they in contact with Drax using your tech?"

Kendrick shook his head. "No, that was his setup."

"And the person who stole the helicarrier wasn't one of the Invisible Commandos anyway. I was just hoping that there was something of Titan's still inside the ship."

"If there was, I wasn't informed. He was trying to sell the helicarrier to me, not the other way around."

Reader's phone beeped. He read it, then showed it to me and Tim. Serene felt that the Vata were all able to determine a real person from either an android or a robot. "Tell her to bring them here," I said quietly to Reader, who nodded and went back to texting.

"We have some people coming to join us," I told Kendrick. "While we wait, Vance, can you get the rest of my immediate team ready to go? Once we deal with this situation we need to focus on what you wanted to do."

"Abner came over with me," Lillian said. "He's downstairs speaking with the Chief Usher, verifying what he can and can't change."

"Good initiative."

She beamed. Still made her look like Joker Jaws to me, but at least the Joker was fully on my side now, so there was that. Wondered if that made Abner Harley Quinn. Decided I'd table that determination for later.

"I'll get everyone else ready," Vance said and started texting. Contemplated getting everyone texting at the same time, just to see if I could, but then decided I had better uses for my efforts. "Including Gideon?"

"Yes, if he's available and you agree with Vander that we should ask him to take an official position with the Cause."

"I do and we should."

Serene came in. "We're here." She had a man with her I'd never seen before. However, he had long, dark hair and it wasn't pulled back. Was willing to bet that he had metal plates at his temples.

The man looked around at everyone, then looked to Serene. "All organic."

"Kitty, this is Tevvik," Serene said. "He was by far the best at determining organic from machine."

"Super, bring in his boss, for want of a better word."

"Ruler," Tevvik said with a smile.

"Ruler number, what, twenty-one or twenty three?"

"On this planet? Number one."

"Good to know."

"What's going on?" Kendrick asked. Drax came into the room. Kendrick jumped up. "Get that lunatic!"

He lunged for Drax, but Culver and Vance grabbed him. Kendrick was still shouting and Drax joined in. Culver and Vance were still having to hold Kendrick back, and Tevvik and Serene were doing the same with Drax. We had a full-on domestic dispute going. Lucky us.

Three more Vata showed up. They also got in on the domestic dispute. Had no idea where Buchanan, Siler, or Wruck were, but if they were around, they were staying hidden and out of the fray.

Leaned next to Reader. "It was a lot less loud when you and Tim were doing this with Vance. Wish Jeff was here. Or a reality camera crew. We could sell this somewhere, I'm sure."

"Oh, I have faith in you, girlfriend."

Clearly it was time for me to represent. Contemplated my options. Sent a text to Jeremy requesting his presence. Pulled out my iPod and speakers. Plugged the speakers in, turned the volume up to eleven. But what song to choose? Jeremy arrived just as I came up with the right choice. Nodded to him and hit play.

CHAPTER 45

PINK'S "TRUE LOVE" came blasting out. Kendrick and Drax both stopped shouting and stared at me, mouths open. Reader and Tim, meanwhile, were cracking up. I still had it.

Once the room was quiet except for Pink and Lily Rose Cooper singing, I turned the volume down to a normal volume. For me. It was probably still loud for others, but oh well, too bad for them.

"Now that I have your attention, I'd like everyone to sit down, shut up, and have a Coke and a smile." Everyone sat. No one requested a Coke and smiles weren't in abundance, either, since Reader and Tim were trying to get a hold of themselves. "Good job. Gustav, the reason you were doing all the testing in the desert was to prove that there is a difference between a human, android, and robot brain, and that you and your people can tell what it is. Per Tevvik, everyone here is a real human."

"Yes, so what?" Drax snapped. "He insulted me."

"We have a short memory, I see." Turned to Kendrick. "Gustav thinks you stole the helicarrier. That's why he's mad at you."

"What? What the hell? I didn't steal anything!"

"Yeah? Jeremy, your thoughts?"

"He's telling the truth."

"Meaning that what took that helicarrier was an android. Gustav, you know that's what we suspected."

"He called me a lunatic!"

"Because you are!" Kendrick was ready to go again. Turned the song back up. They quieted. Turned it back down. "The song is all about love and hate and how they're so closely tied. And all that jazz. At any rate, the bottom line is that Thomas isn't a sneaky thief and Drax isn't a kidnapping lunatic. Basically, you were both screwed over by the same person or persons unknown but definitely suspected. And what we need—and by 'we' I mean the country and by 'need' I mean what I expect you to do—is to work together to help figure out how to get that stupid helicarrier and all the people in it back safely under our control."

"Why was he," Kendrick nodded toward Tevvik, "talking about a ruler?"

"That's a funny story. It turns out that Drax isn't actually a human. He's what's called a Vata, from a distant planet, Vatusus, which is near the Galactic Core. They're really good with electronics on Vatusus. In fact, all the Vata have a really interesting thing that sets them apart from the other humanoid races that we've met so far. Tevvik, if you would?"

He smiled and pulled his hair back. The humans in the room who hadn't known that we had another alien race skulking about all gasped.

"Yeah, organic metal plates in the temples is different, isn't it? That's part of how they commune with electronics. And that's good for us, because we have two androids and one robot under our control now, and they could tell that they weren't humans or A-Cs."

Tevvik shook his head. "Not quite. Organic versus inorganic. We couldn't tell the difference between human and A-C brains, just that the androids had circuitry within the gray matter and the robot had circuitry instead of gray matter, if you will."

"Gotcha, thanks for the distinction. So, Thomas and Gustav, you two need to kiss and make up, because you're not actually each other's enemies. Oh, and by the way, the second part of that funny story is that Tevvik and his friends are here because Gustav is, as it turns out, from the Vatusus Royal Family. Ergo, meet Prince Gustav. He, and I quote, eschews the title, but his retainers really like it. And, Gustav, humans dig royalty, so you get really comfy being called Prince Gustav, 'cause I'm going to be using that whenever I need to."

Both men were staring at each other as the music changed to "Crystal Baller" by Third Eye Blind.

Considering it should have gone to another Pink song, chose to take this as an Official Algar Hint that I needed to be thinking about Crystal Maurer in some way.

Turned the volume lower. "Gustav, Thomas has a Bloodhound Tracker that I think can help us. What I want you two doing is trying to figure out how to narrow down where the helicarrier could be. We'll be helping with that because, as Tim said before many of you arrived, this is my skill."

"What is?" Tevvik asked politely.

"Mind melding with the League of Crazed Evil Geniuses. It's a gift and a curse both, but I find the will to go on." Mostly because sex with Jeff made most of my trials worthwhile. But I decided to keep that one to myself.

Of course, Jeremy blushing meant I probably hadn't kept that quite as to myself as one could hope. Oh well, such were the risks of working for Centaurion Division.

Vance's phone beeped. "Gideon can't make it right now, he has state business he has to deal with, but he's happy to have an official job and title with the Cause. The others on your team are standing by, Kitty. How do you want to handle this?"

"Gustav, did you ever send Stephanie to Titan for any reason?"

"Once or twice, yes."

"Super-duper. Did you ever meet her, Thomas?"

"Pretty girl, blonde hair?" he asked. I nodded. "I did. She came to bring me prototypes a couple of times. We didn't talk too long either time, though."

Stephanie had hyperspeed, meaning anything she wanted to get she could without Kendrick necessarily noticing. "Can we get our paws on any working BTs, Thomas?"

"Yes, I can have the prototypes brought over."

"Make it so." Contemplated all we had to do. Decided I could ignore all the FLOTUS crap and focus on the interesting and important stuff, like finding the flyboys and our other missing people, just like Tim wanted.

My music changed to "Break Your Plans" by the Fray. Interesting. I was ready to roll into a full on Get Our People Back meeting. But since it appeared I was on the Algar Network, took this song to mean that Algar wanted me focused on the FLOTUS stuff for some reason. The reason probably being that Mom and Vance were right—the peace talks were the top priority and my handling them well was the way to go.

Heaved an internal sigh. Now was not the time to argue with the King of the Elves. "Okay, Serene and Tim, you need to get Thomas, Lillian, Gustav, and the rest of the Vata focused on trying to determine if there's a way to track any of our missing people or the helicarrier itself via Titan and Vatusan means."

"What about you?" Reader asked suspiciously.

Heaved an external sigh. "I'm going to be working with my team to prepare for the peace talks."

Everyone in the room stared at me. "She means it," Jeremy said finally. He sounded as shocked as the rest of the room looked.

"Wow, thanks for that. I just know that we don't have a lot of time and with Team Technical on the case, I can't honestly imagine that I'm going to come up with the right stuff. So, you guys do that, the rest of you go back to the meetings you were having, and let me try to get my FLOTUS house at least somewhat in order. If I have an Evil Genius Mind Meld Moment, I'll call or text."

Serene looked the least stunned and she recovered the quickest. She ushered those I'd named out and took Jeremy along with her for good measure. Leaving me, Vance, and Reader in the dining room.

Reader kissed my forehead. "I'm proud of you, Kitty. That wasn't an easy decision for you to have made."

"Yeah, well, please be sure to tell Jeff and Chuckie about it. I doubt they'll believe you, but a girl can dream."

"Where will you be going?" Vance asked Reader. Pointedly.

Reader gave Vance a long look. "You'd better be ready to tackle this on your own, because if she blows it because you didn't prep her enough or correctly, I'm going to make sure there's blowback on you."

Vance shrugged. "I live in fear."

"Good." Reader went to the doorway. "Kitty, I'm headed back to discuss strategy with Jeff and Raj. Try not to burn this part of the White House down while we're otherwise engaged."

"Wow, you're really taking all the fun out of my new job."

CHAPTER 46

ONCE READER WAS GONE, Vance sent a text to those waiting down below or wherever they were. To his credit, Vance didn't say any of the nasty things I could see him thinking about Reader aloud.

He and I stayed at the table and munched on donuts until the rest of my team arrived, meaning Colette, who arrived first, hyperspeed being what it was, and Nancy Maurer, who was being escorted up by Abner. Got up and gave her a hug. "Thanks for joining the team."

"I was so honored you asked, dear," Mrs. Maurer said. She had a very high-pitched voice I'd originally thought was faked. It wasn't, though, and I was used to it now. Still called her Squeaky half the time, but she'd accepted the nickname with grace so we were good.

Colette was in, of course, the Armani Fatigues: Female Version—black slim skirt, white oxford, black pumps. Abner and Vance were both in extremely fashionable suits. And Mrs. Maurer was in a very sensible, clearly expensive dress and jacket combo. Basically, my team was Dressed to Impress and I was Dressed to Play Hoops.

Got everyone beverages, requested more donuts, put them in the middle of where we were sitting, then we started in on the fun that was my new job. Dreaded the day that I'd be expected to do this in my official FLOTUS office—just knew that I wasn't going to be able to put my feet up on an extra chair and lounge there while scarfing donuts and Cokes.

"Kitty, do you want anything changed in here?" Abner asked. "It strikes me as a very warm room already, but, while we're brainstorming, I'd like to get an idea of what you do and don't like about it."

"Vance, I must say that the mind reading classes have been a huge success. Abner, I like this room a lot. But, sadly, since I have an official office somewhere, I'm fairly sure that most of our meetings are going to be there, so this is probably not an area you need to focus on."

Mrs. Maurer patted my shoulder. "You'll get more comfortable in the White House, dear, I promise. Feeling awed and out of place here is natural."

"It's set up to make us feel awed." Vance looked around. "We're fine for an informal working session that happens to include food. I think you can get away with us meeting here more often than you think, Kitty. You can always use needing to be near the kids as an excuse, too."

"That's me, Mother of the Year."

"I like it cozy," Abner said, clearly going for the Sucking Up Tactic. I had no issue with this tactic. "This is a lot more relaxed than everything yesterday. I'm all for this room as the official team meeting place."

Colette was clearly wondering why she'd bothered to join my team, but to her great credit, she didn't mention that aloud. "We need to focus on keeping the First Lady's reputation and image strong yet accessible."

The others picked this line of thought up and ran with it. We were at this for a couple of hours. Everyone else had way more to offer than I did. So while I tried to help and listen as attentively as I could, I also spent some time running things over in my mind. Didn't get much of anywhere, but at least I felt like I was trying, and that was something.

Heard nothing from Team Technical, but one of the many random A-Cs we had brought in a BT prototype for me to stare at. Per the A-C it was the Multiple Target Model and it had been loaded with the flyboys' DNA. Not that I could tell, but I chose to believe.

Stared at it. It looked a lot like a hockey puck or one of those weird not-really-a-coaster things some restaurants gave you when you were waiting for your table. Whatever it was, it was dressed up for Christmas, since it had a lot of colorful lights on it. Had no idea what any of them indicated, but they didn't seem excited, so the flyboys weren't nearby. Which I already knew, but confirmation was something, right? Dropped it into my purse to go over with Kendrick at a later time.

Lunchtime loomed then passed and no one suggested getting anything to eat. We'd polished off the donuts at least an hour prior and I was hungry again.

"No one's going to expect Kitty to be a Stepford Wife," Vance said, based on a suggestion from Colette that we focus me on typical First Lady Activities, like throwing parties and being nice to the spouses of visiting dignitaries. Wondered if anyone had bothered to brief Colette on how I actually rolled.

Well, time she learned. "You know, I think we have some Stepford stuff going on. All top-secret, high-level stuff." Looked at Vance.

"Everyone's already got the clearances."

"Awesome." Filled them in on what had gone on with the Kitty-Bot and Janelle Gardiner. "So, I have no idea if that woman's alive or dead, but she's definitely got a robotic version of herself hanging out at her house."

"We can't go there," Vance said flatly. "Again, in your case, at all in ours."

"Oh, I wasn't going to suggest that, actually. I'd just like you guys thinking about it, keeping your eyes and ears open and all that jazz. No, what I was going to suggest was lunch."

"I can't believe you're hungry," Vance said.

"I like food. Sue me."

Mrs. Maurer cocked her head. "You know . . ."

"Squeaky, I know looks like that. What are you about to suggest?"

"One of the things that the country needs is the feeling that things are returning to normal. Your husband has to be seen working. But you . . . you just have to be seen being relaxed and normal. And what's more normal than going out to luncheon?"

"I love this plan! Can I wear what I have on or should I change to match the rest of you?"

Vance didn't look excited. "Not sure. Depends on what kind of image we want to you to portray. Nancy, are you sure about this?"

She nodded. "Yes, dear, I feel strongly about it."

"Choose wisely," Abner said. "Wherever you pick is

going to essentially be anointed as the first place the new First Lady ever ate."

"Kitty, you have a favorite place, don't you?" Mrs. Maurer asked.

"I do. The Teetotaler."

"Excellent. As Abner said, this will help them, too."

"You two don't know her like I do," Vance said. "This sounds innocuous. Something's going to go wrong."

Colette nodded. "Per my briefing from Raj, trouble follows Kitty closely."

"I'm in the room. Look, we'll take Len and Kyle along. And one more A-C, if he's free." Sent a text, and within seconds White walked in the room, Len and Kyle in tow.

"Missus Martini, thank you for the invitation. As always, you know when I'm peckish."

"I live to serve, Mister White. Boys, it's time to get out of this joint and head over to the place where everybody knows our names."

Len grinned. "The Teetotaler will be glad to see us."

"I recruit and hire so well. Okay, so, are we okay to take a limo? And, again, do I wear this or do I change?"

The new arrivals had views on my outerwear, just as the rest of my team did. Stopped listening after a few minutes and instead sent texts to Jeff, Chuckie, Raj, Doreen, Reader, Tim, and Serene, letting them know that I was being a wild woman and taking my new team out to a late lunch.

The responses were essentially the same—everyone told me to have fun and stay out of trouble. Chose not to be bitter that my nearest and dearest didn't think I could handle one meal out without creating an incident. Jeff's message included the admonition to leave the kids in the White House with Nadine. Nice to know that he already trusted her more than me. Actively chose not to be bitter, but it took effort.

"It's her first public appearance since she took down Cliff Goodman," Abner said. "She needs to look nice, not like we dragged her off the track."

"I was on the track team, but yeah, I kind of think Abner's right. Everyone else looks great. This is lovely for being inside, but for going out I think it's too casual."

"We'll get the car while you change," Len said.

"I don't think you get the Beast," Kyle added, referring to the Official Limo of the President. "But we'll also do you a favor and let your Secret Service unit know that you're planning to leave the White House."

"Like you need to remember to do every time," Len said.

"When did you guys trade sides on me?"

Len winked. "Every time we're being good, is what I meant."

"Oh. So not often."

"Right. Or, as we call it, routine." Len and Kyle trotted of and I trotted across the hall.

Went into the dressing room and looked over my options. I had a lot of them. Many suits, many variations of the Armani Fatigues. Many pairs of jeans and concert t-shirts and such that I couldn't wear today.

Chose to mix it up. Put on a black slim skirt but chose a blue blouse. Sure, this was a little reminiscent of what I was wearing during the National Convention when all hell had broken loose. But it was also nice and, at the same time, unremarkable.

Put my hair up in a big banana clip, so I once again looked like I'd put time into the 'do, and made sure that the special goggles were in my purse along with my Glock and several clips, my phone, iPod, speakers, and hairspray. Never knew when a superbeing would show up, after all. Sure, we hadn't had one for a few years now, but that just meant we needed to remain vigilant.

Checked in on the kids before I left the area. To find that my kids were not here.

CHAPTER 47

LIZZIE WAS AROUND in her room, lying on her bed reading. But Nadine, Jamie, and Charlie were nowhere to be seen. "Um, where's everyone?"

Lizzie shot me a look that said she feared I was getting too old for this stuff. "They're at daycare. Nadine took them over late because you and Jeff were sleeping in. They have six Secret Service agents with them, too. Nadine's staying to help Denise. That's basically her job, after all. The agents are staying to guard because that's their job."

"Thanks for the refresher course. And you're here because?"

"Because I'm totes too old for daycare." It was official — Lizzie felt I was far too old for this stuff. "And school doesn't start for a month or something."

"Huh. Has anyone told you about the gates and how to work them?"

"Everyone. The red dab of paint low and sort of behind a toilet indicates a gate. All gates other than those in the White House complex are set for the Dome. All gates in the White House complex are set for the Embassy. Only A-Cs can calibrate the gates because only A-Cs can see through the cloaking. In an emergency, run through one. Don't go through otherwise because the gates are all monitored and they aren't playthings and severe punishments exist for any child who is stupid enough to use them incorrectly." She sounded totally bored as she recited this litany. "Denise says all the kids learn this from Day One. I think Charlie's already clear on it, so why you think I'm not is totes beyond me."

I hadn't learned all of this for years. Lizzie was with us under two weeks and she had it down already. Actively chose not to be bitter. And resolved to give her the Briefing Books of Boredom so she could get all caught up. Sure, that was likely to be viewed as a punishment, but that's what happened when you were a mouthy teenager.

"Super. Guess what? We're going out to lunch. Grab whatever and meet me in the hall." I wasn't as old as Lizzie thought, and I knew better than to leave a teenager alone in a place like this. I knew what I'd have done, and it was safer to assume that Lizzie would also try to get into every room she shouldn't and plan accordingly than to be too trusting and have an "incident."

"I don't need to prep." She heaved a sigh, but dragged off the bed and grabbed her messenger bag. I approved. Of the bag, not the attitude.

"Some kids would be excited to go out to lunch with the First Lady and all that."

"And some kids were reading a really great book the First Lady's dragged them away from."

"Oh, my God, pardon the hell out of me. Bring the book along, I won't be offended that you want to read instead of help, add in, or join a conversation." Definitely was going to give her the Briefing Books of Boredom, and soon. Maybe as soon as we were back from lunch.

She rolled her eyes, but grabbed her book anyway. Caught the title. Lizzie was engrossed in Sun Tzu's *The Art of War*. Interesting choice. Decided not to mention it. Right now.

We met up with the others in the hallway and headed down to meet the boys. Evalyne and Phoebe were waiting for us. "Thanks for actually letting us know what you're doing," Evalyne said, sarcasm knob only at about seven on the scale.

"Lunchtime. Are you guys able to eat?"

"No," Phoebe said. "We're on guard, if you'd care to remember. But we ate already, so your timing is good."

"Go me. By the way, I have no idea how you guys plan on rolling but I don't think we want to clear out the Teetotaler just for me."

"Noted," Evalyne said. "We'll see." She spoke into her lapel. "Cyclone and Entourage are leaving the Crown.

Heading down to the Carpet, then off to the Golf Course. Note that Cutie-Pie and Challenger are in the Playroom, but Comet is going with Cyclone. Cosmos is in the Castle."

"Wow, the Teetotaler gets a nickname? Rosemary and Douglas will be thrilled. What's the Playroom, the Embassy?"

"Obviously," Lizzie muttered. Apparently she was in a mood. Or else was just testing to be sure she could be herself around her new full-time adult guardians. Gave it even odds for both.

Evalyne didn't grace this with a reply. Instead she headed us for the underground parking garage. There was a whole world under this complex that almost rivaled a typical A-C structure. Almost. But even the White House complex didn't go down fifteen stories like Dulce. A-Cs were number one with a bullet when it came to burrowing.

With Lizzie there were nine of us, plus my Secret Service team of six. Meaning we needed to take two limos. Because Len and Kyle were approved at the highest levels, they could still be my driver and shotgun, which I insisted on.

The President had some impressive limos. However, we'd also incorporated A-C limos into the motor pool, because, frankly, the idea of not having a laser shield was one I was no longer comfortable with, and that went double for Jeff. The invisibility shield was also a nice touch, though we almost never used that. My brain nudged. Something about this bore more thought, but Phoebe was assigning who was sitting where, and I lost whatever it was.

Evalyne insisted that at least one Secret Service agent had to be in my limo. Put my foot down and insisted that the Secret Service car had to have an A-C in it, just in case. Since she didn't need to brief me on a speech, Colette offered to go with the Secret Service limo. Agreed, but felt underrepresented in the Speedy Getaway Department. Sent a text to Manfred, the head of my A-C security detail, asking him to join us, which he did.

So Evalyne in my car with the rest of my team, Colette and Manfred in the other with the majority of the Secret Service, we finally headed out in two limos packed to the gills with people. Thanked God that I'd had all those donuts

or I'd have been fainting from hunger by now. On the plus
side, we'd absolutely missed the lunch rush.

The trip to the Teetotaler was uneventful. Lizzie took
the time to keep on reading.

"No Club Fifty-One protestors out," I mentioned.

"They're still confused as to whether they're now on
your side or not," Vance said.

"I'll take whatever reprieve we can get."

We pulled up in front of the restaurant and the real dog
and pony show started. Manfred and two of my male Secret
Service agents went in and secured the restaurant. Phoebe
and the other agent in that limo who wasn't driving got out.
He came to relieve Len, who got out along with Kyle. They
joined Phoebe at the curb, waiting to escort the rest of us
inside.

Two of those who'd gone inside came out now and stood
outside the doorway. This was Evalyne's cue. She got out
and indicated that Abner was up first. He got out, and Kyle
took him and hustled him inside.

As this was going on, Evalyne had Mrs. Maurer get out.
Len helped her and took her in as Kyle came back to the
car. He took Vance now, as Len came back. He took Lizzie
and hustled her inside. Kyle waited at the car.

Looked at White. "We could have just linked up and
used hyperspeed to get inside without being seen at all."

"Well, the point of this is to be seen, so that wouldn't
work." White indicated that I was up, since Len had returned.

Len helped me out, but White came out right after me,
and the two of them flanked me, with Kyle on White's other
side, while Phoebe took the lead to the door and Evalyne
brought up the rear.

Our Impressive Display of Super Security Measures
over, I looked around the Teetotaler. Thankfully, there were
some people in here who hadn't been run off by my security
detail, meaning that we hopefully hadn't ruined anyone's
afternoon. Manfred was stationed at the back door. Evalyne
and Phoebe took opposite sides of the room and sat at tables.

True to expectations, the owners, Rosemary and Douglas, looked as if all their dreams had come true. I liked them
and gave them both hugs. Introduced them to everyone
they might not know. Turned out they knew everyone other

than Lizzie, who Rosemary fussed over. Lizzie was sweet and charming to Rosemary. Filed this away for review later.

We had a regular table and it was available, so we were ushered there. Tried not to pay attention to the fact that the people in here were staring at us. That was part of the point of coming out, after all. Made sure to sit with my back to the wall, though, and kept Lizzie next to me. For some reason, all this security made me feel far less secure.

We ordered, then I heaved a sigh and did my best to relax. "So, what do we want to cover?"

"I spoke with the Secretary of State while we were driving," Colette said. "She wants us to have an inauguration party."

"Is she high? There is no reason to throw a party. I know for a fact that the Johnson Administration did not party like it was nineteen-ninety-nine after Kennedy was assassinated. I don't think the Martini Administration should party down after the Armstrong assassination, either."

"Vince's death isn't being called an assassination," Vance said.

"Well, I'm calling it that, and I know Jeff is, too. Cliff was trying to kill everyone, but he succeeded in killing our President. And a ton of other people, too. This is not a reason to throw confetti and cheer."

"It's okay," Colette said. I could tell she was using her troubadour talent to calm the situation down. "It doesn't have to be elaborate, but the widow of the late President is the one requesting this."

"Why? And I mean that seriously, as in I want an answer that makes sense."

"She wants us to show our enemies that even though we had a tragedy, we can still find joy. Officially. Unofficially, she thinks it will help encourage the peace talks, because if we set up the party to happen after the peace talks, then they do double celebration duty."

"Ah. She's being sneaky. Now that I can get behind. But doesn't it leave us open if the peace talks don't go well?"

"It does," Mrs. Maurer said. "But possibly not as badly as it might. The party will have to be sold to the American people, though. You can't just throw it. Normally inauguration celebrations are huge affairs. This can't be that, but it can't be something too small, either."

"Because that would seem sad and pathetic, yeah. Please tell me this is your job."

Mrs. Maurer laughed. "It is. Your team will handle it, dear. We'll consult with you, of course, but all the details will fall to us."

"If there is any way in the world to get Aerosmith to play, I will do whatever you want."

"I'd imagine that if the First Lady requested them," White said, "and they were available, the band might be willing."

"Make it so." There was apparently more than one way to keep hope alive.

Our food arrived and we discussed the potential party while we ate. If done right, it could be fun. Lizzie seemed a lot happier with tea and delicious foodstuffs in her, too, so another one for the win column.

"So, should we combine Raj's Club Fifty-One Thank You Ceremony with this?"

"I'm not sure that we should wait on that," Colette said.

"Could be a great way to get a triple," Vance said.

Mrs. Maurer nodded. "That could actually help sell the inauguration party to the populace—it's really celebrating the human spirit and all those good things."

"I'm not sure," Abner said. "I really think we want to think it through."

"Oh, that's not our style," White said with a laugh.

"Traitor. But I agree with Abner—anything we're doing needs to be thought through."

"Include the announcement of your Cause," Kyle said.

"Might be too much," Len said. "It's going to be a fine line for what will fly and what will flop."

"You guys need to solve the problem of how you get all of them to Washington first," Lizzie said. The table looked at her and she looked defiantly back.

"Lizzie has a good point," I said, because she did. "We discussed it briefly before, but since this probably falls under my office somehow, we need to figure out a way to bring in those who want to come in that doesn't break the bank—theirs or ours."

"Some of them will be coming to protest, too," Lizzie added.

White nodded. "True enough. We may be able to use our

empaths to determine who should or shouldn't be included."

"That seems to be a very . . . nonactive role for the Field agents," Colette said.

"Not if it keeps Club Fifty-One from turning the President's thank you ceremony into an anti-alien protest," White said dryly.

Everyone spent the rest of the meal discussing the pros and cons, Lizzie included. I was too busy stuffing my face to add much, since White and Lizzie were representing my concerns quite well. Besides, what I wanted was to ensure that we could get Aerosmith. Probably meant I'd need to save the world again, but that was how it went for us anyway.

During this, people came and went. We got looks, but no one seemed offended or freaked out that we were here. Decided taking everyone out had been the right plan. Maybe we'd do it weekly. I'd done that before, when Naomi was still alive—gone out with some of my Embassy staff regularly. Since she'd died I'd done it much less, probably because, to me, Operation Infiltration had sort of started when we were here at the Teetotaler.

Well, no time like the present to change it up and be retro at the same time. Sent a text.

The reply came quickly. They were available, bored, and on their way. No sooner had I read this than two women came in via the back door—Abigail and Mahin.

Douglas hustled another small table into our mix while Rosemary raced their favorite teas over. The gals sat down while I received long-suffering looks from Evalyne and Phoebe, presumably so they could keep in practice.

Abigail was the youngest Gower, and, like her eldest brother and late older brother and sister, she was gorgeous. Beautiful dark skin, great hair, sparkling eyes, smart as a whip—Dazzler all the way.

Mahin was also a hybrid—but with a Middle Eastern mother and Ronald Yates as her Secret Father. She wasn't Dazzler stunning, because hybrids took after the human parent externally. But her mother hadn't been ugly, and while Mahin wasn't gorgeous she was attractive, with olive skin and long dark hair that was as black as Abigail's but completely different at the same time.

Mahin had been the person who'd made us aware that not all hybrids were exactly full A-C on the inside, since she only had one heart. Because of this and other discoveries, we'd determined that Ronald Yates was a "sport" in terms of genetics—there was no predictable outcome when he mated. And he'd mated a whole heck of a lot.

As per usual, the gals were in the Female Standard Issue. Mahin looked apologetic for their arrival, but Abigail grinned at everyone's surprised expressions. "When the First Lady says she'd like you to join her party, you join her party."

"I just figured that we were going to want to ensure that whatever we came up with was coordinated with the American Centaurion Embassy. So I asked the Cultural Attachés to join us."

"Nice spin," Evalyne said, as she came over. "Next time, please run these requests through me so we have some idea of what's going on."

"Oh, will do." Vance was on my other side. "Is there a role we can give Lizzie?" I asked him quietly, while the others quickly filled Abigail and Mahin in on what we'd been discussing. "One that's official, one that a teenager can do, but one that keeps her officially on my team?"

He nodded. "Youth Ambassador is always a good one."

"Ambassador of what?"

"Whatever we want. I'll speak with her about it when we're back and not in a group meeting."

We were done eating and having final pots of tea when a slender bleached blonde came in. Mrs. Maurer was next to Lizzie, and I saw her stiffen.

Took a closer look as the woman looked around. "Who is that?" I asked quietly.

"The last person I expected to see here," Mrs. Maurer said, voice like very squeaky ice. "My daughter-in-law."

CHAPTER 48

CRYSTAL MAURER made quite the show of "spotting" us. It was an act, and I could tell it was an act easily. Wasn't sure if that was intentional or if she was just a terrible actress.

She headed for our table and Evalyne and Phoebe both got up and intercepted her. "I need to speak with the First Lady," Crystal said rather imperiously.

"No, you don't," Evalyne said nicely, but with steel in her tone.

Looked at Mrs. Maurer. She was shooting daggers at her daughter-in-law. Couldn't blame her. But we needed to hear what Crystal had to say.

"Let her come," I said.

Crystal smirked at Evalyne and Phoebe. Decided her death would be slow and painful. "Thank you," she said as she stepped up to the table and shoved in between White and Kyle. "I need to speak with you on matters of state."

"I'll bet. Where are your children?"

She blinked at me. "What?"

"Your children. You have some as I recall. Where are they?"

"Not here. Why? My children aren't why I came to see you."

"Not here in Illinois or not here in D.C.?" Wished I'd brought an empath with us but we hadn't had room in the car for Jeremy. Then again, among Abigail's talents were that she was a reverse empath—if someone around her was angry, she got angry, and so forth. So congratulated myself on my prescience.

"What does it matter?"

"See, it matters to me, and you came to talk to me. Ergo, ipso facto, and that's the fact, Jack, you're going to tell me where your kids are, or this conversation is over."

Noted out of the corner of my eye that Lizzie had a pad and pen out, presumably taken from her messenger bag. She appeared to be doodling.

"Where are *your* children?" she countered. Had to hand it to her—she'd clearly heard my Dad's advice about answering a question you wanted to avoid with another question.

"My children aren't what we're talking about."

She smirked. It was fast, but I caught it. Confirmation, as if I'd needed it, that she was in on one or more of the Bad Guy Plans du Jour. "My children aren't what I came here to talk about, either."

Yawned. It was a fake yawn, and I made sure it was exaggerated. "Um, yeah. Losing interest fast."

"Why are you so interested in my children?" Crystal glanced at Mrs. Maurer. "Oh. Someone's been whining about how she doesn't see them much? She's full of it. She could see them all she wanted if she and my husband came home and stopped hiding here."

Mrs. Maurer actually hadn't mentioned her grandchildren to me recently. She'd had to choose between keeping her now-android son safe or risk rescuing them, and she hadn't been sure that Crystal was in on anything, just that Crystal hadn't cared at all when Maurer had become a different person, literally and figuratively.

"What would they be hiding from?" Colette asked. Her voice was sweet and she sounded fascinated. And I could tell she was using troubadour influence.

"They think that people are out to get them," Crystal said dismissively.

"Oh dear. Maybe that's why the First Lady is so worried about your children's whereabouts," Colette said, oozing innocent concern that just begged for a reply.

"My children are fine. They're at the Mayflower, as a matter of fact."

Managed not to make a Mayflower Madam joke, but it took a lot of self-control. Just didn't think it would go over well with this particular crowd. Noted Lizzie was now fiddling with her cell phone.

"When were you going to tell us you were in town?" Mrs. Maurer asked quietly. Well, as quietly as someone who had a squeaky, high-pitched voice could manage. That voice was also trembling.

"When it was convenient," Crystal snapped.

Made eye contact with Colette. She nodded almost imperceptibly. "Goodness, are the children old enough to be left alone all by themselves?"

Crystal heaved a sigh. "They're ten and eight, so yes, they are."

Didn't consider a ten-year-old old enough to be left alone in a strange hotel room, but then again, Crystal hadn't confirmed that they were alone. "You didn't get a hotel babysitter?" I asked.

"No. They're fine alone. They're used to it now, since I had to go to work because my husband quit his job, his life, and his family to come be a mama's boy."

"And yet you haven't divorced him." Or mentioned that he was actually an android now. "Standing by your man, I see. Sort of. From several states away. But whatever, it's good to know about your kids, I feel better about all of that now. And since you've answered my question, what is it you wanted to see me about?"

"Finally, I have an offer for you."

"Gosh, how exciting. What is it?"

"I have information you want. You have information I want. I figure we can do a trade."

"What information could I possibly have that you'd want?"

She stared at me for a moment. "Why are you more interested in that than the information I have?"

"Why does the order of this matter to you?"

Her eyes narrowed. "You're tricky."

"I am, you're right."

Maybe it was because I'd dealt with androids before. Maybe it was because I'd recently considered that androids passed as humans so well because they were normally so unpleasant. Maybe it was because she was focused on the order of something innocuous. But it was probably because her husband had revealed himself to be an android—complete with showing exposed circuitry—on national and international news a few days ago, and Crystal hadn't mentioned it even in passing.

I was now certain Crystal Maurer had joined her husband in the Land of Circuits and was an android.

Wished I'd dragged Chuckie along with us, because I had no idea how to slam a pen or pencil into an android ear in the correct way to keep them from self-destructing. And I knew without asking that if I gave away that I knew Crystal was an android that her self-destruct mechanism would go off. And, A-Cs with us or not, I didn't like our odds of survival. Besides, coming here was supposed to make Rosemary and Douglas even more successful, not destroy their business.

Decided that giving her what she wanted might be wise. "What information do you have for me that I'd want?"

"Wouldn't you like to know?"

"Um, yes, that's why I asked." Either she was an android without the best programming or she was an idiot.

Poor programming meant that it wasn't Cliff or LaRue who'd done it. Or whoever they had on staff wherever they still happened to have staff. So, that might mean that Crystal had been made without Cliff's knowledge. And I knew just the person who had the access to not only Cliff but to Crystal, seeing as she'd been Gideon Cleary's assistant when Maurer was his running mate—Stephanie.

"Oh. Yes. Right. Sorry." Crystal seemed to be blipping. She blinked several times in rapid succession, shook herself, then looked back at me. "Sorry. I want a guarantee that you'll give me what I want before I give you what you want."

"Sorry, I don't make stupid deals. Tell me what you have and tell me what you want, and we'll go from there."

"Fine. I know who broke into the White House. And I want to be at the peace talks."

"Ah. How interesting." Sipped my tea, which had gone cold. Poured more hot tea into my cup, added sugar and milk, stirred it, sipped again. Then I looked up. "You're still here?"

"Yes. I want to confirm our deal."

"I don't care about your information and I'm not inviting you to the peace summit."

She stared at me. "What? Why not?"

"I already know who broke in." Because I frankly figured it was Crystal herself. Had a guess for how she'd been invisible, too. Shrugged. "Give me information I'm really interested in. If you give me what I want, what I really, really want, then I might let you come to the peace summit."

"What is it that you really, really want?"

"If you don't know, then we have nothing to discuss. Call me when you've figured it out."

"I don't have your number."

Couldn't help it, I snorted. "Sure you don't. Get it from whoever you're working with, for, or around. I'm sure they've got me on speed dial."

"Fine." She glared at me, then looked at Mrs. Maurer. "Give my husband my regards." With that she spun on her heel and walked out.

"Someone pay our bill as fast as possible." Ensured my voice was low but urgent. White got up and went to find Rosemary. I stood up. "We need to follow her."

Len waved his phone. "Sit back down, Kitty. I contacted Mister Buchanan while you were verbally sparring with her. He sent Mister Falk, who's just told me that he has her and is tailing. He has a team of P.T.C.U. agents with him."

"Great." Sat back down as requested, though what I wanted to do was run after Crystal and follow her to whatever lair or base of operations she was using. "Tell them not to approach her, because she'll self-destruct."

"She's an android?" Vance asked, sounding horrified. But not as horrified as Abner looked. Colette, on the other hand, got up, nodded to me, and went and got Manfred. They disappeared. Hoped they'd find Falk and his team, and Crystal, quickly.

"Yes," Abigail said. "Chuck's been having me work with John and Cameron to see if I can pick up emotional nuances between full humans or A-Cs and androids. It's hard, but I've been working at it since we all got back from Beta Eight, and I'm sure that she's an android."

Mrs. Maurer was pale. "I need to get to my grandchildren."

"Don't worry, it's totes handled," Lizzie said. We all

looked at her. She shrugged. "I sketched her picture and sent it to my dad, along with the hotel name and that the kids are ten and eight." She held up her notebook that she'd been doodling on—there was quite a good likeness of Crystal drawn there. "He's with Mister Buchanan, who got in touch with Jeff, who said that he was against child endangerment. So the Secret Service went over and got them. They're at the White House, 'cause the Secret Service rolled with some A-Cs."

"Awesome. We need to get Nancy back there immediately."

"What are we going to do when Crystal calls the police?" Mrs. Maurer asked, voice squeakier than usual.

"She won't." Stood up again and indicated that everyone else needed to stand, too.

"You can't be sure of that," White said as he rejoined us.

"I can be, actually." Headed for the door. "She's not nearly as good as the androids that Antony Marling made, meaning she's not from that factory, so to speak. I was sure she was an android before Abby confirmed it. I think someone with a lot of skills and a hell of a lot of connections made her. No idea if Crystal was willing or not, but it doesn't matter. Her programming is better than the Fem-Bots I've seen, but not nearly as good as the other androids I've dealt with."

Zipped through the door before Evalyne or Phoebe, which earned me a couple of really loud sighs from the two of them. "The cars aren't here yet," Evalyne said, as she got in front of me. "Meaning you should still be inside." Phoebe was talking into her lapel, demanding our cars step on the gas.

"I'm a rule breaker, me."

"Tell me something I don't know. We're not going to allow you to go after her, so don't plan on trying."

"I wasn't." Looked around. Didn't see Falk, Colette, or Manfred, let alone Crystal. "You know, this makes at least the third time our enemies have essentially ambushed us at the Teetotaler. If I didn't love the place so much I'd say we should never come back here."

Had a tingling in between my shoulder blades, like you can get sometimes when someone's watching you. Spun around. No sign of Buchanan. Then again, I'd never really felt him watching me unless he'd wanted me to know he was there. Didn't see Mister Joel Oliver or Bruce Jenkins or any of their compatriots.

Looked up and around. Still didn't see anyone. "Think there are drones around here?"

"There shouldn't be," Evalyne said. "Why?"

"I think we're being watched."

One of our limos arrived. "What the hell kept you?" Phoebe asked as she opened the door.

"No parking across the street, no parking anywhere nearby," the driver replied. Checked. He was definitely one of the Secret Service guys who'd driven us here.

"Get Nancy back. And Abner and Vance, too." Looked at Lizzie, who gave me what I assumed she felt was a steely gaze. Decided that I'd let her win this one. "Richard, Lizzie, Abby, Mahin, the boys, and I will take the next car."

"That leaves agents stranded," Phoebe said.

"Call for another car. I want these three people guarded. So send the other dudes along with this car. Colette and Manfred will either rejoin us, stay with Falk and his team, or simply use their A-C ability to get home faster than anyone else and be waiting for us. We'll divide up into the next two cars."

Another limo rounded the corner, so Evalyne and Phoebe stopped arguing. Instead, Evalyne sent the two Secret Service agents who'd been guarding the door into this car.

"Stay at the White House, all three of you," I said to my staff. "See you soon."

Evalyne closed the door and they drove off. The next limo pulled up.

And, because I knew how my life worked, the driver was definitely not one of my Secret Service detail. But it was someone I knew, in that sense.

Thomas Kendrick was behind the wheel.

CHAPTER 49

IT LOOKED LIKE KENDRICK, at any rate. But he was either in the White House complex or somewhere else with the rest of Team Technical. Then again, I was 99.99 percent certain that there was an android of Kendrick running around. And that the android could drive was not a shocker.

"That's our vehicle," Evalyne said, voice strained. "How did he get into it?"

"I don't think that's the real Thomas Kendrick. Mister White?"

"Agreed, Missus Martini."

"Abby?"

"Need more time, Kitty. Stall if we can risk it."

The passenger's window rolled down. "Get in, please," the driver who did sound like Kendrick said. But there was no real recognition in his expression, not that this was a surprise. He also wasn't wearing what Kendrick had been. Sure, he was in a suit, but his was gray, and the real Kendrick had been in navy.

Looked into the car, despite Evalyne trying to keep me from doing so. There was no one else inside. "Where's the driver? The original driver?"

The Kendrick Android stared at me. "I'm the original driver."

"No, you're not. I want to know what happened to him. Or we're not getting into the car."

"I've been driving this car all day."

"You tell me where the original driver of this car is, or I'm not doing anything you want."

The Kendrick Android stared at me for a bit. "Around the corner, four blocks down, in a dumpster."

Phoebe was talking into her lapel, advising others that we had a man down. Meanwhile, I was already angry, which was good. Rage, not fear, was my friend.

Our options were likely limited, though with A-Cs around we could run and be safe. Or I could find out what the Kendrick Android wanted. And with Stephanie incarcerated, had to figure the only person—to use the term loosely—who had any idea where our missing helicarrier and people were was this android. Crystal might know, but the Kendrick Android knew for certain.

"Thank you for the information. Who do you want in the car?" I asked.

"You're not getting in that car," Evalyne said strongly.

"She is or you'll all get shot," the Kendrick Android said. "We have snipers on the rooftops."

"Told you I felt like we were being watched. Give us a minute," I said to the android. "Need to confer on who's getting in with me."

"The kid and the old man," the Kendrick Android said without missing a beat. "The two women who aren't Secret Service can get in, too. The others will be shot if they try to get into the car with you or try to get you away from the car."

"He's bluffing," Phoebe said.

No sooner were these words out of her mouth than a bullet hit the ground just in front of her feet. Grabbed Evalyne and Phoebe both as they both started to move to cover me. "Don't react and don't try to shield me. That was an intentional miss." Looked up and around. Didn't see anyone.

"Our job is to shield you!" Evalyne sounded as upset as I figured everyone felt.

"Yeah, it is, only I never asked for someone to take a bullet for me, and you and the boys aren't on a short list for that option as far as I'm concerned." Besides, the android wanted to have me bring along two powerful A-C hybrids, my normal kick-butt partner, and a kid who'd been trained by three top assassins. Clearly I was going to be rolling with a strike force.

Decided I didn't want to risk it and sent a strong mental message to any of my stealth strike force that might be around that I could use some backup. Felt something nudge my leg, but didn't look down.

"Get in or we start shooting," the android said.

"Connect with Falk," I said quietly to Evalyne. "He'll know what to do to coordinate." Nodded to White, who opened the passenger door and ushered Abigail, Mahin, and Lizzie inside, then got in himself.

I opened the front passenger's door. "What are you doing?" the Kendrick Android asked, sounding shocked.

"Riding shotgun. I like it, rarely get to do it anymore, and want to ensure that you don't try the old Gas Them Unconscious Ploy. In fact, roll down the privacy window, or I don't get in and my people already in get out."

The android tried staring me down. It's difficult to stare down a machine, but I'd learned stare-down techniques from Mom, and so far she and Chuckie were the only ones who could beat me.

My record remained intact. The android dropped its eyes before I had to give. "Fine." He hit a button and the privacy window rolled down.

Looked back at the boys. "Get the four of you inside where it's safe," I said to Len. "Remember, this is just like when I first met you guys."

Len blinked, nodded, grabbed Evalyne and started to pull her back. Kyle looked uncertain, but he grabbed Phoebe and did the same. "You're sure?" Kyle asked worriedly. Len nudged him.

"This is just like when we were in Vegas, Kyle. I promise."

Saw the light dawn for Kyle, too. Waited until the four of them were inside, the boys willingly now, the women far less so. Made sure my team was still conscious and alive in the back, then got into the car and closed the door. "Where are we going?" I asked as our android driver pulled us away from the curb and I rolled the window down. The windblown look was always in fashion, especially because I had to figure an android could release gas and not be affected by it. Besides, the banana clip was doing a great job of holding my hair in place so far.

"Somewhere we won't be found," he replied as we

headed off and the others in the back followed my lead and rolled their windows down, too. Ensured I was turned sideways in the seat, with my seatbelt on, so that I could keep an eye on our driver and my team in the back.

Lizzie was texting away, as was Abigail. Sadly, my looking back meant he looked in the rearview mirror. "Turn off all your phones and give them to me," he ordered.

Found it interesting that he'd taken so long to ask for our phones. But then again, he wasn't one of Marling's Top Models. Stephanie had clearly followed the schematics, but creating something like androids so lifelike as to fool humans and empaths both required artistry as well as scientific knowhow. Marling may have been one of the Original Board of Directors for the Crazed Evil Megalomaniacs Society, but he was definitely an artist. And Stephanie wasn't.

No one handed their phones over. He put his arm out and grabbed me by the neck. "I'll crush her windpipe if you don't." Everyone's phones from the back dropped into the front bench, between him and me. He let go of me immediately. "You, too," he said. "And turn the phones off."

"Thanks, gang." Turned their phones off. "So, what do we call you?" I asked as I dug my phone out and massaged my neck. He definitely had the Android Grip.

"Thomas."

"No way. You're not him."

He shot me a snide look. "I'm truly Thomas Kendrick."

"He's definitely not," Abigail said.

"See? You're truly not, though you may not know it for sure. You are his android. So, you can choose between the names I'm willing to use. Kendroid or, if we're playing nicely, TK."

"I don't understand why you want to give me different names."

"You'll adjust. Can we use my phone to listen to music?"

He glanced at me. "I have a GPS scrambler."

Decided not to ask him if the scrambler was in the car or inside of him. That was me, using the old diplomacy skills like a boss. "Super-duper and whatever. Does it affect music? Because if it doesn't, music would be nice."

He shrugged. "Go ahead. Just don't try to send a message or answer a call."

Pulled out my adapter and plugged it into the dashboard. Hit random and Mötley Crüe's "Same Old Situation" came on. Had that right. "So, TK, why do you want all of us?" Figured it might be wise to keep him talking. My experience said that keeping your enemies monologuing was the only sure technique for short- and long-term survival.

"You're all important."

Waited. This appeared to be his entire thought on the matter. "Yeah? Important to whom?"

"Various interests."

We were on Independence Avenue, heading for what turned out to be the 295 going north. Apparently we were heading for Maryland. Wondered if we were heading to Camp David, but didn't have a real guess—I'd never been there, and since I was driven more than did the driving these days I tended to not pay a lot of attention to where we were going. Probably needed to pay a lot of attention right now.

Looked around to see if I could spot anyone following us. That someone was or would be trying to follow us seemed likely, since I doubted that Evalyne, Phoebe, Len, and Kyle had all decided to say the hell with us and just declare that it was now Miller Time. They might have wanted to, but had to figure their sense of duty would have overridden those desires.

Didn't spot any limos. Well, that wasn't true—we were in the D.C. area and it was a typical day for most people, so there were limos and other nice cars with official drivers about. But none of them were swerving in and out of traffic. The only vehicle doing so was a motorcycle—a black crotch rocket. The rider was all in black, too, helmet included. But that was how most people rode on a sport bike—like they were on a racetrack.

The music changed to "Machine Slave" by Front Line Assembly as the Kendroid put the pedal down. Really hoped that there weren't any cops nearby—knew without asking that he'd kill them if they tried to pull us over. Looked around for cops. None. No limos, either, or big burly SUVs, or anything else that seemed like it might be carrying the cavalry.

"Would those interests have names?"

"Yes."

"Wanna share them with me?"

"No."

Interesting. Most of the androids that I'd interacted with couldn't stop running their yaps. This one was, naturally, Mr. Curt And To The Point. Figured.

"Why did you take Drax's helicarrier?"

"Because we need it."

"Who's we?"

"You'll find out."

"Can't wait. What about the people who were on that helicarrier?"

"What about them?"

"Where are they?"

"You'll see."

Promising. But no guarantee that we were really heading to where the flyboys and the others were. "Are they okay? As in unharmed and unchanged?"

"For now."

That boded. "Who's making the decisions on whether or not they'll remain unharmed and unchanged? Stephanie?"

He pushed a button on the dashboard. "Go to sleep now."

Prepared myself for gas. There was none that I could tell. But I started to feel sleepy and I could tell that Lizzie did, too, by the way her head was bobbing. Noted the three A-C's looked tense.

"Sonic wavelengths," White said.

"I don't hear anything." Well, other than Front Line Assembly.

"Subsonic." Mahin sounded tense. "They can kill us if they go on too long."

Considered options. Had no idea if it would work, but it had worked in the past. Grabbed my phone and turned the volume up to high just as the song changed to "Bring Me To Life" by Evanescence.

Results were happily immediate. I felt more awake, Lizzie jerked and seemed more conscious, White and the girls looked less pained. The Kendroid, on the other hand, looked like he was having some issues.

He was jerking and twitching. Revised "issues" to "seizure." While we were driving down the highway at a rather high rate of speed. Right toward what looked like a traffic jam.

Always the way.

CHAPTER 50

DECIDED I'D HAVE trouble wresting the steering wheel away from an android who didn't want to let it go. Found the button on the dash that the Kendroid had pushed and pushed it again.

"Subsonic sounds have stopped," Abigail shouted. "Now we're just all at risk of going immediately deaf."

"Everyone's a critic!" Checked the android. He was still jerking. Lowered the volume until he stopped jerking. This timed out for him to stop twitching and slam on the brakes.

The team in the back ended up on the floor. Heard a lot of complaining and what sounded like quiet bird squawks of anger and Poof grumbling. Well, at least I knew my Stealth Backup was here.

"That was foolish," the Kendroid said. "I almost lost control."

"I feel so ashamed of myself. I'll just keep the music ready to go up to eleven, though, and you, Kendroid, can keep your fingers off of anything that's going to incapacitate anyone else in this car."

"I'll agree but only if you turn the music off."

"For now, sure." The song was almost over anyway.

"Why did you call me Kendroid instead of TK?"

"Because I didn't like what you did to us. Do you prefer TK?"

"I'm . . . not sure."

"Well, feel free to ponder that and let me know your preference."

"I will. Thank you."

The traffic jam was over fast and we were back to racing

along. Decided to accept the détente and stop trying to question him—for all I knew he had more nasty buttons he could push.

This worked for a few minutes and several miles, but the scenery, while pretty, was kind of mundane. Besides, I wasn't really all that great with silence. Presumably this meant I wasn't comfortable with myself. Not true. I was all about the wonder that was me. I just liked sharing that wonder with others. Also, I was starting to get sleepy and it wasn't due to anything that the Kendroid was doing—the movement of the car was enough. Clearly I was totally calm and cool in the face of danger. Also clearly I needed to stay awake and alert and all that jazz.

There was nothing for it—I had to run my yap or die. Time to see if the interrogation skills were up to snuff. "Why did you want Lizzie?"

"She's your daughter."

Caught that Abigail had her hand over Lizzie's mouth. Managed not to blow it myself, but only just. Frankly, if I hadn't been sleepy, I'd have blurted out that he had seriously wrong information. As it was, this woke me right up, so that was one for our meager win column.

"Ah, so it's the usual grab my daughter ploy?" It always was, when you got right down to it, or at least had been since Jamie had been born. Was now glad that Nadine had been totally on the case and taken the kids to daycare and that Jeff had insisted I leave Jamie and Charlie with Nadine. Because if they'd been in the White House, they'd have been with us.

"Your daughter is very powerful."

"So everyone likes to point out." Looked out the side view mirror. There was a motorcycle behind us, a black crotch rocket. The rider was all in black, helmet included. Couldn't be sure if it was the same one I'd seen back in D.C. or not. "Why did you want Richard?"

"He's important."

"You said we were all important."

"True."

"So why him and the other gals? Why was it okay to bring them along and not the others?"

"The others are humans."

"You could tell?"

"Yes."

"Single heartbeats," White said.

"That's one way, yes," the Kendroid agreed. "Though only two of you in the car have two hearts. The others were all security. That's the other way."

Picked up the sarcasm. But if he was susceptible to being sarcastic, then he might also be susceptible to flattery, meaning now wasn't the time to point out that we had A-Cs working security, too. "Wow, you can hear heartbeats from far away?"

"Yes. Can't you?"

"Um, no, not really. I can if I'm leaning my head on someone's chest. Otherwise, not so much."

"Can't the others?"

"No," White said. "We can't. It takes very specialized hearing."

"Jeff could pick it up." At least I remembered that he had when we were in Vegas.

"Jeffrey has been enhanced," White reminded me. "And that had happened prior to the time I believe you're speaking of. It's also possible to hone listening skills to that extent, but it takes training and focus, which he also had. The average A-C can't hear heartbeats any better than you can, Missus Martini."

"As always, I learn something new every day. So, Kendroid, you've got some cool skills. What else can you do?"

"What everyone else can." He sounded uncomfortable. "I don't like Kendroid."

"Noted." Not sure what it meant, but I was happy to take whatever I could get.

"You're not like everyone else," Mahin said gently. "That's why we're interested."

"Of course I'm not like everyone else! I'm Thomas Kendrick. That makes me an individual."

"What do you do for a living?" Abigail was getting in on this with the rest of us.

"I . . . do things." The Kendroid looked like he'd just realized how lame that sounded.

"Yeah, but what things? Exactly? We're just curious." Ensured my tone was interested and friendly.

"I . . ." He was quiet but not having a seizure or pushing buttons to knock us out, so decided we were still doing okay. "I have a heartbeat."

Exchanged the WTF look with those in the back.

"But you know it's not a real heart, don't you?" Lizzie asked.

"I have thoughts and feelings."

"You do," Abigail agreed. "But like Lizzie said, they aren't quite like ours, are they?"

"What do you do for a living?" I asked as gently as I could, because Abigail's question had been the one that had thrown him and he'd avoided answering.

"A living? I . . . I don't . . ." His voice trailed off as he moved the car over. Either our exit was coming up or he was thoughtfully going to park before he had another seizure.

"Why did you take the helicarrier and the people?" I asked as we did indeed pull off the parkway onto route 198. Per the signs we were entering Laurel, Maryland. Had no idea what was here or nearby, but sincerely hoped it was an invisible helicarrier.

Also sincerely hoped we had no state police nearby, because the Kendroid wasn't slowing down.

"Because we needed them."

Was going to ask another question but chose to look around and check the side view mirror. There was a black motorcycle coming off the 295 and onto this highway. Wondered who this was and if they were our backup or if they were just heading wherever we were for whatever reason.

We'd gone in and out of wooded areas along the way here. If we'd gone to the left we'd have been in what had, from the parkway, looked like a typical little city area. But we'd gone right and were in more woods. Heavy woods.

"Are we near Camp David?"

"No," White replied. "Not close, really. We could get there from here, but from where we started there's a far more direct route."

We made a sharp left, almost a U-turn, tires squealing impressively since the Kendroid clearly wasn't in the mood to slow down for anything other than a traffic jam, and headed into even more forest on a much smaller road.

"I think . . . I think we're heading to somewhere bad," Mahin said, as we made a right, with slightly less tire squealing but still far more than anyone in the car probably enjoyed. "I've been studying this part of the country under your father's direction, Kitty. And I think we're heading to an abandoned area." She looked worried, and more so as we made another right onto a really bad road, one that was clearly not on the repair schedule.

"Well, that would make sense for what's been going on." Stephanie was merely using the time-honored bad guy move of making an abandoned building her base of operations. "Lots of areas get abandoned. What's bad about this one?"

Looked around. There were a lot of big buildings and not a lot of other cars. In fact, I saw no other cars at all. There was a lot of scrub and overgrown bushes and trees and the like.

"What's bad," Mahin said as we pulled into a circular drive that had definitely seen better days, "is that this entire complex is part of the Forest Haven Insane Asylum."

CHAPTER 51

"**O**F COURSE IT IS!** Because that is exactly, and I do mean exactly, how my life works. What's the skinny on this place, Mahin?"

"It was closed due to horrific treatment of patients. If there's any place that could be haunted in this region, we've just arrived there."

"Of course it is! Maybe we're just passing through."

The Kendroid parked the car. "Here we are." He took the keys and got out.

We were parked in front of a dilapidated brick building that had four stories with a weird attic-looking thing on top. Everything around it was overgrown, and even though we were here at the start of summer, all the plant life looked like it was at the turn of fall to winter—alive but mostly dead or dying.

Most of the many windows looked black, but I realized they were open or broken, because I could see window frames dotted about. In addition to this, there was debris and, of course, graffiti all around, too.

If there was a competition for Creepiest Building, this place was going to take the blue ribbon.

Looked back at the others. "So much for that passing through idea. Haunted, you say, Mahin?"

"Nothing confirmed," she said tensely.

"Horrible conditions inside?"

She nodded. "Among the worst. They literally just left it, and no one will buy the property. For reasons."

"I don't believe in no ghosts. But, let me also say that I didn't really believe in aliens until I met all of you, so . . ."

"Ghosts can't hurt you," Lizzie said. "It's the living you have to watch."

"My 'daughter' makes a good point."

The Kendroid poked his head back into the car. "Get out now. We're here."

"Gotcha. We're just all being Cowardly Lions right now. Give us a mo."

"What do you mean?" He sounded confused. Stephanie was definitely not up to Marling's level.

"It's a popular culture reference," I said as I unplugged my phone stuff from the car and put it into my purse. Did a purse check while I was doing so. Had a few Poofs on Board but they had something on top of them, meaning the Poofs were giving me a message. It was the BT tracker prototype the real Kendrick had sent to me. And unlike before, when it just looked like a weird "waiting for your table coaster thing" decorated for Christmas with a bunch of different colored lights, it was now blinking as if our table was ready.

Looked more carefully at the Poofs in my purse. They weren't Harlie, the Head Poof who was ostensibly Jeff's but who hung with me most of the time, nor Poofikins, which was my Poof. They weren't the other Poofs who usually stayed with me. But I recognized them, because I somehow knew who each of the Poofs were, even the unattached ones.

Only, these Poofs were not unattached. These Poofs all belonged to the flyboys.

The fact that I could have and should have just asked the Poofs where the flyboys were dawned on me. Then again, none of the Poofs had demanded I find their owners. So either the guys were okay, or the Poofs had no idea where the guys actually were. Of course, the guys were in alien tech, and not necessarily tech the Poofs were familiar with.

Tabled beating myself up for another time when I was feeling cocky. "We're not alone," I said quietly to the others, then got out of the car. They followed suit.

Looked up and around, in case there was an aircraft of some kind that had been tailing us. The skies were nice and clear. Interesting. In a worrisome way.

"It's already totes creepy here," Lizzie announced without a trace of fear in her voice. "And we're not even inside yet. Will he let me take pics, do you think?"

"Why do you want to take pics?" the Kendroid asked. Had the distinct feeling he didn't know what Lizzie meant.

"Pics is short for pictures. Lizzie is a creepy places aficionado, so she'd like to commemorate our exciting visit."

"Oh." The Kendroid seemed confused. "I suppose that's alright."

White and I exchanged a look. This was not typical android or robot behavior.

"I totes need my phone to do that," Lizzie said.

"Ah. Then no. No you can't." With that, the Kendroid spun on his heel and walked off.

"Nice try," White said to Lizzie.

Who shrugged. "I really wanted to take pics. But yeah."

Abigail stepped close to me as the Kendroid headed for the creepy building, which still had a weathered sign— Forest Haven Asylum—on it. Someone had sprayed over the "aven" with red paint and put "ell" in its place. Told myself it was just kids being kids. Didn't stop the shiver that ran down my back, however. Unlike Lizzie, I wasn't all about thinking being scared was fun.

"What's going on?" Abigail asked softly. "I can't really feel anything here, but I know you and I can tell you're excited. As well as creeped out."

Opened my purse and pulled out the BT as Kendrick opened the front doors. Naturally they creaked loudly, because the only thing that would have been worse was them opening inward silently. The lights were amber and blinking.

"This is a Bloodhound Tracker from Titan. It's got the flyboys' DNA programmed in. Not sure, but I think the BT feels that at least one of them is within ten miles of us."

"Ten miles is a lot."

"Yeah, but not when you're looking for a needle in the entire hay field. Now that we're here, it's just a nasty haystack we have to look through. I call that progress."

"I call this not my idea of a field trip, but if we can find the guys, I'm all for it."

White didn't let any of us go through the doorway until the Kendroid was several steps in. "Ladies, I'd like to remind you that good Field Agents, which as of right now we all are, like to look before they leap. For traps and triggers and the like. Missus Martini, I stress that this is a place where I feel caution must be exercised."

"Stephanie didn't have him bring us here to play nicely." Abigail nodded her head toward the Kendroid.

"Honestly, I think he's acting alone right now. But yes, Mister White, I'll be cautious."

"I'm sure you will." He took my hand. "Because I'm your partner."

Mahin took Lizzie's hand. Lizzie gave her an affronted look. "I'm not a baby."

"You're also not an A-C. I'm not a full one, either, but I've learned that hyperspeed is a good thing."

Abigail nodded and took Mahin's free hand. "Field Team Why Are We Here is ready for action."

"I love you, Abby. Okay, let's step in all cautious-like so Mister White doesn't give us a severe talking to."

Moving like scared rabbits, we entered the insane asylum. And all got to see that Mahin hadn't exaggerated anything. In fact, she'd been extremely low-key in her descriptions.

The place was trashed. Some due to vandals, some due to age, most due to what it had been like in here when it was a functioning place. There was filth and debris along with old magazines, office furniture, even a dentist's chair and a computer. This place had it all. It was as if Stephen King and Dean Koontz had written the screenplay for a film by Guillermo del Toro, George Romero, and Wes Craven.

It smelled of death, decay, and mold, along with other fetid scents I actively chose not to try to identify. Some of them were probably recent, since there was enough graffiti on the walls to indicate that teenagers came here at least infrequently. But most of the bad smells were, like the rest of this place, old and getting older by the minute.

It was, naturally, dark and creepy, though there was enough light coming in from the open, cracked, and/or dirty windows that I could see well enough. There was also a heavy layer of dust, though not through the main corridors. Those were still cluttered with garbage and debris, but they weren't nearly as dusty. This was definitely a deserted place that was being used.

The Kendroid walked along and we followed, Mahin sharing her information about this real-life House of the

Damned. Nothing she said made any of us happier about being here.

"There were kids in here?" Lizzie asked in horror, as we passed a room that had a dilapidated crib in it.

"Yes," Mahin said. "There were all ages. The mentally ill, the mentally retarded, anyone accused of such, epileptics. Anyone someone wanted to get rid of along with people whose families thought they were here getting good care. This place was even worse when it was active than it is now."

"How charming," White said, sarcasm knob heading for nine on the scale.

"Well, I know what I'm nominating for next Halloween's Winning Haunted House."

"We should cleanse this place with fire," Mahin said angrily. "There is nothing good here."

Looked at the BT. It was still flashing, but the color had changed from amber to a sort of yellow-green. "No, I think there are definitely some good things here."

Dropped the BT back into my purse just as the Kendroid turned around. "What are you doing?" He didn't seem to have caught the BT, which was all for the good.

"Taking in the sights. Where are we going?"

"To where you're going to be staying. Well, you four." He indicated the adults. "Your daughter will be coming with me."

"The hell she will."

The Kendroid shrugged. "I'm stronger than you, and faster. You won't have a choice."

"There's always a choice. Even for a preprogrammed android such as yourself."

"I'm a real person."

"No, you're not. You're an android." It was heartless, but he truly wasn't real. This wasn't the same as Cameron Maurer or Colonel John Butler—those men had been turned into androids against their will. But the Kendroid had been created. Had no idea if Stephanie had used some poor person's body or if she'd just created him from scratch, but since Thomas Kendrick was alive and well, voted on the latter.

"I'm as real as you."

"Real, yes. A real person? No. Where are the real people you kidnapped?"

"They were already kidnapped."

"They were, but at that time they were safe. Right now I'm worried that someone's trying to turn them into not-people, into androids that just look like them but aren't them anymore."

"That's what they want to do to all of us," Abigail said. "You and Uncle Richard in particular, Kitty. Change you into androids, program you to destroy us all, because everyone trusts the two of you. Mahin and I are just along to make sure Uncle Richard doesn't fight it, just like Lizzie's here so you won't fight it."

"Where are you getting this from?" I asked her in as low a voice as I could manage and without moving my mouth.

"We're not alone with him," she replied in kind. "Not sure if I'm feeling humans, A-Cs, or androids, but they're all waiting to attack us. They're the only things I've been able to really feel since we got here, by the way."

The Kendroid cocked his head at us. "You're right," he said to Abigail. "We do need you in order to make the others do what we want."

"Who is this 'we'?" I asked again, using Mom's Voice of Authority. "I want an answer this time." Heard steps around us and took a look around. "Oh. Wow. I guess it's easier to just make one prototype and stick with it than branch out, huh?"

There were eleven other Thomas Kendrick androids surrounding us.

CHAPTER 52

THE ADDITIONAL KENDROIDS weren't dressed alike. Four were in uniform—representing Army, Navy, Air Force, and Marines—one was dressed like an A-C, two others were in different suits, including a gray one. The rest were in various forms of casual dress.

"Interesting army of one you've got going here, TK. So, who came up with it, Cliff, Stephanie, you?"

"I have no idea who Cliff is."

"But you do know who Stephanie is." The other Kendrick Androids stepped closer. "Wow, it's really Stepford around here. Did Stephanie just not get enough Barbies or, in this case, Ken Dolls when she was a child?"

"Stephanie is not your concern," the Kendrick in the Air Force uniform said.

"Why are you afraid of us knowing about Stephanie? I mean, we actually know all about her, but I'm just curious what you're afraid of telling us about her."

"We're not afraid," the Kendrick in the Marines uniform said. "We just don't need to tell you anything."

"You do if you want my cooperation."

"We can make you do what we want," the Kendrick in the Navy uniform said.

"So you think, but you actually can't. TK, you can't tell me that you think you have eleven twin brothers. I mean, there's a proper word or phrase for that, quadruple times three, maybe, but I don't know what it is and frankly don't care. Surely you can see that you're not humans. Even the best breeding dogs and rabbits have a challenge birthing a dozen at a time."

He did look around. "We are real."

"Again, yes, you're real, as in you're here and we can touch you. But you're not human. None of you are."

"Why do you discuss with them?" the Kendrick dressed like a total preppy asked. "Just take them. We need them to finalize the processes."

That definitely boded. "We don't plan to go quietly into that good night or crazed Frankenstein lab or whatever."

The TK Kendroid looked back at me. "It will be easier if you don't fight us."

"Yeah, I'm all about not doing it the easy way." Looked around. Whoever had been on that motorcycle apparently hadn't been following us. Pity.

While they could and did ingest things whole and cough them up again, the Poofs couldn't safely eat something non-organic, and that was how they handled enemies. The Peregrines were tough but not android tough, meaning they'd get hurt. So my Animal Backup was out.

Meant I was going to have to shoot eleven androids with my Glock. This was not our prime option, really. I was good, but reality said I wasn't *this* good. Plus, experience reminded me that it took a lot of bullets to take an android down. Even if these weren't up to the level of Marling's creations, they were going to take a licking and keep on ticking.

The androids moved closer to us. "Ah, Kitty? Any ideas?" Abigail asked.

"Use your talents is all I've got."

Mahin was already concentrating, I could tell. Her talent was being our own earth bender—if it was dirt, she could make it do what she wanted. And there were a couple of little dust devils forming because lord knew there was more than enough dust in here for her to work with. However, they'd need to be full-on dust tornados to have a hope against an android.

"Missus Martini, may I suggest that it's high time you used the crazy?"

White had a good point. But the only crazy I could come up with was using rock and roll. After all, loud music had affected the Kendroid in the car, and it hadn't stopped when I'd turned off the sub-sonic stuff.

"Need my iPod and portable speakers, please and thank you," I whispered to the Poofs inside my purse. The requested items were shoved to the top. "And any earplugs you might randomly find in there." Hey, Algar had made my purse a Request Portal during Operation Civil War, and I lived by the cat motto of asking for what you wanted.

Five pairs of earplugs surfaced. "You're all the best." Shoved a set into my ears and handed the rest to the others using hyperspeed. However, there was nowhere for me to safely put the iPod and speakers. "Out of the purse if you value your hearing." My purse was Poofless.

Spun the dial to my Everything Louder Than Everything Else playlist, turned the volume up to eleven, and hit play. "Bellend Bop" from G.B.H. came screaming onto the airwaves, just as the androids started to attack.

Happily, music was saving my day again, because the androids had some severe issues with it, at least at this volume. The Kendroid, having experienced this before, spun and ran for the back door to this place, as far as I could tell.

"Animal Enforcers, go after the TK Kendroid!" That might mean the Poofs and Peregrines were going to find the flyboys, or they might just all tackle the Kendroid as one, but it also meant they were safe and not at risk of getting smooshed, stepped on, or worse by the Army of One.

The others hadn't dealt with us before, and apparently there was no shared hive-mind. I'd take the wins wherever we got them, no matter how small. They were herking and jerking while trying to walk, looking like so many men I'd seen without rhythm trying to do cool dance moves. I'd find the funny in this in retrospect, I was sure. Presuming I got to a point where I was able to reminisce.

"It's like they're android zombies!" Lizzie shouted with far too much enthusiasm in her tone. The Preppy Kendrick managed to stagger near to her. She ducked into a crouch and kicked its legs out with a really good sweep. Of course it got up, but she swept it again. She was doing a good job of keeping it at a distance.

Meanwhile, Mahin had managed to get the dust to cooperate, and she had two of the Casual Kendricks surrounded with it. The dust and music seemed to be causing them problems. I could but hope that the dust was getting into their circuitry and causing them annoyance if not trauma.

That left the other eight for me, White, and Abigail.

Pulled out my Glock, aimed, and fired at the head of the

nearest, which was the Army Kendrick. Got two good shots into its head before it herky-jerked its way over to me and tried to knock the gun out of my hand.

Meaning it was time for the fun of hand-to-hand combat. Managed to hold onto my Glock while I did some kung fu moves that were good, but not my best. Because I wasn't angry. I was creeped out and worried and all that jazz, but enraged I was not.

Tried to focus on the dead Secret Service agent. I'd been mad enough over an hour ago. But I'd had to think and talk in between then and now, not kick butt. Took a hit to my stomach that sent me flying into Abigail. We went down. On top of the Marine Kendrick, but still, down.

Said android tossed us up and off. While we were flying through the air to, thankfully, land on our feet in impressive cat-like stances I knew Abigail had been practicing with Tito and I just lucked into, the music changed to "Bomber" by Motörhead. Nice of the loudest rock and roll band in the world to join the party.

Abigail and I went back-to-back as the Marine Kendrick went for her and the Army Kendrick kept after me, presumably because I'd been the one who'd shot him. Or else I was closest. Decided the nuance didn't matter.

Shot him again, several times in the torso. Had some effect but not enough, especially as he flailed about and knocked my gun out of my hand. It skittered off away from me and my team. Interestingly, none of the androids tried to pick it up and use it. Hoped the music was scrambling their brains.

Now it was a lot of wild android swinging and a lot of dodging, kicking, sweeping, and leaping on my part. Had to body-slam an android away from Mahin so that she could keep on doing her thing, and another away from Lizzie's back. She was holding her own against the Preppy Kendrick, but didn't need another one attacking.

"Abby, can you do anything with them?" We were all having to shout to be heard over the music and through the earplugs, but since the music was still causing the androids issues, decided to leave it on.

"Not really. I can't affect their minds or their emotions." She ducked and I slammed a front ball kick into the Marine Kendrick then did a back kick into the Army Kendrick.

Managed to stagger them both back a little, but not nearly enough. It was hard to fight in these clothes, too, my attractive yet sensible pumps in particular. Couldn't speak for the others, but I wasn't going to last like this forever. I needed to get mad.

"What about shields?" One of the things Abigail and Naomi had been able to do was to create a protective shield around people and things. But the Gower Girls had burned themselves out protecting people and landmarks during Operation Destruction, and it was in the regaining of her powers that we'd lost Naomi. However, after our trip to Beta Eight, Abigail could create shields herself now, with some creativity, too.

"Per Tito and Chuck, I need to reserve power until it's necessary." She'd used a lot of power during our time on the Murder Train, more than she'd had on her own before. But that was a reason we were all still around to talk about it.

The A-C Kendrick knocked me down. "Kind of feels necessary!" Managed to shout this as I rolled into a somersault, but decided not looking at my clothes would be a wise choice.

"Not if you were really fighting," White called. "Missus Martini, this is one of your areas of expertise."

"I *am* fighting." This said as I landed an upward elbow on the A-C Kendrick that staggered him back, just in time for the Army Kendrick to get back into my action.

"Not like you could be," White said.

"Everyone's a critic!"

"Remember that they want to do terrible things to your children," Abigail called. "If we don't stop them, who will protect Jamie and Charlie?"

Thought about how every bad guy wanted to take my little girl and do horrible things to her. Some of them had. And who knew what plans they had for my infant son? Thought about what had been done to Chuckie. About all the terrible things done to Jeff. What had been done to Serene. About all the people we'd loved who we'd lost because of these murderous lunatics. Sure, these androids hadn't done any of that. But they'd been created by people who had.

The music changed to Fall Out Boy's "The Kids Aren't Alright." Which wasn't on this playlist. Meaning I was again on the Algar channel. And he was telling me my children were in danger, and I was here, fighting androids, not there, protecting them.

The rage hit.

Grabbed the Army Kendrick, ripped one of his arms off, and started beating him with it. That, combined with all the bullets in him, finally did the trick. He stopped moving, and I was pretty sure he was offline or whatever we called a dead android.

Spun and grabbed the Marine Kendrick's arm as he was swinging at Abigail. Flung him face-down onto the ground and jumped onto his back. Wrapped my arm around his neck and pulled. Hard. With all the anger I had.

Managed to wrench his head off. He didn't explode and, happily, there wasn't much blood. Lots of circuits and such, but not a lot of blood, bone, or sinew. Enough blood or whatever liquid was inside these things to wreck my clothes, naturally, but that was par for my particular course and I figured the ruined outfit was worth it.

While I'd been thusly engaged, Lizzie and White had finished off the Preppy Kendrick, and Mahin had stopped her dust devil because the two androids she'd had trapped were also down. Couldn't tell if they were dead or deactivated or just so filled with grit that they couldn't move, but they weren't attacking.

"Go team!"

"Yeah, Kitty," Abigail said. "About that . . ." She nodded her head toward the front entrance.

Took a look and realized there were just two problems now. The first was that this particular song wasn't nearly as loud or screamy as the prior songs had been, meaning that the remaining six androids weren't being affected nearly as much.

The second problem was that the Kendroid hadn't run away so much as he'd run to get reinforcements. Lots of them.

CHAPTER 53

THE NEW ARRIVALS were more copies of Kendrick. Since they'd all come in through the front door, our exit to the car was blocked.

There were a good twenty of them, but they clearly weren't done. I could tell because they were all naked. And while they should have been ashamed, they clearly weren't.

"It's like we're in a *Matrix* movie only Agent Smith is really and truly a Ken Doll." There were no reproductive organs on the Kendrick Ken Dolls. "Clearly Stephanie had a serious Barbie issue that has never been resolved."

"Gross." Lizzie looked as repulsed as she sounded. "Parts or no parts."

"This is reminiscent of when we were in the hidden lab many years ago," White said. "Only there's nothing for you to 'check out,' Missus Martini. I'm sure your disappointment knows no bounds."

"I'm with Lizzie on this one." But at least these weren't made up of A-C body parts. At least, I sincerely hoped not. Didn't voice that just in case I'd be proven wrong.

Our group of five clutched together. The remaining six androids that we'd been fighting looked pretty fresh, since all but the A-C Kendrick had hung back for whatever reason. Possibly because Stephanie hadn't programmed them to be smart. However I wanted to spin it, though, we basically had close to thirty enemies facing us now.

"Are you guys thinking what I'm thinking?"

"That we should turn down the volume?" Abigail shouted.

"That we're all dead?" Mahin asked.

"That we should run?" Lizzie suggested.

"That these models aren't as far along as the ones we've already met, and that our driver is the most complete of all of them?" White asked.

"Maybe to Abby, not yet to Mahin, yes to Lizzie and Mister White." The new additions started for us. The music chose this moment to switch to "Nine Lives" courtesy of my Bad Boys from Boston.

Screamin' Steven Tyler really was a lifesaver. The Kendroid turned and ran again. The six clothed androids started to do the herky-jerk thing. The third Casual Kendrick slammed himself into a nearby wall repeatedly until he stopped moving. The other five were doing better but not great. So yay on that front.

Sadly, the new arrivals didn't appear to have any issues with the music.

"They're not as advanced for sure," Abigail said, voice tense. "I can't feel anything from them at all."

"Meaning they aren't affected by the music?" Lizzie asked.

"Meaning they may not be affected by much of anything other than complete destruction," White replied as the Naked Smith Army—which would be a cool name for a rock band—started for us. Slowly, but then, they once again had us surrounded, so could take their time and savor the moment.

"Time to use the shield?" I asked hopefully.

"When do you want me to burn out?" Abigail countered. "Seriously, I'm still kind of depleted from everything we just went through. I have enough, but not enough to last if this goes long."

"I'd counsel waiting," White said.

"I want to live to at least be old enough to drive," Lizzie shared.

"Whine to Abby and Mister White, then, 'cause I've been overruled."

"What does that mean for us?" Mahin asked.

"That we need to get out of here!" Ran for my Glock at hyperspeed while the others linked hands. Got my gun and got back in time to grab Abigail's hand as White took off.

Hyperspeed allowed us to get past most of them, but there were a lot of them and they were fast. They were blocking and pinning our group in no time. "Scatter!" I shouted.

We dropped hands and all took off in different directions. Dawned on me that Lizzie couldn't scatter like the rest of us and Mahin probably couldn't either. Turned my music off and ran back. Mahin wasn't in sight but Lizzie was there, running and dodging. But there were six of them around her. Body-slammed two of them to clear my way to her, grabbed her hand, slammed through two more, and we took off again, down a nearby corridor.

"I thought you sent the animals after TK," she said as we stopped and I listened for pursuit. Took the earplugs out and dropped them into my purse. She did the same.

"I did. Doesn't mean that they were able to do anything." Hoped that I hadn't, once again, sent my pets into a trap.

"Totes hope they didn't get trapped."

"The mind reading classes can officially stop now. I'm terrible with mazes. How are you at them?"

"I'm okay. Why?"

"We're in a maze and I have no clear idea where in that maze we actually are."

Lizzie stared at me for a moment. "Oh. I guess a place like this is a maze, isn't it? Okay, I'll pay attention from now on."

Managed not to ask her why she hadn't paid attention so far, but she was the kid and I was the adult and supposedly trained professional.

Decided that as the trained professional, I was going to do what always worked for me. Got out my phone and headphones, clipped my phone to my waist while wishing I was in jeans and Converse. There was no way I wanted to run around here barefoot.

"Hey, you could call someone," Lizzie said.

"Wow, and duh, you're right." Looked at the phone. "Only I have no bars. We may be at a creepy deserted hospital but it's not *that* far from civilization."

"Maybe the ghosts are blocking the signal."

"There are no ghosts."

"In a place like this? Bet me."

"Later. We have enough problems with those living you mentioned earlier. Or at least sort of living. Though there's always a good shot that this place has some kind of shielding or scrambling or whatever going on."

Went back to what I'd been planning originally—playing music. Kept the volume low so I could still hear things around me well and hit play. Flo Rida's "Run" came on my personal airwaves just as I heard someone coming. I was not going to complain about being on the Algar Channel.

Grabbed Lizzie and headed off again. Heard shouts. She looked behind us. "We have three of them after us!" We came to stairs before we came to an exit and I didn't hesitate, I ran upstairs.

The stairs weren't in as bad of a shape as I'd figured they'd be, but they weren't in great shape, either. We didn't fall through or get stuck mostly because of hyperspeed and the fact that I was a hurdler and so able to leap the holes effectively.

Reached the landing on the second floor. "Think this place has more than one staircase?"

"Probably, yeah."

Decided the androids were too close and headed us up the next two flights of stairs, which were just as bad as the first set. However, it did put us farther ahead.

"I heard what sounded like some of them falling through," Lizzie said quietly as we reached the fourth floor and moved toward what I hoped was the other staircase.

It was far worse up here—rooms and offices filled with both the mundane and the horrific, all abandoned, all decaying. And shoes. There were shoes of all kinds, including skates and the like, left all over the place. Took the time to reload my Glock and handed Lizzie some clips. "Since I have no pockets, you're going to be holding these for faster access."

"Sure, I totes did that with my dad and the uncles." Her face fell. "I miss them."

Gave her a quick hug. "I do, too. So, let's try to think like them, stay safe, get rid of our enemies, protect our friends, and rescue our missing people."

"You really think they're here?"

Looked out a window that had bars on it. We were on the back side of the building. There were a lot of dilapidated buildings scattered about, some bigger, some smaller. There was also even more trash and debris in the back than in front, though inside was still winning the Hoarder's Horror Challenge.

But there was an area, a big area, that didn't have any buildings on it. And all the scrub that I could see from here looked very flat. "Oh yeah. I think they're really here." Pointed toward where I was looking. "What do you see?"

"You mean other than all the crapola and junk and stuff? I see . . . oh, wow. It's sitting there, isn't it? That's a smooshed tree for sure."

"Yep."

She grinned at me. "Quick Girl's ready to take on the bad guys, Megalomaniac Girl."

I grinned right back. "Stick with me, Grasshopper, and I will show you the Way."

CHAPTER 54

OF **COURSE,** there were a lot of buildings, and there was no way for us to determine where all the people we were looking for might be. But the Kendrick Android Army had arrived from somewhere, and it wasn't in this main building.

However, standing around admiring a sad and ugly view wasn't really in our best interests. We took off again, this time at human normal. Figured saving my hyperspeed strength might be wise, especially after all the conservation lectures from Abigail.

We passed several rooms with the remains of hospital beds. All of them had straps. Suppressed a shudder every time. In the fifth room like this the bed was broken apart. Stopped running and took a closer look.

"Why are we stopping here?" Lizzie asked, sounding nervous for the first time.

"Because I think we can use stuff from in here. Do you hear something?"

She shook her head and pointed. Looked where she'd indicated, just as "Creeper Kamikaze" by The Exies came on. Couldn't swear to it, but it looked like someone had just walked outside by the small window. Only we were on the fourth floor.

"It's a reflection of a tree or something," I said as firmly as possible. Even if Algar was telling me this place was haunted, so what? We still had to survive the androids.

"I think this place is totes haunted."

Really wanted to ask that the mind reading stuff cease and desist but I controlled myself. "Probably is. And so what? You said they couldn't hurt us. However, we have androids after us who definitely can. We have to deal with the immediate threat first. So, grab one of these metal bars, pointy ones for preference."

Dropped my Glock into my purse and ripped the pieces that would work best apart. Wasn't hard, since the bed was pretty much already destroyed.

Lizzie took the bar I handed her. "We going to try to skewer them with these?"

"Indeed we are. I have no idea if it'll work, but be sure it's an android."

"That'll be easy." She made a gagging face. "This Stephanie chick is weird."

"Truer words and all that. Now, let's get going. We need to ensure that we get all of these androids offline and find the others and make sure they're okay."

We turned around to find that one of the Naked Army had found us. We were both startled and we both jumped. Almost lost my hold on my metal rod, but held on. Based on where we were in the room, I was closer to the doorway, meaning I was going to be leading our attack.

My track coaches in high school and college both had probably been the most sadistic and dedicated in the entire country. Not only did they make sprinters run distance and make distance runners do stair charges with the sprinters, but they'd made us all learn how to do every, single event, in case anyone on the team was out due to illness or injury. This meant that I was decent with the javelin, a skill that had come in very handy since meeting the Gang from Alpha Four.

The android was just far enough away that I could throw the bar into him, which I did. He tried to block it, but I was revved up again, not necessarily on rage, which didn't seem to be sticking around long right now, but on nerves and adrenaline. The bar went through the stomach.

In an organic creature this would be a really bad hit. In an android, not so much. The bar went through, but he didn't stop. Well, he did stop, looked down, then kept coming. So much for my brilliant idea.

On the other hand, while he was thusly distracted, I'd gotten my Glock again and, because he was a very close and convenient target, I was able to get five headshots off in rapid fire.

Once I stopped shooting, Lizzie started slamming her bar against his head. He went down and wasn't moving, though because of the bar he was down like he was part of the creepiest lean-to ever built.

Flipped him onto his side and he remained immobile. Put my foot on his chest and pulled the bar out. "I think he's dead, or at least immobilized."

"Are we going to have to do this for every one?" Lizzie asked.

"No idea, but probably."

"This was totes easy 'cause he was just standing there, but I don't think the rest will be."

"I'm with you on both thoughts." Got ready to run again when my music switched to "Change Your Mind" by The All-American Rejects. Pondered this then had a thought and dragged the body to the far end of the room. "So, let's turn the tables and stop being the game and instead become the hunters."

Lizzie cocked her head at me. "You want us to, what, stay here?" She looked around. "We have plenty of bars, I guess, if we need them. But why? If they catch us, we don't have anywhere to go."

"Right, but running around just means we're attacked or caught in a place that isn't loaded with additional ammunition." Ripped the rest of the bed apart and put the rods into a pile that was easier for the two of us to grab from. There was a sturdy footboard and an even bigger headboard that I put in their own pile. Pulled out my iPod and speakers again and hit pause on my phone's music. "Get ready, we're going to lure them to us."

Put my purse on the floor and hit play. The sounds of "How You Like Me Now" by The Heavy came on. This was a good song to fight to, and I put it on repeat. It wasn't loud and screaming like the others had been, but the music hadn't affected the Naked Army anyway—with my volume all the way up it would draw them to us, and it was more important that I was in the groove than anything else.

We didn't have long to wait. Another of the Naked Army arrived. This time Lizzie happened to be closer so she slammed her bar at an upward angle so that it entered the stomach but went up and out through the top of the back.

As before, the android kept coming, though it was having issues. Ensured it had more by shooting five shots into its head. It went down. Lizzie pulled out the bar, I dragged the body to what I was hoping would become a pile.

Was really glad that we were using the stab then shoot technique, because the next person through the door was Mahin. "Do you need help?" she asked, looking wild.

"Not yet but potentially." Shared Mission: Duck Blind details. "So, what have you been doing?"

"Running mostly." She cocked her head and ran behind me. "There were three after me and I think they're here."

Put my gun into my left hand and hefted a bar with my right while Mahin grabbed a bar, too. The first of the Naked Army came running in and impaled himself on Lizzie's bar.

Couldn't shoot him because the next one was right behind him and I had to use my javelin skills again. I was a little high, but the good news was that even though I missed the android coming through the door, I speared the one behind him right through the face.

Lizzie meanwhile had pulled out her bar from the first one and was slamming it against his head. Mahin was in a really good horse stance, bar up like a spear, so when the unharmed android came at her, she was able to stab him through the gut.

I got my Glock back into my shooting hand and proceeded to empty the last five bullets in the clip into the android Mahin was dealing with. As it went down, I dropped out the empty clip. "Refill!"

Lizzie, still hitting the android with the bar one-handed, reached into her pocket and tossed me a new clip. Slammed it in, then shot the android that was pulling the bar out of its body. It went down, Mahin grabbed her bar back, then she and Lizzie dragged their androids to the pile, while I went to drag the one in from the hall.

Which was a mistake, in that I didn't have a bar on me and six more androids were converging on us from both sides.

On the plus side, I had a mostly full clip. The ones on my right were closest. Emptied said clip into them, one, two, three. Literally. They seemed to have no self-preservation and less intelligence about doing things like ducking or dodging. Had no complaints—I liked being alive.

Luckily for me, Lizzie came out and rammed a bar into the nearest android on my left while Mahin dragged the one in the hall back into the room. Dropped the clip as Lizzie and I ran back into the room. She slapped a new clip into my hand and grabbed a bar while I put the clip in and turned to shoot the next android.

He obliged by walking into the room, taking five bullets to the head, and going down.

"You know, I don't remember androids being this easy to kill," I mentioned as the third one came in and I shot him, too. "Think it's because they're not really 'done' yet?"

"Possibly," Mahin said as she dragged the two in the room to our pile. "But they may not be 'dead', so to speak, just immobilized."

Went outside with more caution this time. No one else was in sight, so I dragged our last android in, pulled out the bar in his head, and tossed him onto the pile.

"We totes have over half the naked creepers down," Lizzie said. "Should we stay here? Doesn't seem like anyone else is coming."

"Give it a couple of minutes and enjoy the brief respite. Trust me, it won't last long."

True enough, it didn't. Only this time what came through the door wasn't one of the Naked Army. It was the Navy and Air Force Kendricks.

Fortunately for us, we were all getting good at the Stab and Shoot Method. Unfortunately for us, these androids were a lot harder to take down.

Lizzie skewered Army Kendrick while Mahin did the same to Navy. Put five bullets in Army Kendrick, Lizzie tossed me a new clip, then I put five bullets into Navy Kendrick. They were still up. Not doing great, but still up and swinging. Army Kendrick pulled the bar out of his middle and started swinging it around.

Lizzie dodged and fell against Navy Kendrick, which was good because she hit his side where the metal bar was not and made him lose his balance so the kick he was aiming toward Mahin missed.

Navy Kendrick went down, Lizzie managed to keep her balance, though she was staggering. I had to back up to

avoid being hit by Army Kendrick, so I used the time to
shoot him some more. He went down, but he wasn't out.

Mahin grabbed another bar and started slamming it on
Army Kendrick's head. Meanwhile, Lizzie had pulled the
bar through Navy Kendrick's back and was hitting him with
it as well.

Put my last bullets from this clip into Navy Kendrick,
then dug around in my purse for another clip. Found one,
and only one. Couldn't remember how many clips Lizzie
still had on her, but had to figure it wasn't all that many.

We dragged the finally down androids to the pile. Looked
out the window. There were several of what looked like either large metal shipping crates or portable classrooms or
stranded rail cars some ways away from the back. There
were ten of these—two sets of two to the right and left, a set
of three in the middle, another set of two to the far left near
a larger building that was even farther away, and one that
was sitting at an angle and alone, kind of in the middle to
the right.

It was between this angled smaller metal building and
the larger normal, for this place, building that I was pretty
sure the helicarrier was sitting.

However, there was something more important much
closer to the building we were in. White and Abigail were
standing back-to-back, and they were surrounded by the
remaining dozen androids. And it didn't look like Abigail
was using her shield, which probably wasn't wise at this
juncture.

"We need to get out of here. Grab our ammunition, such
as it is, and let's get going."

Put my Glock back into my purse and hit pause on my
iPod as Mahin picked up the remaining metal bars. Lizzie
and I took the footboard and headboard—which were far
heavier than they looked—just in case.

We were heading for the door when I heard a weird
sound, sort of like white noise. Turned around. To see that,
unfortunately, Mahin had been right—the androids had
been down, but they weren't out.

The pile was moving.

CHAPTER 55

THE THREE OF US FROZE. Some things make you stop in your tracks. Some, like seeing Jeff on our wedding day, were great reasons. Some, like what we were watching right now, were not.

The pile was moving, as if the androids on the bottom were trying to move the ones on top of them. My iPod started up and I knew I hadn't jostled it. Instead of the song I'd had on repeat, we now had "Electric Worry" by Clutch playing. Loved this song, but memory shared that it had been used for a video game—one about killing zombies.

"I think they've rebooted or whatever," Lizzie said, her voice only shaking a little bit.

Mahin opened her mouth, but whatever she was going to say was interrupted by the pile sort of exploding out, as the first android we'd taken down crawled out and over the pile of his duplicated brethren.

"Kill it!" Mahin screamed. "Kill it with fire!" Then she started really yelling, but in Farsi. I had no idea what she was saying, but I was pretty sure that the words "kill" and "fire" were in there.

Adrenaline is a funny thing. When it came to fight or flight, I was usually on the side of kick 'em in the tenders first, run away later. Right now, though, I really wanted to run. Only Mahin was freaking out in the doorway and, due to all the metal she was holding, was actually blocking any escape Lizzie and I could hope to make.

Looked at said teenager. For the first time she looked terrified. "They really *are* zombie androids," she said, her voice heading to the level where only dogs would be able to hear her. Normally I thought of that as my personal register, but couldn't really fault Lizzie for going there.

Lizzie was a kid, and she was, for all intents and purposes right now, *my* kid. Sure, I hadn't given birth to her, sure she had an adopted father, but she was my ward, and besides Batman hadn't birthed any of the Robins, either, but they were his wards, and that meant Batman was going to do all that he could to save whichever Robin, even though he'd put said Robin in danger in the first place. Apparently I had a *lot* in common with Batman right now.

However, I also had zombie androids, and they were terrifying my friend and my kid.

Rage hit, in all its She-Hulk and Wolverine's Berserker Rage glory. Pulled the footboard and headboard out of Lizzie's hands, let the headboard fall, then took one end of the footboard and started slamming it against the android as if the footboard was a baseball bat and the android was good ol' Beverly, who'd tried to do horrific things to Jeff during Operation Fugly.

They might have been tough, they might have been rough, they might have been made of metal and wires and nothing else nice, but these androids didn't stand a chance against me right now.

I was slamming what appeared to be an indestructible piece of metal and wood against these things, to the song that was now on repeat, and I just made sure that they were splattering as much as androids could splatter.

Slam, spin, slam, kick, slam, jump up and down on the body, slam some more. Lost count of which one I was destroying and just kept on. Realized that Mahin and Lizzie were helping again, beating the androids with the metal bars. They were also kicking, stomping, and jumping on the bodies.

I was going faster than either one of them, though, and not just because Lizzie was a human and Mahin was a hybrid without the double-hearts. I was revved to the top of my adrenal rush and everything else around me was in slow motion, just like it had been during Operation Confusion, when my husband and friends had been chained up and tortured.

Was glad Jeff wasn't around because my rage and our terror would have really affected him badly. Just channeled worry about what he'd be doing if he was here into smashing more androids.

Sooner than I'd have thought, we had no more moving parts in here. It looked like a horrific murder scene, which was to say that it still fit the entire motif of this House of Horrors and didn't even look out of place.

We stopped and backed away.

"Wow," Lizzie said finally. "I guess they do die."

"When you turn them into separate parts and make the parts mush, yeah, they do."

Mahin was muttering about how this place should be burned to the ground. Had never realized she had arson in her veins, but clearly she was Old School and believed in setting the monsters on fire. Couldn't argue with the logic, just didn't want to turn a gigantic building to ash because I knew that wouldn't play out well for us.

"Let's get out of here and help the others."

"Should we turn off the music?" Lizzie asked.

"Um, yeah, I guess." I mean, clearly Algar was going to turn it on anyway. Felt something brush my cheek, and looked around. No one was there, but I thought I saw movement out of the corner of my eye again. But when I looked, nothing. Okay, so maybe the music wasn't Algar, but was a helpful spirit. I'd ask Algar later. And take whatever help we could get, ghostly or otherwise.

We gathered up our makeshift yet extremely effective weapons—the footboard was banged up and dented, as were some of the metal bars, but they were in useable shape, and the headboard hadn't been touched yet.

Put the iPod on pause but put my earbuds back in and started my own music up. Band of Horse's "Is There A Ghost" came on. Nice to see Algar was keeping his sense of humor.

We headed downstairs carefully and cautiously, but as quickly as we could. Naturally, I got lost, so Lizzie ended up taking point, though I kept close to her. However, having destroyed the zombie androids seemed to have emboldened her, and she wasn't nearly as freaked out as she had been.

Other than seeing more decay, desolation, and a variety of horrific things in every room we passed, we didn't come across any more androids. Since I'd seen the remaining dozen surrounding White and Abigail, this wasn't a surprise, but it confirmed that we didn't have even more androids out after us. At least not yet.

We found the back doors and slunk through them. To hear the sound of what I was pretty prepared to say was a rocket launcher.

CHAPTER 56

SHOVED MAHIN and pulled Lizzie back against the wall. "Stay down," I said quietly. It wasn't hard to stay hidden—there was a ton of trash back here, including what looked like old refrigerators, vending machines, and beds. Truly, Forest Haven was a little slice of heaven.

Of course, all the crap made it hard to see. Wanted to get out there, but also didn't want to get hit. Hyperspeed seemed like the obvious choice but, with all the stuff we were holding, it was out of the question. And while some might have just dumped their weapons and done the running thing, I didn't have faith that said weapons would be here when we got back. I also couldn't guarantee I could find them again in all the trash.

Handed Lizzie the footboard, then held the headboard up as a sort of makeshift shield. "You two stay behind me and be ready to run." With that, we started off toward the sounds of explosions, hiding behind the Mighty Headboard Shield, "Rocket Queen" by Guns N' Roses in my ears.

The convenient thing about there being explosions is that it gave us a direction to head for. Shoved aside the thought that only lunatics headed toward the sounds of explosions, since I ran toward stuff like this all the time.

The building was a long rectangle, and we'd come out in the middle of it. The action was ahead of us, but on the other side of a gigantic pile of trash. So, around the trash we went, crouched down like we were trying to win the Duck Walking Championship.

Of course, using the headboard as a shield that we were all ducking behind meant that we couldn't see anything.

And because I was the one holding it, I couldn't peek around either side. Either I had to keep going blind or I had to lower the headboard and expose my head. Neither option seemed all that brilliant.

"Can you hold this?" I asked Mahin quietly.

She nodded, put down the bars, and took the headboard from me. We still had the pile of trash on our right, so the only option was for me to peek around the left, which I did, wondering if we were actually being stealthy or if we weren't being attacked because our enemies were laughing so hard.

There wasn't anyone that I could see. Though there were what looked like some destroyed android parts nearby.

Took the headboard back and, while Mahin picked up the metal bars again, decided that, even though explosions were still happening, we could walk upright and all that jazz right now. Still held the headboard in front of us, but with my head exposed so I could see.

We could move faster this way, which was good. Once we were near them, it was easy to confirm that the parts were indeed android and they weren't going to start moving on their own any time soon.

"Where are Richard and Abigail?" Mahin asked.

"No idea. They were in this area, but I don't see them."

"Maybe they're with whoever's blowing the androids up," Lizzie suggested.

"Maybe they're the ones who are blowing them up," Mahin added.

"They weren't looking like they were winning when I saw them, and they didn't have weapons with them. And until we see who's got the rocket launcher or bazooka or whatever, we don't assume they're our friend."

Looked around. Other than trash and android parts, I didn't see anything else that shouldn't be here. The explosions now sounded like they were on the other side of the metal boxes that, now that we were near them, did appear to be metal cargo containers. Had no idea what they were doing here, but decided that if we could avoid ever going into them, it would probably be in our best interests.

There was enough room between the sets of cargo containers that we could still use the Mighty Headboard Shield, so we did. As we neared the end of the middle set of three and could therefore see the lone, off-kilter one, I spotted White and Abigail. They were using the cargo container that was at an angle as a far better shield than we were working with.

There was a figure dressed all in black, wearing a black backpack and a black helmet, and this person was at the near end of the building shooting what was indeed a bazooka of some kind. My time with Centaurion Division had taught me that there were many kinds of personal rocket launchers, but I wasn't close enough to name the make and model of the one in current use. They kept shooting, reloading, and shooting again, in a very fast and efficient manner.

"Who is that?" Lizzie whispered.

"I'm not sure—"

Would have said more, but my music changed to Aerosmith's "Dude (Looks Like A Lady)" and I stopped talking and did a closer examination. The person wasn't large, but they were very comfortable with the weapon. White and Abigail weren't trying to get away from this person, either— as near as I could tell, they were being protected, not held captive. And that backpack looked vaguely familiar.

The person stopped firing and turned to those two, indicating they should come with. They did as requested.

Decided we'd waited long enough. Besides, we had our Mighty Headboard Shield. We were safe. Trotted across the little clearing—looking both ways for incoming androids— and followed the others as they took off for the two other containers diagonally across this clearing from this oddly angled one.

Checked the clearing—lots and lots of android parts. No functioning androids were standing, running, attacking or even visible. "Did you guys get them all?" I asked as we took cover, just in case, behind these last containers.

All three of them jumped, but the person in the motorcycle helmet nodded. Good, enemies accounted for, at least for now.

White and Abigail looked relieved to see us. "I didn't realize you were behind us, Missus Martini. We were about to start searching for you," he said.

Abigail nodded. "We had a little difficulty that delayed us. Like, you know, being surrounded by hostile androids."

"Yeah, I saw you from an upstairs window. Where we were having to beat and shoot our androids into submission, seeing as we didn't have the snazzy rocket launcher."

"Our rescuer only had the one," White said.

"Yeah, well, I'm sure she didn't have time to grab a lot of things. Adriana, let me say with all sincerity that it's really great to see you."

She flipped the visor of what was absolutely a motorcycle helmet up. "Grandmother says that she'd like you all to come by and have some refreshments when we're done here. And yes, all the hostiles are down."

Adriana was the granddaughter of the Romanian Ambassador, which, since their embassy was across the street from ours, was why we'd met. However, though her grandmother, Olga, was currently mostly confined to a wheelchair due to MS, she was former KGB and had been training Adriana in the Old Ways. Adriana had saved my life more than once, and was considered a vital part of the team.

Olga was also the Oracle. From the vantage point of her second-floor office that had two windows that looked out onto two rather mundane streets, she knew everything that was going on. Figured the invitation to drop by was a hint that indicated that Olga felt we were all being too slow to catch on to what was really going on. Was sure she was right, so looked forward to the upcoming mental gymnastics, since Olga liked to make you work for it.

Therefore, Adriana being our rescuer wasn't a surprise. What did surprise me, though, was that everyone else looked surprised by this reveal, White and Abigail included.

"Really, gang? Okay, I admit that I was watching for pursuit and saw a motorcycle several times on our trip here. But she's too small to be Malcolm, Siler, Len, or Kyle, and our A-C Field agents can't ride a bike. At least, not yet. And let's face it—Adriana's amazingly well trained. Why are you keeping the helmet on, though?"

Adriana shrugged. "I figured it was more important to figure out what was going on and do what I could to rescue you. Besides, extra protection doesn't hurt."

"Truer words and all that. By the way, I think Lizzie and I know where the helicarrier is."

"Across from these containers, yes."

"Show-off."

Adriana giggled. "I like to keep you impressed."

White cleared his throat. "Sadly these aren't containers, though they do look like it. Abigail and I thought we might find either hostages or weapons in these. We've been inside. These were classrooms. Of a sort."

"I thought they looked like those portable classrooms we had when I was in grade school. Never my favorite place to be."

"Trust me when I say that these are worse than anything you've experienced, Missus Martini, and leave it at that."

"Gotcha."

"Why are you holding that headboard?" Abigail asked. "I mean, I think it's a headboard."

"It is, and, as Adriana said, extra protection never hurts."

"How is that protection?" White asked.

"I'm holding it as a shield." Decided I could put it down for the moment. "The footboard that Lizzie has was amazingly effective when we had to smash androids that we thought we'd already taken offline." Lizzie kept a hold on the footboard, though Mahin put the metal bars down.

Adriana nodded. "Len said you'd been taken by an android. That's why I brought *vechi de incredere*, here." She patted the bazooka.

"What does that mean in Romanian?"

"It would translate to Old Trusty for you."

That was what I called my purse and what Olga apparently called her personal bazooka. Didn't know whether this made me more normal than Olga or less prepared and realistic. Probably both.

"Aha. Nice to see that Olga kept some mementos from her KGB days to pass down to you. So, did Len call you or something? Or is Olga even more prescient than even I think and you called him?"

She laughed. "No. He'd texted me, to ask me to drop by, when Crystal Maurer arrived. I was on my way to meet up with all of you when he called me, right after he and the others went back into the Teetotaler, after you'd been taken. He felt that I was the only one likely to react with the kind of speed he wanted, especially since I was already on the way."

Considered this. Why would Len think everyone was acting slowly? He'd texted with Buchanan earlier. And Buchanan had sent Falk immediately. Nothing wrong with those actions. Other than the fact that Buchanan hadn't been the one to come. But I'd assigned him and the others to a job, and maybe Jeff had sent him to do something, too.

None of that said too slowly, though. So, maybe Len had called someone else before he'd called Adriana, and whoever that was had told him that a political response was going to be necessary.

"Ah. They're trying to minimize fallout and not get the press involved."

"So Grandmother believes. Though she wasn't entirely convinced and feels that more could be going on."

"I'll take the obscure hint under advisement. Did you get your ammo from us?"

"No. It's all ours. But Grandmother said to tell you that it was on the house."

"I love Olga. So, you guys just happen to have personal rocket launchers lying around the Romanian embassy?"

"Yes. Don't you?"

"Honestly? Yes." Maybe every embassy in town was armed to the teeth. The Israelis and Bahrainis certainly were. Or maybe it was just the embassies we hung with. "And you were bringing it with you to come have tea with us?"

"Yes. Len said there was something wrong with Crystal and that I should assume she was an android. Therefore, I came, as you Americans like to say, armed for bear."

"Trust me, I am *not* complaining. So, is anyone else planning to come rescue us? Just asking and all that."

Adriana shook her head as she took her helmet off. "I don't know. I was focused on finding you and then tailing you so that I wouldn't be noticed. I have no cellular service here, though, so I assume we're being scrambled or dampened in this area."

"Yeah, that's my guess, too. I was able to keep my phone on while we were driving, but I have nothing here, either. So, we work under the assumption that if a bigger cavalry is on the way, it's going to take them time to find us."

"Possibly much time. It was hard for me to tell, by the way, but I believe that I lost coverage sooner than when I arrived here. I believe I lost it once I was near to your car."

"Fantastic. Maybe once we're farther from the car we'll get service again, but I never count on things working out that well. Okay, so, are we sure all the androids are destroyed?"

"There were twelve that had Mister White and Abigail surrounded," Adriana said. "And I've destroyed all of them." She nodded toward the android carnage in the clearing. Recounted. Yep, there were twelve android heads, or what was left of them.

"Go team. We took care of our thirteen. So that means that, with the first ones we hopefully put out of commission, we got them all. But what about the Kendroid?"

White shook his head. "We haven't seen him, and believe me, we looked."

"Though we didn't get far," Abigail added. "We checked all these containers first, since Uncle Richard felt they'd be prime holding cells."

"I'd agree. But no?"

"Not for a long time." White looked ill and Abigail shuddered.

"Put it this way," she said. "Uncle Richard was right, but they were used decades ago. Our prisoners aren't in them. Thank God."

"Yeah, I think I'll pass on taking a look-see."

"Should we go back to the car and get our phones?" Lizzie asked.

Checked my phone. "Nope, still have no coverage here, and per Adriana we probably want to get farther from the car, not closer." Was about to suggest we try to determine where the cellular blockage or scrambling or whatever was coming from, in case it wasn't coming from the limo, when my music changed to "All the Pretty Ones" by the Exies. Clearly this was a hint. Looked around. "Have you seen the Poofs or Peregrines?"

Before anyone could answer, heard a whole lot of squawking and bird screaming coming from the other side of these containers.

Didn't hesitate, just ran for the sound of my Peregrines in trouble.

CHAPTER 57

RAN INTO THE AREA littered with android parts, but no Peregrines were in evidence, or Poofs for that matter.

However, the screeching was still going on, but as I listened, it was clear that it wasn't coming from one area, but from all over. And it was echoing, which made determining where the birds were more difficult. Stopped running and tried to focus.

The others reached me quickly. "I hear them," Mahin said. "But they don't sound like they're in any one area."

"That means we have to split up." We all looked at each other. No one was excited by this idea.

"Hyperspeed handles so many things," White said as he took Lizzie's hand. Abigail grabbed Mahin and Adriana.

My music switched to Cher's "Living in a House Divided." Chose not to argue or question Algar's musical choices right now. "Look, the Peregrines are either in trouble or they've found something. I'm with you on the idea that we should use hyperspeed. I just think that we should split up. And, since we're already in teams, let's go with that."

"You don't have a partner." White took my hand. "Two teams is fine. But no one goes off alone here," he said firmly.

"I agree," Adriana said. "I'd prefer we all stay together, but I agree that the birds seem very upset. We'll take everything to the west, you take the building ahead of us and everything to the east."

"Ah . . ."

"We're taking all the buildings near the basketball courts. You go the other way."

"Gotcha."

"How do we stay in touch?" Lizzie asked nervously.

Adriana dug into her backpack and pulled out two walkie-talkies. "These should work. They're already set to the right channel to communicate." She handed one to Lizzie and kept the other for herself. Then she took out two flashlights and gave me one and Mahin the other, after which she put her helmet into the backpack.

"Room in there now that you used all your ammo?"

She smiled. "Of course. We like to be efficient." She took Abigail's hand again and they zipped off toward the left.

Examined the building ahead of us. It was another brick building, though nowhere near as large as the main building we'd had so much "fun" in. Probably a quarter of the size, if that. Only one story, decrepit like every other building I'd seen since we'd arrived.

"Remember that the invisible helicarrier is around here somewhere," I said to White.

"Yes, we spotted where we believe it is based on the flattened foliage. We considered trying to see if we could feel it, but since it's truly invisible and we have no idea what we'd be touching, discretion became the better part of valor."

"So it's not cloaked with what Centaurion normally uses?"

"No, it's not. Which, since it's from Vatusus, isn't that much of a surprise, though I'll admit to disappointment."

"Can all A-C's see through the Invisibility Shields?"

White gave me a look that said he felt I might be overtired. "Not the ones used for the vehicles. Not normally, at any rate. Those shields are a more concentrated form of the cloaking we use. Why?"

"I think I know how Crystal Maurer got into the White House at o-dark-thirty this morning."

"Does it matter for this situation?"

"I have no idea."

"Good to know. At any rate, duty awaits. Shall we?"

Lizzie and I both nodded, and we took off at the slow version of hyperspeed, I presumed to avoid slamming ourselves into the helicarrier, and headed for our first target. White circumnavigated us carefully and took us far wider than probably necessary to avoid the helicarrier, but who was I to complain?

The doors were open, so we went in.

To discover, as "Haunting the Chapel" by Slayer came on, that we'd indeed found the chapel. There was graffiti and lots of dust, but it wasn't nearly as destroyed as the main building. We searched quickly but found nothing, though there were a couple pairs of shoes here and there. Still heard the Peregrines squawking, but they sounded farther away now.

"I don't think any kind of God was ever here," Lizzie said quietly.

"Too true," White replied. As the former Supreme Pontifex, I had a feeling that he, even more than the rest of us, found this entire place upsetting on a deeply personal level. "May they all be in the embrace of a loving deity now."

We left, and now it was time to choose where we went next. There were buildings across the street, so we went to them. The one directly across from the chapel was two stories. The doors were ajar, though they did say that there was No Trespassing. We chose to ignore that and ran inside.

It was dark in here, not that there weren't windows and such, but if the main building had been murky and foreboding, this one took those elements up to eleven. Couldn't hear any birds as well once we were inside, but we did a fast run through the place just to be sure. This building was easily two-thirds the size of the main one but it contained no Peregrines.

Besides all the horrific elements we'd seen already, this one had even more hospital-type stuff, though it was loaded with shoes, too. Wondered if there was some horrible reason for it and had to figure there was. Maybe the ghosts kept the shoes around so they could escape or something esoteric and creepy like that.

Bottom line, though, was that we'd either found the infirmary or this place had really been the Home for Aspiring Dr. Mengele Wannabes. Had a feeling that I should bet on both, especially when Van Halen's "Somebody Get Me A Doctor" came on my airwaves.

There were stairs going up and down. We went down first. The basement appeared to be more medical and what I was pretty sure was a morgue. It was in horrific shape, and parts were impassable. Didn't know whether to be grateful or not that Adriana had given us a flashlight. Was hugely happy we were going through it at full hyperspeed.

Nothing other than old horrors discovered, we headed upstairs. Most of this floor was just the usual decay, debris, garbage, and shoes, but there was a big room on one side that, when I entered, was really reminiscent of all the Labs of Horror I'd seen in the past few years.

The walls looked thicker, as if they were reinforced, and there was weird medical machinery, what looked like a small assembly line, and what looked like a freestanding room or giant freezer or similar.

"What do you think?" White asked.

"I think we open that freezer and get prepared for what we'll find."

White nodded, let go of me and Lizzie—who I shoved behind me—and pulled the door open.

Nothing leaped out at us, and I took a careful look inside. There were a lot of what looked like standing coffins, only they were made of glass. They were all open and empty. Counted. There were twenty.

"Looks familiar, doesn't it, Missus Martini?"

"Yeah, similar to the cloning lab we found under Gaultier, but it's not quite the same. My guess is this is where the androids sleep or rest or are programmed or whatever when they're made. But I don't think this is where they hang once they get clothes." My music changed to "Déjà Vu" by Iron Maiden. Decided Algar was enjoying himself again.

White cocked his head. "There's something else ... familiar about this."

"What?"

He shook his head. "I can't remember what it is. The tickle of memory feels quite . . . old."

"Well, it'll come to you, I'm sure."

"Think we'll find something like this but made for twelve?" Lizzie asked.

"Not sure. Honestly, I think that once they get clothes they go elsewhere. But since there are no androids, hostages, or Peregrines, it's time to check out another *Cabin in the Woods* and see what we luck into."

As we were ready to leave, Lizzie looked out the far window. "Is that civilization?" She pointed off to our left, where there was a flash of something that didn't look brick.

"I suggest we find out," White said. We linked up and

headed downstairs and out. It was still cruddy outside, but so much less horrible than inside.

"Hey, it's totes quiet again," Lizzie pointed out. "What's happened to the Peregrines?"

"I'm going to hope that Adriana's team found them and that they're okay."

"We should still continue to search, however, regardless of the Peregrines' potential situation," White said. "Or shall we see if we can get help?"

Social Distortion's "Prison Bound" hit my airwaves. "I wonder if that's a detention center or something."

"Meaning we can get help," White suggested.

Lizzie grimaced. "There's no way we're supposed to be here, not after what Mahin said about this place. You know what they'll do if we ask for help."

"No, I don't," White said. "What will they do?"

She shrugged. "Tell us we aren't supposed to be here, lock us up, and wait for our parents to come get us. Totes metaphorically speaking, of course."

"Of course. Lizzie's right, though, I think. Let's see if we can find our hostages first. I don't really know how we're going to explain that we think there's an invisible helicarrier sitting here without causing some kind of incident that's only going to hurt Jeff's presidency."

"While us trotting around in an abandoned mental asylum won't cause any problems, I'm sure." White's sarcasm knob was going well past eleven.

"Right. So, where to next?"

"Next door, so to speak, seems the most prudent."

We were about to head for the building that was east of this one when Lizzie jerked. "Hey, has anyone checked to see if the car that brought us is still here?"

CHAPTER 58

WHITE AND I looked at each other. "I doubt it," White said.

"Adriana's team is doing the same thing we are, searching, so probably not."

"With all haste, then," White said, as we headed down what claimed to be 2nd Street, at least per a very old, very bent street sign. This street was as badly maintained as the one we'd driven on when we'd arrived.

Reached the curved driveway to discover that, yes, the car was still here. Lizzie took the opportunity to retrieve her cell phone and turn it on. Like me, she had no bars, no service, and an attempted text to me was not received.

"We need to find the Kendroid, don't we? I mean in addition to all our missing people, Poofs, and Peregrines."

With the main building to our left, there were three buildings on this street, and we were in front of two of them. The one that was farther away down the street to our left was quite large, and there were two matching buildings that were, for this complex, smaller. We headed for the rightmost of these, since we were practically in front of it.

White nodded. "We have no idea how to get into the helicarrier, let alone fly it. He could be inside it for all we know."

"It's not firing at us, and I'm sure we'd know if it had or was taking off, so my money's on no. However, I don't see any scorching on the ground, so who knows?"

"Perhaps it's a Vatusus specialty."

"We can but hope." We reached the rightmost building.

Another three-story brick monstrosity. Could not wait to see how many pairs of shoes were on display here.

As with the other building, we ignored the No Trespassing sign and zipped through. Unlike the other one, there was no basement here. There was also nothing that indicated that anyone was hanging out here for any length of time. Severely lacking in anything resembling our hostages, Peregrines, the Kendroid, or Stephanie's actual Evil Villain Lair.

Still, we checked every room on all three floors. Other than feeling like I'd never want to go out in the dark by myself ever again, there was nothing of note unless you counted the many shoes that were in rather neat piles here, all things considered. Decided I didn't want to note them and moved on.

Out of this one and onto its twin, as "Slaughter House" by Front Line Assembly appropriately provided my soundtrack. This building was the same—debris, shoes, dirt, graffiti, broken windows, creep factor up to eleven—only it was clear that people had been living here.

Well, "people" was too strong a term. There were several rooms on the top floor that appeared to be lived in, to use the term loosely. But they were slightly less filthy, dusty, and decrepit. "I think we've found the Finished Androids Bunkhouse."

"There's only eleven rooms that look sort of lived in," Lizzie pointed out. "Where was TK sleeping?"

Had some suspicions, but kept them to myself for right now. "No idea. Presume we'll find out." My music changed to "Bright Lights" by Matchbox Twenty. Checked the BT. It was the same yellow-green as when we'd gotten here. Dropped it back into my purse.

Out again and down a wide path at the other side of these buildings that led us to the bigger building off this street. This brick building was shaped like a cross, with four wings of equal length spreading out from the center. It also had three arches and kind of looked interesting, at least as compared to the other buildings we'd seen so far.

We discovered this was the cafeteria. Considering how gigantic this place was, that the cafeteria building was huge wasn't all that shocking.

As with the others, it was murky, creepy, and had shoes scattered all over. Unlike the others, this place looked like there had been a riot inside before it had been abandoned. However, by comparison to everything else we'd seen, it was kind of innocuous. It also didn't look like it possessed a lot of hiding places.

My music changed to "Look Around" by the Red Hot Chili Peppers. Clearly Algar felt that I was being too quick to judge.

There was nothing of interest on the main floor, but there were stairs going up and down. We went up first this time, because the building didn't look like it had two stories from outside.

Turned out that it had a weird attic where they stored nonperishables. And naturally it was someplace where not even Lizzie could stand upright.

"Do we need to go in there?" Lizzie asked.

Realized that "Look Around" was on repeat. "Yeah, unfortunately, I think we do."

There was a clear path between all the expired foodstuffs and, go figure, we could easily walk side-by-side, but we had to walk like we were pretending to be furry apes. So we had both uncomfortable and unsafe going for us.

"Do you hear something?" Lizzie whispered as we crept in at human regular, because White wasn't confident that the floor was going to hold and we didn't want to slam our heads onto something.

"Sort of a ... scrabbling?" Made sure to keep the flashlight aimed firmly in the middle of the path.

"Yeah." She sounded as nervous as I felt.

White cleared his throat. "If anyone's here, please speak out or make some noise," he called, definitely projecting his voice. "Other than scrabbling."

There were some thumps. And also some scrabbling. Thought about where we were and how long this place had been abandoned.

"There are rats or woodland creatures or both nesting here, aren't there, Mister White?"

"Oh, possibly."

"You saw some, I know it, don't even try to lie."

"Fine, yes. However, the thumping is continuing, and I don't believe that rats or woodland creatures are quite advanced enough to be making that noise in response to my request."

"Ghosts would be," Lizzie pointed out.

"But we don't believe in ghosts," White said, as we walked very carefully toward the thumping, which was coming from the farthest end of the attic from where the stairs were because the cosmos just wouldn't have it any other way in my experience.

We reached an intersection where we could go right, left, or straight when the thumping stopped, because naturally. It was a shorter walk to the end going straight, so that's what we did. We went as far as we could to find another door.

"Oh, goody. Who gets to do the honors?"

"I will again, Missus Martini. Please try to only scream if flight is necessary."

"Oh, roger that and I'll do my best and all that jazz." Considered our situation and that I wasn't the only one ready to scream. "Quick Girl, that goes for you, too."

"Check." Lizzie sounded a little better, so congratulated myself as I ensured that I had a firm grip on the flashlight and Lizzie both.

"Go for it, Mister White."

He pulled at the door—it appeared to be locked, but after some serious straining the door sort of burst open. And I managed not to scream. But only just.

CHAPTER 59

"JERRY!"

Jerry was tied up and gagged and lying on the floor. But the room was so small that even though he, like the rest of the flyboys, wasn't tall, his shoulders and head were against the wall. He was positioned in such a way within this room that moving would be close to impossible. He'd done the only thing he could—lifted his legs and banged his heels on the floor—to make the noise we'd heard.

Dropped Lizzie's hand, shoved the flashlight at White, and ran into the room as fast as someone walking hunched over could. I pulled the gag out of his mouth and helped him move into a normal sitting position.

Jerry worked to talk and I realized his mouth was too dry to speak. Looked into my purse. The BT was flashing green. Nice to know it worked. "Hang on, let me see if I have any water in here." My hand hit something that sure felt like a water bottle. Pulled out a bottle of Dasani, got it opened, and got some into Jerry's mouth.

He swallowed, nodded, I gave him another drink, he swallowed that, then he heaved a sigh. "It's really good to see you, Commander."

The flyboys still called me Commander in part because they knew I missed that job so much and also in part because they still considered themselves my team, even though they were loyal to and loved Tim just like I did. They also called me Commander when we were in active or danger situations, and this was both.

"Let's get you untied."

Lizzie was on the walkie-talkie while White and I got

Jerry untied, which only happened because I audibly searched for my Swiss Army knife in my purse and Algar again delivered. "We've found someone Kitty called Jerry, over."

The walkie crackled. "Excellent," Adriana replied. "We have six P.T.C.U. here, over."

"We still have totes more places to look, over."

"Us too. All prisoners are suffering from exposure and dehydration, over."

"Totes same here, over."

"Still no phone coverage, over."

Looked at my phone and shook my head. "We don't have any either, over," Lizzie shared.

"Continue looking, we'll determine what to do once we have everyone found. Out."

"How long since anyone gave you water or fed you?" I asked.

"Days," Jerry said. "When Drax had us we were fine. I mean we were prisoners and pissed as hell, but we weren't mistreated. In fact, we were treated really well. But he kept us captive in the helicarrier, and when that got taken we were turned into real prisoners." His eyes flashed. "Thomas Kendrick—"

"Isn't the guy who took you guys. It's an android version. There were a dozen of him, and twenty more, but we've destroyed all of them. Well, other than the one that took you guys."

"Let's get you out of here," White said, helping Jerry up as much as we could under the low roof circumstances. "We can discuss things outside."

Realized that the Chili Peppers were still on repeat. "I think we need to check down the other paths here."

Jerry nodded. "They split us up so no one could work together."

"Listen," Lizzie said. "Do you hear more thumping? It's really faint, but I think I hear it."

"Yeah, I do." We were back at the intersection. Pulled the BT out of my purse. It was still bright green. Of course, Jerry was with us. Realized that Kendrick wasn't wrong—this thing still needed refinements. Dropped it back into my purse. "Let's go right first. Jerry you want to wait here or come with us?"

"I'm sticking with you, Commander."

"Can't blame you." We hunched our way down this way and came to another door. White had Lizzie help keep Jerry upright, then he pulled the door open.

"Chip!" Walker was in there, in the same trapped position that Jerry had been in. Whoever had put them in here had been both methodical and very clear about what to do to keep them basically immobile without actually harming them.

We raced in and did the same thing—I got the gag out of his mouth, gave him a couple sips of water, then White and I got him unticd.

"Commander, it was Thomas—"

"No, it was his android. Long story, will catch you up when we've found everyone."

Walker managed a weak grin. "Gotcha."

Lizzie kept Jerry and White took Walker. The flashlight and I led the Hunchback Way and headed for the other side of this path. Did my best to ignore the scrabbling—getting the flyboys and the others was worth wading through God alone knew what and being watched by rats and/or worse.

Last door, and this time I held Walker while White pulled the door open. "Matt!" Hughes was in the same position the other two had been, not that this was a surprise by now.

White took Walker so I could go in first and get Hughes ungagged and give him water. Had to untie Hughes on my own, but was getting good at it by now.

"Commander, Kendrick is—"

"At the White House with Jeff. He's not who took you, his android did and he wasn't aware that he had one."

"Why isn't Jeff with you?" Hughes asked, sounding worried.

"Long story. Which we'll go over once we're out of here. Are the three of you injured in any way?"

They all shook their heads. "Just our pride," Jerry said.

"Yeah, we all feel that, trust me. Okay, let's get going."

Helped Hughes up and we made what now felt like a long, hunched trek to the stairs. Getting the flyboys down was a little dicey, but they hadn't really been roughed up, just tied up, so while they were having some difficulties, they didn't seem injured.

Standing upright felt awesome, but we needed to get them out of here and into fresh air. Which we did, and at a faster speed since we could walk like humans now.

Once outside, we got them to a reasonably uncluttered spot and got them sitting down normally. Well, after White and I both hugged each of them tightly. The flyboys were wincing against the sunlight. My rage was building again, which was good, since we still had a long way to go to find everyone else.

"Guys, did you happen to see Camilla, Rahmi, or Rhee at all since you've been captured?"

They nodded. "Camilla found us at Drax's," Jerry said. "She didn't think we were in danger and she was gathering intel, so she and the princesses were staying on the helicarrier with us, only they were hidden. She was working for Drax already, apparently, but she didn't let him know she was there."

"Yeah, she's our Cinderella Undercover." Sadly, Algar didn't give me a tune change.

"Everyone was okay with that," Walker said. "At that point, we just figured that we'd all get whatever information we could and report back if we were traded for other prisoners."

"Or we'd just take the helicarrier when Camilla gave the okay," Hughes added. "But when the android of Kendrick took us, he found them. I don't know what happened to them after that, but I know they were captured, too."

My stomach clenched. "Do you know if they're hurt or . . . worse?"

"I think they're still alive," Walker said. "No idea if they're in bad shape or not, though. But I don't think they were able to put up a fight."

"There was some sort of stasis thing I guess Drax had created," Hughes said. "I think it was like what was used on us when we were captured by the Rapacians, only more sophisticated."

"I'm officially sick and tired of being captured, by the way," Jerry added.

"I'm sure the others agree." Wanted to ask Lizzie to contact Adriana but "Look Around" was still on repeat. "Mister White, we need to go back in there and search the lower floor."

"We can't leave these guys here alone," Lizzie said.

"Good point. Guys this is Lizzie, aka Quick Girl. She's Siler's adopted daughter. Lizzie, Jerry Tucker, Matt Hughes, and Chip Walker. They're Navy pilots assigned to Airborne for Centaurion Division, so they report to Tim, who I'd love to be able to reach, but we still have no cellular service around here."

"I think the helicarrier does," Jerry said.

"And if we could figure out how to get into it, that might be viable. I can see the suggestions and questions forming, please save them. I think everyone who was taken will have the same questions, and I'd just love to tell you all the answers at one time, versus over and over again. Plus, I want to find everyone or confirm that we can't find them before we worry about the helicarrier. Just know that Lizzie's fourteen, on our side, quite the little butt-kicker, and is on the other side of the walkie from Adriana, Abigail, and Mahin."

"I could totes catch them up while you two go do your thing."

"Or there's also that option. But, Lizzie, remember that they and the others don't know about anything that's happened since before we got on the Murder Train, so save the big reveals for me and when we're all together."

"Why?"

"Because I said so."

She shot me a dirty look. "You're not my mom."

"Yeah? Just think of your other code name as Robin and take any issues up with Vance."

With that White and I headed back into the cafeteria.

CHAPTER 60

WE DID ANOTHER fast but more intensive search of the main floor and still found nothing and nowhere someone could be stashed. Then we headed downstairs, with me hoping that the Romanians used the extra-long-lasting batteries in their flashlights.

The lower level didn't match the upper ones, so there was only one long corridor. Naturally the stairs going down were in the exact middle of this corridor and also of course it was pitch-black, smelled of death and decay and other horrible things, and was the creepiest place we'd visited yet. On the plus side, it was a normal-sized floor, so we could walk upright like we were all evolved and everything. On the not plus side, the BT was back to its yellow-green, meaning it was unlikely the other flyboys were in the building.

"I feel so lucky," I muttered to White as I played the flashlight around to make sure we weren't about to walk into the Creepy Bat Cave or the Viper's Nest. Thankfully, saw no slitheries of any kind, for which I was profoundly grateful.

"Truly." White had a firm hold on my hand, which was nicer than the death grip I had on his. "I believe I'll hold off on shouting down here, unless you think it prudent."

"No, let's just go to each end and see if there are small rooms or whatever."

We went at human normal speeds. Slow human normal. Not to extend our stay in the lovely Basement of Doom, but because it was so dark that the light from the flashlight just seemed to be swallowed up, and tripping around here was not something either one of us was looking forward to.

"What's with the shoes, do you think?" I asked as we went past yet more pairs. The ones down here were work-boots, ballet slippers, and ice skates. "I mean, none of this is normal, but the shoes thing is beyond weird."

"No guess," White said. "I'm trying not to focus on them, and I suggest you do the same."

"Do I even want to know what you've noticed about them and haven't shared?"

"No," he said firmly, "you do not."

"Okey dokey. On a different but still not cheery note, any guess as to what's happened to the Peregrines or Poofs?"

"I have no idea. That's your area of expertise. However, I don't believe this is the place where you want to try to have them gather to rejoin you."

"No, not at all."

We didn't talk for the rest of the way, in part because it was suffocating down here. Was hoping we wouldn't find anyone here because I was even more worried about how they'd be doing than how Jerry, Hughes, and Walker were doing.

Reached the end of the corridor. No special room, but there were four metal cabinets that looked heavy and also like they were blocking something. There was just a little space between the top of the cabinets and the ceiling, meaning there was some air coming in. So to speak, in this particular atmosphere.

White and I moved them—tons of fun since I had to put the flashlight into my purse because the cabinets were heavier than they looked, so the light was moving around and not shining anywhere we needed it—but we were re-warded.

There were two men here, gagged of course, and tied back-to-back, sitting with their legs out straight and also tied at the ankles and knees. This was reminiscent of how the Dingo and Surly Vic had tied up Amy and Caroline during Operation Sherlock. However, these people were jammed into the walls in such a way that they couldn't move.

Mr. Flashlight shared that one was white and one was black, but both were in black Armani suits. Hard to tell with gags in their mouths, but I was willing to bet that they were both really great looking.

This meant either of them could have based out of half of the Centaurion bases around the world. However, since I knew we'd lost four Field agents during Operation Epidemic, that they were assigned to D.C.—and therefore that I should know who they were—was a given.

Didn't recognize either one of them. This meant nothing, of course. They could have been working with me for years and I probably wouldn't have been able to pick them up out of a lineup.

"Their necks are tied, too," White said quietly.

"It's because they're A-Cs. They needed more control than the humans." Which truly boded for the princesses.

Pulled out the Swiss Army knife I hadn't owned until we'd found Jerry, and White and I went to work. Carefully took the gags out of their mouths while White started to cut the bonds around their necks.

"Don't try to talk. I'll give you water as soon as it's safe for you to drink it."

"These aren't rope," White said tensely. "The knife has dulled already. They seem to be a metallic alloy of some kind."

Looked into my purse. "I wonder if I have some kind of metal cutters just stashed away in here for a rainy day." Dug around and, sure enough, a pair of sturdy metal cutters came up.

White shot me an appraising look. He didn't say anything—he couldn't even if he'd wanted to, since Algar wouldn't have allowed it—but I got the distinct impression he'd figured out that Algar had turned my purse into a portal.

That he wholeheartedly agreed on this course of action wasn't in question, of course. White took the cutters from my hand. "I'm so glad you always come prepared for any and all eventualities, Missus Martini."

"Let's just say that I've learned to roll with anything and everything possible and leave it at that. I'm hoping I have more water in there, too." The A-Cs were clearly going to need more than the three flyboys had. And I had no idea if Adriana had any water with her, or if all the people they'd found and hopefully were still finding were out of luck.

White got the steel bonds off of the agents' necks and I gave them both a couple of sips of water. Then let them each take a slightly larger drink. "Sort of swish that around in your mouths before you swallow."

They both nodded and did as suggested and White introduced them as Daniel and Joshua, who was the white guy, both from South Africa. "How did you find us?" Daniel managed to croak in an accent that was probably really adorable when he actually had saliva around to help out.

"Long story. We're still finding the others, so everyone gets to get rescued, get into the fresh air, and once we're all together, I'll share our Campfire Stories."

It took much longer because thick wire didn't cut any faster than rope did, and there were a lot more bonds on these guys than we'd dealt with so far. But finally it was done. White took Daniel, who was the empath and therefore the bigger guy of their team, while I took Joshua, who was the imageer.

Both guys had trouble standing and more trouble walking. We were able to go at hyperspeed, though, so that was a huge help. I was definitely angry enough that the skills were working just fine.

Left them outside with the others who were, thankfully, exactly where we'd left them, then White and I headed back to do the other half of the lower corridor.

"Do you think we'll find others here?" he asked me as we made our way as carefully as before, but much more quickly.

"Yes. Our people were stashed by androids, and machines definitely like symmetry and things being even and so forth."

Sure enough, we got to the end and, after moving the heavy metal cabinets, we found our other set of Field agents, bound exactly like Daniel and Joshua had been. These turned out to be Lucas, the imageer, and Marcus, the empath, both from Spain and based originally out of Euro Base. As with Daniel and Joshua, they'd been assigned to the D.C. duty because they were considered a top team.

Got them topside without too much issue, but still it had taken a while. And yet "Look Around" was still going on. Seriously had to wonder if Algar thought I was an idiot or couldn't count.

Then it dawned on me that he might be trying to tell me something else. So, I did as the song suggested and took a look around.

"What are you looking at?" Lizzie asked.

"Everything. Nothing. Just looking around."

"Adriana's team has found the ten Secret Service agents who were taken. They're moving them to the car. They can't use hyperspeed, though, because none of their rescued folks have taken the cure. Think we should move our people there, too?"

"Probably, yeah." The Kendroid had taken the keys but the car could be hot-wired. It couldn't hold everyone, but it could take the worst to the nearest hospital if nothing else, and they could call for help. "Help. You know, seriously, why isn't the cavalry here?"

"Because they can't find us?" Lizzie asked.

"Yeah. And yet, they should be able to, wouldn't you think? I mean, my phone was on for the entire drive here . . ."

"What?" White asked me. "I know that look."

"He said he had a GPS scrambler. And I was all kinds of polite and didn't ask if it was inside of him or not."

"You mean the Kendroid?" White asked.

"Yes, and once again, let me mention how much I love that you embrace my names for things. I think the GPS scrambler is inside of him, not inside of the car. Meaning he's sent is and is continuing to send our people on a wild goose chase of some kind."

"Adriana agrees with you," Abigail said as she appeared out of nowhere. "Meaning that if we want help, you, me, or Uncle Richard have to literally run for it and hope to get some help, or we have to find the Kendroid and make him turn off the scrambler and cellular obstructer we're all sure he has on him, too."

"We still have five people missing, too. We have to find them first." And the song was still going on. Thankfully I really liked it, but obviously I was missing something and Algar was going to play this song until I freaking figured it out.

There were at least three huge buildings to check, and probably more, since this place was surrounded by forest. Even with hyperspeed it was going to take us time to find the others. And the people we'd found didn't seem to be doing that well, the A-Cs in particular, faster healing or no faster healing.

So maybe I needed to look around at the entire complex. After all, there might be a building that screamed Hostage Center more than the others. Or maybe I'd find someone to help us. Or the Kendroid.

"You three get everyone to the car so we're all together. I'm going to check the perimeter and see what I can find. But I'll need the walkie."

Lizzie handed it to me. "You sure you should go alone?"

"Yeah, our people need help. I won't enter a creepy building alone." Everyone around me snorted. "I think I should resent that. Look, I'll have the walkie, and I'll keep in touch."

"I don't like the idea of you going alone," White said.

"I know. I'm not thrilled with it. But I just know we need to hurry up. I'll stay in contact, I promise." And with that, I took off running.

CHAPTER 61

GOT OUT OF SIGHT, stopped, and looked in my purse. "A pair of jeans and a pair of Converse, please and thank you." Reached in, was rewarded. "Socks, too. You really and truly are the best."

Quickly pulled the jeans on, then took my skirt off, just in case we had the most unhelpful paparazzi in the world lurking about. Then I put on the socks and thankfully changed my shoes. My feet might have loved Algar most of all.

What to do with the skirt and pumps was now the issue. Wrapped the skirt around the pumps and put them on the top of my purse. They could come in handy. Weirder things had been before, after all.

Checked the BT. Still the yellow-green color. Of course, three of the five flyboys were in the vicinity. However, it had definitely shown green when we were near them. For all I knew, it had done so outside of the building they were in and I just hadn't paid attention. Decided to keep the BT out.

Headed off again, as if 2nd Street went on, which it didn't. There were several buildings that were clearly part of Forest Haven since they were in horrible decay. A couple of them were near what looked like a brand-new facility that was what Lizzie had spotted. But the fencing seemed quite high and even though I was sure those of us with hyperspeed could get in, Lizzie's point about getting out again was key. I didn't want to use the FLOTUS Card here, for a variety of reasons.

The decrepit buildings were bordered by dense forest and what I was now certain was a detention facility. The high wire fencing that went around what looked like a track or a football field as well as the rest of the place was something of a clue. The BT didn't change color by any of them. So, nothing else to see here.

Headed back to where I'd started, essentially, this time following a street that proclaimed itself Forest Haven Avenue, going what I kind of thought was east. There was the one building to my left that we'd been headed to when Lizzie had thought to have us check the car, and three big ones to my right—the BT remained yellow-green.

Ahead of me the street turned into a path. Followed this and finally came to a really creepy building surrounded by forest. Did a fast run around. No signs of anything or anyone, but that meant nothing. Looked at the BT. It wasn't full green, but it was definitely less yellow-green.

Really wanted to go in here and not just because the BT might be indicating Joe or Randy were here. I also wanted to check it out because I felt in my bones that if Stephanie had chosen one of these buildings as her Supervillain Lite Lair, this was the one. However, I'd promised I wouldn't go into the creepy buildings alone and, frankly, the idea of going into even the chapel by myself was a lot more than I felt able to handle unless it was absolutely necessary.

Ran back and this time went to the south, behind the three big buildings. Hit the street we'd come in on, though I was on a part I hadn't seen before. The biggest building yet was on the other side. It looked like ten large interconnected buildings, really. This also had three of the big metal containers near different doors. The BT remained yellow-green around this section.

There was something about this place, though—any time I was near it, the sun seemed to disappear even though it was right there in the sky. Decided I was getting far too spooked and now wasn't the time to bravely do things I'd promised not to.

Went the rest of the way down this street and was rewarded with the sun not disappearing for no good reason. The street dead-ended at some trees. But it started again on the other side of the trees—and the even higher double fencing topped with barbed wire that was on the other side of the trees, just before the road started again. Lovely neighborhood.

Could see buildings beyond the trees and there were cars and diesel trucks parked there. Decided to check in. "If you guys checked all the buildings to the so-called west, then I think we have eight left to go through." Waited. Nothing. "Oh. Over."

"You're new at this, I see," Adriana said. "But yes, we checked all the buildings, including the one that seems to be a part of the prison but is not. Over."

"Aha, so you guys saw that, too. We vetoed going there for help. What did you guys think? Over."

"We think that we are not supposed to be here and that no one is going to believe we are who we say we are until it becomes an incident that will make your enemies very happy and your husband miserable. Over."

"Nice to be on the same page. I'm by what looks like another prison. Or detention center. Or something else that requires a lot of barbed wire and such. Though the barbed wire could be there to keep that place separated from this one, since it's more along what I think is the property line as opposed to around the facility. Over."

"Mahin says that we are actually quite near to NSA headquarters and feels that where you are might be related to that. Or it could be benign and merely trying to ensure that whoever comes here doesn't go there. However, as with the prison, going there for help might be inadvisable. Over."

"Yeah, that was going to be my question, so thanks for anticipating. We need more water. And a rescue. Are you all still with the car? Over."

"Yes. Over."

"Great, coming back. Over. Um, sorry, out." Contemplated if I should change back into my skirt and pumps, but my feet said that there was no way they were going back into the FLOTUS Shoes. Decided I'd come up with some lame story, kicked up the hyperspeed, and rejoined everyone.

Seeing over twenty people sitting in, on, or around the limo really brought two things home—one was that we needed to get help, pronto, and two was that we needed to find our remaining missing people sooner than we needed to get help.

Interestingly, no one mentioned my change of clothes. Figured that either they were all too stressed and such to notice or that Algar was ensuring that they couldn't notice. Chose to totally not care.

"What's our game plan?" Jerry asked.

"Find the others and get the hell out of here would be my recommendation," Hughes said dryly. Everyone else nodded.

"We have one car and it won't hold enough people, so until the cavalry arrives . . ." Looked at the A-Cs. "Hey, Dan and Marc, what are you feeling around this place? I mean, can you pick up anything other than those of us here?"

"I can't feel anything," Daniel said, clearly trying not to wince at his new nickname.

"I can't, either," Marcus added, while trying less hard to hide the wincing. "I was thinking that our kidnappers must have done something to us."

"Drax didn't," Daniel said. "I could still feel everyone when he took us. I didn't stop feeling until we got kidnapped by what Missus Martini is insisting is an android."

"Oh, my God, it's Kitty, period. Commander if you must have a title for right now. And he's definitely an android, and that would mean that said Kendroid has emotional overlays and blockers inside of him, too, which makes sense. But that means there are more of them here, because the Kendroid wasn't at this location all the time since you guys have been taken."

"What does that indicate for assistance?" White asked. "Again, I know that look."

"I've been really enraged a couple of times. And I'm sure some of us were scared. In fact, I'd think everyone we've already rescued and those still missing were and are mad and scared as hell."

"And?" one of the P.T.C.U. personnel asked.

Abigail jerked. "And why hasn't the strongest empath in at least this part of the galaxy—who was actively looking for his missing people—picked up anything?"

"More to the point," Mahin said, "why hasn't he picked up where Kitty is?"

"Because he can't, because whatever Stephanie has going on here, she's already set it up so that her uncle can't find her or anyone she takes captive. I'll wager that she has something here that affects imageers, too."

"We're all still affected from what they hit us with three

years ago," Joshua said. "But I'm willing to bet that if I tried to read anything, I couldn't." Lucas nodded his agreement.

"So no one is coming to help us," White said. "Meaning it's up to us to find the rest of our missing people and that helicarrier."

Decided to go with my gut. "I think I found the place that's most likely to have the rest of our people. I could be wrong, though. There aren't enough of us to search every building at once, and we don't have enough walkies for more than two teams. Thoughts?"

"Missus Martini, myself, and Adriana as the strike team. Everyone else here."

Adriana nodded. "I agree with Richard." She handed her walkie to Lizzie.

"Should one of us try to find a store or something?" Lizzie asked. "Everyone needs water and they're all totes hungry, too. And most of them are at least a little hurt. And maybe we could, you know, phone home or something."

The "little hurt" observation looked to be a gross understatement. Had no idea what the conditions the Secret Service captives had been in, but they looked flat-out awful. The P.T.C.U. folks looked like the flyboys—they'd seen better days. And it was a tossup as to whether this had actually damaged the A-Cs' healing factors or if they were so badly injured that natural repairs were taking a long time.

"I'm worried about leaving, honestly."

"Why?" Adriana asked.

"Because I don't want to, say, send Abigail off so that the Kendroid can grab her. Then we're waiting for rescue that won't come or we have to send someone else, who gets captured, and so on."

"Why do you think I'd get captured?" Abigail asked.

"Because the Kendroid is still at large and I think he's slavishly trying to get Stephanie's takeover bid back on track."

"Kitty, you're probably right, but everything we'd need is in the helicarrier," Jerry said. "Food, water, medical—it had it all. And our jets."

"Super. Anyone know how to get into an invisible thing we can't see?"

"I say we just go back to where it is and start feeling

around," Abigail said. "What are the chances we'll actually hit something dangerous?"

"High," the flyboys said in unison.

"I don't think it's where you all think it is," Daniel said. Joshua nodded. Nice to see they were a synced team.

This earned him the group's attention. "Beg pardon?" I asked for all of us.

"It's bigger than the space you all think it's in. We've been discussing it, so I know where you think it is, and we looked as we came to the car. I know everyone's basing their idea of where the helicarrier is due to crushed trees. But other things could have done that."

"How do you know how big it is?" White asked.

"When we were captives with Drax we weren't really shackled up," Joshua replied. "We had free run of the helicarrier. We couldn't touch anything we weren't supposed to—the ship was set up to prevent that and it did, effectively."

Daniel nodded. "So we," he indicated Joshua and himself, "ran it. And we timed ourselves. We know how fast we run, and we did tests. It's too big to be where you think it is."

"Then where is it?" Hughes asked. "It's not hovering in the air or something."

"Are you sure it's here?" Walker asked. "I mean that seriously. Just because it took us here doesn't mean they left it here."

"There's only one guy who can fly it right now. Trust me, it's here." Thought about it. "Dan or Josh, has either one of you seen *The Avengers*?"

They both nodded. "Yeah," Joshua said, clearly as enamored of his nickname as the others were. "We both saw it. Why?"

"Would you say Drax's helicarrier is around the size of the S.H.I.E.L.D. helicarrier?"

"A little smaller, actually," Daniel said. "But along those lines."

"Awesome. I know where the helicarrier is, then. And probably where the Kendroid is as well."

CHAPTER 62

"WONDERFUL," White said with enthusiasm. "Where are they?"

Everyone looked at me expectantly. "We need to save the others first." This earned me looks of confusion and frustration, depending.

"Not that I'm arguing," Abigail said, "but why don't you have the rest of us get the helicarrier while you and Uncle Richard get the others?"

"Because I think it's going to take subterfuge to get it, because I'm pretty sure that's where our missing android is hiding out. It's probably helping him send out the GPS scrambling and cellular dampening, too. I think that if we wander over there and seem to be searching that he'll zap us or grab us or something. And, since we're in a danger situation, I'm going to be brutally honest—out of every person here, the one most likely to get the Kendroid to see our side of reason is me."

Lizzie nodded. "My dad says that's one of your skills—flipping enemies."

"Out of the mouths of children and all that. And before you say whatever retort I can see forming, Lizzie, just know that it's an old saying and let it go."

Lizzie closed her mouth, shot me a glare, then grinned. "Fine, fine. But I think you're right." She swallowed. "And I think you guys are going to need me on the strike force team."

"Why is that?" White asked, sounding like Christopher normally did when I suggested White do something dangerous.

"Because I'm the smallest, so I can get into places you guys can't. And because my dad and the uncles trained me."

"Speaking of which," Walker said, "when do we get to find out what the hell is going on?"

"Fine, fast update, I'll do a recap when we find the others. Cliff Goodman launched a bioterrorism Doomsday plan that ended up backfiring, but not before it killed a variety of people, including President Armstrong."

Everyone stared at me. "That means Jeff is the President," Jerry said finally.

"Yep."

"Wow," Hughes said. "That means you're the First Lady."

"Yep." Saw the Secret Service and P.T.C.U. folks all get a hell of a lot more alert, feeling awful or not. "And while I can see that many of you are about to try to give me the old wheeze that you now need to stagger up and take the bullets for me, my reply is simply this—hells to the no. This is my turf, in that sense, I'm in charge, and I'm staying in charge. Period."

"There are other ramifications," White said.

"Like the fact that the uncles died to save me." Figured using that term wouldn't freak out the Secret Service and P.T.C.U. folks but would tell the flyboys what was going on, which, based on their expressions, it did.

"But a goodly portion of the leadership of this country was killed," White added, "along with many other innocents."

"New people are in the roles now, and while Cliff got away, again, he was unmasked as the Mastermind on national and international TV. Guaranteed the person behind you guys getting taken by the Kendroid is Stephanie. There is another plan going, too, that involves robots, but that you're going to have to wait for until we find the others. Drax isn't actually a bad guy, he's just from a planet far, far away and unclear on how to actually do a good sales pitch. Thomas Kendrick is also not a traitor as far as we've been able to tell. Abby, Mahin, if they must know details, enjoy sharing."

Lizzie handed her walkie to Abigail and took White's hand. Adriana took her other hand.

"Anything else you want to share?" Abigail asked me.

"Don't get separated. Don't leave this area. But someone

try to hot-wire the car. Team Terror, let's head to where I think the rest of our people are being held."

"I'll provide the speed?" White asked.

"And I'll steer because, don't faint, I actually know where we're going."

"I remain impressed."

"You need to work on your lying skills, Mister White."

"I'll keep it in mind."

We zipped off to the building that had given me the distinct feeling that something was going on inside of it. The building was a large rectangle, one story, with forest and scrub growing closely around it. There was also a broken-down, ancient bus at the start of the woods on the side where the entrance was. The entrance faced away from the rest of the vast complex, which might have been why it seemed suspicious to me.

"Well, this place is beyond totes creepy." Lizzie looked around. "Think there are things in the woods?"

"Define 'things.' Just kidding, don't. And I'm sure there are. The question is, what's inside of this place?" Checked the BT. Couldn't swear to it, but it looked more green and less yellow. Handed the walkie to Lizzie, then got my Glock in my right hand and the flashlight in my left. "I'll take point, Adriana, you bring up the rear. Lizzie in front of you and behind Richard."

Everyone nodded and we walked through the doors that, interestingly enough, did not say No Trespassing. The interior was possibly the worst we'd seen yet—there was an accumulation of so much ancient junk that it was hard to identify what most of it was. Old computers, chairs, desks, sports equipment, medical equipment, beds, and more. And, of course, shoes. More and more shoes.

The shoes here weren't in neat piles. They were thrown everywhere and no pairs were together. Actively chose not to focus on this, because I was sure it meant something horrible.

The others linked up, then White and I trotted us through at the slow version of hyperspeed. Fewer windows here than in some of the other buildings, and less breakage of said windows. They were all filthy, so it was darker than many of the others we'd visited.

Mr. Flashlight was still going strong, however, so it was

relatively easy to see. The entire place was the same as the first room we'd come into, and most of the walls were down or so broken that they might as well have been down.

The ceiling didn't look much better and was sagging in places. Trees had managed to grow here, too, and a few had broken through the roof, letting light filter in in ways that managed to make the place even eerier than I'd have thought possible.

But there was one thing missing. This place didn't stink.

Oh, sure, there was the smell of decay and such, but for the amount of ruin here, it should have been as bad as the other buildings, if not worse. But it wasn't.

"You sure this is the place?" Lizzie asked.

"Yes. Look for a way to get underground."

"Do we have to touch things?"

"Since when did you get so dainty?"

"Since we went into that cafeteria."

"Good point. Let's hope not." Wondered if I had any of the evidence gloves Serene's team used with me, or if I could or should ask for some. Decided to cross that bridge when we discovered it burned down.

Midway between the two biggest trees that had broken through was an area that was relatively clear, except for a broken-down wheelchair that looked like it had been used to beat androids dead. It was sitting almost bathed in light.

"It's under that," I said to White. "I'm positive."

He nodded. "I don't see any signs of a trapdoor, however."

Went up to the wheelchair and shoved it out of the way with my foot. Nothing happened. But I noted that the floor moved in a way that floors didn't normally. "I think there's a tarp down here, or something like it, that's camouflaged to look like the rest of this place."

Adriana also had a flashlight, and she played hers around the area. She shoved the wheelchair back with her hip. "I believe that the wheelchair does not mark the doorway, but rather we should look where it was facing."

Did as she suggested. The chair had a great view of the biggest tree to break through. "Huh." Went over, paying attention to how the floor was reacting to my footsteps. The tarp was still under my feet.

Reached the tree, kicked the various pieces of crap that

were here away, and found the edge of the tarp. Used the Glock to flip it back. Sure enough, there was a wooden door here. "Score another one for Adriana."

"It's a team effort," she said as the others joined me. "Who goes down first?"

"Me, but Mister White, if you'd be so good as to carefully open the door?"

He nodded, pulled a handkerchief out of his pocket, and used that on the handle. "I'm not dainty, but I don't know what might be on this."

"You think she'd put a toxin on the handle of her own trapdoor?"

"I think she would if she'd already taken the cure. Our recent brush with infectious disease is still quite fresh in my mind."

"Hang on. Let me see if I have any of the evidence gloves Serene had me using earlier." Dug through my purse. Sure enough, four pairs were available. And the BT tracker was a brighter green. We put the gloves on while I mentally thanked Algar, ACE, Naomi, Sandy and the Superconsciousness Seven, and any other powerful beings who might be taking note and helping out.

White still used his handkerchief to open the door, but the extra protection of the gloves was appreciated by all. Sure enough, there was a stairway leading down. Sniffed. Didn't smell anything like we'd found in all the other underground rooms here.

"Reminds me of Bizarro World. I'm definitely going first, and Mister White, no worries, I'll be looking for traps like you wouldn't believe."

So saying, I headed down at a very slow and cautious pace.

CHAPTER 63

FLASHLIGHT OR NO flashlight, visibility was close to nil. We were back to inky blackness that swallowed light, meaning even though I was being extra-cautious, I could easily miss something.

However, I made it all the way down without issue. We were in a short corridor that appeared to be made of cement. It was decently wide, though the ceiling was low, but not so low that White had to hunch.

We walked about fifty feet with no incident and reached a door. It had an old-fashioned door handle, one where you had to push down on a lever with your thumb to open it.

I handed the flashlight to White and touched the handle lightly and quickly. Nothing happened. Took the handle in my hand. No electroshock. So far, so good. Then I pushed the lever down. The door didn't open.

Heaved a sigh. "I think it's locked. Adriana, who's faster at lock picking, you or me?"

"Me." She stepped forward, pulled something out of her backpack, and got to work. Heard the click of the lock opening. Adriana stepped back. "You have the gun, you go first."

"You didn't bring a gun?"

"I brought a rocket launcher."

"Good point." Took the flashlight back from White, made sure the safety was off on my Glock, then nodded to Adriana. She opened the door.

Another dark corridor. Went down it cautiously. No traps, or if there were, we didn't trigger them. Reached heavy black drapes. Moved one part of them slowly aside.

And turned off the flashlight. Because it was well lit in here. Lit with fluorescent lights.

As we stepped into the room my music finally changed. "All the Right Friends" by R.E.M. came on.

This was definitely a Secret Lab/Villain's Lair combo, but I had to hand it to Stephanie—she certainly had her own style.

First off, it was one gigantic room, with some circular walls that I was pretty positive were encircling the tree trunks. Oh, sure, there were lots and lots of various kinds of equipment with lights merrily flashing, a few big servers, also very active, and all the other Mad Scientist Lab bells and whistles. There was what looked like a throne at the far end. Either that or it was a super-duper massage chair. Really couldn't tell from this distance.

There were other rooms within this room, but they were all glass or Plexiglas. These rooms were scattered throughout—some were for medical, based on their equipment and things like hospital beds, some were for the Business of World Domination, based on their computers and phones and other items.

It was easy to see into everything. Meaning it was easy to see where Joe and Randy were. They were in their own rooms, next to each other, lying on hospital beds, next to other hospital beds that had what certainly looked like android innards on them. The guys were naked, except for a small towel to provide some modesty, and tightly strapped down. Each of the beds was hooked up to what looked like a big light board but what I was pretty sure was a computer of some kind.

The guys had thin tubes inserted into them in various places—elbow joints, knee joints, belly button, and nipples, with five tubes going into their heads. The tubes were very thin—so thin that it was unlikely that a mark would be left if they were removed. And I definitely wanted to remove them.

"Wait," White grabbed me before I could take off running. "Be sure it's them, be sure it's not a trap."

"Good point." We walked over. Took a lot of effort to walk, but we did it. Reached Joe's room first. The glass door slid open when we stood in front of it. Looked for traps. Saw none. Went inside.

Joe appeared to be unconscious but he still looked alive. Touched his wrist. Felt a pulse, but he didn't react. His breathing was shallow.

"Joe," I said quietly. "Joe, it's me, it's Kitty." No response. Shook him. Nothing. "We need a doctor, Tito, Melanie, Emily, Lorraine, and Claudia for preference."

Lizzie nudged me. "There are phones here."

"Duh, and good catch. You and Adriana go see if they work. Call your dad, tell him what's going on."

She nodded and the two of them trotted off to a clear room a couple away from where we were.

"Mister White, any guesses for how we wake Joe up?"

"None yet. I suggest we see if Randy responds better."

We went to his room. Same thing. There was a pulse and he was breathing shallowly, all his tubes were inserted into the same places Joe's were, but he gave no response. "We need to see if Camilla and the princesses are here."

White nodded and zipped off. Because I could see hyperspeed I was able to watch him for the most part. He was back quickly. "No, only Joe and Randy are in this room."

Lizzie and Adriana came back. "The phones require a code to dial out," Adriana said. "We tried several obvious ones, but they didn't work."

Resisted the urge to really curse a lot. "Fine. That means we need to do something, and there's no one we can ask for help." Considered the situation. It sucked. Forced myself to think. "Why did Stephanie go back to Drax? She had the helicarrier, she had a nice android army starting, and she had people she was going to turn into androids who would easily infiltrate our defenses." And cause heartbreak, but I didn't say that out loud. "So, why go back to him?"

"He had something she needed to do the transfer," White suggested.

"Yeah. And she didn't get it, or if she did, it's incarcerated along with her or still at Drax's place. So are the guys brain-dead yet, or are they still themselves?"

White studied the computer walls. "If I assume the lights on these boards are similar to what we use in the isolation chambers, then their brains are still active."

Lizzie stepped closer to the boards and examined them. "The uncles used to say that even the most complicated computer in the world has an off switch."

"But if we turn the machines off, the guys may die."

"Or they may wake up." Lizzie looked at me. "We have to do something."

Before I could reply, the walkie crackled. "Kitty, we have a situation, over." Abigail sounded tense.

Lizzie handed me the walkie. "So do we, what's your sitch? Over."

"Several of the hostages aren't doing well. They need water and medical treatment. As in, we have to get them to a hospital pronto. Over."

"She lives here," I said, not into the walkie but to the others with me. "That means she has food and water here. Maybe first aid stuff, I mean, there's enough medical here. The androids don't need any of that, but Stephanie does. Scatter. See what you can find." Went back to Abigail as the others took off. "Searching to see if we can find anything helpful. Over."

"What's your situation? Over."

"Um . . . we've found Joe and Randy." Gave her a fast update. "So, I don't know if we turn off the machines or what. Over."

While I waited for Abigail to respond, I tried to focus. I could ask ACE what to do, but Jamie would be awake and that meant I'd be asking my little girl to make a life or death decision for two men she loved whose children were her friends. Out of the question. Naomi couldn't really intervene here—she was being watched by the Superconsciousness Police, and taking direct action here would be something they'd really hurt her, and probably us, over.

"I don't know, either," Abigail said finally. "I just know we need to do something. Over."

"Yeah. I'll keep you posted. Out."

Went back to thinking. Algar was already helping me, probably as much as he was willing to, which had been an amazing amount, really. We wouldn't have found the flyboys and Field agents without his musical clues. But as I thought this I realized that my music had stopped once the R.E.M. song had finished. Checked my phone. It had turned off. Now wasn't a great time to run out of battery.

The others arrived, laden with water. "We found her stash," Lizzie said. "She has tonnages of water and food and supplies."

"It's definitely a bunker here," Adriana agreed.

"Great. You guys get that water to the others. Don't argue — we have people who are in terrible shape. Let's not lose the people we came here to save. I'll be fine down here. Just, you know, come back as soon as you can."

White didn't look happy, but logic won out. Adriana emptied her backpack and they filled it with water bottles. Lizzie ran off and came back with a box of food bars and another case of water. White put the backpack on and took the case of water in one hand, Adriana took the box of food bars from Lizzie, then she took one of Lizzie's hands while White took the other.

"We'll be right back," he said. "Try not to cause me to regret having to do this." And with that they took off.

Did a fast run through the entire giant room. Realized I was thirsty as well as stressed, so I grabbed a water bottle and drank it down.

Tried to wake Joe and Randy up again. Didn't work. Tried to make myself unplug their computers from the walls. Couldn't do it. Contemplated turning on my iPod but figured I might need it later and if my phone had run out of juice, it wasn't unlikely that my iPod would, too.

Took a look at my iPod, though, just in case. It was on. And the song that was playing on repeat was Oingo Boingo's "Return of the Dead Man 2."

CHAPTER 64

"**A**LL PRAISE the Great God Algar," I said under my breath. "And yes, I'm kidding. But only sort of."

Didn't need to hear the song, it was an instrumental. It was clear what Algar was telling me, based on the title. Took a deep breath, focused on the Inner Me, then took a look at the light boards behind Joe and Randy.

The lights meant nothing to me, but I ignored that. Instead I looked for patterns, to see if there was something different happening. As far as I could tell there wasn't.

This meant that I just needed to either try harder or think right. Per ACE I always thought right. So, without the assistance of our benevolent observer and with only one musical clue to go on, had to determine the right course of action to bring my two dead men back.

White, Lizzie, and Adriana returned. "We need to bring more supplies to the others," White shared. "I'm pleased to see that you haven't done anything rash in our brief absence."

"Don't expect that to last. Um, do you need Lizzie for the next run?"

"Why?" Adriana asked.

"I think I need help here."

"With what?" Lizzie sounded confused, not that I could blame her.

"With waking Joe and Randy up."

The others exchanged the "oh dear" look. "Are you sure you should try?" Adriana asked gently.

"Yes, I am. Look, I just want someone to bounce ideas off of, and Richard has to provide the hyperspeed. And, in this case, I think Lizzie will help me more than you, that's all."

White nodded slowly. "Just remember that your choices will have ramifications."

"They always do."

He gave me a quick hug, then he and Adriana went off to get more water and such and I turned back to the guys.

"They look dead," Lizzie said quietly.

"Yeah, but they really aren't. They're sleeping like it, though. So, maybe we look at this as how do you wake someone up from a hibernation sleep?"

"No clue."

"Tito knows how. He got Malcolm out of a sleep like this. Dammit, I wish we could get a call out."

"I have no bars in here. I can try more number predials to see if we can get the phone system to work."

"No, I'm sure the predial is long and complex, because to an A-C, having to punch in twenty numbers before you dial the real number you want isn't that big a deal."

"At least they don't look sick," Lizzie said, clearly trying for the optimistic spin. "The other people we've found don't, either. I mean, they look like crap, but they don't look like they have the Alien Flu."

"Yeah, if they did we could keep them going with adrenaline." Jerked. "Oh, wow. Think it could be that easy?"

"Well, if you have adrenaline and you want to give it to them, maybe?" Lizzie sounded doubtful. "But what if it hurts them?"

"I don't think it will." Dug around in my purse to find the container I always carried with me—the case that held adrenaline in case I needed to slam a needle full of it into Jeff's chest. Happily, I hadn't had to do that for a while, but the possibility was always there, and so I was always prepared. And I'd filled it up just the other day, because when it came to adrenaline, I lived the Boy Scout Motto. This stuff had saved the day during Operation Epidemic and I saw no reason why it wouldn't save the day here and now as well.

"Choose who we try first," I said to Lizzie.

"Huh? Why?"

"Because these guys are married to two of my best friends, and if I'm wrong, I want to be able to say that I didn't make the choice."

"So you want me to be the one who picks who might die? Thanks for that."

"Oh. Good point. Never mind."

"You're in front of one more than the other, so that's the guy to choose."

I was more in front of Joe. Okay, Joe would go first then. And I prayed I was right and wouldn't have to tell Lorraine that her husband was never coming home.

We went inside his glass room and took a closer look at things. "I think we want to unplug the android parts," Lizzie said finally. "Just in case."

"I agree." The wires ran into the computer board. I ripped them out and that side of the board seemed to turn off. "Can you go do the same for Randy?"

"Sure." She trotted off to take care of this and I readied my needle. White and Adriana returned again, but I ignored them. This was either going to work or it wasn't, and any more delays helped no one.

Waited one more moment—in case the Various Powers That Be decided to send me some kind of sign to stop. There was no such sign. So, I did what I'd gotten really good at over the years—I slammed the needle into Joe's heart.

Results were immediate.

His eyes flew open. "What the hell?" he shouted. Then he blinked several times and I saw him focus on me. "Kitty? Kitty, is that really you?"

"God, am I glad you're not dead. Yes, it's really me. Hang on." Ran out of the room. "Mister White, get Joe unstrapped and unplugged." Pulled out another needle, ensured that Lizzie had Randy's android innards wires ripped out of the computer board, then slammed the needle into his heart.

Results were again immediate as Randy did pretty much the exact same thing as Joe had. Managed not to cry with relief, but it was a close thing.

White had Joe unstrapped and sitting up and came in and did the same with Randy. "I haven't removed the wires," he told me quietly. "I believe we want to be careful doing that."

"I agree."

"Where are my clothes?" Randy asked. "I mean that seriously."

"No idea honestly."

"I think I found them." Adriana trotted in with what

looked like the uniforms the flyboys wore when they were in the air on a mission, which would be what they'd have been wearing when Drax captured them. "They were in what I think is the room where she does the finishing touches on the androids."

"I don't want to know, do I?" Randy asked. He went pale. "Am I . . . am I still fully human?"

"Yeah, I think you and Joe both are."

"Only just." Lizzie pointed to the android innards lying on the bed next to Randy's.

He shuddered. "Thanks, kid."

"Oh, right, you haven't met her. This is Lizzie." Gave him and Joe, who was holding the tiny towel around him while White helped him into this room, the quick update on Lizzie though I left out what else was going on. They both seemed disoriented, not a shocker, and I figured they should take in all the happenings slowly right now.

Both of them still had the wires in them, too, but they didn't mention it. "These are our clothes," Joe said, sounding relieved. He looked around. "Where are the others?"

"Jerry, Matt, and Chip are with the others we've rescued. We don't know where Camilla and the princesses are."

"On the ship," Randy said. "The helicarrier. They were hard for our captors to control, and I remember seeing them in stasis. The last thing I remember is hearing someone say they were leaving them there because they didn't want to risk letting them escape."

"I heard that, too," Joe confirmed, "and it was a woman talking."

"Stephanie."

They both nodded. "Probably," Joe said. "So, uh, can we get dressed?"

"Oh! Yeah, sorry. We'll turn around." We all did. The glass was reflective. "And close our eyes. We'll all close our eyes."

"You've already seen them naked before anyway," White said, sarcasm knob set to eleven.

"Blah, blah, blah. But that does bring up a good question. Um, guys? Can you confirm that you, ah, have all your important man parts?"

"I do *not* want to know why you're asking that," Randy said, sounding freaked out. "But yes, I do. Thank God."

"Same here," Joe added. "Should we assume we were about to lose those?"

"No, because you were supposed to infiltrate us and you couldn't have done that if you took your pants off in front of your wives. But under the circumstances, just felt it was wise to check." Cracked an eyelid. They had their underpants on. Good enough. Turned around. "Sorry about the bruising on your chests, by the way."

"I'll take it," Joe said. He looked around and, like Randy, shuddered. "How long have we been here?"

"Probably about a week. Finish getting dressed. We need to formulate a plan for how we rescue the last of our team."

"Wait to get dressed," Lizzie said, sounding urgent.

The guys looked at me. "Okay, hold on," I said, as Lizzie tugged at my hand and pulled me into Joe's room.

"What's up?"

"Tito has that thing that proves if someone's fully human, right?" she asked in a low voice.

"Right, the OVS. It determines organic from inorganic."

"Yeah. I don't think these two guys are as organic as they were a week ago."

"How do you mean?"

"I don't think the stuff we thought were plugs actually are plugs. They didn't unplug when I pulled them out of the board—they ripped."

"So? I'm not following you."

"It's not plugs or needles or tubes, going into them. What's in them are wires. Thin wires, like landlines use."

"You know what the internal workings of landlines look like?"

"Yeah, most of the infrastructure out there is landline based, and the uncles wanted to be sure I knew how to tap a phone line from a distance."

"Gotcha. And it's a great skill. But I don't see how these wires being thin wires like old phones use is relevant."

She heaved an impatient teenaged sigh. "I don't think this board is a computer so much as it's a transference device. I think that the wires from the android side were being inserted into the human side."

CHAPTER 65

"THAT SOUNDS IMPOSSIBLE." But even as I said that, I knew it wasn't. The Alpha Centauri system had things that were so advanced that to us they seemed like magic. What could a galaxy core planet have? Things that definitely seemed magic. And while this could be Drax technology, Marling had created realistic androids for years.

"Yeah? Then explain how the wires here," she indicated the stuff that was making up the android innards, "are the same color and shape as the wires going into those guys."

"There could be a noninvasive reason." Though I doubted it. Our luck didn't run that way.

"Well, I think that if we check we're going to find out that they have wiring in them already."

"How much?"

She shrugged. "I have no idea, but I don't think we should let them pull the wires out or cut them or anything. They may have to be surgically removed."

"If they *can* be removed." Looked up to see Joe and Randy watching us. Took a deep breath and went back into the room they were in.

"How bad is it?" Randy asked before I could say anything.

"We know it's bad," Joe added. "We know you, Kitty, and your expression says it's really bad."

"We're androids already, aren't we?" Randy asked, sounding calm in the way someone is right before they totally lose it.

"No. See all those wires? They're all supposed to be inside of you. You're not a full android with all of that still outside of you."

"But we're partial," Joe said flatly.

"Maybe. Lizzie suggested that we not remove or cut the wires that are in you guys. Just in case."

Both guys looked ready to ignore that and pull the wires out. In fact, their hands were moving—Joe's toward his inner elbows, Randy's toward the back of his knees.

"I thought you said these guys were smart," Lizzie said, her Derisive Teenager Tone set to eleven.

Both guys stopped and stared at her. "What?" Joe asked finally.

She rolled her eyes. "Your commander just told you to leave that stuff alone. Me, I'd totes love to see you guys, like, pull your brains out through your skulls because how cool would that be? But Kitty likes you and besides, we don't have a camera, so I can't take footage and be sure I can afford to go to any college I want."

There were a long moments of silence while Joe and Randy stared at Lizzie. I'd known these guys a long time, and I had no idea what they were going to do right now. Also didn't know how much wiring was already inside of them and how it might be affecting their thoughts and actions.

The silence went on, and I knew that it had to break in some way. Decided Lizzie had given me an opening and I should take it. "I'm ordering you both to leave that crap alone right now."

They both looked at me now, but they straightened up and put their hands to their sides. "How do we get dressed?" Joe asked stiffly.

"Really?" Lizzie shook her head. "How are we a superpower? You wrap the stupid stuff around your legs and around your arms. We find a way to cover your heads and keep those wires covered and safe. How is it that you even have to ask?"

"Fear affects everyone," Adriana said softly. "Even those trained for years to ignore it. I believe I've found head coverings." She was holding two knit caps. "The weather is a little warm for these, but they should do what's necessary."

White took one of the hats from her. "Let us help you," he said gently, as he went to Joe and gathered the wires up, twirled them together in a way that looked like it wouldn't tangle, then slipped the hat onto Joe's head. Adriana did the same for Randy. They looked kind of dorky in a cute way, but the wires were definitely hidden.

"What was Stephanie doing with knit caps?" I asked as the guys seemed to get themselves under control and started to put their pants on. White and Adriana helped them with the wires around their knees and they didn't object.

Adriana shrugged. "It gets cold here, and you think she's been here a good while."

"Good point. Did she have any long-sleeved men's shirts lying around?"

"Not that I saw." She cleared her throat. "I did find women's clothing, though. I believe you should take a look at it—it didn't appear to be clothing for Stephanie."

"I'll do that in a bit."

Joe shook his leg a little and a wire slipped out from under his pant leg. "This isn't going to work."

"I know!" Lizzie ran off.

"That kid reminds me a lot of you," Joe said quietly.

"In good ways," Randy added loyally.

"I'm sure. She's been through a lot. More than you guys, really."

"If she's been adopted by who you say, she's been through a ton." Joe sighed. "I don't feel like myself."

"Because of real reasons or because you're freaked out?"

"Probably freaked out," Randy said with a grin. "You know how much of a scaredy-cat Joe is."

Joe grinned. "Yeah, just like you, farm boy."

Lizzie returned with four elastic elbow braces and four knee braces. "The chick running this place likes to be prepared, I'll say that. These were with the first aid stuff. She's totes set up for a siege of epic proportions."

"Whatever works."

White and Adriana again helped the guys get their wires tucked safely and the elbow braces on. "Kind of restrictive," Joe said, flexing his arms.

"But not too bad," Randy added as he took his pants off and started to redo the wires around his legs. "We'll be fine." He cleared his throat. "Thanks, kid."

Joe nodded as he followed suit. "Yeah. Appreciate the help. And the ass-kicking. Normally Kitty's the one doing that."

"She likes you guys a lot more than I do. Though, to be fair, I don't really know you. Jerry's funnier, though."

"He always charms the ladies," Joe said with a sigh.

"But we're the ones who are married to the hottest women around." Randy grinned. "Present company excepted."

"Nice to see you two feeling more normal. I hate to ask this, but did anyone find their shoes and socks?"

"Socks yes," Adriana replied as Joe and Randy waved their socks at me. "Shoes, on the other hand, no."

"God, we've got more shoes to pick from than at a DSW outlet," Lizzie said. Accurately.

"I just don't think we want the guys in some dead person's ancient shoes. Plus, finding their sizes isn't as easy as just walking out and picking a pair of shoes at random."

Lizzie shot me a look that said I was getting older than was good for me rapidly. She trotted off again.

"Should you be letting a kid wander around her by herself?" Joe asked. "Even a kid as competent as Lizzie seems to be?"

"Pick your battles and all that."

Lizzie came back, holding two pairs of shoes. "These were by the tree near the entrance to this Cave of Wonders."

"I love her, I really do." Took the shoes from Lizzie and stared at them. "Um, guys? I think these are actually your shoes. They look like government issue for officers." They also didn't look like they were part of Forest Haven's Shoe Department. These shoes were used and well cared for, not filthy and filled with despair.

Handed a pair to each of them. Sure enough, the flyboys took one look at the shoes, traded, and put the shoes on. "Definitely mine," Randy said.

"Mine, too. Thanks for finding them," Joe said to Lizzie.

She shrugged. "Wasn't hard. They were just sitting there."

Managed not to mention that there had been no shoes near the entrance when we'd first come down here. Managed also not to look around for helpful ghosts. Might never sleep again, and would definitely need to go with an entourage the next time I needed to buy shoes, but I was damned if I was going to point out how freaking spooky this was.

"You want me to look at the clothes?" Lizzie asked Adriana. "If you think they weren't for Stephanie, I have a guess whose they are."

"We'll both go," I said firmly. I was still the one in charge.

Lizzie shrugged but we both trailed after Adriana. "This is the room where I found Joe and Randy's clothes," Adriana said when we reached yet another glass room. It was far away from where the guys had been and blocked by one of the tree trunks.

There were what I thought of as Washington Wife Clothes hanging neatly on a rolling rack. "Oh yeah, I think they're even Crystal Maurer's size."

"I think she was wearing something that looked just like this, only in a different color," Lizzie added. "So, that proves she's an android, right?"

"Well, no, but it ratchets the likelihood up to at least ninety percent."

"What do we do with these clothes?" Lizzie asked.

"The same thing we're doing with most of what's here — nothing."

Adriana nodded. "We will need to have personnel come back and raid this facility, but for right now, what matters isn't this. I just wanted you to see it." She cleared her throat. "I also want you to see something else."

She led us to the far side of the room, an area blocked from sight of the rooms Joe and Randy were in. There were a wide variety of rooms here that looked just like the ones the flyboys were in, complete with two beds, computer light boards, and what definitely appeared to be android innards on one of the beds in each room.

The other beds held photographs of the intended androids. Me, Jeff, Christopher, White, Gower, Reader, and Tim were all nicely represented.

"So, the little Abigail got from the androids was right — Stephanie has definite plans for who she wants to destroy and control."

"She's one wacked out bitch, isn't she?" Lizzie asked.

"She is."

"I don't know that you want the others to see this," Adriana said. "I don't think Joe and Randy will be able to emotionally handle it right now."

"I'm sure you're right. Lizzie, is your phone working to take pictures?"

"Yeah, gotcha." She pulled her phone out and took a few snaps of each of the rooms. "You're going to need to show these to Jeff to make him accept that Stephanie isn't a good person, right?"

"Got it in one."

Creep Out Time and Picture Time both over, we headed back and rejoined the men. White looked like he'd just finished a short counseling session. Considering the circumstances, he probably had. But the guys looked a little better, so the time and effort hadn't been wasted.

"Now that we're all ready to go, I wonder if we should take the computer boards with us," White said, looking worried. "If there are foreign objects in the boys, it might be best to have all the data."

"We need to bring supplies more. Besides, unless we can figure out how to make a phone work around here, we aren't taking much."

"We can come back if needed," Adriana said. "Stephanie is incarcerated, so she won't be returning any time soon."

"As long as we find the Kendroid, I agree with Adriana." Looked at the flyboys. "But that decision's up to you two."

"I don't want to cart that thing around," Joe said. "It looks heavy and it's not made for carrying."

"I'm lazier than Joe, so I agree we leave them here and take our chances."

"Super. Let's hope that decision goes better than most we make. Let's get back to the others."

Lizzie took some pictures of the computer boards while Adriana put her stuff back into her backpack and the rest of us gathered more water, more food bars, and more first aid supplies.

White pulled me aside as we gathered stuff. "I feel it again."

"Feel what?"

"That I should be remembering something about this place. It came on when we saw those glass chambers, and it's stronger here."

"Maybe you're thinking of the underground lab at Gaultier." We headed back with our cases of water.

He shook his head. "I felt nothing like this there. It feels almost like déjà vu, but it's not because you aren't in the memory. That much I know. I don't believe anyone here is in the memory."

"So, it's a memory from before I joined up?"

"No. I believe it's a memory from Alpha Four."

Was going to say more but the others were back with their supplies as well, and getting out of here was more important than White's memory concern. I insisted that all of us drink a bottle of water each, and I made Joe and Randy drink a second one each as well while Lizzie went off to search for something to use to carry the stuff in. She scrounged a sturdy box and we put all the supplies in it. The box needed two to carry it, so Joe and Randy took a side each.

"You sure you two should be carrying anything?"

They both shrugged. "I feel okay," Joe said. "The disorientation from waking up here was bad, but now I feel normal."

"Me, too," Randy said. "Well, as normal as we ever get."

We headed off at a walk since the flyboys had that box of stuff. I was prepared for the trapdoor to be locked, locking us in here, but it was open. White closed it after us and put the tarp back, then we continued on.

Giving credence to Lizzie's theory, and unlike the other hostages we'd found, now that they were up and dressed, Joe and Randy didn't seem to be having any ill effects. Tried not to worry about them. Failed. Utterly.

However, I had other people to worry about more. Camilla, Rahmi, and Rhee were most likely in the invisible helicarrier. Conveniently, I was about ninety-nine percent sure I knew where it was. Unfortunately, I was about one percent sure that I could get into said helicarrier undetected.

Meaning I was going to have to request entry. Oh well, supposedly I had a way with diplomacy.

CHAPTER 66

ONCE WE WERE out of the building I insisted that White use hyperspeed to get the supplies to the others. He agreed, took the box, and took off. The rest of us took off our evidence gloves and I had the others link up and we headed after him. Well, with one small detour.

I ran us around the entire gigantic complex, pointing out the buildings where we had and hadn't found people, and had Adriana do the same. I also showed the guys where the Presumed Detention Center was. We stopped by one of the buildings nearest to the other facility, but one we hadn't searched.

"You two are in uniform and you're in better shape than the other flyboys. If worse comes to worst, you two may have to try to get help for us from whoever's in here."

Joe's eyes were narrowed. "Mahin said we're close to the NSA?"

"Yeah, she did. Not close enough to be able to get everyone there safely, though. At least, I don't think." I had no idea where NSA headquarters was from here, and I also had no idea who there was friendly toward us or not. Sure, I was the FLOTUS now, but that didn't mean anything. In my experience, it was just going to make me a better bargaining chip.

"You thinking it's an NSA facility?" Randy asked him.

"I think it's possible. And if that's the case, then I think it's a good thing you guys didn't go there trying to get help."

"Thank Lizzie. She's the one who thought it would be easy to get in but hard to get out."

She tried not to preen, but she couldn't hide that she was pleased with the praise. "My dad's advice."

"He's a smart man," Randy said. "Joe's right, we need to steer clear unless it's our last option. We'll be treated as enemies, not people to help. And while that will stop the moment they know who we really are, the wife of the Vice President shouldn't be making unplanned visits to an NSA holding facility."

"Oh. Um. Right. You guys didn't get the last update. Um . . . I'm not the wife of the Vice President anymore."

Both guys stared at me. "What the hell happened to you and Jeff in a week?" Joe asked, sounding shocked to his core.

"Is Jeff dead?" Randy asked, sounding horrified.

"Oh, no. Others are, but not Jeff. Stop panicking, Jeff and I are still married." Barring him divorcing me for not calling him, which was not my fault. Gave the guys their CliffsNotes version of the past many days' events.

"You're the First Lady now?" Joe didn't sound like he believed it. Yeah, I didn't really believe it, either.

"Believe it," Lizzie said. "And she hates the job, but the house is nice. So far. I miss the Embassy, though. It's a lot cozier."

"I've never thought of the American Centaurion Embassy as cozy," Randy said. "So I can only imagine how you're doing, Kitty." He hugged me. "Thanks for coming to save us."

Joe hugged me, too. "What Randy said. A lot."

"Well, we were kidnapped, in that sense. I was happy to get the double, though, and rescue everyone. Which, by the way, we are not done with. Mission: Save the Rescue Team needs to roll, and roll soon."

"Yeah." Randy looked around and shuddered. "I can't believe Stephanie stashed everyone here."

"You know about Forest Haven? Are you taking the same course with my dad that Mahin is?"

"No, I watch *Ghost Hunters*, and this is one of the most haunted places they've ever been. Joe, you and Lorraine watched that episode with us."

Joe nodded. "Yeah, the people on that show were spooked to the max. They felt this place was bad news."

"And they felt it was genuinely haunted," Randy said firmly. "And by malevolent spirits as well as just trapped souls."

"Told you," Lizzie said smugly.

"What's with the shoes? Did they say?" I sincerely hoped they'd said.

Both guys shook their heads. "It's just how it is here," Randy said. "Some of them think the ghosts pile the shoes up because they can't leave."

"No one knows," Joe added. "No one's supposed to come here, but you know how people are—this place sees a lot of ghost-hunting and thrill-seeking activity. Some people who come to investigate move the shoes. The shoes are always moved back when they aren't looking."

"Officially creeped out, thanks so much. But, that begs a question—if the *Ghost Hunters* were here, and other people come here all the time, why hasn't anyone spotted us and come over to ask what we're doing here?"

"My guess is that they," Joe jerked his head toward the presumed NSA site, "just ignore anyone here. It's usually going to be ghost hunters, teenagers, or the homeless. As long as they don't jump the fence, who cares what they're doing here?"

"Adriana used a rocket launcher," Lizzie pointed out. "She used it a lot."

Joe shrugged. "If they're well-soundproofed, they might not have heard it."

"Or they heard it and didn't care," Randy said.

"Or they don't care about what happens here, even if a bomb drops," Lizzie suggested.

"Which makes them even more suspicious. Or lax in their security since anyone over here could be here spying on whatever's going on in this facility, though."

"Yeah, so let's get moving," Randy said. "Why give them a reason to check us out? Besides, the sooner we leave Forest Haven the better."

We linked up again and this time I took us back to the others. The flyboys had quite the reunion, and the rest of us ignored whatever manly tears were going on. Jerry, Hughes, and Walker were freaked out and furious about what had been done to Joe and Randy, but White kept the situation under control by reminding them that whatever was going on with Camilla and the princesses was potentially worse. That was us—keeping things calm by pointing out how much worse they were probably going to get.

I insisted that everyone here have water and food bars if they hadn't already and made those who had drink and eat more. Abigail and Mahin were already doing first aid on those who needed it, and Lizzie and Adriana started helping out. Despite the dire situations everyone had been in, a little water, food, and TLC seemed to be going a long way.

I'd been most worried about the two Field teams, but water and food had worked wonders for them and they were looking pretty close to what I considered normal for an A-C.

Once the flyboys had finished their reunion and had more food and water at my direct order, Jerry pulled me aside. The other flyboys, Lizzie, White, and Adriana came along, too. We left Abigail and Mahin riding herd on the security personnel.

"The P.T.C.U. folks can hot-wire the car," Jerry said. "I've had them wait, though, so we don't burn gas for nothing. But considering no one can make a call and, as near as we can tell, no one cares that you've been kidnapped, I think we might want them to go for it."

"I can agree with that, only we're going to have to stuff that car full of people."

"It's a limo, Kitty," Hughes pointed out. "We can get a lot of people into it."

"And they don't have to be comfy," Walker added. "Refugees get to pack in tightly, whoever's getting out of here in the car can pack in tightly, too."

"But we can't get all the people into it. And, before anyone suggests it, I'm not going to be one of those heading off for safety, because I'm not leaving until I find the team I sent to rescue you guys, not to mention my Poofs and Peregrines."

"Where do you think the animals are?" Adriana asked.

"Honestly? I think they're in the same place our last three people are—inside the helicarrier. But let's get back to the car situation first. How many people can we fit into that limo, squished up and breaking all traffic laws and rules of decorum?"

"At least a dozen," Hughes said. "Hopefully more."

"If we have people willing to get into the trunk, we could probably fit even more," Walker said.

"By the way, the Secret Service agents aren't clear on

how you roll," Jerry said. "Despite what you said earlier they want to get you under control and 'protected.' The P.T.C.U. folks don't work that closely with us, so they're more on the side of that mindset than not."

"And there are more of them than there are of us," Hughes added. "And I'm pointing that out because the moment you say what you plan to do next—which is raid that helicarrier, I'm sure—those people are going to do everything in their power to stop you."

"Thanks for helping make the decision. Have them hotwire the car. I want all the Secret Service and the P.T.C.U. personnel jammed in there. They're the ones most likely to get immediate assistance as soon as they check in anyway."

"You got it, Commander," Jerry said cheerfully. He nodded to the other flyboys, and all five of them went off to handle this. Doubted they were going to win on the first attempt but hope did like to spring eternal.

"You're sure?" White asked me.

"I am. I'd love to shove all of you into that car, too, but, frankly, I'm going to need the backup, and it needs to be backup I can count on."

"So, where is the helicarrier?" Lizzie asked. "You've been all mysterious about it."

"And I'm remaining that way until we get everyone shoved into the car." One of the P.T.C.U. guys got the car started and, the moment he did so, the arguments started too.

"They aren't going to want to go," White said. "They're going to insist that you and the other women get in, and then insist that I get in."

"Women, children, and gentlemen of a certain age first. Yeah, I know." Heaved a sigh. "Let's get over there and see if we can't get them to listen to reason."

"The First Lady saying that she plans to try to raid the invisible helicarrier that's manned by her kidnapper isn't going to sound like reason to them, Missus Martini. It barely sounds like reason to me."

"Et tu, Brute White? Really?"

He chuckled. "I'm used to you and the level of risk you find acceptable."

"Stop trying to pretend you're not an adrenaline junkie by now."

"Oh, I'd never try to pass a lie like that." We reached the car and the dispute. Wasn't quite violent enough to be called domestic, but it was heading there. "Gentlemen, if I might have a moment?"

The arguing didn't stop.

"Shut the hell up!" I didn't bellow this, though I could have. But I ensured that my voice was loud and projecting and that I was channeling Mom. The arguments stopped and I received a lot of shocked looks. Whatever. "Thanks so much. Save your breath, if you've been told you're getting into the car, you're getting into the car. Period."

Mouths opened to protest. Put up the paw. Amazing—it still worked, they all froze. "I'm not kidding. If we have to knock you out, we will do so. Frankly, it will be easier to pack you into the car like unconscious sardines, so don't push it. Many of us are in bad moods for a variety of reasons and we've never been against knocking heads. You will be getting into that car, getting the hell out of here, and getting help. This is an order and it's non-negotiable."

A big, burly Secret Service agent shook his head and stepped forward. "Ma'am, I'm sorry, but if you're going to force us to physically remove you for your own safety, then that's what we're going to do." He was possibly the biggest guy here. Did a fast comparison. Yep, definitely the biggest guy here.

"Yeah? Just how are you going to achieve that?"

He sighed. "I'm going to pick you up and put you in the car."

"Well, you can try." Moved into a fighting stance. "Come at me, bro, and feel free to bring it."

CHAPTER 67

THE BIG SECRET SERVICE AGENT looked uncomfortable, but he also didn't look like he was going to back down. "I apologize in advance." Sure enough, he charged.

I sidestepped and tripped him, because hyperspeed was awesome. Then I picked him up, because I was pissed and super strength wasn't so bad, either. Tossed him into the trunk that Walker had thoughtfully opened. This took about three seconds.

Looked around at the rest of them. "Who's going to try out their insubordination skills next? Or, to put it another way, whose ass am I going to next be kicking?"

"She's not kidding," Jerry said cheerfully. "She's used to giving orders and having them acted upon immediately."

"Which is why her team is staying with her, and why all of you are leaving," Hughes added.

The agent in the trunk had the good sense not to try to get out of it, but he did sit up. "Why are you willing to risk yourself?" he asked me. "That's our job."

"Yeah? You risked yourselves at the train station and got kidnapped, left without food and water in horrific conditions, and a lot worse was planned for you, trust me. I, on the other hand, got away from my kidnapper and got the rest of my team away from him, too. And that's just for starters. I could continue to brag on myself and my team and our awesome skills, but I'm sure that my husband is really wondering just where in the world I am, and it might be nice, and I'm just spitballing here, if the people I'm *ordering* to get the hell out of here and go bring us help would actually, you know, do what they're being told. Right. Damn. Now."

The guy who'd hot-wired the car shrugged. "You know whose daughter she is. I say we do what she's requesting." He nodded to me and got into the driver's seat.

"One person who's seeing reason. How refreshing. The rest of you? I can seriously imitate my mother if I have to. In all ways. And you're really making me want to."

The other P.T.C.U. agents apparently needed no other threats. They indicated listening to me was the right choice and most of the Secret Service agents grudgingly acquiesced.

"I have never seen people so freaking willing to get hurt as our Secret Service," I said to White while the various agents were shoving themselves into the car and who else was getting to ride in the trunk was being discussed. "I don't get it."

"They're protectors," White said, as if this answered everything.

"Yeah? I get them protecting a position, I do. But I don't get them being willing to die for someone who just wants to get them to safety."

White was clearly trying not to laugh. "And now you understand how Jeffrey, Christopher, Charles, Malcolm, Leonard, Kyle, and many others feel about you."

"Whatevs. I'm going to make Lizzie my new partner. She's less likely to toss shade like this my way."

"I'm willing," she said. "But my dad probably won't allow it."

"Lizzie, hon, as you can see by our day today, what we want and what we get are not necessarily the same things."

The big Secret Service agent I'd manhandled, whose name turned out to be Keith, gave up his place in the trunk so two smaller guys could fit in there. Other than Keith, the rest of the Security Gang was able to fit into the car, so to speak.

Had a thought and trotted over to the driver's window. He rolled it down. Handed him the BT. "As near as I can tell, this is the only electronic that's not being affected by the android who kidnapped everyone. It's dialed in to the flyboys' DNA and it gets greener the closer anyone is to them. I have no idea what's going to happen once you leave here, but in case no one can find us again for some reason, use this."

He nodded and put the BT into his vest pocket. "Got it."

"What's your name, by the way?"

"Devon Jones."

"You have any relatives named Casey?"

He snorted. "Casey Jones? Ah, no. No one in my family is that twee."

"Works for me." Hoped he wasn't lying. Then again, had to figure that if he was P.T.C.U. then Mom and Kevin had done a very thorough background check.

The guy next to him nudged him. "She's testing to see if you're related to that nutjob Club Fifty-One terrorist." Refrained from making a mind reading comment, but it took effort.

"Oh." Devon snorted. "Your mother's already checked that. And, in case you didn't know, Jones is a pretty common name."

"If we weren't so pressed for time and needing to save tons of people and probably the world somewhere along the way I'd give you a really sarcastic reply and then we could banter for a while. As things stand, my only reply is no duh and stop smart-mouthing the First Lady lest I go all FLOTUS on your ass. Now, get going. Drive carefully, at least until you're out of this area. As soon as someone has cell service, make sure they phone home."

"Thank God you're here to tell us that," Devon said. "That would never, ever have occurred to any one of us."

"Dude, I look forward to getting to banter with you at another time, I truly do."

He grinned. "Feeling's mutual. Try not to die. It'll piss your mother off to no end and, since I'm driving, I'll get the blame."

"Duly noted and I'll do my very best."

"Good plan." He rolled his window up and started off.

"Everyone's a critic." Headed back to the others as the car drove off slowly. "Fifteen men on a dead man's chest."

"Let's hope not," Keith said.

The car made it to the end of the street, then turned right. "Why are they going that way?" I asked everyone and no one.

"Where should they have gone?" Jerry asked.

"Left. At least, I think."

"No one gave them directions," Keith mentioned. "And we were all unconscious when we were brought here."

"My bad. Well, hopefully they won't stop at the NSA's detention center and all will be well." Felt it was important to remember that we needed to tell Jeff and Chuckie that no one trusted what the NSA was doing right now. But also didn't think now was the time to ask someone to take a memo to that effect.

Turned to see if I could tell if there was any action around the helicarrier. There was a good chance that the Kendroid would blast the limo to smithereens. Wasn't sure if those of us with hyperspeed would be fast enough to save them if that happened.

But there were no shots fired that I could see or hear, so decided that the Kendroid either wasn't paying attention to the car or else he had something else going on that boded for us. Figured I should bet on the latter. Either that or the limo was heading for a dead end and the Kendroid just figured he'd hit it on its way back.

Well, no time like the present and all that. "So, gang, we're going to raid a building that has an invisible helicarrier on it. I'm wide open to suggestions for how we figure out how to get inside something we can't see and which the flyboys feel is dangerous to be trying to touch."

"That's your plan?" Keith appeared to be channeling Christopher for this experience, only without Christopher's speed, strength, or experience. Lucky me. "That's your entire plan?"

"Oh, no. Not my *entire* plan. I have more. I'm just not sharing it."

"We used to think she just liked to keep everything close to the vest to keep an air of mystery," Hughes said.

"Then we found out that she has no idea of what she's doing, but likes to work on the fly," Walker added.

"It keeps life interesting," Joe said.

"We all work better when we're terrified and have no idea of what's going on," Randy shared.

"So," Jerry patted Keith on the back, "you should fit *right* in."

Keith shot Jerry a glare. Nowhere near up to Christopher's standards. I'd have given a lot to have Christopher here glaring at me right now—he'd probably be able to get into the helicarrier simply by being so fast that he could find the door in less than a minute.

"You guys complete me. Anyway, let's head on over and see what happens, though I suggest we take the remaining food, water, and first aid stuff with us, just because who knows when we'll see food and water again and because we spent a lot of effort to get this stuff here."

"And the captives will probably need it as well," White pointed out.

"And that, too. Keith, you're elected to be the pack mule. Try not to make me wish I'd tied you to the roof of the limo."

Keith shot another dirty look my way, but he loaded up the box with the remains of our stores and hefted it onto his shoulder. "I can't believe we're spending more time at Forest Haven," he muttered.

"You watch *Ghost Hunters*?"

He nodded. "This is one of the most haunted sites in the country. The thing with the shoes is the worst, but there's not a spot here that isn't filled with evil."

"I know," Randy said enthusiastically, finding the common ground of a shared TV experience. "It's even worse in person than it was watching the show."

"Just leave the shoes alone," Joe suggested. "Leave what you find where you find it."

Chose not to mention that we'd blown that one already and sincerely hoped that Lizzie and Mahin wouldn't mention it, either. Mahin didn't say anything to the others, but I was pretty sure I heard her muttering about cleansing with fire again.

"What about the trash?" Lizzie asked.

"Normally I'd say we should throw it away like good citizens, but this entire place is a garbage dump, so just leave it."

Keith nodded. "I doubt the ghosts will mind."

"Thanks for that, Keith." Considered calling him the Cowardly Lion, but that wasn't really fair. I was as creeped out here as he was, after all.

"So where is the helicarrier?" Joe asked.

"Based on what Dan and Josh said about its size, and based on things I know about its creator and things I did and didn't see, I think it's on the top of the biggest, though not the tallest, building here, the one that's just down the road a ways."

Started off with the others following me. Sadly, the

flyboys were right—I was flying by the soles of my Converse right about now. I knew where our target was, but I had no idea of how to get inside of it.

Lizzie trotted up next to me. "So, when I'm stuck writing about what I did on my summer vacation at this new school I'll be going to, any chance I can write about this?"

"No. Let's pretend that we're all conscientious guardians and that we took you to Europe or something."

"They'll totes know that's not happening. Unless we're going to Europe once we get inside the helicarrier," she added with far more excitement than I felt the suggestion warranted under the circumstances.

"You're acting like this is a summer holiday." My brain nudged. There was something about this that I needed to look at more closely. Not in regard to Lizzie, but in regard to what had happened since Crystal Maurer had shown up.

She shrugged. "So far? It kind of is. We've found everyone and they're all basically okay. We're investigating this totes creepy place, kicking butt and taking names. Honestly, it's pretty fun. I'm kind of hoping we get to go somewhere else interesting when we take over the helicarrier."

"I'm hoping we're going to Andrews Air Force Base once we get inside the helicarrier."

"Will they let us in? Or even know we're there?"

"If we radio them to let us in, yeah, they will."

"I wouldn't let us in. We could totes be bringing in shock troops or something."

"Like the Trojan Horse . . ." Stopped walking "Okay, that's it."

"What's it?" Abigail asked.

"How we're going to get inside the helicarrier."

"How?" White asked.

"We're going to give the Kendroid a present."

CHAPTER 68

"THIS IS INSANE," Keith said for, by my count, the fourth time.

"Most of Kitty's plans are," Jerry said. "But they work out. Somehow."

"I feel the love. Look, time's always of the essence and unless one of you has a better, foolproof way for us to get inside, my idea's the one we're going with."

"I'd appreciate a more thorough recap myself, Missus Martini. Mostly because I have no faith that our cavalry is coming any time soon."

"Fine, Mister White, but only to make you happy. Okay, we have to figure that the Kendroid has been monitoring what we've been doing from inside his Helicarrier Fortress. So either he didn't care that we've found and freed all the captives—which seems unlikely—or it doesn't matter to his plan."

"His plan to turn us into androids?" Joe asked.

"No. I realized when Lizzie was looking at this as a fun field trip that I was looking at the entire situation incorrectly. I was looking at it as just what you said, Joe—that we were being taken to turn us into androids or similar."

"Can't imagine why you'd think that," Randy said dryly. "Since that wasn't happening to the two of us already or anything."

"Dudes, seriously, think for a minute. The whole reason the androids work is that they're slipped in to fool people. My team was kidnapped in broad daylight. Ergo, when we come back, we can't 'slip in' and act like things are normal."

"Joe and Randy could have," Abigail said thoughtfully. "Since everyone was separated, no one could say that something did or didn't happen to anyone else."

"Exactly."

Mahin cocked her head. "This is like when we met, isn't it? We think it's one thing going on, when another is the real goal."

"Yes. Crystal Maurer wanted to go with me to Camp David. Why? Why would she even think I'd allow that?"

"She wasn't really there to find out if you'd agree to her demands," White said. "She was there to see who was with you."

"Exactly. And, you were with me, as were several others who matter to Jeff and Christopher, and that meant that they'd have not one but several hostages to discuss in terms of trade."

"Trading you for what?" Keith asked.

"Not what, who. Trading us for Stephanie. She's incarcerated and her top two androids want her back. The Kendroid in particular. The Kendroid in very particular. He thinks he's a real person, and I think I know why he does."

Lizzie made a face. "Gross. You think he's her boyfriend, don't you?"

"Yeah, I do. And I'd like to point out that only Lizzie made that leap with limited clues. So, everyone else needs to feel ashamed. Anyway, he's got the best hostages he could have in order to get Stephanie released. And we can't reach Jeff and the others, meaning that they don't *know* that we're actually all free."

"And your mother and Jeff are the ones who would approve the release," Jerry said.

"Meaning they'll be making a deal," Walker said, voice tight. "Because they'll be willing to trade her for you."

"Especially because they don't know what she's got going on here like we do," Hughes added. "Let's get this rolling."

"Shouldn't we go for help?" Lucas asked, indicating himself and the other three Field agents.

"No, Luke, because we're probably going to need your help inside the helicarrier. You and Marc were in there and Dan and Josh examined it." On cue, Lucas winced. As if he was going to escape the Nickname Game while I was rolling? "We're going to need you guys there. Plus, androids are hella strong—we need the A-C muscles."

"Should all of us really give ourselves up, though?" Mahin asked nervously. "He could just blast us."

"We're useless to him dead. He needs us as hostages to trade."

"No, he said he needed you and Uncle Richard to turn into androids," Abigail said. "The rest of us are along to make you cooperate."

"That was so Multiplan Man's Army Plan ago, Abby. He did want us for that. We've destroyed all his backup. Ergo, he can't trade android versions of me and Richard back for Stephanie. Trust me, the Kendroid has switched to the simple hostage exchange plan."

"Getting fancy hasn't worked for him," Lizzie said.

"Exactly. So, let's do what Matt said and get Mission: Be Re-Kidnapped rolling."

The others nodded in agreement, even Keith. We headed off again at a walking pace. No reason to rush, in part because that might cause the Kendroid to think we were attacking, when I wanted him to think we were surrendering or similar. The sun was starting to think about setting, meaning we'd been gone for hours now.

"I think I saw the limo go back the correct way," Lizzie said.

"Good." Waited for laser fire or whatever. None. Breathed a small sigh of relief. Gave it a shot to see if my phone would turn back on. It did and I had plenty of battery left. Decided that Algar had His Mysterious Ways and I wasn't going to argue with them. Put my earbuds in, put my music on low, and slid my phone into my jeans pocket. John Mayer's "Bold As Love" came on. Took this to mean that Algar approved my plan.

Checked my purse to see if I had any Poofs on Board. I was quite Poofless. "So, did your Poofs not stay with you guys for some reason?" I asked the flyboys.

"They disappeared right before we were captured," Jerry said. "I know because Flyer sort of said goodbye."

"Like forever goodbye?"

Jerry shook his head. "No," Hughes said. "I mean, we can't talk to the Poofs like you do, but they get their points across. They took off, I think, because they weren't sure they could get out of the helicarrier. At least that was the impression Razzle gave me."

"Dazzle did the same with me, too," Walker said.

Joe and Randy nodded. "Foo seemed stressed when it left me," Joe said.

"Yeah, Fighter didn't seem happy to go," Randy added. "But I haven't seen any Poofs, mine or anyone else's, since we were taken."

"Yeah, if Camilla and the princesses have Poofs, they weren't in evidence," Jerry said.

Rahmi and Rhee both had Poofs. Had no idea if Camilla did or not, but it wouldn't hurt to find out.

One way or the other, though, this was good information but it boded for the Poofs, since they weren't around and if they'd tried to help the Peregrines, Camilla, and/or the princesses, that meant they were trapped on the helicarrier just like all those others. And we had proof that there were things the Poofs couldn't get out of—the Poof Traps that had let Annette Dier kill Fuzzball during Operation Infiltration were Evil Exhibit A.

Thinking about how she'd murdered not only the Poof but the person said Poof had been attached to—Michael Gower—made me angry. This was good, because I had a feeling I was going to need rage, and I was having trouble getting and staying enraged around the Kendroid and this location. Had no idea if it was because I was creeped out, if there was something dampening talents or emotions or whatever like our cell phones and all the empaths' talents, or if it was simply that I kind of felt sorry for him.

Not that I was willing to give the Kendroid a lot of slack, but he reminded me a lot of The Clarence Clone—simple and innocent. Though the Kendroid was far more dangerous to us than TCC had ever been.

"Is that it?" Mahin pointed to a large building on our left.

"Nope." Led the others off the main street onto the circular drive that led to this building's official entrance. Forest Haven seemed to use these grandiose drives to indicate their top places. Or where there were the most haunts and ownerless shoes. Wasn't in the mood to place a bet, honestly.

We reached the entrance as "Knock Knock" by the

Hives came on my airwaves. Nice to see Algar keeping his sense of humor. "Oh," Abigail said. "Look at the shadows."

The sun was low behind the building, and while the invisibility or cloaking or whatever on the helicarrier was good, it wasn't quite good enough. The shadows weren't right for a building. Well, not for just a building.

"Unreal, it's really on the roof," Lizzie said.

"I love how no one believed me until now. There's a road that's just as great as all the others we've seen that encircles this place—it connects to Center in two places, not counting the two for this drive. So, if we get separated for some reason, just get to a road and follow it and it'll take you back. Once you hit Center go left to get back to the main haunted building. If you go right you hit some nice fencing with barbed wire."

"We shouldn't separate," Keith said sternly. "Especially once inside."

"No duh, which is why I said 'if.' Because it helps to have contingency plans."

"It's a good location to hide the helicarrier," Adriana said, presumably to stop our bickering. "And it allows the aircraft to take off without causing damage to the ground."

"I'd be a lot more worried about it destroying this ancient building than damaging the ground," Keith said, clearly determined to do his best to keep the bickering going.

"Keith has a good point," White said. "Every building we've examined so far has been ready to collapse. We need to exercise caution—even hyperspeed won't help us if the floors fall out from under us."

"Thanks for that, Mister Sunshine."

"What do you think crushed the trees, then?" Mahin asked. "Could there be more invisible equipment?"

"They could have played around with our jets," Jerry said. "If they landed one in the area we're talking about, it could have taken out trees."

"Not without damage to the jet," Joe said darkly.

"Dudes, damage to your pretty planes is, currently, the least of our worries." Well, it was the least of mine, since now it was time to figure out how to get in. And I had no really clear idea.

However, showing weakness and indecision wasn't a

good leader trait. "Up From Under" by the Wallflowers came on. Clearly Algar felt I needed the none-too-subtle hint.

"Let's go in. As Richard said, we need to move quickly and carefully. We're heading for the roof and I have no idea which way to go once we're inside."

"Ah," White said. "So, routine."

CHAPTER 69

AS PER USUAL, there was a big No Trespassing sign on the doors, which we ignored. We weren't linked up yet, but we ensured every human was close to an A-C. Kept Lizzie right next to me as we stepped gingerly over the threshold.

"Yay, more shoes," she said as our eyes adjusted and Adriana and I pulled out the flashlights. Heard Keith and Randy muttering about ghosts. Actively chose to ignore them.

"Yeah, I'm thrilled." The shoes were in the usual scattered piles. Nothing like the top floor of Stephanie's Secret Lab, but definitely in keeping with the Myriad Forsaken Shoes Theme the rest of this place kept to.

Daniel and Joshua took point, while Marcus and Lucas brought up the rear. This building had clearly been dorms and classrooms and such. It looked more modern, to use the term loosely. And it had the usual horrors that we'd seen elsewhere in full evidence—abandoned everything, crap everywhere, enough dust to choke a herd of elephants if the smell of decay didn't get them first, prevalent and unrelenting signs of horrific abuse, and shoes, shoes, shoes.

"Did they make shoes here or something?" Keith asked quietly. "Could that be why the ghosts pile them up all over?"

"I believe it indicates that the residents were not allowed to wear footwear as often as they might have wanted," Adriana said carefully.

"Try to ignore the shoes," I said in a tone I hoped sounded authoritarian. "Keith, Randy, and Joe, I mean you guys especially. They won't go away if you ignore them, but paying attention to them isn't in your best interests." Considered our options. "I think I'm going to have us break my 'stick together' rule already. Dan and Josh, are you guys feeling up to doing a quick run through the building? Be honest."

"I am," Joshua said.

"I as well." Daniel looked around. "Can we take one of the flashlights?"

"Sure." Handed him mine and they zipped off. They were back quickly, but not as quickly as I was used to. "Wait In the Dark" by Memory Tapes came and went and "I Have Waited So Long" by Foreigner started before they were back. "Wow, for A-Cs that took forever. Are you guys really okay?"

"Yes," Daniel said as he handed the flashlight back to me. "It's just as dangerous in here as Former Pontifex White said it would be."

"We found a variety of options to get upstairs," Joshua shared. "We weren't sure if you wanted us to test them or if you wanted us to go as a group. It could be a lot of stairs—this is a two story building."

"Three stories in some places." Looked at White. "Your thoughts?"

"We go as a group," he said firmly.

Since we knew where we were going now, we linked up and all enjoyed the benefits of hyperspeed. Happily, the Hyperspeed Dramamine that Tito had created way back when was continuously being improved.

Originally every human had had to take a dose a day, then a dose a week. But now it was a dose a month, so the flyboys were still okay with the hyperspeed. Mahin took it just in case, Adriana regularly took the same dose as all the other humans who worked with us, and Siler had given some to Lizzie the moment we'd all gotten back together at the Embassy after Operation Epidemic ended.

Keith, however, wasn't dosed up. From personal experience, as long as we didn't go too fast—which we couldn't in this building—the effects of hyperspeed would only hit once we stopped.

Unfortunately for Keith, we were having to stop a lot, since Daniel and Joshua hadn't been kidding—there were a lot of stairwells, sensible in a building this size. Some were impassable, some took us to the top but were without roof access, some we thought might have roof access but were blocked by too much stuff we didn't want to move, even though I was pretty sure I had more evidence gloves in my purse.

We hit all of the likely options, while I enjoyed the vocal stylings of Iggy & the Stooges singing "Search and Destroy" courtesy of the Algar Channel, and found we couldn't get outside. My music changed to "Look Sharp!" by Joe Jackson as we reached the last impassable stairwell.

"Let's double-check the more passable ones and look for something you guys might have missed," I said as Keith dry-heaved, having tossed all his cookies several stairwells earlier. Which was okay, because he wasn't adding anything different to the overall mix of this place, including smell.

Only a few people with me sighed, but we headed off again, me looking intently for clues in the dark, the murk, the mess, and the footwear. Was rewarded for this diligence—spotted a faded sign over a door that said Administration.

Headed us through this door, which led to an office that, in turn, led to a short hall that had three doors on either side and one door at the end. The door at the end was entitled Maintenance. Well, it was if I ignored all the graffiti that indicated it was the entrance to Hell and similar, which I actively chose to.

"We searched here," Daniel said.

"Yeah, well we're going to search again. At human speeds."

We left Keith heaving into a wastebasket that was somehow still here and, for this place, in decent shape.

The six office doors led to a variety of offices that looked medical in nature, but could easily have been secretarial. There was so much random junk in all of them that I refused to try to guess. The Maintenance Portal to Hell, however, was more promising, since it had stairs. That went down.

"Did you guys check these?"

"No," Joshua replied. "Because we wanted to go up, not down."

"You guys really don't understand how humans think, do

you? Get Keith—we're heading down and I don't want to leave anyone behind to miss whatever horrors we're heading into."

Keith was retrieved, and we started down. In this case, I insisted on going first. Not because I was so very brave or anything, but because that was my job as the leader. And also because my music changed to "Where It's At" by Beck, and I had a feeling we were close to what we wanted to find.

The stairs were concrete, and the walls weren't all that bad. For Forest Haven, this was a pretty good descent. I didn't race down, but we were moving faster than we'd been able to anywhere else in here.

The one flight of stairs led to the basement, which had boilers, laundry equipment, and other maintenance-type stuff that made sense to be here. If this place was really Hell, then Hell was the only place in Forest Haven that made sense. And, best of all, there were no shoes in evidence. I perked up considerably.

I also found what we really wanted—another stairwell, going up. This one, like the one we'd taken to get down to the basement, was concrete and not all that bad. It also had four landings and went up, by my count, three stories.

Reached a door at the top landing. Tried to open it but it was stuck. Stepped aside and allowed Daniel to give it a go. It didn't budge. He and Joshua both slammed their shoulders against it and got it to give.

They couldn't get the door opened all the way, but got it open far enough that we could all get through, though Keith had to really squeeze himself to manage it.

"Everyone be careful, the taller guys especially, because we don't want anyone to get knocked out by the huge hunk of metal we can't see."

"Okay, we're up on the roof," Joe said. "And I can tell, by the way we're not really seeing all the sun we should be, that there's something above us."

Keith put his hand up slowly until his arm was extended as far as it could go. "I can just feel it. My fingertips are touching something that feels like metal."

"Hand down," Jerry said. "Just in case." Keith nodded and did as ordered. So he could be taught.

"So, we're here," Randy said. "Now what? Do we knock?"

"We could try to get in," Walker said, sounding like this wasn't his preferred plan in any way.

"No, it's too dangerous," Hughes replied. "We don't know what security is on this thing, but we're safer if we assume a lot."

"I thought you had a plan," Keith said to me. He sounded expectant, not snide. Which was a pity, in that sense, since I'd been a lot more focused in getting us up here than in formulating what I'd do once we were.

Thanks to Keith's comment, everyone was now looking at me just as expectantly as he was. Heaved a sigh. It was not time to say I had nothing sane planned. No, it was, as always, time to go with what worked. In other words, it was time to go with the crazy.

And, apparently, Algar approved. Because my music changed to Pete Townsend's "Let My Love Open the Door." It was time to roll Mission: Trojan Horsey.

CHAPTER 70

CLEARED MY THROAT. "TK, we're here to surrender."
Everyone stared at me. "You were serious about that plan?" Keith asked.

"Keith, trust me, you can be replaced. Yes, I'm serious. TK," I said in a louder voice, "we don't have all day. It's getting dark and this place is creepy enough in the daytime. We'd like to take refuge in the helicarrier with you." Waited. Nothing. "And that way, you'll actually have us to trade for Stephanie instead of lying about it."

Heard a noise. It was right above our heads.

White took my hand and Lizzie's and started moving us back. "I believe that your request wasn't immediately reacted to because we're standing under the ramp."

Sure enough, as soon as all of us stepped back about ten feet—a precarious proposition up here, since the roofs were no better than the floors, in that sense—instead of nothing we saw something. A ramp was indeed lowering, and we could see the interior of the ship. Not that there was much to see. The ramp and what looked like dark metal walls once you got up the ramp.

"I have a really bad feeling about this," Jerry said.

"Blah, blah, blah. As long as our friendly neighborhood Kendroid doesn't immediately put us in stasis, we'll be fine."

"Again, that's your plan?" Keith sounded outraged. "That you're hoping that our enemy doesn't immediately immobilize us?"

"Well, most of us, Keith. I'm currently A-Okay with the Kendroid immobilizing you, especially if he immobilizes your mouth."

"Shall I go first?" Keith asked huffily.

"I'd love to say knock yourself out, but I can't. No, I'm going first. Everyone else, if I do get frozen or whatever, link up and run like hell out of here."

"We're fast enough to do that anyway," Lucas said quietly.

"I doubt it, honestly." They'd been captured at Rocky Mount, and while they might have been surprised by the attack, Camilla and the princesses had gone in prepared. "You know, how *did* you guys get captured?"

"We flew into something we couldn't see that slowed us down, forced us to land inside it, and held us immobile," Jerry replied. "It's not tech we have or any other country has, and before you say it, yeah, I caught that the creator is from out of this world. Just saying that we had no defenses against it."

"Well, the creator is supposedly on our side now, so there's that. What about those of you on the ground? What happened at Rocky Mount?"

"I think we were gassed," Keith said. "One moment we were watching for any signs of threats to the President, the next we woke up as captives in the helicarrier."

"Was that the same for the A-Cs?"

"Yes," Daniel said slowly. "Only . . ."

"Only what?" White asked.

"Only I remember a girl," Daniel said. "Blonde, youngish, pretty. She looked familiar. I noted her because she seemed out of place. I was going to point her out to the others when," he shrugged, "I woke up as a captive."

"It was Stephanie."

"You're sure?" White asked.

"It makes sense," Abigail said as I scrolled through pictures on my phone. "She was working for Drax at the time, and who other than an A-C could be fast enough to knock out our people?"

Finally found the snap I was looking for and showed it to Daniel—a Martini Family Gathering shot from a few years ago where Stephanie was front and center. "This the girl?"

He nodded slowly. "She was a few years older, but if that picture is from a few years ago, then the woman I saw could be her now."

"That's her. Okay, so Stephanie helped Drax capture everyone, which makes sense. Presumably she carted you off in a bus or something." Then retrieved her motorcycle, or had it in the transport vehicle or some such, maybe the helicarrier had an invisible shuttle, too, but that wasn't important now. "So, no one remembers coming into the helicarrier via the entrance we've been provided?" All heads shook no. "Always the way. Fine, weapons at the ready and remember to run if it looks bad."

With that, I took a tentative step onto the ramp. It didn't do anything and nothing happened to me, either. So far, so slow, so good. "Creepin' In" by Norah Jones came on. Wasn't sure if Algar approved of my cautious speed or if he was teasing me about it. Decided not to care and continue to make discretion the better part of valor.

Moving one very slow step at a time we entered the helicarrier. We weren't in a loading bay, which I'd expected, but rather in what looked like a wide hallway. The ramp didn't move until the last of us was on the ship, then it closed slowly and with little noise.

We were in the middle of this hallway, so we could go to the right or the left. "Anyone have a suggestion for which way we go?"

"Yes, but it depends on what you want to do," Joshua said. "If you want to search the ship or if you want to find our kidnapper."

"Let's find the Kendroid first."

Daniel nodded and started off toward the right, as my music switched to "Homesick At Space Camp" by Fall Out Boy. Algar was definitely amusing himself right now. "I think this will take us to the command center."

We went at a cautious pace, so everyone was able to take a good look around. It was all *Star Wars* and *Star Trek* and such inside—lots of flashing lights, impressive consoles, what looked like space-aged weapons, futuristic chairs, and on and on.

Moving on we saw areas that looked a lot like the inside of a S.H.I.E.L.D. helicarrier—bays and computers and all sorts of snazzy electronic things galore, and lots of hallways and such—only there were no people or androids in evidence.

Unfortunately, that meant that Camilla, Rahmi, and

Rhee were also not in evidence. Nor were the Poofs or Peregrines. "Poofies," I whispered. "Peregrine Enforcers. If any
of you are here, can you give Kitty a sign?"

Waited. Nada.

"I still think we should have just run for it," Lucas grumbled quietly, as my music switched to "Stay Close" by Sub-
iza. Not that I was planning to run off, but it was nice to
know that Algar didn't want us taking off yet.

"That would have been a bad decision." It was the Kendroid's voice, but he wasn't anywhere in sight. Clearly he
was speaking through the ship's internal communications
system. "I'm able to target anything in this, including fast-
moving beings."

"Super," I said quickly, before anyone else decided to
talk, while still walking along so the others would have to
follow me. "So, are we heading the right way to meet up
with you?" Indicated that Daniel should continue leading
us, which he did.

"Why does that matter? You surrendered. You're now
my prisoners."

"Yes, yes, surrender Dorothy and all that jazz. But I'd
still like to talk to you. In person. So to speak. Person on my
side, at least."

"I don't understand you and I am a person."

"Again, we need to discuss that. Face to face, how about
that?"

"I don't trust you."

Wise, really. Chose not to say that aloud. "Why not? You
let us in."

"You killed all my brothers."

"No I didn't."

"They're all dead."

"Machines can't die. In that sense. But yes, we destroyed
them. Because we had to. Because you told them to attack us."

"You want to do the same to me."

"No, I don't. I do want to talk to you. But I don't want to
destroy you." I didn't, for a variety of reasons, really, the fact
that he was the one with the answers being only one of
them.

We rounded a corner and found ourselves in what
looked like the main point of operation—there was an obvious command deck and just tons and tons of computers

and such in here. It looked amazing to me, but apparently Algar wasn't of the same opinion, since Shania Twain's "That Don't Impress Me Much" came on.

Kind of disagreed—this was impressive-looking stuff and definitely advanced beyond what anyone outside of Hollywood had created. And it was clear that the computers were linked, meaning that Drax was right—the helicarrier didn't need a lot of people to be able to fly.

However, there were five stations up on the command deck area and the Kendroid was sitting at one of them. So the helicarrier did need more than one person to operate it. Which was probably why it was still sitting here—the Kendroid couldn't fly it to the Pentagon and demand they release Stephanie or he'd blow them up. He was stuck here.

"Guys," I asked in a very low voice, as we came to a halt, "do you remember if you saw more than one man when you were captured?"

"No," Marcus replied in kind. "We saw the same man. But he changed uniforms constantly."

"Army, Navy, Air Force, Marines?"

"Yes," Lucas said. "And regular suit sometimes, too."

Nice to have the confirmation of my suspicions—that the Kendroid had had his best copies with him when he'd stolen the helicarrier. And now they were gone.

"What do you want from me?" the Kendroid asked.

"Well, it's more what I can offer you. Because, hold onto your hat, I have a once in an android lifetime offer for you."

CHAPTER 71

"WHAT'S THAT?" The Kendroid asked. "And I'm not wearing a hat."

"Figure of speech, but the that that I'm offering is a that you'll be excited about." Time to bait the hook. "Guaranteed. Or your money back."

"Yeah, what that is that you're talking about exactly?" Jerry asked in a low voice. "I'm asking for all of us."

"I'm talking about you, Jerry. Keep it down."

Abigail nudged me. "For once, I think I'm thinking what you're thinking."

Mahin nodded. "What do you need from us?"

"Follow my lead. TK," I said in a louder voice, as I started walking toward the stairs that led up to the command deck, "I have a way for you to fly this thing."

"What makes you think that I can't fly it by myself?"

I snorted as I trotted up the stairs, the others behind me, "Learn to Fly" by the Foo Fighters in my ears indicating that Algar approved of my plan. "Dude, if you could do that particular that, you'd have already done said that. I realize this machine is set up to run with a very limited crew. However, unlike the ship Drax used to get to our neck of the galactic woods, it does require more than one person to fly it. And I realize we've destroyed all of your copilots." Time to dangle the bait. "But, and you're going to be so glad when you hear this, I have that special offer I just mentioned."

"What special offer is that?"

"I'm so glad you asked! The special, one time only, limited time offer, is . . . wait for it . . . hold onto that metaphorical hat and . . . it is . . . replacement pilots for you!"

"What?" The Kendroid sounded shocked.

"What?!?" This was echoed by all five flyboys, the four A-C Field agents, and good ol' Keith. The girls and White were all blissfully silent.

"I know! It's too amazing to be true, isn't it? And yet, it *is* true! But wait . . . before you decide, I have even *more* for you." Get the hook securely into the fish's mouth. "In addition to pilots, I've *also* brought along additional crew so that *you* can actually focus on the bigger picture and all that." I was talking very fast—not A-C speed, but definitely at Ginsu Knife *Now* How Much Would You Pay Speed.

"The bigger picture?" The Kendroid sounded completely confused. "Fish Out of Water" by Tears for Fears came on. I really enjoyed it when Algar and I were in sync.

"Dude! Yes! The bigger picture is *you* rescuing your lady love all impressively, isn't it? Picture it now—you swooping in to save her just before the firing squad can shoot. Heroism at its finest. And a sure way to stand out from the competition." Give the hook a gentle tug.

"What firing squad? What competition?"

"Metaphors aren't your thing, are they? But, I get it. I mean, what was she doing, hanging out with Drax anyway, am I right? Something was definitely going on there, as I'm sure you've realized. What better way to impress her than by doing the big rescue? And here we are to help out! Guys, take a look at the controls, I'm sure you can manage them."

"Ah," Hughes said. "Gotcha, Commander." He jerked his head at the other flyboys. "To your posts, men." The rest of the flyboys lurched into action. I was used to them catching on a little quicker, but it had been a rough week for everyone.

The Kendroid's eyes narrowed. "Wait. What do you mean about Drax?" Let the fish hook itself more securely.

Prayed that everyone else with me was keeping their expressions neutral or at least looking at the floor or something. Coughed delicately. "Um, I mean the obvious." Let the fish play out a little bit.

"What's obvious?" The Kendroid was definitely not on solid ground here.

Lizzie snorted. "Oh, come *on*. You'd gotten the helicarrier and all the hostages for her. Why would she need to go back to him? Unless, you know . . ." She shrugged.

"She . . . she needed something from him for the android process on full humans." The Kendroid sounded confused and defensive.

"Oh, of course. I'm sure she did." Ensured I didn't sound like I was sure at all.

"Do Americans still fall for that excuse?" Adriana asked, sounding sad for all of us.

"Only the ones not, you know, programmed to notice the clues and such."

"What do you mean?" The Kendroid was definitely upset and out of his element. "She was missing vital parts in order to properly create."

"Is that what she told you?" Adriana asked, sympathy dripping. "I guess the old lies are the easiest to pass."

"She wasn't lying!" He didn't sound angry—he sounded like he needed us to believe him.

Randy stepped away from his piloting console and closer to the Kendroid and pointed to the metal railing we were near. "Is this necessary for the safe running of the ship?"

"Ah, no," the Kendroid was clearly shocked by this sudden conversational shift. "Why?"

Randy slammed his fist onto the railing. It bent. A lot. "That didn't hurt, because I think that my arms and legs are already fully androidized. Joe?"

Joe took his cue, trotted over, and straightened the metal out. "Yeah. Mine, too."

They both nodded to me, then went back to their posts. I'd worry about what had been done to my guys later. Had to save us all first. On the bright side, if we needed to destroy the Kendroid, it appeared that Joe and Randy were going to have little trouble with it.

Cleared my throat. "Ah, TK, I think that sort of indicates that there is nothing Stephanie needed from Drax in order to make humans into androids." Tug on the line.

"She . . . she lied to me?" He sounded shocked and lost.

"Well, you know how it is." Abigail shrugged. "A girl likes to keep her options open and all that. Play the field until you're sure you've found the right guy."

"Playing the field can be quite fun," Adriana added. "Many of us enjoy it, though most are looking to settle down with Mister Correct."

"And it's not like Stephanie had a great track record,"

Mahin said. "I mean, just look at the men she was involved with. Before you, I'm sure," she added politely.

"Well, I don't know that it was before TK," I said conversationally to the girls. Let the fish think you're not paying attention to it for a while. "I mean, she was sleeping with Cliff and, clearly, she was sleeping with Drax, and I'm still not convinced that she wasn't canoodling with anyone and everyone in Gideon Cleary's campaign, and I'm not sure when she made TK. She might have made him while she was with Cliff, after all."

"Oh, gross thought," Lizzie said. "Do you think she made all those other Kendroids so that they could be, like, her harem?"

"Wow, I hadn't thought of that," I said, as "Let It Play" by Poison came on. "Sure seems possible to me. After all, he's good looking, so why not make a ton of him, right?"

"Oh!" Abigail sounded totally excited. "Maybe she wanted the real Thomas Kendrick and he turned her down."

"I had not thought of that," I lied. "But that makes a hell of a lot of sense. Can't get the guy you really want? Make a replacement that won't turn you down. Genius, really." Turned back to TK. Yank harder on the line. "Sorry, got off on a tangent there. Anyway, so the plan—"

"Stop! Stop trying to avoid the question! Why did Stephanie lie to me?" He sounded a little like Jeff when Jeff was having jealousy issues. He sounded a lot more like his heart was breaking.

Felt bad, but not bad enough. I had people and animals missing and presumed to be in extreme danger. The feelings of an android were going to have to come second.

"Ah," I said gently. "Um, TK, well . . . I think she lied so that you'd do what she wanted. I mean, isn't that why people lie?"

He nodded. "But why lie to me? I love her. She loves me."

Lizzie snorted quietly. "Sure she does," she said under her breath, but so that he could definitely hear it.

He spun toward Lizzie. "What do you mean?"

She rolled her eyes. "Oh, nothing. Nothing at all. I mean, why would she want a real person when she had you, right?" Lizzie really had her Teenaged Sarcasm Meter up well past eleven.

"What? What do you mean? I'm real!"

"No, Pinocchio, you're not a real boy yet." And I wasn't sure if he ever would be. Though, as with Cameron Maurer and Col. John Butler, the possibility was there.

"What do you mean?" he yelled. "Why do you say things that don't make sense? Why are you doing this to me?"

"Doing what?" I asked nicely. Yank harder on the line, be sure the hook is set.

"Making it all confusing! Nothing makes sense. *You* don't make sense."

"Humans don't make sense. A-Cs rarely do, either. Frankly, most organic beings don't make sense. It's just something we all do. All of us. Machines, on the other hand, they make sense. And Stephanie isn't a machine, she's organic, so she won't make sense. And maybe she wants someone else who doesn't make sense, either."

The Kendroid was shaking and it seemed that tears might be a possibility. Had no idea if he could cry—an Antony Marling Android would have been able to, but so far I wasn't as impressed with Stephanie's workmanship—but if he could, tears were going to be arriving soon.

"Why is this happening? Why are you doing this to me?" he asked plaintively.

"You have my friends and my pets. I want them back. But I want to help you out, so that's why we're here. To help." Put my hand onto his arm. Pull hard on the line. "We're here to *help* you, TK. Tell us what you need us to do for you."

"I . . . I . . . I want Stephanie back."

"Even after all she's done to you?" Start reeling in the line slowly.

He stared at me. "Done to me? What . . . you mean cheating on me?"

"Yes, and lying to you and whatever else she's done. I mean, how do you know that you really love her? Maybe she just programmed you to love her, you know?"

"That's so unfair," Lizzie said. "I mean, he should be free to make his own choices."

Abigail nodded. "To just make someone love you . . ." She shook her head. "Talk about removing free will."

Adriana sighed. "Unrequited love is a terrible thing."

"Unrequited, what do you mean? Stephanie loves me." He was pleading with us to agree.

Time to reel in faster. "Then why did she leave you for Drax?" I asked.

The Kendroid stared at me. He was still shaking. "She did, didn't she?"

Flip the fish onto the deck. "She did. I'm sorry you couldn't see that before. I guess it's because she doesn't see you as a real person."

"What . . . what do I have to do?"

"To achieve what?" I asked.

"To become real, to be the man she wants? What can I do?"

"Nothing," White said from behind me. "Nothing at all."

There was something in his tone. Turned around to see White, the Field agents, and Keith surrounded by Poofs and Peregrines. But they weren't alone.

CHAPTER 72

CAMILLA, RAHMI, and Rhee were there. Keith was sup- porting both princesses, but Camilla was standing on her own, though it looked like Daniel and Joshua were ready to catch her if she happened to fall. All three women looked seriously pissed.

"You guys okay?"

Camilla nodded. "No thanks to him."

Turned back to the Kendroid. "We call this checkmate. What do you call it?"

He gaped. "How . . . how did you find them?" he asked White.

"It's amazing how distracted Missus Martini and the other young ladies made you," White said. "The rest of us felt that we would be of more help putting our natural tal- ents to use." He smiled at me. "We searched the ship, found where everyone was being held, and released them. It wasn't as difficult as it could have been, since Daniel and Joshua had already examined the entire ship and had good suspicions as to where the animals would be. Once they were released, they led us to the chamber where Camilla, Rahmi, and Rhee were being held."

The Field agents looked pissed. "They were in stasis for sure," Joshua said. "No air, no water, no food, just frozen."

"How are you guys doing?" I asked the women. "For real, this time."

"We will be fine once we can avenge ourselves," Rahmi said. Rhee nodded.

"I'm with the princesses," Camilla said. "I assume you've figured things out?"

"Yeah, you guys have been gone for over a week. We've probably figured a lot of things out, but no guarantees that it's everything you know." Looked at the Kendroid again. "Your ship is officially commandeered. Matt, do you guys know how to fly it by now?"

"Pretty sure we do, Commander," Hughes said cheerfully.

"What heading do you want?" Jerry asked.

"Get us to Andrews on the double. Colonel Franklin has a nice parking place reserved for us."

Hughes barked orders and the ship shuddered. The Kendroid was shuddering, too.

"You tricked me," he said.

"No. I'm just better at salesmanship than you are." My salesmanship professor and former boss would both have been proud of me right about now, since I'd used their techniques to the letter. "I gave you exactly what I said I would. I have five guys here flying this thing for you. I'm going to take you to Andrews, and you're going to get to go see Stephanie in her cell. Maybe they'll let you stay there with her."

"Not that I'd think you'd want to," Lizzie said. "Because we weren't making it up—she's cheating on you."

"Because you're not a real person," Mahin added.

The Kendroid again looked like he was ready to cry. "I'm real," he said plaintively.

"No. You're not. I could possibly help you become more human, but you haven't given me a lot of reason to want to. However, if you do want to try to become a real boy, then I'll help you. As long as you come over to the good guy's side. You know Stephanie's wrong to be doing what she is."

He was shaking even harder. "She might be wrong, but she's all I have."

"You could have more," Adriana said. "But you have to choose to want more."

"I . . . I . . ." His face fell. "I can't. I can't change my programming." He blinked several times in rapid succession, and my music changed to "I'm Blowin' Up" by Kool Moe Dee.

"You can fight it," I said urgently. "Other androids have fought the self-destruct sequence, and you can, too."

"I don't know how!"

Grabbed his hand. "Look at me and just focus on being you. Not your programming, on you, on the person, the being, you think you are. You're more than the programming someone else gave you. That's what being human is—being able to overcome your programming when you have to, when it's right to."

The Kendroid stared at me for a few long moments while he continued blinking. Then he squeezed my hand, but not too hard. "Thank you for trying. But . . ." He shook his head, leaped over the railing, and ran off the way we'd come.

"Commander, he's heading for the same hatch we entered through," Walker called.

"Open it."

"Have grounds on viewer," Joe said. Ran over to see what he had. We were pretty high up already, which was good for us if the Kendroid self-destructed. But only if he did so when he wasn't inside the ship.

"Android has left the ship," Walker said, as we continued to rise up. "Hatch is closed and secure."

Joe had a good view of the grounds and I watched the Kendroid avoid hitting any of the buildings and fall to the ground. He didn't explode. "Think he's dead?" Joe asked.

"No. Stay on him."

Sure enough, as we rose up, I watched the Kendroid jerk and sort of bounce on the ground. Then it stopped. And, as we started forward, he stood up, looked up, and waved at us. Then he ran off, headed toward the main house and Adriana's motorcycle. Knew without asking that he could hotwire and ride it.

"Do you think he knows you're watching him?" Joe asked.

"Yeah, I think he does."

"What do you think he's going to do?" Randy asked.

Heaved a sigh. "I have no idea." My music changed to "Home Tonight" by Aerosmith. "But I know what we're going to do. Whoever has external communications, contact Andrews and the White House. We're going home."

Everyone cheered, Poofs and Peregrines, too. Even Keith.

At least we did until Jerry shouted over everyone else. "Commander, we have a situation!"

CHAPTER 73

"**WELL,** that success was short-lived."

"So," Abigail said, "you know, routine."

"Yeah. Jerry, what's up?"

"Need you to confirm countersigns." His voice was very tense. "They don't believe we're who I'm saying we are. I'm on with low-level at Andrews. They've supposedly hooked in someone at the White House, but I can't determine who. Whoever I'm talking to, they don't seem to know that American Centaurion or the Office of the President are missing any people, yourself included and in particular."

"Fan-freaking-tastic. Everyone, see who you can reach on your phones. Guys, see who else you can reach via the ship's telecommunications." Took my own advice and checked. I had bars. Called Jeff.

"Hello!" He sounded hearty and cheerful.

"Jeff, it's me—"

"You've reached Jeff Martini. I'm unavailable right now, but please leave a message and I or one of my team will get back to you as soon as possible." The phone beeped. "Mailbox is full," the automated female voice shared.

Stared at the phone. Hung up. Tried Chuckie. "Charles Reynolds, here." He sounded all business and no nonsense.

"Chuckie—"

"I'm unavailable. Leave a message." The phone beeped. "Mailbox is full," the same automated female voice shared. Well, we were all on the same A-C Carrier System, so that made sense. Only that so far, but one thing was better than none.

Called Reader, Tim, and Mom. Got the same thing—hit their voicemails and couldn't leave a message.

"Kitty," Abigail called, while I tried Buchanan, "no one's answering. I've tried Paul, Walter, Kevin, and Serene and all I get is voicemail with no way to leave a message. And I can't get a call through to my parents." Same response from Buchanan's phone—no answer and the mailbox was full.

"I can't reach Doreen, or Raj, or Pierre," Mahin said. "I tried William but I can't get the call to connect."

"My wife's phone is the same," Joe said darkly. "Voicemail and you can't leave a message. I tried my mother- and father-in-law, too, and Tito as well. Same thing." Rahmi looked stricken and Rhee looked confused. Felt their pain.

"Mine, too," Randy shared. "Wife and in-laws both. Along with the main Embassy phone. Same lack of anything. Nice to know they missed us."

Camilla waved her phone. She looked pissed. "Can't reach anyone who matters, same thing as everyone else."

"Like Mahin, I can't get through to Dulce," Jerry said. "Not hitting voicemail, for which I guess we should all be thrilled, but literally can't connect to their number. Any of the Dulce numbers. That goes for all A-C Bases worldwide. Cannot connect."

"Maybe we're still being dampened," Abigail said.

"Or we have limited range for some reason. Guys, see if you can fiddle with our communications. Maybe we're blocking ourselves in some way."

"I can't reach my dad," Lizzie said. "And I tried your dad, too, Kitty. And Denise and Nadine." She looked frightened. Well, that was a change from the adults who all looked as upset and angry as I felt. Abigail put her arm around Lizzie and hugged her.

Tried not to worry about the kids—mine and everyone else's. If we couldn't reach the Embassy, there could be a bad reason as to why. Tried Vance. Got nothing—couldn't connect to his line.

"Christopher's phone is the same—voicemail with no way to leave a message," White said. "The same with Amy's. I've tried all other Embassy personnel, including Magdalena." Since White and Nurse Carter were dating, this was the same for him as my calling Jeff. "I believe the phones are all turned off. The quickness of both the answer and the send to voicemail is indicative."

The others nodded. "Have tried all White House personnel we know that Chip, Jerry, Joe, Randy, and I have numbers for," Hughes said.

"That's a lot of numbers," Jerry added. "We're popular, or at least I thought we were. We know everyone."

"Ship's telecommunications system says that Richard's determination is correct," Walker shared. "It's not on our side. Phones appear to be turned off. Voicemail systems are either full or also turned off. There's a way to do it so that the system will give everyone a 'mailbox full' response even if the mailboxes are empty."

The Field teams were having the same luck as the rest of us. Keith, however, had a different issue. "My phone won't connect to anything or anyone."

"He's not on our system," Daniel added. "That might be why."

"The A-C's system is stronger than the normal carriers'. I just tried Vance, who I don't think is on our system yet, and couldn't connect. So, if I'm understanding our situation correctly, we can reach most of the very people we want to reach, but they've set things up so that we can't actually reach them."

"Or someone's hacked our system," Mahin said.

"Hackers! Everyone try to reach Hacker International!"

"Tried that already," Jerry said. "Same for them as all the others."

"I've reached Grandmother!" We all turned to stare at Adriana, who started talking quickly in what I assumed was Romanian. Her look of elation changed to one of worry. "I understand. Yes. I love you, too." She hung up. "Grandmother says that no one has hacked the phones. If the phones are off, they were turned off intentionally by the Office of the President, the Director of the CIA, or the Head of Field."

We all stared at each other. "Wow," I said finally. "I guess we know where we stand."

"Grandmother is as unable to reach anyone as we are. The American Centaurion Embassy is in full lockdown—Romanian Embassy personnel were not able to contact anyone, and were repelled away from the door, so were unable to knock or gain entry. Grandmother is concerned for us and suggests that we be prepared."

"For what?" White asked.

Adriana swallowed. "To fight."

"Commander, Adriana's not wrong. I've managed to stall while we wasted time trying to reach our loved ones who apparently don't miss us at all," Jerry said. "But you need to get involved or we need to fly far, far away as fast as we can."

Went to Jerry's station and put on the headset he gave me. "Hello, to whom do I have the pleasure of speaking?"

There was a pause. "Identify."

"This again? You first. Jerry, did we get a name from those we're speaking to at Andrews and the White House?"

"Negative, Commander, and I did ask. We're supposedly on a conference call with both locations, however."

"Super-duper. Jerry, make sure the others can hear this, just in case. To whoever's on the other end of this line, I have no idea what the password is when you've been kidnapped, then escape, save everyone else, and recapture the stolen invisible helicarrier, but whatever that password is, we're saying it."

"We need proof of who you are." Did not recognize the voice. This boded. "You are in a foreign craft above American soil. Identify or we will shoot you from the ground."

"You decloaked us?" I asked the flyboys.

"Unintentionally," Jerry said, voice tight. "It was closely connected to communications. If we'd been able to leave in a normal way, we would have been able to avoid decloaking."

"And we're just learning these systems," Walker reminded me.

"Fine, fine, these things happen. Look, whoever I'm talking to, I'm the First Lady. Kitty Katt-Martini. Also known as Cyclone to the Secret Service. Perhaps you've heard of me?"

There was a pause. "The First Lady is confirmed to be safe and not in an enemy helicarrier. Per the President of the United States."

"Excuse me? I'm in the airship you're threatening."

"Negative. The First Lady is on the White House Lawn,

with the President. Both confirmed by top-level White House staff and on the news right now. So, your plan to fool us isn't working."

Randy waved me over. The headset was cordless so I went. Sure enough, he had a viewing screen up and it showed Jeff and "me" on the lawn, doing a photo op. Sure, it was Francine doing her Double Me Duty, and you could tell because she was far prettier than I was in real life. However, no one seemed to note this.

"According to the news, this is the President and First Lady announcing that the peace talks are back on and scheduled for three days from now," Randy shared. "They were out earlier, too, a few hours ago, apparently to just sort of wave at reporters and announce that things were just peachy in the White House, but it was televised."

"What the literal hell is going on?"

"You were kidnapped," Camilla said quietly. "That's what Richard told us. Something must have happened to force a press conference, so they trotted your double out. But they clearly haven't told anyone on the front lines that the actual First Lady is really missing."

Decided it was time to think hella fast. No one had come to rescue us, and we'd been at Forest Haven for hours. Meaning whatever scrambling had been put into effect had truly been exceptional. Drax's stuff had been good, after all, and we'd have never found him if not for Wruck. Chose not to ask where Wruck was right now.

Instead, focused on the here and now. It seemed clear that Jeff and everyone else either thought we were somewhere far, far away or were so hidden they couldn't find us. Or else they were glad we were gone. Yesterday I'd have scoffed at that option. Right now, however, it seemed very possible. Time to return to my call and see what I could salvage of this situation.

"Look, I realize that you think you're seeing the real FLOTUS, but I need you to tell the President, my husband, and the Director of the CIA, my best friend, that whatever intel they have is wrong. We're near some NSA black site, I think. We're literally less than an hour away from D.C."

"Are you threatening enemy action against our capital?"

"Good lord, is Keith's twin on the other end of this line or something?"

"I resent that!"

"Not now, Keith. Look, I'm Wolverine and I'm trying to reach Nick Fury. Does that help?"

"Not at all."

"I want to speak with the President, Jeff Martini, my husband, aka Cosmos."

"You are not the First Lady and therefore not authorized to do so."

"Really? Then give me the Director of the CIA, Charles Reynolds."

"You are not authorized to do so."

"How about Tom Curran, the Director of the FBI?" Didn't know Curran at all, but figured I'd have a better shot with him than whoever was holding down this fort.

"Again, you are not authorized. You are not authorized to speak to anyone other than me."

"Who are you?"

"You are not authorized to know my name, rank, or serial number."

"Of course not. Where is Rajnish Singh?"

"Nowhere you need to know about."

"I want to talk to Colonel Arthur Franklin and I want to do so right now."

"Identify. The President has protocols in place to determine if you are actually who you say you are. Meet those, or we will be forced to shoot you from the air."

Camilla took a headset from Walker. "This is Agent Ninety-Nine."

"Seriously?" Went over to where she was. Walker had type on his screens. Looked like he was trying to reach Hacker International via a method other than cellular. I approved.

Camilla shot me a look that said she'd heard all the jokes and had been sick of them before she'd heard them. She also tossed out some numbers and words and such so fast I couldn't catch them.

"Those protocols are old," whoever was on the other end said. "Agent is not confirmed."

Camilla looked shocked for what I suspected was the first time in her life. But she gave it the old college try. "Supersede protocols due to state of emergency. New protocols are sign countersign. Romeo."

"Negative. You are not authorized."

Camilla looked worried. "What did Jeff change while I was gone? And why?"

"I have no idea, but whoever we're talking to doesn't seem to think I've been kidnapped. Well, I was, most of us were. But we got better. Which is why we're trying to get to you there at Andrews."

"Identify or we will shoot you from the sky."

"Oh, my God." Had nothing else. Went with the things that worked best—the crazy and channeling my mother. "I am the wife of the President of the United States, and the daughter of the Head of the P.T.C.U. and you *will* put me on with one of those two people immediately or I will personally come down there, kick your ass into the Atlantic Ocean, and then ensure that you do the rest of your active duty in Siberia using our nice exchange program with Russia. Do I make myself clear?"

"You're clear, but we still need identification."

"How's this? I am the former Head Ambassador of American Centaurion. I have the Former Supreme Pontifex with me, along with the current Cultural Attachés. And if you do not immediately put us on with the President of the United States I will ensure that I ask my friends from other worlds to blow your facility to high holy hell, with specific attention paid to you and your entire family line."

"That might not be the right tactic," Hughes said quietly.

"Warheads are arming," Walker said.

Looked over at White. "A little help?"

He shrugged. "There are many ways to prove it's you. But I suggest you take your earphones out."

Stared at him for a moment, then realized that I probably wasn't the only one Algar assisted every now and then.

"Gotcha. Whoever's on the line, I'd like you to listen to this very, very carefully."

Turned my phone's volume up to eleven, hoped that this was going to work, and hit play. And "Back in the Saddle" came on, with Screamin' Steven Tyler doing some of his very best screaming.

CHAPTER 74

"WARHEADS HAVE DISARMED," Walker said, sounding relieved.

"President has left the photo op, though the 'First Lady' is still there," Randy said.

Let the song continue to play because I was really annoyed. Could hear someone shouting over the music. Decided they could shout a little longer.

"That sounds like Jeff," Jerry said.

"I don't care who it is," I shouted into the headset. "I am seriously pissed with every, single person in charge of whatever the hell you all think you're in charge of! And that includes my husband, best friend, and mother. Especially my husband!"

The shouting on the other end stopped. Good. Turned the volume down, though I let the song play on.

"Now, I'm going to try this one more time. Then, quite frankly, if I get the same responses I've been getting, I actually will declare myself, this helicarrier, and all those on it as our own sovereign nation, and we will go invisible, disappear, and become America's worst nightmare."

"Ah, Kitty?" Not Jeff. Not Chuckie, either. Definitely not Mom. But the voice was familiar.

"Kevin?"

"Yes, it's me. I believe I have things under control now."

"You believe. What do you base this faith upon? Exactly." The song ended and I turned the music off. Wanted to hear everyone very clearly now.

"Your mother is on-site now and is angrier than you are, if you can believe it."

"Currently I cannot, and that's not because I'm selling Mom short. Someone had better explain how no one in the entire government could find us when we were literally less than an hour away from the White House, and why we cannot reach anyone at all, or I'm going to decide that everyone wanted us to stay missing."

"Trust me, that's not the case."

"Really?" Had a horrible thought. "Has anyone wanded Jeff and Chuckie and everyone else? What if they've been replaced by robots or androids?"

"No," Kevin said soothingly, "we're all really ourselves."

"How would we know that?" Camilla asked dryly.

Kevin heaved a sigh. "Countersign Protocol Alpha. Do it fast." He and Camilla shared words back and forth quite quickly.

She shrugged. "As long as we can trust that this is really Kevin Lewis, then he's confirmed that everyone is who they should be."

"Well, that's good news. Then, since we haven't been infiltrated, why was whoever took our call at Andrews and the White House *convinced* that I was safe and sound?"

"You're the one who suggested having your double in place."

"Don't try logic with me right now, Kevin, I am not in the mood. They armed warheads and aimed them at the ship I'm in after I'd told them who the hell I was. After Camilla gave them every sign and protocol known to mankind. And after all Centaurion phones other than ours, apparently, were turned off, with no voicemail possible. I'm currently wondering if this is an Alpha Four divorce ritual that no one told me about. I'm very seriously wondering."

"It isn't."

"Yeah? Prove it. This isn't the kind of reaction I expected when I was kidnapped. Everyone calmly putting my double in place and going on as if nothing bad has happened while *simultaneously* not having anyone look for me doesn't say 'I love you.' It says 'problem solved, get lost and stay lost' in my world."

"No, it's not that at all, Kitty, I promise. We had to do something, because the media got an anonymous call about the First Lady being in peril and we had to show that this wasn't the case. So Jeff was forced into a press conference literally at the same time you were taken. We locked down the phones so that no one could make a mistake and share classified information."

"Who is the person who authorized shutting down all the phones and who authorized keeping my phone and the others' phones active?"

"Ah ... Jeff, Chuck, and James authorized the phone shutdown. Your mother overrode and kept the phones of those known to be missing active."

"I'm no longer totally pissed at my mother. Everyone *else* on the other hand ..."

"The Administration can't reveal that the first time you walked outside of the White House you were snatched or there will be no faith in the leadership and we'll spend the next few years battling everything and everybody."

"I don't care. Let me be more accurate. I not only don't care, but I'm literally so angry that I'm about to go break Stephanie out of whatever hole she's in and join her side."

"See, that's part of the problem."

"Oh, don't tell me, let me guess. You all listened to the freaking android who gave you demands and did what she said to do, didn't you?"

Kevin coughed. "They did. I'd like to be on record that I said not to do it. I had full faith in you."

"Suck up. I like that, but still. Did anyone find the sniper that was on the roof somewhere near the Teetotaler?"

"No."

"Did anyone *try* to find said sniper?"

"Ah ... no. It was believed that the sniper went off after the limousine you were in."

"Believed. What was this 'belief' based on?"

Heard someone talking in the background. Kevin cleared his throat. "Someone saw a black motorcycle with a rider all in black and what looked like a weapon leaving the area around the same time as you."

Exchanged the "really?" look with Adriana. "Congratulations. Whoever 'someone' is, they spotted the only person who actually came to rescue us. Said person is not American or an A-C. By the way. So, let me get this straight. I'm kidnapped, along with several others, and someone sees who they think the sniper is going after me, and ... then what happened? I'm asking because the answer is clearly not 'we followed the motorcycle and found where you and the others were being held,' so I'm just excited to discover what actions were actually taken."

Kevin cleared his throat again. "I'm not totally clear on why, Kitty, because I wasn't involved in any of this, but pursuit was not allowed. Under the feeling that it would put you in more danger. There appears to have been a breakdown in protocols."

Not allowed. How interesting. "Well, we're just overrun with that, aren't we? Where are you and where are James and Tim?"

"I'm at Andrews, and so is your mother. Now, for both of us. James and Tim are at the White House along with Chuck, Jeff, and everyone else. They're hooked into this call, though."

"Awesome. My men? I'm so very, very beyond angry with you that I cannot adequately express it. I strongly suggest you stop whatever stupidity you're doing and figure out how to apologize to me for, oh, the next year, year and a half. Jeff? If you want a divorce, there are easier ways, and if you do, trust me that if this is how you're asking, I'm going to use this ship to make you really sorry about your breakup delivery method. Kevin? Get me Arthur Franklin and get him *now*."

"Here, Missus Martini, ma'am."

"Oh, I'm not mad at you, Arthur. Yet. You can continue to call me Kitty. The rest of my men had better be following your lead and calling me ma'am, however. Is my parking space still available at Andrews?"

"Yes, it is. Would you like an escort?"

"I will have my flyboys shoot any aircraft near to us out of the sky. I was not joking. It's been a very long and trying day and I'm just overjoyed to know that my men were morons and not only didn't tell anyone we might contact *that* I was kidnapped but also left some stupid protocol crap that I knew nothing about *and* that Camilla knew nothing about as the only way to confirm who I was. Just peachy. At least when Chuckie did that before it was a code I freaking knew."

"Those protocols were put in place due to a terrorist threat." Mom had joined the group call, and she was truly as pissed as I'd ever heard her. "I cannot adequately express how displeased I am that this Administration's first acts were to ignore my counsel and do something this remarkably stupid. I cannot express it at all because if I try I will be cursing from now until the Fourth of July."

Heaved a sigh. "Fine. Mom, I'm so angry. We save the day and this is the thanks we get?"

"Get used to it, kitten."

Camilla snorted. "Yeah, trust me, get very used to it."

"Already am. So, Mom, is this my husband's not-so-subtle way of saying he wants a normal wife?"

"Not to my knowledge, kitten. Though if it was, there won't be enough of him left for you to hurt. I'm easily as angry as you and I'm far closer to where he is than you appear to be."

"I love you, Mom. Of course, I have a big helicarrier I'm now dying to test in a variety of ways. But, presuming Jeff isn't going for the Grandiose Breakup Plan—and nothing that's happened so far is convincing me that he isn't, by the way—I suppose I shouldn't kick him, Chuckie, James, and Tim as hard as I can in their personal parts?"

"No," Mom said. "Not as far as I've been able to tell." Camilla's expression said that she was all for kicking and that she'd like to help kick. "Their reactions appear to be based out of stupidity and fear."

"How about their shins? Can I kick those?"

Mom laughed. "Maybe. See how well they grovel."

"I'd just like to say, in my defense, that we were all worried about you," Reader said as his way of letting me know he was also hooked into the call. "Ma'am. And all our intel said you were out of the country. Which was confirmed since we couldn't find you anywhere and Jeff couldn't feel you or any of the others."

"Try it in person, James. Still too angry to want to hear about it. So, do tell me this—you all released Stephanie, didn't you?"

"Yeah, we did, girlfriend. Getting the feeling that was also a mistake you're going to be really angry about."

"You have no idea. Why?"

"We were told that you and the others would all be killed. And we saw, ah, proof. Same reason we didn't follow the sniper and all the phones went off—if any of us tried to follow him or you or shared what was going on, you'd be killed."

"And never once did anyone ask themselves if that was a realistic version of events to be believing. Wow. Just . . . wow. Mom, did you verify that Jeff, Chuckie, James, and Tim—and, realistically, everyone else—are fully organic?"

"We did, because of the fact that we've already had robotic and android attacks. Per Tito and the rest of the White House and Embassy medical staff, everyone's who they should be."

"Didn't believe me?" Kevin asked.

"Let's just say that I felt getting a confirming second opinion was wise. Speaking of which, Mom, when did I stop believing in the Tooth Fairy?"

She chuckled. "At age five, because your father tripped putting the money under your pillow and accidentally woke you up."

"I feel remarkably reassured that you're really you, Mom. So, where are the security personnel we sent off in the limo?"

"They're at a bar called Charlie's a few miles away from where you were. Per Devon, it was the first place they found where they had phone service and since it's your son's name, he felt it was prophetic."

"I like Devon. Let's keep him around."

"I plan on it. Charlie's is a gay bar, apparently quite a fun place, and everyone there was incredibly helpful. Once those folks found out what had happened, they got our people food and drinks and have basically been taking care of them. I told the team to stay there and expense it until we could safely pick them up."

"They deserve the break. And who knows, maybe someone will make a love connection."

"Most of those teams are straight, but you never can tell. So, leave them there, don't try to add them into your new nation."

"Hilarious. Though you'd be the Queen Mother."

"I'm touched, kitten, really."

"Why are you less mad at Angela than the rest of us?" Reader asked.

"Because she's my mother, she's the reason our phones

are on, I can now say with some confidence that she didn't approve the moronic plan you all agreed to, and she gets more of a pass than any of you ever will. My husband and two best guy friends in particular. Megalomaniac Lad in also particular. Because you didn't send anyone to look for us even in more particular. Actually, let me list out all the things you didn't do—you didn't send anyone after the sniper, you didn't follow the motorcycle, you didn't think that maybe the terrorists were bluffing, you didn't think I would be anything other than a victim, and you didn't bother to let anyone know that I might be calling for help. Anyone still wondering why I'm furious should just review that list."

"Coming up on Andrews airspace, Commander," Hughes said.

"Awesome. Are my children safe? And do they now think they have a new mother?"

"They're safe," Mom said. "The moment we found out you were taken the Embassy went into lockdown."

"Yes, that was confirmed by Romania. Who were not allowed entry into our Embassy during a time of emergency. Which, let me mention, makes me even angrier than I already was, as hard as that is to believe."

"The only counsel of mine that was followed was turning your phones back on, kitten. And that only happened recently."

"Unreal. So you guys are why we couldn't call out for hours?"

"Possibly. On the plus side, your children aren't thinking of Francine as the new you."

"Guess we'll have to give Jeff more time for that, then." Heard someone shouting in the background. Was fairly sure it was Jeff. Ignored it. My phone rang. It was Jeff. Ignored it. "So, I have another question. Was Christopher involved in this stupidity in any way?" Phone rang again. Chuckie. Ignored it.

"Actually, no," Mom said. "And if it helps, he, like Kevin, also felt that you and his father were probably more in control than anyone else believed."

"Excellent! Nice to know that there were three whole people who actually could look back at past events and take a wild one that we weren't going to roll over and play scared. Christopher, and only Christopher, can meet us wherever Arthur is having us land. I am not in any mood to do the Happy Reunion Dance and, frankly, after this reception, I find it hard to believe anyone else in this ship with me is, either. Christopher can come and get us and, if the rest of you are lucky, convince me why I should speak to any of you ever again."

Lizzie sidled over next to Walker and whispered something to him. He nodded.

"What are you two chatting about?"

"Lizzie would like her father to come with Christopher," Walker said. There was something about his tone that made me choose my next words very carefully.

"Is he able to do that?"

There was silence on all ends of the line.

Cleared my throat as I saw the color drain from Lizzie's face. "Let me rephrase that question. Where are Benjamin Vrabel, John Wruck, and Malcolm Buchanan?"

More silence. Finally broken by Mom. "We don't know."

CHAPTER 75

MAHIN WENT TO Abigail and Lizzie and they did the group hug. I censored the variety of things I wanted to say. "When did they go missing?"

"They went after you," Kevin said.

"Well, it's nice to know they cared. Against orders, too, I'd have to guess, based on how little activity was centered on finding me and the others. Against the direct order of the terrorists, too. After I divorce Jeff, I'll see if any of the three of them are looking for a solid relationship."

Heard some more shouting on the other end. Was sure it was Jeff. Continued to ignore it.

So did Kevin, since the shouting didn't sound like it was on his end of our many-lined conference call, which made sense since he'd said Jeff was with Reader. "They went based on intel that we received from Crystal Maurer. And yes, we know she's an android, because half of your team made it back to the White House."

Half. More than half should have made it back, really. I'd rolled with a huge entourage. "Where are Colette, Manfred, Len, Kyle, Evalyne, and Phoebe?"

More silence. I was going to hate this answer.

"Again, we don't know," Kevin said, having obviously drawn the short straw or being the only one willing to man up. Censored myself again so that I wouldn't share that I was, if possible, even more angry than I'd been before.

"I'm out of communication for a little while and things just go to hell in a handbasket, don't they?"

"Pretty much." Kevin didn't sound any happier than I felt.

"I feel your pain," Camilla said.

"Ready to prep for landing," Hughes shared.

"Belay that, Matt. Kevin, Mom, when was the last time anyone saw or heard from Len and those others?"

"Right after you were kidnapped," Mom replied. "Len contacted Malcolm and was told to follow you. Then he was contacted by Jeff and told to ensure that he and the others returned to the White House immediately. They haven't been heard from since."

"They were supposedly with Burton Falk and his team. Has Falk checked in?"

"No," Mom said. "And no one from his team, either. Not since they went to follow Crystal Maurer."

"I appreciate Malcolm, Len, and the rest of these folks so much right now. And I'm going to say that if any of them are hurt, the men who didn't support them going after me are going to pay for it." Looked at Adriana. "What are the odds that they followed you or us in some way?"

She shrugged. "Len knew I was coming, what I was driving, and how I was dressed. And Manfred is an A-C, yes?"

"Yes, and so is Colette. Nice to know my Second Marriage Pool is even larger now. Those listening in can just guess who I like more than all of you right now and potentially forever after, and if you need it spelled out for you, which I'm sensing that you do, it's the people who actually cared enough to try to find us, orders or no orders."

Heard more yelling and my phone rang again. Jeff. Continued to ignore both. "And, oh, wow. I think I know where they are, and kudos to everyone currently living in the Sovereign and Flying Nation of Kitty Land who prevented us from checking out that 'detention center' nearby for help. Matt, turn this puppy around. Mom, Kevin, when you lose contact with us, and you will, trust me when I say that it's not us or the helicarrier doing it or, amazingly enough, our side blocking us."

"I thought you said the Kendroid was why we couldn't make calls," Abigail said.

"And I thought your mother said it was our own people," Mahin added.

"Right, well, trust me, based on the fact that Keith couldn't make calls, it's more than the Kendroid or our own people. So, when you lose us, Mom, trust me, it's not us doing that. James, are you still on the line?"

"Yes, and cringing with anticipation."

"Good. Tell Chuckie and Jeff—who I am refusing to speak to directly right now—that there is an NSA black site right by the abandoned Forest Haven Insane Asylum. And I do mean *right* by. That's where we were, by the way, and also by the way, I'm going to suggest to any man of mine who is even considering making the weakest joke about me and the insane asylum that you should consider just how far your charm isn't going to get you in this situation and keep any and all witticisms to yourselves."

"Check," Reader said. "Speaking for all your men, who are all incredibly sorry."

"Save it, James, I'm too angry to forgive at the moment. My husband for potentially not much longer least of all. Mom, tell the security team at Charlie's that their R and R is over. I need them to commandeer or simply borrow cars and get to the NSA site. Trust me, they all know where it is because we all avoided it in case we could get in easily but not get out in the same way."

"Kitty, there is no NSA black site where you're saying," Reader said, voice tight.

"Yes, there is, and at least some of our missing people are there. But, you know, feel *free* to argue with me. I think I'm the angriest I've ever been with people who are not my sworn enemies, but I'm always interested to see if I can go even higher on the rage scale. She-Hulk definitely wants to smash, James, and Wolverine's Berserker Rage is all set to go off, so go for it."

"Got it, not arguing with you. Just saying we have no record of this."

"We freaking looked at it. It's not a small facility. And I can guarantee that it's not showing up on grids because it's got the most sophisticated GPS scrambling and cellular blocking in the world going on. As in, whoever's running it is very possibly not our friend. And by 'our' I mean America's and by 'friend' I mean is probably an enemy of the state. You know, just like I am, apparently."

"Kitten, is that level of sarcasm necessary?"

"Yes, Mom, it is. It's part of my process."

"Well then, carry on. Be careful. I'll be busy putting intelligent protocols back in place."

"I love it when we're in Rage Sync together, Mom, but not with each other. I feel so bonded."

"That's my girl."

Was going to say something else, but heard static, then nothing. "We're in range of the NSA black site," Jerry said. "Clearly we have no more outside communications." The rest of the team chimed in that their phones were back to being good for taking pictures or listening to music and that was about it. Mine, too.

"Not that our communications were all that successful."

Jerry nodded. "Good point. And before you take my head off, I figured out how to put the cloaking back on when we were over Andrews. No one can see us, presumably whoever's at that site included."

"Yeah, I'm sure, because they'd have taken this ship, or at least investigated, if they'd been able to see it somehow."

"Tossing me, Matt, and Chip into your Marriage Pool, by the way. We're all willing to be Prince Consorts." He looked at Abigail over his shoulder and winked. She snorted a laugh while the other flyboys all chuckled. "What about you, Richard, you adding your name in, too?"

"Oh, I insist on always being on Our Sovereign Leader's Options List, Jerry."

"You complete me, Jerry. I love your confidence, Mister White, though you're not wrong." Rhee cleared her throat. "Yes, the Pool is open to the available females, too. Kitty Land welcomen everyone." Rhee grinned, and Rahmi and Camilla laughed.

"If our wives are as 'concerned' about us as Jeff appears to be about you, Kitty, count me and Randy in, too."

"Thanks, Joe. Maybe we'll just have a multiple marriage or something. Though until this experience, I'd have told you guys that Lorraine and Claudia were really worried and wanted you home safely. Same for Tito and your mother, Rahmi and Rhee."

"Fear makes many people incredibly stupid," Camilla said. "Meaning the terrorists probably had compelling evidence. I'm not suggesting we give them a pass for being morons, but if they acted out of fear and reasonable doubt, then it's a little more forgivable."

Took a deep breath, held it, let it out slowly. "You're probably right. But I'm still upset."

"That's normal." Camilla managed a smile. "Use the

anger now, just remember that you may want to lose it once we're back."

"Will do, Agent Ninety-Nine."

Camilla rolled her eyes. "I knew I shouldn't have shared that."

"Your mother sounded proud," Lizzie said. She sounded shocked, though I doubted it was with my openness toward my second marriage.

"She is." Heaved a sigh and went to Lizzie to take her from Mahin and Abigail and give her a hug of my own. "We're not really a line of women who bow and curtsey and weep and hide. We're a line of women who get mad and get even." Lizzie hugged me back. I could tell she was trying not to cry. Kissed the top of her head. "And you fit right in, Quick Girl. Let's see who all is being held against their will. If Mister Dash is not amongst them, I'm just betting that Falk will have some guesses as to where he, John, and Malcolm are."

"You think they're together?"

"Yeah, I do, I really do."

"How do you want us to do this, Commander?" Hughes asked, getting us back to business. "Raining fire from the sky, landing on the roof, or a stealth attack?"

"What do you guys suggest?"

"We get to offer suggestions?" Walker asked.

"Yep. I'm not mad at any of you, not even Keith."

"Thanks," he said, sarcasm knob easily at nine on the scale. "But if you mean it, I think a combination of obvious and sneaky is the way to go."

"Keith, you may have quite the future after all. So, who's going to go with me to be the distraction?"

"You're not doing the sneaking in?" Mahin sounded shocked.

"Nope. Adriana's here. She'll be Sneak Team Lead. And before anyone even thinks about giving me an argument about it, she's KGB trained and better than all of us put together. Matt, can you fly this without Joe and Randy?"

"Yes, if someone else can handle simple controls. But why?"

"The why is because I want our personal Six Million Dollar Men with the raiding party. Keith, my man, you're up. Time to learn to fly. Try not to do something that will make me mad at you."

"You got it," he muttered, as Hughes directed him to cover Joe's position. Joe gave him some quiet instructions.

"Need one more, Commander," Hughes said.

"Has to be a human. Lizzie, while I'd love to take you with me, it's going to have to be me and Richard knocking on the front door. Abby and Mahin, want you two with Lizzie and the flyboys in our Sovereign Nation Ship because if we need cavalry I'd like said cavalry to be together and actually coming for us. Plus, the security folks know you both and you'll have to coordinate with them when they get here."

Lizzie nodded and went to Randy's seat. He patted her shoulder then did the instructions thing.

"Commander," Jerry said, "I think you're forgetting one key thing."

"Only one? What are you referring to, Jerry?"

He grinned at me over his shoulder. "This is a helicarrier. Created for battle. As in, we have weapons that can leave the ship."

Stared at him for a long moment. "Giving myself the 'duh' on that one. I honestly didn't think this was equipped since no one used anything to escape."

"We couldn't access the weapons," Daniel said. "Trust me, we tried."

"The security repels with painful force," Joshua added.

"It does," Jerry agreed. "When you don't have control of the ship. But we do now. So . . ."

"Gotcha. Gang? Let's weapon up."

CHAPTER 76

DANIEL AND THE other A-Cs led us to an area some-where rather close to the command deck. Couldn't have said where it was—the helicarrier, like so many other things, was a rat maze to me already and I was completely lost.

The room we arrived at was clearly an armory, however. Glass or Plexiglas or Vatusus' version of either made up the top half of the walls. The bottom half was metal. And inside were an array of weapons and body armor that would make the armed forces of every country on Earth drool with desire.

"We couldn't even open this door before," Lucas said as Daniel quite easily opened the door.

"There are at least ten others like this scattered around the ship," Marcus added as we went inside and everyone, even those I'd have said were slightly more pacifistic than the others—namely White, Abigail, and Mahin—were running around like kids in the most dangerous candy store in the world.

"Commander," Walker said over the intercom, "have spotted the security forces. Do you want to try to get them into our Floating Fortress of World Domination?"

"Yes, because those guys deserve to be armed for bear and protected just like the rest of us. Drax Industrial definitely has the contract for Kitty Land. See if Keith can give you numbers so you can try to call them first. Who knows, maybe we can get through even though we're cut off from our supposed friends at Andrews and the White House." Had another thought. "Chip, I'm going to give you a phone number. See if you can make contact."

"Will do."

Gave him Drax's number that I'd saved to my phone, then went back to equipping myself and everyone else.

The body armor actually conformed to each individual, kind of like a wetsuit but without being as hard to put on. Wasn't as easy to use as the stuff Alfred in Bizarro World had created, but, if it worked, it was a lot less bulky than Kevlar and a lot more maneuverable than actual armor.

The guns were lightweight and came in a wide variety of sizes and magazine loads and, unsurprisingly to any of us who'd been on the Murder Train, there was also a huge assortment of knives available.

Before we were done choosing our weapons of personal destruction, Walker was back on the com. "Commander, have connected with the other security forces via text, which we still seem able to use, though only via Keith's phone. They're at what Devon insists is the entry to the area we were in. Will be picking them up shortly. There are some civilians asking if they need to come along, too."

"Tell them thank you but no. I think we have enough people in danger right now. Be sure someone gets contact info for all the nice people at Charlie's who helped out, though. Then tell them to leave the area immediately."

"Already handled on the contact info and will do on evacuation order. Also was able to connect your call, mostly because I think he has the ship wired for it somehow. You now have Mister Drax on the line."

"Awesome. Gustav, how goes it?"

"I'm deeply confused about how your government handles things, but otherwise, I'm good. How are you?"

"Oh, no longer kidnapped, about to do a raid, just as confused as you are about what's been going on, and really pissed off at my husband and close friends."

"Interesting. I'd relay a message but I and my retainers have been put into lockdown in your embassy for the duration."

"Why ask why? Clearly there's a distinct need for my input over at The Big House."

"Possibly. So if you're hoping I can assist you, I'm limited. I'm under guard, but they did allow this call."

"Super. The Sovereign and Flying Nation of Kitty Land is hella impressed with your skills. You're officially our weapons dude. We have no money, but we've already got your stuff, and we'll definitely be giving you sterling recommendations."

"You found the helicarrier?" He sounded elated. Good.

"Yes, we did. Long story that I'll tell you later, but rest assured, it was not the real Thomas Kendrick who took it, so you two can remain friends and business partners. Here's the thing. Can this puppy extract people from either the ground or a secured facility?"

"I don't follow you." Heard voices in the background, then heard Drax relay my request. "Sorry, Tevvik says that he does follow you. Call is now on speakerphone."

"Missus Martini, are you asking if the ship can 'beam' someone up?"

"Hey, Tevvik. Let's go with Commander Kitty right now. And yes, I do mean that. How did you know?"

"Your father is with us and is providing any interpretation we might need."

"Hi, Dad! Please don't let Jeff have Francine impersonate me to the kids."

"That's not what's going on, kitten, I promise, though I understand why you're upset." Dad was oozing parental support. Clearly Mom had told him how angry I was. "We'll get it straightened out once you're home. The children are fine and missing you. But I'll let you get back to Tevvik. The Vata are fascinating. Did you know—"

"Dad, love you, but you're not Tevvik who you said you were giving me back to."

"Sorry, kitten, you're right. Go ahead."

Tevvik chuckled. "Thank you. Plus, Commander Kitty, we've been searching for Prince Gustav for two years. Radio waves carry, and in this part of the galaxy, there's not a lot of interesting things going on. We've received all communications from Earth and the Alpha Centauri planets for over a year while we made our way to you."

"I thought you could travel hella fast."

"We can. There are a lot of planets to check, Commander Kitty, inhabited and uninhabited. Vata are thorough people."

"Good to know. Prince Gustav seems . . . less thorough."

"I resent that."

"But you can't deny it, my prince. You're right,

Commander Kitty. The royal family has less need to be thorough—that's what their retainers are for. At any rate, to answer your question, no, I don't believe the ship is equipped with 'beaming' technology."

"Bummer. Okay, then we get our people out the hard, yet much more exciting, way."

"There's body armor and weapons in the ship, or there should be," Drax said.

"Ahead of you and speaking to you from one of your armories. Anything we should know about any of the tech we're about to start using on a raid to rescue our captured people?"

"Not really. I made them for humans and A-Cs to use. I could tell you how to use the small invisibility irradiation chamber that's on board if you'd like."

"No, I'm with Thomas Kendrick on that—I'd prefer an easy on and off way to do the Invisibility Mambo. Which, by the way, I think one of our enemies has. Why I'm calling and what I'd like you to do is to contact Serene somehow and tell her that I think that Stephanie has figured out how to use the A-C's invisibility shielding—which is on all their vehicles and around the Crash Site Dome, for your info—and made it something that a human or android can wear and turn on and off and that no A-C can see through."

"Tevvik has a direct line to Serene and is contacting her now." Heard quiet speaking. "Ah. And your father already asked her to come over."

"Great. Your job, Gustav, is to help her figure out how Stephanie did it and how to combat it. And I'd like that done quickly."

"I'll do my best."

"Works for me. Not sure if we'll be able to contact you again. If we can't and if they ask, yes, I'm still furious, though trying really hard to see their side of things. If anyone cares, I'm certain the sniper was using this invisibility stuff, and if we discover that Burton Falk and all of that team decided to come after me because they lost Crystal Maurer's trail—which I assume they did and plan to find out the moment I rescue them—it's because she's using that tech, too. The biggest question is who the sniper was. My answer is that I'm going to bet cash money that it was someone Stephanie's worked with before, and it's also someone willing to play one side against the other. Ergo, my money is on Casey Jones, she of Club Fifty-One and Cliff's Crazy Eights and probably more besides."

"You're sure?" White asked.

"Not a hundred percent, but to get someone onto the payroll this fast, it had to be someone Stephanie already knows. The other Crazy Eights are mad at her, but Casey was already running a double game. Who's to say she's not running a third?"

"Commander Kitty, your father hooked Commander Dwyer into this call via his phone and she says that she got all that," Tevvik shared. "She'll be to us momentarily and will take control of this situation and will hunt down any other connections to Stephanie that might have been the sniper."

"They'll let her in the Embassy when it's in full lock-down?"

"They will because I shared that I'm as mad as you are," Serene said.

"Nice of you to join the party."

"I'd have been here sooner but I've been busy screaming at Jeff, Chuck, James, and Tim."

"You complete me."

"Doing my best."

"Commander Kitty," Drax said. "I realize this may not help, but the ship can 'see' into buildings. Are your pilots wearing the helmets?"

"Guys, I know Chip left this line open 'cause I know how you guys roll. So, are you?"

"What helmets?" Walker asked.

"Push the button that says INT—it's short for interactive." Said with a tremendous amount of static.

"I think we're losing you guys. We're going to the presumed NSA black site next to the abandoned Forest Haven Insane Asylum. If we don't come back soon, send an army."

"Have lost the connection, Commander," Walker shared a few moments later.

"Figures."

"Believe they did receive your last comment. Need you back here at command, as well."

"On my way." Looked at White. "Well, sorta. Richard, are you equipped?"

He took my hand. "Yes, and I know the way back." We zipped off and were back at the command center quickly.

All five pilots, which included Lizzie and Keith, were wearing helmets. They looked like what I considered a typical jet pilot's helmet, but with an amber visor that went over the top half of the face. From what I could see of their faces and from their body language, the flyboys looked intent and relieved. The three of them were doing whatever it was they were doing with a lot more confidence and authority.

Lizzie and Keith, however, had gone from looking worried and nervous to looking like they'd had an infusion of Can-Do Attitude and as if this was now the most exciting thing ever. Clearly the helmets were helpful. "What's up and I presume the helmets are good?"

"Oh, my God," Lizzie said. "They're totes amazing! You wouldn't believe what you can see with this thing on!"

"They help tell you what to do to fly the ship," Keith added. He glanced over at me. "Can I request permanent assignment to your security detail, Commander Kitty?"

"Keith, welcome to Team Adrenaline Junkie, and yes, you can." Went over to where Jerry was, since he was the one beckoning to me.

"We don't have a totally clear spot to land to pick the team up. I realize you want to equip them, but they're already in position, just outside of what we think would be the black site's visual radius. Keith's been in constant communication with them, and the thinking is that we either bring down equipment for them or they're the fallback team."

"Makes sense. So, can we see inside the buildings like Drax said we could?"

"No idea yet, Commander," Hughes said. "We haven't tried over any buildings we've passed since they were civilian and we're not the NSA."

Every station had at least one viewing screen. Jerry had three, and one of them was aimed at the road beneath us. We were high enough that we had a good view of the entire area we were headed for, so I got to see Forest Haven in all its glory. It looked a lot better from above, in part because it was almost fully dark out.

Which meant that I noticed the headlights. Lots and lots

of headlights. All heading out of the black site's parking lot and out to the highway. There were other headlights, too, coming from down the road. "Where are those other cars coming from?"

"School for underprivileged youth," Keith answered. The helmets were clearly as impressive as the team had said. "Meaning it's a nice juvenile detention center. That complex shows clearly as what they are, and we've cross-referenced. They're legit, and while some of the students live there full-time, and therefore so do some administration and security staff, plenty come and go."

"Interesting. Wish we'd run that far."

"No, you don't," Keith said. "Devon said they checked it out when they went the wrong way to leave. The team decided it was a risk—to us and to them—to ask for help, based on the site we're going back to now. By the way, Devon's certain that's an NSA black site, and half the team with him agree. Whatever we're going to find there, no one expects it to be good."

"Gotcha. Well, I'm hoping we find our missing people. Our team on the ground is hidden?"

"Waiting in the trees just down the street," Hughes said. "Civilians dropped them off as requested. The limo was out of gas, so it's a good thing they found help."

"It's always nice to have friends in all the places, high, low, and otherwise. Right now, I think we have friends in that black site. So, equipped as we are now, I'm going to ask again—how do we approach?"

Jerry looked up at me and grinned. "Well, Commander, we do know this beast lands well onto a roof."

CHAPTER 77

WHILE THE FLYBOYS were maneuvering the helicarrier into place—with Joe and Randy choosing the wiser course and, helmets or no helmets, talking Keith and Lizzie through what they needed to do—I took a couple of moments to pet the Poofs and Peregrines. It was a fast pat for each, but I could tell the animals appreciated it.

Wanted to tell the animals to stay in the helicarrier and also ask them for help. Decided it was time to let them exercise their free will and let them do what they felt was best.

The rest of the team had arrived with Joe and Randy, and everyone was definitely dressed to raid and armed for bear. They'd also found goggles and brought some for me and White as well. These weren't like the goggles that allowed you to see invisible people—these were goggles that let you see in the dark.

"Commander," Hughes said as we moved above the roof of the largest building, which was shaped like a big, thick letter L, "can verify visually that there are only a handful of vehicles left at the site, and they appear to be parked in the back portion of the lot."

"Ninety-five percent certainty they're in the lot reserved for security personnel," Jerry said. "Meaning work's done for the day."

"Long hours, really. It's around seven in the evening, isn't it?"

"Normal hours if you're running twelve-hour shifts," Walker said.

"So they're not a twenty-four-seven operation? That seems . . . odd."

Randy shrugged—interesting that I could see it through the body armor. "It keeps your cover better in some ways if you look like everyone else. I think that they leave when the school personnel leave, so that it's obvious to anyone going to or from the school that it's just a regular kind of workplace."

"The other facility we were blocked from at Forest Haven is an adult retraining compound," Keith shared. "Totally legit, not a detention center, just a place for adults out of a job to go to learn new skills. And they're letting out now, too."

"So that means that if there's another shift at the black site, they won't be here for a few hours."

Got the room's attention, go me. "What do you mean?" Mahin asked.

Heaved a sigh and saw Camilla clearly trying not to laugh. "They're faking out the normal people nearby. But I'm still betting they have a nighttime crew. Those people just arrive probably around nine in the evening and most likely leave somewhere between four and six in the morning."

Camilla nodded. "I'd assume so. That gives us what we hope is a two-hour window to do this raid and rescue. I'd suggest we do it faster than that, because there's no guarantee that the next crew will be here at nine. They could be here at seven-thirty."

"Ah, Commander?" Keith sounded concerned. "Devon reports that someone's joined their team."

"Who?"

"Christopher White."

"Ah, no worries, we're not mad at him. Does he want to join us?"

"He wants to lead that team. He brought weapons for them with him."

"How?"

"In a big bag, apparently."

"How Santa Claus in the Summer of him. But yes, tell them that they should absolutely follow Christopher's lead. He's done this kind of stuff a lot more than they have, and I'm saying that with the assumption that everyone down there has been in this kind of work all of their lives."

"Roger that, Commander."

Looked at White. "I guess he didn't want to wonder how you were doing anymore."

White chuckled. "I appreciate his concern over my welfare."

"Yeah, it's nice to know that someone cares." Of course, I'd told Jeff and the others to stay put, so it wasn't fair to compare them to Christopher, who I'd asked to have meet us.

"While we'll be landing, you can leave the ship earlier," Walker said. "And I'd recommend it. There are cables at the hatch I'm sending you to—they'll help you get down safely."

"Commander," Hughes said as Walker gave Daniel some quiet instructions, presumably about how to find the right exit hatch. "We are in position over the roof. As soon as we lower, I expect anyone there to be aware of us, so suggest away team preps for departure."

"Gotcha. Until I'm back, Matt's in charge. Matt, ensure that you don't move onto the side of the men I'm angry with."

"Roger that and no fear, Commander. I know who my ultimate commanding officer is. And it's you, in case you weren't sure."

"That's the spirit. Lizzie, that means you obey Matt's orders. Within reason. Same for Abby and Mahin."

"Got it. If they totes try to leave you guys here or something I'll handle it."

Abigail grinned and Mahin nodded.

"Excellent. Daniel, lead us to our exit point."

The raiding party followed Daniel to a hatch that looked just like the one we'd entered through. The surrounding area was different, though. It resembled the interior of a plane that was being used by paratroopers. As promised, we found the cables—and lots of them. The paratrooper comparison got a lot stronger. Happily, there were gloves here, too. Nice to see that Drax thought of everything.

We all put on gloves and grabbed a cable. Joe showed us all how to hold onto the cables to go down like we'd want to in order to avoid going splat.

"Who's lead now?" Adriana asked. "Kitty, you're here, so it should be you."

"There's enough room that we can go two at a time," Randy said.

"Good, but this isn't my area of expertise, at least not until we're down. Joe and Randy, you lead, then me and Richard. Camilla and Adriana, you bring up the rear. Everyone else, no shoving, play nicely, go in teams like you're already used to—Field, princesses, Field."

Joe grinned. "Sounds good. And before you ask, yes, we'll catch you, Commander."

"Thanks, I'm certain that'll be an issue."

"Everyone should put on their goggles then hold onto the straps," Randy indicated straps all around this area. "Make sure your weapons are strapped, too. Check each other to be sure. Even though we're low, when the hatch opens, there's going to be some backdraft."

Did the weapons check with Randy, who was in front of me, and Daniel, who was behind. We were all secure. Checked my purse which, body armor or no body armor, I still had over my neck. My skirt and pumps were gone as if they'd never been with me, but I had something in their place—Harlie and Poofikins. Poofs on Board made me feel a tad better.

As I thought this a third Poof arrived—Murphy, who was Jeff's special Poof. Harlie was supposedly his, but had bonded with me. But Murphy was definitely Jeff's Poof now. Interesting. Patted the Poofs. "Kitty's never mad at any of *you*." They all purred at me, which made me feel better and a little less upset with Jeff and the others.

We all got our goggles in place and hooked on just in time, because backdraft there was. Though it wasn't all that bad, it probably would have knocked me or Adriana down and possibly out. And it wouldn't have been fun on the eyes, either.

We were much more than a few feet over the roof, however. But my Six Million Dollar Men didn't hesitate. "Go!" Joe said, and he and Randy jumped. They whizzed down their cables just as they'd shown us how to do. But they were easily ten feet above the roof when the cables ran out.

Both guys flipped into somersaults in the air and landed on their feet in lovely cat-like crouches.

They stood up, turned around, and waved.

"We're up, Missus Martini," White shouted.

Nodded and we jumped onto our cables.

Couldn't pay attention to White because I was too focused on myself. I was whizzing down the cable a lot faster than I'd been prepared for—the end came a lot sooner, too. Tried to flip in the air like Joe and Randy had done, but didn't manage it. Sort of flailed around like I was trying to do the backstroke in the air, which probably looked hilarious.

Managed to tuck my head so when I landed I might not knock myself out. But I didn't hit hard—I hit White, landing right in his arms.

"Wow, you're impressing all the girls again, Mister White."

"It's what I do. I landed close to where it looked like you were going to hit. I must say, when you make Jeffrey suffer later, do tell him about this. But please make sure I'm far away."

Laughed as he put me down. "Yeah, this is normally Jeff's job. Wish I didn't feel like today he wouldn't have done it, though."

"Let's get through this raid, then we'll find out what really happened on their end of things. I'd imagine we'll understand once we know."

"Hope so. Or I'll go on a rampage, so, you know, fun times either way."

All the rest of the teams had absolutely no issue landing and were all on the roof by the time White had put me down and we'd finished bantering. Actively chose not to be bitter.

Joe indicated it was my show now. Made the "after you" sign. "You and Randy take point. You've had more experience. But I'll be right behind you."

"Please remember to keep a wary eye open for traps and such," White said to them and me as we all pulled our big guns off of our backs and I shifted into place behind Randy, White right behind me, clearly ready to yank me back if necessary.

Nodded, then Joe made the "moving out" and "be quiet" signals, and we started off at a trot. There was a doorway ahead of us, and Joe had us go to the right and left so we wouldn't be in the line of fire. Randy pulled the door open. "Clear!"

They headed in and downstairs and the rest of us followed, going quietly. Not for the first time, I was glad that I'd asked for and received jeans and Converse—there was no way I could have been quiet in pumps.

We reached the top floor, and Joe motioned to Daniel and Joshua. Those two took off at hyperspeed and were back quickly. "Clear," Daniel said. "Two sets of stairs heading down, both clear when we checked."

"Looks like a combination school and scientific think tank," Joshua added.

Joe nodded, and we headed for the nearest stairs down. Heard what I was pretty sure was the helicarrier landing as we did so.

Reached the ground floor and Daniel and Joseph zipped off again. This time they weren't as fast to come back.

"Found some security," Daniel said when they returned. "Subdued and contained. Left them near the main entrance, so we may want to move them."

"We found these on them." Joshua handed me some keycards and four walkie-talkies. Dumped them into my purse, doing my best not to disturb the Poofs in there.

"Any guess for who's running this place yet?" The keycards and walkies hadn't had any logos on them.

"Not yet," Daniel said. "We caught them unawares and they're knocked out, tied up, and gagged. We didn't do interrogations, but we can later if necessary."

"Okay, you guys and Luke and Marc—do fast searches of all the buildings you can access." Handed them the keycards back. "Only subdue if it's safe for you to do it. Otherwise, come back and we'll full-on raid. We'll be moving the prisoners."

The two Field teams took off. Joe led us to the front door, which was accessed through a long entry hallway. Took a look at our unconscious prisoners. No one looked familiar to any of us, and they just looked like normal guys doing security. They were dressed that way, too. If this was the NSA black site we all thought it was, these guys were definitely providing the Normal Person Camouflage.

The princesses dragged the bodies into a nearby office that Camilla indicated. "We need to give the fallback team a heads up if we're able to," Joe said. "They can't help us if they don't know what we're doing."

White nodded. "That will fall to me. Be right back. Start firing weapons if you need me sooner." He took off.

Looked around. Nothing exciting to see, though the goggles had adjusted to the fact that we had light. They did some interesting stuff, but nothing that mattered for what we were doing right now, unless I cared about how thick the walls here were, and currently I did not.

The Field teams were back shortly after White had left. "Nothing and no one," Marcus said. "Anywhere on the above-ground levels. We found a stairway leading to lower levels but figured you'd want the full team before we headed down."

"It's a think tank, I believe," Lucas said. "Classrooms, offices, rooms devoted to science and engineering."

"And so far it looks innocuous," Joshua added. "So let's hope you're right, Commander, because if not, we've attacked without provocation."

"I'd be a lot more worried about this if anyone could have found this place listed. That they couldn't means that I'm not wrong, but that they're really smart about hiding their real work here." I sincerely hoped.

"We checked what we could of the grounds as well," Daniel said. "Nothing of interest. There are three smaller buildings that were only accessible by going outside. Look like dormitories, but there's nothing in them to indicate that anyone's sleeping here right now."

White returned now, but he wasn't alone. Christopher was with him.

Who grinned at my shocked expression. "You didn't think I was going to stay hiding in the trees all the time, did you?" He nodded to the others. "Not here to cramp your style, and love the outfits, by the way, but I figured I'd be more useful on this team. Devon has things under control and they know that if one of us doesn't come back to them within thirty minutes, they signal the ship that they can't see but is on the roof and then they come in after us."

"We're dressed for a commando raid, thank you very much. But, to your point, let's not stand around talking. We've searched the entire complex and, other than four normal security guys that the team knocked out, there's no one and nothing." Considered asking Christopher if he wanted a weapon or body armor, then figured he was in the Armani Fatigues and probably felt that was all he needed.

Christopher's eyes narrowed. "Were all four at the main door or were they on patrol?"

"Guarding the door and entry hallway," Daniel said, as the others nodded. "And they were here on duty, not hanging out."

"Then there's something suspicious going on. If you only have four guards for a complex this size, they should be on different floors and areas. That they were here indicates they aren't guarding the complex so much as they're guarding the door."

"I'm so proud."

Received Patented Glare #1. Considered offering him a pair of goggles. "I was the Head of Imageering for over a decade before you ever met us, if you'd care to remember."

"Oh, I remember. You're just thinking like a sneaky human, and I call that some serious educational growth."

He rolled his eyes. "Thanks a lot. But, before we head off, I just wanted to tell you all what I already told the fallback team—I'm really thankful you're all okay." Christopher hugged all of us, one at a time. A-Cs liked group hugs, but there were too many of us do to one smoothly, and our armor, goggles, and weapons made a group hug far too unwieldy and probably dangerous.

"Thanks," I said as he hugged me. "Of course we're okay with no thanks to anyone else. And almost no one else seems to care."

"I know. They care, Kitty, though I can see how it didn't look that way to any of you. But they were frightened. And I understand why you're all upset."

"Probably not all of the reasons," Joe said, "For example, Randy and I aren't all right. In that sense."

"Technically we might be better," Randy said. "Only not fully human."

"What happened?" Christopher looked worried, then horrified, as I gave him the fast recap of the fun we'd been having. He hugged Joe and Randy again once he had the full story. "We'll figure out how to fix it."

Joe shrugged. "Right now, I still feel like me but I can do things I couldn't before."

Randy nodded. "Kitty's calling us her Six Million Dollar Men. I kinda like it."

Christopher looked blank.

Heaved a sigh. "It's a popular culture reference. I'm so not surprised you don't get it. But the guys are dealing and we need to roll because you gave Devon a timeline."

Christopher nodded and heaved his own sigh. "You're right, let's go see what's hiding in this facility."

CHAPTER 78

CHRISTOPHER ACTUALLY zipped out to tell Devon when to start timing us, meaning we waited about a minute before he was back and we were able to start off again, this time heading for the staircase the Field agents had found.

There was only one stairway going down, and it was at the far end of this main building. Per Daniel they'd found elevators in every building, but none of them went underground and they'd tried the keycards in them, just in case.

"I'm going to mention that there being only one way down is suspicious."

"It is," Christopher agreed. "I checked the area out before I joined up with the other team. The insane asylum looks exactly like I imagine Hell looks like."

"I think it might be creepier."

"No argument. In addition to how the security team was stationed, the fencing all around this place really indicates something shady going on, since we checked and it's not a listed prison or similar. It's not listed as anything. Like James said, there's no record of any building like this being here. The only things listed on this part of the property are all part of the insane asylum. And no, I'm not going to make any jokes."

"Nice to see you've learned and matured. Fatherhood is good for you. But, let's be real—something this size didn't build itself."

"Again, no argument, but there's no record of it, meaning it's definitely a black site of some kind. By the way, I told Amy and Serene where I was going, but didn't check in with

Jeff and the others. Mostly because I didn't want to be the messenger."

"I have no interest in their messages."

"I've never seen you this mad at Jeff, let alone Chuck, James, and Tim," Christopher said.

"I've never had them literally approve the arming of warheads aimed at me."

He nodded. "I don't think that's the real reason. But I understand."

"Do you?"

"Actually, yeah. You just got written off as helpless by four men whose lives you've saved more than once."

"Got it in one. I'm insulted for me and your dad, let alone for Mahin, Abigail, and Lizzie, that the assumption was that we were so incapacitated that they needed to instantly capitulate to terrorists."

That was it, in a nutshell. If I stopped to really consider it, I was still angry because I felt written off as helpless and I expected better from the guys I loved the most. Not the most mature reaction on my part, though.

White nodded. "Yes, and I understand the frustration. I share it, as well. However, son, we do need to remember that anger is what Missus Martini uses to fight."

Of course, White was correct about why my being immature right now might be the right plan. Not an issue — the warheads aiming for us were still a very recent memory. "Oh, trust me, not a problem. Explanations for why I'm upset don't make me less upset. They just confirm the anger, you know?"

"Yeah, I do." Christopher looked around. "I'll be right back." He zoomed off at Flash level and was back before we'd reached our destination. "I just checked everything out. You guys really think this is a think tank? It looks more like a school, especially since it has dormitories."

"Maybe that was the cover story when it was being built." I might be mad at him, but Chuckie had trained me really well in how to spot the conspiracies and the lies used to cover them up. "Build a school, then claim that there aren't enough students to justify staffing it, shuffle some papers around, and you've got an excellent facility to use for whatever nefarious thing you're planning."

"If this is NSA run as we all suspect, and is hidden as

well as it seems to be from a paper trail standpoint, that indicates a high-level government official or officials are involved," White pointed out.

"Despite Cliff's best efforts to kill everyone in Washington, I'll bet we still have plenty of options for who's behind it."

"You know what this reminds me of?" Christopher asked. Rhetorically, since he answered his own question. "Gaultier Enterprises. Dad, doesn't it seem like it's laid out similarly to the building we visited with Amy?"

White nodded. "Yes, son, you're right. Only it also resembles a school."

"Or a think tank," Lucas said. Clearly he was going to stick to that idea regardless. Couldn't blame him—I tended to stick to my ideas, too.

"What I find most interesting is that it has a very limited number of windows that face the streets and it's decently lit inside," Camilla said. "As in, no one's having trouble seeing because there are lights on. Why? There were all of four men in here, and they were all stationed by the front door."

"No idea," Randy said. "But I'm sure we're going to find out."

We reached the area that led down. It was blocked by a thick glass wall and door. There was a keycard entry box on the concrete wall that the glass wall connected with.

Camilla snorted. "I think we can stop assuming school *or* think tank. No one blocks off an entrance like this and requires keycard entry for benign reasons." She tapped the glass. "Bulletproof. And I knew that without the goggles to tell me. Whatever's going on downstairs, it's top secret."

Looked at the glass more carefully. Yep, the goggles shared that it was bulletproof, they just did it in my peripheral vision, and I'd ignored it. Needed to not do that—if we had cool tech, we should use it. My brain nudged.

"You know . . ." Had to arrange my thoughts, because my brain was nudging rather urgently. I was missing something I needed to pay attention to and it was a Megalomaniac Girl something—a leap I needed to make that my brain felt was the correct jump to take.

"What?" Christopher asked. "I know that look. Well, what I can see of that look, I mean."

"I'm leaving the cool goggles on, but yeah, I have a look

going, I'm sure. The Kitty-Bot was created by YatesCorp, but by their robotics division, meaning the tech side of either Titan Security or Gaultier Enterprises. Probably both, since they were all in bed together for so long. And you said this place reminds you of Gaultier Research, right?"

"Yes, so?" Christopher sounded like he was trying to be supportive even though he had no idea why I was talking. More personal growth. Go team.

"So, in any raid that Chuckie and Mom have ever done, they've never found the Kitty-Bot or any other Fem-Bot. To the point where we all forgot that there was a Kitty-Bot until yesterday."

"Yes, and again, so?"

"So where would you build Fem-Bots? I mean that seriously. They have to be done in some kind of secrecy, and I'd imagine they need a decent facility of some kind—the Janelle Gardiner Fem-Bot was certainly clean and well made. And wouldn't female robots be something that would sound amazingly awesome to those politicians who are always wanting to stay a few jumps ahead of any other country in terms of espionage and warlike behavior?"

"That's kind of a leap, Kitty," Christopher said. The Field agents all nodded. Well, none of them were all that wet behind the ears—they'd probably served under Christopher at some point, so it wasn't shocking that they were in agreement with him.

"Is it? The lab where the clones were being made at Gaultier was deep underground. The lab under the Embassy was deep underground. Every Centaurion Division base goes deep underground. Some because of convenience, but mostly because it's harder to spot what you're doing if you're doing it deep enough in the earth."

"I don't see how you get a robotics factory here from that," Christopher said.

"Because Stephanie's Lair is underground right here in Forest Haven and she was making androids there. Maybe there's a special power grid in this area that she tapped into, because she had full power in her Lab of Doom. Meaning she probably piggybacked from this place."

"Wouldn't that be noticed?" White asked.

"Yeah, but not if your power needs are sky-high already and you're not actually paying a bill. The only way anyone notices if they're using too much power is because the power company shares their monthly usage numbers on their bill. No bill, no usage information."

"I'm sure something shady's going on here," Christopher said. "But I think you need to keep an open mind, because I doubt that we've found the robot factory."

"Oh, I will, but I think we should be prepared to find a robotics factory somewhere. Because those robots pack a punch and take a licking and keep on ticking. They aren't up to most androids, but they're tougher than any human and most A-Cs."

"We'll remain ever-vigilant," White said. "I, personally, am waiting for the next attack, since I have a clear memory of how our luck works out. And, armed to the teeth or not, assuming this facility is mostly empty or not, I don't expect the next part of this offensive to go as smoothly as this portion has."

"That's why you're the best Field agent we have, Mister White." Looked at the four Field agents who all looked a little hurt. "Don't mean to diss your skills, boys, but he really is the best."

"Oh, I'm sure they're not any more insulted by the insinuation that they're not up to my dad's level than I am," Christopher said, sarcasm knob heading for eleven. "I see what Jeff means about the hero worship."

"Yeah, well it's going to be a bit before I can go back to worshipping my other heroes."

"I'm sure you'll forgive them," White said. "Ultimately."

"They really feel awful about it," Christopher said as Joe took the keycards from Marcus and tested to see which, if any, would open the door. "If that helps any."

"It does, but as the hero I'm in no way upset with just said, let's let me stay angry until we've rescued everyone. I've had trouble keeping the rage going today, so stop being reasonable for a while."

Christopher grinned. "As long as you're not mad at me, fine, they're all panicked idiots. Until we're home."

"Deal."

Third card was the winner. The lock clicked and Joe opened the glass door cautiously. Nothing happened. "Who's holding onto the card for this door?" he asked quietly. "I'd like us to keep them separate so that we don't waste time trying a key that's already worked its lock." He pointed to the other side of the wall, where another keycard lock sat. "I think we need to use it to get back out as well."

"Give it to Adriana. She's bringing up the rear, meaning she'll be in the lead if we have to run like crazy for some reason."

The first keycard handled, we went back into formation. White put Christopher behind him, despite Christopher's arguments against this. "I'm bigger than you, son, and I'm wearing body armor and you're not. Just accept that I don't want to see my only child hurt and roll with it."

"Kitty's rubbing off on you, too, Dad."

"I take that as a compliment."

"Hence why I'm never mad at your dad, Christopher."

The stairway was unremarkable. Concrete all the way around—per the goggles it was at least twenty feet thick on either side—and decently lit. We went down the equivalent of two stories, based on the number of steps and landings. And came to another door. This one wasn't glass but metal, only six inches thick per the goggles. However, it had the keycard entry pad as well.

Joe tried the three cards he still had. Third one was again the charm. This one we handed back to Camilla, since she was next to Adriana.

Through this door we entered a long hallway, also concrete as thick as the other area had been, also well lit. Refrained from making any *Get Smart* jokes, mostly because I doubted Camilla would appreciate it. Because of Jeff's old TV shows obsession, I'd probably seen every TV show ever made by now, and I was fully up on Maxwell Smart and his gang. However, had to figure we weren't going to find much to laugh about at the end of this corridor.

Took what seemed like forever but was probably only a couple of minutes for us to reach the end of the hallway, which was, naturally, another six-inch-thick metal door. The first keycard Joe tried was the winner. This one he gave to Randy.

Through this door and, lucky us, it was time to go down another couple of flights of well-lit and thick concrete stairs, which indicated to me that we were now at least three stories underground. And, at the bottom of these stairs we got to meet Door #4.

It was metal, too, the now-standard six inches, and Joe's last key worked. Nice to know that the security guys had been able to get down here if they'd wanted to.

"Everyone get ready," Joe said softly. "And be prepared for attack."

With that, he opened the door cautiously and stepped through.

CHAPTER 79

ABSOLUTELY NOTHING happened, and Joe motioned for the rest of us to come inside.

We entered into a dark area, but that was because we were behind heavy curtains. Had a feeling that whoever had designed this place had helped Stephanie out with her lab as well.

Rejoiced that we were finally using the night vision part of our goggles, but it was underwhelming since I wasn't deeply into curtains.

Joe waited until we were all in, with Adriana still holding the door open just in case, then he slowly drew back a tiny bit of the curtain. He looked back at me and jerked his head. Went forward.

"Need you to take a look and tell me what you think," he said softly.

Nodded and took that look.

It was a brightly lit space, large as far as I could tell and the goggles shared. It was also clearly a factory. There were assembly lines and similar, but it was sparkling clean, like an Intel commercial — I expected that anyone we would see in here would be dressed in the white clean room suits, complete with hoods.

Only there was no one that I could see.

The goggles were having issues, though. They were no longer telling me anything. Had no idea what that meant, but figured it meant something bad.

Went back to Christopher. "I see no one. Need you to do the Flash reconnaissance, with me, so we can see what's

going on. Be careful—the goggles aren't working past the
curtain as near as I can tell."

"Glad I'm not wearing them, then." He grabbed my
hand and took off.

On the plus side, we were going fast enough that even an
A-C couldn't see us. Of course, on the negative side, the
moment we stopped I was going to be retching unless I got
lucky. Tito's Hyperspeed Dramamine didn't work for anyone in terms of Christopher's Flash Speed. So in addition to
looking at what was going on and who might be where, I
was also looking for my Vomit Target.

I was spoilt for choice.

The space was as large as I'd first thought, all bright
white walls, floors, and ceiling, with industrial lighting and
glass anywhere white walls were not. The place screamed
Clean Room, and it was definitely a factory where delicate
things were being created. Delicate, feminine things that
were still going to pack quite the punch.

There were what I sincerely hoped were synthetic limbs
all over the place, each in their own section along a winding
assembly line. The parts were all feminine, at least based on
what I saw at this blurry level. Giving me hope for synthetic,
the parts looked more plastic than person.

What there weren't were any whole people, synthetic or
organic.

We did a full circuit of the room, then Christopher
started to really examine it. Decided not to complain, because as long as we were moving I wasn't barfing.

"Christopher, I'd like to point out that we're clearly in
the Fem-Bot Factory." Said this softly just in case.

He grunted. "Yeah, good call. I don't know how you do it."

"I'm able to think like the crazed evil geniuses. It's such
a thrilling gift, believe me. Speaking of which, I see no one
here."

"I'm going to slow to regular hyperspeed because I
don't, either."

At this speed I was still able to hold off the barfing, so
that was good. In addition to the winding conveyer belt assembly line and the baskets and bins of body parts hanging
or sitting at stations, depending, we were able to spot what
was labeled the Art Room, which, based on a quick inspec-
tion, was where the bodies were spray-painted to look

lifelike. It was a large room and it resembled a car body and paint shop, presumably for similar reasons.

There were offices as well, lining the far walls. All their walls were made of glass, and I was certain whoever had created this place had also had the contract for Stephanie's Fixer-Upper at Forest Haven.

There were a bank of what looked like gigantic closets or similar, also all white, near to the offices that looked the most important, if I based importance on the size and sleekness of the desks and the size and apparent comfort of the executive chairs behind them, which I did. The closets or whatever they were were about eight feet tall, came out about ten feet from the wall, and were at least thirty feet wide. But those thirty feet were broken up into ten three-foot sections, at least based on the lines that seemed to indicate doors.

We headed back to the others, me grabbing a handy wastebasket along the way, and, while I barfed into that, Christopher shared our findings with the others.

Barfing done, I straightened up and shared my thoughts. "We need to search this place as fast as we can, meaning the A-Cs are going to have to do most of the detailed searching. There are a lot of offices in there—we're looking for anything that shows who's involved and what's actually going on. Anything suspicious, as well. If you're not sure, run it by me or Camilla. Christopher can show you where to start."

"What do you want the humans, princesses, and semi-androids to be doing?" Joe asked, as the seven A-Cs headed off.

"We're going to do a general search, just in case, and examine what looked like closets near the executive offices."

"You don't want us doing the hyperspeed search?" Rahmi asked.

"Nope. I want you two with us in case there's something bad hidden somewhere in here. Link up, it's a long way from here." So saying, I took Joe's hand, the others linked up as requested, and we headed off toward the giant closets.

I was revved and angry and not creeped out in here, so the skills were working just fine, meaning I was able to go at the slow version of hyperspeed, mostly so the others could see what Christopher and I had seen already. Still, it didn't take us long to find the closets. Had to say this for these giant white rooms—they were hard for me to get lost in.

"Any guess for how we open these?" Randy asked once we arrived at our destination. "I don't see any door handles or locks or anything."

"It's definitely a room or rooms," Adriana said. "But the goggles are telling me nothing."

"Yeah, I care a lot more about what's behind Door Number Three here than I do about how thick the concrete around the stairs was."

Rhee cautiously touched part of the closet. Nothing happened, so she pushed against it.

And it swung inward, just a bit. Nothing happened, other than the door swinging back quickly. So she pushed it again, harder, and it opened fully.

"Come in," a man's voice snarled. A man's voice I recognized. "Don't just stand there gloating."

"Malcolm?"

Went to the doorway and looked in, using my body to keep the door opened. This wasn't a closet—it was a cell. An all-white, brightly lit, but ultimately rather tiny cell. And the door was definitely trying to close itself automatically. If I hadn't been enhanced I'd have probably been pushed back.

Buchanan was sitting on a bench that was part of the back wall. He looked shocked. And like he'd been in a fight, but that wasn't a surprise. Really didn't figure the people we were coming to rescue had been taken without a struggle of some kind. He also wasn't alone. There was what looked like a bright, white Roomba in there with him.

"Missus Executive Chief?"

"In Drax Industrial's finest in body armor and weaponry."

"Don't stand there, get the hell out of here!" Buchanan wasn't getting up. In fact, I wasn't sure if he could.

"Um, we're here to rescue you. I mean, if that's okay and all." I took a step in.

"Don't come inside!"

"Why not? Will the walls explode or something?"

"No, the doors only open in and they're impossible to open from the inside. Believe me, I've tried. But that thing," he pointed to the Roomba, "will shoot you if you come any closer."

"What will it do to you?"

"It's why I look like I've just had a vacation. Prisoners get electric jolts of increasing intensity if they don't behave. These rooms are also soundproofed and they have limited air. I had no idea you were here."

"We were stealthy."

"Sure you were."

"Huh. I'm choosing to ignore that." Considered my options. "What happens if I shoot the Roomba of Evil there?"

"No idea."

"Rhee, want you ready. Rahmi keep the door open. Rhee, when I fire, you go grab Malcolm and get him out, using your fastest version of hyperspeed."

The princesses nodded. Rahmi locked her arm against the door. "It won't move, I promise."

Nodded, then took another step in so that Rhee would have some room to get past me—a three-foot-wide space didn't leave a lot of room for maneuverability. As I did, the Roomba of Evil spun toward me. Didn't hesitate. Shot it, and jumped back as Rhee ran inside.

Drax made good guns and I only needed one shot. The Evil Roomba exploded as Rhee picked Buchanan up, spun, and ran out of the room. Pulled Rahmi away as soon as those two were free and got us both to the side. Some debris did come flying out before the door closed itself, but Joe blocked it from hitting anyone else. He wasn't even knocked down.

"Body armor works great," he said. "That explosion packs a punch, though, so we need to be careful."

Rhee nodded. "I am uninjured, but I don't know if Mister Buchanan was hit."

"I was, but not badly."

"Same thing all over again. Adriana and Camilla, get Malcolm out of range and patched up somehow—it's a factory but there must be med kits somewhere. And be sure the others know we've found at least some of our missing people. Randy, want you ready in case things go badly here and to handle rescued captives transport. Otherwise, princesses, Joe, let's do it again."

Rahmi opened the next door. Looked inside to see Falk. He looked as bad as Buchanan had. "Burton Falk, nice to see you. Sit tight, we're here to rescue you."

"Missus Martini?"

"Getting tired of those I'm here to rescue sounding shocked about it, and you're only our second of this particular foray. Everyone else I rescued after I'd been kidnapped was hella grateful."

"Get me out of here without getting yourself hurt and I'll fall onto that side of things."

"Will do. Team, let's rock and roll." Stepped inside so I had a clear shot at this Roomba of Evil, took it, and we all did what we'd just done before. Rhee had Falk out and Joe blocked the rest of us from being hurt. Randy carried Falk off to find where Buchanan and the others were, even though Falk insisted he wasn't hurt.

We waited for Randy to return, which was pretty quickly. "I think I can go almost as fast as an A-C now," he said. "Joe, you probably can, too. Want to switch jobs and test it?" Joe nodded so they traded places while Rahmi opened the next door.

Kyle was in here. "He's the biggest guy, most likely," I said to Rhee. "Will you have any issues?"

She snorted. "We practice carrying two of our people, one over each shoulder, as battle drills. Kyle will not be an issue."

"Kitty, be careful," Kyle said. "That thing is evil."

"The Roomba of Evil, I know. However, it's toast against Drax Industrial's laser blaster." Hey, I'd taken the gun with the coolest sounding name, so sue me.

Our extraction process worked smoothly again, though Kyle was hit with some debris. Joe picked him up. "And we're definitely as strong as an A-C now, because there's no way I could have hefted Kyle before."

"Do I want to know what happened to you?" Kyle asked, sounding worried. Rightly.

"Tell you later." Joe ran off while Randy brushed himself off.

"Joe's right, the body armor's top-notch."

"Good to hear, Randy. Let's get the next captive out, shall we?"

This prisoner was Len. "Kitty! I knew you'd find us!"

"Len is my favorite, I'm just sayin'." Joe returned and nodded to me. Gave him the nod right back. "Gang, let's lock and load."

Once again, we did our thing and once again it went smoothly. Decided not to question this. If we had a rescue that was actually going smoothly for once, I, for one, was not going to complain about it. Besides, it was only going smoothly because we'd found the helicarrier and Jerry had had the brains to tell me to weapon up.

Len was lighter than Kyle and Rhee was faster therefore, so he wasn't hit with shrapnel. However, Joe took him to the others anyway.

"This is going remarkably well," Rahmi said.

"I cannot express how I seriously hope you haven't just jinxed us." We opened the door. "Dammit. Girls, this is why we never mention when things are good. Because it always explodes in our faces."

Just like the Roomba of Evil had on the prisoner in this cell.

CHAPTER 80

ON THE PLUS SIDE, such as it was, the Roomba of Evil had literally blown up, so we didn't have to deal with it. We just had to deal with a body with its head blown off.

Fortunately, I'd already barfed my guts out a little earlier, so I could keep myself to just a little gagging. The flyboys and the princesses were all battle trained, so they handled it stoically.

The bright white room was splattered with blood and gray matter. Actively chose not to look at it. Actively chose not to look at the headless body. Therefore, actively chose to look at my gun. It was far less upsetting.

Rhee retrieved the body. "Who is it?" she asked.

"I have no idea." The guy was in a black Armani suit, or what was left of it. Every man who'd been captured wore the Armani Fatigues because the P.T.C.U. agents who worked closely with Centaurion dressed to blend in, so it could be anyone. It could be Siler—it was his body build. It was Manfred's body build, too. Tried not to freak out, because that wasn't allowed to the leader. "Take the body to wherever the others are. We'll get everyone out then determine who this is that way, if the others don't know."

Joe helped Rhee—he took the shoulders because he was a gentleman—and they headed off.

"What happened?" Rahmi asked softly.

"I'd assume he was trying to get out or he was trying to disarm the Roomba of Evil and hit its self-destruct switch. It's clear they're loaded to explode because they're sending out far too much shrapnel for the single shots I'm hitting them with."

Joe and Rhee returned, looking solemn. "Falk's going through the guy's pockets. Hopefully we'll know soon enough who we lost."

"Okay, on to the next." Tried not to sound grim. Failed.

The next one was also not good. We had another man down. On the positive side, he had his head. On the negative side, he didn't have his middle, and the room looked even more like a scene out of a slasher film than the last one had. He wasn't someone I knew, but he looked familiar. "I think he's one of Falk's team." Meaning one of Mom's people.

Randy helped Rhee take the body away this time. Joe patted my shoulder. "Hang in there, Commander."

"They died because they came to save me. And because no one else did, so no one got here in time to save them." The rage hit, and it hit harder than ever before. "Speaking as the FLOTUS, I'm glad Jeff can't feel how angry I am because it could kill him. But, speaking as the Commander, this makes me never want to forgive him or the others."

"No, that's not what you want," Joe said gently. "Not really. I understand why you're so angry. I'm angry, too. This is war, though, Kitty, and I know you've been through this before. The higher-ups screwed up and our forces paid the price for it. It happens all the time. It's not good and it's not right, necessarily, but it is part of how things go. You focus on who you can and did save, and try to honor who you lost."

"What else?"

"That's it. Other than making your enemies pay for their part in it. Which you do all the time. But Jeff and the others aren't our enemies, and I know you know that, no matter how upset with them you are."

Took in a deep breath and let it out slowly. "I've never been this mad at Jeff or the others before, but you're right. I don't really want to never speak to them again or anything. I want to yell at them a lot, though. I just never want anything like this to happen to anyone on my team."

"I know you get told this all the time, but that's both your strength and your weakness. And as someone who's willingly followed you since pretty much you started, I follow you because you care and you've never not cared. But I don't want you turning to hate. I don't want you to become like the people we despise. I want you to be angry because someone on our side or an innocent was hurt. But I don't want you to want to hurt the people who love you, even if they really screwed the pooch on this one."

Managed a laugh. "They really did. And I really wonder why."

"Camilla said fear. I'm sure she's right. I have to think that whatever they were told, it terrified not just Jeff, but Chuck, James, and Tim, too. So that has to be pretty bad, because those guys don't terrify easily." Randy and Rhee returned. "So, let's keep on saving who we can, Commander, and we'll deal with the fallout once we have all of our people back, whether it's safely or to bury them with honor."

Didn't care, hugged Joe, body armor and weapons and all. "Thanks. I really needed that little talk." Heaved a sigh. "Let's get to the next one, folks."

"There are only ten of these," Rhee said as we went to the next door.

"Right, and we've done six of them, so only four more to go."

"And only one to a cell."

"Thank goodness—it's barely wide enough for one."

"Yes, but we had thirteen missing, if I counted correctly."

Did the math fast in my head. "You did count correctly. So, either we find people doubled up, or when we're done here we're not actually done. Always the way. Let's get these last four out, then, as fast as we can do it."

The only change was that Rhee and Rahmi switched, so Rhee had the door and Rahmi had the excitement, so to speak. The next cell didn't have a dead body in it, for which I was hugely thankful. It had Manfred, who looked even worse than Buchanan had. Figured he'd tried to game the Roomba of Evil with hyperspeed and it hadn't worked. At least he was alive, for which I was even more hugely thankful.

We did what was now actually feeling a little like a routine maneuver and got him out without issue, with Randy prepped to take the shrapnel hits.

Joe took Manfred off to the others, and Christopher came back with him. "We've found things I think you're going to be interested in. Need my help here?"

"I'd say yes but if Rhee is right, and so far there's no reason to think that she isn't, we're still going to be missing people when we're done. Need you to search around here for anything that could be a door or something we've missed. Take your dad with you—he's got the most exposure to my methods, and I can guarantee that you both need to be thinking like me and trying to spot what a sneaky person would have created to hide the rest of our team."

"Will do." Christopher zipped off and we got into position again.

This one was another tragic discovery. Another agent, another head blown off. Joe was right—I needed to focus my anger on the people who'd done this, not on Jeff and the others. Which I sincerely planned to, once we could figure out who they were.

Joe and Rahmi took this corpse, who again might or might not have been Siler, to the others. "It'll be okay, Kitty," Randy said. "We'll make them pay."

"What if one of these guys is Nightcrawler? Then Lizzie's out another parent. Of course, whoever's dead probably had family who are now going to get the lame letter that doesn't bring your loved one back."

Randy nodded. "Just like Bill's parents did." He hugged me. "And just like way back then, that you care about people you may not even know and are angered by their death and mourn their loss means you're still the person I'll follow to Hell and back."

"Thanks." Hugged him back as Joe and Rahmi returned. "Already went into Hell to get you guys. So, technically, does that make this place Purgatory?"

"No," Joe said. "It's too clean and sterile to be either Purgatory or Hell."

"We say that Hell is an absence of anything," Rahmi shared. "There is nothing to do, and you will never interact with anyone ever again."

We all agreed that sounded horrible. As we went to the ninth cell, considered that this was the fate that awaited Algar should he ever be caught by the Black Hole People's Police Force. Didn't feel he deserved it, but then again, that was because he was on my side. Something to remember— the bad guys rarely saw themselves as evil. They saw themselves as in the right and being expedient.

This cell had our first female—Colette was inside. "God am I glad to see you."

She was sitting on the bench and looked far less beaten up than the men. "I'm glad to see you, too. Don't enter the room—"

"We know about the Roomba of Evil."

"I have more than that." She pointed up, so Rahmi, Rhee, and I all looked.

Colette did indeed have more going on. There was what looked like strong netting hovering at the ceiling. And it was hovering, as in staying up under its own power.

"Wow. What is that?"

"It's a stun net. If I try to get away or try to hurt myself, it'll come down and wrap around me, stunning me into unconsciousness."

"And you know this how?"

"Our captors explained it to me. And, sadly, I saw it work. Evalyne and Phoebe didn't believe them."

"Are they still alive?"

"As far as I know, but I have no idea if anyone other than me is alive."

"Many are."

"But not all." She looked ready to cry and to kill something, both. I could relate.

"No, not all. Hang on while we confer on how to handle this."

"I'm faster than the net, but there's nowhere to go," Colette shared. "And the, ah, Roomba of Evil is set to block me and slow me down."

Rahmi and I looked at each other. "I'm willing to risk it," she said.

"I don't know." Rhee looked into the room. "The issue isn't beating it out of the room. The issue is getting the door closed before the net can escape."

"Good point." Had a thought. "Did anyone happen to bring a flamethrower?"

Randy pulled a small tube out of his back pocket. "I did. At least, that's what I think it is."

The tube was marked as Personal Flamethrower. "Only one way to find out." Pointed it away from everyone and anything and hit the red button with my thumb. A long flame shot out. "Okey dokey, Randy, great call. Rahmi, I'm going to shoot the Roomba of Evil and then flame the net. Get ready, because this one's going to be a lot harder."

We were in position. I shot the Roomba of Evil, no is-sues. Rahmi ran in and grabbed Colette while I shot the flamethrower at the net.

Had to keep the button down to keep the flames going. Fire was good because it was definitely hurting the net and it also melted the shrapnel, though some of it still made it out and hit Randy and me, too, this time since I hadn't jumped back and out of the way. The guys were right—the body armor was great. Still not as good as what Alfred in Bizarro World made, but pretty damned awesome other-wise.

Fire wasn't as good, however, because even flaming the net could fly and follow its target. Which it did, just manag-ing to slip past the closing door.

Was ready to scream and start running when someone came up behind us and blasted the net with a fire extin-guisher. The net crumbled.

"Wow. Nicely done." Turned to see Adriana grinning at me. "Got tired of playing Florence Nightingale?"

She shrugged. "Someone saw you testing your flame-thrower. I just went to the logical assumption."

"Great. Let's open our last cell and see what we've got."

Opened the cell and felt my jaw drop. Wasn't sure who was more shocked—me or the prisoner.

CHAPTER 81

JANELLE GARDINER stared at me, as openmouthed as I was. I recovered quickest. "Wow, you're still alive. Up until these past few days I wouldn't have thought I'd say this—but thank God."

"Who are you?" She sounded exhausted and frightened.

"Um, sorry, though we've met I guess we haven't actually talked a lot and I know we're all hard to see with the gear on. I'm Kitty Katt-Martini." Figured now wasn't the time to play the FLOTUS Card.

She jerked. "It's really you?"

"Last time I checked."

"Last time I checked I was watching you lying in wait for the President while my so-called friends were telling me that I should be honored that I was chosen to be one of the three main prototypes of Personal Robotic Anti-Terrorism Units."

"Yeah, that wasn't me. It's what I like to call the Kitty-Bot. There's a Janelle-Bot, too. I've already tangled with her and ran away so as to live another day and all that jazz. So, you want out of this cell or are you content to hang around until your 'friends' kill you?"

"I want out. Please."

"Okay, gang, it's the usual fun. Adriana, please have that fire extinguisher ready."

We did the same maneuver as we had for Colette. Worked better this time because we'd done it once before and because Adriana was a lot closer to the flaming net and put it out of its misery and ours before it could get through the door.

We all took Gardiner to our impromptu medical area. The A-Cs had found water bottles, and everyone was having some, the prisoners in particular. While Camilla checked Gardiner for injuries and everyone had a water and a smile, we conferred about the rest of our missing team.

"Siler's not here, and neither is Wruck," Buchanan said. "I did the approach here, because we thought it was a government agency."

"It is, but it's an illegal one."

"We'll argue semantics later, Missus Executive Chief. I was literally dragged inside by four guys. I have no idea where Siler and Wruck are, but I'd imagine Siler did his blending thing and ensured the two of them disappeared."

"Huh. I have no idea where they went, but they sure didn't come over to visit us at the insane asylum."

Buchanan nodded. "Wruck literally refused to set foot on those grounds. That's why I tried this place to see if you'd come in here. I had no idea the others were here, but I think they got here before we did, because I didn't even get a 'hey, how are you' out before I was grabbed."

"We followed Adriana," Len said. "As well as we could, anyway. I was tracking her on GPS but her signal was going in and out and then disappeared. Manfred and Colette searched all the businesses in this area."

"We overheard someone talking about the insane asylum," Manfred said. "So we figured that could be a good hiding place."

"Right you were. But why didn't you go there first?"

"We thought the newer building was a school or a detention center," Kyle said. "It seemed like a good spot to go to get help, and we figured we'd need it." He shrugged. "We got in the door, explained who we worked for, and were knocked out fast. I woke up in the cell."

"Same story for the rest of you?" Everyone nodded, other than Colette.

"They spent some time with me, Evalyne, and Phoebe, after we woke up. That's how I knew the net was dangerous. Otherwise, I woke up in the room where the cells are and was shoved into one because I chose not to fight after seeing what happened to the others."

"Lovely. Did they plan to ransom you guys or anything?"

Colette shook her head. "We were told that no one

knows this site is here and they want to keep it that way. They wanted the women as prototypes. That's why we had the nets—it was to prevent us injuring or killing ourselves." She nodded toward the three dead men.

"Do we know who they all are?" I asked Falk.

"The rest of my team." He sounded furious. There was a lot of that going around. "They must have been close to getting out."

Chose not to argue or support this mindset, since I had no idea, and Falk, and Buchanan as well, was already upset enough. The others were, too, but I understood how their chain of command worked, and also how it felt when you lost someone you'd accidentally put into danger.

"So Siler and Wruck are MIA and Evalyne and Phoebe are presumably still in the building?"

Buchanan nodded. "Not that we have any idea of where they are."

"We do," Christopher said, indicating the A-Cs. "We also found proof that Monica Strauss was in charge of this."

"Not a surprise. Anyone else incriminated?"

"Ansom Somerall and Talia Lee," Gardiner spat. "My colleague and my best friend."

"Yeah, well, when you side with the bad guys, you get betrayed. That's in all the rulebooks. Why'd they hook up against you?"

"Ansom's sleeping with her." Gardiner shrugged. "It won't last, his liaisons never do, but Talia thinks she's special. Ansom wants complete control of Gaultier and it doesn't matter that I haven't cramped his style—the moment Quinton died I was no longer protected."

"Quinton Cross was your guardian and/or benefactor?"

"Yes. He actually had limits. Ansom has none."

This was a complete reversal of how I'd seen those two men, but it wasn't that big a surprise, really. Different levels of evil were still evil, when you got right down to it.

"Wow. I'll contemplate those ramifications later, and you'll be helping me to do it." Pondered our options. "Malcolm, are we allowed to treat this site the same way we did the Gaultier black site?"

Noted that Gardiner didn't look surprised at this question, nor did she look chagrined. She looked like that was old news, which it was. But I did have to remember that she'd most likely been involved in everything Gaultier had done against us since Amy's father was killed and factor that into things.

"No, the P.T.C.U. needs to take control, because this is a homegrown terrorist operation, and while I'm sure the evidence you've found is good, I'm also sure that we'll find more. And you're going to need it. While the former Secretary of State is the easy 'high-ranking individual' responsible, I'm sure there are others."

"Monica Strauss' involvement is confirmed," White said. "And yes, we've found the proof. And a large cache of diamonds."

"Really? Then why did Strauss and Villanova yank their diamonds from their settings and why did Villanova hide them in her ice cube trays?"

"As you say so frequently, I have no idea who makes these plans up or why, we just have to foil them. And it appears we have the proof to do so."

"That proof needs to be exposed," Buchanan said. "If we turn this place to rubble like Missus Chief would like, we lose the proof. And 'we say so' doesn't hold up in courts of law or public opinion."

"Good points. Here's the two things I want most right now. One is to find the rest of our missing people. Two is to get whatever cellular dampening and such that this site has running turned off."

"I can handle the second one," Camilla said, "Give me a minute to find the source."

"That source could be anywhere."

She shook her head. "It'll be down here, in the secured area. I was fairly sure I'd found it when you pulled me onto medic duty." She zipped off.

Turned to Christopher. "Any ideas for where the others are?"

"No, but I think we found an alternate exit. It took us a while to find it, too."

"Show me."

He grabbed my hand and we went back toward where the cells had been. Followed that wall along until it looked like we were reaching the far wall and a dead end. Only it wasn't a dead end. The wall was an optical illusion in this area, with a small L-shaped hall that, due to the white on white of this entire room, didn't show unless you were right on it.

"Great. Let's get everyone and check this out."

"Speaking of everyone, we're at our time limit. Should I get Devon or just tell him to continue waiting?"

"Depends on how fast Camilla's working." Checked my phone. Even this deep underground I had bars. "I think she's worked fast. Do you have Devon's number?"

"Yes." Christopher pulled out his phone and dialed. "Hey, it's Christopher White. Yeah, we're all alive and we've found most of the missing." He barked a laugh. "Yeah, I'm amazed, too. Listen, I want you taking command of the facility."

While Christopher shared the news of what was going on with Devon, I called Jerry. "Commander, it's amazing to hear your voice via this old-fashioned means."

"I know. Revel in the wonder. Look, I need you to contact my mother, and only my mother. She needs to call Malcolm so that he can give her his thoughts on what the P.T.C.U. should be doing."

"Roger that. I see your backup team is heading inside."

"Yeah, they're taking over the upper portions. We're in the secret underground portions."

"I miss all the fun."

"Truly." Filled him in on everything. "I do not want to see any of the men I'm mad at." Because I needed to stay mad and I wasn't quite ready to forgive them yet. And because, when I got down to it, I didn't want them in danger and right now, who knew how safe any of us outside of an A-C protected facility were? "When you share information and request the backup that Devon's team is going to need to ensure that this facility remains under our control, please make sure that this is extremely clear. None of them will enjoy me right now, and I have a lot of weapons that work really well."

"Clear, and I'll relay. Should we have Abby and Mahin get the recovered teams into the helicarrier?"

"I don't think they can. We have what appeared to be the only keys for this level, and while Devon's team can definitely breach the front door if they have to because it's normal, I don't think they can breach the ones we had to use to get down here. Everyone's ambulatory, in part because this is a workplace and the folks down here have water and such for themselves. We'll get everyone out with us."

"Now that you've gotten the blockage down, we can monitor you from here. Your signal's faint, but we've got it on the ship's system."

"Great. Lock onto as many of us as you can. We're heading who knows where right now. Also, contact Drax—our goggles stopped being awesome the moment we entered the room we're in right now. I'd like to see if he can determine what might be in this room that would affect the goggles in this way. And while you're at it, just for grins and giggles, see if you can locate Siler or Wruck. I don't think they're in this facility."

Jerry and I got off at the same time as Christopher's call with Devon ended. We headed back to the others at a human trot. Hoped Christopher was merely reserving energy, because if he was running low, we could be in trouble, especially since he hadn't exerted that much energy so far. That I knew of, at any rate.

"They're in and met no resistance," he shared. "They picked the lock without issue, by the way. And the security guards we captured are still captured."

"Amazing."

"Isn't it, though?"

"Yeah. There were more than four cars in the parking lot."

He nodded. "Not a lot more, but yeah, I think we're going to find more people wherever the last of our team is being held."

Camilla was back with the others, looking smug, as everyone enjoyed being able to contact people past their arms' reach. We took stock. Pretty much everyone could walk under their own power, albeit only if they allowed someone to help them. The women didn't argue, but the men only agreed to this after both Christopher and I pulled a wide variety of ranks and Camilla made some cutting remarks about men and their overabundance of stupid pride.

So, Daniel had Buchanan, Joshua had Falk, Lucas had Len, Marcus had Manfred, White had Kyle, and Adriana had Colette. Camilla took Gardiner, which I approved of— Camilla wasn't going to let any form of pity affect her if Gardiner tried something.

Joe and Randy had the unenviable job of taking the dead bodies. The wiser course would have been to leave them, but it was clear that Falk wasn't going to be able to handle that and Buchanan probably wouldn't be good with it, either. The flyboys were strong enough to carry all three bodies.

This left me and Christopher in the lead and Rahmi and Rhee bringing up the rear, while also handling muscle and fighting as might be needed and carrying the two boxes the A-Cs had filled with incriminating evidence. Thusly set up, we set off for the hidden doorway.

The bright white of this area gave way pretty quickly once we were through the illusion doorway. We were back to normal lighting and a reasonably normal corridor, which we walked down cautiously and stayed quiet, just in case. For no need, apparently—if we triggered anything anywhere it was impossible to tell.

The goggles were working again here, leading me to really believe that the room we'd been in was lined with something odd. Once again, I got information about the concrete. Still twenty feet thick, go design team.

After walking about the length of a football stadium we reached another doorway that was hidden in another blind corner. As Christopher and I peeked cautiously around the corner, it was clear that we'd found another Clean Room. It was bright white and the goggles stopped doing their thing.

This was a smaller room, with a lot less stuff in it. Of course, what was in it was what mattered.

This was a hospital setup, and it was kind of normal, at least more normal than anything we'd seen so far. There were beds and hospital-type equipment all over. There weren't any medical personnel, but there were a couple of people in here.

Phoebe and Evalyne were on gurneys, strapped down, with various needles and tubes in them. They each had a weird white tube that encircled them and their portable beds. The tube was like a donut that was mostly hole, and it was on a track that attached to the sides of the gurneys. The tube was moving slowly up and down the length of their bodies, from head to toe. They were either both asleep, both unconscious, or both faking it. We were too far away for me to be able to tell.

There were six large men in here as well. And unlike the guys at the main entrance, these dudes didn't look like regular security. They were all in suits and had a look I was familiar with—the Secret Service and the P.T.C.U. all had this look—these were dudes On The Job. Meaning they were likely to be actual NSA agents, albeit among those working against the government.

I'd thought we were being quiet, but whether we'd made noise, they'd had some kind of warning, or we were just lucky, two of the men turned around and stared right at us.

Then they pulled their guns.

CHAPTER 82

I DUCKED AND SHOVED Christopher back and behind me at the same time—I had the body armor and he didn't.

"Freeze," one of the dudes said, as he moved his gun to aim right at me, just like his buddy already had. The other four spun around and joined the Aim At Kitty Party.

Considered freezing, then remembered I had hyper-speed. Flipped into a somersault and came up ready to start shooting. Only I didn't have to.

Poofs leaped out of my purse—Harlie, Poofikins, Murphy, and a few others—the Poofs of everyone here.

The dudes didn't shoot. They stared. Then the guy who'd told me to freeze started to laugh. "You're kidding, right?" he asked in between snorts of laughter. His pals were snickering, too. "You aliens are idiots. What are those going to do? Fluff us to death?"

"Laugh it up. Poofs Assemble!"

Harlie went large and in charge and roared. The other Poofs followed suit. The six dudes went from laughing to screaming quickly while they aimed their guns at the fluffy monsters that had just appeared. They didn't get a chance to shoot the Poofs, though, because their guns were snatched out of their hands before I could blink.

"Thanks, Christopher," I said as he stopped next to me, holding six guns.

The Poofs knocked the men down and sat on them, growling and drooling. I found that an impressive touch—it added a lot to the overall horror effect.

"So, dudes on the floor, you get one chance each to be helpful. If you're not immediately helpful, I'm going to let my Poofs here eat you. Alive. But don't worry—it'll be over fast because my Poofies are starving, I'm sure."

"Wha- . . . what do you want?" the Spokesdude who was definitely not laughing now asked.

"I want so very many things. We'll start with what's going on with these women—are they hurt, unconscious, or being kept asleep?"

"They were hurt," the Spokesdude said. "They're being repaired."

"I need Camilla," I told Christopher. He nodded and zipped off.

Camilla arrived a couple of seconds later. "What do you need?" She looked at the men on the floor. "They're all NSA."

"Yeah, I figured. You're the only one of us trained in medicine. Need you to check out the gals. I've been told they were hurt and are being 'repaired.'"

She nodded and went to the beds, though it was clear she was examining the machines that were still moving slowly over Evalyne and Phoebe.

"These aren't doing 'repairs,'" she said finally. "They're copying both women's physical structures."

"What a pity for you," I said to the Spokesdude.

"Wait, wait!" he shouted as Harlie lowered its face toward his. "They're being fixed at the same time. It does both."

Looked at Camilla. Who shrugged. "It's possible."

"Fine. Next question. Where are all the people who work in this facility?"

"Day shift goes home at seven," one of the other dudes said quickly. "The night shift comes on at nine. They'll find you then," he added, presumably because he liked living on the edge.

"Oh, they'll find someone, I'll grant you that. And it's always nice to be right. So, next question. What's really going on here? And by 'here' I mean this entire black site."

All the dudes were quiet. "Many things," the Spokesdude said finally, presumably because Harlie growled at him.

"Vague replies will not be tolerated. But we'll try a different question. Is this a secret factory making female robots that are to be used to infiltrate an enemy's defenses and then explode?"

The six guys all stared at me, a couple openmouthed, which was a mistake, since the Poofs sitting on their chests drooled right into their open yaps. Those guys gagged and choked, but the Spokesdude nodded. "Yes, that's exactly what it is. Underground. Aboveground we do research and development on a variety of security measures."

"Is this site the one from which you spy on everyone?"

"No."

"Fair enough." And not my current problem. "Where are the completed Fem-Bots?"

"We don't know. Our jobs are need-to-know, and where the completed robots are sent isn't part of what we need to know."

Had my doubts, but the Poofs were really giving it their all with the threatening and no one else shared anything more or different.

"Why did no one come over to check out all the people running around all over Forest Haven next door?"

"Freaks, losers, teenagers and 'ghost hunters' are there all the time," the Spokesdude said, clearly happy to be talking about something other than what they were doing at this site. "We ignore them unless they try to come onto our property."

"Interesting. What happens to those few who do? Do they get the same treatment my people have gotten?"

"They get told to leave because they're trespassing, here and at Forest Haven, and we'll call the cops. Only your people demanded entry after that."

Had more doubts about this, but since we hadn't found any stray teens or homeless people trapped here, this could possibly be the truth.

"What other ways out of this room are there other than the way we came in?" They were silent again, which was an interesting time to be so. "Dudes, trust me, I've been seriously pissed off at men I love for quite a while now. I have no qualms taking out my frustrations with them on all of you, and I'm sure they'd appreciate it if I did so. Answer my question or I let the Poofs eat you."

Murphy opened its maw and leaned toward the head of the guy it was sitting on. "Oh, God, there's a secret exit over there!" He pointed toward the far side of the room from where we'd come in.

"Are there security measures on this pathway?"

"Nothing deadly," Murphy's Potential Dinner said. "It's secret, only high-level people know where it is. We know because we work high security here. The path lets out in the forest behind us and Forest Haven. There are other paths out from other parts of the facility. They all lead into the forest."

"Nice of you to offer information without my having to drag it out of you. Who normally uses that path?" Silence again. "Seriously? Do I say it's Chow Time now?"

"No," the Spokesdude said. "We're just afraid to tell you the truth."

"Be more afraid of lying."

"We don't know. There is no normal here."

That I really couldn't argue with. "Okay, I'll let that one slide. Who used that path *last*?"

They were quiet again, but Murphy's Potential Dinner finally broke because Murphy drooled right onto him. "Gah! Our bosses. There's another tunnel that branches from the exit in the forest and goes to our main offices."

"I'm supposed to believe that whoever's in charge hoofs it all the way from there to here and back again?" A-Cs would do it, but to an A-C, a few miles was the same as a few steps for a human. Well, as long as said A-C was in shape and all that. "Pull the other one, it has bells on."

"No," the Spokesdude said. "They use Segways."

"Including on the stairs?"

"No, the path is a gradual slope."

"Hang on," Christopher said. He left before I could tell him not to.

"If there's something that you didn't tell us about, and he gets hurt, I'm going to have the Poofs eat you all slowly."

"It's nice to know you care," Christopher said as he returned. "Amazingly enough, they're not lying. There's a network of tunnels down there, all paved, gradual slopes to the surface. I followed the one they said. It took me right to NSA headquarters and there were several Segways there."

"They use them all the time," the Spokesdude said. "The main day-to-day people come here several times during each shift. The bigwigs come by when they feel like it."

"Were any of said bigwigs here today?"

"Yes," the Spokesdude admitted after Harlie growled a

deep, hungry growl. "They left after these two were in-jured."

Was about to ask if said bigwigs had left with anyone like, say, a Fem-Bot or two, but my phone rang. The shock of hearing it almost made me jump, but I controlled the reflex. Dug my phone out and answered on the third ring. "Hey, Mom, where are you?"

"NSA headquarters."

"That was fast. In force?"

"Yes, I prefer to raid with a large number of people."

"Me too!"

"Good to know. I have P.T.C.U., Centaurion, and Air Force personnel with me including Colonel Franklin. Your Uncle Mort is heading to your location with Kevin, some Field agents, and a lot of marines. And yes, we used the Field agents to get us all here quickly, but no, the men you're angry with are still at the White House awaiting your triumphant return."

"Is the sarcasm really necessary, Mom?"

"Yes, kitten, it is. It's part of my process."

"I love you. Christopher will meet Kevin and Uncle Mort at the glass doors going down to the level we're at. I think we have the only keys." He nodded to me, gathered the keycards from the folks on the team who were holding onto them, and took off.

"You might, but I'm sure we'll find plenty of keys. Kitten, once your Uncle Mort is on-site, cede authority to him immediately."

"Gotcha. Mom ... Evalyne and Phoebe were hurt." Described what had happened and the contraptions they were in and mentioned the Poofs' prisoners. Also mentioned that we had three dead P.T.C.U. agents who'd been with Falk. "So, what do we do?"

Mom was quiet for a few long moments. "Leave their bodies with the women. We have a medivac on the way anyway. We'll take them all at once."

"We're like three floors underground and a long walk away from the entry point for the Underground Labs of Evil."

"James authorized all the help we need, Kitty, I promise."

"So, what do we do once Uncle Mort takes over?"

"I can't speak for the others, but you need to go back to the White House."

"Don't wanna. Want to stay in the Sovereign and Flying Nation of Kitty Land."

"I'm sure you do, but you're the First Lady and, once the Chairman of the Joint Chiefs of Staff arrives, you need to go back to *being* the First Lady."

"Why do I think that I'm going to look back fondly on being kidnapped?"

Mom laughed. "Because you know how your life works."

CHAPTER 83

KEVIN AND UNCLE MORT were on-site quickly, which wasn't a surprise. Christopher had met them upstairs with the keycards and they'd stationed people at every door so that no one needed to worry about being stuck.

Didn't want to leave Evalyne and Phoebe, but Kevin insisted on it while Uncle Mort had his marines take the six security guys into custody while I forced the Poofs to go back to small and adorable. Which they did. Then they went back into my purse, grumbling about the unfairness of them not being able to eat the bad men. I felt their pain.

Refused to go until the medivac team—which turned out to be a lot of Dazzlers with one human pilot whose expression said he'd scored the best duty of his entire career—had come down and claimed them.

Then we gave Kevin the boxes of incriminating information we'd found and did the reverse tour so we could point out where our people had been held and killed.

Devon and his team wanted to stay on-site. Some were deemed by the Dazzlers to be in need of medical care, so they were also put into the medivac helicopter, which was military and therefore big and able to take everyone. Devon and about half of those with him were able to remain, however.

Falk and Manfred both insisted on riding with the bodies and the women, and no one argued with them about that, least of all me, in part because they both needed medical care, too, and in other part because that way the dead and Evalyne and Phoebe would be protected.

Gardiner was another point of contention. The Dazzlers

wanted her to go back to Dulce for medical treatment. Uncle Mort wanted to arrest her on general principles. I wanted to keep her with us. Called Mom, who sided with me, though recommended we keep a guard around her, which appeased Uncle Mort. Promised the Dazzlers we'd have White House medical look at Gardiner, and since they knew that meant Tito, Melanie, and Emily, they were appeased as well.

The rest of us, including the two Field teams who I wanted with us anyway, in part so they could keep Gardiner under guard, were ready to go home. Insisted on going in the helicarrier, mostly because I didn't want to lose it again. And I was stalling. I was still angry, but Joe and Randy had made good points, and now that everyone other than Siler and Wruck were accounted for, I knew I had to actually find out why Jeff and the others had caved so fast and easily.

Of course, Siler and Wruck *were* missing, and that meant I had to share that with Lizzie. I was not looking forward to that conversation, which I'd be having in about ten minutes or less.

"Do you think they're okay?" I asked Buchanan, who was definitely not deemed able to stay on-site but who had also insisted on staying with me.

"I think that it's going to take a lot to kill either one of them, let alone both of them together. My guess, based on working with Siler off and on for several years now, is that once he knew this site was compromised, he looked for alternate ways in."

"You think they found the secret paths?"

"Probably. Or they spotted someone coming out in the forest. I'll figure out how to reach them."

"That won't reassure Lizzie."

"Lie to her."

Stared at him. "Excuse me?"

He sighed. "Lie to her. Tell her that they're off doing exactly what I just said."

"What if that's not true?"

"They aren't captured because if they were, they'd have been brought back into the black site, guaranteed. Your mother's taken over the NSA and, trust me, the CIA is right behind her, she just didn't tell you because you're still mad at Reynolds. So if they're there, she'll find them. If they're not there, then they're both doing what they've done successfully for decades."

Heaved my own sigh. "Fine. I don't like lying to her, though."

"Channel your parents. Tell her what she needs to know to get her through." Buchanan grinned. "The ability does run in your family, you know."

"Hilarious. True, though."

We got onto the helicarrier from the roof. Made a stop at the armory and, with a great deal of regret, put our weapons and body armor back. I hadn't wanted to, but White and Buchanan both insisted on it.

Once we were back to looking like civilians, others headed off. But White held me back and let the others head back to the command center ahead of us. "I felt it again. When we were in the lab under the black site."

"What, the déjà vu?"

"Yes."

"Why is it bothering you so much?"

"I don't know, honestly. I just feel that it's vitally important that I remember why all of these areas seem so familiar. Vital to our safety important."

"I've got nothing, especially if this is an Alpha Four memory. Did your people use labs like these?"

"No, not really. You've seen our labs—they don't resemble these so much."

"Unless you like to give birth and take meetings in a fishbowl, sure they don't."

He cocked his head at me. "What do you mean?"

"You guys use a lot more glass than any humans. Gaultier's Lab of Hot Zombies was nothing like this, and the Gaultier Facility Underground Clone Lab wasn't nearly as glassy as these places or even as glassy as the Science Center. So, I can buy an Alpha Four influence if we're talking about labs that are all see-through. Humans do windows, A-Cs do glass walls."

He closed his eyes. "It's there. Right there." He opened his eyes. "But I can't access it."

Patted his hand. "We'll figure it out, Richard. Let's just get back to the others."

We rejoined the others in the command center. Joe and Randy had taken their places back from Keith and Lizzie,

and while the others shared what had happened with those
who'd remained on board, White showed Christopher, Buchanan, Len, Kyle, and Colette around the ship, Daniel and
the others made Gardiner comfortable in the command
center then sat with her, and I talked to Lizzie and patted
the Peregrines, who had felt they needed to stay onboard
just in case.

"Your dad's fine. He and Wruck are following the people
who left the facility via secret passages."

She squinted at me. "You're lying. You don't know where
my dad or Mister Wruck are."

Time to treat Lizzie as if she was Mom. I had difficulty
passing any lie to my mother that she'd believe, but sarcasm
was the best chance of it. Rolled my eyes. "Seriously, you're
telling me that the man who has been alive for decades doing just this kind of work, and the other man who not only
can shape-shift but who was hiding with his and our enemies for years, aren't following the bad guys in order to infiltrate or assassinate? Really? And you think I'd have left
either one of them inside? Really again?"

She sighed. "No. You're right." She hugged me. "I'm just
worried about him. You know how it is."

"Honestly, I don't. At your age I thought my dad was
only a history professor and my mom was a consultant who
traveled a lot because she was so good at helping businesses
improve their bottom-line cash flows."

She looked up at me. "Really?" She sounded unimpressed
with my gullibility. Then her face fell. "Yeah. When I was
younger I thought my parents loved me for me and all that."

Pulled her back and hugged her more tightly. "Your adopted father loves you. He loves you so much that he's altered his lifestyle that he's had for decades in order to keep
you safe. And your kind of second adopted family loves
you, too. No matter what happens, like Jeff and I were saying, God, was it only last night? But whenever, you're with
us forever now, so you'd better get used to it. Miss Mouthy
Teenager."

She laughed. "Yeah, okay, I was totes testing you."

"I knew it! Little Sneaky Pants."

"Commander," Hughes called, breaking up our Batman
and Robin Moment. "Coming up on Andrews. Figured we'd
all want to be ready in case it's déjà vu all over again."

"True enough, Matt. Let's have it on speakerphone or whatever."

"Andrews, this is Sovereign Nation One, requesting permission to land in our reserved, high security clearance parking place."

"I love you, Matt."

"Sovereign Nation One, this is Andrews. We have your space all reserved and ready to go. Please pass along my apologies to Queen Kitty for how people who will be scrubbing toilets for the next several months treated your request the first time."

Recognized who this was. Franklin's adjunct or whatever he was called, Captain Gil Morgan.

"Gil! It's awesome to hear the melodious sounds of your voice."

"Nice to be heard, Queen Kitty." He chuckled. "You have four men who have asked me that you please let them explain what happened before you beat the living crap out of them."

"Wow, they're really worried. Good. They should be."

"They are. In their defense, and in the defense of the toilet scrubbers, too, the situation was definitely out of control and, from what I've seen, confused enough that making decisions out of fear seemed logical."

"They pay you off to support them, Gil?"

"No, I just understand how angry you are and why. But I think I understand how frightened they were and why. However, I enjoy a good show, so, once you're here, I'll be meeting you to escort you and your people to the White House so you can have a Meeting of State and I can watch what happens."

"I like you. You shall have a place in the Sovereign and Flying Nation of Kitty Land should you so choose it."

"Excellent. I've heard through the grapevine that the Prince Consort position may be open and I'm tossing my hat in for that as well."

"Awesome. It's nice to have a position that's considered so desirable."

"Oh, I think your current husband is going to lock that one up, but you can't blame a guy for trying."

"Yeah, well, we'll see. Right now, I'm at war with my current husband. Technically."

The rest of the landing went smoothly. The building we were landing in was gigantic and its roof opened up, just like the baseball field in Pueblo Caliente, so we were able to literally hover over our spot and lower into it without issue.

"Drax makes great ships," Jerry said as we completed landing and he turned off the invisibility shield. "I mean really great. If you do defect, take him with you. If you don't, ensure that he can't sell to any other country."

"And if he's already sold to someone else," Walker added, "we want to buy those ships from them or steal them away. And I'm saying that in the interests of national security. We spent the time waiting for you learning what this ship can do. It can do it all. Whoever was flying it when they captured us and raided Rail Force One either was under orders not to be impressive or was an idiot, because they could have taken over the country using this."

"I wish there was a way to lock it, turn on Lojack, put on the Club, and take the keys, so to speak."

"There is," Hughes said. "And we've done it. I assume that Drax didn't because the ship was at his facility and why lock your car when it's safe in your garage? But don't worry, My Queen, we've got the safety on your ship set to high, and the three of us are the only ones who can access it."

"Three?"

He nodded. "Joe and Randy are concerned about what was done to them. In case they can be triggered by enemies somehow, they didn't want to be able to access this ship."

"I love all you guys so much."

We headed down the ramp to indeed be greeted by Captain Morgan. Resisted the urge to salute and lift my leg up, which was always the urge any time I saw Morgan, just 'cause. Proving he was either insane or just the most relieved person on the planet, Tim was there, too.

"Don't kick me," Tim said as he grabbed me and hugged me. "Long story. Once you know it, you won't be as mad. You'll still be mad, I think, but not *as* mad."

"Why weren't you the voice of my brand of insanity? It's part of your job description."

"I tried, Kitty. The evidence, when I saw it, was extremely compelling." He grabbed the flyboys and hugged each of them. "God, am I glad to see you guys. Not as glad as your wives will be," he said to Joe and Randy. "And, trust me,

they aren't to blame for any of this. None of the women felt
we should do what we did."

White and I exchanged a look. "I suggest we go to the
White House with all haste," he said. "This sounds like
something everyone will want to see."

Morgan nodded. "It will be. We have a gate installed in
this hangar. We can get right to the White House as long as
someone can calibrate. It's normally set to go to Area Fifty-
One."

Christopher nodded. "Not a problem. You ready, Kitty?
As in ready to go over and not try to kill your husband and
two best friends?"

"I dunno. Let's take a vote among all of us who were in
the ship when the warheads were armed against us. Everyone ready to play nicely for a bit, raise your hands." The
hands raised. Slowly in some cases, but they raised. "So be
it, I think we're good."

"You didn't raise your hand, Kitty," Christopher pointed
out.

"Can't put anything past you, can we?"

CHAPTER 84

I WAS ACTUALLY still angry enough that I could walk through the gate without a ton of nausea. My stomach was still empty, too, which probably helped.

We exited the gate in the last place I'd been in the White House complex—the underground garage. No one we were mad at was there to greet us. No one was there at all, Secret Service included. "Where's the welcoming committee?" Joe asked.

"I think they're being smart."

Christopher nodded. "I went through first for a reason, and not just because it's part of my job, since Doreen already said that whatever you were choosing to do was what the Diplomatic Corps was going to support. I've already told Jeff to get everyone in one place. I know where they are, and I'll take everyone there."

"Where are we going?" We had time to kill, since I'd been forced through the gate relatively early in terms of our numbers and I'd insisted the Peregrines gate it home as well, so we had a lot of birds coming through. The Poofs were, as far as I knew, back with their owners or in my purse. "Or is it a surprise?"

"No surprise. Nowhere exciting, either. But under the circumstances, Chuck suggested I not tell you in case you wanted to run on ahead and scream at them in private."

"Oh, no. I want an audience for it."

He laughed. "That's exactly what I told them."

"Are you still speaking to me?" Tim asked as he came through. "Just checking."

"Possibly. The flyboys seem to have forgiven you."

Hughes shrugged. "He's our commander. Right after you, Commander."

"I'd make nasty comments about insubordination, but I'm not crazy." Tim managed a grin as the flyboys laughed. "I just kind of want to suggest that you let them tell you what went on before you launch into a tirade. I think you'll be happier in the long and short run that way. Oh, and Alicia said to tell you that she also suggests this course."

Alicia was Tim's wife. They rented my parents' house in Pueblo Caliente because Alicia still liked her job with the airlines and therefore wanted to keep it, and gates meant that Tim's commute to work was short and easy. "Was she involved in this?"

"No, but we pulled everyone's spouses in and families were put into Centaurion bases. So, she knows what went on and told me to tell you, girl to girl, that you wanted to listen first."

"Okay, I'll follow her, and your, recommendation." I'd gotten to scream while on the helicarrier, after all.

Finally, our huge group was through. Before we went anywhere, had Christopher confirm that my children were fine. They were, though they were still at the Embassy, because it was still in lockdown. Refrained from asking why—after all, my husband had released Stephanie, meaning we weren't safe.

Resisted the urge to tell Jeff and the others to wait and instead go to the Embassy to verify that my children were safe and well. Mostly because I was still upset with the guys, and Jamie didn't need to feel that from me. Parents and friends fought, it was natural, but there was no reason to stress my little girl out because of it. And who knew what Charlie could or couldn't feel? Better to get things straightened out with the guys and then get the kids.

Next, had Christopher call for Secret Service to take Gardiner into a pleasant form of custody, complete with a visit to White House Medical, a nice meal, and a safe, well-guarded place to sleep. She didn't object.

"So, where are we doing the reunion meeting?" I asked Christopher after the Secret Service had taken Gardiner off, I'd sent the Peregrines to their regular duties or the Animal Luxury Suite, and the rest of us had linked up, the better to hyperspeed to our destination in one long daisy chain.

"The Situation Room."

"Really?"

"Yeah. They're going for someplace that seems neutral. And there's video and it's where we were as this unfolded, so the video's set up there."

"Dinner and a show." My stomach rumbled. Did my best to ignore it.

We arrived quickly, though Christopher was nice and didn't go at Flash level. The Situation Room had a variety of TV screens, a large oval table, and a lot of cushy chairs. Not enough cushy chairs for everyone we had, but the floor was available and looked clean, though had a feeling only Lizzie and I would consider that a viable option.

It also had a very worried looking Jeff, Chuckie, and Reader. All three of them looked older than when I'd seen them last, and considering I'd seen them in the morning, that was saying a lot. Decided I'd take Tim and Alicia's advice.

They weren't the only ones here. Gower, Serene, Claudia, Lorraine, and Raj were all in attendance as well. Everyone was sitting but stood up as we arrived. It was the most formal any of them had ever been with me, meaning they were clear on how angry I was. Though perhaps I was a test run for the upcoming peace talks. That was me, going for the bright side.

"Are you alright?" Jeff asked as my team spread out in the room, though none of us sat.

Managed to refrain from saying what I wanted to because I was trying to follow Tim and Alicia's advice. So I said nothing, because I was having to censor myself so much.

Could tell that everyone in the room was looking at Joe and Randy and trying to figure out why they were wearing knit caps at the start of summer. Did a fast check. All five flyboys were doing their Stoic Members of the American Armed Forces bit. So was the rest of my team. Meaning they were going to follow my lead.

White cleared his throat. "If I may?" he asked me.

"Go for it."

"We're all uninterested in pleasantries and extremely interested in what happened, Jeffrey. I suggest you all sit down and get to the pertinent details quickly. It's been a long day and we have people dead and injured."

"We thought you were among them," Chuckie said as those on Team Administration did as White suggested and put their butts in their chairs. He nodded at Raj, who pushed a button on a remote. A video came on.

It was me, only I wasn't dressed like me. Well, I was in a bra and panties. That I'd wear, since they looked like Elf Standard Issue. There were obvious signs of torture, and I was crying. "They killed him," I sobbed out. "Richard's dead. And I'm next. Help me, Jeff. Do whatever they say. Help me, please, please, help me."

I sounded terrified and helpless and more scared than I'd ever been in my life. And never in my life had I ever acted like this.

"That's not me."

"Well, we know that *now*," Jeff said. "But we didn't know it then."

"So, someone sent this and you immediately did what they asked? What did they ask? And why didn't anyone read the image? Christopher was around."

"The message was that they had killed Richard in order to impress upon the rest of you that they were serious," Chuckie said. "We were told that you were out of the country via gate technology, and that the video had been blocked so that no empath or imageer could read it."

"Christopher and I couldn't read it," Jeff said. "Therefore, that seemed truthful."

Refrained from comment. Just barely. "When did you get this?"

"You were kidnapped, and almost immediately the press was contacting us to ask where you were and saying that they'd been tipped that the First Lady had been kidnapped," Reader said. "We activated Francine and had her and Jeff do a photo op outside."

"Then we got this," Chuckie said, nodding toward the screen. "We were told that because we'd lied about your whereabouts you were going to pay for it."

Interesting, though not surprising. "What else did they want?"

"The immediate release of Stephanie Valentino," Reader said.

"Who asked for the phones to be shut down?"

This question caused the three of them to look really

uncomfortable. "Your captors suggested it," Jeff said finally. "But it made sense, since we thought it would protect us and you."

I was back to wondering if these guys, the three men I thought knew me and understood me best, actually knew me at all.

"We couldn't risk anyone who wasn't cleared sharing that you were actually nowhere around," Jeff added, sounding kind of desperate. "And we had to leave the line free for your kidnappers."

"Wow. Just . . . wow. I literally don't know where to start. I mean, I see it, it looks like me. But since we *just* had a Kitty-Bot attack not two days ago, I'd have thought one of you would have suggested that this was faked."

"There's more intel and data than we've shown you," Chuckie said, also sounding and looking pretty stoic, though I knew that he was upset because I knew him so well. Hoped this wasn't going to trigger a mood swing and migraine session and wondered if that was a side benefit that Stephanie and her team were hoping for.

Of course, they could be hoping for Jeff to have an empathic collapse, too. Should have probably had all of my team get emotional blockers from Kendrick before we'd taken this particular meeting, but too late now.

"We're unbelievably sorry," Reader said, not even trying to hide the fact that he was upset. "Does that help at all?"

"Sort of." Not really.

Jeff closed his eyes. "No, it doesn't." He opened his eyes. "I've felt you truly terrified, and it was when Leventhal Reid had you in the desert and you were convinced you were going to die in a horrific manner. And, before you say it, you didn't cry and beg. You fought, but you refused to let him make you helpless."

Chuckie jerked. "Oh. Oh, God, Kitty. I'm sorry. None of us were trying to make you into a victim, in our minds or in reality. We just . . . ."

"Panicked," Reader finished.

"That is why I'm upset," I said quietly, for which I was quite proud of myself. "I didn't cry and beg when the most terrifying man I've ever met had me. And I'm beyond hugely offended that the three of you, and Tim, all felt that I was crying and begging now. I'm not sure what male fantasy of me that video fulfilled for all of you, but if I'm honest, I'm more disappointed than angry." Well, now, at least. "I thought you guys knew me. And the others. None of us have ever rolled over and begged."

Got up close to the screen and examined the image. "Play it again." Raj hit the rewind and we watched me play helpless. Really and truly looked like me. "Huh. I didn't think Stephanie had an android of me ready."

White joined me. "I believe that's a Kitty-Bot. There are some slight differences around the eyes and hairline from the androids we've seen."

"Which begs so many questions, doesn't it?" Stephanie had certainly had the android creation room for me ready, but that hadn't indicated there was a Kitty-Droid ready to go. "I want to see everything, not just this impressive fake of me acting like I never have. All of it. Show us. Oh, and then, in case you're interested, I'll be happy to share all that we did while being kidnapped. You know, like rescue ourselves, rescue our missing teams, then go and rescue the other missing teams. That sort of thing. Things that the chick in this video would never even think of doing, let alone manage."

Raj hit another button and a different screen came to life. This one had a man's voice sharing pretty much exactly what the guys had said—Richard was already dead, I and the others would be if his demands weren't met, he wanted Stephanie released immediately, no contact with anyone regarding this, we couldn't escape because there were tons of people pointing guns at us off-screen, and anyone searching meant immediate dismemberment that they'd get to watch.

"So, where's the scene of them taking a digit or a limb?"

"How did you know?" Jeff asked, sounding strained. Worked to keep my hurt, anger, and disappointment in him and the others to a minimum. Doubted that having to give him adrenaline right now was going to be good for anyone. And the last place I wanted him was in isolation.

"You ordered Len and Malcolm both not to search for me, which is hugely out of character for you, at least for the you I'm used to. So, let's see it."

"It's graphic," Raj said.

"It's a freaking movie, gang. It's not me. It's not even a

real person. Corn syrup with red dye number two is what the blood is, trust me."

Another screen leaped to life. Sure enough, there I was, losing all five fingers, then my hand, then the arm to the elbow. Slowly, done for the supreme effect of torture and gore, finished off with a hot poker to cauterize the wound. By the end of that, I was a shrieking, blubbering, incoherent mess. Interesting. Whoever had made this video had paid attention to Hollywood for sure, because I recognized some techniques.

Turned away from the screen. "You know why Reid could hurt me?"

The room was quiet. Serene broke the silence. "You weren't enhanced."

"Bingo. I *am* enhanced now, but amazingly enough we've managed to keep that kind of hidden from most of our enemies. I'd like you all to note one very important thing—the Kitty-Bot there is not actually being contained. Because they didn't have to do that, since she's programmed for an Impressive Hollywood Death Scene. If that had really been me, I'd have kicked up the hyperspeed and handled things, guns or no guns."

"Do you recognize the voice in the recording?" Chuckie asked hopefully.

"Nope. No idea who that is. He sounds old, though. Like older than my Papa Abe or Nono Dom old."

White jerked. "Play the message again, please." Raj did. White listened intently.

So did I. This time around, noted that the speaker was in love with a catchphrase. Wasn't what the Mastermind had loved, but still, it was repeated a lot. Couldn't argue—I had things I liked to say frequently, too. But it wasn't one I'd heard any of our enemies say before, at least not repeatedly. Wondered if it was to throw us off, make us think he wasn't whoever he actually was. But since no one seemed to have any idea of the speaker's identity, probably not.

"Missus Martini, I believe I remember what about the labs we visited today was so familiar. Just as this voice is familiar, but familiar in a way I don't recognize. It's the speech patterns that are familiar. However, I'm going to need Paul's help to retrieve the memory. Or Abigail's."

"I'll do it, Uncle Richard," Abigail said. "Just in case

we're still our own nation and all that." Was pretty sure she was joking, but Jeff, Chuckie, and Reader all winced.

Gower sighed. "You realize that we need to put aside personal anger right now, don't you?"

She sniffed at all of them, her big brother in particular. "Almost everyone in this room who came in with us was on that helicarrier when you almost allowed it to be blown up. Kitty's not blaming you, Paul, but I am—your job as our Supreme Pontifex is to try to solve issues like this."

"This was the peaceful solution." Though Gower didn't sound like he totally believed that himself.

Abigail rolled her eyes. "I'm with Kitty—do you know her, or the rest of us, at all?"

White sat down and Abigail stood behind him, her fingers gently on his temple. "This may take a while," White said. "It's a very old memory."

"Okay, while we wait, I want someone somewhere making dinner for us. We have a lot of people who haven't had a normal meal in a long time and if they're not at Dulce getting medical care and, therefore one assumes, decent food, they're in here with me and, like me, would like a meal." Had to figure that if I was hungry, everyone who'd been a prisoner in some way was starving, especially those held at Forest Haven. "Crap."

"What?" Chuckie asked.

"We forgot to have anyone take over Stephanie's Lair at Forest Haven. For some reason, those warheads aimed at us wiped that to-do out of my mind."

"We'll handle it," Chuckie said.

Decided to let him have that one because the mistake of forgetfulness was mine. "If she's out, she's already gone back, taken what she might want, and left again. How long has she been out?"

"Since we saw that," Jeff nodded toward the dismemberment scene. "Look, I know you're mad at us, and I get it. But I thought it was you. It sounded like you."

"No, it doesn't. It sounds like my voice. But it doesn't sound like *me*. Speech patterns matter. Cliff Goodman likes to say 'part to play' so much that his minions say it now, too. It's part of how we figured out he was the Mastermind. The old dude threatening to kill the Hostage Kitty-Bot there has a figure of speech, too. He likes to say 'imagine the possibilities' as if he's working for Mattel on their latest New Barbie launch. He said it at least five times in that one threatening message. That's a heavy reliance on a phrase. But the Hostage Kitty-Bot said nothing like I would. Not one, single thing."

"Got it!" Abigail said. "Thanks for that, Kitty, that phrase triggered the memory enough for me to grab it." She stopped looking triumphant and color drained from her face. "Oh dear."

CHAPTER 85

"WELL, THAT GOT the room's attention. What's wrong, Abby?"

"Uncle Richard knows who the speaker is. But . . . it seems impossible."

"I have it now," White said. He, too, looked ashen. And shocked. "I also want to say that it's not possible, but I've learned over the years that anything is possible, even people returning from the dead."

"Who just resurrected for you?"

White sighed. "My father's old adjunct."

"Wouldn't he be dead by now?"

"No, he was young." White shook his head as if to clear it. "Let me start from the beginning. I was very young the last time I ever saw or heard him. He was young, too, though. Probably just in his early twenties, maybe even late teens."

"And he was your father's adjunct?"

"Yes, because he was incredibly talented in terms of science and math and creation. He wasn't being groomed as my father's replacement—I was. However, he was definitely helping my father lead our people farther into the sciences than we'd ever gone before. And he always said 'imagine the possibilities' when they were discussing science and, well, anything, really."

We all exchanged the Oh No look. "I'm going to hate this, aren't I?" Jeff asked.

"Probably." White cleared his throat. "I was named for him."

"His name is Richard?" I wasn't used to A-Cs utilizing names repeatedly. Humans seemed more into that.

"No, Trevor. I was given his name as my middle name. After my mother was murdered, Lucinda and I spent quite a bit of time with him, both with my father and without. Trevor didn't seem to mind when it was just we children with him, either. He always had something for us to amuse ourselves with and never did anything untoward. When my father remarried, we children visited him less frequently because our stepmother was there to care for us, and though Trevor still came over to our home, it wasn't as often as it had been. But ... I thought he was killed when my stepmother was murdered."

"If that's him on the message, he wasn't."

"Correct. But I remember ... my father was so upset at losing another wife. But losing Trevor didn't seem to upset him at all. That was when I realized that my father had been altered somehow."

"Let me just take the Megalomania Leap. Trevor didn't die. Trevor took off for Earth. And your father knew about it."

"Why would he do that?" Christopher asked. "If he was so tight with our grandfather, why leave him alone?"

Chuckie sat up straight. "To pave the way. You all had gate technology longer than you've been here."

"Much longer," White agreed. "We created it so that we could easily travel to the other planets in the system without wasting resources. Gate use for on-planet reasons was a later refinement."

"Again, I learn something new every single day. So, I think Chuckie's right—Trevor comes out here first. Like ... like Alfred or Robin going to set up the Vacation Bat Cave for Batman."

"Makes sense," Reader said. "You think he's the one who found the underground tunnels?"

Thought about Bizarro World. The Alfred there who was Jeff's father here had been the only alien on Earth, and he'd definitely gone searching for a hiding place. And A-Cs were burrowers, so he'd looked underground. "Yes, I think we can go with that assumption. So, he gets things set up for Yates—things like a business that can take off as soon as Yates arrives."

"Why would they assume Yates would be exiled?" Abigail asked. "The Royal Family had already tried to kill him twice, right?"

"Right, and they weren't succeeding. A-Cs like efficiency, you know that. Let's say that Yates and Trevor had insider information. I mean, it's not like only Earth utilizes a spy network."

"There's definitely one on Alpha Four," Chuckie confirmed. "And per Leonidas, it's been around for centuries."

White nodded. "Humans didn't invent deceit, sadly."

"So, no one's mentioned Trevor, ever."

"I haven't thought of him in decades, really," White said.

"The memories were buried deeply," Abigail confirmed.

"Right, well, I didn't actually mean you, Richard. I've spent a lot of time up close and personal with most of the Megalomaniac League, and no one's ever said there was some adjunct guy hanging around doing the laundry."

"He wasn't like that," White said. "He was a creator, a tinkerer, if you will. He created the prototypes and then my father had our people work on them. Trevor is who likely came up with the idea for the ozone shield. I don't believe he created the gates, but he certainly refined them. He favored open laboratories like the ones we were in—clean white walls and glass partitions with a great deal of space. He felt it allowed the creativity to flow without being obstructed and also allowed him to work on multiple projects at once."

"Leonardo," Lizzie said.

"Excuse me?" Jeff asked.

"Leonardo da Vinci," she explained for the Slow of Wit in the room, which I had to admit my husband and best guy friends were amongst right now. "He created, like, all this stuff, totes amazing things, especially for his day and age. But he didn't mean for them to be used for bad, even though a lot of them were. He just couldn't stop creating, even when he tried."

"Does that sound like Trevor the Tinkerer?" I asked White.

"It does. My father was quite proud of him. I'd venture to say that he considered him more like a son." He looked down. "More like the son he wanted than I believe I ever was."

"And thank God for that, Richard. I think I can speak for every person on Earth when I say that we're all thankful you're nothing like your father ever was. But was Trevor an Apprentice or even a Mastermind himself?"

"No," White said slowly. "He never craved the limelight. He insisted that my father claim the credit for his inventions. I can just remember them arguing about it, with my father wanting him to have his rightful due. Trevor was uninterested in that. As Elizabeth just compared, he was more like Leonardo."

Managed not to make a Teenaged Mutant Ninja Turtle comment, but as with so many things this evening, it took effort. "So, we have the Tinkerer here. And I think we can safely say he's still alive and well. For all we know he's created an antiaging pill or chamber or something. God knows who he's been assisting from the shadows all these years, but I'm willing to bet it was everyone against us."

"Maybe some for us," Christopher said. "If he really cares more about the creation than anything else."

"Possibility noted. He's definitely working with the great-granddaughter of his former benefactor, presumably happily and willingly. And, based on what triggered Richard's walk down Memory Lane, he's also helping out those working on the Strauss Initiative. Meaning he's playing whatever game suits him. So, right now, I'd like us all to take a moment and think very hard and very honestly about Stephanie."

"Why?" Jeff asked. "And before you yell at me, I'm fully on the side of Stephanie's not a good person anymore, based on this entire day. They clearly had this contingency plan in place for the next time she was captured. And it was just as clearly set up to literally torture me and anyone else who cares about you. I'm still having to process all of my and everyone else's emotions from seeing that video, let alone the rest of the day, and there are no blocks in the world that can keep how angry you and the others were with us from me. I also appreciate very much that all of you are trying not to be mad at us now. Most of you are still upset, but I can feel you trying to not be, and I'm grateful."

"You make a good point. That was definitely set up to hurt you. And if the Kendroid had been successful in coordinating their Plan B, they'd have returned me, minus an arm, back to you guys in my new and improved android version, and if I was 'off' in any way it would be placed on my having been so horribly tortured and maimed."

"Sounds about right," Chuckie said morosely. "And,

seriously, I'm not an empath and I can feel everyone's anger. We all feel stupid and awful enough."

Took a look at my team. "I don't think we're all still as mad at you guys as you think we are, but, as a warning, you're going to feel worse shortly."

"Why did the Kendroid say he wanted Uncle Richard to be turned into an android, too?" Abigail asked. "If the whole plot was that he was killed to make us cooperate?"

"Because they could pass the 'he wasn't quite dead' line and resurrect him, too." I'd done that, with the Chuckie, Reader, and Buchanan in Bizarro World, after all. It wasn't a new or even surprising technique. "Then you send both of us back, only we're androids."

"That sounds far-fetched," Jeff said.

"Does it?" Joe stepped forward and took his knit cap off. There were gasps throughout the room. Lorraine looked like she'd been punched in the stomach.

"Told you it was going to get worse."

"Oh, that's not all," Randy said, as he, too, took off his knit cap. He also took off the stretchy arm braces Lizzie had found for them. "It's like this on our legs, too."

"What . . . what did they do to you?" Claudia whispered. She looked ready to faint.

"White House Medical will get to make the full determination, but as near as we can tell, Stephanie's using a very intricate process that inserts the android wires into the body. While the person is alive but in a sort of coma. I woke the guys up from that by slamming adrenaline into their hearts. Nothing else worked."

"I took pictures," Lizzie said. "So we'd have something to look at in case the site was destroyed or cleaned out."

"Just so we're all clear, Joe and Randy seem to be more like the new Six Million Dollar Men than androids. While Butler and Maurer had to work to regain themselves, Joe and Randy are still Joe and Randy. And they're under their own mental control."

"Barring someone flipping a switch we don't know about," Randy pointed out.

"But our legs and arms are definitely stronger," Joe said. "We think we can run as fast an A-C, or close to it. We don't know what's going on with our heads, and we also don't know if our lungs could keep up with us running like A-Cs."

"We've been a little too focused on being rescued, getting other people rescued, and not being blown up by friendly fire to test ourselves out. Otherwise, we both feel okay," Randy added.

"They still have all their boy parts, too," I reassured the girls. They didn't look reassured.

"You checked?" Jeff no longer sounded upset or freaked out or anything. He sounded jealous. Which was, all things considered, kind of nice. We might have just had what was probably the second worst fight of our relationship—because nothing was likely to top the end of Operation Drug Addict—but he was still jealous that I might be looking at other guys. Then again I'd kind of mentioned that I was planning to divorce him and look at all my available options. Maybe I'd apologize for that. Later. And in private.

"Oh, I had lots of things to check out, trust me. We were spoilt for choice."

"They were all like Ken Dolls," Lizzie said, making a face. "That's why Kitty made sure Joe and Randy were still intact." Adults coughed and looked embarrassed. "What? Geez, I'm almost fifteen. I've seen the internet."

"I had them look themselves, just in case everyone thinks I took the time to gawk at guys on my team when we were in life-threatening danger."

"Precedent has been set for that," Chuckie said dryly. Reader grinned. Strangely enough, this seemed to be making them both feel more normal, too. My men were weird.

"I mentioned that too," White said with a chuckle. "She wasn't amused."

"Oh, blah, blah, blah. Look, we have a ton to catch everyone up on and I want us fed and Tito and his team to take a serious look at everyone who was a prisoner who's here with us, starting with Joe and Randy. So, let's get back to my key point about Stephanie that I want you all to really listen to and internalize."

"Why is this one thing so important?" Reader asked.

"Because I think it's important to the Tinkerer."

"I'll ask, especially if it keeps you getting less angry with me," Jeff said. "So, what's the key point?"

"Simply that Yates cared about having an heir. A real one. So I think that Trevor the Tinkerer would care about that, too. Richard wasn't his heir, not as Yates wanted. You

certainly aren't and neither is Christopher, and not just because you're good guys and follow Richard's lead, but because, as far as Yates was concerned, your bloodline was
impure. Ronaldo Al Dejahl was close, but, let's face it, he
wasn't enough like Yates to be the true heir."

Waited. Nothing. Not even from Chuckie. Clearly today
had affected them badly.

"So?" Jeff asked finally. Sounded like he was trying to
make me happy and not share that he had no idea what I
was talking about. Expressions in the room said he wasn't
alone.

Heaved a sigh. "Stephanie may have impure blood due
to your mother, Jeff, but I'll wager that the Tinkerer is willing to overlook that, since her father was a traitor to Richard and therefore loyal to Yates. Ergo, Stephanie is the true
Yates Heir based on bloodline and desire to take over the
world both. Meaning that if there's anyone the Tinkerer is
going to support, when push really comes to shove, it's her."

CHAPTER 86

MY PRONOUNCEMENT was met with a lot of non-reaction. Had a strong feeling that everyone was just too exhausted to think anymore. I certainly felt that way. The adrenaline high that fury had given me and I'd ridden for hours had already faded. I couldn't stay angry with them because I did love all three of them still, even if they'd almost ended up getting me and the others killed.

"I get it," Jeff said finally. "And I agree. It makes sense."

"You don't have to agree with me in order to appease me, you know."

"I don't think that's ever worked, let alone would work right now, baby."

Had a feeling that Jeff was picking up that my anger was ebbing, because that was the first time he'd called me baby since we'd gotten in here. Knew why Alicia had wanted me not to come in with guns blazing—she'd seen the video and therefore understood the fear reaction. She might have found their reactions flattering; some women would, after all. I just wasn't one of them.

However, right now, I was definitely the leader for anyone who'd been in the helicarrier, and I also had two children I wanted to see who didn't need to get involved with their parents' fight. And we had Lizzie, too, who was already involved but who, perhaps, should see that even though you can be mad enough to want to literally strangle your husband, there comes a point where you have to break down and accept that he was fallible just like anybody else. And just like anybody else, if your husband and best friends made a mistake that you lived through, perhaps forgiving them was the right course.

"Okay, I'd like to confer with my people from Kitty Land. Give us a mo." Jerked my head toward the door and we all stepped out into the hallway and closed the door behind us. "So, have they groveled enough?"

Abigail snorted. "Not for me. But then, I'm mad at my brother."

"I can tell they were terrified," Mahin said. "And we did not get blown up."

"No thanks to them," Buchanan said. "However, in the interests of national security and familial harmony, not to mention avoiding a hostile working environment, let me make this easier for everyone. They love you. You love them. Kiss and make up."

"Really, Malcolm? You were in the running for Prince Consort."

He grinned. "Yeah, like Gil here said before, I can guarantee that Mister Executive Chief's going to get that job."

Morgan nodded. "I think you handled it with a lot less screaming than anticipated."

"Go team."

"I'd still like to understand why they did all that they did," Camilla said. "But whatever you want is fine with me."

The flyboys nodded. "I think your wives really want you to hold them," Jerry said to Randy and Joe. "I've never seen them look that . . . stricken."

"Do you want to make up with the girls?" If they didn't, wasn't sure if I should be worried, try to fix it, or just go live in the helicarrier.

Joe nodded. "Tim said none of the women made the decisions."

Tim had come with us, wisely choosing to stick with the people who had control of the helicarrier. "They didn't. They all sided with Christopher."

Christopher had also stepped out with us. "I want to take a moment and revel in being so very right and having everyone point it out. I'm really enjoying it."

"Anything to make you happy."

He hugged me. "Make me happier. Forgive them. They screwed up. It happens."

"Not saying I don't want to do the group hug, but three

men are dead because of that screwup, and two women might be."

"And, not to sound callous, that makes today like every other day for us. You know that. We lose people every day. We lose people you don't know about every day. This was one of those days."

"It sure was."

White nodded. "Mistakes get made. We should, perhaps, not compound those mistakes out of righteous anger."

"To err is human," Adriana said. "To forgive, divine."

"I'm going to let all the comments I could make right now slide, but I get the point and, as I said, I'm not against it. But we were all almost killed, so everyone's vote counts. Show of hands, who wants to go back and forgive them?"

The others backed Team Forgiveness with varying degrees of enthusiasm, but all the hands did raise, so we went back into the Situation Room.

Jeff looked worried and hopeful and like a big cat who'd just ruined an expensive item by breaking it, clawing it, and peeing on it, but still hoped for petting, cream, and cat treats. Yeah, Anger was definitely heading for a nap and Libido was coming to the main stage.

"The Sovereign and Flying Nation of Kitty Land is willing to end the civil war as long as food, medical care, and families are produced pronto."

Lorraine and Claudia got up and hypersped to their husbands. The girls were crying. "We'll get them to Tito," Hughes told me, as he, Walker, Tim, and Jerry moved the two couples out of the room.

Serene winked at me. "Thank you, Queen Kitty. We appreciate it. While you were conferring with your subjects we called for food. It should be ready for you shortly." She, White, and Gower ushered everyone else out, heading for a dining room somewhere.

I tugged Camilla back and indicated to Jeff, Chuckie, and Reader that I wanted them to stay. Raj noted this and he stayed, too. Christopher wisely decided not to push it and left with the others. "I'll make sure my dad and I do the recaps," he said quietly to me as Camilla shut the door after him.

"What's wrong?" Jeff asked, trying hard to look confused.

"There's more you didn't tell us. I assume you didn't want to say what else went on in front of the others. However, you're telling me and Camilla because we're the two who expected to get through to Andrews or the White House and didn't. She's the person one or all of you are going to send right back into deep cover danger, and I'm the one who could flip right back to amazingly pissed, despite all three of you doing the best puppy eyes known to mankind, if you try withholding. So we're the two who need to know what the protocols are now, and why you changed them."

"And before any of you try to lie, remember that she knows you and I know how you work," Camilla added. "Panicked by that video and inundated by the press or not, that all three of you, and Crawford, reacted in the ways you did indicates a lot more going on."

"Camilla's my favorite. So details. Full details. Now."

Jeff looked at Chuckie, who nodded. Jeff looked back to us. "Fine, but please sit down. You two looming over us in a threatening manner isn't good for any of our stress levels."

She and I exchanged the "Men" look, but we sat, me on Jeff's right and her next to me. "What Queen Kitty said. No more stalling."

"No, you're right." Jeff ran his hand through his hair. "We had what Chuck called a perfect storm today. When you went to lunch, your mother was briefing us on intel she'd gotten from Mossad."

"Yeah, Mom had said something about that."

"It's more than something," Chuckie said. "Mossad feels that there's something wrong with both their Prime Minister and the President of Iraq. They can't say what, but neither man is acting in character. What were supposed to be peace talks a week ago look more like they're going to blow up in our faces, literally and figuratively."

"They don't want to talk peace but war?" Camilla asked.

"As near as we can tell." Jeff shook his head. "They're gung ho to have their time at Camp David, though. Peace talks have been moved up by a day. We have tomorrow to prep, then we're heading to Camp David the day after. And yes, I know you're both coming. I realize our entire teams are coming, not just Alpha. Doreen's insisting that, if you're still speaking to me, the Diplomatic Corps is on-site too."

"Do we have any intel we can look at on the two Head Dudes Behaving Badly?"

"They aren't behaving badly so much as not behaving like themselves," Reader said. "But yeah, we do have some. Not a lot."

"Roll it here."

"I thought you wanted to eat," Jeff said.

"Bring the food here, too. I know this isn't the Embassy, but the White House appears to have its own kind of Elves, and right now, not arguing with what I want remains in your best interests."

"I'll handle it," Raj said. "Back in a bit." He took off, but not before he passed a sign to Camilla.

"So, what else?" she asked as soon as Raj was gone. "That's not enough to change protocols like you did."

Jeff looked uncomfortable. Chuckie sighed. "We were told by a variety of sources that there would be people attempting to access us during a time of crisis in part to attack us, in part to stop the peace talks. The suggestion was that all protocols be immediately changed and allow all active duty agents to fend for themselves for a brief period of time."

"Wow, for the first time I really know what it's like to be left out in the cold and, trust me, it truly sucks. It's like we were in *Burn Notice* but without Bruce Campbell. So, who were these sources? As in, did Mister Joel Oliver tell you this?"

"No, he did not. These sources came via intelligence from all agencies, not just mine."

Camilla heaved a long-suffering sigh. "All agencies are infiltrated. You know that," she said as Raj returned.

Chuckie and Jeff both looked ready to have migraines. In Chuckie's case, that he wasn't having one at this moment was probably a miracle. Reader just looked like he wanted to go back to modeling and pretend the last many years of his life had never happened.

"Stop," Raj said calmly. "Camilla, you and Kitty are both right. We screwed up. You almost died because of that screwup. We lost people because of it, too. However, we were inundated with all of this at once, and no, we didn't tell most of the others what was going on. Tim, Serene, and your mother knew, and that was about it."

"It's a steeper learning curve than any of us were prepared for," Chuckie said. "In part because of how we moved into these positions."

"And it's a learning curve for Alpha Team, too," Raj said. "Kitty, I want you to pay attention to this next statement. The men who love you enough to die for you fell for the charade and, therefore, were not exactly in their best minds to make decisions. Yes, many of us counseled against their actions. We can all congratulate ourselves for knowing you so well and having our confidence in you confirmed. Jeff, Chuck, and James also have confidence in you. They just were hit with so much, so fast, and the evidence was so damning, that they acted like people, not leaders. It happens. To everyone at some point."

Pondered all of this. "They threatened the kids, too, didn't they?"

All four men sort of stared at me. "Ah, what?" Jeff said finally.

"Our children and the other children. That's why the Embassy locked down so fast and why you pulled everyone in also so fast. They threatened the kids and you had to make the choice between leaving people out in the cold or keeping the children safe. And this is me, Raj, being forgiving instead of extremely pissed that you guys withheld this information."

Reader nodded. "We got a video that showed Denise and all the kids in daycare. Pretty much the statement was that they could get our children regardless of how safe we thought they were. We have Field agents literally in every room of the Embassy right now. Peregrines and ocellars are there, too, on patrol. We have no idea how someone got into the Embassy. And we told no one else, to stop panic in the A-C community. If they can get into the Embassy, they can get into Dulce, and we all remember the last time that happened."

"Roll what they showed you, right now."

Raj hit his remote and one of the screens showed the kids and Denise doing colors and numbers utilizing the animals. It was short, but I took notice of all the kids, Jamie and Charlie in particular, including the naptime area. Paid attention to what my kids were wearing, too.

Waited until it was done. "Note who is not in that picture."

"Everyone is in that picture," Jeff said. "Every single kid in daycare. Other than Lizzie who was with you."

"Right, and you know why Lizzie was with me? Because our A-C nanny was with our children."

Jeff looked pale. "You're saying Nadine took this?"

Really controlled myself from rolling my eyes or making an exasperated statement—clearly the guys were not on their top game right now, and just as clearly it was due to emotional distress, so my causing more wasn't going to improve the situation.

"No. I'm saying that this was taken before Nadine was on the case. Not too much before, by the way. Based on what Jamie and Charlie are wearing, it was taken yesterday, probably when Lizzie went to her room then called me in a panic because her things had been moved. The dude, the Secret Service guy who almost shot me whose name I never got. Where is he at? And, more importantly, where was he stationed before?"

"His name is Cody Boyd, and he was on general rotation," Raj said, texting away. "Confirming his status and his past week's schedule with Joseph and Rob."

"Okay, barring them saying he was never in the Embassy, he's the one who took those pictures. He was far too willing to shoot me, and dedicated or not, shooting someone in a bathrobe with the Presidential Seal on it says Trigger Happy Loose Cannon or Stealth Assassin."

"Confirmed," Raj said. "He was in the Embassy on duty yesterday. The past few days, really. He was one of those coming and going with the kids. He'd requested night guard duty, too, and was given it because the Secret Service is all hands on deck due to this administration's penchant for taking the fight to your enemies directly."

"Fabulous and blah, blah, blah. This is proof that he damn well knew who I was. Also, I'm sure that he wanted night duty to help the Crystal Maurer android get onto the White House grounds safely and cover her escape if she was caught. Christopher may be able to confirm the timestamp, so to speak, if this wasn't tampered with."

"Doesn't matter if it was," Jeff said. "That makes sense. Where is Boyd now?" he asked Raj.

Raj was staring at his phone. Jeff cleared his throat meaningfully. Raj sort of jerked. "Sorry. Just having to process this."

"Why?" I asked flatly.

Raj looked up and he looked shaken. "Because he's gone."

CHAPTER 87

WE ALL STARED AT RAJ. "What do you mean, gone?" Chuckie asked finally.

"I mean Boyd was put into lockup per the President's instructions. This morning, when someone came to give him breakfast, he was gone. The cell and facility were searched. No sign of him."

"I'd complain that no one told me this," Jeff said, "but I honestly think that it could have been the last straw for my sanity if I'd learned this even an hour ago."

Patted Jeff's hand. He moved at hyperspeed and grabbed my hand before I could take it away. Decided that I'd basically forgiven him anyway and let him hold onto it. Interestingly enough, not only Jeff, but Chuckie and Reader relaxed a bit.

"So, he was equipped with an off and on invisibility shield, which, trust me, Stephanie's team has, most likely courtesy of the Tinkerer. He switched it on when he heard food arriving, and sauntered out while they were searching for him. And now I'm willing to say that he's the sniper on the roof. Though Casey Jones should not be counted out of the running in terms of participation."

"It makes sense." Chuckie rubbed the back of his neck. "I need to know, Kitty—are you still speaking to us beyond formal meetings?"

Camilla nudged my foot, but she didn't have to give me the suggestion. Let go of Jeff's hand, got up, and went around the table. Hugged Chuckie. He clutched at me. "The beauty of being best friends since ninth grade is that we can get mad at each other and still love each other and get over it."

Let go of him and hugged Reader. Also got clutched. Felt kind of bad now. "No one can stay mad at the hottest guy in the world forever, James, no worries."

Straightened up and looked at Jeff, who looked extremely hopeful but still worried. "You I'll make up with once the kids are in bed."

A look of relief washed across his face as he grinned. "I'll hold you to that, baby."

"Good. So, what are our next steps, besides dinner, which I was not joking about wanting, and watching videos of our potential political troublemakers, which I was also not joking about."

"I'm putting the protocols back in place," Jeff said. "Though if you and Camilla have thoughts on that, let me know."

"My thought is turn them back on right now," Camilla replied. "Because who knows how many of our people are dead because of this situation."

Raj pulled out a phone that didn't look like a phone I'd ever seen before. He made a call, then handed the phone to Jeff. "This is Bravo One. Revert to systems." He was quiet. "Yes. Confirmed. Yes. Immediately, please." He handed the phone back to Raj, who finished up with whoever.

"So, I can use the old codes?" Camilla asked.

"Everyone can. I've also authorized that all areas that had someone calling in using the old codes should send backup now."

"Hopefully that will work," Chuckie said.

"Field teams are also being requested for those areas," Raj said, as he hung up. "Other than Kitty and Camilla, agents calling in for anything other than routine checkpoints were few. We should be able to get to those who did call in for backup or extraction quickly. And yes, I'll advise if anyone was compromised unduly."

"I'm going to Camp David tomorrow," Chuckie said quickly, presumably to keep me from asking what they considered an undue compromise. "Taking Alpha Team and a variety of other security personnel with me. We want to be sure that the area is prepped and safe. We'll stay there overnight, so we're there when you and the rest of the dignitaries get there."

"Said dignitaries are flying in tonight," Raj said. "We can

get away with letting them rest up tomorrow, but that's why we have to get things rolling the next day."

"Where are they sleeping?"

"Blair House, where all foreign dignitaries stay. We don't have room for them in the White House right now, and we can't show favoritism by letting one into the Lincoln Bedroom and not the other."

"Considering Mossad thinks there's something off about them, I think Blair House is plenty close enough."

Staff with food came in now, and we ate. First Camilla and I donned our Recap Girl capes and filled the guys in on everything that they'd missed. Camilla went first, filling us in on what had happened to her and the princesses. She felt that the androids had been prepared to find her and the princesses at Drax's, though no one was certain how they'd known to look. The assumption was that Stephanie knew Camilla was a double agent and figured she'd be there.

I picked up where she left off, giving them the other prisoners' recollections as well as the high-level for what we'd done and where we'd done it. Neither one of us was actually trying to make the men feel bad again, but we definitely were succeeding without effort by the time I was done with the full day's report.

Suggested we watch the stuff Mossad had sent over while we ate dessert in hopes that it would, somehow, make everyone feel better. Couldn't say with any kind of confidence if there was something funny about the two leaders or not. Imageering had already tried reading the images, but they were digital and no one got anything. Not for the first time I cursed Cliff and his cronies for releasing whatever they had onto our people and taking away most of our imageers' talents.

Asked White, Abigail, Mahin, and Adriana to join us, mostly because we'd all seen a lot of androids in action recently. Tim and Serene came with them, presumably to help out, versus to keep me from getting mad again. Buchanan also joined us. Jeff pointedly didn't tell him to leave or act annoyed toward Buchanan or anything. Wasn't sure if this was good or bad, so chose to not worry about it. There was so much else to worry about, after all.

No one else felt that they could tell much, though White paid particular attention to eyes and hairlines. However, comparisons to older pictures showed that the men looked pretty much as they always had.

We were about to give up when Chuckie got a call. He stepped out to take it while the dishes were cleared. Chef had done himself proud again and I finally felt full, which was nice.

"So, while we wait for Chuckie to come back, let's try to wrap up some loose puzzles. First one, any guesses as to why Crystal Maurer was breaking into the White House?"

"To make you a sitting duck for Boyd?" Jeff suggested.

"No way. Who could have known that you and I would be in the Oval Office, in the dark, at that time?"

"Anyone who knows you," Reader said. "Oh, sorry, was that my Out Loud Voice?"

"It was, and I see you're feeling better about yourself. But let's be honest—there was no way to predict that we'd be in there and would chase whoever broke in out. There was no reason to think anyone would be there."

"Then why was Boyd ready to shoot you?" Jeff asked.

"Convenience," Tim answered. "For all we know he was supposed to kill her at another time and you two just made yourselves easy targets. He could kill her and claim ignorance, that he couldn't see clearly in the dark, whatever. Maybe he thought he'd win points with Stephanie or whoever that way."

"Sounds right to me." It did. Boyd was too well equipped for escape to think otherwise.

"Are you certain it was Crystal Maurer who broke in?" Jeff asked. "You think Casey Jones is involved, too, and, frankly, we have plenty of women who are willing to do whatever for Cliff. Or Stephanie, I guess."

"I'm sure Chuckie thinks Cliff is behind all of this, and will do until we have Cliff incarcerated or a dead body that's really his to show off. My question isn't if I think Cliff's involved—I don't, because I'm sure that Stephanie's behind this and I'm equally sure that she's no longer working for or with him." Plus, Algar had told me Cliff wasn't involved. Not that I could share this. "My question is—why have anyone break into the Oval Office to begin with?"

"To plant bugs?" Tim suggested. "Why is that the loose end you want to focus on? Nothing blew up, nothing was taken, nothing was left."

"Most likely, again, because Jeff and I were there."

Buchanan nodded slowly. "It's a good question. The intruder seemed . . . benign. While Goodman might have been willing to be hidden before, now everyone knows he's the Mastermind. Why bother with finesse? If you can get an invisible person into the White House, why not kill everyone and be done with it?"

"Same with Stephanie."

"No," Adriana said. "She and Cliff are no longer the same."

"What do you mean?" Jeff asked. "Technically they're both domestic terrorists."

"Not really in the same way. Stephanie is a traitor to your people, but in her mind, she's following in her father's and great-grandfather's footsteps. Cliff is looking only for power. Stephanie is also not willing to pretend. Cliff lied to Charles for years because he enjoyed that kind of game. But Stephanie has made it quite clear that she hates all of you, and anyone who likes you."

"You think Stephanie wants us to know it's her," Buchanan said.

Adriana nodded. "From all I've seen, this is more her style. It's not Cliff's. Besides, normally after a defeat of the magnitude that the Mastermind experienced, it would be expected that he'd go somewhere to lick his wounds, regroup, and plan anew. At least, that's what Grandmother said."

"Huh. I did hurt Cliff."

"Yes, we watched on television. Grandmother was quite impressed."

"You hit him with something, before he got onto that chopper," Tim said. "We *all* saw it on the news and the corresponding continuous loops that the news media played."

"So bitter. Yeah, I had those used hypodermics in my purse. I rammed four of them into his butt." Hard.

Serene looked thoughtful. "Used hypos? Was it the adrenaline you carry for Jeff? And used on whom?"

"Yes, adrenaline that I carry with me, and they were used on me, Tim, Siler, the Dingo and Surly Vic. Siler, the Dingo, and Surly Vic were all infected with the bioweapon." No way in hell I was willingly calling it the Alien Flu, not even just among us.

"Interesting." Serene looked thoughtful. "We don't have enough data to be sure, however."

"Want to share? Or are you waiting for Chuckie?"

"No, I can share now. We don't reuse needles because they can spread infectious diseases. It's why so many intravenous drug users get horrible illnesses—they're sharing dirty needles. Disease is also really happy to travel through the blood stream."

She sounded like she was finished. "And?" Hoped I'd asked that in a FLOTUS versus a Queen Kitty way, but couldn't tell if I'd managed it.

"Oh! Sorry. I thought it was obvious."

"Most of us didn't get our medical degrees in grade school, Serene."

She laughed. "Gotcha. Okay, you said you had five spent needles and hit him with four?"

"At least five were used, yeah. Kind of blurry on the events right now."

"Not a problem. All the needles were contaminated, and at least three of them had been inside people with the disease."

"Kitty and I had symptoms," Tim said. "Pretty sure we were infected by that time, too."

"Even better. So you hit Cliff with four dirty needles that had been inside people with the disease."

"I'm not getting it, other than that he probably can't sit comfortably right now. Cliff gave himself the vaccine."

"Yes, but while that's great, there's now the DNA of those who were injected on those needles. Any diseases you have would transfer. Cliff took the vaccine, but that doesn't mean it's able to fight off what would be four different blood samples, all infected in some way."

Chuckie chose this moment to return. "Interesting development. Homeland Security sent me a missing person report this morning, seeing as it was something they'd planned to pass to the CIA anyway and just were waiting for whoever was taking over to get named. The report was verified by the FBI and confirmed by operatives in Cuba and Florida."

"Well, we're trying to figure out the small stuff right now, so your timing's good. So, who besides me and our folks got snatched?"

"A Doctor Tagle."

"Never heard of him." Looked around. No one else appeared to have heard of him, either.

"I'm not surprised. He's the top infectious disease physician in Cuba. Considered one of the best in the world."

"Sounds like people in Cuba or those who are very sick should be looking for him, then."

"And I'd like to know why Homeland Security or the FBI care about this," Jeff added.

"They care because he was known to work for underworld figures and politicians the U.S. doesn't like, if the price was right."

"Willing to bet cash money that when you guys find him he'll be using Cliff Goodman's money."

"That was the thinking, which was why we had the Agencies searching for him. The hope was that if they found Tagle they'd find Goodman. He *is* considered Public Enemy Number One right now, by us and Interpol."

"That was good initiative," Jeff said. "Make sure whoever put that in place gets a meeting with me."

"Will do. But my call wasn't from one of the agencies, it was from an agent who'd been locked out, just like Kitty and Camilla were. She wasn't in danger, but she did have something vital to report." He sighed. "As it turns out, we don't have to look for Tagle any longer. His body was found in the middle of Iraq. Quite mangled, but positive ID was made during the time between when she found the body and when she was able to reach me now."

Let that one sit on the air for a moment. "You know what's funny?"

"What?"

"While you were taking that call we were just discussing how Cliff is probably quite sick because I slammed four dirty needles into his butt. Hard." Hey, I knew Chuckie would appreciate that last fact, and it might make him feel better about the day's continuing disasters, too.

"The price of failure can sometimes be high," White said.

"You think he was killed because he couldn't cure Cliff?" Jeff asked.

"I believe it's very likely, Jeffrey. Now that he's been exposed as the Mastermind, the false face is gone. We all saw it either live or on television."

"Plus, all we have to do is look at how he's treated the women in his life to see that he's not a nice person," Camilla added, sarcasm meter at eleven and climbing. "But, other than confirming that Cliff's sick and, we can hope, dying, how does this help our current situation?"

"No idea, however, we're certain Tagle was never in and was not killed in Iraq." Chuckie heaved a sigh. "As far as we can tell, the body was dropped out of a helicopter. The helicopter has been found. It was local and was stolen the day prior."

"So, Cliff and his gang went to Cuba, which makes a lot of sense. They find Dr. Tagle who maybe doesn't want to work with the guy who's just been unmasked on international TV as the man trying to kill half the world. So, they force him to work on Cliff. He doesn't succeed. He's killed for his trouble."

"How would they get the body there?" Mahin asked. "They have no gate access."

"They've found a way." And that was probably related to the Tinkerer or Stephanie or both. "Maybe their water bender can see the dials on the gates. Besides, they created random floater gates when they had us all trapped in the quicksand in Groom Lake during Operation Defection Election, remember? Who's to say they didn't do it again?"

She nodded while Tim shuddered and muttered something about *The Lion King*. "Oh, I do remember, Kitty," Mahin said darkly. "Believe me. But why leave the body in Iraq?"

Chuckie jerked. "Oh. I'm really off today. It's to disrupt the peace talks, to create another international incident. Cuba's not going to be happy when they find out what's happened to Tagle—he was considered a shining light there."

"And they'll find a way to blame us," Jeff said.

Mahin nodded. "If it's made public, this could easily turn into an incident between not only America and Cuba, but America and Iraq, and potentially the rest of the Middle East."

"That means Cliff's alive." Everyone looked at me and they all looked surprised. Refrained from heaving a sigh. I was Ms. Self-Control tonight. "That's a Screw-You Move, not a strategic move. He's not involved in anything else that's going on—if they've killed Tagle, then Cliff's too sick or hurt to really get involved. Otherwise, Tagle would still be with them, caring for Cliff. But Cliff can have his people dump the body in a place that will cause issues for us and the rest of the world, too."

"Makes sense, and I'll relay your thinking." Chuckie sat back down, though he looked like he wanted to pace. "So, what other loose ends do we have?"

"So many," Jeff said, as he leaned his head on his hand. "And I get the feeling they'll be never-ending."

Decided tomorrow was another day. "You know what, let's just get to bed early and go over this stuff tomorrow."

"We're at Camp David tomorrow," Serene said, indicating herself, Reader, Tim, and Chuckie.

"Fine. Camilla and Malcolm, are you with Chuckie or us tomorrow?"

"I'm with you, Missus Executive Chief. As always."

Camilla looked thoughtful. "I'll go with the security team."

"Why so?" White asked.

She shrugged. "I could use some rest."

CHAPTER 88

THE MEETING BROKE UP and everyone headed to their rooms or to the Embassy, depending. Chuckie went to the Embassy as well, based on the fact that we were technically still in a state of emergency. Camilla went there as well. Had to figure the Embassy's guest rooms were filled up and Doreen, Christopher, and the others who lived there had every room in their apartments taken, too.

Jeff and I called down to medical to check with Tito about the status of his variety of patients. No one seemed permanently hurt other than Joe and Randy. He was keeping them under observation, and he was also consulting with Drax and the other Vata about possible implications.

The Planetary Council, in the meantime, had made a love connection with Tevvik and the others who'd come after Drax, and were making plans for visits of state once Earth's business was taken care of. Nice to see adversity and lockdown bringing everyone together.

"So, do you want to go to the Embassy and get the kids or have Nadine and the security team bring them over?" Jeff asked, as we headed for our rooms. At least, I was fairly sure that's where we were headed. The stairs and hallway looked familiar at any rate.

Actually gave this some thought. "How will we do that normally? I mean, say, a month from now?"

"I have no idea. I can barely think a week in advance right now." He sounded exhausted and very down. Was pretty sure my being angry with him hadn't helped anything and felt bad. Because I wasn't angry now—there was too much going on to stay mad at the people I loved the most.

Took his hand and squeezed it. "I'm sorry I was so upset with you."

"You had every right. That's the worst of it, baby—you had *every* right to be angry. None of us have a legitimate leg to stand on in regard to this. We ignored counsel from people with more experience and those who weren't as emotionally involved and we messed up, big time. And the ultimate decision rested with me, and I did what you said—I let fear control my responses." He shook his head. "Yesterday I felt like we were in some sort of control. Now? Now I truly feel like I should resign and let someone, anyone, else handle all of this."

"No."

"No what?"

Stopped walking in the middle of the stairway and made him look at me. "No, you don't get to quit. No, you don't get to wallow. And no, you don't get to keep on blaming yourself. The only things I'm mad about that you did were canceling the protocols, which allowed some guy at Andrews to aim warheads at my ship, and letting Stephanie out, and I understand why you did both. You did it because you love me."

"Yeah, but I hurt your feelings, and I could tell."

"I'm hurt because you guys caving based on that video made me feel like you didn't know me, didn't respect that I have skills, and somehow were more willing to believe I was helpless than on top of things and turning the tables. But, I get it. I can honestly say that I have no idea what I'd have done if our situations had been reversed. When you're watching the person you love being tortured and hearing them begging you to save them, it's damned easy to give in."

"You didn't give in way back when."

"You mean when Beverly had a needle to your throat? Or when Taft was aiming a gun at your head? Or tons of other times like that? I was there, right there, and I knew I could save you. It's a different situation, Jeff, and now that I'm no longer upset, I can see that."

"But it was still a mistake that almost cost you your life and me everything that matters to me."

"Look, every President has had to make a decision that he regretted, and all of them have had to make hard decisions—some, like Truman, had to make the hardest—and every one of them has second-guessed themselves. You made mistakes when you were the Head of Field. Just like James made today. Chuckie made mistakes when he was the Head of the E-T Division, just like he did today. Mistakes aren't what matter. What you do after you've made those mistakes is what matters."

"You really don't think I should resign?" I heard the fear, hurt, and self-doubt in his voice, and I recognized it because I'd heard it before. As Reader had told me more than once and as I knew myself, Jeff wasn't as cocky and confident inside as he seemed to the rest of the world. Inside, he was still a shy little boy who didn't think that anyone other than his Aunt Terry and Christopher really loved him or believed in him.

Hugged him tightly and he, like Chuckie and Reader before him, clutched me to him. "No, Jeff. I may have threatened divorce when I was furious with you, but I really will leave you if you've suddenly turned into some guy who lets one setback destroy him. That's not you. You're a leader, Jeff, a natural leader. You're the best man for any job you want to take, and right now, this country needs the best man leading it. The world does, too, because if the wrong person is in the White House, then it affects everyone negatively."

"But I almost killed you. And all the others, too."

"Yes, you did. Because you were deceived. Because Stephanie's a bitch and she knows just where to hit you and Christopher. You think it was an accident that they took Richard, too? The Kendroid thought Lizzie was my daughter—Stephanie's not as good at this as Antony Marling was, and for that we should be grateful. But they took Lizzie to use against you, too. Abby and Mahin were along because they're family. And Stephanie wants to hurt her family as much as she can."

"Why? You think it's because of that Trevor guy?"

"No, and you need to stop giving her any benefit of any doubt. I think Trevor the Tinkerer is helping her because he's finally found The One—the person in the right bloodline who is exactly like Ronald Yates. But this is all Stephanie. I recognize her signature, if you will, just like Adriana does. And she did it all, like you said, to hurt you. To destroy you, if possible. And you quitting, you giving up, means she wins. And I refuse to let any of our enemies win, the kid who smugly told me you and I would never be allowed to be married most of all."

His body was still tense. "But what if I make a mistake at these peace talks? What if I'm the reason another war starts?"

Couldn't help it, I snorted. "Oh my God, Jeff, there's never been peace in the Middle East and there probably never will be until or unless we're invaded again by the Z'porrah. Mossad says the leaders coming aren't acting right, meaning they're either trying to use all that's gone on in America as an excuse to fight or someone's gotten to them. But your job is to mediate, to be that voice of calm authority. And that's all you can do."

"You're sure I can and should be doing this?"

Hugged him as tightly as I could. "Yes, Jeff. I know you're the right man for the job. And as long as you stop doubting yourself, you'll do the job I know you can." Looked up at him. "I chose the pick of the litter, remember? And just because you piddled on the carpet and I stepped in it and rubbed your nose in it, you're still the pick of the litter and I still love you."

He laughed and I felt his body relax. "You compared me to a cat in your mind earlier, when you all came back and decided not to secede from our nation. Not sure which one I like better."

"I like when you're the jungle cat best myself."

Now his eyelids drooped a bit as his eyes smoldered and he got a very sexy smile on his face. "That's good to hear," he purred. Then he pulled me to him and kissed me, deeply and a little frantically. Something like how he had at the end of Operation Drug Addict, right before he proposed.

We were like this for a good long while, as both of us relaxed and remembered why we were together. Jeff didn't stop kissing me until I was grinding my whole body against his. But then he did end our kiss, slowly. "We'll discuss the rest of this later, after the kids are asleep."

Heaved a sigh as we separated a bit. "I see how you're getting back at me."

He laughed and put his arm around my shoulders as I put mine around his waist and we continued on upstairs. "No, though I'm incredibly relieved we're back to our version of normal. But we do have two children and a teenager to wrangle into bed. And since I wasn't sure that they'd ever see their mother again, I kind of want to get our family together and just be normal. Well, our version of normal."

"Works for me." Pulled out my phone and sent Lizzie a text asking where in the White House she was. She replied as we reached our well-guarded rooms. "Huh."

"What?"

"Lizzie went to the Embassy after dinner to check on the kids. Apparently Christopher okayed it and went with her, since he was going back to his family anyway. So, she says that Jamie and Charlie are fine and that she, Nadine, and the gang on Animal Duty will come over shortly."

"What about the animals on guard duty over there?"

"It's nice to see you embracing our Animal Kingdom." Continued to text. "Lizzie says that as far as she can tell the Peregrines on duty there are staying, other than Lola, Mork, and Mindy who are coming back with them." Bruno was back on duty here, since I felt a gentle nudge at my leg.

"Any idea if Buchanan's heard from Siler or Wruck yet?"

"None, but I imagine Malcolm will let us know when he does. They're on a mission, I'm sure they're not going to be checking in regularly." And Jeff was a terrible liar, so decided to change the subject, because I didn't want him accidentally freaking Lizzie out. "Where are Crystal Maurer's kids?"

"With their grandmother and father under heavy guard." He sighed. "I feel like that was the last right decision I made today."

"Stop it. Again, I'm sorry I was so mad that I've affected you this badly, but stop. You made plenty of right decisions today, including telling me to leave the kids at daycare with Nadine. So, let's focus on what we need to do to get through these peace talks. The rest will undoubtedly take care of itself."

"Sure. There's a first time for everything."

Lizzie confirmed that I had time to take a shower and change clothes and, in fact, insinuated that would be a great idea so that I didn't freak the kids out. Chose not to argue. Chose instead to insist that Jeff shower with me.

Also chose not to care if our guardians outside could hear us having sex or not. Jeff clearly needed to know that I truly forgave him. Happily, we were out of our clothes fast, in the shower faster, and he had me up against the wall and yowling happily even faster still. Felt he could be sure that I'd forgiven him by my fourth orgasm, but went on to have two more just so that he could be certain.

Cleaned up, dried off, dressed in clean clothes, and sexually fulfilled—not necessarily in that order—we were ready just in time for the return of our children and their entourage. Jamie had insisted the animals stop by to see us, and after the day we'd had, I figured it really couldn't hurt.

"The pets and I are all glad you're home, Mommy," Jamie said cheerfully as I took her from Nadine and Jeff took Charlie from Lizzie, while the pets prowled around our suite, presumably looking for evildoers or a place to mark their territories.

"What about Charlie?"

"Oh, I guess he is, too." She shrugged. "You know how it is with babies. I don't think he understood what was going on."

Managed not to laugh, mostly because, as always, Jamie's comment seemed far too knowing for a four-and-a-half-year-old. Well, for someone other than my four-and-a-half-year-old. "What do you think was going on, Jamie-Kat?"

"Bad people were trying to do bad things." She hugged me tightly. "I'm glad you're okay, Mommy, and that you found Ross and Sean's daddies. They were worried about them, just like I was worried about you." Ross was Joe and Lorraine's son, and Sean was Randy and Claudia's. They'd been born about a minute apart and while they weren't as talented as Jamie, Charlie, or Serene's son, Patrick, they were still showing more abilities than most hybrid male children ever had before outside of the direct Yates bloodline.

Didn't ask Jamie how she knew Joe and Randy were back, because I was afraid that the answer wouldn't be that Lizzie had told her. "What about the other kids? Were they worried?"

"Well, Patrick was because he's my best friend," she said seriously. "But his mommy and daddy were okay. Raymond says he's always worried, but Rachel said it would all work out. And she was right! She's usually right because she's older and knows more." Since Rachel was eight and Raymond ten going on eleven, this was both hilarious and worrisome. All of our kids had way too much stress in their lives, and I saw no way to protect them from it.

"What about Raymond?" Jeff asked. "He's the eldest. Does that mean he knows the most?"

Jamie gave Jeff what I could only think of as her version of the "Men" look. "No, Daddy," she said patiently. "He's a boy. They don't know more than the girls. Almost ever."

Jeff looked at me. "Based on today, I'd say that's basically right."

"Some boys know more and some girls know more. Everybody's different, Jamie-Kat."

"I know Uncle Charles knows a lot, but no one knows more than Nona Angela. Or you, Mommy." She looked up at me quite seriously. "Girls are better. Though I like the boys. But they aren't as smart as me and Rachel." She looked over at our Resident Teenager. "And no one's cooler or smarter than Lizzie, Mommy."

Lizzie blushed. "I totes didn't pay her to say that."

I laughed. "I know. Not gonna lie, I totally agree with you, Jamie-Kat. But still, boys are good, too. What would we do without Daddy and Charlie? And Raymond watches out for all of you, Patrick's your best friend, and you know that Ross and Sean would do anything for you. The other kids in daycare are all your friends, too, aren't they?"

"Oh, I still love them all, Mommy, don't worry. Especially Daddy." Charlie gurgled in what I truly felt was a hurt manner. "Oh, and Charlie," she said looking right at him. "You know I love you, even if you drive me crazy."

Charlie gurgled happily at that and snuggled into Jeff's chest.

"So I think we should all sleep together tonight," Jamie added. "Even Lizzie and Nadine."

"Um, why so?" Had no idea where this was coming from.

Jamie looked at me again, once again with a very Serious Little Girl Face on. "Because you and Daddy had such a bad day."

CHAPTER 89

JEFF AND I actively chose not to question this. Couldn't speak for him, but I wasn't emotionally prepared to hear Jamie's answers.

Lizzie and Nadine were far less shocked than we were, however. "She's been suggesting that since I got over there," Lizzie explained reassuringly, presumably because our expressions told her we were freaked out, which I certainly was, and a quick glance at Jeff said he was possibly more so.

"I think the children are aware when we go into lockdown," Nadine said. "Therefore, they know that things are . . . tense."

"Raymond says that lockdown means all our mommies and daddies are busy saving the world again and we need to stay put and stay safe in order to help them."

"Wow, Raymond is totally on top of all of that and he's also completely right, Jamie-Kat." Wondered which child's innocence I should feel worse about having somehow taken away, my daughter's or Kevin and Denise's son's. Had to lean toward Raymond in this case, because he was just an amazing and awesome regular human boy.

"Oh, we know Raymond is right about being safe. But Rachel's right about things that will happen."

Then again, maybe there was more going on with the Lewis kids than I realized. However, tonight was not the time to find out.

"Well, that's all good to know. Are you suggesting we all sleep in the same bed? Because I think that will be weird for Lizzie and Nadine."

"Oh no. Charlie and I should sleep with you and Daddy

and Lizzie and Nadine can do a sleepover here in the living room."

Lizzie shrugged. "That's cool. All the animals are in here anyway."

Looked around. She wasn't wrong. "Nadine?"

"Where the children sleep, I sleep, unless we're all in our rooms like normal."

"I'll call for cots for you two," Jeff said, as he stood up and handed Charlie to me. "I'm sure we have them or the Operations Team can get some to us here."

"Okay, then let's get you two ready for bed."

Nadine, Lizzie, and I started the bedtime ritual. Jamie and Charlie had already had dinner and baths at the Embassy, so it was only getting them into their nightclothes that required any effort. We were done with that by the time Jeff was off the phone.

Cots arrived quickly via some White House staffers. Apparently cots were kept on hand just in case. Had to hand it to this setup—without Algar running things, they were still pretty awesomely efficient and prepped for anything.

Went to the Family Dining Room and got cocoa for all courtesy of the Elves. Took it back and we all had our treat while sitting with the pets in the now fully packed and crowded living room.

Once that was done, Lizzie and Nadine did the cot sleepover thing and the rest of us got into bed. We put the kids in the middle, Jamie next to me and Charlie next to Jeff. We sang songs to Charlie, and Jamie sang them, too. Somewhere in the middle of the third song he drifted off to sleep, and by the end of it Jamie had joined him. Jeff wrapped around so that he had an arm protectively over my and Jamie's heads. We snuggled our feet together and, in this sort of odd but ultimately very cozy way, we both fell asleep.

Mercifully, my sleep was deep and dreamless. Though I could have used some hints from the Great Beyond or from ACE, I needed the rest more. Woke up to the melodious sounds of "Wake Up" from Two Door Cinema Club, which started the day pleasantly enough.

We had breakfast with Nadine and the kids, then they and the animals went to the Embassy with a lot of security personnel, all of whom had been triple-checked overnight and who, therefore, were presumed not to be traitors in our midst.

Jeff had the fun of having to go meet the visiting dignitaries. I got out of it by being the wife who had to get things ready for the trip to Camp David. Was totally willing to play housewife in this case.

My core team arrived to help out and, I suspected, reassure themselves that I and the others were actually really alive and unharmed. Colette seemed far more comfortable with the team and her position after our Day O' Fun, which was definitely one for the win column.

Vance and Abner both expressed their appreciation for being sent home in the first limo. Len and Kyle, who were back on as my shadows, were totally in control of themselves and made no snide comments about this, though I could tell they both wanted to.

Mrs. Maurer had brought her grandchildren along, since Maurer himself was at Dulce this morning, undergoing more tests that Serene wanted. They were nice kids, clearly a little confused about what was going on, but happy to be with their grandmother. A brief teleconference with Denise and Pierre, a quick trip down to White House Medical for Tito to confirm that the children were still fully organic, then we had a security team take them to the Embassy and join the other kids in daycare. Reassured Mrs. Maurer that, as long as things went smoothly, her grandchildren were now part of our Embassy's daycare system.

Vance then shared that all Embassy children of school age were now enrolled in Sidwell, and he added the Maurer kids to that list. Was still working with the idea that what Vance wanted Vance was going to get, so had no complaints.

We'd actually caught Tito right before he was headed over to Dulce with Joe and Randy for more tests to see if they could or should remove the wires and what to do with them if the wires had to stay. Rahmi was with him, though Rhee was at the Embassy with Queen Renata. Lorraine and Claudia were already at Dulce prepping their husbands' rooms and filling in their doctors. The other flyboys were with Tim doing whatever in terms of security for the international bigwigs.

Packing I left to the Elves after a polite request to my

hamper produced an SUV's worth of luggage that was apparently for the four of us, plus Lizzie and Nadine.

Checked in with Mom, who was taking Janelle Gardiner into protective custody and getting her statement about what had gone on. There was no sign of Stephanie, and Mom and Chuckie had sent teams to Forest Haven, but they'd found no one. True to my expectation, her lair was cleared out.

Spent the rest of the day checking on various things and worrying about the fact that the prior day's escapades meant I was even more woefully unprepared to FLOTUS Up than before. But the team really rallied and ran me through a variety of scenarios. It was a lot like being back in the Washington Wife class, only this time the cool, perfect students were working for me, not against me.

Just before dinner, Buchanan called me. "I haven't heard a word from Siler or Wruck, but we have some interesting intel."

"Can't wait."

"No, you can't, I don't think. Marcia Kramer hasn't been seen wearing diamonds for at least two weeks."

Let that one sit on the air for a moment. "So, we know the Kramers are involved in the Strauss Initiative. And we found a ton of diamonds at the Strauss Initiative Fem-Bot Factory. So, why did Strauss, Villanova, and now presumably Marcia all have to sacrifice their jewelry to the cause?"

"You asking rhetorically or do you want my thoughts?"

"I always want your thoughts, Malcolm."

"Good to know. I think we have a schism. I think that, now that Strauss is dead, whoever at the NSA approved her Initiative has decided that he or she doesn't need Zachary Kramer underfoot. My guess is that Kramer's team—which I'm pretty sure will include his driver, Evan, and Villanova—have managed to get their hands on a bot or two and therefore need their own diamonds in order to make them run."

"I agree with that theory. Can you take it to Hacker International and see what they can do?"

"Already have, and I ran it by Reynolds, too. He agrees that the theory makes sense."

"How are things at Camp David?"

"No idea, I'm not there."

"Why not?"

"Like I told you last night, where you and the Babies Chief are, so am I. Both of your talented children are far less work than you."

"Don't expect that to last. Did Chuckie say how things were?"

"In a way. As a suggestion, when you get to Camp David tomorrow, I really recommend you pull him aside for a few minutes and reassure him that you still respect him, because I truly believe that he thinks that you don't."

"I thought we'd made up."

"Missus Executive Chief, we're delicate creatures, men, and our egos shatter easily. My intel shares that while you and Mister Executive Chief have had big fights like this before, you and Reynolds have not. His faith in your everlasting friendship is now shaky and his ego is shattered and isn't back together yet. Mister Executive Chief has the advantage of getting to have sex with you in order to reassure himself that all's well. Reynolds does not."

"Look at you, Malcolm Buchanan: Relationship Guru."

"It's all in the job description."

"I know who hired you, so I truly bet it is."

"And the Secret Service agents really enjoy gossiping amongst themselves in the name of keeping the team apprised of potential security issues."

"They're humans, that's not a shock, really." Considered things. "How is James?"

"Also in need of reassurance, but not to the same extent. Your forgiving Crawford quickly and him and the others officially indicates you'll really forgive him next. For Reynolds, that's all meaningless. He's relieved you've forgiven Mister Executive Chief, but it's your relationship with Reynolds himself that he feels is fully damaged."

"I'll fix it, Malcolm, I promise."

"Oh, I'm sure you will. Just do it sooner as opposed to later. Anything else you want to go over before I sign off?"

"Yeah, actually. What do you think Stephanie's next move is going to be?"

"Sadly, Siler's the Stephanie expert. I just want the go order to kill her."

"Can't give it to you, much as part of me wants to. It will hurt too many people in the A-C community if we just assassinate her the next time one of us lays eyeballs on her."

"That's what your mother said, too." He sighed. "They know your weaknesses. The Mastermind played on them for years, and he helped train her. She knows people care about her and she's going to use that against all of you."

"Well, we'll figure it out when we get there. Speaking of figuring things out and getting there, what's your take on Mossad's concerns?"

"I think that either they're right and something's going on, or the recent upheaval in the U.S. government has given both countries the idea that we're currently weak and therefore, instead of playing nicely with us, they're going to try to use us to better their own ends. Either way, we'll be ready for them."

"I hope so."

"Oh, we'll be fine. You'll be there to cause your personal form of havoc. And I recommend that you demand that the Vata and the Planetary Council be there, as well."

"Really? Why so?"

"Because, as you've pointed out more than once and did again last night, nothing brings enemies together like a bigger threat."

"The Vata and the Planetary Council aren't threatening us."

"Not yet. But don't count on that lasting."

We hung up and I did my best not to worry. Failed.

Jeff and the others came back to the White House for a few minutes, but only to share that they needed to entertain the dignitaries. While Jeff, Antoinette, Vance, Abner, and Mrs. Maurer handled the details, I grabbed Reader and pulled him aside.

"I'm not mad at you anymore."

"Ah, good. Girlfriend, we're in the middle of a delicate political situation. Paul, Doreen, Raj, and Richard are entertaining the two leaders while Jeff's here. They think he's so interested in them that he's ensuring that things are right personally. He's actually taking a break. And I need to go over things with him during this break."

"Huh."

"Huh what? Tell me that didn't make you mad at me again."

"No. Malcolm just really seemed to think that you didn't believe I'd forgiven you. So I wanted you to be sure that I had."

He flashed the cover boy smile. "Good to know." Reader kissed my cheek. "A part of me doesn't believe you could forgive us because we were idiots. The rest of me knows that you have."

Hugged him tightly. "Everyone's an idiot sometimes, James. I was when we first got to D.C., remember?"

He hugged me back. "Yeah, I do. I'm good. Though you should probably have this talk with Chuck."

"Yeah, that's what Malcolm said. You were here, though, and he's not."

"Nice to know where I stand." He grinned. "I'm just teasing you. This dinner and meeting are likely to run late. So don't give Jeff a hard time about it if he misses putting the kids to bed. This is his first big job as President and he's really focused on doing it all right."

"I know you all are. I'll be the good FLOTUS and not the pissed-off warrior tonight, promise."

Confirmed with Reader that my request for the Vata and the Planetary Council to be in attendance tomorrow was one he was willing to forward to Jeff and the others. Then he took off for Important Meeting Central and I took off for our suite, which I actually found without help.

Had Nadine and Lizzie bring the kids over—mine and the Maurer kids—and we all had dinner with my team in the Family Dining Room. Chase was ten and Cassidy was eight. They'd had a good time with the Lewis kids, so I had hopes that they'd fit into our extended family without too much issue.

Dinner done, we had the usual security folks take the Maurers back to their home. Despite my wanting to have someone with the dainty skills around, it wasn't right to ask Mrs. Maurer and her grandchildren to come with me to Camp David. Besides, I had Vance for that.

"What do you mean I'm going tomorrow?" he asked after we'd sent the Maurers home in one of the A-C limos.

"I mean that I need to not blow it and that means I need you there. Not Guy, though. I think we don't want lobbyists there if we can help it."

Abner looked worried. "What if something happens tomorrow like it did yesterday?"

"See?" Vance said to him. "I told you—it sounds safe but things blow up around Kitty."

"Dude, you're going. Abner can get out of it because I don't think I need a decorator or designer there. But you cannot."

He heaved a dramatic sigh. "Abner, if I don't return, please ensure that my funeral is fantastic and that I get a decently sized memorial stone."

"I will." Abner looked even more worried. He hugged Vance, then me. "Be careful, Kitty."

I reassured him that I'd be the soul of discretion and tucked him into his own limo with his own security.

"So, you staying here tonight or going home tonight? I think we're leaving at some hideously early time, as a warning."

"I'll spend tonight in my own bed, because it might be the last time I see it."

"Wow, thanks for the vote of confidence."

Vance grinned. "I'm confident that there will be trouble. Just know that I'll be behind you all the way."

"Of that, I have no doubt."

CHAPTER 90

THE REST OF the evening was uneventful. As Reader had said, Jeff might have been "in" the White House, but if I considered our rooms to be "home," then he was home late.

The kids were asleep in their rooms and Lizzie and Nadine were in for the night, animals with all of them, well before Jeff finally dragged in.

"God, that was exhausting," he said as he went into the closet to get undressed.

Followed him in. "Want to talk about it?"

"Honestly? No. I just want to not have to think for a couple of hours and relax with my wife. Is that okay?" he asked, sounding worried all of a sudden.

"It's great." After all, I'd find out how things were soon enough.

We snuggled into bed and Jeff found an old Godzilla movie. For whatever reason, if it was an old and totally kitschy movie or TV show, Jeff loved it. We fell asleep before Godzilla had defeated Mechagodzilla, but I knew how the movie ended, and while Godzilla did visit me in my dreams, he was mostly benign and took me for a fun ride on his shoulders, where we surfed from Japan to Hawaii while the Beach Boys sang "Surfin' Safari" as our soundtrack.

We woke up to the rocking sounds of "Wake Up" by American Hi-Fi. Same title but much more rocking than the song from yesterday. Of course, the lyrics were kind of foreboding. Chose to ignore that.

Vance was already on-site and he and Raj had everything organized before we were out of our suite. There were some real advantages to being the President and First Lady. Knew they weren't going to outweigh the disadvantages, but we did soldier on.

We were required to ride up to Camp David in the Beast, though Len was our driver and Kyle had shotgun. Literally our family group, which was six what with Lizzie and Nadine, was all that could fit into this limo comfortably. Didn't share that Bruno, Lola, Mork, and Mindy were also in the car, or that I'd checked my purse and I had a lot of Poofs on Board. By now it should be assumed that Poofs and Peregrines were coming along.

Our luggage went in a burly SUV driven by Secret Service, just like everyone else's luggage. Lost count of the number of SUVs carrying luggage versus people. Lost count of the number of cars overall that we had in our impressive convoy, but it was a lot, many more than we'd had when we were heading into Operation Epidemic and onto the Murder Train.

Jeff spent the entire hour's drive on the phone with my mother—who was still at NSA headquarters and would join us tomorrow—and a variety of others. He did a lot of grunting, and anytime he actually spoke it was about foreign policy, international diplomacy, or equally exciting topics. Len was focused on driving and Kyle was on his own headset having his own grunting conversations. Clearly the men were Occupied.

Requested music, so we listened to the All-American Rejects album *When The World Comes Down* played not nearly loud enough, but a girl had to take what she could get. Spent the drive playing word games with Lizzie, Jamie, and Nadine, while we all entertained Charlie to keep him from trying to lift the car or anything in it. Settled for him merely lifting some of the Poofs out of my purse and juggling them without using his hands. The Poofs didn't seem to mind, so chose not to stress out about this. Much.

So the time passed in a rather conventional manner. No one tried to run us off the road, shoot at us, bomb us, or kidnap us. Was texting with people in various cars in the convoy, and everyone reported that it was all work and serene driving. Had a glimmer of hope that this would end up being a really boring camping trip combining work and awkward small talk and Poof juggling that I'd have to explain as a magic trick.

We finally reached Camp David, where I discovered it had an official name—Naval Support Facility Thurmont—and I was impressed. It was large, and rustic, and staffed by Navy and Marines, making it nice and secure. The tall wire fences looked remarkably like those around the NSA black site and enhanced the feeling of security. My hopes for a good few days rose.

We were installed in the Aspen Lodge, where the President always stayed. Because we were rolling with so many people, we had a lot more in here than was probably recommended. However, while this was supposed to be where the Pres and his family went to relax, we weren't even trying to pretend that this was anything but work for everyone.

Unpacking took a short amount of time. Fortunately, because we were "camping" in cabins with hot and cold running water, indoor plumbing, and central heat and air—for which I was incredibly thankful—I'd been allowed to be in jeans and Converse. I was even allowed to wear an Aerosmith shirt, since my love for my Bad Boys from Boston was, apparently, well known. Decided that meant I was known as a fun girl and refused to worry about it.

In addition to Alpha Team, who were supposedly already on-site, Doreen, White, Mahin, and Abigail were representing for the Diplomatic Corps and our key White House Staff and Cabinet members, the Vata, and the Planetary Council were also along for the ride, as requested. Happily, Uncle Mort was here, too, representing as the newly minted Chairman of the Joint Chiefs of Staff.

Totally shocking me, Abner was here as well. Grabbed him while Jeff talked to Uncle Mort about their plan for how the next few days should go. "It turns out you can make changes here if you want to," Abner told me by way of nervous explanation. "And I . . . decided that I should be here in case you . . . need me."

"Abner, I'm honestly touched. But, and do not take this the wrong way, where are you sleeping?"

Was prepared for him to tell me he was going to be on our couch. "I'm bunking with Vance."

"Works for me." Felt that I'd managed to hide my relief,

since he didn't look hurt. Of course, for all I knew, Vance was in our cabin. Now wasn't the time to worry about it, though.

While Lorraine and Claudia were here with the rest of Alpha Team, the flyboys were all at the Embassy, seeing as air support was not needed, since we'd driven. It was felt that the five of them deserved the rest, Joe and Randy especially. Based on how many people we had here, I was actually glad they'd stayed at home, so to speak, though they'd all probably have bunked in the barracks.

Camilla was around somewhere, as was Buchanan. Not that I saw either one of them, but Reader insisted they were on-site so I chose to believe him.

Mister Joel Oliver and Bruce Jenkins and their camera crews and assistants and such were the only reporters allowed access, as per usual, and they both seemed quite thrilled. The teams with them seemed almost giddy. Decided not to ask where they were bunking, since I figured they'd all be too busy taking pictures and doing interviews to actually sleep.

With all the people coming with us, wasn't sure that we actually had enough space to house the Israeli and Iraqi contingents, but it turned out that a lot of our people were going to house at the barracks on-site.

The Shantanu had thought ahead and brought a very small portable city with them. This one was actually small enough that it should have been called a portable two-story extra-large suburban home, but I wasn't going to argue with the wisdom of Rohini's people ensuring that those from their system along with the Vata would all be housing together, so as not to put the humans and A-Cs out. That they could fit it onto the grounds when there were so many trees around was the real surprise.

Confirming that everyone was everywhere they should be fell to Raj and Vance, apparently. This was made much easier thanks to hyperspeed.

The Israeli and Iraqi contingents, who didn't have the luxury of hyperspeed, were still getting settled when Raj and Vance returned to share that everyone was where they were supposed to be and we were due to have our first casual meet and greet by the pool, wherever that was, in around thirty minutes.

Nudged Jeff who had finished with Uncle Mort. "Want to see what this place is like?"

He looked around. "Sure, I think we can do that, baby. Raj, we're going to take a quick look at the entire grounds."

Raj didn't argue. "Just be back in time for the reception."

Jeff swung Jamie up onto his shoulders. "Ready for a ride?"

"Yes!" she squealed.

I put Charlie onto my hip and took Jeff's hand. Looked at Nadine and Lizzie. "You coming?"

Nadine shook her head. "I'll pass and take the short break."

"I'd like to," Lizzie said hesitantly.

"Hang onto Daddy, Jamie-Kat," Jeff said. "I have to hold onto Mommy and Lizzie."

"Okay, Daddy!" Jamie sounded totally excited. "It's so pretty here!"

"It is, isn't it?" It was. Felt myself actually relax. We could do this.

Jeff started off at the slow version of hyperspeed so we could see what was here. There was a lot, really. Including a gigantic trench that had the familiar fencing on both sides, effectively making it hard for anyone to casually get in here.

We did a fast run around the perimeter by following the paved path right next to the trench and discovered that this area was really big, easily larger than the area around and including Forest Haven. Turned out to be a sort of an asymmetrical pentagon, though one that was sort of elongated, with ragged, uneven sides, and there were so many trees it would have been hard to tell without doing this at hyperspeed.

The lowest corner, which was to the left of the main entrance, had a helipad, a skeet shooting range, and a building that I thought might have been housing a basketball court, but we didn't go in so I couldn't confirm.

Going up from there were just a lot of trees but, as we turned to go along the "top," we spotted the military barracks, which was actually a small complex. And a back entrance or exit. The rest of the sides were all trees, trees, and more trees, though we did spot horseback riding trails. On a total positive, apparently there were horses to ride if we wanted them. Figured that if things went well, maybe I'd have Jamie try riding while we were here. There were also some trails that led outside of the compound, most notably one at the rear near to Laurel Lodge.

Took a look at Laurel Lodge, where most of the meetings and meals were going to take place. Seemed nice, but we had the kids so we didn't really go inside.

Now we did a run through the interior. Somehow they'd managed to fit a small golf course in the lower right corner of this area. There were also tons of cabins in the "middle"—which gave me a feeling of great relief—tennis courts and a fitness center up near the barracks, the Evergreen chapel near to Laurel Lodge, areas for archery and horseshoes, and, per Jeff's briefing, there was also bowling, movies, a trampoline somewhere that we'd missed, the swimming pool outside of our cabin which only I had missed, billiards—or as I and the rest of the normal people called it, pool—hiking, biking, fishing, and, in winter, lots of other sports.

This place was both totally outdoorsy and a Jock's Dream Palace. Seriously considered if we could get a small football field in here for Len and Kyle and so I could start training all the kids in track and field. Not that I was anti-tree, but there were so very many of them that if we had to knock down a couple of dying ones I wouldn't feel too guilty. Decided to wait to suggest that until we'd been on the job for at least a couple of weeks and my Dad, who was totally ecologically focused, couldn't hear me suggest destroying any of the lovely trees and such.

"It's totes beautiful here," Lizzie said. "So much less creepy than Forest Haven, too."

"It's like you read my mind."

Jeff stopped running and pulled us all in for a family group hug. "I can't tell you how relieved I am that you two are back with the rest of the family, safe and sound. I want the two of you to try to focus on having fun with Jamie and Charlie more than anything else. Especially you, young lady." He grinned at Lizzie.

Who grinned back. "Will do, Commander."

Jeff looked sort of wistful. "Not a commander anymore."

Couldn't help it, the Inner Hyena released. "Are you kidding me? You're officially the Commander in Chief of the entire U.S. military. Stop kidding yourself, Jeff. Like I said last night, you've been prepping for and doing this job for your entire adult life."

Jeff gave me a very loving smile. "I'm glad you still think so, baby." He sighed. "I think it's time for us to get back."

We headed back for Aspen—which was neither in the center nor near Laurel, but was quite close to the golf course, go figure—and got there as people were starting to gather. Jeff zipped us into the cabin so we could walk out at human normal. So it was kind of a shock to see that some-one other than Nadine or our Secret Service teams were in here. Not that it should have surprised me.

CHAPTER 91

"JAKOB! OREN! LEAH!" Let go of Jeff's hand and raced over to give our friends from Mossad stationed at the Israeli Embassy hugs. "Feels like I haven't seen you guys for ages."

"Well, it's been a busy time for all of you," Leah said. She took Charlie from me. "He's grown so much since I saw you last, and it was really probably only a couple of weeks ago."

"Feels like a lifetime," Jeff said, as he shook Oren and Jakob's hands and gave Leah a kiss on her cheek. "This is Elizabeth Vrabel," he said. "She goes by Lizzie."

"Or Quick Girl," I added. Leah raised her eyebrow and I nodded.

She turned to Lizzie and offered her hand. "It's always nice to meet a sister."

"Sister?" Lizzie asked, sounding confused, though she took Leah's hand.

Leah laughed. "Sister in the Kick Butt Club. Kitty's mother is our Founding Member."

Lizzie beamed. "Oh, that. Yeah, I guess I'm in."

"Trust me, she's in. So, are you guys here officially or did you sneak into this secured area somehow?"

"We managed to get onto the Prime Minister's protection team for this meeting," Oren said. "His staff is concerned. He's definitely not acting like they're used to."

"We watched the video," Jeff said. "Honestly, because we can't read it, nothing seemed really off to us."

"It's not what they're saying or doing, it's how they're saying or doing it," Jakob said. "And I'm saying they because the Iraqi President is off, too. And in his case, it's getting more noticeable."

"He's acting erratic," Leah said. "One moment he's pleasant, the next he seems almost possessed."

"Drugs?" Everyone stared at me. Resisted the urge to roll my eyes. "Seriously? Come on. It's not like no leader in the world has had addiction problems. That sounds a lot like drug addiction or withdrawal."

"Not that we've discovered," Jakob said. "But we'll search for evidence of such again."

Raj came in. "There you are. We need you outside." He nodded to Mossad. "Are you three done in here?"

"Yes," Leah said. "And before you ask, we were installing bugs."

Stared at her. "Excuse me?"

"Requested by the Head of the P.T.C.U. and the Director of the CIA," Oren explained. "They want us monitoring here, just as they are."

So much for having sex at Camp David. Actively chose not to be bitter, but it took a lot of effort.

Jeff grunted. "Take the bugs out, put the bugs back in. You people need to make up your minds." He nodded to Raj. "We're coming."

Mossad left by a door opposite the one we were going to walk out of so that they could look like they hadn't been in here.

Jeff swung Jamie—who was in jeans, pink tennis shoes, and a bright pink shirt—down and held her hand. I took her other hand while Lizzie took Charlie—who was in a cute green jumper and shirt set—and stayed on my other side. Lizzie was in tennis shoes, jeans, and a t-shirt. And Jeff was, of course, in the Armani Fatigues.

Would have suggested he put on jeans, but decided to see how everyone else was dressed first. So, thusly ready, we headed out to the pool. Aspen was only one story high, but it had an upper terrace and a lower terrace due to the slope of the terrain around it. The pool was near the lower terrace and was quite nice, a sort of figure-eight design with pretty flagstones instead of boring concrete around it.

There were people I was pretty sure were Field agents passing around drinks and light hors d'oeuvres. People appeared to be mingling. So far, so good.

We reached the Israeli prime minister first. He was rather short, only a little taller than me, balding, but not trying to hide it, which was refreshing. He wore glasses and had nice brown eyes. He was in slacks, a long-sleeved, buttoned-down shirt, and loafers. "Eitan, this is my wife, Kitty. Kitty, this is Prime Minister Eitan Harpaz."

"Shalom. It's an honor to meet you," I said as we shook hands and he beamed at me. Amazing, my father's teaching and the Washington Wife class came through in pressure situations.

"And I you as well." He smiled at the kids. "A beautiful family. You both look too young to be parents to this lovely young lady, however."

"True enough. This is Elizabeth Vrabel. She's my ward."

Lizzie bobbed her head and rattled something off in what I was pretty sure was perfect Hebrew.

Harpaz's eyes lit up and he responded in what I was certain was Hebrew. They had a short, animated conversation, then he smiled at me. "A wonderful young lady indeed."

"Yes, we think so. This is our daughter, Jamie, and our son, Charlie."

Harpaz bowed gravely to Jamie. "It's a pleasure, miss." Jamie giggled. Then he chucked Charlie under his chin, making Charlie giggle, too. "And what a fine boy. You have a wonderful family, Jeffrey."

We made some more small talk, then Raj and Vance both came over to move us off to our next stop. "If that's off, I wonder what he's really like," I said softly to Jeff. "That man was totally charming."

Lizzie nudged me. "They're not wrong. His Hebrew is off."

Didn't have time to ask her how she knew this before we were meeting the Iraqi President. He was taller than Harpaz but not as tall as Jeff. He was stout, with a full head of hair. I'd expected him to be in something traditional, but he was in a regular business suit. Clearly Jeff and the others in the Armani Fatigues weren't going to stand out badly in this crowd.

Jeff did the same introduction here as he had with Harpaz. The Iraqi President's name was Faiz Samara. For him I bowed my head and pointedly didn't offer my hand. "Peace be with you, President Samara. We are honored to welcome you to our home."

He smiled gravely. "And peace be unto you, Missus Martini. Your hospitality has already been a gift."

Since I hadn't done a thing yet, figured either he'd loved it at Blair House or he was just being extremely polite. Decided I'd follow that lead and introduced Lizzie, who again showed that the school Siler had put her in was amazing, because she said a greeting in what appeared to be perfect Arabic. Like Harpaz before him, Samara seemed pleased and impressed and replied in kind. Once again, they had a brief, animated conversation, and once again we received compliments on Lizzie the Teenaged Diplomat Extraordinaire.

When meeting Jamie and Charlie, Samara gravely handed Jamie a small gift. She thanked him profusely. "May I open it now, Mommy?" she asked.

Vance and Abner had run me through this particular gauntlet when we'd practiced the day before. "No, sweetie. That's a special present to open later."

Samara smiled at Jeff. "Your family is thoughtful to our ways. I look forward to our time here together. I believe we will make great strides."

More small talk, then we were once again led away. "Again, I think that man was totally charming," I said quietly to Jeff and Lizzie as we managed to get to an area without people. "Was his Arabic off?"

"No, not at all," Lizzie said. "The Prime Minister's accent is wrong, though. It's like he learned Hebrew in a country other than Israel. But not on every word. Just some of them."

"Maybe he's just got a weird way of speaking."

She shook her head. "It's like when you hear a Canadian talking. They totes sound like Americans until they hit a word that's got an O-U in it. Then they sound wrong, you know? It's like that, only different."

"I don't see what Mossad sees in regard to Samara," Jeff said. "He didn't seem odd to me at all yesterday. But Harpaz . . . I'm with Lizzie. There's something just a little off about him. But I can't put my finger on what it is, since he's not doing the wrong word things in English, or if he is, I'm not noticing."

"Maybe he's an android," Lizzie said jokingly.

Jeff stiffened. "Maybe he is. I remember . . . last night at dinner, he blinked a lot. He said he had something in his eye, and I was focused on something Samara was saying so I didn't really pay much attention. Raj offered him eye-drops, which he didn't take. *Could* he be an android?"

"I don't know if eyedrop refusal and some odd pronunciations are enough to declare him an android. He seemed far more human than the Kendroid."

"Is that Stephanie chick the only one who made androids?" Lizzie asked. "I thought you said there were other people doing it."

Jeff and I looked at each other. "Chuck never felt that he'd found all of them."

"And Antony Marling was an artist. Was Harpaz unpleasant?"

"Uh, no, why would that matter?"

"I've just noted that the Marling androids seem so human because they're always nasty. But that could just be the ones I've had the misfortune to deal with." Looked around. Spotted who I was looking for. "Lizzie, go grab Chuckie and ask him to come over here, would you?"

"Sure." She trotted off while Jeff sent a text.

Nadine arrived. "You ready for me to take the kids inside, Jeff?"

"Can't we go into the pool?" Jamie asked.

"Not without water wings, Mommy and Daddy, and a lifeguard." Hey, Jamie had learned to swim while I was pregnant with Charlie, but there was no reason to take risks. And Charlie certainly had never been swimming.

Jeff chuckled. "Mommy's right. Why don't you open your present now and then you and Charlie can go play with Nadine. We saw lots of fun things for you to do, remember?"

"Okay, Daddy," she said cheerfully. As she started to carefully open her gift, Lizzie came back with Chuckie. He was dressed like all the other men from our side of things—Armani Fatigues all the way. Chose not to mention that I knew he owned jeans. Now wasn't the time.

Quickly told him about our conversation with Mossad and Jeff and Lizzie's concerns about Harpaz. "So, what do you think?" I asked him as we finished up.

He shrugged. "No idea." He sounded off and looked off, and I recognized his expression. I'd seen it any time he'd thought that I was dumping him to be with cooler kids. I never had and never would, but it had taken him a few years to believe it would never happen.

"Stop it," I said gently. "I'm not mad at you anymore. You can stop beating yourself up. You're still the smartest guy in any room, still my best friend, and still one of the most important people in the world to me, and I still love you as much as I did two days ago. I'm not leaving you for the cool kids, Chuckie, because you're still the coolest guy I know."

"She's not lying," Jeff added. "Trust me, her emotions, I can almost never block. She still firmly feels you walk on water."

Chuckie managed a small smile. "I don't like failing, let alone failing you, Kitty."

"You didn't. I promise. I'll talk to you about it more when we can be in private, but I just want you to know—"

Was interrupted by Bruno going visible and squawking and Chuckie moving in the superfast way he'd learned so well that he was a rare human who could take down an A-C. Only he didn't take anyone down—he snatched something out of Jamie's hands.

She stared at him openmouthed. "Uncle Charles, that's mine."

He shook his head. "Jamie, Uncle Charles will give you a better present later, okay? This one you cannot have. Nadine, get the kids out of here, *now*. I want them underground as fast as possible. And all the Peregrines with them, too. On high alert," he said to Bruno. Who bobbed his head.

"Underground where?" I asked.

"What's going on?" Jeff asked.

Bruno squawked. He wasn't arguing with Chuckie—he was saying the Peregrines agreed.

"Under this cabin. Your security personnel know where it is. And what's going on is trouble." He opened his hand. There was a round chocolate candy in his palm, mostly unwrapped.

"Um, are we worried about diabetes or Jamie getting a sugar rush or something?"

"No." Chuckie's voice was tight. "Nadine, this is an order. Get the kids out of here."

Decided that we had two choices. I could argue with

Chuckie and pretty much say that I didn't trust his judgment for whatever he thought was going on, which, per Buchanan, would ruin our relationship and Chuckie's ego permanently. Or I could do what I'd done pretty much as long as I'd known him and do what he said when he was adamant like this.

Kissed Charlie and handed him to Nadine. Bent down and hugged Jamie. "Let's do what Uncle Charles says, okay? Maybe he knows that's a candy you won't like and doesn't want us to be rude to the man who gave it to you. Plus, you know Uncle Charles will get you something really special to make up for it."

She nodded. "Okay, Mommy." She looked up at Chuckie worriedly. "You'll all be okay?"

"Yes," he said firmly.

Jeff kissed Charlie, then picked Jamie up and hugged her. "Be good, Jamie-Kat." He put her down and Nadine took her hand. They headed into the cabin. All four Peregrines went visible, Bruno ushered the other Peregrines in, nodded to me, then went back to stealth mode. But he was definitely with the kids. "You should go, too," Jeff said to Lizzie.

"No way. I want to know what the heck's going on."

"This isn't a candy," Chuckie said, voice tight. "I've seen these before. It's an explosive."

CHAPTER 92

"YOU'RE SURE?" Jeff asked, Commander Voice back on Full.

"Positive, though I'm not going to test it here. But if Jamie had bitten into it, it would have killed her and all of you as well."

"And it's rude in Iraqi culture to open a gift right when it's given to you. Vance and Abner drilled all this into me yesterday, that's why I didn't let Jamie open it when she got it." It was amazing how fast I could go from angry, stressed, and confused to enraged and laser-focused. "Can I kill him now?"

"Not yet. If you'd told her it was okay, I'm sure whoever gave it to her would have shared that it was culturally improper and had her wait." Chuckie sounded furious but in control again, as if the wheels were turning properly. Good. The three of us were primed and ready. "Who did give that to her?"

"Samara." Turned to look back at him. Samara's back was to us. And I could have sworn his back moved as if it was undulating. Which human backs didn't do as a rule. "There's something wrong with him."

"He gave Jamie a bomb as a present," Lizzie said. "There's totes something wrong with him."

"No, I mean . . ." Was still looking at his back. "There, see it? It's like his spine is moving." My memory nudged. I'd seen something like this a long time ago now. It had been my introduction to my new life. "Think he's a superbeing?"

The others looked. "I don't see anything," Jeff said. "He'd have to be an in-control one if he is, and we'd have found out about that well before now. We destroyed all of the ones in existence when we met, baby. But we need to be certain this is a bomb, Chuck. And I don't want to find out by making it go off."

Pulled out my phone and sent a text. Serene joined us quickly. Explained the situation and Chuckie showed her the candy.

Serene's eyes narrowed as she examined it. "Definitely an explosive. It's coated in a thin layer of chocolate, but, as Chuck said, we've seen these before. So, do we tackle him, arrest him, or what? Since this can be qualified as an assassination attempt on the President and his family."

"You know, I somehow foolishly thought that this would be dull and boring and just something to get through. I thought that we'd at least have to get to the first night before things went haywire. And I also would have thought that the opening salvo in terms of whatever's going on wouldn't be to try to kill us by giving our daughter an explosive."

Chuckie stiffened. "What if it wasn't to kill Jeff like Serene said, but actually to kill Jamie? As in, they can't steal her away from us, so they'll get rid of her permanently instead?"

"There are a ton of possibilities. I think we also have to remember that Lizzie and Jeff both think Harpaz is off, too. Meaning Mossad is right and something's happened to alter these two men. And it happened recently."

"We have to have proof," Jeff said. "Otherwise we'll—" He stopped speaking as Harpaz came over to us. Chuckie took the bomb from Serene and put it into his outer suit pocket.

"Is all well?" he asked politely. "You all seem . . . tense."

"Oh, just a little jittery due to the importance of this meeting," I said quickly, since Jeff couldn't lie and there was no need to show Chuckie that Serene could. "We so want to help make a positive difference."

Harpaz nodded gravely. "I understand." He looked around. "Where did your little ones go?" As his head was turning I noted that he was blinking. A lot. And I wasn't distracted like Jeff had been the night before, and I'd definitely seen blinking like this before. When androids were trying to reset or not go off or glitching or whatever.

"Lizzie, honey, would you please go get your Uncle Richard?" I asked in the motherliest sugar-sweet tone I could manage. "I know he wanted to ask the Prime Minister a couple of non-high-level questions and now seems like a good time."

"Of course," Lizzie said, sounding like the politest and most well-behaved teenager on Earth. Good, she'd picked up the clue. She trotted off to find White, who I sincerely hoped was nearby.

"Why didn't he ask these questions of me last night?" Harpaz asked.

"We were focused on other things," Jeff said.

Harpaz nodded then turned to Chuckie. "I don't believe we have met yet."

Chuckie put out his hand. "Charles Reynolds. Pleased to meet you, Prime Minister Harpaz."

Harpaz shook his hand and held onto it. "And what do you do, sir?"

Something made me answer before Chuckie could. "He's my best friend. Here for moral support. And extra help with the kids."

Jeff and Serene managed not to react. Chuckie smiled, and I saw him shift into his Wealthy Jet-Setting Bachelor mode. Bruce Wayne was now representing. "It's nice to have influential friends. And this way I get a different kind of vacation and the rare opportunity to meet world leaders." He chuckled. "I live half the year in Australia, so I do my best to avoid winter around the world."

"Ah." Harpaz seemed slightly thrown. Sincerely doubted that the head dude of Israel wasn't clear that Australia's weather was opposite of America's. Also sincerely doubted that the head dude of Israel hadn't paid total attention to who the new players in America's government were. Mossad was definitely not wrong. Sincerely wondered what Harpaz's explosion trigger was and had a feeling we were going to find out.

Lizzie returned with White, who gave me a small nod. Good, she'd briefed him on what was going on. "Mister Prime Minister, how good to see you again. I hope you're finding Camp David pleasant?"

"I am. The First Lady said that you had questions for me?"

"I do." White launched into religious queries, basically

doing a religious studies comparison course. I knew he could do this in his sleep. Could tell that White was examining Harpaz as I'd seen him do with the Kitty-Droid and others.

Chuckie was paying rapt attention to this exchange, and while I wasn't the clearest girl on all aspects of Judaism, particularly as how it compared to the Annocusal view of things, I was pretty sure that Harpaz was representing some things incorrectly. Not the big things, but the little ones. The ones you wouldn't necessarily bother to program in if you weren't Antony Marling.

Meaning that if Harpaz was an android or a really amazing Man-Bot then he wasn't a Marling creation, or if he was, his programming was faulty. Didn't think he was a Man-Bot—he was too good for what I'd seen so far from the Fem-Bots. Considering how much the man was blinking, an android software crash was what my gut wanted to go with.

Raj joined us. "I'm sorry, Mister President, but it's time for your welcoming speech."

Jeff grunted. "Right now?"

Raj nodded. "Our limited press is in position and we need to allow them to send your opening words to the media. It's in the best interests of the administration."

My Megalomaniac Girl cape was already on and I knew, now, without a doubt, that Jeff needed to stall starting that speech for as long as possible.

Nudged Serene where I hoped Harpaz couldn't see. "Oh, Raj, can't they wait a little longer?"

Serene passed an almost imperceptible sign to Raj that I only caught because I was desperately hoping to see it. Raj's eyes opened just a little wider. "Well," he said slowly, "I suppose we can start really whenever the President and his honored guests are ready."

Realized we were missing people. "Where are the Planetary Council?"

"Still prepping," Raj said, "and they didn't feel that they should attend the opening speech, lest they overshadow what this meeting is about."

"Kitty, why don't you go and ensure the press are where you want them and nowhere near the kids?" Jeff suggested. "Check in on the Planetary Council, too, would you?"

Didn't really want to leave them alone with an android,

a candy bomb in Chuckie's pocket, or what I was pretty sure was an in-control superbeing currently chatting up Claudia and Lorraine. But arguing about that with Jeff right now could tip Harpaz off. "Sure."

"Chuck," Jeff went on pleasantly, "why don't you help her do that? You know how she doesn't want to put anyone out or push her ideas forward."

Chuckie nodded. "Happy to give Kitty moral support."

Harpaz chuckled. "I see you're a traditional wife, Missus Martini."

"Oh, very much so. Lizzie, you come too and let the grown-ups talk."

Raj headed off and the three of us went with him. "What's going on?" he asked me quietly. "Other than the Prime Minister clearly hasn't been briefed about you at all."

"Samara gave Jamie a candy bomb, I think Samara is an in-control superbeing, and Harpaz is most likely an android or possibly a robot. Waiting for Richard's thoughts on that."

"Mister White already said that he votes android based on what he saw last night," Lizzie said. "As in, he didn't see the hairline and eye issues that he's noted with the Fem-Bots."

"I'm sure he told you to call him Uncle Richard."

"We're on the job now, Megalomaniac Girl," Lizzie said. "You call him Mister White when you're rolling, so I'm doing that, too."

"Well chosen, Quick Girl. So, Raj, my guess is that the main attack is going to happen the moment Jeff's feeding live to the news media."

"It would have started sooner if Jamie had eaten that candy," Chuckie said darkly.

"So that means they're not working in tandem. No idea if that's good or bad for us, but since my little girl wasn't blown up by the Iraqi President, I think the next trigger will be when Jeff's on a live feed."

"We can't stall forever," Raj said. "The media expects to get this story from our two reporters."

"We can tell them what's going on. They're both trust-worthy."

We were at the far side of the pool from where Jeff was now, near to where Oliver and Jenkins were set up. "Unless there is an attack," Raj said worriedly, "we have to be

incredibly careful about accusing anyone of anything—
these are supposed to be peace talks, not the start of World
War Three."

Chuckie looked at me. "What are the odds that this is
Cliff's doing?"

"Low, honestly. If we're right about him being hurt, and
those with medical knowledge seem sure of it, he's too busy
to do more than that screw-you move he already managed."
Looked around. It was beautiful and calm here. But it
wasn't impregnable, and not just because we'd literally
brought in bad things ourselves. It wasn't protected from an
air strike, at least not one that Drax's helicarrier could manage.

"This is literally the worst thing that could happen," Raj
said. "Your kidnapping was bad enough, but we were able
to survive that because of Francine and your ability to get
out of trouble. But this? If we have an incident at what's
considered a potentially historic event, and the first event
of Jeff's presidency, then he truly might as well resign."

Lizzie's eyes narrowed. "So, whoever's doing this hates
Jeff, right?"

"What do you mean?"

"Really?" She gave me the You're Getting Too Old For
This look. "That man gave Jamie, Jeff's daughter, an exploding candy. That would have killed her and probably the rest
of us, too. And there's an android and an in-control superbeing here, too? And the men who we think are those bad
things were normal until a couple weeks ago? That sounds
like someone making sure that Jeff's ruined."

"Then it's Stephanie. Probably being assisted by the Tinkerer." Pulled out my phone and made a call. "Hey Brian,
it's Kitty."

"I thought you were at Camp David with my wife and
everyone else important."

"I am. Need you to grab The Clarence Clone and get him
here pronto. Use a floater gate and have them mark on
Jeff."

"Want to tell me what's going on?"

"Hopefully stopping World War Three or ending it really
quickly. When you get here, tell TCC that he needs to guard
Leoalla."

"Gotcha, and I'm on it."

We hung up and Lizzie waved her phone at me. "I just told Denise to lock down the Embassy. She's got it handled and alerting the other Bases that something's wrong."

"Well done, Quick Girl. Contact Malcolm. I have no idea where he is, but we need him getting our forces here on alert." I dialed again while Lizzie texted like mad. "Jerry, we're at code red. Need you and the rest of the flyboys to get our helicarrier here, in invisibility mode, ASAP."

"Joe and Randy, too, Commander?"

Chuckie was also on his phone but he jerked, stopped talking midsentence, and pointed. His expression said that whatever he was seeing, it wasn't good.

Stopped talking to Jerry, too, and turned to see what had Chuckie horrified. Turned out it was Abner, who'd clearly tripped on the flagstones around the pool. His drink went flying through the air, and I projected its trajectory—was pretty positive it was going to hit Harpaz.

Abner was trying to regain his balance and not go down. But he was near Samara and was waving his arms around as you do when you're trying not to fall. Abner continued to represent for my side of things by knocking into Samara, which shoved Samara into the pool. A couple of Samara's staff jumped in to help him and Vance managed to keep Abner from going down or going in.

"That can't be good," Lizzie said.

Proving that Lizzie was well trained in understatement, what surfaced out of the pool wasn't Samara. And while it wasn't a shock, at least to me, it certainly was a gigantic surprise.

CHAPTER 93

"JERRY, I'M BACK, and hells to the yeah, I want all five of you." Heard him relay the order to Hughes. Could just hear him over the screaming and shouting from around the pool. "Definitely grab Tito and the princesses, regardless of where they are. Have them take floater gates here if you can't get them into the ship within a minute. Frankly, bring anyone who's good in a fight, but take no time to grab them. Floater gates are everyone's friends right now."

"Give them the override protocol," Chuckie said. "The phrase is 'Kitty's mad as hell and not going to take it anymore.' That should work for any and all US and Centaurion personnel."

"Seriously?" Chuckie nodded emphatically. "Okay, Jerry—"

"I heard him, Commander. Love it."

"Me too. Make your arrival faster than fast and arm the ship for bear. Or in this case, giant squid."

Well, it might have been a giant squid coming out of the pool. Or a giant octopus. Was having trouble counting the arms or tentacles or whatever they were since they were flailing around so quickly. It was big, Kraken-sized if I was any judge, and a sort of glistening black. The glistening seeming to come from ichor and mucus, not pretty skin. It had claws at the end of each tentacle, along with myriad suckers on each tentacle that looked like round mouths full of teeth.

The bulbous head portion had the monster look with a caricature of Samara's face in the middle along with giant eyes that were, naturally, doing the glowing red thing so popular with the in-control superbeing set. Had no idea how long Samara had been combined with the superbeing, but if Jeff was right and he wasn't one of the old ones, then someone had found a parasite and infected him and managed to keep him in control of the change. Neither option was comforting.

"What do you mean?" Jerry asked.

"Superbeing formation. Seems like old times. Literally."

"God. On it!" He hung up. Just in time for us to watch one of the Iraqis who'd jumped in to save Samara get speared through the middle by one of the claws at the end of the tentacles.

"Oh, my God," Raj said. "Can this get any worse? They're filming." He pointed to the news crews who were foolishly not running. Well, Oliver was dragging Jenkins away and shouting at the others, presumably telling them "run, you fools," but they weren't listening.

Figured the speared person would be dead. That's what normally happened when a superbeing hit someone, be they human or A-C. The Samarapus dropped the body into the pool while everyone else was dodging tentacles and claws.

The body didn't float, it went under. And came up a slightly smaller version of the Samarapus. "It's worse," I shared as I pulled out my earbuds, plugged them in, put them into my ears, and pulled up my music. "I'd like everyone to not ask if it can get worse because it always can. We need to get all civilians down into that tunnel thing you talked about, Chuckie. And that includes you and Lizzie."

"The hell it does," they both said in unison. Chose to ignore the unison thing. Bigger issues were at stake, including that Samarapus, Jr. had speared someone in the Israeli entourage and dropped said person into the pool. Sure enough, that person came up as a superbeing. An even smaller Samarapus. At this rate, in about six more spearings, we'd have a Samarapus that was about Jeff's size. That was me, going for the positive outlook.

The Samarapus caught the other Iraqi who'd gotten into the pool and was desperately trying to get out. Speared him, too. He went down and came up a Samarapus, Jr. Our luck held firm.

All of this had taken less than two minutes. What would happen in the next minutes wasn't pretty to contemplate.

"We need to get people away from those things. They're making new ones without issue and that's technically impossible. Avoid getting speared, please and thank you." Put my purse over my neck, hit play on my phone, shoved it into my back pocket, heaved a sigh, and ran. "Victorious" from Panic! At the Disco came on. Sincerely hoped I was on the Algar Channel.

Headed for one of the Secret Service who was too near to the edge of the pool and tackled him. A tentacle just missed him.

"Everybody get away from the pool!" Jeff bellowed. No one bellowed like my man, and if there were people elsewhere in Camp David, was sure they'd heard him. Good, hopefully that meant the marines were coming.

"Get civilians underground," I told the Secret Service guy I'd saved. "And get yourself underground too."

"You have to be protected," he said.

"The hell she does." Keith stepped through a floater gate, followed by Daniel, Joshua, Marcus, and Lucas. The A-Cs went into automatic Superbeing Containment Mode. Daniel shouted some orders, and the other A-Cs who'd been on service duty dropped that act and leaped into the action they'd been trained for. "You do what the Commander says, and you do it now!" Keith bellowed. He was quite good at bellowing, too. Not up to Jeff's standards, but then, none were.

The agent Keith was shouting at scrambled to his feet, looked around, saw someone screaming, grabbed her, and dragged her toward the door for the cabin.

Keith pulled me to my feet. "What do you want me doing?"

"Making the Secret Service lose their death wish. Anyone those things hit is going to turn into a superbeing. We have to kill them, and that takes a lot." And we'd have to find where the parasite was. If there was one. "Get them and anyone else you can underground if at all possible."

Keith nodded and started shouting orders. Amazingly enough, the other Secret Service agents listened to him. Apparently it helped that he was the biggest.

We split up, because I needed to hit the hyperspeed and knock Jeff out of the way of three tentacles he wasn't aware of, because he was too busy grabbing Elaine Armstrong and getting her out of the way of a huge tentacle from Samara-pus heading right for her. I also had to grab my Uncle Mort, who was calmly firing at the Samarapus but who was, there-fore, the focus of a lot of tentacles.

Hit Jeff and Elaine first and kept going, ramming all of us into Uncle Mort. Thankfully, my speed and momentum propelled all of us out of tentacle reach. At least for now. Took all of us to the ground but the tentacles missed us all, so chose to see this as a total win. "Uncle Mort, get Elaine to that bunker thing."

"I know where it is," she said, voice shaking. "It has tun-nels that lead to Raven Rock."

"I heard that was a myth." Though, as I thought of it, Chuckie had only said it was a myth after we were out of college, meaning after Mom had recruited him into the CIA.

"It's not."

"Get everyone there, to Raven Rock," Jeff said to Uncle Mort. "And that's an order. You take my children, Elaine, and whoever's down there already, and get them to safety."

"I'm a Marine son, I don't hide."

"You're the Commander of the Joint Chiefs and we're under attack," I said. "And the Commander in Chief just gave you a direct order."

Uncle Mort shot the hairy eyeball at me. "I can still turn you over my knee, young lady."

"Only when I'm wrong, and you know I'm not." Looked at the pool. We had a couple more Samarapus the Thirds and at least another Samarapus, Jr. "We're too slow. And, oh joy, they're getting out of the pool." Without issues, which wasn't that big a surprise, really. Superbeings were hella hearty.

Jeff looked around. "Raj!"

Raj hypersped over, dodging tentacles like a pro. "What do you need?"

"We need an A-C in the tunnels," Jeff said. "That's you, your job right now. I also want Doreen, Paul, and Richard down there."

"Doreen and Paul, yes. Richard stays here." Pointed. White was busy tossing civilians to Daniel and the others, who were running them off to the cabin. Saw something unsettling. "We need to protect the cabin!"

"What?" Jeff asked. But I didn't stop to explain. Harpaz was being hustled into the cabin by some well-meaning but uninformed Secret Service agents, meaning he was going to get underground. Where my children were.

Hit Harpaz at full hyperspeed and knocked him out of the hold of the agents, which was what I'd hoped for. Knew that he was likely to explode soon because Abner's drink had indeed landed on him and he was blinking like a strobe light. Considered using him to blow up a Samarapus or two, but knew that our luck never ran in that direction. Noted that "Victorious" was on repeat. Meaning I was missing something that Algar wanted me to pay attention to, and it surely wasn't that he wanted me to win because that was a given.

Kept on running. Was really glad we'd taken the time to tour this place, even if it had been at hyperspeed, because I had something of a clue as to where I was going. Oh, not a big clue, but a clue, nonetheless.

Harpaz was fighting me, and he was strong, far too strong to be a human, and too strong to be an A-C, either. Just right for an android. But I was fully enraged and the skills were working perfectly, which included strength. What to do with him was the issue. Because, right now, I was trying to kill someone who hadn't identified officially as a threat. And, as Buchanan had pointed out at the NSA black site, "I say so" wasn't going to hold up anywhere, let alone in a court of law.

Happily, found what I was looking for with only a few detours. Reached the barracks to discover that, as always, things could get worse. There were indeed marines and sailors here, and they were armed. But they weren't fighting superbeings and, based on what was going on, they weren't going to be able to.

They were fighting a Fem-Bot army. A Fem-Bot army made up of me. And there were fifty of them at least.

CHAPTER 94

THEY'D DONE A good job with this set. Whatever the Original Kitty-Bot's issues, her choice of clothing being out of date had definitely been one of them. These Kitty-Bots were all in jeans, Converse, and t-shirts. No purses, though. Adding insult to injury, they were all in red band t-shirts. The same shirt and the same band—the Rolling Stones.

So, whoever had created these Fem-Bots had a sense of humor, knew that I'd mentioned that Aerosmith was better than the Stones more than once and always at inopportune times, and was also wanting to ensure that, should I be around, the other Fem-Bots would know because I'd be wearing the wrong shirt.

Too sophisticated for Stephanie, who didn't have a sense of humor I was aware of, but potentially just right for either Strauss or the Tinkerer. Or whoever was actually now running the Fem-Bot Project, since the idea that there was a schism between whoever was left on Strauss' team and the NSA seemed very likely.

On the plus side, they weren't alone. My Uncle Mort was there, shouting orders, telling the troops that these weren't real women. Which was going to suck for me, but that was so par for my natural course. Of course, reality said that Uncle Mort was either still arguing with Jeff, speared by a tentacle, or, hopefully, getting everyone to safety in the hollow mountain. Meaning this wasn't really Uncle Mort.

Meaning Wruck was here.

Ran right to him. "John!"

He turned and smiled. "Good to see you."

"Not really. This is an android. And he's going to blow soon and we can't have him die without being revealed to be an android first."

Siler appeared out of nowhere and grabbed Harpaz out of my arms. He held him while Wruck changed one finger to look like a pencil and stabbed it into Harpaz's ear. The android stopped struggling and went still.

"God, am I glad you two are okay. And here. How'd you all get in here?"

"Same here," Siler said, while Wruck bellowed that the marines needed to note that I was in a black Aerosmith shirt and therefore the real woman to be protected not killed. Hoped they'd heard him, but there was a lot of gunfire, so it was hard to be sure. "There's a back gate. The Fem-Bots used one as a decoy then overwhelmed the gate guards. The guards are all dead, it happened too fast for us to stop it."

"They aren't the only dead we have." Filled them in fast on the superbeing situation. "Think these attacks are coordinated?"

"No, not at all," Siler said as he dropped the Harpaz android to the ground as I grabbed a Kitty-Bot. He took one arm, I took the other, and we played tug-of-war. "They're not supporting each other properly. This is just a prime opportunity that your various enemies are capitalizing on."

"We're just so lucky, aren't we? Plus, I'm sure Strauss gave whoever's in charge of the Fem-Bots the heads up that the peace summit would be a great place and time to attack, since they had to know that was when she was planning to use the Original Kitty-Bot."

"We've been trailing this platoon since Malcolm was taken. They walked here from the facility, or, rather, from the woods behind the facility, which is where we caught their trail. We all only arrived a few minutes ago. Have you found him?"

"And the others who were taken, yes, we have."

"Good. Glad to see you got out of wherever you were and seem unscathed, too." He looked worried as we ripped the Fem-Bot's arms off. "Legs next. Is—"

We both grabbed a leg while the Fem-Bot tried to kick us, unsuccessfully. She fell forward and her face smashed into the ground. Chose not to take this personally. "Quick

Girl is fine. Refusing to go underground, though." Decided not to share that I had no idea where she was—why make Siler as worried about her as I was?

He flashed a half-smile. "She's the bravest kid I know."

"Ditto. I need to get back to the superbeing situation, though." And hopefully find Lizzie, Jeff, and Chuckie unscathed somewhere.

Noted a few Fem-Bots had broken through the marines and were heading off, presumably for the Aspen Lodge. The marines were riddling the Fem-Bots with bullets, but these were better made than the Kitty-Bot apparently, because they were taking a licking and definitely still kicking. Usually kicking a marine's gun away from him or her, slamming them into the ground, and moving on. Maybe these were Level Five Fem-Bots. Whether they were or not, there weren't enough marines to hold out unless they started using bazookas.

Yanked hard on the leg I had and Siler and I each ended up with another limb. "We'll hold them here if we can," he said. "And will come help if we get them contained."

"We need to preserve that android." Pointed to Harpaz as I put a knee onto the Fem-Bot's back and, using all my strength, ripped her head off. "Without proof that he's an android, we'll be at war with Israel in a day. If the superbeings get over here, keep away from the tentacles. The very last thing in the world we need is either one of you turned into a superbeing."

Mephistopheles had been stronger because he'd combined with Ronald Yates, a powerful A-C. Did not even want to contemplate what could happen if Wruck were to turn into a superbeing, mostly because I wanted to have a hope of sleeping again in the future.

"Which part explodes, head or body?" Siler asked.

"No freaking idea, just be sure you find out without blowing you and John up." Ran after the loose Fem-Bots who were indeed heading for the Aspen Lodge. There were five of them, and they were fast. And there was only one of me.

As I thought this, four people landed from the air next to me and started running with me. Looked up in time to see a hatch closing. "Joe, Randy, Rahmi, and Rhee, it's good to see you guys."

They were in the battle gear we'd used during our NSA

raid, and they had big guns with them, too. Was totally jealous.

"We'd have run here if we'd had to," Randy said, "but Colonel Franklin is now on all of our speed dials, and he got us into the helicarrier in less than a minute."

"Who's up there flying it with the other flyboys?"

"Gil Morgan and Thomas Kendrick," Joe said. "The real one."

"The Great Tito is aboard as well," Rahmi said. "I felt he should remain above leading the attack."

"In other words, you're doing the time-honored thing of doing your best to protect your man. Well done, that, princess. And I'm impressed with everyone's reaction time."

"We are always ready for action," Rhee said. "We used hyperspeed the moment Jerry called us."

"Kendrick was there because Morgan was showing him the ship," Randy said. "With Drax's permission."

"I'll never, ever argue when things go our way."

"Victorious" was still on repeat. The Algar Channel was big on repetition recently. Couldn't focus on whatever the clue was that Algar wanted me to get, though, because the five of us caught up to and tackled a Fem-Bot each.

These were definitely Fem-Bots, and not just because they looked like me. As with the Original Kitty-Bot, they were harder than humans or A-Cs, but not as hard as androids. Of course, that still meant they were difficult to contain. But I had a lot of practice.

The princesses had their battle staffs out and activated and they were using them effectively to destroy their two Fem-Bots. Joe and Randy were literally ripping their Fem-Bots apart with their bare hands. Show-offs, all four of them. I was actually having to fight with mine.

On the plus side, I had the Fem-Bot's back. Wrapped my legs around her waist, got her in a headlock and, as I'd done with the other one, pulled at her head. She had all four limbs intact, though, and I hadn't really done much damage to her when I'd knocked her down, so she was fighting me.

She grabbed my arms and tried to flip me over her head. It hurt, but I had a good lock and didn't lose it. She was spinning us around, not fast to throw me off, but because of being off balance.

"Kitty," Randy called, "she's blinking a lot!"

Pulled harder. Her head remained attached. This was truly disappointing. She ran us toward the others, presumably to explode and kill all of us at the same time.

"Jump off," Joe called. "Now!"

Did as requested, but I didn't have a good way to propel myself, so I basically let go and fell onto my butt. This worked out, since Rahmi swung the glowing end of her laser staff and took the Fem-Bot's head off while Rhee did the same but took her down at the knees.

Scrambled to my feet. "Think she's going to explode?"

"No idea," Joe said. "Do we go back and help the marines?"

"We had at least six superbeings the last time I checked, I think we go to them." "Victorious" was still on, and could have sworn it was louder somehow. Paused for a moment and listened to the lyrics. Realized that Panic! was saying to turn up the crazy during the chorus of this song. Meaning I knew what to do.

Hit speed dial. Happily, he answered right away. "Kitty, what's going on? We got some garbled report from the TV news then it switched to a rerun of a Godzilla movie, and Lizzie has somehow put Centaurion into worldwide lockdown."

"Serene must have gotten Imageering on the case, thank God. But no time for that right now. I need the Flash and the former Head of Imageering when it was busy fighting superbeings, aka you, at Camp David like five minutes ago. But don't come alone. Get Adriana and tell her we need Old Trusty. And bringing a rocket launcher yourself wouldn't be a bad idea."

"We have a superbeing?"

"We have a plethora of superbeings that create new ones just like themselves, only a bit smaller, when they stab their tentacle claws into their victims. Avoid those. Get here. Now." Hung up. My music went back to "Victorious," though it had been midsong when I'd made my call.

"That's impossible," Randy said. "Superbeings don't do that."

"Yeah, well, we passed impossible a little while ago. And, trust me, this one does."

"Anything else we need to know?" Joe asked.

"The original superbeing was the Iraqi President. I just

dropped off the android Israeli Prime Minister with Siler and Wruck who are, thank God, alive, well, and here, fighting alongside the marines who are fighting a ton of these Fem-Bots."

"Let's move," Rahmi said. She reached behind her and unslung the big gun she'd had on her back. "Here. I'm happier with my staff and you were, ah, not as effective as you could have been in that last skirmish."

"I agree on the moving and the skirmishing. Thanks for the big gun, Rahmi, I appreciate it. Joe, Randy, you guys need to grab a hand to do the hyperspeed?"

"Let's find out," Joe said, as he started running faster than I'd ever seen him do before.

The rest of us caught up with him, and I took the lead since I knew where we were going. Was about to turn to my left to get back to where I was pretty sure Aspen was when my music changed. The band was still Panic! At the Disco, but the song went to "Emperor's New Clothes." Chose to grasp the clue and looked around. Spotted the small Shantanu portable city that was sort of to our right and relatively far from the Aspen Lodge. There was a Samarapus, Jr. and two Samarapus the Thirds flopping their way toward it.

Turned and headed for them. "If they get the Planetary Council or the Vata, God alone knows what kind of superbeing will form. We need to destroy these before we can help the others."

"Are you sure they're in there?" Randy asked. "Weren't they at the thing everyone else was at?"

"No, they were staying inside so as not to create a spectacle."

Rahmi snorted. "What do they call this?"

"I have no idea. I'm not sure if they realize that things are dire, it hasn't been going on all that long, really." Seemed like forever but probably wasn't more than fifteen minutes, maybe less. Time moved slowly when you were fighting for your life and totally high on adrenaline.

The Samarapusses weren't making a lot of noise, really, though they were leaving a trail of what looked like black ink. And the sounds of fighting weren't carrying all that well. Probably due to all the trees or something. But if I listened hard I could hear the gunfire and the screams, but both were far away from where the Shantanu had set up their portable quarters. And Christopher had indicated that the news wasn't covering this, thanks most likely to Imageering, and I doubted the Shantanu had brought a television along in the first place.

"Any guess for how to kill them?" Randy asked as he got the big gun he'd chosen off his back.

"Shoot them a lot. I have no idea if these are parasitic superbeings or if the Samarapus was lab created. I put nothing past The League of Evil Supergenius Megalomaniacs."

Joe did the lock and load thing. "Then let's go hunt calamari."

We lined up abreast and started firing at one of the Samarapus the Thirds, since it was closest to us.

Felt like we were in a Michael Bay movie, where the heroes are doing the slow walk toward their destiny. Our destiny happened to include giant cephalopods with claws and teeth in their suckers. We were lucky like that.

The Samarapus was hard to kill, not that this was a surprise. We were using guns that shot lasers, and they were somewhat effective, but not as effective as I'd have liked. All the other in-control superbeings we'd killed had required something other than a hail of bullets to destroy them. Only I had absolutely no idea what killed a giant octopus or squid other than a fisherman's net.

Interestingly enough, these particular superbeings didn't smell. I'd spent time with all the in-control superbeings during Operation Fugly and they'd all stunk to high heaven. The superbeings I'd killed during my tenure as the Head of Airborne were also no perfumed delights. I'd have expected the Samarapusses to smell like fish or stagnant ocean or something. But they didn't smell like anything. Not even when we managed to shoot a tentacle off—no smell at all.

A rocket launcher went off and another one of the Samarapus' tentacles blew off. Turned to see Adriana and Christopher had joined us, both with bazookas. Christopher had a big bag over his back, like he was the NRA's version of Santa Claus. In this case, I was definitely on the side of Ho Ho Ho.

"Nice of you to join the party," I called out.

"You said a plethora," Christopher said as he reloaded from the Sack O' Goodies. "This is three."

"These are three that broke off from the pack. And I

note that you're only sort of denting them with our new weapons." As I said this my music changed to John Mayer's "Split Screen Sadness." Kept on shooting while I pondered this particular clue. Considered the options and realized I didn't have to think that hard. "Crap. I think Jeff and the others need me. Can you guys kill these three without me?"

"Not sure that we can kill them with you," Christopher replied.

"Good point. Think you're fast enough to get the people inside this thing out without them all getting turned into intergalactic sushi?"

"I can try." He tossed his rocket launcher to Rhee and took off.

Could wait and see what happened or get to Jeff. Decided that Christopher was actually the most experienced person here with this situation other than Jeff, and made the choice.

"Someone tell Christopher and Adriana about the Fem-Bots. Don't get stabbed, killed, or," looked at where the Samarapus trail was, "inked, because I think that stuff is acidic." The ground certainly didn't look as good as it had when we'd arrived.

Then I spun around and headed for the Executive Kraken's Swimming Pool.

CHAPTER 95

REACHED MY destination quickly. It helped greatly that the helicarrier had decloaked and I had to figure it was hovering over the main superbeing population, so I navigated based on the giant ship in the sky.

Took stock of the situation once I reached the perimeter. On the plus side, there were fewer people around. On the negative side, there were more Samarapusses around. And many of them were, like the three I'd left the others fighting, out of the pool and trying out for new sports.

Despite the chaos, spotted Jeff easily—he was the one shouting orders to the other A-Cs and the human Centaurion agents, like Reader and Tim who weren't complaining about rank or responsibility right now. No one was. This was one of those situations where you wanted the most qualified people in charge, period.

The Clarence Clone was on the scene, keeping close to Jeff, but I didn't see Brian. Then again, I didn't see Serene, either.

The gun I had had a heavy-duty pulse feature, so I engaged that and started shooting at Samarapusses randomly as I ran around, jumped over, and dodged under far too many tentacles.

Reached Jeff in time to blow off the end of a tentacle that was about to hit him. "You need to move more," I said by way of hello.

"We have these things all over," he replied as he pulled me back and we both leaped to avoid a tentacle that was whipping along the ground. "And you're the only person with a gun that's effective at all."

"We should have the flyboys drop some weapons down to us."

"They tried that already. The superbeings caught them in the air and ate them. At least I think that's what they did with them. They shoved the guns up inside them, where an octopus' mouth would be, so I'm saying they ate them."

Someone slammed into us right as my music changed to "Duck and Run" by 3 Doors Down. "Stop standing around chatting," Chuckie said, as he dragged us away from some more tentacles that had just missed us.

"Why aren't you underground protecting my kids?" I asked as Jeff grabbed us both and ran off at hyperspeed, dodging tentacles and claws and teeth, TCC following right behind us.

"Because Mort saw reason and he's with them. I verified that, then stayed up here to help you and keep an eye on your older kid."

"Where is Lizzie and is she okay?"

"I have no idea. I lost her along with Brian, Vance, and Abner when one of these things leaped between us. I heard Vance and Abner screaming as they ran into the cabin, so I'm pretty sure they made it underground. Brian and Lizzie, though, I haven't seen since."

"Where's Serene?"

"I sent her to Imageering Main," Jeff said. "Right before all hell broke loose. She called for a floater, so I don't know if she knows what's going on."

"She knows. Per Christopher, she's stopped this from getting onto the news. Speaking of which, where are the news crews?"

"Oliver and Jenkins are underground," Chuckie said. "Only because Oliver's not an idiot. The rest of their crews, though . . ." He pointed at the Samarapusses. "They really didn't listen and fell under the spell of being behind the camera, where you can tell yourself you're not part of what's going on, you're just observing it."

"Fan-freaking-tastic."

"James suggested we beat these things to death with the camera tripods," Chuckie said. "I'm worried about him."

Jeff managed a chuckle. "It's all right, he's just having a nostalgic moment."

"What about the Iraqis and Israelis? And where are Leah, Oren, and Jakob? Not to mention Abby and Mahin?" And Lizzie. She was brave and trained, but I doubted that she'd ever faced a superbeing before. Tried not to worry about her. Failed utterly.

"No idea," Jeff said. "They probably went off after some of these things."

"There are more wandering the camp?"

"Yeah, lots more. They're really good at reproducing, and we had a lot of people here for them to grab." Jeff picked me up. "I'll hold you, and Chuck and I will handle the dodging. You shoot."

We did so, Jeff holding me in essentially a sitting position so I'd be able to aim. The gun had unlimited firepower because it wasn't shooting bullets and was self-charging, but it didn't matter—we weren't going to stop all of these superbeings with one gun, even a gun made by Drax.

My music switched again, right back to "Victorious." Figured that meant that Algar felt I wasn't utilizing my crazy enough. Pity that I had nothing.

Spotted a Fem-Bot that had gotten through. So did Chuckie. "What the literal hell?"

"Oh, yeah, there's a Fem-Bot army that the marines onsite are fighting. Siler and Wruck were there, too. You can tell it's not really me because they're all wearing Rolling Stones shirts. Otherwise, they're not as hard to kill as androids or superbeings, but they're really bullet resistant. We had the best luck tearing them apart, and so far, none of them have exploded, so there's that."

"Wish they'd explode over here," Jeff muttered.

"Put me down." He did, and I headed for the Fem-Bot while dodging tentacles, Jeff and Chuckie behind me.

Got up close and put some real effort into my shot placement. Ten to the head, ten to the torso, strafing fire to the legs. She went down. At this rate I could take care of all the Fem-Bots in three hours, four hours tops.

The music got louder. Clearly I wasn't thinking right. So—while I spun around and tried really hard to blow away a Samarapus the Third that had followed us and didn't succeed in doing much other than removing one whole tentacle, which didn't slow it down so much as piss it off—thought about why the music had gotten louder.

"What are the chances that the Samarapusses can turn a Fem-Bot into a robotic version of themselves?"

"No idea," Jeff said.

"Ditto," Chuckie added.

Tossed Chuckie the gun. "Let's find out." Grabbed the Fem-Bot's head and tossed it at the Samarapus the Third. It ignored it. Tossed the Fem-Bot's body at the Super Squid. Ignored it again. "Well so much for that."

"Wait," Chuckie said, as he aimed and shot, not at the Samarapus but at the torso I'd sent over. He fired a lot, but it finally exploded. And another tentacle came off.

"It's a good idea, but taking too much firepower to be effective," Jeff said, as he grabbed the two of us and ran us to where Reader and Tim were standing back-to-back in a battle between them and their handguns against two Samarapus the Thirds.

"Wish we had more of those," Tim said, as Chuckie shot at the Samarapus nearest to him.

"Let's get out of here," I suggested as we all just missed being speared. I grabbed Reader, Jeff had Chuckie and Tim, and we hightailed it toward the portable city.

We arrived just in time to see the Samarapus, Jr. wrapping itself around the portable house and engulfing it. On the plus side, as near as I could tell, Christopher had gotten everyone out. Those with weapons were in a circle around those without.

"Why aren't they shooting from the air?" I asked Joe as we joined the circle.

"No idea. I'm down here."

Stepped into the circle and hit speed dial. He answered on the first ring. "Jerry, why aren't you guys shooting?"

"We already tried that. The targeting is good, but we've got too many people around. We caused three sailors to become superbeings because when we shot one of the small superbeings, its death throes flung it around and it stabbed them before we could shoot its tentacles off. Maybe if the Vata were flying this, things would be different, but we're still learning."

"Is there a safe place to land or hover?"

"Miles away, yeah. We can't get any lower than we are — the bigger ones are big enough to reach us and we were almost grabbed. The best we're managing is keeping them within the confines of what we're laughingly calling Camp David."

"What about the Fem-Bots?"

"Too small, too human-looking, and before you say that they're not you, we know. But we're not A-Cs. People down there are moving too fast for us to see in many cases, the Fem-Bots among them. And I think there are more people aboveground than you realize, too. Some we know went into the underground passage to Raven Rock—Matt's on with your Uncle Mort, so I can reassure you that Jamie and Charlie are okay."

"Well, there's that." And thank God, Algar, ACE, and all the other Powers That Be for that.

"Yeah, but there are more troops nearby than I think you know about, and most of them are armed with only conventional weapons. There are a ton of Field agents down there, too. Meaning that we can't just shoot into the crowd because we can't risk killing one of you, Kitty. Not yet."

Knew what that meant. If this wasn't able to be contained, I'd literally have to give them the go order to drop a bomb onto everything, or Uncle Mort would, in order to protect the world. Well, it would be a showy way to go. Thing was, I didn't want to go, and I didn't want anyone else going, either.

Checked my phone. My music might be paused, but it still hadn't changed. "Jerry, I'm failing on the crazy thinking."

"I got nuthin'. We tried to give you guys weapons. Those Krakens grabbed them in the air and ate them."

"I am not fond of the Samarapusses, especially how they reproduce. Or really anything else about everyone attacking us."

My music changed. Couldn't hear it because I was on the phone, but per my screen, B.O.B.'s "Bombs Away" was now supposedly waiting to be played. "We tried to toss the Fem-Bots to the Samarapusses, but they wouldn't eat them. I don't know why."

"Maybe because they came from the ground," Jerry suggested. "Or because however they eat, or think they eat, they grab from above. I mean, on the plus side, they haven't tried to eat anyone on the ground, just spear them and create more."

While I stared at my phone, the music changed again. To "Bomber" by Motörhead. Then, a second or so later, to "Here Come The Bombs" by Ima Robot.

"Oh. Wow. I'm an idiot. Jerry, I know what I need you guys to do."

"Great! What?"

"I need you to arm and drop every bomb you have on board."

CHAPTER 96

"**KITTY, ARE YOU HIGH?** Or being impersonated?" Jerry sounded worried.

"No, I think I just figured it out." Memory nudged, presumably because my Crazy Gene was working again. "By the way, what about the helipad? I know it's here, we looked at it."

"It's far from where you are, relatively speaking. We could try it, but we have no A-Cs on board, so we can't get anything to you guys that way. Including bombs."

"I don't want you to get something to us, I want to get something to you. How long will it take you to go invisible and land?"

Heard Jerry asking this of Hughes. "Three minutes, tops."

"Great. Make it so. The moment you land, lower the boarding ramp. I'm sending the Vata to you. Then, get back into the air, which should give me time to get the people more out of the way."

"Oh, good luck with that."

Outlined what I wanted the helicarrier to do once the Vata were at the controls while I tugged at Jeff and the others. "We need to get the people out of the way. Either by getting them underground or just out of blast radius. And once we have, I want those bombs dropping and dropping hot."

Everyone who could hear me stared at me. They all said that I was obviously giving up and doing the grand last stand. The only ones who weren't were Jeff and Christopher.

"I'll call you back to give you the bombing go-ahead. If you don't hear from me in five minutes, tops, Jerry, then start your bombing run." Hung up and put my phone back into my back pocket. My music changed to "My Girl" by Aerosmith, so I knew that Algar approved. "Seriously, gang, the Vata need to get to the helicarrier and the rest of us need to get people underground or out of the way. Now."

Jeff looked at me. "Going with the crazy?"

"God, I hope so," Christopher said.

I nodded. "It's what I do."

Jeff grinned. "Everybody, underground or out of the way, now!" Potentially his best bellow yet. "The only targets we want are robots or superbeings!"

Grabbed Christopher's arm. "Get all the Vata to the helipad. Do you know where it is?"

"No idea."

Jeff shoved through the small crowed and grabbed Drax. "Get your countrymen to you now."

Drax shouted something I didn't catch and Tevvik and the others moved to him. "Link up," Christopher said, as he grabbed Tevvik's hand. He nodded to Jeff. "You steer." He grabbed Jeff's hand and the seven of them disappeared.

Spent the time they were gone shooting the Samara-pusses and doing a fast headcount. "Where are Rohini and Bettini?"

"I think in the tunnel," Randy said. "Christopher got them out just before the superbeing encircled the portable city. They insisted on going last. I think he took them straight to the tunnels because he didn't want to deal with them self-sacrificing."

"Good man."

"Thanks," Christopher said as he and Jeff returned. "The Vata are in the helicarrier, but they're being watched by the humans on board, and by watched I mean that all the humans have weapons at the Vata's heads."

"They're our allies."

Christopher shrugged. "Maybe, maybe not. They know it's just in case."

"The weapons are being aimed casually," Jeff said.

"I'm sure that's so much better. Fine, I'll worry about the diplomatic issues later. Okay, Christopher, I want you to get the foreign dignitaries underground. You're the only one who's going to have the best chance of that."

"I know where it is—I had to take the Shantanu there because—"

"Randy told me. Wise choice."

He snorted a laugh. "Thanks. I can get the others, but I know Renata won't go and I also know I can't make her." He nodded toward the queen who was fighting with her daughters. The battle staffs were effective against the tentacles, so one for the win column.

"Fine. Renata's the exception. Get all the others underground. We cannot have these people killed on Earth soil."

He grinned. "Got it. I've got the diplomatic part of this job." With that he grabbed Alexander and King Benny, who were nearest to hand, and took off.

"Everyone, I now want anyone with hyperspeed backing toward the outer perimeters of the compound." Might as well keep the fighters who could go fast out and available. "Humans, link up. You're going underground, regardless of who you are."

"That means you," Jeff said to Chuckie, Reader, and Tim. "I need people we can trust underground. And that's an extremely executive order."

Grabbed Chuckie's hand and took the gun from him. "One at a time or all together, guys. What's going to be best in the long run, do you think?"

Reader took Chuckie's hand while Jeff picked up one of the bazookas that was on the ground—hard to shoot a rocket launcher safely when you were in a protective circle. "Hurry up," Jeff said. "We have a lot of people in danger right now. Joe, Randy, link up."

"Six Million Dollar Men get to stay," Randy said.

"We're not fully human anymore, Jeff," Joe added. "So we're not going."

Reader grabbed Tim's arm and I took off. In the time we'd been discussing this, Christopher had gotten at least six of the visiting aliens into the underground area.

Was able to shoot and run, which was all thanks to the high level of rage and action-driven adrenaline I was riding on. Spotted some other groups scattered about. Shoved the guys into the Aspen Lodge and did a fast check to make sure nothing bad was inside here. Chuckie had the elevator ready. "There are stairs under the service porch if you need them. Be careful, Kitty."

"I will do, and you guys do the same. Please don't sneak out—I gave Jerry the bombing order and I know the guys are going to follow it. And I'm not mad at any of you anymore so I don't want you to die."

They all managed to smile, nodded, and got into the elevator as Christopher shoved two more into it and took off. The doors closed and I pulled my phone back out. "Kitty, you okay?" Jerry asked. "We're ready to bomb. Should we hold off?"

"Yeah, glad I got through, we still have too many people out to let you start dropping bombs. I'm going to keep you on the line, okay? You can talk me in to find missing people, then you'll know for sure when we're all out of range. Or would you prefer I do this with Tito?"

"Nah, do it with me. Tito's in charge of the Vata. They like him more than us."

"He's not aiming a gun at their heads."

"True. They also aren't aware that he can kill them with his bare hands."

"Works for me. I'm probably not going to be chatty."

"And that works for me. I know how this rolls, Commander. When you get out, go to your right." Shoved my phone into my back pocket again and took off, too.

Headed toward the area Jerry had said, which was one where I'd seen people on the way over. These were fighting Fem-Bots and some were A-Cs. "All Centaurion Personnel—get all the humans you can grab and either run for the perimeters or the underground entrances. That's a direct order." Shot a couple of the Fem-Bots for emphasis. The agents looked at me, then at the Fem-Bots. Heaved a sigh. "Aerosmith rules, guys. Figure it out or I'll go all FLOTUS on your asses."

They grinned, nodded, grabbed the military personnel they were with, and took off for the cabin, since they were closer to that. Shot the rest of the Fem-Bots they'd been fighting. Made some dents, but not enough, and decided it was time to get back to my program, especially since Jerry suggested that stopping to kill things they were hoping to kill in a minute or two wasn't smart.

Had to dodge around a group of Samarapusses that were

fighting Fem-Bots. So far, the only battle that I felt was going great regardless of outcome.

Not just the portable city was down or damaged. Amazingly enough, Aspen Lodge was basically unscathed, but
could not say the same thing for a good number of the
buildings I passed. Tried not to contemplate just what this
would mean for Jeff's Presidency—we had to survive this in
order for him to actually have a Presidency.

Managed to find Siler and Wruck, who were still dealing
with Fem-Bots but also trying to handle a couple of Samarapusses. "Where are the marines?" I asked as I skidded
to a stop next to them and blasted a Fem-Bot.

"Dead, moved off, or turned into superbeings," Siler said
shortly.

Someone blasted the Samarapus nearest to us with a bazooka. "Why are you stopping everywhere to chat?" Jeff
asked as he reloaded from the Santa Ammo Sack he was now
carrying and sent another round into the closest Samarapus.

"I'm a friendly person. Where's the android body of Harpaz?"

"Got it underground," Siler said. "Via an A-C named
Colette. She said she worked for you. The three Mossad
agents with her vouched for her."

"She does." Relayed this info to Jerry, who confirmed
that Colette and the frozen Harpaz android were underground. Our Mossad friends, however, were not.

Wruck, who was in human form, looked up. "Did you call
for air support?"

Looked where he was. There were helicopters in the air.
Squinted. They didn't look military. "I think those are news
helicopters. I've got an open line with Jerry—can you confirm?"

"Sadly, I can confirm such indeed, Commander. No military, all cameras."

Relayed the happy news. "Of course they are," Jeff said
as he fired the bazooka, reloaded, and fired again. "What
else would they be?"

"So much for Screne being able to keep media under
control. I assume that whoever tipped off the press that I'd
been kidnapped tipped them off for this, too."

"Probably. Let's get anyone without hyperspeed underground." Jeff fired the bazooka then looked at Siler. "I have

no idea where Lizzie is. I'm sorry, she wouldn't go underground and we've lost track of her." Tried not to let my
stomach clench. Failed.

"We'll find her," Siler said. "Are we sticking with you two?"

"Probably for the best." Looked around. "Where did The
Clarence Clone go?"

"I have no idea," Jeff said as he hit the Samarapus a sev-
enth time with the rocket blast and it sort of blew apart. Only
sort of, though. "Why did you have Brian bring him, anyway?
And I have no idea where Brian is, while we're at it."

"Lizzie and I think Stephanie's behind most if not all of
this, meaning he might be all we can use against her."

"Won't help if you've lost him," Wruck said.

"Based on what I'm hearing, Commander, I can't identify anyone specifically. We still have to stay too far up and
everyone's moving around too much. There are a ton of
people still around, so if you want us to start bombing, get
them out of there."

"Jerry said there are a lot of people here. We need to
keep moving and get them all to the perimeter or underground."

Headed off, Jerry directing me to the nearest sets of people, the men following behind me. Cabins weren't the only
things damaged by now. Trees were down, foliage was tram-
pled or stained with black acid, and if there was wildlife it
had hopefully all scrambled off for safer pastures. Individ-
uals we passed, Jeff ordered to disengage and get to the
perimeter or Siler used hyperspeed to take them to Aspen
and the underground, depending.

"There's something wrong with the Samarapusses," I
said as we reached a clutch of A-Cs and military that were
penned in by a Samarapus, Jr.

"Beyond how they reproduce, you mean?" Jeff asked as
he shot a tentacle off with the bazooka and Siler ran in to
grab the humans. "Get out!" Jeff bellowed, since some of
the A-Cs were just standing there, clearly not sure if they
should run or fight.

"Yes. They don't smell." Focused on shooting off another
tentacle. "And I haven't seen a parasite, have you?"

"Got a good look at the first one's mouth when it was
eating the guns I was trying grab and there was no parasite
that I could see. But that just means it's internal."

"Or that these were created in a lab."

"Don't tell me you want to preserve these for study."

"No, but I think we'll want to ensure that Dulce gets the remains."

"Love your optimism, baby." He shouted orders and the A-Cs seemed to get it. They grabbed humans and took off. Hopefully for safety.

We left the still-fighting Samarapus and headed off again. It tried to come after us, but the tentacles didn't make it easy for them to move fast on land. One small favor in a giant pool of acidic ink.

We wove in and out of the area at hyperspeed, systematically clearing out people while Jerry directed me. Christopher joined us when we were about halfway done. We linked to him and did the rest of the area at the really fast hyperspeed.

Cleared the entire Camp David area other than the helipad and skeet shooting range without finding the people we knew were here—like Lizzie and Whitc. Hughes had the open line to Uncle Mort who was confirming underground arrivals as they happened, so we knew who we were missing.

"Jerry, what's our status for people still aboveground?"

"There are several groups along the perimeter, all hugging the fences, and all moving toward the main entrance, meaning they're heading for the helipad where we landed. Cannot confirm anyone's identity via visual, though."

We were back by Aspen, and it was time to wonder if I needed to have Christopher, Siler, and Wruck force Jeff into the underground. The Original Samarapus was there, still trying to spear anyone it could. And it had people to spear, since this was where Leah, Jakob, and Oren were.

They were doing damage, but it was so big and there were only three of them. It was miraculous that they weren't hurt. Watched them all leap, dodge, jump, and roll away from the various tentacles. Okay, it was skill. But all it was going to take was one mistake.

"We need to get them."

Christopher let go of us, ran off at his Flash level, and grabbed the three of them, depositing them with the rest of us. "Get underground," Jeff said as Christopher brought Jakob over to join Oren and Leah, all of them looking dazed from the speed. "That's an order. We need you alive to verify that the android wasn't something we created."

Grabbed Leah's hand and ran her to the service porch. "There are stairs under here. Supposedly." Not that I saw any.

"There," Oren said, as he joined us and pointed to something that Jakob pulled up. Sure enough, what looked like a floor was a trapdoor with stairs leading down.

"Be safe and guard my kids. And my parents. If, you know . . ."

"We know," Leah said. Then they all hugged me quickly and ran down. Closed the door. "Jerry, I think it's time. Let's test my plan on Samarapus, Senior, shall we?"

"With pleasure, Commander. Please run if one's falling toward you guys—they will go off in five seconds."

Sure enough, bombs started falling from above like giant, nasty hail. Started counting to five. And, happily, Samarapus, Senior saw them.

It grabbed them out of the air in its tentacles and shoved them up under itself, where its mouth was.

"Four one thousand. Five."

Jerry had been quite accurate. And results were immediate.

CHAPTER 97

THE SAMARAPUS' body started doing that thing where it looks like the giant monster who's swallowed the explosives is blowing up inside first. Presumably because that's exactly what was happening.

"Time to go," Jeff said. Christopher nodded and hit the hyperspeed button. The Samarapus exploded as we ran off, spraying parts all over the place. We just missed getting splattered.

"Boy, is the pool going to need cleaning."

"That's the least of our worries," Jeff said. He pointed. More bombs were dropping, and the helicarrier was also firing at the Samarapusses and the Fem-Bots.

"Get underground, Commander," Jerry said.

Looked back. "Ah, can't. There's blown up Samarapus, Senior all over the place and it looks dangerous."

"Head for the helipad, then. We'll pick up all aboveground personnel when we're done with the bombing."

"Will do. Christopher, get us to the helipad."

We zoomed there, avoiding a couple of Samarapus the Thirds I told Jerry about. The rest of those aboveground had headed here, too, as Jerry had said. Most of them were A-Cs, including Daniel, Joshua, Marcus and Lucas, but thankfully Len, Kyle, Adriana, Joe, Randy, and our Amazon Family Fighters were there, too.

"Need to check out this area to see if we have any stragglers," I said to Jeff.

He nodded. "Christopher, keep everyone here, but get them out to the main gate if needed. We're going to do recon."

Christopher nodded and started getting everyone into

formation in case they had to run away or run onto the helicarrier.

There was a newer, sturdy-looking building here, as well as a parking lot where most of our cars were. "Well, we can drive out if we have to."

"Only if they left the keys."

We searched the building quickly—and it was a basketball court, go me for the accurate guess earlier—but found no one. We got to the far side of it to be rewarded by actually finding the rest of the people we were looking for. Lizzie, White, Abigail, Mahin, Brian, and TCC were in a circle with their backs to each other. None of them looked hurt, but none had weapons, either. Would have been relieved, only they weren't alone.

They weren't surrounded by Fem-Bots or Samarapusses. They were surrounded by androids. Naked ones, but still, androids. The androids all looked like Thomas Kendrick, sort of, but without boy parts, which was so very familiar. And they all had guns and they were aimed at the people in the inner circle.

The Kendroid was here as well, as was the Crystal Maurer android. He looked at me. "I'm glad you're finally here."

"Why am I not surprised? How'd you get in? Climb the fences?"

"No," Crystal said. "We killed the guards at the main entrance." Noted that all the androids appeared to have bullet holes in them. Wasn't stopping them, but then the guards had probably been thrown seeing human-sized Ken Dolls coming at them.

"The icky naked ones are really rudimentary," Lizzie called. "Like have to be told what to do rudimentary."

"I can tell them to shoot you," Crystal said nastily. She was a very believable android.

"But you won't," I said. "Because your boss isn't here and I'm pretty sure she doesn't want any of these people dead until she's around to watch."

Crystal shrugged. "Oh, we won't have to wait long."

Heard a sound that wasn't bombs bursting in air or, rather, in Samarapusses. It was a sound I recognized—a Harley was motoring up. Sure enough, Stephanie—in her full black leather Huntress gear, including crossbow—rode up.

She parked the bike and smirked at us. "Hi, Uncle Jeff." She took the crossbow off of her back and aimed it right at him.

"Stephanie, what are you doing?" he asked, rather kindly, all things considered.

"I'm ruining your life. Like you ruined mine."

"They didn't do that," TCC said.

Stephanie looked at him. "I know my mother wants to believe you're really my father. I'd like to believe it, too. So, if you are, leave those people and come to me."

TCC cocked his head at her. "What will you do to them if I leave them and go to you?"

"What I'm going to do if you stay with them. Have my soldiers shoot them."

"Why would you kill any of us?" TCC asked. "These are all good people. You're a good person. You weren't raised like this."

A look of disgust came over her face. "You're not my father. My father, my real father, raised me to hate them. And I do." So much for the hope that TCC would sway her. Maybe if we'd kept her incarcerated and had had the time to devote to her rehabilitation. But we hadn't, and we didn't.

Meaning it was time to do what I did best. "Feeling's totally mutual, Steph. Of course, you're saying that the man who covered you with his own body when Cliff was trying to have us all shot isn't your father. Interesting viewpoint. But, you're probably distracted by all the weird fake manflesh around. You know, I had no idea you had such a crush on Thomas Kendrick."

Her head snapped toward me. "Don't call me that."

Never failed to amaze me, how the majority of A-Cs reacted to nicknames. "Right. So, Thomas turned you down or what, Steph?"

"He was convenient."

"Right." Looked at the Kendroid. "You know she made you because she can't have him, right?" Really hoped that Jerry had the real Kendrick listening in, in case he could add something helpful.

The Kendroid looked at Stephanie and I could see uncertainty in his expression. "She loves me."

"No, she doesn't," Abigail said. "I think she loves Thomas Kendrick, though, lucky him."

"She definitely does," Mahin added.

"What would you know about it?" Stephanie asked.

"Women can always tell," Mahin said dismissively.

"Kitty," Jerry said softly while Abigail and Mahin continued to play on the Kendroid's fears and occupy Stephanie's attention, "we're almost done, and I think we've gotten all of the superbeings and robots, too. We're already back to invisible. All aboveground personnel seem to be at the helipad. We're going to try to land and get the others on board. I'll let you know when to grab the hostages and run."

"You know," I said conversationally, "these androids aren't all that well made. Well, Crystal and TK there are, but the Naked Ken Dolls, not so much. A really good shot through the head and the middle takes them out. You clearly weren't trying very hard when you made them."

"I had to work fast," Stephanie said to me. Mahin and Abigail continued baiting the Kendroid. "For some reason."

"It'll be tight," Jerry said. "We're worried about hitting you guys or the hostages. And it's harder to fire accurately the way you're all grouped when we're on the ground, and we're going to be on the ground shortly. And this is me showing how serious the situation is that I'm not making a comment about how Stephanie clearly didn't get enough Barbies when she was growing up."

"Always the way and I so know what you mean. Meaning you have a secondary lab somewhere nearby, Steph, that's all. Is that where Trevor is?" It was hard having two simultaneous conversations, but I was the girl for the job.

Stephanie stared at me, in shock as near as I could tell. The Kendroid turned away from the girls and stared, too. As did Crystal Maurer.

Saw Lizzie disappear. Then White. Then Brian. Abigail, Mahin, and TCC disappeared at the same time. Meaning Siler had either come looking for us or been advised that we were here, had slipped through the Naked Ken Doll Line, and grabbed everyone. If he was blending, then, as with hyperspeed, anyone with contact would also blend. But that was a lot of people to get out of danger, since he had to sneak them through the androids. So he'd probably need a couple of seconds of stalling time.

"Who?" Stephanie asked, trying to sound cavalier and failing.

"Wow, you're as terrible at lying as the rest of your clan. Trevor the Tinkerer. The man who really likes you because you're so much like your great-grandfather."

"Thomas says that Stephanie seemed shy around him," Jerry whispered to me.

Her jaw dropped. "How . . . ? How do you—"

Loved it when my Megalomaniac Girl theories were proved to be true. The Crazy was always right. Go team.

"Know about him? You'd be amazed at what we know." Looked at the Kendroid. "Like, I know that androids can overcome the programming." Looked back to Stephanie. "Like, I know that you were actually really crushing hard on Thomas Kendrick, so much so that you couldn't bring yourself to actually approach him. So you made a copy. And you liked that so well, you made a ton of other copies."

Stephanie and the Kendroid were focused on me. But I hadn't held Crystal's attention, and she turned to look at the hostages. Who were not there. She opened her mouth.

"Now," I said calmly, as I knocked Jeff down to the ground and covered him.

Laser fire came from what seemed like nowhere, and it sliced the Naked Ken Dolls up fast and efficiently. "Boy, Lizzie wasn't kidding, those things were really badly made. Thank God."

Siler appeared behind Stephanie and got her in a hold that looked well practiced and efficient.

The two fully functioning androids hadn't been hit, though, and they both attacked Siler, pulling him off of Stephanie while she tried to shoot Jeff.

Fortunately, Jeff rolled us out of the way. As we scrambled to our feet and headed for the skirmish, someone else slammed into the group. Lizzie.

"Get away from my dad, you freaks!" She kicked the Kendroid in the nuts and he went down, just like a real man would.

Had no idea how she'd gotten out of the helicarrier, but it was time for me and Jeff to get in there. "I'll take Crystal, you take—" Well, I was going to tell him to take Stephanie, but she'd managed to turn to attack Lizzie. Who roundhouse kicked the crossbow out of Stephanie's hands.

It flew into the air. Jeff jumped and caught it. He turned it on the Kendroid. Who put his hands up.

Meanwhile, remembered that I had a gun and that I hated Crystal Maurer's guts. Started shooting as she ran toward me, using the rapid-fire techniques my mother had taught me for use with my Glock. Happily, they worked with Drax's guns, too.

Ten in the head, ten in the torso, strafing fire to the knees. She went down.

Siler was trying to get into the girl fight, but he had no way of doing so, because Stephanie and Lizzie were really going at it.

Stephanie had A-C speed and strength, but Lizzie had been trained by the Assassination League and she was seriously pissed. They were doing martial arts moves so fast I almost couldn't see it. Wondered if Lizzie was part A-C somehow, or if Siler had slipped her an enhancement, but figured that if Chuckie could move that fast, so could Lizzie.

However, even the best human was at a disadvantage against an A-C. Stephanie sent Lizzie flying through the air. Jeff and Siler both started for her, but she landed in Thomas Kendrick's arms. He put her down. "Get into the ship," he said nicely. "You, too," he said to Siler. Who looked at me. I nodded. I wanted Lizzie safe, and that wasn't going to happen if Siler wasn't holding onto her.

Kendrick didn't step any closer. "Stephanie, is this really the way you want to tell someone that you like them?"

She stared at him. "I . . ." For a moment, she didn't look vicious, triumphant, haughty, supercilious, or anything else like that. She looked like a young woman who was looking at what she wanted but could never have.

"Do we shoot her?" Jerry asked. "Camilla's on board with us, by the way, and she really wants us to."

Stephanie spun and ran off at hyperspeed, leaving her motorcycle, her crossbow, her family, her crush, and the android she'd made to love her behind her.

Looked at Jeff. Who was watching his niece with one of the saddest expressions I'd ever seen him have. "No," I said quietly. "No kill order. Let her go. Tell Camilla we'll find her. I promise."

Looked at Kendrick. He looked sad, too. "When I first met her, I thought she was beautiful but too young for me. And I never gave her another thought in that way." He shook his head. "What a waste."

Jeff gasped and grabbed me. "The android's going to explode."

Looked at Crystal's body. "Not that I can tell."

"Not that one." Jeff turned me toward the Kendroid. "*That* one."

Sure enough, the Kendroid was jerking and blinking in a way that indicated the self-destruct was about to go off. "You can fight it!"

He looked at me and shook his head. "I don't want to. You're right. I'm not real." He looked at Kendrick. "He is. He's who she wants."

"But you're who she has."

Jeff tried to drag me away, but I pulled out of his hold and stepped closer.

"Thomas," Jeff said, voice steady, though I heard the concern, "get into the ship and don't let anyone else out."

"You could have killed all of us at any time. When you kidnapped me, and right now. But you didn't. That's not your programming. That's you."

He shook his head. "I'm not real."

"You're as real as you want to be."

"Let me die."

"Only people who are alive can die."

"Why do you care?" he wailed.

"I'm asking that question, too," Jeff said quietly and urgently. "It's time to *go*, baby."

"I care because you want to be a person, and I think that you can be. I care because people like Stephanie and Cliff and Trevor and Antony Marling and all those like them don't. That's my weakness, according to everyone. That I care, and I care about people who maybe I shouldn't."

"You said I'm not a person."

"You weren't. But the first step in becoming a full android person is the acceptance that you *are* an android, and the realization that, if you do it right, it doesn't matter. You're still you."

The Kendroid's shaking slowed a bit. "But I'm him, too."

"You don't have to be. You don't have to be what Stephanie made you to be. You can be yourself and make your own choices. I promise that you can, TK."

He stopped shaking. "I like that name." He smiled at me. "I'm going to keep it."

"Come into the ship with us, and we'll help you."

The Kendroid shook his head. "I don't know if you can trust me. And until I know that you can, I'm not going to let you trust me."

"Works for me," Jeff said, as he picked me up bodily. "Don't explode on your way out," he called to the Kendroid over his shoulder as he ran us into the ship that we could now see.

We got in and the hatch was raised. Jeff didn't let me go until it was closed. "Put me down. Please."

He did and I headed for the command center at a run. It was easy to find—just headed for the voices.

Got there as we were raising up and ran to the terminal Tevvik was at, which was the one Jerry had been manning. Shoved past Wruck and Tito to get to the screens. "Let me see the ground." Tevvik switched the view to below.

The Kendroid was standing there. He looked up and waved. Then he got onto the motorcycle and rode off.

"Do you believe that he knows you're watching?" Tevvik asked.

"Yeah, I believe he does."

CHAPTER 98

"**WHERE TO, COMMANDER?**" Hughes asked.
Almost answered but stopped myself. Looked up
at Jeff and smiled at him. He gave me a very personal smile,
then turned to Hughes. "We need to get to Raven Rock and
get everyone there out."

"Yes, sir," Hughes said. He relayed the order, but not
before he winked at me.

"You did well," Wruck said quietly. "I realize the others
may not understand why you tried, but Benjamin and I do.
And we both thank you for it, in our own ways."

Hugged him, hugged Tito, then headed over to Jeff.

Spent the time waiting to get there, which wasn't all that
long, showing Jeff around the ship. He was as impressed as
the rest of us. "I think it's a fantastic war machine, baby. But
I'm worried about what we're going to be facing when we
get back. It's been seen on TV by the entire world by now,
I'm sure."

Queen Renata had joined us midway through. "My people would have conquered the entire galaxy with a ship
such as this. I know what you fear, Jeff. This is a dangerous
thing."

"It doesn't have to be. But I have no idea how to make it
seem cuddly, either."

Evacuation of Raven Rock took some time, due to having
to double-check who was where and who was missing. But
Raj and Uncle Mort made sure that Nadine and Colette got
Jamie and Charlie to us right away.

We each hugged both of them, then Jeff took Jamie and
I took Charlie and we all cuddled together for a little bit.

While we were waiting to get everyone loaded and confirming those considered missing in action, who were going to be presumed dead via superbeing for this crowd and dead due to classified reasons to their loved ones, we went looking for Lizzie and Siler. They were in what appeared to be a dining area in the ship and were in the same parental clutch that we were.

"I should bawl you out for that attack," Jeff said, as Lizzie looked up at him a little guiltily. "But I'll save it, since I know you'll listen to it as much as Kitty would, which is to say not at all."

"Right you are," I said without any guilt at all.

Jeff grinned and kissed me. "And I wouldn't have it any other way."

"Mommy," Jamie said, "this ship is so pretty!"

"Is it?" Looked around. Hadn't thought of this as attractive, other than in a saving our lives more than once kind of way.

"It is. Can we ride in it some more?"

"Not sure about that," Lorraine said, as she and Joe came in.

"I'm all for it," Joe said. "I like this ship."

"Hey, just realized that you guys don't have the wires sticking out anymore."

"Nope," Randy said, as he and Claudia joined us. "Tito had them burned off. Didn't hurt, we still seem okay."

"Other than I think we may all have to move to Kitty Land," Claudia said.

"No, I don't think so." Elaine, Raj, and Chuckie joined us. Christopher, White, Reader, and Tim came in right after them. Fortunately, it was a big room. With no signs of actual food. Which was a pity, because I was hungry.

"Why not?" Jeff asked. "I'm pretty sure there's going to be a call for my impeachment or resignation after this. And the less said about how we've left Camp David the better."

"Rohini and the rest of the Planetary Council may be able to assist with that," White said.

Reader nodded. "We talked to them while we were underground. The Shantanu are even better at reconstruction than A-Cs are."

"It's more than that," Elaine said. "Fritzy was at the

White House, and he's been handling things in coordination with Serene."

Raj nodded. "The evil alien attack that was attempting to kill the President and all of the Planetary Council was thwarted."

"Nice spin," Jeff said dryly. "How do we explain the President of Iraq and the Prime Minister of Israel?"

"Mossad will handle the situation with the Prime Minister," Leah said, as she, Jakob, and Oren came in. We were back to our usual room filled to Marx Brothers capacity. And this was a pretty big room. "And what's left of the Iraqi mission is willing to corroborate our stories."

"Which are?" Jeff asked.

"That there was an assassination attempt on your life," Chuckie said. "Before the alien attack. All agencies are determining if it was a coordinated attack or not and will, of course, be working with other world intelligence agencies."

"Oh, of course." Jeff's sarcasm meter was definitely heading for eleven.

Chuckie was unfazed. "Prime Minister Harpaz was injured protecting the First Lady and is in a coma. We'll have Dulce see if he's a salvageable android or if he's going to have to be destroyed. And President Samara was killed protecting your children."

Managed to refrain from saying that this was hilarious, since he'd tried to kill them. Only managed it because said children were right here. Go me, Mom of the Year.

"That's going to fly in political circles, let alone with the regular people?" Jeff sounded as skeptical as I felt. "And it's somehow also not going to finally make the Middle East cohesive by making them all declare war on the United States?"

"Yes," Chuckie said. "Because the truth—that Israel was being led by an android and Iraq by a literal monster who tried to blow up your child—is worse for both countries than this story. I still have the candy bomb, and they know about it. In this spin, their leaders are tragic heroes. They'll stick with it. And their people will, too."

Heard a throat clear behind us and turned to see Alexander there. "Sorry to intrude," he said, "but I feel that you're all missing a very key opportunity."

"Excuse me?" Jeff asked.

Alexander smiled and looked at me. "A common enemy is so very helpful when your families are fighting, don't you find?"

The light dawned. "You want us to blame this on the Z'porrah."

"Yes."

"But they didn't do it," Jeff said.

"If they could have, they would have," Drax said, as he arrived. Figured Hughes had taken over his part of the flying. "The Z'porrah are all of our enemies. You've had their spies here. Those spies affected your people. Who's to say that this is *not* due to the Z'porrah?"

"He has a point, Jeff. I can easily make the case for LaRue being a focal point for all of this, including Stephanie and Trevor the Tinkerer."

Alexander came over and put his hand onto Jeff's shoulder. "Instead of looking at this as a disaster, cousin, why not look at it as the opportunity it is?"

"Opportunity for what?"

Alexander smiled. "World peace."

Opened my mouth, but Chuckie put up his hand and I shut up. "He's right, Jeff," Chuckie said. "The world has been different since the first Z'porrah attack, but because we didn't choose to capitalize on it, we're still mostly where we were prior to that attack—carefully at each other's throats. This kind of event can tear the world apart. But, if it's handled properly, it can be the event that brings the world together."

"The cohesion may not last," White said, as Gower came in and nodded to him. "But Paul has been speaking with several key religious leaders around the world, and the consensus seems to be that if we're being dragged into the galactic community, then we'll go as Earthlings, not as disparate races and nationalities, and that includes we A-Cs. I assume that the political world will follow, in part because we are in this lovely ship that, according to our Navy pilots and Air Force Captain, could take over the world all by itself."

"That was fast."

Gower nodded. "The talks have been going on since the Planetary Council came, Kitty. They were just at a need-to-know level. And none of you needed to know."

"I feel the love," Jeff said. "But how do you convince the common man that this is a good idea? How do I tell the people of this world that they're safe and we're on their side?"

"We'll figure it out, Jeff," Gower said. "We always do."

As he said this, Oliver and Jenkins came in, trailed by Vance and Abner. "I'd love to take pictures," Oliver said. "Only my cameras are all destroyed. As are the poor people on my team."

"You told them to run," Jenkins said with a sigh. "I wish mine had listened, too."

"We listened," Vance said loyally. "Mister Joel Oliver's never wrong."

"Does the hero worship make him sick, or just everyone else?" Abner asked.

"Oh, I like it," Oliver said. "Believe me."

Jenkins managed a laugh. "I'll take it, too, should you want to spread it around. Mister President, we're clear on the spin, so you can count on us to ensure that we stick to the party line."

"Alien attack will get bigger headlines than successful peace treaty," Oliver said. "As my entire career can attest."

Looked at Elaine. "So much for your idea to make the successful peace treaty a part of the inauguration party I'm even more sure we shouldn't have."

"We still need it, more so now." She sighed. "I think the issue of how to thank the Club Fifty-One people is even more vital after this, though. We can't forget them just because another attack happened."

"And another homegrown terrorist attack, too. Though I realize we're not going to mention Stephanie and her androids, nor the Fem-Bots. The Samarapusses and the Harpaz android, aka the 'alien attack,' are more than enough. We're going to have to spend money to fix up Camp David, too, Shantanu and A-Cs or no Shantanu and A-Cs. I can just imagine the complaints if we pay to get people to Washington, and I can imagine the bigger complaints if they have to come on their own dimes."

Keith popped his head in. "There you all are. All personnel are accounted for or listed as missing. We're about to head for Andrews. Should be a short trip."

Handed Charlie to Lizzie, who cuddled him as she

leaned against Siler, and stepped over to Keith. "Where's Malcolm?" I asked quietly. Realized I hadn't seen Buchanan for ages. Couldn't remember when I'd seen him last, or if I'd even seen him once we'd gotten to Camp David.

"Buchanan?"

I nodded.

"He wasn't underground. I thought he was in the ship or with the teams on the ground."

My throat felt tight. "No, he wasn't. At least, I don't think he was."

"I'm sorry," Keith said. "I know you care about your people."

"Yeah. I do." Turned back to my family, doing my best not to cry, when my phone rang. Checked the number. "Malcolm?"

"Missus Executive Chief, it's good to hear your voice."

"Where are you?"

"Watching over you, like always."

Looked around. Someone shoved off the wall at the back of the room. "You freaking amaze me, Doctor Strange."

He grinned. "Camilla grabbed me when the ship was landing to get the Vata. She felt that the two of us would do more good in the air and hypersped us onto the ship right after the Vata. But I appreciate that you were looking for me. Just didn't want you upset. I'm fine."

"Good. Me too."

"Good." We hung up and I went back to my family, feeling a lot better.

Jamie heaved a sigh. "I want to stay on the pretty ship. It's so fun here."

Drax smiled at her. "Thank you very much. I designed it to be as aesthetically lovely as it is efficient. It burns clean energy and is self-sufficient on fuel. The reactor creates the power and the power charges the reactor, with no emissions other than oxygen."

We all stared at him. "Wow," Joe said finally. "I got to get me one of these."

"You technically already have it," Drax said. "The five of you have flown it without issue. I'm sure with a little practice you'll be as comfortable with it as if you were a natural Vata."

Keith popped his head in again. "We're here."

"Seriously? It took longer to load people than it did to fly this to D.C.?"

"The ship goes faster than it feels like."

"*Does* it?"

"I know that look," Christopher said. "What crazy are you coming up with?"

"I think I've figured out how to get everyone to the inauguration while showing off the might of our new allies in a super nice way."

Chuckie and Raj both looked at me, then at each other. "It could work," Raj said. "But we'll have to scan for weapons."

"That's already built in," Drax said, sounding slightly offended.

"Iron Man, don't worry, no one's dissing your mad skills. We're suddenly just all kinds of thrilled that you're here."

"What's the plan everyone else but me seems to know?" Jeff asked.

While Chuckie explained that we were going to use the helicarrier to transport the Club 51 members who wanted to go to the inauguration, we followed Keith back to the command center and the rest of our friends and family. Did a fast head count of my own. Everyone I thought should be here was, including Uncle Mort.

I hit play on my music. "The End Has Only Begun" by Lifehouse came on.

Leaned against Jeff and relaxed. He wrapped his arm around me, and I turned so that Charlie and I were snuggled into Jeff's chest and I could put my hand onto Jamie's back. We stayed like that the whole way home.

CHAPTER 99

THE NEXT TWO and a half weeks were a whirlwind of activity. I didn't even argue about the FLOTUS stuff I had to do, because I was too busy, and everyone else was too busy to hear me whine anyway.

Amazingly enough, the party line was holding. Mossad had come through, and Israel wasn't mad at us or the Iraqis, but were instead mad at the aliens who'd sent the attack to try to destroy them and us.

The two Iraqis who'd survived the attack happened to be high-ranking in government, and they'd done the same thing—focused their people on the alien attack that was centered on the U.S. and clearly done to cause the Middle East to declare war on us. Meaning, therefore, that in order to show their strength, they would not declare war on either the U.S. or Israel.

Of course there was a lot of anti-alien hysteria going on. But it was shifting away from the A-Cs and even the Alpha Centauri residents toward the Big Bad that were the Z'porrah. No one had forgotten Operation Destruction, after all, and having more people than us saying that it was the Z'porrah's fault, not ours, didn't hurt. Knew this was going to come back and bite us hard in the butt later, but right now, it was the best option we had so we were taking it.

It also didn't hurt that Raj was trotting out Alexander, Drax, Queen Renata, King Benny, and Rohini constantly. Alexander was an emperor of an entire solar system that liked Earth a lot and was also, like all the A-Cs, handsome. Drax was a royal prince and also good looking as things went. Renata was a queen, and she'd shifted just a bit to ensure that she looked exotic but not alien. And King Benny and Rohini were flat-out adorable.

These five were our Interstellar Ambassadors, and it was working. Alexander shared that Alpha Four was prepared to give Earth what it needed to join the galactic community. Drax discussed how even at the Galactic Core the Z'porrah were a threat and that they'd heard of Earth's bravery. Renata shared that her planet considered Earth their allies because of our might and our A-Cs. King Benny shared that we'd saved his planet and the entire Alpha Centauri system from Z'porrah spies and a Z'porrah invasion. And Rohini shared that his people were this part of the galaxy's version of the Red Cross and would be helping fix things at Camp David, making it as good as old.

Club 51 was in chaos, because this created a schism. Many of those who'd helped during Operation Epidemic wanted to fly on the helicarrier and go to the inauguration party. Those who didn't were, of course, led by Harvey Gutermuth and adamantly didn't want the others to go at all. The Church of Hate and Intolerance led by Farley Pecker naturally sided with the haters, but reports shared that there were less of them.

Hacker International set up a registration system for those who wanted to attend via helicarrier. As soon as someone registered, the hackers tracked it back and determined who the person was. Felt like we were doing the NSA's dirty work, but it was helpful in determining if we were getting grunts, high-ups, or people who weren't even involved in Club 51 signing up. Had a good percentage of all of them, and a small but significant percentage from the Church of Hate, too. Casey Jones, however, was not among them.

Mom still had the NSA under investigation, but that was going to be a long, drawn-out process. Sadly, the main incriminating evidence for the black site and the Fem-Bots was Monica Strauss. Other information had been redacted and Mom and her team were having to do a deep dive, assisted by some FBI and CIA personnel handpicked by Chuckie and Tom Curran.

Congress did as expected and approved all of Jeff's nominations. Photo ops with King Benny and Rohini helped a lot. It was amazing how many congresspeople had kids who wanted to meet King Benny.

My team, working with Elaine and Raj, had the party setup and prep. We were able to get the National Mall. Because Elaine was right—once the idea was tentatively put forward by Colette, as her first official act as my Press Secretary, the media whipped it up into a frenzy of patriotic puffery and suddenly everyone wanted a party to cheer on our first President with two hearts.

By the time the inauguration was looming and the registration for it was closed, we were expecting a huge number of people. We had five stages because we had so many people coming. And I was in charge of the bands.

Of course, we had things like budgets and schedules to accommodate. Meaning we weren't able to get every band I'd have liked. Of course, I'd have liked to have about a hundred bands, versus the five we could have. And we were down to the wire with a couple of them.

Mrs. Maurer came into my office. "Dear, I've heard from the band for the third stage."

"Are they in or out?"

"In. Very happily in, dear."

"Awesome. So we have Metallica on stage two, Smash Mouth on stage three, Panic! At the Disco on stage four, and Flo Rida on stage five."

"Yes. We're still waiting on stage one. They're on tour, so it's quite complicated."

"Do you think I should have R&B represented? Or classic New Wave, meaning Tears for Fears? We could always add a sixth stage."

"Not really, dear. I think you need to come up with another band in case this one can't make it."

"Fine. Don't want to, but fine. Amadhia and Aaron are going to do the national anthem and the opening song for Jeff's speech, right? And any other songs that we need during the other speeches?"

"Yes, I have that handled, they're clear on what they're singing and when. They've arrived, as well, and Antoinette has them settled into the Lincoln Bedroom. Lovely couple. They seem devoted to each other."

"Yeah, they're cool." And Jeff had insisted on having them. Couldn't argue, Amadhia did have a beautiful voice.

Vance trotted in. "This just came in, and I know you'll want it." He handed a printed email to Mrs. Maurer.

She read it and smiled. "You'll be happy, dear. They were able to do it."

Jumped up and high-fived both of them. "You know what? Sometimes it's actually good to be the FLOTUS."

CHAPTER 100

"THIS IS THE GREATEST PARTY EVER!"

"I can barely hear you," Jeff said. "Thank God I had the kids wear earplugs."

"Whatever! Duuuuude looks like a laaaady!" Yes, of course I was singing along. Not that anyone could hear me over the band and the screams from the crowd. It was nice to hear screams of excitement and happiness.

Jamie was on Siler's shoulders and Charlie was on Lizzie's. Everyone seemed to be having a fine time, earplugs notwithstanding. We were on the side of the stage, so in one of the coolest places in the world to be. Being married to the President had its advantages after all.

"I thought there was more to an inauguration than rock bands."

"Did you? Choose another First Lady then."

"No, I've got the one I want."

"Good to know. I'm pretty happy with my Commander in Chief."

"Thankfully. You know the speeches were supposed to matter."

"You were awesome as always, Jeff. Very moving, totally Presidential. The crowd loved you."

"I don't actually care about the crowd."

Stopped singing along and looked up at him. "Well, I love you. Is that good enough?"

Jeff smiled, his sexy jungle cat about to eat me smile. "It is for me, baby." Then he bent down and kissed me all through the rest of the song.

I didn't mind at all.

Available December 2016,
the fourteenth novel in the *Alien* series
from Gini Koch:

ALIEN NATION

Read on for a sneak preview

"**W**ILL OTHER ALIEN FLAGS** soon be flying all over our country?" the Serious Newscaster asked. "And are these aliens the reason the Z'porrah attacked our world again? Stay tuned for the first of our twelve-part investigative report: Aliens Among Us."

Charles Reynolds cleared his throat as the show mercifully cut to a commercial. Chuckie was my best guy friend since 9th grade, always the smartest guy in any room, and also now the Director of the CIA. "It's not an issue for us to share that the photos were shown out of context," he said, sounding calmer than anyone else had so far. "And I'm sure we can get someone at the UN to share that the flag was their idea. However, this is highlighting one positive thing—the press and therefore the public at large have bought that the attacks at Camp David were caused by the Z'porrah."

The Z'porrah were an ancient race of nasty dino-birds who had the longest running feud ever going with the Ancients, who were an ancient race of shapeshifters. The Ancients were on the side of Earth and the Alpha Centauri solar systems—and by "on the side of" I mean "had meddled with everyone's evolution but because they cared" versus what the Z'porrah were doing out this way, which was still mourning the death of our dinosaurs and wishing the rest of us were long gone.

So, during our last frolicsome fun of less than a month ago, we'd taken the advice of the Planetary Council and had blamed the created in-control superbeing and android attacks at Camp David on the Z'porrah. That our spin for the events of Operation Madhouse had started biting us in our butts far sooner than expected was just par for our particular course. We were, as always, stuck in the sand trap with only a miraculous hole-in-one likely to save us.

Serene Dwyer, who was the strongest imageer after Christopher White, a stealth troubadour, and the Head of Imageering for Centaurion Division, nodded. "That the press is attacking is no surprise. That's what they do these days. However, what Alexander and our other galactic advisors told us is still accurate—LaRue Demorte Gaultier was, is, and always will be a turncoat Ancient and a Z'porrah spy, and every action against us can be traced back to her, directly or indirectly."

"Can we honestly confirm that?" Jeff asked.

Serene nodded. "We can, Jeff. Believe me."

I believed her, since I knew that Serene was the head of the very clandestine Centaurion CIA, made up of troubadours around the world. I was the only person not involved in their operations who knew they existed. Therefore, if Serene said she had proof, we had proof.

"However, some of that proof can never be shared with the general population," James Reader said. Reader was the Head of Field, a former top international male model, and the handsomest human I'd ever met. In a room full of A-Cs he looked normal, because the A-Cs were truly the hottest people on Earth. So far as I'd seen, they were the hottest people in the galaxy, but I was prepared to find other alien races just as good looking out there. That was me, always willing to take one for the team.

"Leave the spin to us," Doreen Coleman-Weisman said. She was now our Head Diplomat for American Centaurion since I was the First Lady and could no longer get away with doing that job. She'd grown up in the Embassy, and though her parents had been traitors, Doreen was loyal to Earth and the rest of us. However, she was the best qualified to be doing the Ambassador's duties. Well, other than one other person.

Richard White was the former Supreme Pontifex for the A-Cs of Earth, meaning their Pope With Benefits. He'd retired to the active lifestyle when my daughter, Jamie, had been born, and he'd been my partner in butt-kicking ever since then. However, due to the events of Operation

Epidemic, where one of our most virulent enemies had launched a bioterrorist attack that had killed half of our country's leadership, White was now the Public Relations Minister for American Centaurion.

White nodded. "Yes, Jeffrey, this falls to us. Doreen and I have been preparing a statement to counter most of this. With the help of the Planetary Council, of course." He nodded towards the other aliens in the room, of which we had a lot, since the Alpha Centauri Planetary Council had come to visit at the start of Operation Epidemic and literally hadn't had time to finish their business and leave yet. We liked to keep our guests busy, go team.

The news came back on. "Welcome back. In a related story to the one about alien flags flying over the White House, our next story deals with the religious summit taking place in Rome right now." We switched from the bald-faced lying Serious Newscaster to a shot of Vatican City. "We've learned that the Pope and religious leaders from all parts of the world are indeed in agreement that they will be encouraging their flocks to join together in order to face the 'brave new world' we find ourselves in."

The Pope was outside along with a variety of other religious leaders, including ours—Paul Gower. Gower had been groomed by White for this position and he was reasonably comfortable with it these days. He was also Reader's husband. The camera zoomed in on him. Sadly, it probably wasn't because Gower was big, black, bald, and gorgeous, but because he was the A-Cs' Supreme Pontifex and, therefore, the person getting all the "blame" in this situation.

Sure enough and right on cue, the Serious Newscaster shared his so-called thoughts. "Is the Pope being negatively influenced by the head of the aliens' religion?"

"Where is this coming from?" Jeff asked. Though this time he wasn't asking the room at large. He was asking the two members of the fourth estate who had unlimited access to us—Mister Joel Oliver and Bruce Jenkins.

Oliver had been the laughingstock of the media for decades, because he'd insisted that aliens were on the planet. He was and remained the best investigative journalist going, and these days, he actually had the respect of his peers.

Jenkins was known as the Tastemaker, and he had

tremendous influence therefore. He'd been after us in a bad way during Operation Defection Election, when Jeff had been running as Vice President to the late Vincent Armstrong. But events of that particular frolic had made Jenkins switch sides in a very fast and permanent way. Discovering that one of the candidates you're supporting is an android did that to some people.

"I believe that the answer is simple," Oliver said.

Jenkins nodded. "Follow the money."

"Excuse me?" Jeff asked.

The answer dawned on me. "Oh. This station is owned by YatesCorp, isn't it?"

Oliver nodded. "Yes. Recently added into that media conglomerate."

"Recently as in the last two weeks," Jenkins added. "You know, right after the attacks on Camp David that we managed to spin well, and the inauguration gala and Club Fifty-One Gratitude Ceremony, which also went far better than could have been expected."

"Mergers happen all the time," Elaine Armstrong said. She was Armstrong's widow and now Jeff's Secretary of State. As such, she was fully on Team Alien. "Not that I am for one moment suggesting that this isn't a concerted effort against us."

"YatesCorp is trying to gather as many affiliates as possible," Oliver said. "And as Bruce pointed out, that's only started since the last actions against the A-Cs were salvaged."

"So, Kingsley Teague is making his move." Looked down the table to Thomas Kendrick, the head of Titan Security and one of the newer additions to Team Alien. "Thomas, your thoughts?"

He shook his head. "I realize I was sort of 'in' with Kingsley and the others, but I don't think they ever trusted me fully, since I came over from the Department of Defense. None of this is something I know anything about."

Based on what had gone on during Operation Madhouse, I believed him. That the others did, too, was confirmed by heads nodding around the room, including Jeff's. Barring Kendrick and others in the room wearing emotional overlays or blockers, if Jeff felt that Kendrick was telling the truth, then Kendrick was telling the truth.

"However," Kendrick went on, "I can guarantee that they want to harm your ward. That they never tried to hide from me."

My ward was Elizabeth Jackson, now Elizabeth Vrabel. Lizzie had been adopted by Benjamin Siler, who was the first human-alien hybrid, being the son of Ronald Yates and Madeleine Siler Cartwright.

Yates was the exiled former Supreme Pontifex who happened to be White's father and Jeff and Christopher's grandfather. Yates had built a media empire and then some, which was now being run by Teague.

He'd also been an in-control superbeing named Mephistopheles. Mephistopheles had allowed Yates to die, with the idea that he'd then move to me. But I'd killed Mephistopheles before that could happen. Operation Fugly might have been six years ago, but there wasn't a day it didn't find a way to rear its head and add into whatever else was going on.

Cartwright had been one of the many female Brains Behind The Throne we'd encountered over the years. She was dead now, too, thanks to the fact that we had talented allies. But Yates, Cartwright, and her sister and brother-in-law, Cybele Siler Marling and Antony Marling, had done experiments on Cartwright's son.

As such, Siler aged far slower than everyone else and, in addition to the standard A-C abilities like hyperspeed, super strength, and faster regeneration, he could "blend," meaning he kind of went chameleon. That blend could extend to those he touched, and while he couldn't hold the blend for all that long, experience had shown that he could hold it long enough.

His uncle had rescued him from the torture his parents were perpetrating upon him and had raised Siler in his trade—assassination.

Due to a variety of things that had happened during Operation Epidemic, Siler had moved himself and Lizzie into the Embassy and they used the name Vrabel for anything public. But events of Operation Madhouse had put Lizzie into the White House with the rest of us and made her my ward, just because things hadn't been complicated enough already.

Despite all that had happened to her—including her parents being traitors who'd been willing to kill her when she wasn't willing to go along with a plan to murder millions of people—Lizzie was a great kid. She was also a protector. Teague and the others were after her because she'd schooled their kids on why picking on people weaker than yourself was a bad thing to do.

"I get that they don't like that Lizzie kicked their kids' and their friends' kids' butts. But the only reason I can see for them continuing the vendetta is because they want to hurt Amy and blame it on Lizzie."

Amy was one of my two best girlfriends from high school, Amy Gaultier-White. She was a tall redhead, a lawyer, and still fighting to get control of her late father's company, Gaultier Enterprises. She was also in the room, because we were nothing if not the most unconventional and chummy administration the White House had seen in a long time if not ever.

"Well, the Fem-Bot Initiative certainly indicates that." Amy was going to say something more, but Tim Crawford ran into the room.

Tim was doing the job that was still the favorite one I'd ever held—Head of Airborne. "Where have you been?" Jeff asked, before Tim could speak. "I asked you to be here thirty minutes ago."

"Sorry I'm late, but you'll be glad I am. Or at least interested in why." Tim didn't sit. "I was at Andrews with the rest of my team, getting briefed on more of what Drax's helicarrier can do."

"Where is he?" Jeff asked. "He was supposed to be here as well."

Tim rolled his eyes. "Jeff, if you'd let me finish, I'd be happy to tell you. Unless you desperately need someone to berate for some reason."

"He does, we just watched the news and they were, as so frequently happens, mean to us and Jeff's tender feelings are hurt. However, I'm here. Tell me whatever it is, Megalomaniac Lad. I care and currently feel no need to berate anyone."

Tim grinned at me. "Thanks, Kitty. Anyway, a request came through to Colonel Franklin and he felt that we needed to discuss it, so I could brief all of you."

"And that was?" Jeff asked, sounding annoyed. "I'm not

trying to berate you, Tim. I just want to know why you're late."

"Jeff," my mother said sharply, "relax. And that's an order."

That my mother was both in the room and telling the President what to do wasn't so much that she was a meddling busybody as much as it was her job. As I'd discovered six years ago, my mother wasn't a business consultant. She was *the* consultant for anti-terrorism and the Head of the Presidential Terrorism Control Unit, a division almost as clandestine as the one Serene was running, but with a lot more power. The P.T.C.U. reported directly to the Office of the President and most of the other Alphabet Agencies reported dotted line into the P.T.C.U. somewhere.

"Ah, Angela has experience with this, Jeff," Fritz Hochberg, our newly instated Vice President, mentioned. "More than you or I do, frankly."

Jeff ran his hand through his hair. He had dark, wavy brown hair and I liked when he did this, because it managed to make him even more handsome than normal, which, considering he was the hottest thing on two legs, should have been impossible. But it wasn't.

Jeff must have picked up my lust spike, because he glanced over at me and gave me a very personal smile. He also relaxed. That was me, keeping the top man relaxed by wanting to constantly keep him in the sack. This was, sadly, probably the only FLOTUS duty I was actually going to be good at, but at least I had this one firmly in the win column.

"You're right," Jeff said. "Tim, I'm sorry, please go on."

Tim shook his head. "Too much caffeine? Anyway, while I realize that the media attacks are making everyone tense—and yes, I know about them because they have TVs over at Andrews—this may make it a little better."

Resisted the urge to tell him to hurry up. We all liked to own our dramatic moments now and then.

Reader felt no such compunction. "Tim, seriously, stop dragging it out. What's going on?"

"We have a whole lot of people asking to enlist." Said as if this was the coolest news in the world.

That sat on the air for a moment. "Um, in the Armed Forces?" I asked politely. "Don't we usually have that? I mean, I'm sure it ebbs and flows and all that jazz, but people wanting to enlist isn't all that unusual."

Tim grinned. "For Army, Navy, Air Force, Marines, the National Guard, and the Coast Guard? Sure. But that's not what I mean. I mean that we have people, many, many people, who want to enlist to serve in Centaurion Division. And they're all humans."

Gini Koch lives in Hell's Orientation Area (aka Phoenix, Arizona), works her butt off (sadly, not literally) by day, and writes by night with the rest of the beautiful people. She lives with her awesome husband, three dogs (aka The Canine Death Squad), and two cats (aka The Killer Kitties). She has one very wonderful and spoiled daughter, who will still tell you she's not as spoiled as the pets (and she'd be right).

When she's not writing, Gini spends her time cracking wise, staring at pictures of good looking leading men for "inspiration," teaching her pets to "bring it," and driving her husband insane asking, "Have I told you about this story idea yet?" She listens to every kind of music 24/7 (from Lifehouse to Pitbull and everything in between, particularly Aerosmith and Smash Mouth) and is a proud comics geek-girl willing to discuss at any time why Wolverine is the best superhero ever (even if Deadpool does get all the best lines).

You can reach Gini via her website (www.ginikoch.com), email (gini@ginikoch.com), Facebook (www.facebook.com/Gini.Koch), Facebook Fan Page: Hairspray and Rock 'n' Roll (www.facebook.com/GiniKochAuthor), Pinterest page (www.pinterest.com/ginikoch), Twitter (@GiniKoch), or her Official Fan Site, the Alien Collective Virtual HQ (thealiencollectivevirtualhq.blogspot.com).

Gini Koch
The Alien *Novels*

"Gini Koch's Kitty Katt series is a great example of the
lighter side of science fiction. Told with clever wit and
non-stop pacing, this series follows the exploits of the
country's top alien exterminators in the American Centaurion
Diplomatic Corps. It blends diplomacy, action, and sense of
humor into a memorable reading experience."   —*Kirkus*

"Amusing and interesting...a hilarious romp in the vein of
Men in Black or *Ghostbusters*."   —*VOYA*

To Order Call: 1-800-788-6262
www.dawbooks.com